NEW
ENGLAND
WHITE

NEW
ENGLAND
WHITE

—

STEPHEN L.
CARTER

ALFRED A. KNOPF NEW YORK 2007

THIS IS A BORZOI BOOK
PUBLISHED BY ALFRED A. KNOPF

Knopf, Borzoi Books, and the colophon are registered trademarks of
Random House, Inc.

ISBN-13: 978-0-7394-9170-6

Manufactured in the United States of America

For Annette Windom

Why does everybody pick on the economists? They've correctly predicted thirteen of the past five recessions!

—*Familiar campus joke*

NEW
ENGLAND
WHITE

THE LANDING IN SUMMER

RUMORS CHASE THE DEAD LIKE FLIES, and we follow them with our prim noses. None of us are gossips, but we love listening to those who are. So, if you happened to pass through the village of Tyler's Landing in the first few weeks after the investigations finally ended and the last reporters left for home, and you stopped at Cookie's Place on Main Street to buy some chocolate-covered raisins, specialty of the house, you'd have had the chance to listen to chubby Vera Brightwood telling you whose fault it was and whose fault it wasn't and whose fault it could never be.

As far as Vera is concerned, the whole mess started not when that colored professor got himself killed in November, but on an unexpectedly sultry winter night nine months earlier—call it February—when pretty Vanessa Carlyle, sixteen going on fifty if you believe what they say, set fire to her father's midnight-blue Mercedes on the Town Green. Yes, that's right, she says, *that* Carlyle, the very same, the one whose mail, according to Joe Vaux down at the post office, arrives addressed to "The Honorable," if you can believe the airs those people give themselves these days. You smile and listen, enjoying a New England summer's brightness through the wide front window of the shop. The word Vera Brightwood brings to mind is *garrulous*. For Vera, one lament flows smoothly into another, and soon she is assuring you that she has nothing against the Carlyles, even though she has been telling folks for the last six years, and tells you too, that the town should never have let them build that gigantic house on the Patterson lot. Which leads her back to the fire. Okay, so she has a few of the details wrong.

For instance, Vanessa never actually spoke to the professor that night, that's been proved conclusively, even if both of them, as Vera reminds you, happen to be colored. But that's just her way. Stories are like sweets for Vera: you have to make them fancier than the ones available next door or you lose your customers. Her time-tested technique involves fluffing up a minor detail here, folding in a richer grade of rumor there, and—*voilà!*—a delicacy worth every embellishment. She might not always be right, but she is never dull.

Anyway, no harm in listening, right?

Cookie's Place is the Landing's version of the Café de la Régence in Paris, and what they used to say of the second is often true of the first: sooner or later, everybody who is anybody stops by. Not just the three thousand people in the village proper, but somehow half the population of the state has heard of Cookie's. Word is that Woody Allen filmed the interiors for some movie in the shop a long time ago, but Vera isn't saying, so it probably isn't true. Although it should be. The countertops are polished white marble shot through with jagged green highlights. The bright red Coca-Cola sign is half a century old. The single room seems to go on forever, but it's really no more than twenty by thirty, the rest just a trick of the mirrors. The candies all sit in glass cases and jars: peppermint sticks in different colors, lollipops with long red swirls, a hundred varieties of jelly beans, truffles, buttons, straws, butterscotch, little mailboxes and Statues of Liberty and Ford Model T cars that dispense mints, hard candies in rolls and hard candies on sticks and hard candies shaped like animals, eight flavors of fudge, and all the chocolate the addict could wish, including an elegant diet-busting concoction, all Vera's own, called cranberry chocolate.

Something new is always baking. The luscious aromas drive you half mad, just the way they are supposed to. Whether you like candy or not, you begin to salivate as the desire for sinful pleasure snares you, and before you know it you are ordering everything in the shop. Vera, atrociously plump, cheeks puffy and pink, white-gray hair drawn neatly into twin buns, measures a pound of chocolate-covered raisins by eye as she talks your ear off, explaining in her husky smoker's voice the problem with the Carlyle house. And you listen to the story because you really do want those raisins.

Vera talks about the house. She has good, solid reasons why they should never have let the Carlyles build it. Like they should have left the meadow alone, so kids could play softball. Like the house breaks up the view from the road down into the valley. And it's too big and too ostentatious anyway, that house, all those sharp angles and glass walls that catch the sun, so when you drive by the place seems to *wink* at you, especially if you happen to be staring at it, which Vera, who has lived on the other side of the reservoir long enough to oppose every house built for miles around, does a lot more often than she likes to admit. Oh, Vera is in a dither, and beneath that delicate porcelain skin something glows warm with fury.

Certain that the woman is crazy, you begin to inch toward the door, the chocolate-covered raisins in your clutches, but Vera stops you with a word.

So what about the car? she asks, and you remember what she said about the girl—what was her name?—Vanessa. Do you want to hear about the car? asks Vera.

Sure, you say.

Vera is happy to tell you, but, first, maybe you want some fudge with that? Another specialty of Cookie's is the butter-rum fudge, with or without walnuts. Tying your bright-green box with her trademark green ribbon—no cellophane tapes for Vera; no, sir!—she says, oh, by the way, she must have forgotten to mention that while the car was burning, pretty Vanessa tried to open one of her veins with an X-Acto knife.

And when you have heard Vera out, maybe you're still not sure what to think, except that you are swooning with sympathy for Vanessa, to say nothing of her parents, her sister, and her two brothers. Vera talks so hard she leaves you dizzy, but you finally see it as though you were there, because Vera Brightwood has that gift, she always has, she can bring a story to life: the shiny blue Mercedes, brand-new, leased three months earlier, just two thousand miles on the clock, a roaring pyre in the concrete driveway of the red brick town hall as winter dusk falls, and, off to the side, this long, skinny brown girl, intricately woven braids obscuring half her winsome face, sits calmly on a slatted bench and struggles with the knife, sawing away at skin that refuses to break.

Poor kid, Vera finishes, a tear in her good eye.

You are inclined to agree.

And you know, Vera adds, sotto voce, as she tries to get you to buy some Jelly Bellys to go with your raisins, even with all the university folks buying up the land because they've decided that converting farmhouses is smart, there are only five colored families in town.

Surprised, you ask if the town keeps track of these things.

She asks what things you mean.

You frame your objection carefully. The number of African-American families living here, you explain. Do you actually keep track?

Some of us do, Vera tells you.

Why?

Vera leans close to whisper, her breath cloying as though she is fermenting inside, yellowy gaze lifting to the door just in case one of those liberals should come in. Money, she says. We keep track because of money. Nothing against the coloreds, mind, but real estate has been pretty flat around here lately, and I've never heard of a place yet where having colored neighbors makes values go up. You show me one and I'll be for that open-housing thing. Oh, and they should have sent Vanessa to jail after she burned the car: Vera is tired of the way they always coddle the coloreds.

Appalled, you try to speak up, but Vera refuses to feel guilty. She says you have it all wrong, she has nothing against the coloreds and she never did, even back when they were burning everything in sight until LBJ, rest his soul, called the National Guard to make them stop: she's upset about the stupid *house*. Pinheads, she hisses, but it isn't clear just who she is talking about.

You decide it's time to go.

You leave Vera behind, and now you're dizzy in the brilliant summer sunlight, her tirade still ringing in your head, and all you know is that you want to leave the Landing as far behind as you can. You find your car, you blink till your eyes clear, you roar out of town, who cares about the speed limit, that woman is crazy. You figure there is a cop hiding behind a billboard somewhere, but you decide to take your chances, because Vera's story has left you feeling unsettled and reckless. And maybe you get away with it, because the town police are not on edge the way they were back a few months ago. It's almost as quiet now as it was last November, a frozen interregnum, when Vanessa's arson was in the past and the killings were in the future, before time twisted around and history marched into the Landing, demanding vengeance; the second week of November, when everybody in the cheery white village of Tyler's Landing was feeling safe.

Last time for a while.

PART I

MAXIMIZING UTILITY

Utility Function—In economics, a measure of a consumer's preferences expressed by the amount of satisfaction he or she receives from consumption of a set of desired goods or services. Economic theory assumes that people make rational efforts to maximize their utility. Sometimes one person's utility is dependent on another's.

CHAPTER I

SHORTCUT

(1)

ON FRIDAY THE CAT DISAPPEARED, the White House phoned, and Jeannie's fever—said the sitter when Julia called from the echoing marble lobby of Lombard Hall, where she and her husband were fêting shadowy alumni, one or two facing indictment, whose only virtue was piles of money—hit 103. After that, things got worser faster, as her grandmother used to say, although Granny Vee's Harlem locutions, shaped to the rhythm of an era when the race possessed a stylish sense of humor about itself, would not have gone over well in the Landing, and Julia Carlyle had long schooled herself to avoid them.

The cat was the smallest problem, even if later it turned out to be a portent. Rainbow Coalition, the children's smelly feline mutt, had vanished before and usually came back, but now and then stayed away and was dutifully replaced by another dreadful creature of the same name. The White House was another matter. Lemaster's college roommate, now residing in the Oval Office, telephoned at least once a month, usually to shoot the breeze, a thing it had never before occurred to Julia that Presidents of the United States did. As to Jeannie, well, the child was a solid eight years into a feverish childhood, the youngest of four, and her mother knew by now not to rush home at each spike of the thermometer. Tylenol and cool compresses had so far defeated every virus that had dared attack her child and would stymie this one, too. Julia gave the sitter her marching orders and returned to the endless dinner in time for Lemaster's closing jokes. It was eleven minutes before ten on the second Friday in November in the year of our Lord

2003. Outside Lombard Hall, the snow had arrived early, two inches on the ground and more expected. As the police later would reconstruct the night's events, Professor Kellen Zant was already dead and on the way to town in his car.

(11)

AFTER. Big cushy flakes still falling. Julia and Lemaster were barreling along Four Mile Road in their Cadillac Escalade with all the extras, color regulation black, as befitted their role as the most celebrated couple in African America's lonely Harbor County outpost. That, at least, was how Julia saw them, even after the family's move six years ago out into what clever Lemaster called "the heart of whiteness." For most of their marriage they had lived in Elm Harbor, largest city in the county and home of the university her husband now led. By now they should have moved back, but the drafty old mansion the school set aside for its president was undergoing renovation, a firm condition Lemaster had placed on his acceptance of the post. The trustees had worried about how it would look to spend so much on a residence at a time when funds to fix the classrooms were difficult to raise, but Lemaster, as always with his public, had been at once reasonable and adamant. "People value you more," he had explained to his wife, "if it costs more to get you than they expected."

"Or they hate you for it," Julia had objected, but Lemaster stood his ground; for, within the family, he was a typical West Indian male, and therefore merely adamant.

They drove. Huge flakes swirled toward the windshield, the soft, chunky variety that signals to any New Englander that the storm is moving slowly and the eye is yet to come. Julia sulked against the dark leather, steaming with embarrassment, having called two of the alums by each other's names, and having referred half the night to a wife named Carlotta as Charlotte, who then encouraged her, in that rich Yankee way, not to worry about it, dear, it's a common mistake. Lemaster, who had never forgotten a name in his life, charmed everybody into smiling, but as anyone who has tried to raise money from the wealthy knows, a tiny sliver of offense can cut a potential gift by half or more, and in this crowd, half might mean eight figures.

Julia said, "Vanessa's not setting fires any more." Vanessa, a high-school senior, being the second of their four children. The first and the third—their two boys—were both away at school.

Her husband said, "Thank you for tonight."

"Did you hear what I said?"

"I did, my love." The words rapid and skeptical, rich with that teasing, not-quite-British lilt. "Did you hear what I said?" Turning lightly but swiftly to avoid a darting animal. "I know you hate these things. I promise to burden you with as few as possible."

"Oh, Lemmie, come on. I was awful. You'll raise more money if you leave me behind."

"Wrong, Jules. Cameron Knowland told me he so enjoyed your company that he's upping his pledge by five million."

Julia in one of her moods, reassurance the last thing she craved. A blizzard was odd for November. She wondered what it portended. Clever wind whipped the snow into concentric circles of whiteness in the headlights, creating the illusion that the massive car was being drawn downward into a funnel. Four Mile Road was not the quickest route home from the city, but the Carlyles were planning a detour to the multiplex to pick up their second child, out for the first time in a while with her boyfriend, "That Casey," as Lemaster called him. The GPS screen on the dashboard showed them well off the road, meaning the computer had never heard of Four Mile, which did not, officially, exist. But Lemaster would not forsake a beloved shortcut, even in a storm, and unmapped country lanes were his favorite.

"Cameron Knowland," Julia said distinctly, "is a pig." Her husband waited. "I'm glad the SEC people are after him. I hope he goes to jail."

"It isn't Cameron, Jules, it's his company." Lemaster's favorite tone of light, donnish correction, which she had once, long ago, loved. "The most that would be imposed is a civil fine."

"All I know is, he kept looking down my dress."

"You should have slapped his face." She turned in surprise, and what felt distantly like gratitude. Lemaster laughed. "Cameron would have taken his pledge back, but Carlotta would have doubled it."

A brief marital silence, Julia painfully aware that tonight she had entirely misplaced the delicate, not-quite-flirty insouciance that had made her, a quarter-century ago, the most popular girl at her New Hampshire high school. Like her husband, she was of something less than average height. Her skin was many shades lighter than his blue-black, for her unknown father had been, as Lemaster insisted on calling him, a Caucasian. Her gray eyes were strangely large for a woman of her diminutive stature. Her slightly jutting jaw was softened by an endearing dimple. Her lips were alluringly crooked. When she smiled, the left side of her wide mouth rose a little farther than the right, a signal, her husband liked to say, of her quietly liberal politics. She was by reputation an easy person to like. But there were days when it all felt false, and forced. Being around the campus did that to her. She had been a deputy dean of the divinity school for almost three years before Lemaster was brought back from Washington to run the university, and her husband's ascension had somehow increased her sense of not belonging. Julia and the children had remained in the Landing during her husband's year and a half as White House counsel. Lemaster had spent as many weekends as he could at home. People invented delicious rumors to explain his absence, none of them true, but as Granny Vee used to say, the truth only matters if you want it to.

"You're so silly," she said, although, to her frequent distress, her husband was anything but. She looked out the window. Slickly whitened trees slipped past, mostly conifers. It was early for snow, not yet winter, not yet anything, really: that long season of pre-Thanksgiving New England chill when the stores declared it Christmas season but everybody else only knew it was cold. Julia had spent most of her childhood in Hanover, New Hampshire, where her mother had been a professor at Dartmouth, and she was accustomed to early snow, but this was ridiculous. She said, "Can we talk about Vanessa?"

"What about her?"

"The fires. It's all over with, Lemmie."

A pause. Lemaster played with the satellite radio, switching, without asking, from her adored Broadway show tunes—Granny Vee had loved them, so she did, too—to his own secret passion, the more rebellious and edgy and less commercial end of the hip-hop spectrum. The screen informed her in glowing green letters that the furious sexual bombast now assaulting her eardrums from nine speakers was something called Goodie Mobb. "How do you know it's over?" he asked.

"Well, for one thing, she hasn't done it in a year. For another, Dr. Brady says so."

"Nine months," said Lemaster, precisely. "And she's not Vincent Brady's daughter," he added, slender fingers tightening ever so slightly on the wheel, but in caution, not anger, for the weather had slipped from abhorrent to atrocious. She glanced his way, turning down the throbbing music just in case, for a change, he wanted to talk, but he was craning forward, hoping for a better view, heavy flakes now falling faster than the wipers could clean. He wore glasses with steel rims. His goatee and mustache were so perfectly trimmed they might have been invisible against his smooth ebon flesh, except for the thousand flecks of gray that reshaped to follow the motion of his jaw whenever he spoke. "What a mistake," said Lemaster, but it took Julia a second to work out that he was referring to the psychiatrist, and not one among the many enemies he had effortlessly, and surprisingly, collected during his six months as head of the university.

Julia had been stunned when the judge ordered the choice of intensive therapy or a jail sentence. Vanessa cheerily offered to do the time— "You can't say I haven't earned it"—but Julia, who used to volunteer at the juvenile detention facility in the city, knew what it was like. She could not imagine her vague, brainy, artistic daughter surviving two days among the hard-shelled teens scooped off the street corners and dumped there. As her grandmother used to say, there are our black people and there are other black people—and all her life Julia had secretly believed it. So Lemaster had chosen Brady, a professor at the medical school who was supposed to be one of the best adolescent psychiatrists in the country, and Julia, who, like Vanessa, would have preferred a woman, or at least someone from within the darker nation, held her peace. She had never imagined, twenty years ago, growing into the sort of wife who would.

She had never imagined a lot of things.

"Cameron told me something interesting," said Lemaster when he decided she had stewed long enough. They passed two gray horses in a paddock, wearing blankets against the weather but not otherwise concerned, watching the sparse nighttime traffic with their shining eyes. "He had the strangest call a couple of weeks ago." That confident, can-do laugh, a hand lifted from the wheel in emphasis, a gleeful glance in Julia's direction. Lemaster loved being one up on anyone in the vicinity, and made no exception for his own wife. "From an old friend of yours, as a matter of fact. Apparently—"

"Lemmie, look out! *Look out!*"

Too late.

(111)

EVERY NEW ENGLANDER KNOWS that nighttime snowy woods are noisy. Chittering, sneaking animals, whistling, teasing wind, cracking, creaking branches—there is plenty to hear, except when your Escalade is in a ditch, the engine hissing and missing, hissing and missing, and Goodie Mobb still yallowing from nine speakers. Julia pried herself from behind the air bag, her husband's outstretched hand ready to help. Shivering, she looked up and down the indentation in the snow that marked Four Mile Road. Lemaster had his hands on her face. Confused, she slapped them away. He patiently turned her back to look at him. She realized that he was asking if she was all right. There was blood on his forehead and in his mouth, a lot of it. Her turn to ask how he was doing, and his turn to reassure her.

No cell-phone service out here: they both tried.

"What do we do now?" said Julia, shivering for any number of good reasons. She tried to decide whether to be angry at him for taking his eyes off the road just before a sharp bend that had not budged in their six years of living out here.

"We wait for the next car to come by."

"Nobody drives this way but you."

Lemaster was out of the ditch, up on the road. "We drove ten minutes and passed two cars. Another one will be along in a bit." He paused and, for a wretched moment, she feared he might be calculating the precise moment when the next was expected. "We'll leave the headlights on. The next car will see us and slow down." His voice was calm, as calm as the day the President asked him to come down to Washington and, as a pillar of integrity, clean up the latest mess in the White House; as calm as the night two decades ago when Julia told him she was pregnant and he answered without excitement or reproach that they must marry. Moral life, Lemaster often said, required reason more than passion. Maybe so, but too much reason could drive you nuts. "You should wait in the car. It's cold out here."

"What about Vanessa? She's waiting for us to pick her up."

"She'll wait."

Julia, uncertain, did as her husband suggested. He was eight years her senior, a difference that had once provided her a certain assurance but in recent years had left her feeling more and more that he treated her like a child. Granny Vee used to say that if you married a man because you wanted him to take care of you, you ran the risk that he would. About to climb into the warmth of the car, she spotted by moonlight a ragged bundle in the ditch a few yards away. She took half a step toward it, and a pair of feral creatures with glowing eyes jerked furry heads up from their meal and scurried into the trees. A deer, she decided, the dark mound mostly covered with snow, probably struck by a car and thrown into the ditch, transformed into dinner for whatever animals refused to hibernate. Shivering, she buttoned her coat, then turned back toward the Escalade. She did not need a close look at some bloodstained animal with the most succulent pieces missing. Only once she had her hand on the door handle did she stop.

Deer, she reminded herself, rarely wear shoes.

She swallowed an unexpected lump in her throat. "Lemmie."

But her determined husband was up in the road, waiting calmly to flag down the next car, even if it took till spring.

"Lemmie!"

He was at her side in an instant. He could do that. Lemaster was madly in love, her friend Tessa Kenner used to say, with his own reliability. He forced me to fall in love with him, Julia had explained to her disapproving mother, who wanted a man from one of the old families, not a man from one of the islands. I didn't have a choice.

"What's wrong, Jules?"

"I thought it was a deer, but . . . well, there's a body over there."

She pointed. He followed her finger, then strolled through the ditch to take a look.

"Don't touch it!" she said, because he was already kneeling, brushing snow from the face, probably ruining the crime scene, at least from what she heard on *CSI*, to which she was addicted. She waited, sitting half in the car with the door open, the air bag blocking her access to the radio, which she really wanted to shut off.

Lemaster returned, narrow face grim.

"It's not a deer," he said, almost consolingly, small, strong hand on her shoulder. "It's a man. And the animals have been . . . well, you know." Julia waited, reading in his face that this was not the real point her husband wanted to make. At last he sagged. "Jules, we know him."

CHAPTER 2

THE TERRIERS

(1)

THE DETECTIVES WERE SLEEK AND WHITE and very polite, either because that was their nature or out of deference to Lemaster, president of the university, for him just a stepping-stone, as he and his wife discussed but only with each other, and everyone else assumed, to a more impressive sinecure. They arrived at the house on the crest of Hunter's Meadow Road just before ten on Saturday, escorted by a fidgety officer from the minuscule Tyler's Landing force, a doughy man named Nilsson, whose doughy son had been in Julia's basic-science class four years ago—the same year she was fired, or quit, depending on how you looked at it—two eager terriers from the state police, their quiet voices and brush-cut brown hair so well matched that they might have been twins. They reminded her, in their grim and mannerly professionalism, of the Naval officers who came to the house on North Balch Street in Hanover, New Hampshire, in a Reagan-era October to inform her mother and latest temporary stepfather that her twin brother, Jay, a Marine, had died in Grenada. Julia, newly wed as well as newly a mother, had been home by painful coincidence, for Mona Veazie had celebrated her fifty-third birthday the day before, and had spent it dandling her grandson, Preston, named for Mona's father, the architect. So the daughter had the opportunity to sit in the living room and watch her mother die a little, too.

By the time the detectives rang the bell of the house called Hunter's Heights—up here every dwelling had a name—the unpredicted snow was over, and Mr. Huebner from town had plowed the long, snaking driveway not once but twice. Bright morning sunshine exploded from the shimmering whiteness hard enough to make her eyeballs ache. Or maybe the ache had a more fundamental source: although Julia had finished crying for a while, little Jeannie, sniffling from her cold, had caught Mommy raging at herself in the bathroom mirror, where an earlier, happier self smiled sadly back at her. This could not, Julia told herself, be happening. But it could. The detectives were a gray-visaged reminder of the hard truth that death stalks every life. So, when Lemaster summoned her, she washed her face and fixed her makeup and went down to see what they wanted. Over the handful of hours since the discovery of the body, they had done a lot of homework. Just a few details, they said. A couple of questions, folks, sorry to bother you so early, but this is a murder investigation. You understand.

The Carlyles understood.

They all sat in the living room, where Lemaster had stoked a fresh fire in the grate underneath the indifferent watercolor of solemn people on an Atlantic-side beach in Barbados, and, no, thank you, the detectives did not care for anything to drink. Julia, craving a glass of wine despite the hour, followed her husband's sober example and stuck to water. Lemaster's special assistant, Flew, rallying round the boss in the crisis, had put out a copious platter of everything he could find— crackers, cold cuts, Brie—but no one except Julia partook. She felt a glutton, tortured and exposed by her husband's abstemiousness. Jeannie, supposedly resting, was more likely on the upstairs landing listening in. Sleek, competent Flew was probably listening, too, perhaps from the butler's pantry, unless he was scrubbing the kitchen, for he hated all messes, but those that cluttered his boss's life particularly: every time Flew walked into the house on Hunter's Meadow and began to look around, Julia felt hopeless, and judged. Vanessa was in her room, door firmly shut, likely asleep but possibly on the computer, for she had evolved her own methods of burying the pain and confusion of mortal experience. As had stolid Lemaster. The family Bible stood on the mantelpiece, twelve inches high, creamy and intrusive. The Book of Common Prayer, 1928 version, stood next to it, for Lemaster Carlyle ran a traditional Anglican home and took a perverse pride in not caring who knew it.

The twin terriers said they knew how hard this must be, but their matched eyes said they didn't. They sat side by side on the brushed leather sofa, imported from Italy, that Lemaster hated for its ostentation, for he possessed the immigrant's thrift. Doughy Nilsson perched alone on a wooden ladderback armchair of intricate design, one of the few pieces Julia had retained from Mona's house in New Hampshire. Like the Louis XV writing desk in the front hall, the aging chair had as its original provenance her grandmother's famous townhouse in Harlem. There had been a day, as Mona put it, when everyone who was anyone in the darker nation passed through Amaretta Veazie's salon: by which she meant, anyone who aspired to position in what they called the Clan, the heavily fortified borders of which, once upon a time, Granny Vee and her buddies diligently patrolled, lest the wrong sort of Negroes force their way in.

When she tried to explain the Clan to her white friends, they never quite got it. But Julia was not surprised: whenever she mentioned that her family had been architects for seven generations, even most black people looked at her pityingly, as if she had exaggerated a tale of her forebears building their own shanties. Whereas in actuality Veazie & Elden had been, back in the nineteenth century, one of the five largest architectural firms in Manhattan.

The terriers did not seem the sort to take an interest in the social history of the community. Their elaborate questions came with a slowness that was fresh torture. They spent a lot of time flipping through their notebooks. Julia wanted to strangle them, and even placid Lemaster seemed edgy beneath his politesse, but an almost palpable air of impending tragedy hangs over encounters between black Americans and white police, and the best intentions of all sides have nothing to do with it. Nor was Julia certain that their intentions were the best, but her mind just now was in two hundred different places. They pressed on. They kept asking why the Carlyles had chosen that route home, seeming to doubt the whole daughter-at-the-movies story. Vanessa, the skinnier of the terriers pointed out, had driven back to the house with her boyfriend. Julia explained that the teen's decision had defied her father's edict. Lemaster had forgiven the breach because he understood Vanessa's worry at her parents' tardiness. The story felt laborious even to Julia, and the detectives must have agreed, for they interrupted to point out that Four Mile was an old logging road, running over water company property, and posted against trespassing.

"Everybody takes Four Mile," said Julia uncertainly, before Lemaster could stop her.

"Not everybody found the body," said the skinnier.

No, but somebody had to, she almost spouted, feeling like the divinity student she had once been, arguing over the fallacy of synchronicity.

"And that's why we're all here," said Lemaster, with brio.

A break while little Flew stepped in, towheaded and freckly, offering round cups of hot chocolate on a tray. Julia took one to be polite, but the detectives didn't. Their eyes followed him out of the room.

They asked about cars that preceded them and cars that followed them, they asked about whether cell phones ever worked out there, they asked about footprints and tire marks, they asked if the Carlyles had seen anyone else, they asked why Lemaster had taken his eyes off the road, they asked why he had touched the body: as a former prosecutor, surely he knew—

Lemaster delivered a quiet, confident answer to every question.

Sitting in the overdecorated room, surrounded by the sort of ostentation for which the Clan had once been famous, memory tumbling harshly through her head, Julia found herself more than willing to let her husband take the lead. Her thoughts were none too reliable at the moment. She was missing snatches of conversation. Although sitting down, she felt like she was wobbling on her feet. She had barely slept. She had phoned both the boys—Aaron at Phillips Exeter, Preston at M.I.T.—and had fielded easily two dozen calls so far this morning. Reporters she turned over to Flew, who had arrived at the crack of dawn and was expert at delivering a piece of his mind. Most of the rest were members of her club, Ladybugs, who in their fluttery way were drawn to disaster, each Sister Lady, as if reading from a script, announcing that she was "sorry to wake you" but had "heard the news" and "wanted to see how you're holding up"—but, really, to probe for inside information to match against whatever rumors were circulating already through the county's thin community of middling and higher-class African America. That was what the members called themselves, Sister Ladies, emphasizing both their intimacy and their distinctiveness. You had to be *somebody* to get in, the older members liked to say, mainly in reminiscence, because nowadays a black woman could become somebody in a single generation: not exactly the way things had worked back in the day.

Much later, when the winter turned bleak and scary, it was this moment that Julia would remember: sitting in the living room looking out on the early snow, the detectives plodding through their questions, while stray thoughts teased her mind—thoughts of Ladybugs, thoughts of Granny Vee, thoughts of the stories she had heard all her life about the old Harlem days when the Clan still mattered, even to black people not a part of it. It was almost as though, even on the terrible morning after she discovered the body of Kellen Zant, Julia Carlyle knew that the answer to the mystery that would soon coil around her wounded family lay in the darker nation's shadowed past.

(11)

THE TERRIERS MOVED ON to Kellen Zant as flames flickered in the grate. The Carlyles knew him, of course, and admitted it at once: knew him not only from campus, but in the casual way that most members of the Clan knew each other, for they bumped up against the same people constantly, brown skin to brown skin, in the endless spiral of dinner parties, fund-raisers, club dances, book circles—although Kellen Zant, a poor Southern boy of no certain origin, was not born to the Clan, and had spent years battering his way in.

Did you see him often? asked one of the terriers.

Not *often*, answered Lemaster before Julia could think.

But you saw him socially?

Lemaster again, playing games: That depends on what your definition of *saw* is.

Back at their notebooks, unamused. An important man, they said, not quite asking. He was just an economist, said Lemaster, past master of the unspoken campus put-down, implying not that economics was not serious but that Kellen was not serious, for despite his notoriety in the field he had committed little scholarship in recent years, preferring to earn income by consulting for large corporations. Was he good at his work? the twin terriers asked, and Lemaster offered his most charming smile and answered. "He held the Tyson professorship in economics. One of our most prestigious endowed chairs. We don't give those out for good behavior."

Misunderstanding the irony, perhaps deliberately, the detectives asked whether Professor Zant was guilty of bad behavior.

Lemaster had a way of lifting his thick, upswept eyebrows that was supposed to remind you that he was the smarter. He did it now. Julia could not tell whether the detectives reacted. "The entire university community will miss his wisdom and his wit," he said, as if composing the eulogy, or perhaps the statement for the press, for the director of campus information had called four times since last night.

The detectives made a note, perhaps about Kellen's wisdom, perhaps about his wit, and kept punching. They asked about enemies. None known. They asked about scandals and corruption. None known, but Julia had to hide a secret shrinking. They asked about recent fights and arguments and grudges, they asked about how he got along with colleagues and students and neighbors and friends. Oh, and, as long as we are on the subject, had not President Carlyle and Professor Zant had a recent, rather public feud?

Julia sat up straight, as did the detectives, although Officer Nilsson had the grace to look embarrassed. Lemaster's hand tightened on his wife's, who had not realized he was holding it, but his cool voice told Julia that she was the one being reassured. "No. That was media silliness, hunting for stories to make African Americans look bad."

Might he tell them what actually transpired?

"I had a series of private meetings with leading faculty last spring, after I had accepted the job but before I took the reins. In my chat with Kellen, I suggested that an economist of his eminence could do much to change the world if he would spend less of his energy on his private clients, and more on scholarship." A bemused smile. Lemaster's intelligent eyes sought out the shining grand piano rather than the attentive faces of the terriers. "Kellen said he would think about it. That was all."

The skinnier detective, a man named Chrebet, grew interested. "I found some reports saying the two of you hadn't ever gotten along. Some private thing."

"Nonsense."

"I read in the paper where Professor Zant was so mad he was thinking about leaving the university."

An old Lemaster dictum: "I prefer facts to news."

Nobody smiled.

"The meeting was private?"

"Just the two of us."

"Then how did the media find out about it?"

But Lemaster chose to take the question as rhetorical. He looked at his watch, making sure he had their attention first.

Just a few more questions, they promised. Professor Zant was worth a lot of money, right? From those private clients of his? This for some reason aimed at Julia, who dropped her eyes to examine the intricate yet ordinary stylings of the not-quite-Persian rug. She shrugged. Back to Lemaster: He invented some formula or something, right? A better way of estimating past stock prices adjusted for hypothetical events, said Lemaster, playing mind games once more. That was back in graduate school. They waited. Lemaster filled the gap. The Zant-Feldman equation, he said, was one of the greatest advances in finance theory in the past half-century. But perhaps the terriers were aware of a greater, because, unimpressed, they consulted their notebooks and kept on questioning. Not married? No girlfriend, to your knowledge? Boyfriend, then? No? Any idea who would want him dead? The Carlyles professed mystification.

Chrebet said, "You heard we found the car?"

"Saw it on the news," said Lemaster.

"In an industrial park on Route 48. Near as we can tell, he was shot in the car—two bullets in the head—and dumped on the road, and then the shooter drove to the industrial park and left it."

"And no suspects?"

"Not yet." Julia was impressed at how her husband had taken charge of the conversation; but he always did. Just weeks after their move to the Landing, he had wandered into a packed meeting of the zoning board, grabbed a seat at the back of the auditorium, lone representative of what his fraternity called the darker nation, and, within an hour, was all but giving the orders.

"Was anything taken?" he asked now.

"His wallet. Keys. Maybe other things."

"Robbery?"

"Could have been a robbery. Could have been meant to look like a robbery."

Again Julia was on edge. She expected, from what she saw on television, that this was the moment when the detectives would ask where each of them had been between eight and ten last night. Instead, the photographs came out. Chrebet slid two from a folder. He slipped the first to Lemaster, who gave it a quick glance and passed it on to his wife, waiting for the next. Julia looked, and looked away. The gold Audi TT in which Kellen had taken such pride, for he used to say he had all the luxury of the fools who bought more expensive sports cars, except that his cost less, got better mileage, and was more reliable. The seats were of a cream-colored leather, but in the photo the passenger's seat was black with blood.

"He was shot somewhere else and driven to Four Mile," Chrebet said, turning a page. "He bled for a while."

Two bullets, Julia was thinking. Surely only one was needed.

Lemaster spent longer on the second photo as the detectives asked if they had any idea, however faint, about who would do such a terrible thing.

Then the second photograph was upon her, and she understood still less the motive for sharing, unless they intended only to shock. A close-up of Kellen's face, taken presumably at the morgue. Yes, it was he, as best she could tell from what little was left unmarked. Kellen's eyes, usually laughing and dark brown, were tightly closed. There was no such reflex, she remembered from a seminar back in college. When one died slowly, yes, the eyes would close, as in sleep. But in the case of a sudden, violent trauma, they should have remained open. She frowned. Did coroners close eyes? Maybe the killer did it to be nice. Or maybe she remembered wrong.

No, Lemaster was saying, and Julia noticed that the photographs were back in the folder. Neither my wife nor myself would have any idea who would do such a thing, he said, lightly mocking their cadences.

Julia waited again for them to ask where the Carlyles were last night at whatever hour the thing occurred.

Instead, Chrebet asked about what the economist had been working on. Lemaster said that if they meant his scholarship, they should ask his colleagues in the department. The detectives waited. He said that he himself had no idea, and glanced at his wife, who echoed the theme. They asked what Professor Zant might have been working on besides his scholarship, and, again, the Carlyles could offer no assistance: thus pronounced Lemaster, speaking for both.

A signal passed between the detectives. Oh, yes, we almost forgot, one more thing. Would you, Mrs. Carlyle, be able to characterize for us your relationship with the decedent?

Relationship?

Weren't you once close and personal friends?

A speechless moment, only the detectives able to make eye contact with anybody else in the room. History piled up behind her, thick and strong. She recalled a face of quite seductive jolliness, a sparkling delight focused on her alone.

Yes, we were, briefly. But that was before my marriage.

Can you tell us when you talked to him last?

As much as saying they did not believe her.

We have a busy day, gentlemen, Lemaster said, and her appreciation of him quickened, and felt like love.

They sorryed and thanked their way out the door.

CHAPTER 3

KEPLER

(1)

"CITY'S A POWDER KEG," said Boris Gibbs, with satisfaction. "Ready to blow any minute."

Julia, who had noticed no protesters or riot police on her way in to the divinity school this morning, nodded politely, and said nothing. By the city, he meant Elm Harbor, where the university was located, and where she and Boris were having, for the moment, lunch; not the Landing, nearly half an hour distant. The Landing, of course, where they both lived, was nearly all white; and the city . . . wasn't.

"I've been listening to that radio guy, Kwame whatsisname. All right, he's a little bit over the top, but he has a ton of listeners, Julia. A ton of listeners. They hang on his every word, and, believe me, he's riling them up." He seemed to hope something would happen. A lot of white liberals were like that these days, waiting desperately for African America to reawaken and lead the Left out of the wilderness. But Boris Gibbs was no liberal. He owned no politics anyone could discern, and few emotions apart from a stormy self-satisfaction. He lived to slice up events, or ideas, or egos. Pressed, he would concede the sinfulness of the desire to flay others. It was, he often said, the thorn in his flesh. He seemed delighted to have one.

"I believe you, Boris."

"That black professor the campus cops beat up a couple of years ago. Remember? The unarmed kid who got shot in the car chase. Plus all the ordinary bullshit of everyday life. This business with Kellen is the last straw, you mark my words. The racism your people have to face these days is depressing."

Your people. She liked that one, almost as much as calling murder *this business with Kellen.* She said, evenly, "I read the papers, Boris. It was armed robbery, not a hate crime."

Boris shook his head at her naïveté and took a huge and ugly bite of his huge and ugly burger. He was, by his own reckoning, a huge and ugly man, with a bloated pink face and twisted, unhappy features that bespoke a life of misery, but he was one of the happiest people she knew: he always said what was on his mind, and so avoided the stress of holding back. They were deputy deans together at Kepler Quadrangle, the popular name for the div school, even though Boris, something of a campus historian, would rush to tell you that Kepler was the building, not the school. When not busily carping, Boris taught a bit and mainly managed the div school's budget, at which task he was a wiz, but the dean wisely kept him out of public view.

"At least that's what the police say," he smirked.

"Meaning what?"

"Meaning, you're a grown-up, Julia. You get to decide for yourself what to believe."

Julia swallowed the sharp retort that sprang to her throat. It was Tuesday, and she was tired of speculation about Kellen Zant. But the campus could speak of little else. Not many Ivies see a professor shot dead, and never one as popular as Kellen. The college paper had managed to mention six times in two days that the president had found the body of what the articles kept calling his "occasional adversary." Not even Kepler was immune. Little Iris Feynman, the third deputy dean in their underpaid administrative triumvirate—she managed "external affairs," meaning relationships with the university, the few alumni who had money to give, and any reporter who might accidentally wander in while looking for, say, the business school—had been in Julia's office earlier today to report a rumor that a disgruntled graduate student had done it. But the smart money—according to old Clay Maxwell, the New Testament specialist, whom Julia had encountered when she went to the drafty faculty lounge to fill her coffee mug with the vile brew that was all Kepler could afford—the smart money was on a jealous husband.

Julia said, "Can we please get back to the budget?" Because that was the subject of her lunch with Boris at one of the many undistinguished cafés near the div school. Claire Alvarez, their dean, under orders from the provost, had requested proposals for a 5 percent trim, and, like

Scrooge, wanted their memos by Christmas. Everyone at Kepler knew bad news was coming. A cluster of students sat in a nearby booth, eyeing the two deans uneasily, worrying which of their favorite programs would go under the ax. Far more campus energy was spent nowadays placing blame than fixing problems, and it was plain where the blame would fall. Julia carried the portfolios of dean of students and acting dean of admissions—the budget no longer called for separate posts—and collected a single half-time salary for the two full-time jobs. She had prepared, unhappily, three proposals to reduce her chunk of the budget: one that would turn the foreign students against her, one that would outrage the women, and a third that would persuade the minorities that she was an Oreo cookie—dark on the outside, white on the inside—which was what they used to call her in college.

"The budget?" Boris laughed. "They're cutting it again." Gesticulating with one hand, holding his burger with the other. Outside, the sky had gone the color of fresh slate. Julia was Yankee enough to read the signals: more snow was on the way. Besides, the Weather Channel said so. She watched Boris waving his burger, which, piled with every condiment known to man, was leaking. Messy sauces dripped everywhere. Other diners turned away. The waitress swung by the table to mop up the worst, and to bring him another Dr Pepper. He ignored her, as always, but he was a known big tipper. He licked mustard from thick fingers. Two wives had divorced Boris Gibbs. It was easy to see why. "They'll always cut our budget. It's because we're not scientists or capitalists, Julia. We don't splice genes or write software. We don't build huge fortunes. We do God, so we're not important."

"I'm a scientist," she said, forcing a grin, and it was true: her undergraduate degree was in biology, and she had taught middle-school science for years.

Boris raised notched brows like devil's wings. His eyes bulged, but they always did. He grabbed the filthy napkin to wipe his mouth, a simple act he managed to make slurpy and loud. Sometimes Julia suspected that the whole *I'm-so-ugly-and-disgusting* thing was an act, designed less to keep the world at bay than to render intriguing what would otherwise bore. Unlike Julia, Boris also taught a class every semester, and was among the students' favorites, even though his subject was systematic theology, a bear of a course, a rite of passage that left future pastors trembling. Julia and Boris were not quite friends, but she found his obstinate rudeness a source of endless fascination, the same way, as an undergraduate, she had been fascinated by a species of beetle that ate its siblings.

"Well, fine. If you're a scientist, add this up. If it was a robbery, how come they left the car? That Audi must be worth something, right? Right?" In the classroom, he bludgeoned his students much the same way: *Are you talking about Christology or soteriology? Well? Do you even know the difference?* "And how come they drove him out to the suburbs? Well? Why didn't they just dump him in the city? It's not like anybody would notice." Boris sat back, very content with his argument, and immediately ruined the effect by spilling his soda.

"I don't know, Boris," said Julia, as if she had not spent hours puzzling over the same questions. "I haven't thought about it. It was an unpleasant moment, and I'd kind of like to put it behind me instead of everybody asking all the time." A long intake of breath. "Now, can you please look at these numbers I worked out? Because I think I've found a way to keep both of my assistants." For Boris wanted her to lay off her full-timer and keep her half-timer: the last thing Julia intended to do, given that her full-timer was the only black secretary in Kepler.

"Tell you something else. Your friend Kellen? The story is, he was having this hot-and-heavy affair with some married woman." His eyes were greedy. "I wonder who."

"Kellen had nothing but affairs." Her cheeks grew warm. "He liked life to change around him. Nothing excited him except the future and its . . . possibilities. He used to say he never wanted to do anything twice." Julia winced, and made herself stop. How on earth had she allowed her fellow dean to lead her down this path? Kellen had been talking about sex when he made the remark a lifetime ago—sex, as it happened, with her. "Boris, please, if you look at my proposals—"

"Already looked. They're garbage. You're trying too hard to be nice. Face facts, Julia. Somebody's going to wind up hating you, right? Right. So the only way you exercise any autonomy at all is by choosing who." The waitress, who knew Boris's proclivities, had brought a third Dr Pepper without being asked. He downed half in one dribbling gulp. "Anyway, this married woman? I hear she's pretty prominent around town. Or her husband is."

"What are you trying to say, Boris?"

He ignored her indignation. Wiping his fingers on the tatters of his napkin, he hunched closer, increasing the likelihood that he would sputter on her. "So, are you going down to New Orleans or whatever for the funeral?"

"Arkadelphia. And yes." Wondering why she was blushing afresh.

"How about our esteemed president? Showing the flag, delivering a eulogy, weeping crocodile tears?"

"Lemaster has too much work."

"Too bad." A furry grin. "Want some company?"

"Have some, thanks." Now in an even greater hurry to escape him.

"Well, good. You have fun, if that's what one does at funerals. How are the kids taking it?"

"They're fine," she said, not sure whether she was lying. Should she talk about her eldest, Preston, off at grad school, who never called home if he could avoid it? About Vanessa, whose troubles could fill a book? Or Aaron, her ninth-grader, who had fled to Exeter to escape the tension in the house since his older sister's arrest? And what about Jeannie, more determined than ever to prove herself the household's perfect little princess? She felt all four of them drifting away from her, and the pain of loss twisted her mind in sadder directions. "They didn't really know him," she said, a bit faintly. "Or not very well."

He was already on to another subject. "Oh, listen, I'll tell you another thing I heard about your friend Kellen. A few people out in the Landing were pretty angry with him."

Boris lived just a mile from Hunter's Heights and loved to spread gossip, some of it true. Julia was intrigued, finally, in spite of herself. "Angry at Kellen? People in the Landing? What did Kellen have to do with the Landing?"

"No idea, but, whatever it was, it sure got a lot of people's backs up."

"Well, no disrespect, but I don't see how on earth Kellen could have been doing anything in the Landing without me knowing about it. He would have told me—" Julia stopped, confused by her own words. Her colleague's mocking eyes told her that he had spotted her error, but would preserve his teasing for a fitter time. "I mean, I would have heard about it. We all would."

"Unless he didn't want you to know," said her fellow dean, and took another messy chomp on his burger.

(11)

By Sunday afternoon, two days before her lunch with Boris, the gossip-flies had already begun buzzing everywhere. No screen or spray ever suffices to keep them out. Stop answering the telephone and they arrive as television bulletins. Shut off the set and they pop up online as headlines. Get off the computer and the phone rings: in this case sugary Tonya Montez, chief Sister Lady of Harbor County, bearing the breathless news that she was listening to one of the inner-city talk radio stations a little while ago, on the way home from morning worship at Temple Baptist (*Yes, by the way, I'm also more faithful than you!*), and heard the host, Kwame Kennerly, proclaim that the murder of Kellen Zant proved once and for all that it was open season on the men of the African diaspora. She did not often agree with Kwame, said Tonya, which was a lie, but he was right about this one. Julia tried to get a word in, but nothing slows a Ladybug in full flutter. You wait and see, said Tonya. There's gonna be more.

More what? asked Julia, perhaps missing the point.

Next came Donna Newman, whom Julia—shopping with Jeannie— encountered later Sunday, at the deli counter of the Stop & Shop on Route 48. Donna, who ran half the social clubs in the Landing—the Caucasian Squawk Circle, Lemaster called them—had heard that "this Zant" was seen in town the night he died.

"Of course he was," said Julia.

"I mean *before* you found him." A glance up and down the aisle. "They say he was with a *woman*," said Donna, ominously, but he always was.

Then, on Monday, it was Tessa Kenner on the telephone, Julia's roommate at Dartmouth, whom she hardly ever heard from, still less saw, other than on television, where Tessa read the news for two hours five nights a week on one of the cable networks, not because she had been Phi Beta Kappa at Dartmouth and a star in law school but because she possessed the principal qualification producers sought: blond hair. But Tessa had saved her life twice in the bad old days, and Julia was never quite able to hold against her what Lemaster insisted was a hopeless waste of talent.

Tessa, as it happened, did more asking of questions than spreading of gossip, and Julia, despite the warm space her old roommate occupied in her heart, danced around the answers. They agreed that Julia should call when next in Washington, and Tessa would call if she ever passed through Elm Harbor, although nobody ever did. Then Tessa, before hanging up, asked the worst question of all.

"And the two of you were over, right? I mean, like, really over?"

"Of course."

"There wasn't, like, any hint of any little thing?" A professional chuckle, as if laughing was a subject she had studied. "No juicy tidbit?"

"Is that why you called, Tessa? To ask about me and Kellen?"

"I'm not working on a story," she said hotly, denying an accusation Julia had not made. "I'm just worried about you, that's all."

"I'm fine," Julia lied, wondering what tales Tessa might be spreading through the higher echelons of broadcast journalism; and whether her past would come back to bite her after all.

Later that evening, as snow whirled, dervishlike, outside every window, Mona called from France—Mona, who never talked on the telephone, because she knew hers was tapped!—to make sure her daughter was bearing up as poorly as she expected, and also to ask whether she had heard this story that Kellen was some kind of fascist, a turncoat who worked for murderous American-supported dictators all over the world.

No, Julia told her mad mother. She had missed that one. But Kellen was an economist, she said, so she kind of doubted the story. And, by the way, how are you?

"Well, all I can say is, I'm *so* glad you didn't marry him." As if he had ever asked.

Mona had never approved of Kellen, just as she had never approved of Lemaster, neither of them really quite one of *us*, dear—the one too poor and the other too dark—just as she had never approved of her daughter's decisions to raise her children in the suburbs (where their friends would be white) and to take the job at the divinity school (because God was dead). Pressed, Julia probably could not have come up with an aspect of her life with which her mother was pleased; but, as so often, the distaste was mutual, the two of them locked forever in the prison of the animosity formed back in Julia's adolescence, when Mona said it was none of her children's business which of her several boyfriends was their actual father, or whom she married, or how often.

"Thanks for calling, Mona. It's great to hear your voice."

"You'll miss me when I'm gone, Julia Anne"—what Mona called her when annoyed.

"Come for Christmas."

But the invitation brought only a lecture on why it was wrong to celebrate holidays so hegemonic and culturally exclusive. Thanksgiving, too, arriving next week, took its knocks. The United States of America, Mona reminded her daughter sternly, was the source of most of the world's misery, and to offer thanks for the blessings of a nation built on slaughter was not piety but hypocrisy. She said much the same in the steady stream of feverish letters still duly published by the various journals and newspapers whose editors remembered who Mona Veazie was, or once had been.

"Oh, right. I'd kind of forgotten."

"You can take that tone with me all you want, Julia Anne. But you can't change the facts. Your Kellen was dirty. He was a fraud. All he cared about was money." A pause, but the awaited contradiction was not forthcoming. "It's true, dear. You'll see."

"He wasn't my Kellen," said Julia, although, once upon a time, he was.

(I I I)

AFTER LUNCH WITH BORIS, she headed not back to her office but to the parking lot, because she had to see her dentist about the tooth she chipped in the accident. She panicked for an instant when she could not find the Escalade, and then remembered that it was in the shop for a new dashboard, air bags, and bumper. She had come to work in the reliable old Volvo wagon, copper-colored and medium rusty, manufactured back when doors unlocked with keys and air bags were a mysterious luxury. From the day she earned her license to the day she torched the Mercedes, Vanessa had been the principal driver of the wagon. Now Vanessa was not allowed behind the wheel. Julia hesitated before climbing in. The lot was overcrowded: the divinity school shared it with the Hilliman Social Science Tower, the hideous glass-walled monstrosity on the other side of Hudson Street, which ran like a river separating the two ways of explaining the world. Invited a couple of years ago to lecture at Kepler on the separation of church and state, Lemaster had argued that the divinity school should be "an island of transcendent clarity in a sea of secular confusion." She had made the mistake of repeating the line to Kellen, who had laughed. *Every discipline thinks it's a clever little island with exclusive access to the truth, Julia,* he had scolded her. *All that makes the div school different is that not even your own graduates agree.*

Twenty-odd years since Kellen suddenly blurred and burdened. Twenty years of marriage, twenty years of motherhood, fourteen here in the city, and the past six in the Landing. They had built their ostentatious house with Lemaster's consulting income and a good chunk of her inheritance from Granny Vee. Now, with Lemaster six months into the presidency of the university, they were preparing to move to the ancient mansion she could just see, beyond the scaffolding, farther down the hill.

It occurred to her that the mansion, too, stood in the shadow of Hilliman Tower.

Julia gazed at the winking green glass. Kellen's spacious office had been up there, on the sixth floor of Hilliman, where the movers and shakers sat, looking down on everybody else, for Hudson Street ran downhill toward the Gothic sprawl of the campus proper. She had never mentioned to a soul that she could see Kellen's window from her first-floor office, but suspected he knew. She had trained herself not to look too often. But she looked now, wondering what the economist could possibly have been doing in the Landing to get people's backs up; and why he would hide it from her, when, ordinarily, he telephoned on the flimsiest of excuses.

"Excuse me, miss. Are you moving? I'm a little bit stuck here."

She turned. Behind her, a fortyish man waited impatiently, holding the door of his BMW. She recognized him: a famous anthropologist, always on PBS, and a political activist of some note. His tone said he had no idea who she was, or why she was crowding the faculty-only parking lot with her ancient Volvo. If black men were barely noticed on Ivy League campuses, even by the most liberal of their colleagues, black women were invisible. Julia's mad mother, back when she was teaching at Dartmouth, would have taken the time to lash the professor with the rough side of her tongue, after which she would likely have taken him to bed, because she had a thing for white men in general and intellectuals in particular. But Julia at the moment had no thing for anybody.

"Sorry," she said, and climbed into the car.

CHAPTER 4

MARY

(1)

To GET TO ARKADELPHIA, ARKANSAS, you fly into Little Rock, rent a car, and drive pretty much forever, sharing the turnpike with logging trucks and Wal-Mart trucks and construction trucks and produce trucks and those nameless, faceless behemoths that roar up behind you in sudden demand, commanding you to accelerate or clear the way or preferably both, then roll on past you in majestic anger, on eighteen, twenty, it sometimes feels like fifty wheels, the wash of air striking your poky little rental like a thunderclap. Bumper stickers proclaim that the right to bear arms will be the last to go. The radio preachers are louder than you remember from when last you tuned in. There is no obvious speed limit. You pass signs advertising churches, and statues advertising churches, and brightly lighted crosses advertising churches, and most of the signs bear pictures of American flags as well, and an awful lot are indistinguishable from the many banners cheering on the Republican Party, and eventually it dawns on you that you are not anywhere near New England any more.

Julia Carlyle, feeling oddly liberated, would ordinarily have viewed all of this in fascinated absorption, because her undergraduate training as a scientist made observation natural to her. But just now she was distracted, still working through her emotions about the sudden death of a man toward whom she had felt, once upon a time, passionate desire, murderous rage, and most other emotions in between. She had met Kellen when she was barely Vanessa's age, a freshman at Dartmouth. A younger and less distinguished and sinfully attractive Kellen Zant, at that time a graduate student, was serving as a teaching assistant for

Econ 101. Julia dropped by his office one afternoon for help on drawing indifference curves, and, as Granny Vee used to say, dreaming soon led to doing.

"You there, Moms?" asked Vanessa, beside her in the front seat of the rented Sable, lovely brown face with its long, expressive bone structure eerily placid behind the spray of chattering beaded braids.

"Hmmm?"

"You're not supposed to daydream while you're driving."

Julia knew her daughter was half teasing, half complaining, for she had not been behind the wheel of a car since February, or not that her parents knew. Granting her request to travel to the funeral had been Vincent Brady's bright idea, in order, he said, to bring mother and daughter closer together. Her father had opposed the trip, but the three of them had worked on him. In the end, they had not so much worn Lemaster down as given him what he needed most: somebody to blame in case things went awry. As for missing a couple of days of school, Vanessa was smart enough for her absence not to matter, yet marginal enough for her absence not to be noticed.

Perfect Jeannie was sleeping over with friends, a luxury not currently on what Vanessa called her permission list.

"I'm not daydreaming," said Julia, pulling into the right lane to allow a double trailer rig to rumble past. Scudding clouds made the sky's faint blue seem far away. The warmth was an unexpected treat. "I'm just thinking."

"About Kellen?"

"I think you mean 'Professor Zant,' honey."

"Whatever."

Julia almost stopped in the middle of the expressway. "No. Not *whatever*. It's a matter of—"

"Respect for my elders. I know." Vanessa's window was rolled down, and one arm lay along the sill. She wore a dark-blue dress and pearls, but persuading her had been a chore: had her mother allowed it, the teen would have worn jeans and clogs. Vanessa reveled in her own eccentricity. Last fall, until they caught her, she had twice managed to sneak off to school with her clothes on backward and inside out, an idea from some song, as a protest against conformity. "Moms? Did you respect him?"

"Respect him? Kellen?" Here was a new question.

But her daughter, chuckling, gave her no chance to think it through.

"I think you mean 'Professor Zant,'" Vanessa said. "Anyway, I don't think he was all that respectable."

"Come on, honey, you hardly knew him."

"Maybe not, but I've heard how you and Dads talk about him."

Lemaster, Julia told herself as she spotted the exit. Not me. Lemaster. I would never discuss Kellen in front of the children. But another part of her knew that over the past twenty years hardly a day had passed when Kellen Zant, restless, delightful, alluring, indulgent, amoral, had not claimed a secret corner of her thoughts.

(11)

LIKE THE EXPRESSWAY, the small city of Arkadelphia is mostly churches. Not literally, perhaps, but a first-time visitor must be forgiven for gaining that impression, for one seems to stand on every corner, and if most are home to evangelical congregations, the major denominations are also well represented.

Guided by the NeverLost system in the rented car, Julia rolled past grand Victorians and cookie-cutter raised ranches and dwellings so small they might as well be called shacks. On the stoops of the shacks sat the city's unsmiling poor, depressed and overweight, black and white alike. Caucasian poverty was another America in which she had little experience.

To reach the church, she passed a warehouse, squeezed down a narrow side street, and made a sharp left at a red brick elementary school. The building was small and neat and wooden and whitewashed, the mourning rambunctious and weepy. The casket was closed. The scatterings of family sat in the front, pride of place given to Seth Zant, the tireless uncle, hero of every story Kel told of his childhood. That Kellen never knew his father provided a common pain about which he and Julia used to talk, for he lacked Lemaster's abiding faith in the plain virtue of withholding the deepest sufferings of the self. Kellen's teenaged mother died of an overdose, and Seth came into his life. The unlettered auto mechanic, along with his late wife, Sylvia, had raised the remarkable boy, who set records all through grade school. The family relation was distant. Kellen was languid and lanky, with the easy grace that some possess as a gift and others envy all their lives. Seth was squat and wide, built close to the ground, as if to improve his chances at survival in a cruel world. His shiny Sunday suit was of uncertain age, but proudly worn. Aunts and cousins adorned the rest of the pew. Nadia, Kellen's ex-wife, sat one row back, strawberry-blond hair marking the spot, some sort of computer maven in Silicon Valley, clutching the hand of a sullen boy of perhaps ten who had to be the son of whom Kellen often spoke, but whom Julia had never met. Nadia and Kellen had wed at Stanford, where he taught for five years. The marriage had been brief, lasting only as long as it took Kellen to find a job back east, for settling down was never his way; Kellen being Kellen, the inventor of Zant-Feldman, every economics department in New England made him an offer. He chose to move to Elm Harbor, and Julia chose not to wonder why.

"Moms," said Vanessa, mouth almost touching her ear. They were in a pew near the back, wanting not to intrude, although Julia knew Seth had seen her. The small building was no more than half full, but the noise shook the rafters. Having worshiped for the past decade at an austere and traditionalist Anglican congregation, Julia was unprepared for either the length or the enthusiasm of the service. The pastor, a thick-chested man with a limp, had been speaking for what seemed hours, dragging his bad leg as he galloped back and forth in the front of the church—there was no altar, or not as Julia had come to understand the word—and the congregation supported him with loud hallelujahs and amens. There was piano and singing and clapping. A couple of the women held tambourines and used them, constantly and inexpertly. A couple of relatives fainted. Not exactly the Clan at prayer, but Vanessa got into it, up on her feet swaying and clapping and singing even when she knew none of the words. Julia had forgotten how joyous faith could be; or perhaps she had never known, for the divinity school where she had once studied and now worked lived out its days in a fog of ideology and historical-critical methodology, unaware that such excitement over God existed, except as an irrational adjunct, as it was thought on campus, to Republican Party politics.

"Moms!" said Vanessa, louder this time.

"Keep your voice down, honey. What is it?"

"Look."

"Look where?"

Vanessa stretched a slender arm to point past her mother, toward the only white mourner not related to Nadia, a fierce-looking woman with a thick tangle of black hair, and an expensive scarf so sloppily knotted that Julia guessed the woman had donned it in a moving vehicle and made the funeral with minutes to spare: although in truth she had been there when they arrived.

"What about her?" said Julia softly, trying for the sake of politeness not to peek too obviously. The woman seemed terribly angry, as if her day had gone terribly wrong, but tying your violet Hermès silk scarf in a car, poorly, will tend to do that.

"She didn't like him very much."

"She what?" Two pews ahead, a stout dark matron in elaborate Sunday hat turned and glared. Julia cringed. "And keep your voice down."

"Kellen. She hated Kellen."

So did every other woman he ever dated, or tried to. "Professor Zant or Mr. Zant. How can you tell that?"

"Look at her face, Moms," murmured Vanessa, who possessed her mother's talent for reading other people, and her father's certainty that you had to be most kinds of fool to disagree with the conclusions of so brilliant a brain. "That's not missing somebody. That's checking to make sure he's dead, so you don't have to kill him all over again."

"Come on, honey. Why would she be here if she hated Kel— Professor Zant?"

Vanessa continued to stare, ignoring her mother's commands to stop. Twice she seemed about to explain. But, nine months after the fire, there remained moments when, for all her charm and chatter, Vanessa got tangled in the whirlwind of her peculiar mind and could not manage her intended words. She dropped her sharp chin, settled back against the worn polished pew, and shut her eyes in confusion, even if it looked like prayer.

(I I I)

OUTSIDE, in the sunshine, flowing from one group of chattering relatives to the next, never identifying herself beyond her name and the claim of being an old friend, Julia lost sight of her daughter. Vanishing was among Vanessa's specialties. Vincent Brady described the habit as natural, born of a need for control and independence, but Lemaster said she was obstreperous. Julia refused to panic, reasoning that the girl could not go far in an unfamiliar town, and made her way over to Nadia to offer condolences. The ex-wife had hard golden eyes. Whatever her politics back home, she was exhausted from so much exuberant blackness. Julia perceived at once that the woman did not need another hug, and so shook her hand instead. Nadia, upon hearing the name, grew chilly and dismissive. Kellen and Nadia had not even met back when he had whatever he had with Julia, and yet the woman looked ready to fight. Julia wondered what Kellen had told his wife, and when. A part of his charm in a woman's life was that you always believed what he said; a part of his terror was that you always knew you shouldn't.

Julia spoke briefly to rugged Seth, who asked her to come to the house later on: "I got something Kellen would of wanted you to have." He gave a ferocious wink that promised to make the visit worth her while. Now she knew where Kellen had learned it. "Dress casual." Turning, Julia saw Vanessa around the side of the church, laughing easily with a bevy of kids her own age and younger, Nadia's scrawny son among them. Whatever Vanessa was saying had the boy smiling. Julia smiled, too. People always adored her daughter on first meeting and even second, but that third one could be a mess. Her smile faded as she remembered the precocious child who had loved piano and ballet and Sunday school, who devoured books of word games instead of sweets, whose special smile was reserved for her mother alone. Then, although she tried to resist, her mind skipped to the terrible night last February when Vanessa burned the Mercedes.

Lemaster had been out of town as usual, and Julia had to face the early hours without him. The first officer on the scene, a baby-faced old man of thirty who had never seen anything like this in his life because the Landing had no crime to speak of, asked Vanessa what she had done and why she did it, not the way the courts prescribe, and surely inadmissible, but never mind, the case would never go to trial. The former straight-A student, by then somewhere in the B-minus range or worse, shrugged her slim shoulders, never quite looking at him, and said, voice dull with lost hope, *Why not?* Then, gazing at the conflagration, blood smudging her wrists, the hint of a smile tugging at her lips, she added, *Isn't it the most awesome thing?* At the hospital, they strapped her down for two days, trying one sedative after another until they got the dosage right. Waiting for her husband to return, Julia sat in the corridor with a Sister Lady or two, listening as Vanessa begged for somebody, anybody, to please, please come and kill her.

"Julia?" said a soft voice. "Mrs. Carlyle?"

Relieved at the distraction, she swung around, and found herself face-to-face with the wild-haired woman who had sat near them in the pew. The anger had vanished, but the redness in the stranger's sallow cheeks proposed that it was on call twenty-four hours a day. The Hermès scarf was if anything more crooked than before. She looked to be about Julia's age, and her bearing suggested that she had seen a lot of life.

"Have we met?" said Julia, with her mother's hauteur, because strangers had no entitlement to use her first name. "Ms.—uh—"

"Mallard," the woman said, and indeed she displayed a birdlike fussiness, mouth flaring as though she might at any moment quack, satiny hand brushing Julia's like a feather. "Mary Mallard."

"How did you know Kellen?"

"You mean, what am I doing here, given that I'm white?" Julia blushed, and there turned out to be space on Mary Mallard's ducklike countenance for a smile after all. "I'm not one of his women, if that's what you're thinking. No, no, we were working on a project together. We didn't finish. Too bad." A lift of the long flat chin. "You missed the wake."

"We just flew in this morning," Julia explained, unexpectedly apologetic. Whatever Mary Mallard's profession, she excelled at putting people off their ease.

"I know. I expected you last night."

"Expected me?"

At the curb, mourners were piling into their cars for the wailing trip to the cemetery. Mary Mallard fiddled with her scarf. "I only had time to collect one of the pieces. I need the other three."

"Pieces of what?"

"The surplus."

Julia felt like a simpleton at the genius convention, but perhaps it was the sun. "I'm sorry. The surplus what?"

"I'm a writer, Mrs. Carlyle. I'm a little surprised you haven't heard of me." From anyone else this would have been a pouty complaint, but Mary was only stating fact. Her fingers poked at the tangly hair, but it was hopeless. The jutting mouth gave her a comic look that Julia knew to be a deception. Mary Mallard was a very serious woman, whose clear, skeptical eyes knew you were lying before you did. "I do investigative reports."

Julia's tired brain finally drew the name and the face from hundreds of hours of insomnia-fueled late-night talk shows. "You do those scandal books. Who really killed JFK. The plot against Martin Luther King. Things like that. Conspiracy theories."

"I like to take a closer look at things that the rest of the media prefers to bury, yes."

"I'm afraid I haven't read any. They're not exactly my cup of—"

"Please don't pull that Ivy League superiority crap." Tone still calm, as if reporting the weather. Vanessa, over by the side of the church, was sneaking looks at her mother, obviously wishing she could listen in. "Kellen trusted me completely. So should you."

"What am I supposed to trust you with?"

"Come on, Julia. The surplus. Capturing the surplus. That's what Kellen called it."

"I don't follow."

"He said the buyers' utility functions were interdependent, and that was going to help him capture the surplus. He shared some of the surplus with me. He said you'd have the rest of it."

Julia shook her head. "This is news to me. And it isn't even in English."

"Kellen had a scar on his face. About here." Gentle fingers touched Julia's cheek beneath the right ear. She shivered, not from the caress, but from the memory. She knew exactly where the scar was, and where it came from: her fingernails. She had been trying, with reason, to gouge Kellen's eyes out. On television a couple of years ago, busily lying about his childhood, he had called it a souvenir from a gang war. "Just a tiny white circle. You'd hardly notice if you didn't know it was there. But Kellen showed it to me."

"I see."

"I'm telling you so that you'll trust me. I really was close to Kellen, Julia—may I call you Julia?—and we really did work together."

"If you say so."

"The thing is, he only gave me the photograph." Shifting her weight, she drew a pack of cigarettes from her handbag, glanced around, then thought better of the urge. "Well, the photograph isn't enough. It doesn't prove anything. Kellen knew that. He said it was just a teaser. So he slept on the sofa. So what?"

Julia wondered whether she was logier than she thought, from rising so early and driving so far, or whether the journalist really was making as little sense as she seemed to. "I'm sorry, Ms. Mallard. Mary. I'm not sure what we're talking about here."

The ducklike mouth turned down. "Really? Well, that's unfortunate."

"What's unfortunate?"

"I thought you would have the other three pieces. I'm sure Kellen said so."

"If you would tell me what other three pieces you mean—"

Mary shook her head. "If you're lying to me, that's one thing. If you're not—" She shrugged. "Nice meeting you anyway."

"But—"

The writer had already turned away. Now she swung back. "I'm going to skip the cemetery, Julia. I've had as much Kellen as I can take, I think." Bushy eyebrows drew together. "There's just one problem. If you don't have the other pieces of the surplus, who does?" A puzzled shake of the head. "He seemed so sure."

CHAPTER 5

THE ONE WHO GOT AWAY

(1)

FROM THE CEMETERY, Julia and Vanessa made their way to a lovely Victorian bed and breakfast on North Tenth Street, to shower and change in a room of Versailles-like proportions, so sparsely but tastefully furnished it was like being outdoors. Vanessa enthused over the gold leaf on the beveled bathroom mirror, and Julia's practiced eye labeled it nineteenth-century, Louis XVI style, probably made by hand in New Orleans, and, certainly, worth a bit of money. For a moment, she thought of offering to buy it, for antiques were her fifth or sixth love, and she knew quality. The gilding was directly on the glass—a rarely seen process known as églomisé—and the mirror included a transparent panel at the top with another gilded design painted inside. Sometimes life with Lemaster felt like gilding on glass, too: the rest of the Clan envied her perfect marriage, but Julia knew its slick, shining fragility. She peered closer. Mirrors were her thing. Granny Vee bought them everywhere she went, and the collection in her Edgecombe Avenue mansion had once been the pride of Harlem, but most of them wound up in France with Julia's mother, who sold them piece by piece, along with anything else of value she could put her hands on, in order to write checks to organizations pledging to end war, poverty, ignorance, oppression, and hatred, preferably by next month.

Julia ran her fingers along the filigree, wondering, absurdly, if the intricate scrollwork might conceal a microphone. She had no idea why she was thinking this way; Mary Mallard must have really spooked her. Remembering her purpose, she asked Vanessa what she and the other kids had been talking about.

"Oh, you know," she said, the fingers that now and again lived lives of their own stumbling over the fastener of the Mikimoto choker until Julia helped her. To Lemaster's consternation, Julia refused to wear fakes, or to allow her daughters to, because, she said, the Clan would notice. "Just old stories."

"Stories about Professor Zant?" She was still looking at the mirror, studying the lovely églomisé. The Eggameese, Vanessa had called it as a toddler, after once mishearing her mother on the telephone with a dealer, complaining that a particular églomisé was too loud, and had for a time imagined it to be a snarling night crawler who lived in her bedroom mirror: *Mommy, Daddy, I'm scared, the Eggameese was looking at me!*

"About the colleges down here and stuff. History. They have really cool traditions and everything, ghosts, this killer tornado a few years ago, famous battles. Stuff like that. Did you know they evacuated the whole town in the Civil War?"

Appropriate African-American umbrage. "Probably just the white people."

"Yeah." Like the rest of her generation, she could not have cared less. "They have this famous park. Oh, Moms, listen." Vanessa's gray eyes lit up. She was speaking, as she often did when her strange brain leaped into overdrive, much too fast. "They should call it 'A Hailed Park.' "

"Why?"

"It's an anagram of 'Arkadelphia.' " Anagrams being her special talent, and special love.

"You did that just now? In your head?"

Vanessa, bristling, missed the point. "Well, it was the best I could come up with on the spur of the moment." Her irritation faded, and the shoulders sagged again. Vanessa loved playing with words. Lemaster thought she wasted her mind on these games, but Dr. Brady encouraged them. Julia thought of anagrams as ghostly mirrors of words and phrases, some of them gilded. "Anyway, they asked me if there were any stories about where we live, and I told them all we have is snow."

Julia's next question came out nervously, because the Clan taught the presentation of the family to the world as perfection. To air your dirty laundry was a treasonable offense. "You didn't tell them about . . . about Gina?"

Vanessa crinkled her nose and grinned. "Oh, Moms, come on. You know how Gina hates when I talk about her."

"Right. Right. So you've said." Both returned to their dressing, the daughter serenely, the mother uneasily. Julia dared not say more. She and Vanessa quarreled constantly, as adolescent girls and their mothers do, and Julia reveled in these rare moments of peace.

Gina Joule, according to one theory, was the cause of Vanessa's peculiar mania. The other view held that Vanessa's obsession with Gina was only a symbol, a sort of Jungian manifestation of a deeper trauma. Gina was seventeen, like Vanessa, a resident of the Landing, also like Vanessa—and her father, like Vanessa's, taught at the university. As a matter of fact, Merrill Barnes Joule had been the beloved dean of the divinity school: another connection. Merrill Joule had even been a leading candidate for president of the university, but events had overtaken him. Gina was a shy, creative child, as Vanessa was, her only true experience with the opposite sex having begun in the fall of her eleventh-grade year: that is, about the time Vanessa had her own first date. She had Vanessa's height, moderate smile, and slightly gangly grace, for Vanessa kept an enlargement of a newspaper photograph of Gina atop her dresser until Dr. Brady urged her, Julia begged her, and Lemaster ordered her to take it down.

Whenever Vanessa unexpectedly vanished for an hour or two, she would explain that Gina needed her, and leave it at that. True, Gina was white, and Julia had never forgotten her mother's dictum about finding her children black friends. Gina's skin color, however, was very far from being the largest problem in the friendship between the two girls. Nor was the largest problem that Vanessa had surprised everybody, including her teacher, with the last-minute announcement a year ago that she had changed the topic of her term paper for AP United States history— she had decided to write about Gina. No, the largest problem was that Merrill Joule had been in the ground a good quarter-century, and his daughter, Gina, had drowned at the town beach back when a stamp cost eight cents, Cokes were a dime, and Leonid Brezhnev ran the Soviet Union.

(11)

IT WAS THE TERM PAPER, of course, that had started all Vanessa's problems, far too much to demand of eleventh-graders, which was what Vanessa was when she flubbed the paper and burned the car. Advanced Placement American History asked the unreasonable. So Julia believed, anyway, and, less agnostic on the matter of her daughter than on the matter of the God she professed every Sunday at the adamantly defiant Saint Matthias, she clung to this view in the face of contrary arguments by doctors, teachers, her august husband, even Vanessa herself, who insisted, a year later, that she still wanted to finish the research. The paper had earned an embarrassing C+ because, although the text was elegantly written, its use of sources, said Ms. Klein, was thin—and Julia, who had read it, agreed.

A year ago, Vanessa had been an honor student, with ambitions not unlike those of her older brother, who left high school at sixteen to enroll at the Massachusetts Institute of Technology. The intervening months had been painful ones for her résumé. Her test scores were still high, but, between her behavior, her arrest, and her rapidly dropping grades, the college counselors no longer knew what to counsel. Vanessa had said more than once that she would happily attend the state university, or even a two-year college, but Lemaster, the immigrant, was in matters educational a considerable snob; as, for that matter, were Julia and most of the Clan.

At the regional high school, where African Americans were less than 2 percent of the student body, Preston's buddies had mostly been math and computer nerds, but Vanessa hung out with more marginal citizens, as Lemaster in his clever way labeled them. Her activities were eerily eclectic. History Club, coalition for animal rights, trivia bowl team. A strange, conflicted child. Loved hip-hop but sang in the medieval choir. Worked crossword puzzles and anagrams like a demon but suffered from unsuspected misspellings whenever she wrote a paper. Served as vice-president of both Young Republicans and COGS, the Coalition of Gays and Straights. She was a declared and aggressive pacifist but liked to read about war. The shelves in her bedroom sported books on famous battles, as well as plastic models of warplanes and ships built from kits and a collection of yellowing board games from Avalon Hill, unearthed at estate sales and on eBay: Gettysburg, Waterloo, Iwo Jima. Some evenings, she would walk around the house with a volume on some ancient battle in her hands, chanting like a monk from the Middle Ages. Lemaster refused to put up with it, but Julia, when acting alone, could not seem to make her stop. "It makes me happy, Moms," the teen would insist, knowing how to make her mother bend. Julia only wished that fewer of Vanessa's chants had the timbre of funeral marches.

At first it had been all right: Vanessa, in October a year ago, had decided to write her paper on the response in the Landing to the Supreme Court's school desegregation decisions in the fifties, and began dutifully putting in her time at the public library, the archives of the board of education, and, finally, the Harbor County Historical Society. Then Vanessa announced a change in her topic. No longer did the story about the fifties interest her. Instead, she had grown fascinated by the death of Gina, a loner like herself. Julia, by instinct still a teacher of teens, at once raised an objection: what thesis could she possibly craft around Gina? For Gina's story was well known. She had disappeared one night after last being seen in the company of a black teenager from the city who, never formally accused of the crime, was coincidentally slain by police just days later, after stealing a car, an event that led to the only race riot in the county's history. In the meantime, Gina's body washed up. She had been sexually assaulted, police said, and had fought back.

Vanessa answered that she did not care about the thesis, she cared about poor Gina. She would say no more. The Carlyles fretted. Other AP history students over the years had found themselves enchanted by Gina's story, but none of them—Lynn Klein warned Julia—had written good papers. Even Preston had taken a brief look, before abandoning the topic for a richer one. Julia consoled herself, and her husband, with the fact that the term paper was not due until March, and if their daughter seemed a little bit lost at sea, she was at least getting an early start on the journey back to safe land. Then Vanessa began to avoid her friends, her grades began to slip, and Lemaster, to whose immigrant sensibility the report card was everything, was ready, as he put it, to take measures.

But Vanessa beat him to it, torching the car on the thirtieth anniversary of Gina's death, and drawing the family into its current spiral.

"I did it for Gina" was the only explanation she ever offered: to the team of psychiatrists at the university hospital, to her therapist, Vin Brady, to her parents, to her eager classmates, among them That Casey, whose interest in her never ripened beyond casual dating until after the fire.

Vanessa did finally finish the paper, although not until April, the final product every bit as dismal as her parents and her teacher had feared, for she presented little more than a handful of newspaper accounts reporting that Gina had vanished, and that the disappearance remained unsolved. "You need a stronger thesis," wrote Ms. Klein, "and a larger diversity of evidence."

Vanessa asked if she could do another draft. Ms. Klein said of course, but made no promises to change her grade. Seven months later, Vanessa was working on it still. Julia kept a copy in her office cabinet, in what she privately called the Vanessa File, along with the photo of Gina Joule that used to grace her daughter's dresser. Lynn Klein did not know—nobody did, outside the family and Dr. Brady—that now and then Vanessa and Gina sat down for little chats.

(III)

THE HOUSE WAS TWO STORIES HIGH, boxy and blue-shingled, on a sunny side street. Hedges were neatly trimmed, but the faded flower boxes on the front step sat empty. Half a dozen cars jammed the curb, dominated by a wounded truck that sat exhausted in the driveway. The large black dog dozing on the cracked concrete of the walk looked too old to do much guarding. Pretty curtains hung in the windows, and Julia had an instinct that they were homemade. Seth Zant sat on the top step with a Pepsi in his hand, watching Julia squeeze into the last remaining parking spot. She wondered what gift he held in store.

"You made it," said Seth. "Good."

"Of course we did."

He gave Vanessa a long look. "Bet you have to beat the boys off with a stick."

The teenager colored and dropped her eyes and could not get a syllable out. Julia squeezed her daughter's frozen hand and answered for her. "We try to be as gentle on them as we can. We only bring out the stick in emergencies."

Not too funny, but Seth laughed anyway, to tell them both he got the point.

The gathering was the sort that Lemaster handled brilliantly, Julia poorly, and Vanessa not at all, for the teen stayed mostly in the corner next to the punch bowl until one of the endless train of relatives dragged her into the kitchen and pressed her into service refreshing the platters of fried fish and fried chicken and barbecued ribs heaped on the dining room table. Seth Zant also did his share of dragging. Instead of passing along whatever he had invited Julia to collect, he introduced her to various people as "the great love of Kellen's life" or "the one who got away," until, unable to bear any more, she begged him to stop. So instead he sat her on the sofa like the guest of honor and let the others take turns sitting beside her and saying pretty much what Seth had, preceding it always with "So, Julia, I hear you were . . ." Everyone had a Kellen story to share.

A hefty churchwoman named Ellie, who grew up with Kellen and sounded like she might have had a considerable crush on him, described an inquisitive, impatient kid who got into lots of fights, even with children a whole lot bigger than he was, because, Julia, he had such a good heart, always going around looking to protect the weak. He did the Lord's work, Julia, no matter what mischief he got up to once he went North. Julia nodded politely. An ancient man called Old Tim told how, back in high school, Kellen even faced down a fella with a knife who was bothering a girl at a party. "He was just in high school, Kellen, a skinny little ninth-grader, but he almost killed a man that night, and never lost a minute's sleep over it."

Tell her the rest, said Ellie.

Oh, and he also got the girl. That was Kellen, Old Tim explained, while various relatives, Vanessa helping, cleared the dinner dishes and presented the lemon meringue pie and homemade ice cream, which Julia's better angels failed to persuade her to decline. "That's why men do most stupid things," Old Tim said, twinkling. He put aside his empty pie plate and patted his ample gut. "To impress some girl."

"I think it was brave," said Ellie, and Julia wondered if she had been the girl. But another part of her remembered other fights Kellen had picked during their year and a half together in Manhattan, usually with bigger men, bars he had been thrown out of, nightclubs that had banned him. She remembered how one particular battle ended with her standing terrified over the gurney in the emergency room at Saint

Luke's–Roosevelt Hospital in midtown Manhattan while a tut-tutting Indian doctor used tweezers to pull shards of glass out of his shoulder. Your boyfriend, said the doctor, is a very angry man. One reason Julia recalled that episode so sharply was that she was the one who had hit him with the bottle. "Very brave," Ellie confirmed, with a warm glow.

Old Tim was unimpressed. "You know what the difference is between brave and stupid? Brave is when you fight because you have to. Stupid is when you fight because you want to. That was Kellen's problem right there. He loved to fight."

Seth was beside her. "Can I borrow you for a minute, honey?" She glanced automatically at the kitchen, where from her vantage point on the sofa she could see Vanessa scrubbing pots under the watchful eyes of the matrons. The teen seemed perfectly content, soothed by the repetitive motion. "She'll be fine," said Seth, following her gaze. "This won't take long."

Now dressed casually in clean khakis and a stained shirt, Seth led her up a narrow stair to the room above the one-car garage. She knew at once that the room was Kellen's, not so much from the squeaky-clean nattiness of posters and bed and books, or from the economics and math and science texts lining the walls. No, the way she knew was from the delicate silver hand mirror lying atop the dresser.

"That's mine," she blurted, although she had not clapped eyes on it since the final split from Kellen. She rushed across the room and swept it up. "That's my mirror!"

"Been up here for years," said Seth, watching her.

"For years?"

"I figured it was a lady's mirror, not a man's. But Kellen liked to have it around."

"He did?" said Julia, face suddenly warm. She picked it up. It was silver and tortoiseshell, intricately filigreed on the handle and the back, manufactured in the late nineteenth century by the famous British maker William Comyns, whose hallmark was embossed on the handle, hidden within the design. Granny Vee had given it to her just months before her death. Julia had cherished it, but left it behind in Kellen's apartment when Tessa, against Julia's will, had dragged her physically out of Manhattan to save her from further mistreatment. For a while she had been scared to ask for it back, worried that to speak to Kellen at all would be to tumble back into his bed; and then, when she met

Lemaster and grew stronger, she was too embarrassed. The mirror had little value in the antiques market—two or three hundred dollars at most—and until now Julia had assumed that at some point Kellen had tossed it, or sold it, or given it to another woman. "I never knew what happened to it," she said truthfully.

"He wanted you to have it. He told me lots of times. I didn't know it was yours to begin with."

"I don't know what to say."

The dam of Julia's will had held back the tears through the flight and the drive and the service and even the burial, but now they found the fissures and began to flow. Seth Zant, wise enough to say nothing, handed her his handkerchief. She dabbed her eyes. The small window gave on the twilit driveway, where people were packing leftovers into their cars. Laughter, hugs, departures. She blew her nose. She used the mirror to fluff out her hair. She turned it over, rubbed the surface with her fingernail, checking the finish. Kellen had not taken care of the silver, allowing it to tarnish. She glanced at the hallmark. Scratched in several spots, hardly recognizable. In her mind she reduced the value from two or three hundred dollars to between twenty-five and fifty.

Wait.

"Seth?"

"Hmmm?"

"Did Kellen leave . . . anything else for me?" Knowing it would sound greedy, but needing to know. Mary Mallard had put the idea in her head. Capturing the surplus. Whatever that was.

"Anything like what?"

"Wow, Moms," said Vanessa from behind her. "Look at you. You were so gorgeous in those days!"

Julia turned. Her daughter stood smiling in the doorway, studying a photo in a plastic frame atop the dresser. Julia had noticed it when she walked in, and ignored it. Now she walked over and, sure enough, there she was, arm in arm with Kellen, strolling along Broadway, which Kellen, like most black men, despised on principle. But he went from time to time for her sake, as, now, Lemaster did. She was wearing a halter top, and high platforms, and absurd little shorts. Had she really dressed that way? She lifted the William Comyns mirror, looked at herself at forty-three, tried to remember what twenty-three had been like.

"No, I mean, sure, okay, you're gorgeous now, but wow." Fully in the room now, leaning over to study the image. "This is seriously cool. I love that outfit. I want five just like it." Chuckling because she was one up. "So, were the two of you like an item or something?"

"Vanessa, honey, I'm not really comfortable talking about—"

"Your mother was the great love of my nephew's life," Seth confirmed, unhelpfully. "Always called her the one that got away."

"That sounds really romantic," said Vanessa, now at the shelves, pawing through the books as if the bedroom were a library rather than a carefully tended shrine. Outside, a breeze stirred the darkening trees. Winter might be less severe down here, but it was coming. "And so totally cool."

"It was a . . . a long time ago."

"You can have the photo too if you want," said Seth.

Vanessa said, "Does Daddy know?"

"Of course your father knows," Julia said, slowly sinking. Whose idea had it been for Vanessa to tag along? Who had invented children anyway?

"I guess you always had a thing for older men, huh?" Vanessa had taken down a calculus text, riffling the pages as if hoping money would fall out.

"Ah, Vanessa, that's not . . . uh, an appropriate thing to say."

"Not that Kellen wasn't seriously hot. So I can understand it."

"Vanessa!"

Her daughter was not listening. She had started turning the pages faster, glaring at her own hands because they refused to stop, as would sometimes happen, said Dr. Brady, when she struggled to choke off the trauma within—a trauma that remained unidentified, and whose existence Vanessa denied, although Brady assured them it was there. Julia, the mother in her aroused, forgot her embarrassment and, following the psychiatrist's instructions, touched Vanessa on the shoulder and told her gently to put the book back on the shelf.

"Let her be," said Seth Zant. "There's nothing valuable up here." Julia started to explain, but he rode right over her. "I mean, the books and the pictures and the mirror are about all they left."

"They?"

Seth tapped the desk with a fingernail. "Kellen used to come down for a week or two at a time to work. Get away from it all. Had his computer right here, printer, notebooks, I don't know what all. Anyway, that's what they took."

"Who did?"

"Had a little break-in while I was up north claiming the body. Funny, though. Got a fair-sized television downstairs, Sylvia's jewels, and what-not. But I guess the dog musta spooked them or something, because they only did this one room, and all they took was Kellen's work."

CHAPTER 6

INVENTORY RISK

(1)

LITTLE JEREMY FLEW MET THEM at the airport, because Lemaster, who was supposed to have picked them up, was in New York for a meeting of Empyreals, a minor black social club of which he was a dedicated member. He had called Julia to say that afterward he would probably just take the train to Washington rather than come back, because a friend who held Redskins season tickets had invited him to tomorrow's game. Julia scarcely bothered to mask her fury and, in her pique, commanded Flew to carry their bags, which, uncomplaining, he did. He chattered all the way to the parking lot, mostly about the weather, but also about how that awful Kwame Kennerly had been on the radio again, bad-mouthing the university, its new president, and the fact that said president lived in Tyler's Landing. Ignoring this intelligence, Julia snapped out her cell phone to call Wendy Tollefson, at whose house Lemaster had arranged for Jeannie to spend the night: Wendy, who adored Jeannie, being a friend of Julia's from her teaching days. She had no children of her own, and often stayed at Hunter's Heights to look after the girls when both adult Carlyles had to be out of town.

Jeannie asked could she please sleep over anyway, they were playing Monopoly.

Flew had brought a Land Rover owned by the university, for greater traction in the snow, and Julia, in her dudgeon, climbed with Vanessa into the back seat, perhaps to remind him that he was really a glorified chauffeur. She was not mad at Mr. Flew, she was mad at Lemaster, but he was not around to be kicked, so she kicked his aide instead. She hated this side of her personality, wanting to be as warm and informal in everyday life as most people thought she was, but a part of her inheritance from Mona was a need now and then to display her Clannishness—especially around members of what Lemaster's fraternity, the Empyreals, liked to call members of the paler nation.

"Are you hungry?" said Flew from the front as the car ticked through the snow.

"No," said Julia.

"Yes," said Vanessa.

"I have a little something waiting for you at the house, or we could stop on the way if you like. There's fast food, of course, and there's also a lovely seafood place—"

"I've lived in the county since the early eighties," Julia interrupted. All the way back to when Kellen nearly killed her. "I know where the restaurants are."

The little man's mood was impossible to shake. Friendly blue eyes met hers in the mirror. "Isn't it amazing, Mrs. Carlyle, how, no matter how much we know about something, we can always learn something new?"

Julia colored, then colored some more, aware of Vanessa's bemused scrutiny behind supposedly sleeping eyes. Unable to work out a suitable riposte, Julia apologized for her bitchiness, assuring Mr. Flew that he was not to blame even as he assured her he was not offended. She watched the scenery for a while, feeling deserted and lonely, as she often did within the shell of her dutiful marriage. Lemaster preached constantly on the primacy of obligation rather than desire in moral life, and Julia often wondered, but never dared ask, whether he might have in mind his relationship with his wife. Was there something he would rather be doing instead? With someone else? She did not believe he had cheated on her in twenty years of marriage, but one never knew for sure. Her college roommate, Tessa Kenner, had been married briefly to a black man, a historian of some note, who had treated her badly. Tessa, in those days a law professor rather than a television anchor, had forgiven him readily, almost happily, for what she called his peccadilloes, explaining once to Julia, over coffee, that this was simply a need all black males possessed, born of centuries of racial oppression, to liberate themselves from the repressive strictures of bourgeois sexual custom.

I'm sure you have the same trouble with Lemaster, Tessa had murmured with the quick, sloppy racial judgment of the white intellectual, holding her cup in both hands, the way people did in television commercials and nowhere else.

I most certainly do not.

Tessa had nodded, blue eyes full of pity at the romantic self-deception of so many women who, if only they saw the world unadorned and authentic, would toss off the shackles of tradition and false consciousness and build something thrilling and new.

"You can be such a bitch sometimes," said Julia, maybe to Tessa, maybe to herself, maybe even to Mona, because she had been dreaming and now snapped awake as the Land Rover hit the gravel of the long driveway up to Hunter's Heights. She blinked and glanced around. Vanessa was still out, for real this time.

"Thanks," said Julia to Mr. Flew. "That was fast. And very smooth."

Jeremy Flew was not listening. He had slowed at the switchback several hundred feet from the house, the headlights washing over the snow, the thickly huddled trees beyond inky and silent in the darkness. "Was there an accident, Mrs. Carlyle?"

"An accident?"

He had stopped the car. The yellow cone from the headlights picked out two of the smart black coach lamps that lined the Carlyle driveway every twenty feet, both broken off at the base and lying in the snow.

"Oh, that. It happened in the storm last week. The night—the night Professor Zant died. I think Mr. Huebner hit them with the plow. I already left two messages, but he hasn't called me back." Julia wondered whether she was giving too much information, because Jeremy, in the mirror, was looking at her oddly. "You wouldn't know him," she gabbled on, wishing she knew how to change the subject. "But Mitch Huebner is kind of a legend in the Landing, living out there in the woods with his guns and his dogs and never a word to say to anybody anyway. I don't think he's really much of a telephone guy. Maybe I should send him a note."

The silence was deep and thrilling as Julia waited to see how much of this nonsense Lemaster's assistant would choose to believe.

"Are you sure?" said Mr. Flew at last. "That it was Mitch Huebner?"

"As opposed to whom?"

"The newspapers report that there is a good-sized dent in the front left fender of Professor Zant's car. The police have asked anybody who might have had a hit-and-run accident last Friday to call, et cetera, et cetera."

Julia rubbed her eyes. She looked out the window. The switchback where the lamps were down made a little valley, from which you could see neither the house nor the road—meaning that neither the house nor the road could see you. The driveway was a plunging, winding, sliding, death-defying mess. Every winter Mr. Huebner's plow shaved off the gravel, piling it at the top of the hill, and every spring they paid him again to spread the gravel back down. "I still don't get your point," she lied. In the wing mirror demons capered, but it was just a trick of yellow light playing on blowing snow.

"The broken lamps are on the left side of your driveway."

"When Mr. Huebner has been drinking—"

"Perhaps you should call the police, Mrs. Carlyle."

Panic. Had the detectives noticed the lampposts last weekend? But they had not asked. Neither had Lemaster, or any of the many well-meaning visitors. "Jeremy, please. Listen to me. Kellen Zant was not at this house Friday night. Please, don't even suggest that."

"Is it possible that he was here and you didn't notice? You and Mr. Carlyle were at Lombard Hall most of the night."

"But that's just the point." Julia had trouble staying calm. "There was no reason for him to be here." Alongside the switchback was a turnaround, a flat surface where drivers could repair their mistakes. That was where the broken coach lamps were, at the turnaround. Julia drew herself up. "Lemaster and I were at the dinner for the alums. Vanessa had a date. Jeannie was supposed to be spending the night with a friend, but she got sick. Anyway, Kellen would have thought the house would be empty. So why come all the way up Hunter's Meadow in the storm if there was nobody home?"

"That's what I was wondering," said Mr. Flew. He put the Land Rover back into gear, and continued to climb the winding drive toward the looming house. Julia turned her head and watched the switchback until shadow claimed it.

(11)

LATER. Julia stood at her favorite spot in the living room window, looking downhill toward the road, wondering whether Kellen had really been in her driveway the night he died; and wondering, too, why she had not yet shared this possibility with the police, or even her husband. She wore woolen pajamas and her favorite housecoat, threadbare and ankle-length, blue and voluminous, left over from their honeymoon, which she believed to carry the family luck. She wore glasses to rest her eyes from the contacts. She had checked her e-mail and come away suitably uninvolved. She had tried to exchange instant messages with friends, but nobody she knew was on, not even Tessa, like herself a night owl. Surfing the Web had yielded fewer mentions of Kellen than she expected, but plenty of information on Mary Mallard, including Web sites dedicated to promoting her theories and Web sites dedicated to debunking them. An empty box of Vera's cappuccino truffles resided in the kitchen trash, snuggled against an empty bag of microwave popcorn—the unbuttered kind, because she was watching her weight.

She was thinking about her last encounter with Kellen himself, in the shopping mall up in Norport, three days before his murder.

I'm in trouble, he had told her, glancing around wildly as they sat in the food court, Julia wondering if their meeting was just chance. Several bags of Christmas presents circled her feet: she was an early shopper. *I need your help,* Kellen had added, which was what he always said.

Julia invited him to explain.

I can't hold my inventory. I have to spread the risk.

What risk?

The inventory risk. He grabbed her hand. She grabbed it back. *These are dark times,* said Kellen, who ordinarily avoided metaphors conflating darkness with evil. *They're dark times, and the dark matters. You're the only one who can help.*

Julia had started in on her speech about how he had to stop following her around, this could not go on, he had to leave her alone, the same speech she always delivered, and Kellen had started to explain, as he always did, that he was serious this time, he wasn't flirting, he really did need her help, and that was when she had spotted Regina Thackery and Bitsy Farnsworth, both Ladybugs, emerging from Lord & Taylor upstairs, and had leaped to her feet, telling Kellen she had to run, because the last thing she needed was for the Sister Ladies to spark stories about Julia's clandestine rendezvous with you-know-who.

I have to spread the risk. The inventory risk.

Another term from economics. Like *capturing the surplus.* Kellen loved his jargon, to be sure, and squeezed it into ordinary conversation as often as he could, usually to obscure his purposes, as he did back in their Manhattan days, when, after Julia tired of screaming at him, he would describe his flings with other women as rational exercises in maximizing utility. This time, however, she had a hunch that he had been trying to tell her something. Something that Mary Mallard thought she already knew.

Julia watched the snow, wondering if Kellen had really tried to make it up the driveway in that terrible storm the night he died, expecting the house to be empty, and whether, upon seeing the babysitter's car, he had turned in panic, striking the lamps. She did not understand why he would want to come to the house when nobody was home, any more than she knew what he had meant at the shopping mall when he said he wanted her to share his inventory risk; or that the dark mattered.

But maybe it was better not to care.

Kellen Zant was her past, and he had no right to drag her back into his life, even by dying and leaving a puzzle behind: he had wounded her, nearly killed her, and had no claim on her.

Standing in the living room window now, New England night softly alive around her, Julia gathered Rainbow Coalition into her arms, because the children were too big. She had coveted in life, and she had been coveted, and the messy life both produced was, she had thought, behind her. Lemaster was her sanity. Her safe harbor. Nothing else was supposed to happen.

But something had. First Vanessa burning the car, and now . . . all this.

Julia picked up the empty wineglass she had left on the low side table and turned toward the long living room, done in period green wallpaper, where the broad bay windows stretched from the nine-and-a-half-foot ceiling to eight inches above the floor. A grand piano, a vintage Steinway, filled the bay, salvaged from Amaretta Veazie's townhouse, where, in the old days, Duke Ellington would occasionally tickle its ivories. Preston and Aaron played badly, and the youngest, Jeannie, not at all. Vanessa played beautifully. When the extended family gathered last year for Thanksgiving, Julia and her daughter had presented the fruits of six weeks of rehearsal with an experienced coach, Rimsky-Korsakov's "Capriccio Espagnole," among the most challenging piano duets in the classical repertoire, and, despite a couple of flubs, brought tears to every eye, even Lemaster's.

"I hate this," Julia said, speaking of his job, and, implicitly, hers. Probably she was talking to her late brother, Jay, her twin. "I really, really hate this."

Jay did not reply.

She felt lonely and cold. Lemaster's dedication to his tiny fraternity annoyed her afresh. The Empyreals were dying; everybody said so. In the upper reaches of the darker nation, these memberships mattered in a way her white friends never quite understood. Lemaster could easily have joined one of the larger, more prestigious clubs, but had declined their overtures. Tonight of all nights, to go off to New York, and then to Washington—

She made herself stop. He had rescued her. It was as simple as that. She had truly loved only two men in her life, one who had destroyed her, one who had put her back together. Yet she wondered when life would stop happening to her and she would start happening to life.

Kellen wondered the same thing. He used to tease her about wasting her life. Maybe Mary Mallard was right. Maybe Kellen had left her his surplus. Maybe he even expected—

No. No. She would not pursue it. She would stay sane, which meant staying away from thoughts of Kellen. She stood in the window as the wind whipped the snow into high sleek drifts, wondering what had happened to all the rich, surging energy she poured into life. It was her brother's death all over again. Only three Marines died in the Grenada operation, but Jay Veazie was one of them. He received a posthumous Navy Cross for "extraordinary heroism," which Mona had thrown into the pond not far from their house on North Balch Street. After that, her politics went from radical to scary.

As for Kellen, well, as far as Julia was concerned, there was supposed to be a reckoning, not this absolute, this grim, gray wall, the scary firmness of life's end intruding on its middle. Absent a diagnosis of cancer or an unexpected stroke, the physical organism we call human was not supposed to betray the trust imposed by its owner, or not for many years to come. She remembered that last argument with Kellen, at the mall up in Norport, and how she had not let him finish whatever he was trying to tell her about *inventory risk* and how *the dark matters*. When she spotted Bitsy and Regina and jumped up, Kellen grabbed her arm and asked if they could set up a time to talk. Positive that his motives were as always ulterior, Julia had climbed on her high horse and told him that was probably not a good idea, and, by the way, would he please take his fucking hand off her arm?—for she was a different person around him, and a lot of the difference came out of her mouth. He said they really needed to talk, as soon as possible, and that they could meet in some out-of-the-way place if it would make her feel better. Julia, perhaps overwary, experienced these words as an invitation to dalliance, and told him to leave her be. The last thing she needed in her life was any of his nonsense, she told him, and the anger of her parting shot, her decision to turn on her heel and stalk away before Kellen had a chance to answer, was a gnawing pain in her gut: she had not even said goodbye.

CHAPTER 7

TRICKY TONY

(1)

AMONG JULIA'S FAVORITE STUDENTS was a peaceable fellow
named Poynting, a brilliant and puzzled gay activist who found himself drawn by the rigor and learning of Orthodox Christianity, and
hoped to find space within it for one narrow exception to the received
tradition—which he otherwise endorsed wholeheartedly, right down to
what the Orthodox and the Catholics called "fidelity to Apostolic tradition" and outsiders called "not letting women be priests." On the cold
but clear Monday morning following the funeral, Poynting sat in Julia's
office to ask about possible sources of grant funding for a proposed trip
to Bologna over the summer to research the confraternities established
in the thirteenth century to enforce the sexual mores of the Church.
Possibly what Joe Poynting really wanted was a free trip to Italy, but
most of her colleagues would be quick to accept one. So Julia, with a
few minutes to spare before she had to meet with her boss, took considerable pleasure in opening her well-ordered files to find a foundation
likely to support him. In the event, they found three or four, which was
three or four more than she found for most students looking for financial help to do something interesting, because religion in general, and
divinity school in particular, were considered unsexy. Finding ways to
twist student projects into smeary reflections of what the foundations
really wanted to fund was one of her favorite parts of the job: mirrors
were, after all, her thing.

As Poynting, quite happy, was leaving, Julia stopped him.

"Joe? Weren't you an econ major at Vanderbilt?"

"Years ago."

"But you remember some of the terminology?" Neatening her desk, sliding the application forms back into their proper folders, and the folders back into their proper drawers. "Like 'capturing the surplus.' What does that mean?"

Standing in the doorway, her student drummed his fingers on his own mouth. "Oh, well, you know. The consumer surplus, say, is the difference between the value of a good to you and what you pay for it. Theory says you'll only buy when the price is less than the value you place on it. The point is, the seller wants to make that spread as small as possible. That is, the seller wants to capture some of your surplus if he can. He does that by trying to get you to pay a price very close to the actual value you place on the good." Poynting laughed. "Or something like that."

Julia thought it over. As simple as that? "One more question."

"Shoot."

"Why would somebody think that the best way to capture the surplus is an auction?"

"Does this have something to do with that professor who got killed? The one who was your friend?" Diplomatically put. "Is that why you're asking?"

Julia hesitated. She knew that Joe Poynting, like many of the black students at the university, harbored an uneasy respect for Kellen Zant, who was seen, on the one hand, as the consummate race man, always on television decrying discrimination in corporate America; and, on the other, as a kind of racial entrepreneur, building a consulting-and-lecture-circuit empire on the foundation of the guilty consciences of white businessmen. Some of the students even considered Kellen a sellout. Julia was not sure exactly where on the spectrum young Poynting fell, and so, wanting not to offend, she settled for avoiding the question.

"Just help me out here, okay?"

"For you, anything." They grinned at each other. "The answer is what's called the 'winner's curse.' Suppose you're bidding for a good you plan to resell, but you aren't sure what the resale value is. You have to guess in order to bid. And the trouble is, if the auction is contested, you often have to bid more than the resale value to get the good. That is, you can't immediately turn around and sell for what you paid. If your motive is resale, in other words, it's possible for the seller in an auction to capture all of your surplus."

"Does that always happen?"

"Of course not. The market value might not be the most important thing. That is, you might want the good for reasons other than resale. And there are ways to set up auctions that try to avoid winner's curse and some of the other famous paradoxes. But I'm not really up on auction theory." He brightened. "I seem to remember Professor Zant published a paper on auctions a couple of years ago."

I'll just bet he did. "But what if somebody referred to something as his own surplus?"

"If he knew what he was talking about—if he was an economist, say—he would probably mean something he had managed to hold back in an exchange, something he would have been willing to give up but didn't have to." A pause as the young man seemed for a moment to look into her soul with all-seeing eyes. "Something of value to him."

"And inventory risk? What does that mean?"

"Oh, well, that's pretty basic. You're a businessman. You hold inventory for sale. The problem is, it can decline in value. You get stuck with computers nobody wants. Or with dresses that are out of style. You try to reduce your inventory risk. One good way to do it is to get somebody else to hold your inventory, so you're not stuck with it. That way, you order it as needed, and the inventory risk rests with somebody else."

"Dark times? Darkness that matters?"

She had finally stumped him. "New one on me," he said.

Alone again, she tried to read admission folders from the early applicants, but could not get her mind off the conversation with Joe Poynting, and how it fit in with what Mary Mallard had told her. She could not believe she had quizzed poor Poynting about all this, just a few days after promising herself to stay clear of Kellen's little mystery. But Kellen had always had that effect on her. No matter how often she swore off of him, she always stumbled back. Even after her marriage, Kellen would chase her down with his preternatural sense of when Lemaster was away, Kellen with his slow, sleepy, syrupy Southern voice that used to soften her and sweeten her, to melt every barrier she tried to erect, and it was sometimes only sheer luck that had kept her from stumbling back to him.

She checked her watch. Time for her meeting with the dean. Walking through the halls, she reflected that she knew at least a piece of it now. Not much, but some. Kellen was selling something. That was the big mystery. Either he had already sold it, or he was about to; but, whatever the sequence, he planned to hold back the best part for himself.

The trouble was, he had wanted to spread the risk. He had wanted Julia to hold for him—whatever it was. He had told Mary that Julia would have it if anything happened to him. He was killed less than a week after asking her, and being turned down.

What she did not know was whether he had found somebody else to hold it before he was shot.

(11)

"So how's the family?" said Claire Alvarez brightly. "So many children. That's wonderful. Just wonderful. I envy you so."

"Everyone's fine," said Julia.

"Does Vanessa know where she wants to go to school?"

"Ah, not yet."

"Well, I know she'll be a star wherever she goes. She's amazing." The dean of the divinity school nodded. She was a tall, ethereal woman who for the past fifteen years had taught Christian ethics to students who increasingly doubted that there were any. Her sweetness covered you like a blanket. Old Clay Maxwell, already on in years when he taught Julia over twenty years ago, liked to say that Claire could make you feel so warm and fuzzy that you slept through the part where she fired you.

"Thank you," said Julia, although talk of Vanessa and college frightened her.

"Did she enjoy France? She was just in France, wasn't she?"

"She loved it," said Julia, omitting to mention that the trip had been a year ago, Vanessa's sixteenth birthday present, a private visit to Granny Mo, before everything went bad.

"I just adore that girl," Claire said, as if they were discussing a musician or a painter instead of a troubled teen. But Claire found few women she didn't like. She was the nation's leading expert—possibly the nation's only expert—on the holiness theology of the great Methodist evangelist Phoebe Palmer, who, as far as Julia could tell from Claire's frequent and enthusiastic lectures, had distinguished herself in the years leading up to the Civil War, when other Protestant clergy were arguing over the place of slavery in a nation that believed in Scripture, by first skipping the subject and then skipping town, preferring to spend the war years in England. "By the way, are you in some kind of trouble?"

"Trouble?" said Julia, very surprised. "I, ah, I hope not."

"I'm sorry to sound so melodramatic," said Claire, gentle face composed in the half-smile that was her only known expression. "I know we're supposed to be talking about admission and financial aid, and we'll get around to that. But I just had the strangest visit from a lawyer who's also a major donor. It turned out, all he wanted to talk about was you. Odd, isn't it?" Folding her hands alongside the polished silver humidor that was the improbable tradition of her office. "Tice is his name. Anthony Tice. He does those late-night television commercials."

She stopped, apparently waiting for a confession.

"I've seen them," said Julia cautiously, fingers wrapped tightly around the folder holding the presentation they were working up for the provost. "But I don't know him."

"You're not worse off. He's not a particularly pleasant man. Very smart, very good-looking, and knows it. He's given us a hundred thousand dollars each of the past two years. I'm not sure why Mr. Tice thinks us worthy of his beneficence"—looking up at the portraits of past deans, as if the answer might be found there—"but the nation's divinity schools are not exactly awash in money these days."

"What did he ask about me, Claire?"

"Two things. Your relationship with poor Kellen Zant—"

"We didn't have one," Julia objected, too quickly.

"—and, second, what kind of person you are. Do you have integrity? Courage of your convictions? Are you willing to take risks for a great cause?" She rose to her feet, moving slowly around the long, shadowy office, rendered only moderately cheerier by the November sun. "It was as if he was preparing to make you a job offer of some kind. At least that's what I thought at first." The dean had reached the window. She fussed with her hair and watched the view, even if there was nothing to see but the drabness of Hudson Street in winter, and, from the short side of the room, the rich, ugly swankness of Hilliman Social Science Tower, looking condescendingly down on the superstitious rabble of Kepler: the one where truth was measurable but not eternal, the other where truth was eternal but not measurable. "I sang your praises, of course. I told him how proud the school has always been to count you among our graduates, and how delighted we were that you chose to come work with us three and a half years ago."

"Thank you," said Julia, who in fact had never completed her degree.

"And he asked how you were bearing up under the pressure. He meant finding Kellen's earthly remains. I told him it must have been terrible, naturally, but you bear up fantastically well under pressure." Turning back into the room, arms folded. "You do, you know. It's one of your many marvelous qualities, Julia. Things don't get to you. You take the same delight in God's creation no matter what's going on in your life."

Julia dipped her head. This was pouring it on a little thick, even for Claire. The reckoning would surely follow. Nervous, she began nibbling on her lower lip, a habit of which Mona had tried, and failed, to break her by painting her lip with iodine.

"You've been here a little over three years. The students adore you. The faculty respects you. You seem to like everybody. I suspect you'd even get along with Mr. Tice, unpleasant though he can be. He wants to meet you, Julia." Claire made it sound like a blind date. "Yes, the man's self-centered and probably greedy, and he talks a mile a minute. But, Julia, if you can get along with Boris Gibbs, you can get along with anybody."

"What does Tice want to talk about?"

"Kellen Zant, I think. He says the two of them knew each other. They worked on a project together. They didn't have the chance to finish their research. I formed the impression that Mr. Tice might want to recruit you to take Kellen's place."

"Oh, Claire, no. No way."

A kindly palm came up. "Far be it from me to force you, Julia. But think about it. Mr. Tice is a major benefactor of the school, after all, and you are . . . a dean. You might at least talk to him. Or don't. It's entirely up to you." Meaning it wasn't.

"I'll think about it," Julia promised. She owed Claire, and they both knew it, for the dean had searched her out in the miserable months after she lost her job in the public schools. To this day, Julia was not sure why, although Claire loved to give speeches trumpeting Kepler as a showcase of diversity.

"The only strange part came at the end of our conversation. He asked me if you were good at running your office. I naturally said you were wonderful. Well, you are. The neatest, most efficient office in the building, Julia. You know that. I told him, of course. And then he asked me if he could have a look at it. At your office. At that point I had to tell him that, as grateful as we are for his support, there are limits to—"

But Julia missed the rest, because she was pelting down the hall.

(111)

"ARE YOU SURE NOTHING'S MISSING?" said Lemaster, sizzling with fury.

"Nothing I could see."

"I can't believe this. I can't believe it."

"I can hardly believe it myself."

They were sitting in Lemaster's study, a two-story affair separated from the main house by a breezeway. Except for a few family photos, and a flurry of south-facing windows, books covered every square inch of wall. Lemaster had told her back in their courting days that he wished he could live in a library. Now he nearly did.

"I know this Tice. Sat on a couple of bar committees with him. Half his clients are scum. Mafiosi, accused terrorists, ax murderers. Seriously. All right, they all deserve representation, but I get worried when one guy feels he has to represent all of them. Tricky Tony. That's what they call him." A heavy sigh. "Thing is, he isn't a bad lawyer. He's actually pretty good. But he has no sense of morals. None. And he doesn't have an independent thought in his head. He wouldn't cross the street without a client paying him for it. So, if he wanted to see the inside of your office, it was on behalf of a client."

Julia sipped her wine. They were sharing a rather pretentious Napa Valley white. "What kind of client?"

"No idea. But, Jules, the nerve of this man. To come onto my campus, to try to get one of my deans to open my wife's office to him!" On his feet now, striding around the room. "All right. All right. Believe it or not, he didn't actually violate the canons of ethics, or the law, either. Lawyers have a lot of freedom to—never mind. He's not going to get away with this."

My campus, she registered. *My deans. My wife.*

"You just said he didn't break the law and he didn't break the canons of ethics."

"That doesn't matter."

"It doesn't?"

He shuddered to a halt. When Lemaster put on this act, stomping around, Julia had to hide a smile, because, being so short, he reminded her of a child throwing a tantrum. "The rules laid down are not necessarily the proper measure of right and wrong."

"What are you going to do?"

"Make sure it doesn't happen again. Now, trust me." In his run-along-now tone, when he wanted to get back to work. Often she felt like a supplicant in this palatial room. Often she was. "Wait. Jules, wait. One thing."

"Hmmm?"

"Do you have any idea why this Tice wanted to see your office? What he was looking for?"

"No."

"The Vanessa File?" He meant the collection of clippings and memos about their daughter's troubles, which she kept at Kepler in the arbitrary belief that it was safer there than at home.

"I don't know. I don't think Claire is aware of its existence."

"Maybe Tony is." He stroked his graying goatee. "Well, all right. Never mind. I'm sorry you had to go through this, Jules. I'll take care of it."

Julia hesitated. Through two decades of marriage, Lemaster had always promised to take care of whatever problem might arise, and had generally kept his word. She wondered when she had crossed the line from reliance to dependence.

"Thanks, sweetie," she said. Already back at his laptop, he only smiled.

Julia stepped across the breezeway into the house. Maybe Tice had indeed been after the Vanessa File. Perhaps he represented someone planning to sue them for some offense, yet unknown, that the teenager had committed. But Julia had another explanation, even if she was not prepared to share it with her husband.

Mary Mallard had assumed, erroneously, that Kellen had entrusted his surplus to Julia before he died. There was no reason in the world to suppose Mary was the only one who thought so.

CHAPTER 8

MAIN STREET

(1)

THE FOLLOWING AFTERNOON, two days before Thanksgiving, Julia snuck out of Cookie's like a thief, carrying candy for gifts to various friends and colleagues. Snuggling at the bottom of the bag was a diet-busting box of cappuccino truffles for herself. Standing in Vera's shop, she often identified friends according to their tastes: Tonya Montez from Ladybugs was peanut brittle, Iris Feynman from across the hall at Kepler was vanilla fudge, and budget-conscious Boris Gibbs, who spent his own money on less expensive sweets from the CVS but would never turn down a freebie—Boris was smeary, messy chocolate-covered cherries.

Out on Main Street, the day was clear but glowering. Icicles garlanded stores and trees and parking meters. Julia recognized few passing faces, but she was not really looking. She was worrying. Jeannie walked contentedly beside her mother, features swallowed by the fur-lined hood of her pricey parka as, delicately, she popped Jelly Bellys into her mouth. Of course Jeannie was content. She was always content. Unlike her brothers, Jeannie seemed to view her older sister's weaknesses as an opportunity to showcase her own strengths. The mantle of Clan princess, once draped around Julia's shoulders—as, back in Harlem of the fifties, it had been draped around Mona's—had started to slip from Vanessa's even before the fire. Jeannie seemed to think the mantle her due.

In her dreariest moments, Julia gazed in wonder at her four children, and felt maternal failure staring back at her.

"Hurry up, honey."

"Why?" Another Jelly Belly.

"Because it's almost five."

"So?"

"So, we have to go see Mr. Carrington before he closes."

"Why?"

Classic Jeannie. In her leisurely way, she was never quite disobedient, but she always wanted reasons. Still, Julia was not about to explain to her youngest that Vera Brightwood, in the midst of one of her poisonous monologues, had let slip that she had seen Mommy's ex-lover, three days before he died, going into Old Landing, the antiques shop across the street.

Or that he stayed for an hour.

(11)

FRANK CARRINGTON WAS, to Julia's way of thinking, a typical Landinger: white and sturdy and in town forever. In his day he had been everything from deputy constable to school-bus driver to bartender, before discovering that he had an eye for antiques, or at least a talent for fleecing tourists, and opening Old Landing. The village was a good twelve miles from Elm Harbor. Thanks to the wisdom—or recalcitrance—of the zoning board, the Landing, unlike the other shore towns in the county, had yet to be fully colonized by professionals who commuted to the city. It was full of Frank Carringtons, who simmered with resentment toward the university folks who moved in and raised prices and elected Democrats to the town council, but, at the same time, craved the hard cash they dropped into the till.

"What about him?" said Frank, when Julia had stated her business.

"Was he here?"

"I'm a businessman," the dealer explained, intonation Yankee-flat. He was winter pale and New England lanky, and wore his tawny hair in a younger man's style. His shop was long and dark, crowded with antiques, half of them hidden in shadow. "I do business with anybody who walks through that door. Now, some of our merchants up here don't like minorities. I'm not like that. You know I'm glad you folks are here."

Yes, she knew, because he told her every time she came in to make some little purchase, or, now and then, some big one.

"We need more minorities," he announced, in the same tone he might have used to suggest that Pleasant Road needed a stoplight. "All kinds," he added piously.

Julia, examining a girandole, said nothing.

"How's Pres?" Frank asked, still punching, because the Landing still marveled over her firstborn. Four years after Preston's early graduation, the regional high school had not recovered from the discovery that its resident genius was black. Nor had Lemaster, the relationship between father and son forever spoiled, on both sides, by the discovery that the son was the smarter of the pair. "Still doing the Landing proud, I bet!" said Frank, smiling weakly.

"Preston is fine."

"Brightest black kid anybody around here ever saw," he said, meaning it as a compliment. "Now, tell me about the rest of the family."

Julia refused to be distracted.

"What did he want, Frank?" She glanced at Jeannie, who was standing in the front window, admiring the porcelain Christmas village. A sign warned visitors not to touch, but any minute now, her mother knew, Jeannie would pick up one of the pieces and, possibly, break it. "Kellen Zant. When he was in here. What did he want?"

"Same thing everybody wants. To buy something."

"He bought something from you? Kellen?"

"Some reason he shouldn't?"

"What did he buy?"

A moment's hesitation, as if figuring out how much to charge for the information. Frank was tall but hunched, as if his height was greater than his ambition. His eyes kept straying over Julia's shoulder, toward Jeannie, who was now kneeling. "Remember that nineteenth-century cheval mirror you looked at last month?"

"Of course." She also remembered how Frank Carrington had wanted eighteen hundred dollars for it, which was daylight madness.

"He bought it."

"Kellen bought the cheval? Why on earth would he buy the cheval? Kellen didn't know squat about antiques."

"Well, he bought this one." Puffing up with pride. "Paid full price, too."

"But it doesn't make any sense. What would Kellen do with an antique mirror?"

Again Frank's eyes cut toward Jeannie, who, true to form, had lifted the little train station from its base. She held it close to her face and peeked inside. Rules applied to those less perfect than she. "He said it was a gift."

"A gift?" A moment's unreasoning jealousy. "For whom?"

"For you."

Julia glanced at her daughter, not wanting to be overheard. She actually put a hand on the older man's arm, drawing him deeper into the gloomy shop. "That's not funny," she said.

"It's not a joke, Julia. He asked me what you liked, and I told him."

"But—"

She stopped, not sure how to make the point. Yes, sure, she and Kellen had now and then exchanged little trinkets and treats: that birthday fudge, for instance. But Julia could not get her mind around the idea that he would have bought her an eighteen-hundred-dollar mirror. She was a married woman! Who was she supposed to tell her husband it was from? She would never have accepted it, as Kellen would surely have realized, and, besides—

"But he didn't give it to me."

"Well, no," Frank Carrington admitted, rubbing ghostly hands over each other to wash away responsibility. "Sorry about that. It's just that he said he would call me with delivery instructions. Only he never did."

"You mean—"

"It's still here. Would you care to see it?"

(III)

AND SO JULIA, hoping it would all turn out to be a dream, had the chance to examine the second mirror Kellen had left her. "Now, Julia, you understand, I can't give it to you," said Frank, removing the dust-cloth. "It was my *impression* that he intended it as a gift for you, but I don't know for sure. So the mirror would still be his property. The property of his estate, I guess."

"I understand," said Julia, circling the tall oval mirror, noting chips and scratches automatically. It was in poor condition, but something in her loved it for its age. Ever since childhood, Julia had harbored a secret theory about what made old mirrors different from other antiques: if you stared into one long enough, you would begin to see faint outlines of all the women down through the decades who had preened and primped in front of it. Back in Hanover, and even more so at Granny Vee's townhouse in Harlem, the younger Julia used to stand for hours, squinting at the silvered glass, waiting for history to reflect back at her. So far, despite years of staring, no luck, but now and then she imagined Mona behind her, warning in that high voice, self-pitying and self-satisfied, that Julia should stop hunting so hard for whatever she imagined waited on the other side: *If you stare at those things too long,* her mother would say, supposedly quoting Granny Vee, *you'll turn into one of them.*

"It's a beauty, isn't it?" Frank murmured, as if giving her a sales pitch. His voice had crept higher, as it did when he was nervous. She noticed that his hands had resumed their shiver, and wondered why. Maybe he planned to keep the mirror and sell it again.

"A beauty," she lied in agreement. Actually, it was poorly cared for. She tilted the mirror and felt it weave. The glass had been polished, but her reflection was distended in the unsteady surface, like a fun-house image. The more Julia examined it, the more the cheval reminded her of something, but she could not think just what. "One of the finials is broken," she said.

"Chipped."

"That's a big chip." Frank spread his hands, perhaps to indicate that the damage was out of them. Julia studied the joints and the swivels, picked at a scab of glue. "And Kellen paid full price?"

"Uh-huh."

"After you told him I'd looked at it?"

"Uh-huh."

Julia shook her head, completely confused. She did not see why Kellen would buy her an ugly, overpriced antique mirror in such poor condition. But, counting the Comyns Seth had delivered in Arkadelphia, this made two mirrors from Kellen in a week. Even a man as impulsive as Kellen Zant would have a reason for so strange a pair of gifts. Was this what Boris Gibbs had heard about? That Kellen was in the Landing buying her an expensive antique? But why would anyone be angry about it? Could this be the surplus Mary Mallard had asked about, the one Kellen had told her he would be giving Julia? She touched the broken finial again. If she knew Kellen—and she did—he had been up to no good. But the connection between buying the cheval and doing no good eluded her.

She warned herself to stop wondering. What Kellen might have been up to was not her business. He had tried time and again to draw her back into his life while he was alive. She would not permit him to succeed now that he was dead. For the first time since Kellen's death, Julia's anger at him began to dull her pain.

"And that was all he said? That it was a gift for me?"

"Well, not *all*." Frank had retreated so far into the gloom that his voice seemed to float on air. "He said you would like it because you love history."

But history bored her. She must have told Kellen a thousand times that she cared about the future not the past, a sin for which Mona frequently admonished her. She was about to say so, perhaps unwisely, when a tinkling crash sounded from the front of the shop.

Jeannie was on her feet, eyes innocently wide, hands safely behind her back, several graceful steps from the shattered porcelain building.

"It wasn't me," she said.

CHAPTER 9

SURFACE TENSION

(1)

LEMASTER'S SECOND COUSIN ASTRID was in town for Thanksgiving, her pair of serious, distant, gangly youngsters in tow, and she brought as usual a mad, gaunt, chain-smoking energy to the house on Hunter's Meadow. Astrid Venable was dark and tiny and handsome, like Lemaster himself, and every bit as haughty and brilliant. They had both immigrated as teens, and had been raised—along with Astrid's younger brother, Harrison, star investment banker—by the same hard-driving aunt in Chicago. Their aunt sent them to Catholic school, trying to cover two bases at once. Astrid focused, laserlike, on whatever drew her interest, mostly her work on Capitol Hill, and her social vortex, for the club life of the darker nation was her second home, and sometimes her first: she had served as national vice-president of Ladybugs, and was currently national secretary for one of the more exclusive black sororities, and would never skip either a convention or an opportunity to tell you why you should have been there. Astrid thought of nobody but herself. She grew irritated if Lemaster did not answer her e-mails immediately upon receipt, and often called Hunter's Heights late at night, knowing Julia was always awake, to tell her to turn on the television, quick, because Public Broadcasting had a documentary about some obscure black sculptor of whom Julia had never heard, and never would again. If Julia said she was doing something else, Astrid became defensive, and annoyed.

As for Astrid's children, they were slobs as well as snobs, leaving clothes and boots and electronic games and Coke bottles and cookie crumbs distributed around Hunter's Heights in a pattern that suggested propriety, or at least the existence of a servant class, as in their raising there always had been. Before the move to Washington, Astrid had been a partner in a Wall Street law firm, and had more cash stashed away than her cousin, by no means starving, would earn in five years. Lemaster resolutely avoided discussing politics, but, apart from her clubs, Astrid talked of nothing else, and hated every word out of your mouth unless it parroted every word out of hers. There were husbands in Astrid's past, not all of them her own, and perhaps in her future too. Lemaster considered his cousin a screechy, unthinking loudmouth, and a spoiling mother besides. The children, he told his wife, were scarcely recognizable as West Indian, for he possessed the immigrant's combative pride in his heritage, whether it really existed or not.

Julia was secretly scared of her.

Astrid flew in on Wednesday, to kisses and hugs and exchanges of sacks full of Christmas presents, and Julia prepared a tofu-based stir-fry to complement the Thanksgiving turkey, because no one in Astrid's family ate meat or poultry, or not when their mother was around. The children, said Astrid, had brought their homework, although, from what Julia could tell, their tasks consisted mostly of playing hand-held video games, and adjusting their laptops to the household's wireless router, so that they could instant-message their friends.

Thanksgiving dinner itself managed to be boisterous and desultory at once—boisterous because of Astrid's constant yapping, and because the table was full, including Wendy Tollefson, Julia's buddy from her teaching days, as well as several friends from the university who had nobody else to dine with; desultory because neither Carlyle son attended. Aaron had received permission to spend Thanksgiving in Texas with the family of his wealthy roommate, and Preston, mysterious as always in his rudeness, had simply announced, by e-mail and without explanation, that he would not be present. At Julia's urging, Lemaster asked Suzanne de Broglie, a professor at the div school, to bless the food. Suzanne prayed to "God, our Mother" as her president glared at his wife. After dessert, by family tradition, everyone at the table gave thanks for something. Jeannie thanked God for her wonderful Mommy and Daddy and her wonderful sister and both of her wonderful brothers and for everybody else who was alive, and also the ones who were dead. Vanessa's prayer was inaudible. When Astrid's turn came, she gave thanks for the defeat of the latest attempt to destroy the public schools by providing vouchers to poor children, and added her fervent hope that God would soon expose the Religious Right as the Irreligious Wrong.

Suzanne's father, also a divinity professor, had been a stern traditionalist and was one of Lemaster's great heroes. After dinner it was plain that Lemmie was tempted to ask her what Eduard de Broglie would have thought of her prayer. A few years ago perhaps he would have. But he was president of the university now, and so settled for venting, later, at his wife. The problem, he told Julia as they readied for bed, was that people want a God small enough to fit in their hip pockets, to be pulled out only when necessary to gain a secular advantage. Nobody wants a God who tells us what to do, he said. We want a God who commands only what we tell Him to command, and allows whatever we tell Him to allow. We want a God who's smaller than we are, who is never unruly, who falls into line. No wonder nobody goes to church any more. Why worship a Being that insignificant? Julia, like everyone in the family, had heard the speech a hundred times. She agreed because agreement was what Lemaster liked. Lying beside him, she tried to imagine a husband with a sense of humor.

On Friday night, Julia wanted to drag her cousin-in-law, as the children called her, to the monthly meeting of Ladybugs, because Astrid, despite her move to Washington, remained a member of the fabled Westchester County chapter, before which the others all but bowed down, in obsequity as well as simple envy. Westchester sopped up a considerable fraction of the black wealth of greater New York, and its members included one president of a Fortune 500 company, two wives of heads of Fortune 100 companies, two major network-television personalities, four wives of New York sports stars who earned millions, on and on, down to those who, like Astrid, were merely (as Granny Vee used to say) decently off.

To Julia's surprise, Astrid pronounced herself too exhausted, so they stayed home and played three-handed pinochle with Vanessa, which in the great days of Harlem had been practically the official game of the Clan. They ate popcorn and watched an old movie and mostly waited for Lemaster, who had to drop in on a retirement dinner for the senior black lawyer in town; and Julia had the shrewd intuition that it was the desire to see her cousin, not so mortal a vice as tiredness, that had kept Astrid home.

"Are the media out of your hair, dear?" she asked Julia at one point, startling her into playing the wrong card.

"You mean, because of what happened to Kellen?" A nervous laugh. "That's all ancient history, the way the news cycle works these days."

"I wonder if that's true."

"If what's true?"

"If it's ancient history." She looked worried, and in need of a smoke, and Julia knew she would soon be excusing herself for a little walk in the yard. Astrid sensed the scrutiny. "I'm just waiting for the other shoe to drop. It's what I do for a living."

Julia, thinking of the cheval mirror, said nothing, but Vanessa, scribbling the scores, shot Aunt Astrid a worried glance, picking up a nuance her mother had missed. "Is the Senator worried about what Kellen was working on?"

The Senator being Astrid's boss.

"No, no, darling, don't be silly. No. Why would you say such a thing?" And excused herself to take that walk without waiting for Vanessa's answer. Julia, too, wondered why her daughter had asked, but before she could press, Vanessa escaped to her cell phone, because That Casey was calling her. Later on, Julia chatted with her cousin-in-law in the basement guest room, decorated with posters of Broadway shows featuring black artists, and Astrid said what she always said, that she did not understand why Julia did not listen to the authentic music of the community: by which she meant the gruesomely misogynistic lyrics that were Lemaster's secret love. Vanessa waltzed in, wanting to show Aunt Astrid the photograph Seth Zant had given them in Arkadelphia. Julia was mortified. She had thought it well hidden, but trying to conceal anything from Vanessa was a thankless task, as they had learned when, scarcely past toddler stage, she had uncovered the trove of Christmas presents Lemaster had buried in the back of the locked cabinet in his study.

"They were this really hot item," said Vanessa triumphantly.

Astrid's eyes widened. "They were?" Julia saw her future, this juicy item passed along the gossip chain, from one chapter of Ladybugs to the next. Astrid smiled at her. "Lemaster never told me."

"He, um, he's good at keeping secrets," said Julia, feeling the peculiar need to apologize.

"I'll say," said Astrid, her tone disdainful, as though keeping secrets was another vice.

THE VISIT, despite the season, was no social call. This was business, and Astrid's only business nowadays was politics. She served as chief of staff for Senator Malcolm Whisted, another longtime Lemaster friend. Their roots went back to college, when they had spent their final two years on campus as part of a foursome sharing Hilliman Suite, reserved by terms of a long-ago deed for the eldest member of the Hilliman clan then attending the college, and up to three of his friends. The suite occupied most of the top floor of Hilliman Hall, a dormitory, not to be confused with the social-science tower and half a dozen other campus buildings, the Hilliman family being among the university's largest benefactors. The rest of the floor consisted of two smaller rooms, very desirable these days for their proximity to Hilliman Suite, even if they had once been servants' quarters.

Jock Hilliman, who went on to further fortune as a corporate raider, had the suite back in Lemaster's day, and scandalized his relatives by inviting the black man to move in: the first time, whispered his relatives, that a Negro had ever crossed the threshold of Hilliman Suite, other than in service. He added two more of his buddies, known then as Scrunchy and Mal, who grew up to be, respectively, the President of the United States, and a senior Senator planning to enter the Democratic primaries that began in just three months with the Iowa caucuses, and, if things went as planned, to challenge Scrunchy next fall. The press was already fascinated by the possibility of college roommates running against each other. But the relationship was less close than it appeared. Jock, Scrunchy, and Mal had mostly lost touch with each other over the years, but Lemaster, with his eerily efficient power of friendship, had stayed close to all three. When Jock died three years ago—in the arms of his much younger mistress, although the obituaries said only that it was a heart attack while visiting a friend—Lemaster had eulogized him so masterfully that even Scrunchy and Mal, hard-nosed politicians, had managed a few tears for the cameras.

It was Lemaster who had helped Astrid secure her job.

(I I I)

ASTRID SPENT MUCH OF SATURDAY afternoon closeted with her
cousin in his study, their raised voices perfectly evident to anyone who,
like Julia, snuck through the breezeway, stepped into the anteroom,
and pressed her ear to the heavy door. Julia could not make out the
words, but had discerned last night, from the small cues of posture and
glance, that Astrid was for once the supplicant, and Lemaster held all
the cards. She could not linger, and not only because she might get
caught: she had to pick up the kids from the multiplex where, in various
combinations, her children and Astrid's were seeing movies. Driving
over in the fully repaired Escalade, she tried to figure out what the
argument could be about.

Inside, she found Jeannie sitting primly on a bench with Odessa,
Astrid's thirteen-year-old, for they had seen the new Disney; and, striding up and down with a soda in one hand and his phone in the other,
Odessa's brother, Cedric, fifteen and unusually tall for a Carlyle, who,
with his mother's distracted permission, had snuck into an R-rated film
involving vampires and world conquest, the plot consisting mostly of
gore. They were all waiting for Vanessa, who had met That Casey to
see a romantic comedy, and Julia disciplined herself not to wonder what
the two of them were getting up to in the darkness. Theirs was the
shortest film, but Casey had evidently been late, and the couple had
gone to the next show.

Thinking of nobody else.

Burbling Jeannie had loved the Disney, sophisticated Odessa pretended to have found it beneath her, and tall Cedric was too busy on the
phone to greet Aunt Julia. She checked the times, discovered that the
romantic comedy would not be out for another hour and ten minutes,
and suggested that they get some Chinese food at the place across the
street, then come back for Vanessa. While everybody was busily agreeing, Julia spotted That Casey in the vestibule, very cozy with the sort of
girl Vanessa liked to call "trivial blonde," who displayed, even in the
November chill, sufficient flesh to have risked, in Julia's youth, arrest.
Furious for Vanessa's sake, ignoring every sensible rule of parental non-
intervention, Julia stormed across the lobby, tapped the aspiring poet
on the shoulder, and was nearly caught off guard, as always, by the pristine innocence of Casey Wyatt's moist, sensitive green eyes.

"Mrs. Carlyle! Hey, how are you holding up? Was it really terrible? Vanessa says it was really terrible." Elbowing the trivial blonde as he fished for inside information. "This is Vanessa's mom. She found that dead black guy."

The blonde mumbled what might have been a greeting.

"So are you okay?" said Casey, less an expression of compassion than an effort to suggest his own status as insider with what was doubtless the Landing's most talked-about family. Brown ringlets of hair curled boyishly over his forehead. The soft curls gave him a Byronic look, and it was his poetic side that drew Vanessa; that, plus the fact that he was her only suitor at the regional high school, where perhaps twenty kids out of fourteen hundred were black. "Vanessa says it was messy, his head all shot off and everything."

"And where exactly is Vanessa, Casey? What are you doing out here"—eyeing the blonde—"when the movie's in there?"

"It's not my fault, Mrs. Carlyle. She changed her mind. She didn't want to go. She had something else to do. So I saw Melanie here, you know, from school? And I figured—"

"What else?"

"What?"

"What did she have to do, Casey? Where's my daughter?"

He pointed, vaguely, toward the parking lot. Nearby Jeannie's eyes were huge and excited, as they always seemed to be at the hint of Vanessa causing trouble. She reached for her mother's hand. Odessa was now on her own cell phone, joining her brother in ignoring the world around her.

"She said she had to see about something." He began to look worried. "She was acting all weird. I tried to stop her, Mrs. Carlyle. Honest."

"See about what? Where did she go?"

Casey glanced at the trivial blonde, who had backed off a pace to nibble at a fingernail. "She always does this. Whenever we're together." He was whispering now, eyes on the carpet, and Julia, against her will, sensed his bewildered pain. Perhaps he really did care for Vanessa. "We go to dinner, we go to the movies, we go wherever, and everything's fine, and then, all of a sudden, she hops up and runs off. And it's always the same reason." The tortured gaze came up, and, for a moment, they shared the guilty knowledge of being unable to control, or even understand, what they loved. "It's always because Gina needs her."

(I V)

JULIA'S EMOTIONAL RANGE had never quite encompassed panic. Veazie women were planners and problem solvers, organized and assertive and in small ways incautious, willing to risk error in preference to inaction. It was only through the determination and toil of its women, Mona often said, that the darker nation had survived the foibles of its men. When Julia had discovered, just weeks after moving in with Lemaster, that she was pregnant, she neither dithered nor sobbed, but went straight to her boyfriend to tell him the news, taking it for granted that their future would turn on his first reaction. Had he proposed an abortion, she would have slapped his face; had he proposed that the problem was hers to solve, she would have gouged his eyes on her way out the door, hoping to blind a minimum of one; when, instead, he proposed marriage, Julia turned him down, on the arbitrary ground that she did not want to trap him into a rash decision. The decision was not rash, Lemaster had assured her. He had been thinking about asking her for some time, but shyness had held him back. Julia nearly slapped him for that claim, too, because Lemmie had never had a shy moment in his life. Hands on hips, she had invited him crossly to prove it. He smiled and said, "If the baby's a girl, I'm even willing to name her Amaretta." But the baby was a boy, and they named him Preston, after Granny Vee's husband, and Julia's only known grandfather.

Now, planning always, she called neither her husband nor the police. Instead, she called Vanessa's cell phone.

Voice mail.

Think. Plan. Act.

Gina. Whenever Vanessa went roaming, she said she was doing it for Gina.

She piled the kids into the Escalade, made the protesting cousins hang up their cell phones, and began driving along Route 48, peeking around the half-empty strip malls, deserted industrial plazas, and listless car dealerships that seemed to surround every suburban multiplex these days. After a few minutes, everybody got in on the fun, but just as Cedric began speculating aloud about possible disasters that might have befallen her, Vanessa called back.

"I'm at the Historical Society. I saw you were trying to reach me, but I can't use my phone in the reading room."

"You're where?"

"Doing some research. I had an idea."

Forget the idea. "How on earth did you get there? That's four, five miles from here!"

"Called a taxi."

"Vanessa—"

"I know, Moms. I know. I should have asked you." Irritably patient, like a long-suffering adult. "But you would have said no."

"That's right!"

"Well, that's why I didn't ask. I didn't want you to say no. It's okay if you want to ground me, Moms." Giving permission, making it sound like parents punish children for the parents' sake: which, often enough, they do. "I got what I came for."

"Which was what?"

"I'll tell you about it later. They're getting ready to close. Do you want to come get me or what?"

So Julia rearranged the sequence. She picked up Vanessa first, saving the piece of her mind for later. She had planned to take Vanessa to the mall, to look for a dress for the Grand Orange and White Cotillion right after Christmas, the social event of the year for the New England branch of the Clan, but Vanessa wanted not to go. Maybe that was really why she had run off: to avoid shopping with her mother for a dress.

(v)

BACK AT THE HOUSE, Vanessa had homework, Jeannie busied herself writing a poem about a cat who went to the moon, and Astrid's children vanished into the basement to do whatever they did. Astrid herself was fuming in the downstairs guest room. Lemaster was gone, attending a campus dinner, after which he would drop in on a small party the mayor of Elm Harbor was throwing for a few good friends. Actually, Lemaster could not stand the mayor, a pristinely corrupt man named Shea, but the requirements of the job were the requirements of the job. Later, Julia ran out to the supermarket, taking Vanessa along for that long-awaited lecture. The teen listened in stubborn silence, glaring out the window, and, when Julia was exhausted, said what she usually said: "You don't understand."

It was not until later that night, as they lay abed watching a late basketball game from the West Coast, Lemaster still cross from his argument with Astrid, that the two of them had the chance to spend any time together.

"Do you know what Astrid's biggest problem is?" Lemaster asked his wife as she dozed on his hard shoulder.

"Mmmm-mmmm."

"She's the kind of person who thinks nothing's as important as an election."

"Maybe this time around she's right."

"No. She isn't right." Distractedly kissing her forehead, admitting no possibility of error: for, although a good deal more charming than Astrid, Lemaster was no less self-certain. He quoted a favorite maxim: "Winning is not a virtue."

Julia waited, but it became apparent that the subject her husband had barely opened, he had already closed. She steamed a bit, as she always did when excluded. Then, after a couple of commercial breaks, and an unsuccessful effort to rouse him to amorousness, she finally told him about Vanessa's flit, minimizing the teen's disrespect, playing up the role of That Casey in order to give her husband somebody to blame. Lemaster heard her out, then flipped through the channels, finally ending on *Book TV,* where a famous novelist was explaining why men should never write in women's voices. Julia knew better than to interrupt his pondering. Lemaster was the sort of general who would never fire until he was ready to blow the opposition to Kingdom Come.

"Brady is an idiot," he finally said. "An absolute idiot. How was I to know? He's chief of adolescent psychiatry at the med school." Lemaster was answering an objection she did not remember raising. "People sing his praises. So—what does he do? He sits around talking about respecting Vanessa's voice, allowing her—what does he call it?"

"To exercise her agency." Julia shivered in the stifling room—Lemaster, aggressively tropical, especially in New England, loved to turn the heat all the way up, and never asked first—as she remembered the grueling months after Vanessa's arrest. Lawyers, psychiatrists, social workers, judges, more psychiatrists, interviews and reports and courtrooms, on and on, Julia's head whirling until she lost track of which one of them, mother or daughter, had gone off the deep end. And there were times—she would never admit it!—when she was relieved to have three other children, mostly normal, even if the primacy of Vanessa's needs nowadays meant that the rest were starved for their mother's time. Lemaster concentrated on the television, evidently unaware of her growing distress. Julia said, "He says she needs enough space to be an independent agent."

"Exactly. Our daughter tries to kill herself, and Brady says she needs more space. What a moron." Although he never raised his voice, Julia sensed the self-reproach. He made few mistakes, her Lemmie, and hated himself for the few. "They should take his license away," Lemaster grumbled, and she wondered, because her husband knew everyone who mattered, whether he might be planning to give it a serious try.

"What do you want to do? Get somebody new?"

"I don't know. Maybe." Annoyed at his own indecision, he changed the channel again, skipping past the news in search of a better truth. "Vanessa likes him now, I bet. Telling us to let her be a free agent. She sure was a free agent today, wasn't she?"

Julia admired her husband, but sometimes she wanted to smack him. Did he really pay so little attention to the largest crisis in his own household? "Oh, Lemmie, she can't stand him. She wants a woman."

But Barbadian men have trouble backing down, even when, to stay ahead, they are forced to disagree with themselves. "Maybe that's evidence that he's doing a good job: that she doesn't like him. Too much of the world is governed by what people *like*. How people *feel*." As so often, her husband spoke as if to a roomful of people. "I don't want Vanessa to *like* her therapist," he pounded on. "She can hate his guts, for all I care, as long as he helps her. And that's what I don't know, Jules. What we don't know. If he's helping her or not." A sound that might have been an angry snarl. "Gina again. Gina. All we need. Every time she runs off, it's the same reason. Gina wanted her to. Heaven knows what she tells her friends." He meant, what her friends told their parents. "Or writes in her blog."

"She never writes about Gina in her blog."

"Right. Because Gina doesn't want her to." Lemaster sighed, and then, to her relief, Julia felt his body relax in her arms. "I guess nobody can be an idiot about everything. Brady said we shouldn't indulge this Gina business any longer. I wasn't sure before, but I think he was right." This took Julia by surprise. He had bypassed entirely the relatively juicier questions of Vanessa's brief disappearance and That Casey's complicity, landing with both feet precisely where she wanted him not to go. "So—here it is. She cannot spend any more time worrying about what happened to Gina. She just can't. Brady can work and work to get to the source of her obsession, but, meanwhile, he wants us not to let Vanessa pursue it. He's been very clear about that. So let's make it clear to Vanessa that we agree." He gave his wife no opportunity to express an opinion. "And you know something? Vanessa has been doing better. A lot better. Or she was. Until . . . well, until recent events."

Did he mean Kellen's murder? Astrid's visit? Or did Lemaster mean—could he possibly mean—that he blamed Julia for somehow putting thoughts of Gina back into their daughter's head?

"She's still doing better," said Julia.

"We'll see."

"What will we see?" she asked, holding on for dear life, wondering— oh, she hated these moments!—wondering if her husband even liked her, or viewed their marriage, as he did most of life, through the stulti- fying lens of duty.

"We'll see," he said slowly, "if she can give up the obsession again."

"You make it sound like she can choose."

"I think she probably can. Unless events tempt her in the wrong direction."

It was just like surface tension, Julia decided, for deep inside she was still the biologist who used to teach science to middle-schoolers, and she searched constantly for analogies. Her hidden anger was akin to the air inside a bubble, pressing, pressing against the thin skin of self- control, which could contain the expanding gases completely until the moment that it popped. Then everything would come out at once. Feeling cornered and ready to snap at him, Julia stiffened against Lemaster's small body.

"Oh well," he said, sensing that he had pushed too far. "It doesn't matter. It's over. Vanessa is safe. That's the important thing. All right, so she slipped the traces a little. I suppose that's what Thoroughbreds do, isn't it? She's fundamentally a good kid. She didn't do anything stupid." He seemed to be talking himself away from his worst instincts. "Maybe Brady hasn't been a complete disaster. As for That Casey, well, no point in dumping on him. He's just the way he is. A spoiled Caucasian faculty brat."

"At least Vanessa is being more social now," Julia ventured hope- lessly, now that Lemaster was through judging everybody.

"Yes." Cold as steel. "She certainly is."

He switched channels again: an action-adventure movie in which only the hero knows the truth, and is forced, without visible reluctance, to kill anybody who gets in his way. They watched him reload and keep on shooting. Julia, the empiricist, wondered how he dealt with the weight of the ammo.

"Lemmie?"

"Hmmm?"

"Tonight, while we were waiting for you"—she hesitated, not wanting to mention their daughter's name just when the storm had calmed—"I was wondering if whatever it is that Astrid wants—"

"She wants dirt." Voice still chilly. "The President and I were room-mates, we've been friends forever, she figures I must know all his dirty secrets. I told her Mal was his roommate, too, we all shared Hilliman Suite, so ask Mal for dirt. She says the Senator is much too fine a man, et cetera, et cetera, but, really, I think her problem is Mal doesn't know any." A pause. "And, of course, Jock is dead, and Astrid, the way her mind works, says that's proof that there's dirt. Jock died of a heart attack, in bed with his mistress, so Astrid says the mistress was in on it."

It was a moment before Julia realized he was done. "Is there dirt to know?"

"I can't talk about that, Jules."

"I know. I know. I just meant, um, even if you can't tell me what it was? I just kind of wondered if it might have something to do with Kellen."

Another time-out while her husband consulted the odd little referee inside his head. "Same old Astrid. Does what she wants, and devil take the hindmost." Lemaster yawned. "When she's on one of her crusades you can't talk sense to her. Well, don't worry. I'll talk to Mal. He'll have to call her off."

Don't worry? "Will he do that? Just because you ask him?"

"Of course."

Another problem solved: like magic, the way he did it. He kissed her briefly, turned off the television, rolled onto his side, and closed his eyes. He never answered her question about Kellen.

CHAPTER 10

A WALK ON THE BEACH

(1)

IN THE MORNING, Lemaster took Vanessa and Jeannie to the eleven o'clock Eucharist at the adamantly named Saint Matthias, which some years ago had seceded from the Episcopal Church in a fit of traditionalist theological righteousness. Astrid's children slept in. Julia and Astrid went to brunch at the Landing Club, the private and pricey haven of the town's well-to-do, which the family had finally been invited to join when Lemmie went to work in the White House. Kellen had joked that the town was betting that the family would follow Lemaster to Washington, so that the membership would never actually be used: and perhaps it was true.

"You have to make Lemaster see," said Astrid, "that his view of the world is too narrow. You cannot live your life on the fence. You cannot evade the responsibility to take sides. The issues facing us are too vital. People of his caliber, and yours, must not be permitted to hold back."

"Hold back what?"

Astrid played with her Grape-Nuts and soy milk. A few slices of cantaloupe completed her meal. Julia was barely able to touch her poached eggs and sausage, for fear that Astrid would be able to see the pounds adding. "The President of the United States was once your husband's best friend in the world. In college, he got up to all sorts of mischief. Once upon a time, we might have said that the college record of a public official was not the public's business. Those days are over, Julia. The issues are too important." Her mantra, and, in a sense, her ideology. "Scrunchy—what an odd nickname, I would love to know how he got it—Scrunchy told his friends after college he had done terrible things in those years. Now, maybe he just meant he got drunk too often and woke up in a strange bed now and then. But maybe he meant more. We would like to find out." *We* meaning, in Astrid's jargon, the forces of righteousness and truth. But she was confirming Lemaster's account. "Scrunchy would have confided in Lemaster if he confided in anybody. We would like to know what he confided. The fact that your husband is fighting so hard to keep the secrets suggests that they are secrets worth telling."

"Or worth keeping," Julia murmured, thinking again of Kellen, but Astrid pretended not to hear. Astrid wanted Lemmie's secrets. Mary Mallard wanted Julia's. Suddenly everybody seemed to think the Carlyles had inside information. She pushed images of Kellen's two mirrors from her mind: even dead, he would *not* suck her back into his world.

The waiter asked whether there would be anything else.

"These have been terrible years for our country, Julia, terrible years. The Dark Ages all over again, if you will forgive my metaphor. Lemaster talks about honor and loyalty and keeping his word. But you cannot win the battle against evil with one hand tied behind your back."

"I think the President would agree with you."

Prim mouth, looking askance, the way true believers do when their faith is mocked. "This is not a laughing matter."

"Sorry."

"I'm seriously worried about you, Julia. You used to be much more political."

"I think you're confusing me with my mother."

A couple of women Julia knew from town came over to say hello. Julia did introductions, but it was plain that nobody would remember anybody else's name. They did little kissy things, jewelry jangling, and moved on.

Astrid watched them go. "They're afraid I'm moving in."

"Why would that bother them?"

"Too many of us move in and they'd have to move out."

Julia colored, surprised into defending the Landing. "People aren't like that here."

"White people are like that everywhere."

Astrid wanted to pay for brunch, probably to show off her platinum American Express card, but Julia explained that all charges went to a member's account. Astrid tried offering cash for her share, which Julia politely refused, wanting to be in Astrid's debt as little as Astrid evidently wanted to be in hers.

They stood on the front step, forcing diners of the paler nation to excuse themselves in order to gain entrance, a game Lemaster, at odd moments, also liked to play. Off to their right, sloping smoothly white, was the finest golf course in the county. Astrid's flight, a puddle jumper from the Elm Harbor airport, left at four.

"We have the same problem in Ladybugs," said Astrid, as if resuming an earlier conversation. Only it turned out she was. "At the convention in Dallas—you weren't there, were you?—several of us offered a resolution critical of this Administration and its record. Not taking sides in the election—that would of course be illegal for a not-for-profit—but moving as close to the line as we could. Telling the truth about what has been happening in this country, and letting the Sister Ladies decide how to vote. Do you know what happened? They would not even bring it to the floor. They let it die in subcommittee. Laurel St. Jacques gave a speech about how the tradition of the organization was that we stand outside of politics. As if tradition is an argument. The older women, the ones who have been around forever, all nodded and cheered and clapped. All except Aurelia Treene, the writer—you've met Aurie, right? No? Well, Aurie is a gem. She has to be seventy-nine, eighty, something like that. She's been a Ladybug, oh, fifty years. She lived in Harlem in the old days. She's known some of these clubs since they were founded."

Julia tried to say that she knew Aurie Treene, displayed autographed copies of her novels back home on the bookshelf, had met her through Granny Vee when still a child. But Astrid was listening only with her mouth.

"Aurie knew your grandmother. She said this has long been the curse of the best of us, and is therefore the curse of our clubs. The sororities, the fraternities, the social clubs, all of them. The best of our people reach a certain level of success, and they decide that they have moved beyond politics. One reason they become so devoted to the clubs—Aurelia said this—is because it lets them express solidarity with the community without actually having to do anything about it. They can congratulate each other on their achievements, and leave the striving for justice to those they have left behind." During this monologue they had descended the steps. They were crossing the street, because no smoking was allowed on club property, even outdoors, except the golf course. The gutters were thick with slushy runoff. "And Aurie said something else, Julia. She told us that the worst offender of all, the club that in the old days used to have the most successful men, but the men least likely to do anything to risk their standing, was the Empyreals. Lemaster's club," she added unnecessarily, with an angry little bark of laughter. "The Empyreals might not be important any more, but I guess that's one tradition they've stuck with, huh? Not getting involved."

"They're just *clubs*, Astrid."

"Nothing is *just* anything," she shot back, like a divinity school professor explaining Heidegger.

"What I mean is, nobody expects the Boy Scouts to be in politics. The chess club. The . . . the scuba diving association. People need space to relax."

"But they are not permitted to relax for a living. Not in such times as these."

Julia held her tongue. Arguing with Astrid was like arguing with Lemmie: the two of them stored up zingers by the bushel. Including zingers that possessed no zing.

"You're a good woman," Astrid assured her as they strolled toward the town beach. A sprinkling of fresh snow glistened in the noonday sun. A scattering of gulls had lingered for the season and were feeding on the sidewalk. "Lemaster could learn a lot from you."

"I've learned a lot from him."

"You are his wife, Julia. You are closer to him than anybody in the world. You have to make him see sense." A pause, as a terrible idea struck her. "Or does he want this man to be re-elected? Working in the White House—that was just service to his adopted country, wasn't it? Not service to the President?" She seemed to have rehearsed this argument a lot, probably with Washington friends whose judgment she had to avoid. "Surely Lemaster is not a *supporter*?"

Julia chose not to touch that one. "He's your cousin, Astrid. Ask him."

"He *claims* to be neutral." A hissing sound. "As if neutrality is possible." Rubbing her face as if in exhaustion. She was not accustomed to opposition. "Fine. If he's not a supporter, he could prove it. He could help."

"Maybe he just doesn't like to play dirty," said Julia, zipping her parka tightly against the frosty air.

"It's not dirty. It's doing what's necessary."

"Astrid—"

"Or we could go around him." Astrid linked her arm through Julia's and put her mouth close to her ear. Now they were down to the point of their walk. "I mean, all the secrets could get out without Lemaster necessarily being the source. He wouldn't even have to know it got out." A confident throaty smoker's chuckle as, with her free hand, she waved her cigarette. "And he certainly wouldn't have to know *how* it got out."

Julia said, distinctly, "I don't know the President's secrets, Astrid."

"We have to defeat this man. For the sake of the country."

And if Senator Whisted wins, you probably get to be White House chief of staff, don't you? Aloud she said: "Even so, I don't know any secrets. Until yesterday, I didn't even know there were any secrets."

"Well, there are. We're sure of it." *We:* the good guys again. "Scrunchy used to tell Lemaster everything. And Lemaster tells you everything."

Julia's turn to laugh. She kicked through a snowdrift in her high boots. "If that's what you believe, Astrid, you don't know your cousin as well as you thought."

"He would have told you this. It's too juicy to keep to himself."

There are only so many times you can deny a proposition truthfully before you begin to doubt your own story. "Lemaster doesn't tell secrets, Astrid. Period. That's why he knows so many. He believes nothing is more important than our honor." She shook her head, feeling oddly pathetic. She decided not to tell Astrid that she and Lemaster were going to the White House for dinner on Tuesday; although she must already know. "Lemmie always says you have to assume anybody you tell a secret will tell as many people as you told."

"Honor?" Astrid echoed, her voice tinged with the skepticism we reserve for the discovery of a hitherto unsuspected vice.

"Loyalty. Keeping your word even when it costs. That kind of thing. Lemmie will take a head full of secrets to the grave." Julia searched for a way to drive her point home, a way Astrid would appreciate. Thoughts of Kellen and the mirrors intruded again, and again she shoved them away. "Look. Maybe he knows Mal's secrets, too. He's known them both for like thirty years. Did you ever think of that? Lemaster keeps Scrunchy's secrets, and he keeps Mal's. That seems fair."

But Astrid was not so easily deflected. "It isn't the same. One man wants to save the country. The other is destroying it. Fair has nothing to do with it. There is only one moral course: you protect one man and try to stop the other."

(11)

THEIR WALK HAD TAKEN THEM to the parking lot for the town beach, small and white like the Landing itself, and, by common consent, the most picturesque and dramatic in Harbor County. Julia, as conflicted as her famous mother by the competing tugs of the exclusivity of the Clan and justice for The People, had always felt a secret dirty thrill, a delicious frisson, at the thought that residence in the Landing gave the family access to the beach about which others merely fantasized. Bathers from other towns were always trying to sneak in. Kwame Kennerly, the most popular local host on what was called in the trade urban radio, was constantly railing against the "segregated" beach. Before whatever happened to Vanessa happened, the family used to walk here after church on Sunday, even in midwinter, when the sand was hard and the water a defiant gray that secretly thrilled and frightened Julia with its implicit endorsement of eternity.

Thirty years ago, Gina Joule had drowned here.

The two women crossed the snowy parking lot beneath the low slate sky, Astrid still whispering reasons why Julia should get her husband to share whatever dirt he was hiding on Scrunchy. Today's guard, a pimply boy, watched them incuriously. Julia offered a saucy wave, because it was always possible that he was somebody who would be offended if she failed to recognize him. He was opening a box of fudge wrapped in Vera Brightwood's trademark green ribbon, and unless he ate less of it, the pimples would be with him for a long time. Paying a kid to guard the beach in winter struck her as a waste of money, but somebody was here twenty-four hours a day, a tradition that went back to the war— by which the town's old-timers meant World War II—when workers from the ship foundries then located a couple of towns away used to spill into the Landing to eat lunch by the water. A lawsuit challenging the town's policies was currently pending in the state's highest court, the plaintiffs—including Kwame Kennerly—represented by several professors from the law school. Julia, torn afresh between her egalitarian pretensions and her innate snobbery, was not sure how she felt about the prospect of the beautiful beach, so splendid in its isolation, suddenly teeming with humanity.

Astrid, having exhausted abortion and the war, was going on about energy policy and alternative fuels, when the pimply boy stepped from the booth.

"Residents only," he snapped, raising a hand.

Julia swung around, hands on hips, head tilted back, for she never felt quite as Clannish as she did around Astrid. "I beg your pardon?"

"Beach is closed to the general public. Residents and their guests only." He tapped the shiny red-white-and-blue sign in case she was deaf. Usually the guards only dozed. "Town ordinance."

"I am a resident. I've been coming to the beach for six years."

"Residents and guests *only*," he repeated, as if she had missed the point.

"Did you hear me?"

"The beach is closed." His tape seemed to have wound back to the beginning. "Town ordinance."

Julia's face burned. She could not believe she was suffering this humiliation in front of Astrid, whose half-smile suggested that the contretemps was proving her point. A moment ago, in full view of the two women, a teen with two dogs had strolled unmolested past the guard post. A white teen. "Listen to me, young man—"

"Residents and guests only. The beach is closed."

Her cousin-in-law had a hand on her shoulder. "This is why we have to get that man out of the White House. So shit like this will stop."

"Wait." Julia looked past the guardhouse, across the empty parking lot, down to the cold, smooth slope of sand, and the frothy, inviting water beyond. In her imagination she felt the chill. She was a Veazie, and would not accept defeat; looking the boy in the eye, she realized that she need not. "I know you," she said quietly.

"Town ordinance. Residents and their—"

"You're Petey Wysocki, aren't you?"

This shut him up. The pimply jaw gaped. "Uh—"

"I'm Julia Carlyle. Remember me? I taught you eighth-grade general science."

"Oh. Uh. Uh." Like a man lifting a heavy weight. "Right. Right! How are you, Mrs. Carlyle?"

"I'm fine, Petey. I'm fine." Smiling in memory, because she had liked Petey, for all his struggles in the classroom.

"How's your family?" she asked now, still smiling. "Didn't I hear your sister got married?"

He blushed, pleased that she remembered. "Yeah, and she's working on her second kid. Can you believe it?"

"That's great. Give her"—a search of those endless mental lists as Astrid looked on, impressed—"give Doreen my best. And your brother, ah, Mikey. Tell Mikey I said hello."

"I will."

"And your parents, too."

"I will, Mrs. Carlyle. I will. Thank you."

"Thank you, Petey," she said, and moved toward the perfect sand. Despite the season, she might even take off her shoes and socks, roll up her pants, and go up to her ankles in the frigid water.

"Wait, Mrs. Carlyle."

Julia turned. "Yes, Petey?"

"I'm sorry, Mrs. Carlyle. I still can't let you on the beach."

"I beg your pardon?"

"Even if I know you? It's still residents and their guests only." He tapped the sign. "Town ordinance."

CHAPTER 11

PRIVATE DINNER

(1)

"I wonder what he's going to ask you to do," said Julia, smiling at her husband in the mirror as she stood behind him adjusting his collar, although, in truth, it was already lying perfectly. But fixing his appearance was the sort of thing he had been raised to expect his wife to do. As scholar and university president, Lemaster Carlyle was all for the equality of women. In his home, by his own proud admission, he remained a traditionalist; and, whatever else the word implied, it meant that Julia checked his tie and smoothed his collar every morning.

"We don't know that he's going to ask me to do anything. I just started a new job. So it's probably nothing more than a social thing. It's been a long time since we all sat down together." But the fierce ambition in his shining brown eyes conveyed a different message.

"Almost a year."

"Something like that." He smoothed the vent of his suit, turned this way and that, preening in the mirror. He slung a dark formal coat over his arm. Six months as president of the university, and Lemaster was prepared to move to the next thing. Twenty years of marriage, and he was always prepared to move to the next thing. "I think we're ready," he said, and it took her a moment to realize he was speaking only of tonight.

Julia, who never liked the way she looked in evening attire, thought nothing of the sort, but held her tongue. Everything in Lemaster's closet seemed to fit him perfectly. If she did not cut out the vanilla cherries and cappuccino truffles, nothing in hers would ever fit her again. She made herself a fresh promise to stay away from Cookie's: it was just the first Tuesday in December, and there remained time to keep the stern resolution she had made back in January. She sat on the bed to put on her pumps and glanced out the window. They were at the Hay-Adams, a hotel she liked for the way its paneled rooms seemed to breathe history on you, although on this trip their choice had really been dictated by proximity to the White House. Even though the Social Office had offered a coveted on-site parking space, in these days of heightened security they would have had to wait forever for the vehicle search; the only reliable way to get there was to walk.

"Just give me a minute to call home."

"Why?"

Julia was, for a second, stuck on the words. Wasn't it obvious? "To see if the kids are all right. If they need anything."

Lemaster pointed to her shiny Isabella Fiore handbag. She owned several nice purses, from several nice makers, because she had been taught that a special evening bag is the mark of a true lady, and, despite her best efforts, could not stop trying to be one. "You have your cell." He patted his pocket. "I have mine. Wendy is no shrinking violet. She'll call if there's an emergency."

"I'd just feel more comfortable—"

Both palms came up, although he was declaring victory, not surrender. "No, Jules, please, don't get the wrong idea. I'm not trying to tell you what to do. If you need to call, go ahead. We have the time." A grin. "Whatever you need, I'm on your side."

Need. She wanted to slap him, and so kissed his cheek.

In the elevator they talked about their afternoons. Julia had lunched with Tessa Kenner, soaking up Washington gossip, astonished at how much blonder she had become. Lemaster had met alums and lobbyists, but most of his work had been by telephone. As they crossed Lafayette Park in the brisk Washington night, Julia tottering on her heels, grasping his arm more for balance than for show, he said, "By the way, I forgot to mention, that detective dropped by Lombard to see me yesterday. Chrebet."

"What did he want?" Not the lampposts. Please. And not the mirrors. But another part of her knew that Lemaster had never forgotten anything in his life.

"He was wondering—this is going to sound strange—who would have known we were taking Four Mile Road home that night."

"Why?"

Lemaster shrugged. "Chrebet seems to have some idea that Kellen's killer might have left his body there intentionally." Their feet crunched over the salted walkways. "For us to find."

"What?"

"I pointed out that whoever it was would have to be awfully sure we'd stop. How could anybody know we'd have an accident?" A wintry laugh. "Chrebet said he had to pursue every possibility, no matter how unlikely. Then he misquoted Conan Doyle."

She clutched his arm more tightly. "But why—I mean, who—"

"I have no idea who. I have no idea why."

Julia caught the tiny slightest emphasis on the pronoun and felt her fury rise. She stopped watching her feet for a moment. They had almost reached the northwest gate and its guardhouse. "What's that supposed to mean?"

"That I have no idea who or why."

"No. You're suggesting that I might know why."

"Of course I'm not. I told him neither of us had the slightest idea. Oh, good, we're not late after all." He pointed to a taxi a block away, at the corner of Seventeenth Street, depositing the House Majority Leader and his wife. In the park, protesters were beating drums, but Julia could not remember why.

"Lemmie, wait. Wait." Pulling his arm to slow him down, because otherwise he would be busily glad-handing, and she would never get him back.

"What's wrong, Jules?"

"I want you to tell me the truth."

"It is not my habit to tell you anything else. I'm your husband."

Oh, well, that explained everything.

"Please, Lemmie. Tell me you don't think I would have any idea who did this."

The eyebrows did that inverted-V thing that she hated. The night chill nipped a brightness into his dark cheeks. In the cold his sharp face always seemed so handsome, and so impregnable. "No, Jules. I don't think you have any idea. All right?"

"I don't know." She felt sullen, uncertain, ready to scream. Lemmie did this to her, whether by intention or not: took her perfectly reasonable indignation and turned it into a perfectly unreasonable shame. "I guess so." A shake of the head. "I don't know. It's all such a mess. I hate this."

"It's going to be fine, Jules."

"You don't even know what I'm talking about!"

"Interesting."

"What is?"

"How you seem to get awfully riled every time Kellen's name is mentioned."

"And that's an awfully shitty thing to say."

Those eyes, so beautiful and expressive and wise. Reproach. Judgment. Hurt. Lemaster disapproved of vulgarity, and the kindness in his voice made sure she knew it. "Calm down, Jules. Look. I'm sorry. That didn't come out right. I love you. I would not hurt you for the world, or let anybody else hurt you. You know that. So tell me, Jules. Please. Tell me what you're so upset about."

About the fact that I seem to get awfully riled every time Kellen's name is mentioned. About the fact that he broke the lamps on our driveway. About the fact that he left me two mirrors. About the fact that I missed my chance to say goodbye. About the fact that our daughter sometimes freezes up when she tries to eat her cereal in the morning. About the fact that love to you is duty, not choice. About the fact that I got pregnant and married the man who calmed me down instead of trying for one last chance with the man who—

"Nothing." She smiled her crooked smile and, once more, straightened his tie. He was a good man, she reminded herself. Solid and steady. "I'm sorry, sweetie. Let's go see the President, and find out what job he's handing you next."

Except that, once they were inside the White House, she knew that the get-together had nothing to do with Lemaster's career, or, indeed, with Lemaster. Dinner was in the Yellow Oval Room, upstairs in the residence, with its view south between the columns of the Truman Balcony toward the Washington Monument and beyond. The President and the First Lady, Lemaster and Julia, and three other couples: a prominent novelist who had vociferously opposed the President's election, the new head of the second-largest think tank in town, and the Congressman they had spotted outside. The Majority Leader and the think-tank fellow both had spouses in tow; the novelist had brought a girlfriend. Not the floating of a job, then. The sort of mix-and-match party this President was said to enjoy. But, for a moment, all Julia could

see was the novelist's girlfriend, who, according to his laughing intro-
duction, wrote circles around him.

"Julia and I have already met."

"Have you?"

"Oh, yes. And it's so nice to see you again," said Mary Mallard.

(11)

THE TWO WOMEN STOOD on the balcony, shadowed by one of the
massive columns, lights deliberately kept dim for reasons of security.
Inside, the party was into the *oh-do-you-remember-the-time* stage. The
South Lawn was floodlit and, from this vantage, looked like a football
field before the big match.

Mary Mallard said, "I was hoping you would have called me by
now."

"Why would I do that?"

"To tell me you'd found Kellen's surplus." The writer stubbed out
her cigarette, her excuse for wandering out here, with only Julia—who
no longer smoked but, unlike most of her judgmental generation, could
stand those who did—as company. Although Mary's ducklike countenance was softer than Julia remembered from the funeral, the obsidian
eyes had lost little of their fanatical glow. At her neck was another Hermès scarf, this one of a playful plum. "The truth is, Julia, I really think
we should work together. I think we share a common goal."

"What goal is that, Mary?"

"Truth. We're each of us, in our own way, committed to truth."

"I see," said Julia, leaning on the rail.

"You don't think so. But you're the one who got fired because she
decided to let a thirteen-year-old explain to her science class why she
thought the Genesis story was true and God created the world in six
days." Julia was stunned. It had not occurred to her that Mary would
look her up.

"I did *not* get fired."

"There were parental complaints, there was going to be a hearing,
the union ran for cover, and you resigned." The writer was precise.
"You were offered several speaking dates, which you turned down. By
the way, how's your daughter doing? Vincent Brady has such a brilliant
reputation. Would you say it's justified? Or too early to tell?"

Julia was ready to get in her face. "You've made your point, Mary. Now, do you want to tell me what I'm doing here, or do you have some more showing off to do first?"

The white woman's tone remained placid. She lit another cigarette and drew deeply, eyes closed, and Julia remembered the delicious tickling warmth of smoking outdoors on a cold night; and not only tobacco. Early snowflakes, tiny and delicate as newborns, brushed over their faces. "You're here because the President and the First Lady invited you to dinner," said Mary. "Please don't make it into something it isn't."

"I'm here because you wanted to talk to me."

"I'm just a hack writer, Julia. The White House Social Office doesn't exactly dance to my tune. If I wanted to talk to you, I'd drop by Room 118 of the main building of Kepler Quadrangle, or the Exxon station on Route 48, in Langford, where you buy gas twice a week on the way home, or Greta's Tavern on Main Street, where you like to stop for coffee after work, or the bagel shop at the corner of King and Hudson, where you used to have the occasional breakfast with Kellen Zant."

Despite her anger, Julia was dizzied by this casual disclosure of how much information the woman had compiled about her everyday life. Still, she kept on swinging, because Veazie women never quit. "Unless you wanted to meet me where there was zero possibility of being overheard."

"Although they deny it, I've always suspected that the Secret Service has the whole White House wired for sound."

"Probably not the balcony, though."

Mary smiled. Her lips, painted bright red, would otherwise have been nearly invisible, despite her protuberant mouth. "Yes. Probably not the balcony." She stubbed out the second cigarette. Down below, uniformed guards on patrol looked up at them suspiciously. The writer waved, so Julia did, too, on the off chance that waving helped them decide whom not to shoot. "And, yes, you're right, when I heard you were going to be here I sort of had to persuade Mr. Pulitzer Prize in there to bring me as his date instead of somebody else." A glance at the door. "He needed a lot of persuading."

"Am I supposed to be flattered?"

"No. You're supposed to stop attacking me and listen for a minute. I'm joking. Okay, I'm not joking. But, seriously, please, Julia. Just give me a minute. Kellen came to me, not the other way around. That's what

I want you to understand. He was on the track of something important. An old story everybody got wrong. That's what he said. And that the implications would be—earth-shattering."

"He was always the shameless self-promoter."

"Maybe so." She pulled out a third cigarette, pondered whether to light it, yielded to temptation. "But he was frightened, Julia, and I'd never seen him frightened before. He offered me a teaser. That's what he called it, a teaser. He said when he had the story nailed down he'd give me the rest. Not before." She paused. "He said he'd had some help in putting together his inventory. He said the Black Lady had helped him. That's what he called her, Julia. The Black Lady. You could hear the capital letters. Naturally, I figured it was you. Black Lady, Sister Lady—you see the connection. I mean, you are all black, aren't you? Ladybugs?"

"That's actually a contentious issue. The charter doesn't specify skin color, even though it's understood, and a few of the chapters have tried to admit Caucasians to make up the budget, because it's not cheap to be a member and they can't find—" Julia made herself stop. "And that's why you bothered me at the funeral? Because you think I'm Kellen's Black Lady?"

"That was part of it. But Kellen also said that if anything happened to him he'd arranged to transfer the surplus to the girlfriend who got away. That's you, I believe."

"It could be any of a dozen women. He had so many."

"I don't believe that, Julia. You don't believe it either." She flicked the cigarette over the balcony, the red ash arcing into the chilly night, an act Julia found vulgar as well as rude but also endearingly defiant, reminding her, oddly, of Vanessa. "Come on, Julia. He wanted you to follow up his work. All right, nobody can force you. If you choose not to try, that's your business. I understand that."

"I'm so glad," said Julia, irritated by her condescension.

"I know it sounds silly. But Kellen said he had the goods on a major political figure." She pointed toward the glass doors. "Maybe the guy in there. Maybe somebody else. I don't know, and he wouldn't say."

Maybe the guy in there. No. No. Do not think about it. Do not invite Kellen back into your life.

"It's not my fight, Mary." She turned away to look at the Monument, the red lights blinking for the benefit of air traffic, even though air traffic was no longer allowed.

"No. I suppose it isn't."

Julia heard something in the writer's voice, or thought she did. She spun around. "There's more. There's something you're not telling me."

"We should go back inside." Despite the fiery eyes, the voice remained calm as autumn. "They're going to miss us in a minute."

"What did you leave out, Mary? What else did Kellen tell you?"

A beat while the white woman decided how much to tell. From inside came the novelist's laughter, raucous with drink. "He said he would set it up so that the girlfriend who got away had only one, ah, welfare-maximizing choice."

"Choice about what?"

"About whether to . . . follow his footsteps. Search for his surplus. His inventory. Kellen seemed to think he could, ah, force you to help." While Julia processed this distressing notion, Mary scribbled on a business card, which she handed over. "My home and office number are the same. I wrote my cell phone. You give a ring, I'm on the next flight."

"I doubt that I'll be calling."

"Because you're not interested in what Kellen was up to. So you told me." Mary reached for her cigarettes, then changed her mind and tucked them back in her handbag. "Or maybe you're putting on a show. They say you love the theater." The writer delved in her purse for a piece of paper, handed it over. Julia, still in a snit, unfolded it, glanced, then glanced again. She sagged. Snowflakes danced across the floodlit lawn. She was holding a photocopy of a letter from an outdoor electrical contractor recommended by Norm Wyatt, the architect who designed the house—and, as it happened, That Casey's father. The letter, addressed to Julia, contained an estimate for replacing the broken lampposts on the Carlyle driveway.

From far away, Mary Mallard was speaking to her. "I think a lot of people would be very interested in knowing exactly what happened to your lights, Julia."

Julia clutched the rail, all her warring selves, present and past, mother and child, docile and aggressive, defensive and patient, sinner and penitent, hater and lover, roiling around inside. She had no idea which would be left standing when their eerie dance ended.

"You're a considerable bitch," she finally said. "Did you know that?" Mary waited. "So—what is this exactly? Are you accusing me of some kind of—"

But by that time the President himself had flung open the French doors and come outside to see what they were doing, and invite them back in for charades.

Good choice.

(111)

LEMASTER ENDED THE NIGHT in a sour mood, once he realized that the dinner was no more than social, and grumbled about one thing or another all the way back to the hotel. Julia, who had dithered over telling him about Mary, decided that she could not.

Not yet.

So she let her husband run on until he realized for himself how close he was to whining. That snapped him out of it, as she had known it would. Carlyles never complained. Carlyles took charge, turned the tables, grabbed the bull by the horns, reversed the controls—he and Astrid and her brother, Harrison, all three embarrassingly successful in their chosen careers, had so many different ways of describing their shared life philosophy that they sounded like each other's coaches, which perhaps they were.

And so tonight, as usual, Lemaster transformed himself, becoming once more the cheerful and confident man she had known since divinity school twenty-odd years ago. He told her, as they sat at the table in their hotel suite, sharing a snack and a drink and watching a basketball game, how the President had drawn him into a small study for a private conversation, to the envy of others in the room.

"What did he want?"

"Well, he beat around the bush, but, to make a long story short, he wanted me to promise not to endorse Mal Whisted. Apparently rumors have gotten around, maybe because of Astrid's little visit."

She waited, but Lemaster made her ask. "And did you promise?"

"I told him what I told Astrid. I'm through with politics. I told him I'm aggressively neutral." That triumphant smile, tinged tonight with sadness. "I told him that both parties had moved so far from any real interest in the future of African America that I don't much care who wins." The fun faded. "That's true, Jules. I don't care."

"I know," she said, because he told her so often, although, just now, the meaning seemed somehow more profound, a fundamental axiom of his faith.

"You know what the trouble is? The Caucasians aren't afraid of us any more." About to answer, she decided to let him talk his own way out. "Besides," he said, brightening, "it's not like my endorsement is worth anything."

"Oh, Lemmie, it is so," she assured him, and, for a while, they talked sports.

The only uneasy moment came when they lay abed a bit later, after a brief and dutiful conjugality, and Lemaster asked the dozing Julia what she and "that woman" had been discussing for so long.

"Girl talk," Julia tried, playing to his vanity.

"What kind?"

"You don't want to know," she said, guessing, correctly, what his response would be.

Up reared the handsome head. "Please, Jules, tell me the two of you weren't out there smoking. I thought you quit."

"You know the old joke. I'm sure I can quit because I've done it so often?"

Then she pulled him down for a kiss, knowing her husband, in this respect, better than he knew himself. Thinking he had caught her at sin, he would never look for the lie. And, right on schedule, there beside her in the darkness, Lemaster began to explain, as though any living grown-up owned any doubts, all the health hazards of tobacco use. And Julia held him and stroked his back and nodded and promised to do better, because promises were what he liked. It was not, she had once told Tessa, that Lemmie thought he was better than other people. He just got such a kick out of lecturing them.

CHAPTER 12

AN ALMOST NORMAL DAY

(1)

THE YOUNG CHRISTIAN SOCIALISTS were demanding the impeachment of the President of the United States, Professor Helen Bohr sought a student research assistant possessing a working knowledge of Ugaritic, the gay-and-lesbian caucus was holding a potluck for questioners, and the Vesperadoes needed two more tenors: in short, the notice board outside Julia's office was much the same as on any other Thursday afternoon, as was the rest of the shadowy Gothic hallway, with the exception of the thin, sober man in brown suit and soft cap waiting patiently on the fading wooden bench.

At first Julia barely noticed him, far too frustrated from her luncheon meeting with administrators at Lombard Hall who were trying to force the divinity school to become more selective in choosing its students—otherwise, they said, having crunched their numbers, the size of the class must be reduced, meaning less tuition money, and a fresh round of layoffs. Julia had complained to Lemaster last night that some of his people seemed to imagine a world full of twenty-two-year-old geniuses dying to spend two or three years preparing for the ministry, but he had told her that he could not interfere, that Kepler would have to mend its own fences. She returned to Kepler frustrated and embarrassed and probably angry at her husband for his many fussy proprieties, as though, in all the history of the universe, nobody had ever winked at anything. She continued to fume as she unlocked her office. Before Lemaster's triumphant return from Washington last spring to take charge of the university he loved, she had never had to ask his permission for anything. Now the entire divinity school, once her sanctuary, seemed to value Julia principally as a conduit to her husband.

She was angry for another reason, too. The day before yesterday, in Washington, Tessa had pumped her for inside information about the relationship between the President and Senator Whisted back when they were students. Julia, nervous, had said she did not even know if the two men had been friends, and was not comfortable talking about it. Last night, on her show, Tessa had told the world that a source close to both candidates informed her that the two men had probably not even been friends back in college. She added, ominously, that her source was uneasy even discussing the subject. Julia had a call in to Tessa this morning, which her old roommate had not yet seen fit to—

"Mrs. Carlyle?"

She swung around in surprise, because nobody called her that on campus. She was "Dean Carlyle" to the younger students, "Julia" to faculty and, by her own insistence, staff and older students as well.

The man removed his soft hat, uncovering a familiar crew cut and pinched, locked-in face; although not smiling, her visitor looked at her out of pale eyes that just missed sympathetic. Julia said, "May I help you?"—her tone probably too shirty—and then realized who he was just before he spoke.

"My name is Richard Chrebet, Mrs. Carlyle. I'm a lieutenant on the homicide squad of the state police." He offered his credentials. "You might remember speaking to me at your home a couple of weeks ago. I wonder if you could spare a moment."

The mirrors, she thought wildly. Seth Zant told them about the Comyns. Frank Carrington told them about the cheval.

"You visited my husband the other day."

"Yes. And now I'm visiting you." Like a children's game.

"May I ask what this is about?"

"Your daughter."

Maternal panic. "My daughter? Which one? What happened?"

He held up both hands but never smiled. "Nothing has happened. Your children are fine. Nevertheless, we have to talk about Vanessa."

(11)

INSIDE HER SQUEAKY-CLEAN OFFICE, Julia waved him to a chair and then shut the door, a thing she almost never did except when counseling a student, both because Kepler had a long tradition of informality, and also because she liked to project a friendly image. Chrebet sat very straight, like a suitor preparing to ask for the hand of his beloved—a simile, come to think of it, that had led a clutch of students to boycott old Clay Maxwell's course on Paul for a few days last year when he offered it in class. Sexist and heterosexist both, they said. Julia puttered, watering her several plants, taking off her boots and slipping on her flats, shuffling papers on her perfectly neat desktop, doing everything she could to postpone whatever Lieutenant Chrebet had come to tell her. He had arrived at an hour when both of her assistants were out, one at lunch and the other running errands, and perhaps he had planned it that way. Despite his stiffness, he seemed in no hurry, like a man who had in his day outwaited experts.

Finally, she ran out of ideas, and so sat down.

"What about Vanessa?"

"Mrs. Carlyle, let me begin by explaining that I have children of my own—"

"Julia. Please."

"Then call me Rick." But still the investigator did not smile. "I have children of my own, so I understand how fiercely a parent wants to protect them. I have asked my superiors for permission to interview your daughter Vanessa. I would come to you in any case before approaching her, because she is, of course, a minor. I also have another reason. You are her mother. You might be able to explain things that I would miss. Or to help me frame the right questions."

A second's faintness passed. "Just tell me, Rick. Don't prepare me. Tell me."

"I don't want you to get the wrong idea. I am not suggesting in any way that Vanessa had any sort of involvement in what happened to Professor Zant. I do think she might help us shed a little light on what has proved to be more difficult than we expected—figuring out what Professor Zant was working on when he died."

"Why would Vanessa know anything about that?"

"She might not. That's why we want to ask her a few questions."

"Ask me."

"She's under a psychiatrist's care, isn't she? Your daughter. Behavioral issues." He nodded as if to say every teen had them. "How's that going?"

But Julia refused to be drawn. Yesterday Vincent Brady, Vanessa's therapist, had wondered to Julia whether the teen might be suffering from post-traumatic stress disorder—he pointed in particular to her tendency to freeze up and dissociate—to go along with the anxiety and obsessive-compulsive disorders he had previously diagnosed. If indeed a stress disorder was part of her problem, he explained, the initial trauma had predated both the death of Kellen Zant and the torching of her father's car: that was apparent, Vin said, from what he called her behavioral trajectory. He had also speculated, in months past, that Vanessa was showing signs typical of drug or alcohol abuse, or, possibly, withdrawal, but blood screens were consistently negative. He had already ruled out sexual abuse. Lemaster grumbled that Brady was running through the manual like a first-year psychiatry resident.

"Why do you think Vanessa would know what Kellen was working on?" she asked, ignoring the detective's question. "Give me reasons."

He lifted a finger, ticking off a point. A raucous laugh outside the door told her that her assistants were back. "First. Last summer, Vanessa volunteered several hours a week at a soup kitchen at the Methodist church near the campus. Professor Zant sometimes volunteered at the same soup kitchen."

"I'm missing the connection. I bet fifty people volunteered there."

"Seven adults, four teenagers. Those were the regulars, present at least two hours a week."

She shook her head. "Even so, I don't see what this has to do with—"

"Second." Another finger. "In October, on her seventeenth birthday, your daughter received a delivery of maple-walnut fudge from a mysterious admirer."

The rapid-fire delivery, so different from the pace he had set at Hunter's Heights with Lemaster present, brought out in her, as Julia suspected it was supposed to, an urge to pull immediate answers from up her sleeve.

"She guessed it was from her boyfriend—"

"The card didn't say 'love.' It said 'thank you.' Correct?" Stunned by the intimacy of his knowledge, Julia could only nod. "Did your daughter happen to mention whether the fudge was stale?"

The light was growing fuzzy. Perhaps the sun had gone behind a cloud. Perhaps it would stay there. "Stale? Why would it be stale?"

"Did she mention it, Julia?"

"Not that I remember. No."

A knock. The door swung wide open. Latisha, her hefty full-time assistant, the one Boris Gibbs wanted her to fire. "Julia? I got a call back from IT? About what's wrong with your computer?" Because it had started locking up and crashing regularly. At the moment, said computer was not even in the room, but somewhere else on campus, being tested, quarantined, treated.

"Not now. Please."

"But they said it's important—"

"Please. We'll do it later, okay?"

Latisha looked at Julia, looked at the detective, and then, eyes wide, backed out of the room in a flurry of desperate apologies. Like everyone around Kepler, Latisha was dreadfully aware that layoffs were coming, and she was certain that she was to be one of them, for she had not been around long enough to gain protected status under the collective-bargaining agreement.

When the door was shut, Rick Chrebet continued, not missing a beat. "Three weeks before your daughter received the package, you sent Kellen Zant a box of fudge for his birthday, purchased from Cookie's on Main Street in Tyler's Landing."

"Yes. I did."

"It was maple-walnut, wasn't it?"

Julia felt violated. She did not care if some judge had signed a dozen subpoenas. She was going to strangle Vera Brightwood.

"I believe the fudge that your daughter received was from Professor Zant. It was the same box you sent him. That's why it might have been stale."

Pin-drop silence. The room wavered. Julia knew that if she turned, the stained-glass figures decorating her windows would be shivering with disapproval.

She said nothing.

"Third. Most important, we would like to know why your daughter's cell number was in the address book of Kellen Zant's phone."

"You're not serious."

"I'm afraid I am, Mrs. Carlyle. Julia. Not only was her number in his address book, but, during the two weeks before his death, Professor Zant made at least five calls to her phone, and she made at least three to his."

Just weeks ago Julia had been lamenting the awful truth that Kellen had died before she had the chance to say goodbye. Now, for a mad moment, she wished he were still alive, so that she would have the pleasure of killing him. Slowly. Painfully. But she held on to her sanity: a near thing, but she held it and when she answered, was impressed by the calm in her own voice.

"Why are you telling me this, Rick? I would have thought you'd prefer to spring it on us—on Vanessa—as a surprise, instead of warning me. You know I'll ask her."

Chrebet crossed bony legs, folding his fingers over his knee. It occurred to her that the lieutenant was taking no notes. "I am hoping you will ask her, Mrs. Carlyle. I'm afraid it is possible that I won't have the opportunity."

"I don't understand."

"We may not receive clearance to interview her."

"Why wouldn't you?"

The detective measured her briefly with those pale eyes, as if wondering whether to bother. Anger, she finally realized: that was what she had been reading in the pinched, locked-in face. The fury of the athlete tripped up on the final lap.

"Don't you read the papers, Julia? The case is about to be closed. It was a robbery."

Only after he left did Julia take time to puzzle over why the detective had not asked these questions during his visit to Lemaster.

(III)

ALONE IN HER SMALL OFFICE, Julia began the process of not thinking. She tidied shelves that needed no neatening. She straightened the edges of the three stacks of admission folders on her work table, arranging them in razor-sharp lines. Having already watered the plants, she fed them their various magical foods, then stood at the window, watching through the colored panes and involute leading as Rick Chrebet crossed the parking lot, leaning into the afternoon wind whipping down from the north. She respected the bitter fire she had noticed in the pale eyes at the end of their interview: the fierce pain of incapacity to fight what the soul says must be fought. She used to see it in the mirror every morning in the final weeks of her final relationship with Kellen.

Julia slipped into her parka and pulled on her Ugg boots. Most days she left Kepler as early in the afternoon as she could, in order to beat the children home. The buses dropped off Vanessa and Jeannie a little after three. It was now minutes before two. The drive was twenty-five minutes. In the outer office, Latisha handed her a memo the IT people had sent over, summarizing their findings, while Foxon, her white part-timer, who never seemed to do any work and plainly would rather not have had a black boss, whispered importantly on the telephone: Foxon, who, if Latisha went, would get an upgrade.

"Leave it on my desk," said Julia.

"They said to tell you ASAP." Reproach. Confusion. Fear. "You should at least look at it."

"I have to go. I'll look at it tomorrow."

But Latisha, to Julia's surprise, stood her ground. "They said today."

"Please. Just leave it on my—no, never mind." She took the memo, folded it, stuffed it into her pocket.

Trying to slip out of the building, Julia ran into Boris Gibbs and Iris Feynman, her fellow deputy deans. Boris saluted her with his ubiquitous candy bar, offered a smeary wave. She remembered how he had promised to find out what Kellen was up to in the Landing. Their lunch seemed ages ago.

Iris, said Boris, was making trouble again. "*I* say Kepler is too Christian-centric. *She* says it's supposed to be, it's a divinity school. And she's *Jewish*. She should be leading the protest!"

In Boris Gibbs's world, this passed for humor.

"This isn't my kind of argument," said Julia, eyeing the exit.

"Julia's not a God woman," Boris explained, as if Iris didn't know. "She goes to church, but she's not a God woman. Julia's old-fashioned. She goes because her husband takes her. He's a traditionalist Anglican. That's a polite way of saying he likes the reactionary prayer book the rest of the civilized world has abandoned." He took a bite, pointed at Julia. "I have some information for you."

Iris, smiling in relief, said she would leave them to talk.

"Boris, I'm sorry. I can't do this just now."

"He was building a house."

This slowed her down, as perhaps it was meant to. "He what?"

"Your Kellen was building himself a house in the Landing." He took a huge bite. "Looked at a nice lot with a private beach, talked to a surveyor, everything."

After the interview with Chrebet, she had trouble taking this in. "Are you telling me that Kellen Zant was moving to Tyler's Landing?"

"Building a house at least," he answered, very pleased with himself. "Looks like he didn't tell you that, either." He clapped a hand on her shoulder, and she wondered what candy stains she had just picked up. "There's more to the story. But you're in a hurry, so I'll tell you the rest later."

Laughing, Boris stalked off down the hallway. It would be much later before Julia realized that his argument with Iris was the larger clue.

(I V)

"NOT A GOD WOMAN," she said aloud, rankled by Boris's cruel teasing. Heading for the front entrance, trying to decide how to put to Vanessa the question that had to be put, Julia changed course and slipped into Kepler Chapel, the divinity school's own worship space, not nearly as grand as the university chapel, but perfectly serviceable. She glanced around the vast, cool chamber, but had the peeling frescoes and flaking gold leaf and crumbling plaster cornices all to herself. She walked slowly up the aisle. There was a high altar a century old, carved with fading words from the eighth chapter of John's Gospel, and a low altar of younger and brighter wood, offering no statement whatsoever. Along the walls and in various closets were stashed sufficient chairs, crucifixes, altar cloths, chalices, thuribles, and fonts to enable nearly any denomination, saving only the most austere, to arrange matters to the comfort of its members. In a shadowed corner stood a rickety rack of votive candles in copper stands, none lit. Up above, cold afternoon sunlight sparkled through clerestory windows.

This was where she and Lemaster had married twenty years ago, the stunned families bearing the union in shared furious stoicism, each side unalterably persuaded that Julia had trapped him, for by their wedding day she had been in her fifth month, the baby growing within difficult to conceal. She had felt her mother's mute humiliation burning into her back, and, later, insisted that all she recalled of the ceremony was grabbing Lemaster and fleeing for her life. This was a lie. In actual fact, she remembered every painful minute, even the part where she silently cursed God in the midst of her vows for getting her into this situation; for Julia, good American Protestant that she was, could not quite get her mind around the notion that her troubles might be her own fault.

Since returning to the div school three and a half years ago, Julia had developed the habit of coming here when she needed to think, because the chamber was hardly used during the workweek, and she could sit in relative peace. That is, she could sit in peace except on those occasions when Kellen would glide over from his office in the massive social-science building just across Hudson Street, sneaking into the pew beside her to share his latest woes. Or she would return to her office on the first floor only to find him lurking unhappily in the corridor: always, there was some crisis he could discuss with nobody else, because nobody else had ever understood him. When Julia told him to leave her alone, he would slink off in that affecting, soulful way that certain bearish men can achieve at the drop of a hat, only to show up again a week later, by e-mail or instant message or telephone, proposing lunch or coffee or whatever she could spare. He would wear her down. And so they would meet, and Kellen would tell her about a woman who was giving him trouble, or a colleague who had teased him about not having done much scholarship lately, or a potential client who had hired another economist despite Kellen's greater qualifications.

You're going to have to handle it, she would say, quoting Granny Vee. *That's what grown-ups do. They handle things.*

I can think of things this grown-up would rather handle, he would answer, teasing her with mellow eyes.

You can't lead an ordered life if what matters most is desire. She supposed she must be quoting Lemaster now.

So who wants to lead an ordered life?

Kellen was brilliant and accomplished and honored everywhere. He was also a big baby, and wanted Julia to play mommy, to offer a shoulder to cry on, the way she used to, except crying was not what he planned if he ever got his head back on her shoulder. What Kellen told

Julia in a thousand little ways was the same thing Seth Zant kept saying the day of the funeral: she was the one who got away.

Mostly she had kept her distance.

Up at the mall in Norport, Kellen had said he had to spread the inventory risk because he was in trouble, that they were facing dark times, that the darkness mattered. She had dismissed it as another slimy flirtation, for Kellen had been in so many different kinds of trouble in his life that it was hard to imagine any single one could possibly be the worst.

Now she was not so sure.

Not a flirtation. A message.

Boris was right, of course. Julia did not believe in God, not really. Twenty years ago, she and Lemaster had moved in together and dropped out of div school, Lemaster because what he was learning made him fear that it might all be false, Julia because what she was learning made her fear that it might all be true. With time, both had overcome their fears, and reverted to type. Father Freed at Saint Matthias spoke, often, of Heaven. Lemaster listened keenly. Julia indulged him. But when in her secret heart she looked toward the future, two, three, perhaps four decades hence, she saw herself in an uncaring hospital, surrounded by soulless machines, a child or two to hold her hand, her husband long dead, and she herself waiting for the dark curtain to come down, and, on the other side, only blankness.

Time to go. Reaching into her pocket for the car keys, she found the IT memo. She unfolded the single short page, read it once, quickly, then a second time, more closely, key phrases jumping out: . . . *riddled with spyware . . . more sophisticated than the usual commercial . . . not a product by amateurs . . . escaped the antivirus software . . . spoofed Task Manager . . . follow every keystroke . . . every Web site or e-mail . . . of a quality used by federal government, usually with a warrant . . .*

And Kellen had said he had the goods on a major political figure. And had left the evidence to her.

Julia Carlyle was still, as she had always been, a dedicated agnostic. Nevertheless, sitting alone in the empty, dying chapel, she bowed her head and prayed.

CHAPTER 13

MOTHER AND DAUGHTER AND FRIEND

(1)

"CAN I TALK TO YOU, honey?" said Julia, stepping into her second-eldest child's room.

Vanessa, hunched over the computer with her friend Smith, shrugged her shoulders, but also clicked away the instant messages that popped up all over the screen whenever she was online. It was natural, her mother knew, for a teenager, caught in these invented years between the freedom of a child and the burdens of an adult, to protect a private sphere. Still, she worried about the friends her daughter made online and the secrets she shared or discovered. Rainbow Coalition, curled on Vanessa's lap, glared at Julia as she might at an intruder. Smith, pierced nearly everyplace her ghostly-pale flesh showed around her heavy black outfit, did not even look up. Outside the windows, the night sky was clear and beautiful, but more snow was in the forecast for morning.

"Vanessa?"

"Uh-huh." Laconic, even vaguely disrespectful, as she always was around Smith, who had been, a couple of years ago, a mousy white thing named Janine Goldsmith. Her close-cropped head was bobbing as she examined some object held in her lap. Julia wondered if she might be stoned.

"I'm talking to you, Vanessa."

"I hear you."

Julia moved closer, her gown brushing the floor because she had kicked off her heels the instant she and Lemaster had walked in the door. It was Friday, and another fancy dinner, this time a fund-raiser for a college fund for minority students. Julia had mostly danced while Lemaster had mostly worked the room.

"Vanessa," said Julia again. "Vanessa, would you mind turning around? And turning the music down?" For the incomprehensible sounds were surprisingly loud in the room, even if nearly undetectable in the hall.

"Nope." Vanessa swiveled in her chair, grinning at her mother as Smith continued to toy with what Julia could now see was some sort of electronic thing that probably had not even been invented a month ago and would be all the rage a month hence, for her indulgent parents, angrily divorced, believed that they could purchase their way back into their daughter's good graces. Vanessa winked. She wore glasses instead of contacts, as she often did late at night. A robe covered loose pajamas. Her feet were stuffed into bunny-rabbit slippers so ancient and floppy that Julia wondered how she could walk without stumbling. She had asked this afternoon if she could have her eyes lasered. It was Friday, and Smith was sleeping over, but, despite the hour, she showed no signs of readiness for bed.

Julia said, "Hello, Janine. How are you?"

Smith did not budge. Kids today.

To Vanessa: "I'd like to talk to you."

"Kay."

"You're a woman of few words tonight."

"Yep."

This was Vanessa's New England Yankee persona, one of several identities from which she selected when protecting a vulnerability near her core. Vincent Brady had warned them not to be distracted by what their daughter showed on the surface.

"Is everything okay, honey?"

"Uh-huh." Idly stroking Rainbow Coalition's pudgy neck.

"Can we talk privately?" Wanting to put Rick Chrebet's question without Rick Chrebet; but also furious at herself for asking permission. Yet she had no clear way to relate to her daughter. They still had reached no agreement on whether Vanessa would be attending the Orange and White Cotillion after Christmas, and Julia was reluctant to order her to go. She also was no longer sure her orders would be obeyed.

Oh, God, what was wrong with her child?

"Smith *is* private," said Vanessa. Her hand trembled, but she was able to make it stop. "I tell her everything anyway."

Smith let out a small grunt that might have been sorrow or glee, disagreement or excitement or even a snore. The device in her lap had a small screen. A DVD player?

Julia said, "May I see you outside for a second, please, honey?"

Vanessa nodded grimly, as if to say duty called, but Smith looked up briefly, her pallid face sharp and disapproving, as if manners were out of fashion.

When they were in the gallery, the wide balcony between Vanessa's bedroom and the bridge to the master suite, Julia leaned close and said, "Is she okay? Janine?"

"She's under a vow of silence. Until the violence stops."

Oh, well, that explained everything. "Ah, honey, listen. I won't take long. I've been wanting to ask you—"

"Four."

"What?"

"The number of times I ran into Kellen Zant." Grinning. "I've been waiting for you to ask."

(11)

JULIA SHIFTED HER WEIGHT on aching feet. She had allowed herself a full day to cool down before raising the question, because, had she pressed Vanessa in the first hours after Chrebet's visit, she would have been fiery indeed, and her relationship with her elder daughter was difficult enough. Lemaster was downstairs talking to Flew, who had met them on their arrival, fulfilling some undisclosed errand. "Excuse me a sec," she told Vanessa, because she had noticed that Jeannie's door, decorated with her perfect little poems, was open a perfect little crack. Julia crossed the wide landing and knocked. The only response was scampering feet. "Go to sleep, Jeannie."

Julia waited for the muffled acknowledgment, then turned back to Vanessa, drawing her down onto the sofa because standing hurt too much. "Do you want to tell me about what happened with Kellen Zant?"

"I'm *willing* to tell you."

With an effort, Julia withheld a cranky response, refusing to imitate, as she too often did, her own impulsive and short-tempered mother. "Please stop, Vanessa. Tell me."

"If you want." She rubbed her eyes, then cast a glance of almost passionate longing at the door to her room. Julia wondered whether her daughter was thinking of Janine—no, Smith now—or of the computer. It occurred to Julia that her daughter was awfully tired and should probably be in bed. But Vanessa and Smith would stay up until dawn, doing whatever it was that they did. "The first time I ran into him was at the div school library, I think like November. A year ago. I think."

Julia, who could never recall her daughter suffering such memory problems before, was still at the first hurdle. "You ran into Kellen . . . in Kepler?"

"Uh-huh. When I was doing research for my term paper. I was coming out of the archives, and he was in the reading room—"

"Wait, honey. Wait. Are you sure?"

"No, Moms. I'm making it all up." She made a sound. Distress? Anger? "Yes, Moms, I'm sure. I was even kind of surprised, because I figured, you know, he's the big economist, the big bad corporate consultant, and Dads is always talking about how he doesn't really do any scholarship, so what was he doing in the library? Especially the div school library? But there he was. And after that, um, like January. Then maybe in the summer. And then this fall. September or something. One more time at the div school, and one time at the Historical Society—"

"The Harbor County Historical Society?"

"Yes. And I saw him after school one day, too."

"He came to the high school?"

"He was, like, passing by in his car when I came out. He asked if I wanted to get a cup of coffee or something."

"That bastard," said Julia before she could stop herself, wishing afresh for the chance to kill him all over again. "Honey, what . . . what did you two talk about?"

"You know. School. The weather. How good my hair looked today."

"He talked about your hair?" said Julia, sinking fast.

"Uh-huh. And how I was the spitten image of my mother. Only Kellen said *spitting*. Got it wrong." A shy smile danced over her lips and was gone. "How he liked my taste in clothes. How smart I was. Word games. He liked word games. He pestered me, Moms." Shuddering. "He'd e-mail me and IM me and call me up. It got kind of creepy. He was too old to be calling me."

"Oh, honey, he didn't . . . I mean, the two of you . . . Please tell me . . ."

"I didn't sleep with him, if that's what you mean! That's too gross for words!" Vanessa's head tipped forward and she covered her eyes. She rubbed her temples. She had to be sick by now of answering questions all the time, and here was her mother making it worse. Already Julia almost regretted trying.

Except that she needed to protect her daughter from . . . whatever.

"I'm sorry you had to go through that, honey."

"Me, too. It was like he was stalking me. Like I said. Creepy."

"I wish you'd told me or your father. We'd have handled it."

"Well, it's been handled, hasn't it?" said the teenager tartly.

A pause while they thought this through together. Vanessa's face slowly fell as the implications of her own comment sank in, and a wave of revulsion swept over Julia, as a wicked little voice assured her that Kellen had deserved his fate. Then Julia asked the question that had been rolling around in her head ever since Rick Chrebet's visit.

"Honey, did he ask you about your paper?"

"My paper?"

"The one on Gina Joule."

Vanessa dropped her eyes and laughed harshly. "Oh, Moms, come on. He didn't care about my term paper. He cared about getting in my pants."

"Oh, honey—"

"Creepy pervert. He was like forty-nine or something, flirting with a teenager. Wanted me to have *coffee* with him."

Still Julia fought to keep her head above water, not missing the forest for the trees, and as many other metaphors as she could mix, as long as she got her answer. "So he never . . . ah, he didn't ask you about what really happened to Gina that night?"

Vanessa's head snapped up, braids flying. "Nothing *really* happened to Gina, Moms. Didn't you read my paper? It was DeShaun Moton who killed her. Remember?" Retelling the story anyway, another habit she shared with her father. "Gina had this big fight with her mom, she went storming out of the house, she walked around. DeShaun stole the BMW, he spotted this cute white girl near the Green on his way out of town, he pulled over, he flirted a little bit, and Gina, stupid little thing that she was, got in. Probably because she was mad at her mom. Girls do stupid things when their moms make them mad. I mean, no girls we know, but, um, generically. Anyway, DeShaun drove her over to the beach, tried to do what guys do, they fought, she drowned. And DeShaun, well, he got the hell out of Dodge. Only he was stupid, too. Five, six days later he's back, he steals another car, the cops chase him, bang, he's dead. Okay, right, I know, they shouldn't have done that, but he was guilty as sin, Moms. I mean, come on. The evidence was clear. Sure, people wanted DeShaun not to be guilty, because he was black and Gina was white, and, you know, black men getting lynched for killing white girls, that's a pattern as old as—" Vanessa did not seem to be able to decide what the pattern was as old as, and, for a moment, her mouth worked soundlessly. This time Julia had the good sense to let her daughter fight her own way out of it. "Go back and read the paper, Moms. I've seen the records of the case. It wasn't even close. Open and shut. They had witnesses. They had his past record. They had everything. Sure, there was a riot, but the rioters were wrong. I wanted them to be right. That's why I wrote the paper, to prove DeShaun was innocent. But he wasn't innocent." Vanessa stopped again, and brushed at her arms and chest, as if to wipe away the remnants of her tirade. She smiled as if the rest had never happened, and spoke calmly. "Anyway, he shouldn't have been bothering me. Kellen. It was creepy."

"I know. I'm sorry, honey."

"And I honestly don't know what Kellen was working on, Moms. He didn't tell me. But if by some chance he really was looking into what happened to Gina? Well, if he decided it wasn't DeShaun who did it, and told the world? He'd be lying, Moms."

"You're very sure?"

"Hey, remember what Dads told me, before I sat down to write my paper? He said a student who does a research paper is supposed to become like one of the world's leading experts on his subject. Her subject. Well, here I am. I'm the world's leading expert on Gina Joule. And, yes, Moms, I'm very sure it was DeShaun Moton. So was the family, I guess, because they dropped their lawsuit against the Landing. Didn't even get a settlement."

"Did you tell Kellen?"

"Of course not." Eyes wide with disbelief. "We never talked about it. I told you. Kellen didn't care who killed Gina. He cared about looking at my legs. It was creepy."

"So those phone calls—"

"He kept wanting to get together. He was a sicko." Calm again. Like throwing a switch. "Don't tell Dads, okay? He'll have a fit. I mean, the guy's dead. Let him rest in peace."

Julia had been thinking much the same thing. "And that was it? The sum total of your relationship?"

Vanessa's head snapped up again, and Julia knew she had chosen the wrong words. "We didn't have a relationship! I just told you! I mean, come on! That's gross!"

Janine poked her head out the door as if to see if her buddy needed defense. Julia stared at her until, pierces and all, she vanished again. Vanessa, meanwhile, had never stopped reciting: "We weren't even friends, Moms. We weren't anything. I was minding my own business, and he came along and bothered me, okay? Guys do that sometimes, even older guys. I'm sure that happened to you, too."

"That wasn't what I meant, honey. Honestly."

Children, but especially teenaged girls, own a variety of disdainful stares, and Vanessa favored her mother with one of the best. "Sure, Moms."

"Honey—"

"And, see, now that I know you guys were an item? It makes sense. He was bothering me because he figured it would bother you."

Julia was stunned by the profundity of this insight—and its likely truth.

"I'm sorry you had to go through that, honey. Truly sorry. Oh, honey." Offering a hug, which Vanessa, still as a statue, neither accepted nor refused. "He was a terrible man. He was." She wondered whom she was trying to persuade. "He had no business doing any of that. I'm so proud of you, the way you handled it—"

Vanessa's quiet reply withered her. "Oh, Moms, you don't have any idea how I handled it."

A dangerous idea began to form in Julia's mind, an idea she had been beating back and beating back, ever since her conversation with That Casey at the multiplex. She beat it back again.

"Well, I'm proud of you, honey. And I love you."

"Was there anything else?" said Vanessa, with all Lemaster's hauteur. "Because I really am okay, I promise. And I'd kind of like to get back to what I was doing."

"Ah, no, nothing else," said Julia, hiding her exasperation, blaming herself for being so bad at drawing her children into serious conversation. "Oh, by the way, honey, what exactly are you doing?"

"Saving you guys a pot of money with MP3s. But don't worry, I'm mainly ripping CDs I borrowed from Casey and using a file-swapper nobody's heard of, this really cool Korean site. Don't get that look. It'll be fine. My anti-hunterbot systems are enabled. RIAA"—she pronounced it *ree-ah*—"will never find me."

"And how would you describe what you're doing if your first language was English?"

"Downloading music."

"Oh." An uneasy pause. Julia tried to figure out when she had become so powerless over her adolescent daughter. It occurred to Julia, not for the first time, that not one of her children had a single close black friend, other than kids they knew through their parents: exactly what Mona had warned her about when they moved out of the city. "Legally?"

"No."

"Well, don't, then, okay?"

"Sure, Moms."

"Vanessa?"

"Yes, Moms." Hand on the knob, no longer masking her impatience. Julia felt certain her daughter was lying to her, but could not figure out about what.

"What's that thing Janine's playing with? The, ah, the electronic thing?"

"Her name is Smith now, Moms. It's a protest, remember?"

"Tell me."

Vanessa could be punctilious even in describing mischief. "It sniffs cellular networks for ESN and MIN. It's supposed to work even under AMPS and NAMPS. We're testing it."

"In English, please. It does what?"

"Clones the cell numbers. You know, to make free calls." Vanessa saw her mother's face go gray. "Don't worry. She's not using it for profit. She found the plans online and just wanted to see if she could build one."

Julia remembered, with a pang, when Janine Goldsmith took consecutive first prizes in the school science fair. And when Vanessa would not have helped her do . . . whatever she was doing. The other thing she remembered was that Lemaster had opposed the sleepover. Julia had wangled it out of him to buoy Vanessa's spirits.

"Tell her to put it away, okay? It's a teensy bit against the law. And wrong, too," Julia added, but afterthoughts carry little moral heft.

"Okay, Moms." That sweet smile again, like the welcome into a new religion.

(i i i)

She kept her half-promise to Vanessa. She did not tell Lemaster about Kellen's creepy attentions toward their daughter. There was no point, she assured herself, lying beside her husband, willing herself to sleep. Kellen was dead. Vanessa's fragile recovery had been too hardwon. The coming end of official interest in Kellen Zant was the best news she had heard . . . well, since he was shot.

She said, "Lemmie?"

"Hmmm?"

"That detective came to see me yesterday. Chrebet." The darkness was like the inside of the tent at the overnight campouts on which Mona used to take her children when they were small, hoping to keep them from growing up into wimps. "He said they're getting ready to close the investigation."

"So I hear." Sleepily. "Robbery or something."

"That's what he told me."

"Seems awfully convenient." Lifting his head briefly, then settling again. "But I guess it's not our call." A yawn. A way he had, putting behind him what could not be changed. In her mind's eye, Julia could see the campfire, whipping yellow and red as the night rose. "Oh, by the way, I talked to Mal Whisted." A beat. "About Astrid."

Right after you went to the White House and spent a few minutes alone with the President, Julia registered, but choked the thought before it could grow. "Okay."

"He said he'll call her off. He doesn't believe in that kind of—"

"Okay."

"Astrid's just the way she is." Lemaster drew her closer. "You can't choose your family, I guess." A kiss. "Fortunately, you can choose your spouse."

A lovely interlude in the shadows, a little poking and prodding.

Then: "Lemmie? What do you think really happened? With Kellen,

I mean?" Half wanting his remarkable mind turned to the problem because she was tired of speculating alone. Half testing him.

He made her wait so long Julia feared he had fallen asleep. Again the thoughts she dared not think clamored for attention, and, with difficulty, she fended them off. "I suppose whoever did it must have thought there was a good reason."

"But who would hate him that much?"

"It didn't have to be hate, Jules."

"What else could it be?"

Listening for his answer, imagining a sleeping bag, dying embers, stars diamond-bright against dark velvet.

"I know what Kellen would have called it," he said at last. "Rational maximizing of self-interest."

CHAPTER 14

A SURPRISE GUEST

(1)

SUNDAY NIGHT JULIA HAD DINNER in the city with a pair of Sister
Ladies: Regina Thackery, an obstetrician on the staff of the medical
school, and Kimmer Madison, a partner in the biggest law firm in town.
They were, technically, a subcommittee of a subcommittee, charged
with crafting a description of the purpose of a fund-raising dance to be
held in May, because the group wanted a way to support health services
for pregnant teens without taking a position on abortion. Regina volunteered, and also drafted Kimmer, her bosom buddy, who never actually attended the organization's meetings, although now and then she
brought her son to Littlebugs, the children's auxiliary, created decades
ago so that middle-class women of the darker nation could find play-
mates for sons and daughters too precious to be risked among the black
masses, yet too black to be risked among the whites. Julia had no clear
memory of how she had stumbled onto the subcommittee. So far the
trio had met twice and accomplished next to nothing, and this meeting,
at Cadaver's, an expensive if peculiar restaurant downtown, was headed
in the same direction: good food, good wine, good conversation, none
of it on the topic.

Usually Julia enjoyed these get-togethers. But tonight she was distracted, and both her Sister Ladies noticed.

"Are you okay, honey?"

"Everything all right at home?"

They could not draw her with politics. They could not draw her
with gossip, even when Kimmer let slip the juicy morsel that she had
decided, due to the shortage of black men of a certain age and quality,

to start dating her own ex-husband. They could not even draw her into a discussion of relationships, where ordinarily she would dissemble, recognizing how the rest of the Clan thought her marriage ideal; but, having learned at Mona's feet never to air dirty laundry in public, she shared with nobody in the world the chilly truth that living with Lemaster was like climbing Everest every day.

Without oxygen.

"I'm sorry," she said, when their banter failed to rouse her. She sipped her wine, glaring at her barely touched tilapia as if she had identified a new enemy. "This hasn't been an easy few weeks."

They understood, eyes begging for more.

"Maybe we should never have moved out of the city," she continued, surprising herself. And perhaps she was even sharing a piece of the truth, although not, to be sure, her deepest fears. "It's like ever since we got to the Landing—"

"Hey, look who's here," said Kimmer with sudden unenthusiasm, handsome walnut face crinkling with distaste as she gazed across the restaurant. Like Lemaster, Kimberly Madison seemed to know everybody in town.

Julia and Regina turned as a tall, fit man of the paler nation strode happily toward their table, jollity gleaming from friendly blue eyes, not the smallest hair out of place. You had the sense that all of life delighted him.

"Don't get up, don't get up," he said, waving his large hands, although nobody had budged. "Kimberly, my dear, introduce me to your friends."

"Regina. Julia. This is Anthony Tice."

(11)

SHE RECOGNIZED HIM from his television commercials, but he was even more overwhelming in person. He possessed the chipped good looks and fetching smile of a man who spent a lot of time practicing in the mirror, and the broad shoulders of a man who spent a lot of time in the gym. She had heard that Tice developed an amazing rapport with juries, and, seeing him in the flesh, believed it.

"Well!" he said, face alight with a hot joy that made her queasy. "Julia Carlyle. We meet at last. My pleasure. Really."

"Go away," said Julia, and both Sister Ladies turned to look at her. He sat down instead.

"We have a lot to talk about," he assured her.

"Do you *know* him?" said Regina.

The legal Adonis said hello, and that was all it took. Julia gave him a lengthy and detailed piece of her mind, because she had needed an outlet for weeks, and this man's nonsense with her dean was certainly a contributing factor. Tony Tice seemed unsurprised, and unfazed. He bore her vehemence stoically. When she ran down, her Sister Ladies were staring at her; as was her end of the restaurant.

"I only need a couple of minutes." His suit fit perfectly. His shoes glistened. His feet, like his hands, were very long. "If you returned my calls I wouldn't have to bother you."

"I didn't return your calls because I don't want to talk to you."

"Hear that? She doesn't want to talk to you," said Kimmer, switching sides.

His weatherproof smile never wavered. "I won't be long, Kimberly, dear. You ladies can get back to your dinner in a sec." To Julia: "Did you talk to your dean about me?"

"Sure. She said you might not give your contribution this year if I don't talk to you." Her cell phone rang. She ignored it. "Well, now we've talked, so you can pay up."

Again Kimmer tried to interrupt.

"The thing is, I'm representing a client." Leaning forward, trying to get her to lean toward him so he could whisper, but Julia refused to play. "My client was doing business with Professor Zant, and I'm afraid their business was never quite concluded. I'm sort of picking up the pieces—"

Julia held up her hands, not wanting Regina and Kimmer to hear any of this. "Okay, okay, I'll talk to you for a minute. Just for a minute."

She left the table with him, walked to the foyer, where diners without reservations waited. Out on the street, a bitter cold rain had replaced the recent snow, so they stood beneath the awning.

Infuriated by his complacent whiteness, feeling Clannish, Julia went at once on the attack. "How dare you just come up and interrupt our dinner like that."

"I'm a lawyer. I'm rude for a living."

"Well, whatever you're selling, I'm not interested."

"I'm buying, not selling."

"I don't have anything to sell, Mr. Tice. No matter what you might think, I was not Kellen's Black Lady."

She had hoped to startle him, but he startled her right back.

"I see you've talked to Mary Mallard," he said. "I wouldn't trust her if I were you. Professor Zant's dealings were with me, not Ms. Mallard. He was going to sell to my client. Ms. Mallard is an interloper. You shouldn't let her near you."

"After tonight, I'm not going to let *you* near me."

The smile never left his face, and she had to admit the effect was rather endearing. "Let me make it simple, so I won't take much of your time. Professor Zant was in possession of an item that my client was interested in buying. They had negotiated a deal. Zant gave my client what he called a teaser. He promised to deliver the item itself within a couple of weeks, and then somebody shot him."

"Are you finished?"

"Shari Larid," he said suddenly.

"What?"

"It's a name. Shari Larid." He spelled it. "A substitute teacher. Professor Zant said she would have the materials he was selling, and you would know where to find her."

Julia shook her head. "I don't know anybody of that name. I knew a lawyer named Aird when I worked in New York, but that's about it. There. We're done. Now, will you please go away?" When Tice just kept smiling, she tried again: "Who's your client?"

"Privileged. Sorry." He didn't look sorry.

"I'm going to tell you the same thing I told Mary. I don't have any idea what Kellen was doing when he died. He didn't tell me anything. He didn't leave me anything. We didn't have that kind of . . . of, ah, relationship." An unexpected heat in her cheeks caused her to stumble over the words. "And I don't appreciate anybody suggesting anything to the contrary. So go back and tell your mysterious clients you messed up. Tell them you've got the wrong girl."

Still he was undeterred. "You have no idea how important this is. There could be a nice reward if you help. We could make a deal." Waving away her fresh objection. "Just think about it. That's all I'm asking."

"You're out of your mind."

Her cell phone rang again. Irritated, Julia glanced at the screen. Claire Alvarez. Whatever she wanted could wait. "All right, Mr. Tice. You want a deal? Let's make a deal. These are my terms, and they are not negotiable." Finger stabbing the air. "You come near me again, for any reason, and I'll have you arrested. Period."

"I'll be in touch," he said, undeterred, and slipped his card, unwanted, into her hand.

Julia's smile was savage. She did not often give vent to her anger, not in the years since marrying Lemaster. It was like being high, only more natural. Making sure the lawyer saw her do it, she tore the card in half and tossed the pieces into the filthy snow mounded along the street. She strode back inside, trying to project a haughty swagger. Lemaster was down in Florida, fund-raising, but when he got back she would tell him about Tice's harassment, and let him, as he had said, do something about the man. Meanwhile, she felt triumphant. She had told Tricky Tony off. After twenty years of letting her husband solve her problems, she had handled this one herself. As she sat back down, Regina and Kimmer remarked on her changed mood, even going so far as to tease her about her clandestine conversation.

Julia, still high on her success, went along with the fun.

Her cell phone rang yet again. Odd for her dean to be so persistent. She marched out to the lobby to take the call. Claire, sounding shaken, asked if Julia could come to her house right away. Julia looked at her watch. Almost nine. She asked if it could wait until tomorrow.

Claire told her why.

Two hours ago, as Boris Gibbs crossed the crowded parking lot after Christmas-shopping at the big mall up in Norport, a sport utility vehicle, skidding in the snow, had pancaked him, and kept on rolling.

And although nobody believed them—in emergencies people tend to see strange things—a couple of horrified witnesses would later insist that the SUV had backed up and hit him again.

(I I I)

LATER. Julia down in the family room skimming through the channels as the latest storm screeched along the eaves, demanding entry. No snow, but plenty of nasty bone-chilling rain, and already the yard was invisible, despite the floodlights, angry droplets hurtling down like gunfire. CNN. Click. Fox News. Click. MSNBC. Click. Nothing.

Unlike Kellen, poor Boris did not make the networks.

Just a traffic accident, after all, and Boris was white, and known to nobody of consequence beyond Kepler, aside from the tiny handful of scholars in his field, and, in truth, not even to all of them.

Irritated, she turned off the television and went to the kitchen desk to try the online versions. But she kept imagining what it must have been like. The truck hits. You're down, you've never felt such pain, but you're alive. Relief floods through what body you have left. Then the truck comes back. And back.

The police discounted the reports, but Julia knew they would live in her nightmares.

She wondered what Boris heard at the end. An engine gunning. Screams, of course, maybe his own. Then that final click, brightness to blankness. And what Kellen had heard. Would his brain even have had time to recognize the gunshot? She thought not. Just an instant of pain. Or of surprise.

Followed by . . . whatever.

The line between life and death, everything and nothing, was so easy to cross. Leave your car at the wrong end of the parking lot and the inexplicable miracle ceased: no more beating heart, no more breathing lungs, no more thinking brain. Some days Julia believed devoutly in God, the resurrection of the dead, the life of the world to come, and all the rest of the affirmations in the Nicene Creed she recited on Sunday mornings at Saint Matthias. Other days she believed only the evidence of biology: all organisms returned to dust, and, as entropy died, the whole universe would eventually do the same. And yet she was not exactly on unfamiliar terms with death, and not only because she had lost Jay, her twin brother, twenty years ago. Back in college, as nobody knew but Tessa, Julia had attempted suicide when Kellen had dropped her. Stomping back from dinner to her apartment near the bookstore, she penned a scathing note, probably to Kellen, possibly to Mona, then put on her full makeup and most expensive dress, swallowed a bottle of Valium, and curled on the sofa, gleefully imagining the scene after her roommate discovered her artfully arranged corpse. Only Tessa never came home that night, and Julia was astonished to wake the next morning, aching and cramped from the ridiculous position in which she had been sitting, having somehow managed to vomit up most of the pills while asleep, spewing violently enough that she had avoided choking on the residue. She was sitting in her own filth. It was all very Dante. And quite unfortunate: pills always worked in the movies. She felt deliciously incompetent. Standing up was the hardest thing she had ever done. The light made her head churn. She squinted it into sparkles. Outside the window, a fresh snow covered the campus. She threw the bottle away and threw the dress away and showered for about a week, then marched over to the deserted economics department—it was Saturday—where she climbed in through a window and used her keys to scratch the hell out of Kellen's polished door. For good measure, she smashed the little glass window too, but the wires kept it from shattering. Then, plowing through the snow, she dropped in at the house on North Balch Street she had hardly visited in two years of college to tell Mona she wanted to drop out of school for a while, maybe do some traveling: Sri Lanka sounded far enough, although she also thought she might run off to join the revolution in what the smart set in those days called Azania.

Mona, writing hard in her study as the small fire she preferred licked at the grate, contemplated her daughter's scrubbed, peaked face, the weight she had lost, the trembling fingers, the wild uncertainty in her eyes; or perhaps she just contemplated the rumors that had reached her ears; either way, experienced psychologist, she assessed the situation correctly.

"Why don't you just murder the guy instead?" she asked. "Because anybody who would do this to my Jewel doesn't deserve to live." And went back to her work.

As Julia, time and again, had gone back to Kellen. And not only at Dartmouth. When, after graduation, she moved to Manhattan to take a job at an advertising agency—one of Mona's many connections, for in those days, before her radical period, she advised the makers of soap and beer and automobiles on how to hook black consumers—Kellen moved, too, down to Columbia. The salary and benefits were great, and he wanted the New York lifestyle, including the considerable possibilities for consulting income. But when he came sniffing around Julia, he assured her that she was the principal reason, and Julia, despite having sworn never to speak to him again, allowed herself to be assured.

And assured.

During her time in New York, Kellen had been the truck, backing up and running her over, backing up and running her over, Julia lying there, allowing it to happen, again and again, more pain than she thought possible, her days and nights chemically aided, until the weekend when Tessa, in her second year of law school, came down to the city for lunch and a Broadway show, took one look at her former roommate, and made the decision for her. Tessa forced Julia to pack, frog-marched her to the car, and drove her to Elm Harbor, where she refused to let the black woman out of her sight for three days, even in the bathroom, and then, when Julia had run out of obscenities, ordered her to enroll in a department, any department, made no difference to Tessa as long as she did not go back to—

The telephone was ringing. Nearly midnight, and the telephone was ringing.

For a moment Julia experienced a hallucination. It was Boris calling. Who else? Boris finally had his report on what was going on in the Landing, the truck had missed him, he was still alive.

Hand shaking, she lifted the receiver. All right, then, it was Lemaster, she told herself. Lemaster, calling from East Podunk, or wherever he was spending the night, glad-handing and raising money. Some friend of Vanessa's, figuring that, with the storm in tomorrow's forecast, there was probably no school. Or one of the boys, calling to talk about plans for Christmas.

Wrong again.

"Julia, hi, this is Bruce Vallely. Sorry to call so late. You might not remember me, but my wife, Grace, was a member of Ladybugs."

"Of course I remember, don't be silly," said Julia, surprised to hear his leisurely, confident voice. Bruce was director of campus safety and, presumably, trying to reach Lemaster. Guessing that the late call meant a further helping of bad news, she drew the front of her tattered robe together in an unconsciously protective gesture, and made a mental check of the location of each of her loved ones. "Grace was such a lovely woman. I adored her. I'm so sorry." But they had been through this part before, at the funeral a year ago, and neither one of them really wanted to do it again. Presumably this was about Boris Gibbs. So Julia said, "Bruce, if you're looking for Lemaster, he's down in Miami, at—"

"I'm not, Julia. Actually, it's you I'd like to talk to." Bruce was a throwback to an earlier generation of men of the darker nation, cautious and slow-spoken. Every sentence out of his mouth seemed months in gestation. She suspected that it made people think he was not particularly bright, because American culture rewards mostly speed, as in the mania for standardized tests—which Julia entirely hated. She also suspected that Bruce Vallely was smarter than people thought. "Let me assure you, everything is fine. No emergency. But I wonder whether there is a time tomorrow when I might drive out to see you."

"You mean out here? To the Landing?"

"Yes."

"Because I'm right at the div school—"

"I know where you work, Julia. But I think it would be better if we had our conversation away from prying eyes."

Prying eyes? "I get home about three—"

"If it's all right with you, I think it would be better if I didn't come to the house. We should meet somewhere else."

Julia blinked. But Bruce was a serious man, perhaps overly so. Whatever he said, he meant quite literally. "Bruce, what is this? What's going on?"

"It's about Kellen Zant, Julia. It's important, and . . . it involves you."

"What about me?"

That wait again. "I'd rather explain tomorrow. I don't want to bias you."

He wants to know about my broken lampposts. About the mirrors. About the surplus and the inventory risk.

Bruce named a tavern he knew on Route 48, just outside the town limits, and Julia, dazed, said she would meet him there on her way home from Kepler.

Upstairs, later, as cold December rain lashed the windows, Julia struggled to find a position that would enable her to sleep, but it was spiritual not physical discomfort that was keeping her awake. Alone and worried, she tossed and turned, puzzling over those final words. Bias her about what? Bruce was the sort of man who had a good reason for everything he did, so she supposed he must have one now. Yet the uneasy truth remained: although he had been Grace's husband, and Grace was an absolute dear, Julia did not know Bruce very well, and did not really like him. Maybe because he scared her. Before assuming his campus post, he had been a senior city detective. One day he and his partner were sent to pick up an accused serial child molester. There was a fumble, never fully explained, and Bruce wound up going into the house alone. The suspect wound up dead, resisting arrest, although he was unarmed. Bruce Vallely had broken the man's neck. For this act of heroism he received a medal. The following January, on the occasion of the State of the Union message, he was invited to sit in the President's box.

CHAPTER 15

THE SECRETARY

(1)

WHAT BRUCE VALLELY HATED MOST about his job was being summoned, and the director of campus safety tended to be summoned a lot. By the provost. By the dean of students. By the city police commissioner, wanting to work out a better liaison procedure with his old buddy Bruce, even though, if we tell the truth and shame the devil, the commissioner had hated him when they worked in the same building. By the endless campus committees to which, ex officio, he reported. Then there were the truly terrible days when it fell to Bruce, in his official capacity, to notify parents, spouses, siblings—*I wish I had better news for you, but your daughter was at a frat party last night and it seems that . . .*—and he would listen to the screams, the tears, the recriminations, and wonder why exactly he had not retired down south, the way Grace always said they should, when he left the force.

All of those days were bad. But worst of all was a day like the Tuesday following the murder of Professor Kellen Zant, two weeks and six days before he would make his oblique approach to Julia Carlyle. Because on that Tuesday Bruce Vallely was summoned by the secretary of the university, a fussy little old-schooler whose bald pink pate shone in the flat whiteness of the chandeliers, who seemed to whisper all the time, especially when he was at a great distance, and who happened to be the titular boss of the director of campus safety in the chain of command, although, as a matter of daily practice, Bruce reported mainly to the vice-president for campus affairs, and through her to the new president, Lemaster Carlyle, whom he had met half a dozen times and wholly despised.

But today was the secretary's day, and the meeting was on the secretary's turf.

That meant the Admin Quad, as the maps called it, a place into which Bruce hated to venture even on festive occasions, let alone days like this one. The university administration spread over three sepulchral buildings, tile-roofed and marble-faced, at the southern end of the campus, as well as endless floors of rented space downtown. The downtown spaces were in two of the city's several underused office towers, leased at a deep discount, so that the university was able to trumpet proudly yet another investment in the community and, at the same time, save money. The prestige was having an office in one of the mausoleums, which is what they looked like with their marble steps and columns and cornices, fluted windows on the sides, and wrought-iron double doors that looked likely to weigh about three tons each, and probably did. The largest of the three mausoleums, at the south point of the compass, was Marshall Lombard Hall, where the president, the provost, and the secretary, technically the three most senior functionaries at the university, had their offices. As in so many public buildings of the period, the marble front steps were a little too deep to allow one to hurry. Climbing slowly, Bruce assumed that today's summons was related to the murder of Kellen Zant. The university, he had heard from old friends on the force, was exerting enormous pressure on the authorities to solve the killing of one of its own. In the town of Elm Harbor and its suburbs, the amount of pressure the university was able to exert was quite a lot.

He was right—but not in the way he thought.

(11)

THE SUITE OF ROOMS occupied by the secretary of the university was on the second floor of Lombard Hall and occupied most of the back. His eight broad windows—*his* because no secretary had ever been other than male—offered a magnificent view over Harbor Park and, in the architect's original conception, down to the water beyond, although now one saw only the commercial buildings that, from the highway, formed most of the city's skyline. Bruce supposed there must be some sort of message in that, but he was not a man for metaphor. He liked words that had meaning, questions that had answers, and people who refused to offer five different reasons why good was no better than evil.

"I'm afraid we have a bit of a crisis on our hands," the secretary murmured from the far side of the polished desk left over from the old days, too big for serious work, but just the right size to let underlings know just how far under they linged. The walls were covered in soft green fabric, the university's color. Lighted sconces illuminated disapproving portraits of the great dead white males who over the years had run the place.

"I'm happy to help," said Bruce, because Grace had warned him before she died to try to be more polite, especially to those who controlled his budget, and his salary. *Remember, you won't have me to clean up your messes any more, Lee*—which nobody else ever called him, nor did she when anybody was around, a play on his surname as well as an homage to the kung fu films that had fascinated him in the early years of their perfect marriage.

"Are you, then?"

"Of course, sir."

"Community's up in arms. Usual suspects, preaching about racism and how the university is the font of all evil and I don't know what all. People tell me it's a bit of a tinderbox sort of thing, what with Professor Zant being black and so forth."

"Just tell me what you need," Bruce enthused, hoping he sounded sincere, because the job was one he wanted to keep. He was no fool. He knew what part his skin color played. His hiring had been announced with great fanfare after the previous director had resigned under pressure following a series of racial incidents involving the campus police. Probably the most egregious—certainly the one the newspapers liked best—had come almost two years ago, when a black professor had been mugged in the middle of the campus, and the officers who responded let the white muggers escape while holding their guns on the professor. His predecessor was finished after that, and Bruce Vallely got the job. Grace, still the picture of robust good health, had been delighted. He earned almost twice what he had made working for the city, and the benefits were astonishing. If keeping all of that meant occasionally toadying up to the likes of the secretary, then he would do it. "You know you can count on me."

The secretary arched his gruff, graying eyebrows just enough to tell his guest that he was already unpersuaded. The little man's name was

Trevor Land, and his first cousin was some kind of power over at the law school, a former dean, but from what Bruce understood, Land's real constituency was among alumni of a particular kind: the old-monied white kind. He was their champion, their man on key committees, their advocate in the political-correctness wars, and, at the worst moments, their spy. He was whispered to hold a veto over decisions ranging from the selection of a new university president to the siting of a new gym. Over the years he had held a dozen different positions around the campus, but always administrative, never academic. He was probably in his late sixties. With his tiny eyes and rimless spectacles and vested suits with gold watch chain, his delicate chin and soft, inept hands, he looked the part of the foppish time-server. His habit of mouthing nonsense words—*Yes* and *Oh, no doubt* and *I see* formed half his vocabulary— confirmed the impression. But Bruce, eighteen months into the job, knew already that Trevor Land was not a man to be trifled with.

Once, a week or two after he started, Bruce had been summoned, much like today, and asked by Trevor Land to quash the DWI arrest of the daughter of a prominent alumnus. At that time Bruce had not yet figured out the nature of his work. He thought that he was still a policeman, not realizing that he was now a politician. So he pointed out that the arrest was by city, not campus cops, and thus out of his jurisdiction. The minute reptilian eyes, usually so sleepy, were, for just an instant, wide open, and Bruce was startled by the primitive cunning he saw there. And the power. Then the foppish façade closed down again. *Well, yes, I see, if you think there's nothing to be done, well, yes, I suppose I could go back and report that fact*—the tone now dubious: sharing his dilemma, one man of the world to another. *Only, you see, they're accustomed to asking small favors. The alums, I mean, alums are the same everywhere, what? What's the old line? Change is the enemy of memory. Yes. Alums like the status to remain rather quo, Chief Vallely.* A small chuckle, as though this fancy was a joke between the two of them. *Yes, well, what can one do? It's their contributions, after all, on which we rely for our fiscal health. We're not socialists, after all, are we? Private education requires private donation. So there we are. And, yes, well, I'm afraid that when they get crossed, Chief Vallely, they aren't terribly happy, if you see what I mean. The alums. These little things, children, family, you know, are so important to them.* A small, encompassing wave, as though to indicate Trevor Land's understanding that every race has its families. *Which of us doesn't love his family, after all?*

And alcohol, well, high spirits, we all had our day, didn't we? It's not as though it's murder or some such. . . .

Bruce, no fool, had gotten the message. He had smiled and nodded and said he would see what he could do, then returned to his office at the edge of campus, steaming, and read a couple of verses from Paul's Letter to the Colossians to calm himself down. Then he had contacted friends over cityside, as it was known, called in a few favors, gotten the matter quashed. Felt dirty doing it, gave some thought to quitting— the principle of the thing—but Grace, still unaware of what was growing in her pancreas, was looking at new houses out in the beautiful subdivisions they were building in Norport these days, telling him happily that they needed a place befitting his new status, not knowing, because he would never burden her with the knowledge, that his status, on the campus, was about on the level of the people who cleaned the bathrooms, except that they had a union and he didn't.

All of which is to say that, although Bruce Vallely had no earthly idea what Trevor Land had in mind for him today, he knew to a moral certainty that he would hate it.

He was right.

(III)

"JUST A LITTLE HIGH JINKS," murmured Trevor Land, his eyes sleepy and unfocused. "Not a crisis, really, unless we allow others to make it one. You know how it is."

"I know how it is," Bruce repeated, fuming, but only to himself.

"These boys were just having fun. They weren't involved in whatever else might have happened. Terrible business, but one must move on, mustn't one? And look to the interests of the institution."

"Yes, sir." Trevor Land enjoyed being sirred by underlings. "On the other hand, if they saw Professor Zant's car that night near the hockey rink, that makes them witnesses."

"Witnesses. Sounds so formal, sort of thing. Not sure I care for it." Lifting both hands to prove his innocence. "After all, we have our name to preserve, don't we?"

"Yes, sir," Bruce repeated, "but the police have a murder investigation, with which President Carlyle has ordered me to cooperate in every way possible."

"And with which we are cooperating to the full. Oh, yes. But that's my point, you see, Chief Vallely." Bruce controlled his facial muscles. Grace had schooled him carefully not to bristle. Nobody but Trevor Land called him "Chief," which was not his title, and which always sounded, in the secretary's mouth, patronizing: a put-down, reminding him of where he stood. "That's my point," the little man repeated. "One has nothing to do with the other. These are good boys, Chief Vallely. Good boys. Know most of the parents."

"Earlier that night they were drinking in a bar, Mr. Secretary. From what you tell me, at least two of them are underage." He hesitated but had to say it. "One or two of the names are familiar to me. Known troublemakers. I'm sorry, sir."

"Well, yes, I suppose one could put it that way. Breaking into the libraries and so forth." Those innocent hands came up again, soft and pliable, uneasy with absolutes. "But on Friday night, Chief Vallely, they were only having a drink or two. That's all."

Bruce assumed he would in the end be forced to yield, but he was not ready to go down without a fight. "It is against the law, sir. It is also dangerous."

"Well, yes, Chief Vallely, naturally, one wants the law enforced, students protected, and so forth. At the same time, Chief, one has to be a little bit understanding," said the secretary, suddenly the very soul of tolerance. "Not so many outlets these days for manly high spirits, Chief. Fraternities moribund, might as well be dead. One of them just voted to accept women, I hear, if you can imagine. Calls itself a 'social club' now." His prim jaw made a chewing motion, although the pristine chamber offered no evidence that anyone had recently eaten, or was ever allowed to. Trevor Land raised a finger straight up, like a Roman statue, then lowered it slowly until he was pointing at himself. "Not that one is against the women. Join whatever they like, my view. Don't happen to care for sexism, thanks very much. On the other hand, now and then, boys have to get together with other boys and let off a bit of steam. Harmlessly, Chief. Harmlessly."

The secretary paused, and, for a moment, each waited the other out, like poker players unsure of one another's cards. When it became apparent that Bruce was prepared to sit all day, Trevor Land resumed his lecture.

"Not easy being young, my view. Not if you're a person of any quality. Best horse in the world needs to test his reins, Chief Vallely.

Perfectly natural, providing nobody gets hurt, sort of thing. I did it. You did it. I daresay boys will always do it."

"Yes, sir, I quite agree. However—"

The word *agree* was all the secretary wanted. The finger was pointing again, this time at Bruce's hard chin. "Then you see how it is, Chief Vallely. Young men of high spirits, nothing more. But one can imagine, Chief, if the newspapers were to get wind of this, well, given the tragic events of last weekend"—he meant the murder—"one can see, of course, how it might easily be blown out of proportion. To our mutual damage, I might add. Tinderbox." Folding his hands like the contrite if mischievous schoolboy he might once have been, Trevor Land concluded his sermon in a mournful tone. "As secretary of the university, Chief Vallely, I bear the heavy responsibility of protecting the reputation of our institution. You're here to assist in that task, Chief. That's why we brought you in."

Bruce sat back, taking a moment to ponder, and the nicely aged green leather chair settled with a satisfying crackle. He saw the problem that had probably caused Trevor Land a sleepless night. Nobody was saying, yet, that Kellen Zant had been killed on university property; and maybe nobody would ever say it, because there was no earthly reason to think that it was true. On the other hand, the police doubted that he had been killed where he was found. Almost certainly a bizarre robbery. So far, the school was in the clear. On the other hand, these students had seen the gold Audi on campus, or so they claimed. It struck him as odd that Trevor Land knew first, and ridiculous that he should think it important to keep it from the police, but the secretary, by his own proud admission, put the interests of the university first. Bruce saw the way it must have happened. The boys, frightened out of their wits, had gone to some powerful alum—probably a parent—who had called somebody, who in turn woke up the secretary and asked him to fix it. The story, as Trevor Land related it, was vague and implausible, and therefore might, just possibly, be true.

What had drawn their attention to the car? Trevor Land did not feel qualified to offer an opinion. Had they seen anything inside? Trevor Land, alas, possessed no basis on which to say. Had they recognized any person or persons approaching the car? Trevor Land was unable, Chief, to venture a guess. Why had they not gone to the police? There at least the secretary was able to help, in his vague, donnish way. One or two of the boys had been in trouble before, and, well, you know how it is, Chief, when young people begin to worry less about justice than about false accusations . . .

"We should tell the police," said Bruce firmly. "It's the only right thing to do."

"Oh, no doubt, no doubt. I see that, of course."

"I'm serious, Mr. Secretary. The boys are witnesses. Or might be."

"Yes, well, perhaps. Except they didn't see anything."

"We don't know that, sir. You don't know that. They haven't been interviewed." He had almost said *interrogated*.

"Think they're lying? Protecting each other's backsides, kind of thing?"

Carefully, carefully. "I think, sir, that sometimes, when a professional takes the time to interview a witness who is sure he hasn't seen a thing, the witness turns out to be carrying a single tiny speck of information that can break a case wide open."

Trevor Land massaged his fleshy chin. The tiny eyes seemed narrower than ever. "I see. Very well. Good point, Chief, good point. They may not know what they know. But we still have an interest here. The school. Can't have another scandal, too many already in the last few years. Can't offend the families, either. Not these families. Other hand, we don't want to interfere with an investigation. Now, if you could help us here, if you could think of a way to balance both interests, well, Chief, that would be worth a good deal to us. Gratitude, for one thing. Mine. The school's. The families' too. Never know when you might need a favor. Good people to have in your debt, if you see what I mean."

"And by help you mean . . ."

"Perhaps you could give the conversation a first go, Chief Vallely. See whether you might be able to winkle it out of them."

The deal was quickly done, the plan Trevor Land had no doubt had in mind since he received the first telephone call from whoever it was who could light a fire under such a man as he. Bruce was the director of campus safety and a retired detective. He was, the secretary said, beyond reproach. He would conduct the interviews himself, no recording, nobody sitting in, and report his findings to Trevor Land, who would then, as the secretary quaintly put it, take a view. If the boys had information that should be shared with the police, well, then, Bruce would pass it along and the boys would have to take their chances. But if, on the other hand, as Trevor Land suspected, it was nothing but boy-ish high jinks, a drunken bit of revelry, well, then, there would be no reason for anyone to be the wiser, would there?

No reason, Bruce agreed.

And then Trevor Land did a thing he had never been known to do before, not with so lowly a minion as the director of campus safety. He waddled out from behind the smartly polished mile-wide desk, threw a pudgy arm around Bruce's shoulders, and escorted him to the door, with lots of nods and winks and promises of greater things to come, should he conclude this matter in "a balanced and satisfactory manner."

Riding his golf cart back to the office, Bruce thought about the condo in South Carolina that Grace on her deathbed had still been urg-ing him to retire to. He supposed that it wouldn't do any harm to go down and take another look. Then he reminded himself of his daughter still in college, and how much he enjoyed the membership he could now afford at the Norport Country Club, where his rehabilitated Mus-tang convertible was by a considerable margin the most eye-catching car in the lot. But his conscience refused to hide behind the money, and his mind refused to focus on anything other than the Apostle Paul's warning that the real battle in this life was against principalities and powers.

CHAPTER 16

THE OCCASIONAL STUDENT

(1)

BRUCE VALLELY WAS NOT A MAN given to introspection. He was a cautious thinker, but only about the puzzles life laid before him, never about his own motivations. So, when, on the very next morning, he conducted the first of his interviews with one of the students, he did not take the trouble to wonder whether he was being unnecessarily harsh or skeptical because of sour memories of his own Elm Harbor childhood, when young men not unlike the one whose sloppy apartment he was now visiting—in two words, white and privileged—looked down on Bruce's father because he cut the university's grass and trimmed the university's hedges and weeded the university's flower beds; or on his mother because she emptied the professors' waste baskets and washed their blackboards and waxed their floors.

Bruce grew up with the bitter stories. How the more liberal among the students now and then muttered a quick hello to his parents if they happened to pass, eyes averted, in the hall. Not one bothered to learn their names—at least their last names. Students half his mother's age called her "Danielle" to her face because they read it on the embroidered tag on her uniform; his father, a deacon of the church and a stern, proud man, they called "Joe." And thought they were doing the world some good by acknowledging their servants at all. *They can't help it*, his mother used to say. *The Lord has given them so much, naturally they forget how to be human.* But Bruce, even as a child, had thought his mother mistaken. They could help it just fine. They just didn't want to.

Bruce Vallely had enjoyed many aspects of his year and a half as an employee of the university, the salary and benefits and status foremost among them; but, in his secret heart, felt anything but love toward most of the people with whom his job brought him into contact. At his moments of greatest stress, when his ingrained tendency to resort to hostility, anger, or threat grew most pronounced, he reminded himself of his final promise to Grace, to avoid the messes she would no longer be around to fix. The day after his meeting with Trevor Land, still more than two weeks before the call to Julia Carlyle, Bruce Vallely needed every bit of will power he possessed to keep his word, because his meeting with the first of the students the secretary had asked him to interview was . . . not going well.

"I don't have to answer that question," the young man said for the third time, or the thirtieth. He was a wispy white kid, long and thin, brown hair worn long, sporting a tee shirt calling upon the casual observer to perform a sexual act on capitalism. Bruce was not sure how that was done.

"It's in your interest to cooperate with me," said Bruce mildly.

"Why? Because you say so?"

"Because I'm not official. I'm not on the record. What you say to me is safe," Bruce said, knowing it was not precisely true. Not even close.

The kid roused himself, but not much. "Well, we just saw the car. We didn't see the guy."

"How did you know it was the same car?"

"I don't remember."

"Which one of you spotted it first?"

"I don't remember that either."

Bruce frowned, knowing that an unhappy expression on his face struck terror into most white people he encountered. And it had a noticeable effect on skinny Nathaniel Knowland, who shrank physically away from him, scrunching deeper into the plush sofa in the living room of the young man's apartment. Bruce was seated in a straight-backed wooden chair borrowed from the dining room set. Nate Knowland's place was on the twelfth floor of the Rogoff Towers, the closest thing to a luxury high-rise the city possessed. A wall of windows offered a panoramic view of Elm Harbor, stretching over the university, across the park, over the blocky office buildings of downtown, all the way to the water, where, even in the foul weather, sailboats bobbed. Few students could afford to live in such a style, but Nate's father—as Trevor

Land had been at pains to remind Bruce—was among the very wealthiest alumni of the university. As a matter of fact, Cameron Knowland was what the school designated as the "Senior Trustee"—in effect, the chairman of the university.

In Bruce's mind, that was one strike against Nathaniel Knowland right there. His dismissive hauteur was a second. Third, Bruce had simply had a bad day and was not prepared to sit still for much more nonsense. Nate Knowland was twenty-three years old, finally back for his senior year after taking time off to work in Daddy's company.

"You don't remember," Bruce repeated, the disbelief plain in his voice.

"That's right."

"You're a smart kid. You have to remember what happened just a few nights ago."

Nate smirked. On the college campus, the students were royalty and the professors were divine, and Bruce Vallely, being neither, was nobody. To Nathaniel Knowland, he was just a minion. Like the man who cuts the grass. Or the woman who washes the blackboards. Bruce wondered what attitude the young man would adopt if he bumped into the current president of the university. But, given the identity of Nate's father, the chances were they had already met.

Nathaniel Knowland said, again, "I don't remember."

"Friday night. The night Professor Zant was shot. It was a big night around here, Nate. How can you expect me to believe you don't remember?"

"If I told you I don't remember, it's because I don't remember."

And Bruce decided not to take it any more.

(11)

BRUCE VALLELY WAS WELL PAID for his work. He had obligations to his family, and to the university. He had made promises to Trevor Land. But he was still, by instinct, a cop. So he stood up suddenly, startling young Nathaniel Knowland, who had perhaps forgotten that the man with whom he was alone in the apartment was not only black but six foot five and two hundred twenty solid pounds. And had once killed a man with his bare hands.

Once that people knew of.

After ambling easily across the space between them, Bruce leaned over the sofa, close enough to the young man's pale, frightened face to smell his unhealthy breath.

"You're lying to me, Mr. Knowland. No, don't argue. You're lying. I know it and you know it. The only question we have to resolve is what exactly you're lying about. You can tell me right now or you can tell me five minutes from now or you can tell me an hour from now, but you are undoubtedly going to tell me."

Nate Knowland, shrinking further back, as though close contact might infect him, turned his head to the side, giving Bruce a view of one delicate pierced ear, the diamond in the stud certainly a real one. He mumbled something.

"What was that? I didn't hear you, Nate."

"I said I want a lawyer."

"Tough shit."

The bobbing head snapped straight again, the eyes wide. "I know my rights!"

"You don't know anything about anything." Leaning closer, letting the fury bake off his face, the heat searing Nate Knowland. Bruce had been keeping his temper for twenty-four hours, ever since his meeting with Trevor Land, and it felt good to let it out. Sorry, Grace. "You call yourself a student. Do you know where the word *student* comes from? Latin. It means someone who takes pains. Who is careful and works hard, in other words." He used this line with pretty much every student he interrogated. Sometimes it worked, sometimes it didn't. But Nathaniel Knowland did not look tough. Instead of living in the dorm with his fellows, here he was in a three-bedroom apartment. Why a student, living alone, needed so much space, when so many had so little, was a mystery to which Bruce would turn his attention on another day: probably the same day he figured out why four Carlyles needed eight thousand square feet. What he was sure of was that, in Nathaniel's case, Daddy paid for it. And a boy like Nate would want every penny his father could lavish on him but resent his dependence at the same time. Bruce had seen that resentment before, too, in plenty of students, and even some of his classmates at the state university years earlier. Experience made him confident that the resentment, if turned inside out, could break down the young man's resistance. So he said, carefully, taking pains:

"You see, Nate, you might be a student one day, but right now—the way you're acting?—you're a spoiled little rich boy whose daddy pays some flunky to hand you a parachute every time you decide to jump out of an airplane without looking. I've got news for you, Nate. Daddy isn't in the room just now. It's just you and me. Now, you said you want a lawyer. If I were still a city cop, that might make a difference. I'd have to stop questioning you until some guy in a suit worth my annual salary explained to you the most effective way to lie. Well, I'm not a city cop, Nate. I'm a university cop. That means I'm private, and your constitutional rights, as you call them, carry as much weight as the Easter Bunny. Okay?"

Nathaniel Knowland was spoiled, but he was no dummy. His voice climbed a register or two, but he made his point: "Then I have rights under the university rules. There's a whole set of procedures you have to follow."

Bruce nodded. "That's right, Nate, and you can insist on your rights if you want to. You can insist on a proceeding before the Judicial Tribunal. And you know what? That will mean a formal record. No way to keep the police from finding out. We'd have an obligation to make a report." Actually, this was a lie. The last thing Bruce wanted was Nathaniel Knowland before the tribunal, whose proceedings were secret, its transcripts sealed. "Listen to me, Nate. You're scared. I understand that. And you don't think you want to talk to me. I understand that, too. But, Nate, believe me, you definitely do not want to talk to the police. This town is getting ready to explode over Kellen Zant, and the police would love to get their hands on a spoiled rich white kid who withheld information about the crime. They'll leak it to the papers, Nate, and the papers will eat you alive."

"You can't talk to me that way!"

"I'm only telling you what I think will happen."

"You're threatening me." Almost a whine now, but some defiance underneath. Perhaps he was tougher than he looked.

"Just a prediction, Nate." Bruce's voice was soft. "That's all."

"You can't talk to me this way! There's a law or something! You can't threaten me or . . . or coerce me."

"Listen to me, Nate. You have to understand the way it works now. Around the campus, I'm the law. You're the suspect."

"Suspect!"

"Unless you start telling me something, yes."

The young man's eyes flew in every direction, as though he anticipated help. "I . . . but . . . it was a robbery! I read it in the papers! Why would I rob some black guy? Look at this place!"

Bruce Vallely almost smacked him. It was a near thing. The hand came up, big and dark and raw. *Some black guy:* that was the phrase that set him off. But he could almost feel Grace's loving fingers on his wrist, returning it gently to his side. And he saw in Nathaniel Knowland's face a new alertness, less fear now than sheer panic. Because nobody, least of all a rich and skinny white kid, wants to be alone with an angry black man.

"My father will have your job!" Nate announced, but the eyes, still wide open, and the voice, now screechy, gave him away.

"Sure. That's why he sent you to his alma mater, to get involved in a murder."

"I'm not involved!"

"Either you're involved or you know who is." Bruce went into his crouch, slipping a strong arm around Nathaniel Knowland's skinny neck, which, at the moment, he wanted badly to wring. The long hair was greasy. The shoulders trembled. Bruce selected an avuncular tone. "Now, listen to me, Nate. You're in very, very big trouble, you and your pals. You saw something you're not telling me. And you did something you're not telling me. Worse, you're not telling the cops. They get upset about things like that. Do you know what the penalty is in this state for obstruction of justice? I'll tell you for free, Nate, it's not as bad as the penalty for being an accessory to murder, which is what you're looking at right now. It doesn't matter if you're an accessory before the fact or after"—a lie, but never mind, to be followed at once by another—"if you have knowledge and you don't share it, you're still in trouble."

Nathaniel Knowland dropped his eyes and muttered a few words, but only to himself. It was just as well, Bruce decided, that he could not understand what the young man had said, because he suspected that full knowledge of whatever imprecation the boy had mouthed would have left him very angry indeed. Maybe too angry. He said softly, "Come on, Nate, there's never going to be a better time to tell. And if it's just something embarrassing and not something illegal, then you're a lot better off telling me now than telling the police later."

"I won't implicate anyone else," the young man said, surprising Bruce with his pluck. "I'll tell you what I saw. What I did. That's all."

"Sounds like a good place to start."

"Not just to start. To finish. I want to make that clear. I'm not going to talk about any of my friends."

As a city detective, Bruce used to hear this story over and over in the sweaty and dark little rooms set aside for interrogation. Sometimes he would even try a snappy comeback: *Why won't you talk about them? They're right down the hall, talking about you.* Sometimes the ploy worked, sometimes it didn't, but that kind of lying always left him feeling grubby. Now the lie wouldn't even wash. So he said: "Look, Nate. You can put any limits on your comments"—he had almost said *confession*—"that you want. I don't have any power to coerce you to tell me what happened. I just think it's in your interest."

And so the boy started talking.

(iii)

THE THING WAS, said Nate Knowland, they were just trying to have a little fun. They were students, they were young, it was Friday night, and they would be out of here and into serious jobs soon enough. They had been studying all day, except for a little squash in the afternoon, at least for Nate, and now they were looking for something to do. One or two of them had girlfriends, but this was a guys' night out. They were five altogether, a couple of rich kids, a couple of hangers-on to rich kids. They had a couple of beers each down at Nelson's—

"Nelson's on Henley Street?"

He nodded. "Off campus," he added, as if hoping to limit Bruce's jurisdiction. "Anyway, most of us are over the drinking age, and it shouldn't be against the law to get a little sloshed if you don't hurt anybody"—and if Bruce thought maybe the five of them had sampled a few illegal substances along with their beers, he was not about to say so. Or not until mentioning the possibility could bring him some advantage.

"So, anyway, after that, we went over to the hockey game. But Dartmouth was creaming us, so it got old fast. One of the guys was meeting his girlfriend at nine, so we were out on Town Street, I'd say, ah, eight-fifteen, eight-thirty, something like that. We were out on the street, trying to decide what to do next, and that was when we saw the car."

When Bruce, by design, failed to react, Nate tried again. "The gold Audi, the one Zant got killed in, parked right on the street."

"Who said he got killed in his car?"

Nathaniel blinked, less frightened than confused. "It was on the news."

"How did you know it was his car?"

Back to where they had started. Only, this time, Nate answered. "Because we saw him, too."

This was new. Not quite the way Trevor Land had told, or failed to tell, the story. He wondered whether the university secretary had not known, or known and not told. Either way, it was always wrong for an interrogator to show surprise except for effect. So Bruce, not even raising his voice, said, "I'm sorry. Which 'him' is this?"

Nathaniel Knowland was impatient. "Zant. He walked right past us. One of the guys was an econ major and had a course with him."

"And what was the name of your friend who recognized him?"

A shake of the head, as defiant as any child. "I told you, I'm not gonna get the guys in trouble." He raised a forefinger, pointing toward the ceiling, a gesture eerily reminiscent of Trevor Land. "I have my ethics."

"I understand." Patting him on the back, straightening up, striding away across the spacious room. Sometimes Bruce had to be his own good cop and bad cop both. His voice remained gentle. "Okay. So you saw Professor Zant. What was he doing?"

"I told you. He walked past us, and got in the car."

"Where from?"

"I don't know. Behind us. I mean, ah, they came from the direction of the campus. We didn't see exactly where."

This time he could not keep the surprise from his voice. " 'They'?"

"Yes, they. If you just stop interrupting me, I'll explain everything." The student took a long breath. "He was with this woman. At least we think she was a woman. She could have been a small man, I guess. And, no, I don't think any of us would recognize her if we saw her again. I mean, when they walked down the street, she was on the inside and he was on the outside, so he was kind of walking in and out of the glow of the streetlights, and she was more on the fringes. Like she was smart enough not to let anybody see her face. I can tell you she was black. Definitely black. And she was wearing a white rain slicker with a hood, so it sort of hid her face."

"In the middle of a blizzard she was wearing a rain slicker? Not a parka? You're sure?"

He nodded vigorously. "It was a slicker. And it was white. Kind of shiny. Made her hard to see in the snow." He puffed out his cheeks and hugged himself as though struggling to stay warm, then continued. "So, anyway, they got in the car—he got in first, on the passenger side, and she got in the driver's side—they got in the car and she drove away and that was it."

Bruce pictured the image, found it all wrong, for no reason he could articulate.

Nate Knowland was still talking. "We figured, you know, he has a certain reputation. Had. So, we figured, he and this woman—I mean, there wasn't any affection they showed or anything like that—but—"

"Let me be very clear. The car was parked on Town Street, across from the rink."

"Uh-huh."

The rink faced the rear entrance to Hilliman Tower, where Zant had his office. So far, at least, the story was plausible. "And you're sure Professor Zant got in first? And the black woman in the white rain slicker was driving?"

"That's right." Nate Knowland was coming down from the wonderful high of terror. His elegant features had gone slack, and the eyes were moist and flat. "I don't know. I'm just telling you what we saw."

"Of course, you were pretty drunk."

"We had a few drinks. We weren't drunk. And we all saw the same thing."

"The same woman in the rain slicker."

"Yeah."

Bruce made a note in his book, a tiny symbol only he could decode. Nate's story was so simple and dull as to smack of invention by the witness, except for those two details.

"Do you remember anything else?"

He nodded. "She had a British accent."

"So you overheard the conversation?"

"Only a sentence or two. But they were talking about President Carlyle."

Another note. This, too, was well beyond Trevor Land's oddly limited information. "What about him?"

Nate shook his head. "We didn't hear much, I told you. But it sounded like she was trying to tell Professor Zant that he was too big for them to take him on."

"Can you give me the exact words?"

"I think those were the words. 'Too big for us to take him on.' Something like that." A nervous shrug. "That was all we heard."

CHAPTER 17

THE DEBT

"Not enough, Chief, I would think," said Trevor Land mournfully. "A silly story by a drunken schoolboy. Not worth bothering the police about."

"Mr. Secretary, they saw the victim the night he got shot. They saw him on the campus, where the police aren't even looking. Not only that. They saw him with another person, something like an hour and a half before the body was found. How can it not be worth bothering the police?"

A long pause at the other end of the telephone. Bruce wondered whether the secretary was aware that his underling had omitted a detail: the tantalizing comment about Lemaster Carlyle. When Trevor Land spoke again, it was in the same sad tone. "I am not the sort, Chief Vallely, to tell a man how to do his job, especially a man of your qualification. If you think you have to go to the police, well, that would have to be your call, not mine. Delegated authority. My philosophy of management. One asks only that you consider the university's good name. We cannot afford another scandal."

"Yes, sir, but—"

"Just indulge me one moment more, Chief Vallely, if you would. Small point. You heard the young man's story. But so far that's all you've heard. Consider." In his mind's eye Bruce saw that finger pointing up at the ceiling again, so like a statue. "Perhaps he was drunk and cannot remember what he saw, or perhaps his recollection is accurate. We don't know which, or not yet."

"It's the job of the police to figure out which, not ours."

"To be sure. To be sure. But, Chief Vallely, excepting your presence, of course, the police of our fine city are not notable for their discretion. Not where the university might be concerned. Most of the time, in my experience, Chief, telling the police is the same as telling the papers. They can no more keep secrets than Ulysses could resist the Sirens, and nobody to tie them to the mast, you see." Bruce in fact did not see, but was not about to say so. "Now, Professor Zant was a highly valued member of this community, and we naturally would want to give our all to help bring his killer to justice. And that is why we are so fortunate, Chief, to be blessed by a man of your caliber. Now, what you decide to do is your own business. But may I offer a small bit of advice? From my decades, frankly, of dedicated service to the university?"

Orders, he meant. "Of course, sir."

"Well, Chief, were it I facing the dilemma? I would perhaps prefer to firm up the case a bit before I risked the school's reputation at the hands of the local journalists. Rock and a hard place, sort of thing, I admit, but perhaps it would be better to wait. Just until I had a little bit more information."

Bruce waited for more, but Trevor Land was evidently waiting for him. He said, slowly and distinctly, "Mr. Secretary, are you proposing that I undertake a more thorough . . . investigation?"

Trevor Land's voice seemed sleepier still. "Ah, well, Chief Vallely, I would prefer not to place so *intense* a characterization on my advice. Rather, I would propose that you should do as you and I discussed earlier. You should, I think, be about the business of tying up the loose ends. Don't rush to judgment, that's the thing. Get on it, say, after Thanksgiving. Patience. Diligence. Yes. So, Chief, my view? Make sure the loose ends are tied up, that you have your ducks in a row, kind of thing, and then, by all means, take what you have to the proper authorities, with my blessing."

The director of campus safety gazed at the wedding photograph atop the credenza, Grace so beautiful and young, although she only grew more beautiful as she grew older. If only he could have a few minutes to consult her wisdom and humor. But she was dead over a year now, barely into her fifties, and he faced the secretary's slimy cynicism armed only with his own integrity. He made no pretense—unlike a certain university president he could name—to be exceptional in that respect.

"May I ask a question?"

"By all means, Chief. Please."

"Suppose that I agree to do as you . . . suggest. And suppose a moment comes, fairly soon, maybe, when I believe that I have all my ducks in a row, and you don't."

"Pardon me, but I did not get the question, Chief Vallely."

Bruce preferred arguing face-to-face, where he could use his size to advantage, even against his titular superiors; but, aided by Grace's glowing visage underneath the window, he was willing to tangle over the telephone. He had survived the vicious internecine warfare of the police department and, long ago, the vicious actual warfare of the Central American jungle; he could trade insincere, wordy threats with the likes of Trevor Land any day of the week.

So he rushed in where angels might fear to tread.

"Sir, as you know, the charter under which my department operates has as one of its cardinal rules that any evidence we uncover of a felony must be turned over, at once, to the police or the other responsible authorities." A beat to let this sink in. "Maybe I can hold off a few days, but, sooner or later, I'm going to have all the loose ends tied up. Suppose, at that point, you and I disagree about what step to take next. Whose view wins?"

The answer, although surely prepared in advance, was a very long time coming, as if the secretary wanted Bruce to imagine that he was just now working through the options.

"Ah, I see your concern. Yes. But remember, Chief Vallely, it is fully up to you to choose what to do. My small suggestions are only that, suggestions. Naturally, I would consider it unlikely in the extreme that we would face such a disagreement. But if the time came when we did . . . well, let us reserve judgment, kind of thing. Cross that bridge when we come to it instead of burning it in advance, if you get my meaning."

"I think I do."

"Excellent, Chief Vallely, excellent. And, you know, Chief, when all of this is over, no scandal, the university protected, and justice served—when it is all over, Chief Vallely, remember, please, that you will have in me a friend and supporter for life, and I am not without a certain influence in affairs. And you yourself will be taken care of. That I can assure you."

Bruce decided that enough was enough. "Meaning what exactly?"

The secretary, an old hand, correctly judged his underling's mood.

"I'm sure I meant no offense, Chief Vallely. I was suggesting nothing untoward."

"May I ask what you were suggesting?"

"Only that you're family, Chief. And that I think you will find me a useful person to have in your debt." A laugh, because they both knew that he had gone too far, that he could easily, at this very moment, make an enemy of his subordinate.

Bruce asked the secretary to hold on.

He laid the telephone on the sagging desk and swiveled toward the window with its hideous view of empty buses. He remembered a strange conversation with his former partner, Rick Chrebet. The two men had met for a drink Monday night, and Bruce had steeled himself for some joshing, because the city and state cops thought the campus police had a soft life. Instead, a bitter Rick Chrebet had told him that higher-ups in the department had already decided that Zant's murder was a robbery, maybe a carjacking gone awry. They were pressing the investigators to endorse the same theory. Rick thought he could hold them off for a week, maybe even two, but eventually he would have to cave. When Bruce expressed surprise—the man had been dead only three days!—Rick had smiled, downed another beer, and told him that the decision was coming down from the top, not up from the ranks. He would say no more.

It occurred to Bruce now, lifting the phone once more, that he might be able to succeed where his old team had failed, and put the university that had so tortured his parents into his debt. He could say no to Trevor Land and keep his job until retirement. He could say yes, for the wrong reason—personal ambition, for instance. Or for the right reason—getting into position to collect what was due.

"I'll be happy to help," he said to the secretary, not sure why his every instinct for survival was screaming at him to answer the other way.

CHAPTER 18

THE ORIGINAL THINKER

(1)

"GIVE ME A MINUTE HERE," said Arthur Lewin, pacing his vast but spartan office in the economics department. He had another outpost in the math building and a third at one of the endless interdisciplinary programs every university spawns. He was thirty-two years old, but on the campus already a legend. "I mean, this is, you know, a little weird. Weird, but exciting, too." It was Tuesday, December 2, five days after Thanksgiving, and Bruce, as ordered, was continuing to tie up loose ends.

"Is that so?"

"Well, you see, Bruce—do you mind if I call you Bruce?—it's just, I don't think I've ever been interviewed by the cops. Well, you know, if you don't count, like, college."

Bruce Vallely remained seated on the far side of the round table stacked high with papers and reprints that served Arthur Lewin in lieu of a desk. Two casement windows were set into the narrow wall, and two computers—a laptop and a desktop—were on a table just below. On the desktop, numbers seemed to be crunching. The laptop displayed what looked to be the draft of a scholarly article, thick with equations, although the window actually in use contained a game that Bruce did not immediately recognize—something to do with placing colorful counters on squares that shifted. Art Lewin, playing against the machine, seemed to be winning. Near the computers stood a single lonely photograph in an antique gilt frame, a pair of girls with Arthur Lewin's eager gray eyes. No other family snaps in evidence.

"Were you in trouble in college?" Bruce asked.

"Isn't everybody?"

"I don't know if everybody is. I just wondered if you were."

Art Lewin kept on grinning. He wore jeans and scuffed boots and a raggedy brown sweater, and his reddish hair was thick and uncombed. He did not look to have shaved in days. His face was soft and pudgy, as though he had never lost his baby fat. His gray eyes were friendly and excited behind tiny lenses. He possessed the delighted optimism of a personal trainer, and the dressing habits of an exhausted student at exam time. He was an associate professor of economics and, according to a couple of people Bruce had asked, might be the greatest genius in the field since Kenneth Arrow. Not that Bruce knew, or much cared, who Kenneth Arrow was. His field of interest was narrower: he cared about Kellen Zant, and this man, by every account, was Kellen's best friend.

Maybe his only friend.

Zant, some years older, had been Art Lewin's teacher, his guide through graduate school, and his mentor in the department. Most people Bruce had talked to seemed to think mentee had long ago surpassed mentor.

Professor Lewin said, "Believe it or not, it's true. Just about everybody does get into trouble in college. Well, not everybody. But a majority of males are in some kind of trouble with the law before they turn thirty. Listen. There are plenty of data on this. Do you want to know what proportion of young men have been arrested? This isn't a racial thing, by the way. You read all those reports about one-quarter of the black men in Washington having been in the criminal-justice system or something, right? That's a crock. The numbers are all skewy. They have to be a lot higher. Listen. In the general population? All males? The proportion of all males who have been arrested is on the order of one-third to one-half, maybe a little higher, depending on how far back you go—what age you measure—and what you consider an arrest."

"I consider it an arrest when I put the cuffs on."

"Right. Right. But consider this." The economist paid him no attention. The office contained no file cabinets, but one wall was a whiteboard. Art Lewin leaped across to it as though spoiling for a fight and began sketching with a pair of colored markers. He drew a vertical line, and a horizontal line stretching right from its base. Bruce recognized the axes of a graph. The professor drew a squiggly line and labeled it $f(x)$. "This function is, say, the probability of arrest, by age, right? See how it slopes? It's nonexistent for babies—we're just doing males, okay?—and it gets higher in the early teens, and then—boom— here—we have a maximum, in the late teens, early twenties; and then it declines in a fairly regular fashion here. Above thirty, it's real low. Fifty, nobody gets arrested. All this is well known, right? Now. This curve— this is tricky—this represents the population according to age. We're aging fast. We know what that means, I assume. Answer: crime is going to go down. Has to. Inevitable. Because it's all the young men"— tapping the board with his marker—"who are the criminals. Follow the same cohorts as they get older, they stop doing whatever they were doing. No more crimes. Well, okay, not zero, but an arbitrarily small number."

"Because they're in prison."

"Very funny. Good one. But no. No. Why do they commit fewer crimes? Answer: because they're older. Now we can—"

"Professor Lewin, please. Please. We can have the lecture later."

"I know, I know. See, here's the thing. Look. See the multiple inter- sections? Know what that means?"

"Please, Professor Lewin. That's enough. Arthur!"

The economist pivoted slowly, innocent gray eyes, for a moment, not in the room. Then he was back, but sullen, a child genius in the act of showing off, cut short by a callow grown-up. "I'm sorry. I thought you'd be interested."

Bruce did not want to give offense. "It's fascinating, Professor. Really. And perhaps another time you can explain it to me in detail."

"I did a paper on it. I have a copy"—he delved into a stack on a shelf behind his desk, neatly labeled REPRINTS OF PUBLISHED, and pulled out an article of eight or ten pages—"which you can read at your leisure. Then we can talk some more, okay?"

"Sure."

"A lot of the data on this topic are just wrong. I proved it."

"I believe you."

A sheepish smile. "I know I babble. I love my work, Bruce. I just love it."

Bruce smiled back. Smiles cost nothing. "I can see that."

"You know, Bruce, back in the forties and fifties—we're talking about the postwar years, when America stood alone, unchallenged, all that silliness?—the mathematicians thought they could draw the right function and solve every social problem. Even crime. I'm talking about economists who did math."

"And now?"

"Now, I would say, mathematical treatments still dominate. You have to know your theory, but the profession—and I would say properly so—is getting more and more interested in applied mathematics again. A lot of us think it's time to march out and save the world. I know you think I'm exaggerating, but, okay, listen for a minute." Both hands waving now, fingers pointing in all directions, the man's energy amazing, like a third person in the room. "Listen. What is economics, really? The dismal science? No. Answer: it's the study of the distribution of goods and services subject to constraint. Well, what isn't subject to constraint? Answer: nothing. Military strategy, political campaigns, eggs, even sex. Everything is subject to constraint, Bruce. So, in a way, economics is a kind of summary of everything that matters in human existence. We really do hold in our hands the tools to save the world. Pretty cool, huh?"

"Is that what Kellen Zant thought?"

Arthur Lewin's manic energy began to flag. He did not move from the whiteboard, it was plain that he had no intention of sitting, but his narrow shoulders sagged slightly, and he nodded his grizzled chin twice, as though conceding the intrusion of reality.

"Yeah. Kellen. What a bummer."

"Can we talk about him for a minute?"

"About Kellen? Listen. Don't get the wrong idea about him, Bruce. It's not true what people say. He wasn't in it just for the money. He always said economists could make the world better, if we would just turn our attention to the right problems."

Bruce said gently, "That wasn't exactly what I wanted to talk about."

"No? What, then?"

"Well, for one thing, we could talk about who'd want to kill him."

The grin returned, but without the earlier glee that told you how much Arthur Lewin loved his work. This time, he was merely acknowledging an absurdity. "Well, I guess you could say I would."

(11)

THEY WERE WALKING across the main campus, because Art Lewin had decided he wanted to be on the move to talk about this, and he was the kind of man who did pretty much what he wanted: a fully grown Nathaniel Knowland, only with a lot more charm. Slushy dark snow swished underfoot. Bruce reminded himself that Art Lewin was a rising star. His recent predecessor as director of campus safety lost his job because of scandal, and the scandal was worse because he had not properly managed his relationships with the faculty.

"Let me tell you something about Kellen's work. I don't mean Zant-Feldman—"

"Excuse me, Professor. Others have also mentioned Zant-Feldman, but nobody has yet told me exactly what it is."

Art Lewin smiled again, and Bruce smiled back, impressed that the young man had not, as so many professors would have, rolled his eyes. It occurred to the onetime detective that loving a subject was a true advantage in a teacher: if you enjoy talking about your field, you will never treat a question, or a questioner, as dumb.

"It's a formula for valuing securities, especially stock options, except, unlike, say, Black-Scholes, it's backward-looking. What I mean is, it's a way of answering the question, 'In light of what we now know, what was the value of this particular option when it was awarded ten years ago?' It's actually a really clever measure of stochastic volatility, using the differential of—well, never mind. Okay. See, Kellen was in grad school at Dartmouth when he figured it out. Then this guy Feldman at Columbia helped him refine it, when Kellen spent a couple of years there as a post-doc? And, you know, Bruce, it's not true what they say, that Kellen couldn't have finished it himself. That's just racism, okay? But I guess you know all about that, right? So, anyway, the thing is, Zant-Feldman got Kellen lots of consulting work. Okay?"

Bruce found himself no wiser. "Okay."

"But lately he wasn't just doing Zant-Feldman any more. He was trying to use some more sophisticated tools, to build futures markets on events? Try to see if experts could predict what will happen next year or in ten years in, say, commodities markets? Because, you know, this idea that the mass of people might know best is very hot right now. It's an old idea in economics. It's how markets work. Chaos theory touches on it, too. You've seen some of the literature? A lot of it gets into the popular press these days." He made *popular* sound like an obscenity.

"I'm afraid I've missed it."

A dubious nod. This was not, Bruce saw at once, Art Lewin's thing. "Like, say, suppose you want to know how many jelly beans are in a jar? It turns out that the best thing to do is ask lots and lots of people and then average their answers. Even if none of the answers is close, chances are the average will be. The more people who guess, the better the answer. Because the net cognitive errors balance each other out, right? Or—you want to guess the outcome of an election. Should you ask people who they're going to vote for? Answer: No. That's media silliness. No. You get a better prediction if you ask people who they think is going to win. If you put together, say, an electronic market, and let people buy and sell futures contracts on the election? Turns out you'll usually get pretty close to the actual percentage of the vote. Pretty cool, huh?"

Again Bruce called him gently to heel, persuaded that, if not stopped, Art Lewin would go on like this all afternoon. "Professor, this is all very interesting, and someday when we both have more time, I'd be happy to hear the details. But, for now, I'd like to be a little more concrete."

"Concrete?" the economist echoed, with a revulsive shudder, as if to signal that what really mattered were the great abstractions. "Concrete how?"

"Like, say, to talk about Kellen Zant. Not the work. The man."

"The man was his work. You can't understand him if you don't understand his work."

"I'm not trying to understand him just now, Professor. I'm trying to understand exactly what happened to him." He rushed to press his advantage while Art Lewin was still thinking this over. "Why don't we start with the last time you saw him?"

"The last time I saw Kellen—I told this to the police—was the day he died. Friday. We were playing chess in my office, same as we did every Friday. Blitz. Five minutes a side. That way we could squeeze in enough games to have a realistic—" The economist stopped, the child in him erecting a defense against accusations not yet lodged. "Look, Bruce, it was just our way to have fun, okay? Some people play football, some people get drunk. No, wait, I do get drunk, that's not a good example. But some people—I don't know—fly kites or something."

"What time was this? When he came by your office?"

"Oh, probably four. That's what time it usually was. I mean, you know, I didn't look at my watch or anything. But I would guess four."

"Who won more games? On Friday, before he died?" Allowing a light touch, but just that, of impatience to show.

"Oh, well, I won more *games*," said the economist, as if Bruce was missing the point. "But they don't count. Kellen was distracted. His mind wasn't on chess. And, besides, we didn't really finish. Usually we played until about ten. Sent out for Chinese food, talked about work, played chess. But on Friday we stopped early." Standing before a huge snowbank, he turned and held up a hand, forestalling an objection not yet offered. "Wait, Bruce. Wait. I want to make something clear here, okay? It's not true what they say about Kellen. He was brilliant. As brilliant as I am. He didn't just do his consulting work. He did care about scholarship. He wasn't lazy. That's just racism talking. He was working on this book about games, and it was serious for him. He had plenty of projects to keep him busy."

"I'm sure he did," said Bruce after a moment's evaluation and mental filing. The sky glowered, but he had the sense that neither dark nor cold would slow Art Lewin in full excited academic stride.

"And he had this new project, too. Just in the last year or so. Very hush-hush. A new way of looking at an old problem. That's all he would say. He was going to make millions. That's what he said, Bruce. Millions."

"I'm sure he was. But on the night he died, what did the two of you do?"

"We played chess. Then he just left."

"What time was that?"

"It wasn't late. I don't know. Five. Five-fifteen. I asked Kellen—I asked him—I said, 'What's the hurry?' He said he had an appointment. Now, Bruce, I knew his reputation, so I assumed it was with a woman. Probably a married woman. That was his preference, you know that, right? No? He used to say he liked married women better than single women, and preferably with two or three kids at home, the younger the better. It was less complicated, he said. Kellen was a little bit—I don't know—commitment-shy, I guess. You can look at his preference for married women as a rational strategy for maximizing his sexual satisfaction while minimizing the risk of commitment. See, Bruce, commitment entails costs. There are opportunity costs—the consumption value of what you could be doing instead—and there are also considerable risks downstream. What we might call post-commitment risks. The risk of making a mistake, say. Of discovering you hate your spouse. Or that you love someone else more. Now, some people marry or make other kinds of commitment as a way of managing risk. The risk of a lonely life, for example. It's a trade-off either way you do it, of course. Now, in Kellen's case, the risk of being stuck was the one he wanted to avoid. Of course, there are multiple strategies available, and, actually, you can also look at his preference for married women as a form of insurance. Because, if you think about it, sleeping with married women is in certain ways more costly than sleeping with single women. That cost is the value of the risk of being caught—the harm if you really are caught discounted by the likelihood of its occurrence. That extra cost represents the amount that a person who is commitment-averse is willing to pay, we might say, to purchase insurance against winding up in a committed relationship that he—"

Again, very gently, Bruce Vallely brought his witness to heel. "If we could just get back to when Professor Zant left. He said he had an appointment, and you guessed a woman."

"Right. That's what I—"

"Did he clarify matters? Did he tell you if he was meeting a woman, whether married or not?"

They had made it all the way to the Science Quad, the grand, blocky monstrosity on which the university was betting its future as, a little late, it tried to position itself as a center for the new technologies. Students flowed around them in earnest, hurrying groups.

"No," said Art Lewin, towering over Bruce because he had scrambled up a filthy berm of snow heaped against the side of the computer center by a plow driver who had decided, for an unfathomable reason, to remove the clean white blanket from the lawn. "No, he didn't tell me. Except he made one little joke. He said he was thinking he might go to Jamaica."

"Jamaica? That's what he said?"

The economist nodded. "He said he had urgent business there. In Jamaica."

"You're sure he said Jamaica?"

Art was continuing to climb, as though the physical distance would grant perspective; or perhaps he had simply had his fill of interrogation. It wasn't fun any more, and life for the Arthur Lewins of the world, raised to believe that all would be well as long as you just stayed smart, had to be fun, or it was not worth living. "That's right. He said he was going to Jamaica, and that if I had half a brain in my head, I could figure it out. That was the kind of thing he used to say, Bruce. Half a brain."

"He said you should be able to figure out where he was going?"

"Yes. Like it was just another of his games." Art was all the way at the top now, his feet almost two meters above the ground, turning carefully in a small circle, lord of all he surveyed. He said, voice now softer, for Bruce had caught up, "I reminded him, if it was a puzzle, he was supposed to leave me clues to figure it out. Know what he said? He said, 'I already did.'"

(I I I)

THEY HAD TRAMPED back down the snowbank, and Art Lewin's shoulders were freshening their slump. No, this was not fun. Bruce thought he knew what the young man was thinking. That his friend and mentor was really gone. Reliving the good times they had together— the formulas, the chess, the arguments, the competition—had brought home to him how much he had lost.

"Think hard."

"I am thinking hard." Art Lewin's tone was now petulant.

"No note? A last-minute e-mail? Maybe even an equation on a blackboard? Are you really sure he didn't leave you any kind of clue to what he meant by Jamaica?"

"I'm sure. I'm sure."

"Well, how about something anonymous. A note from a source that—"

"There's nothing, Bruce. Honestly. Do you think I haven't been racking my brains trying to come up with one?" A boyish sigh. They had reached the sidewalk, where rushing cars sent up frigid showers of dirty slush. He perked up. "I did have an idea, though."

"Go on."

"Well, you know, he liked women, like I said. So I thought maybe he was planning, you know, to meet some woman. A Jamaican, maybe. At a motel or something, spend the weekend."

"Why would he need to go to a motel? He lived alone, didn't he?"

"That's true." Art Lewin was irritated to have missed the point. Then he brightened. "So—maybe he had a Jamaican woman coming to his house?"

Bruce glanced at him as they walked, an idea forming. The professor, sensing the scrutiny and not much liking it, increased the distance between them. They passed beneath a wrought-iron gate and were back to the Original Quad, as it was called.

"Did you and Professor Zant ever discuss Lemaster Carlyle?"

The economist's Adam's apple bobbed in his scrawny neck. "Oh, well, everybody has, ah, *opinions* about Lemaster. But we would just shoot the breeze."

"Do you know if Zant might have had some grudge against him?"

"Well, Kellen was the kind of man who had lots and lots of grudges, but most of them were about people he'd never met. You know. Politicians, activists, syndicated columnists, people he thought wasted their influence." Back on safe territory, he stood a bit taller. "You know, Bruce, there's this whole political-science literature about the incentives of politicians? What turns out to be the best way to predict their votes? Answer: the desire for re-election. Standing up for an unpopular principle is such a tiny part of politics that most studies can't even pick it up. Kellen hated people who'd do anything to get ahead, and anything else to stay there."

Like Lemaster Carlyle, Bruce was thinking, but he wondered whether his own biases might be playing him false.

"What about Mrs. Carlyle—"

The objection leaped across the space between them as if determined to strangle this idea aborning: "No, Bruce. Don't think that, okay? It was over a long time ago. Kellen liked married women, but he wasn't crazy."

"Crazy?"

"You don't mess around with the wife of a man like Lemaster Carlyle. You don't dare. No matter what rumors you might have heard about what is going on, or not going on, between them. And, besides, I know Julia is good-looking, but isn't she like forty or something? That's kind of old for Kellen. He liked them younger."

"Why not?"

"Why not what?"

"Why don't you mess around with the wife of a man like Lemaster Carlyle? Why is that such a crazy thing to do?"

Art Lewin's facial expression said that perhaps Bruce was the crazy one. "Come on," he said, and, with difficulty, laughed. "He wouldn't take it very well, would he?"

"I suppose not," said Bruce, certain he was missing something. They were standing at the heavy wooden door to the building. The old iron lock no longer functioned. Art was holding his electronic key to the entryway. Bruce had a master that opened every door on campus.

The economist looked up at the sky, and Bruce steeled himself for a disquisition on the causes of weather. Instead, the young man grew wistful. "You know what? It wasn't just Kellen who hated Lemaster Carlyle. I don't think Lemaster liked Kellen too much either."

"Why do you say that?"

"Well, you know, they had that disagreement in the papers. But even before that. I saw them together this one time, at the faculty senate, when Lemaster was still a law professor, before he went to Washington and all that. I was just out of grad school. Anyway, the senate was debating this committee proposal to amend the university's code of ethics, to forbid sexual relationships between professors and students in all circumstances. Lemaster was a big backer. Kellen was one of the leaders of the opposition, because, well, he said grown-ups can make their choices, but let's just say there might have been some spark of self-interest. Anyway, at the break, they ran into each other in the hallway, and Kellen asked Lemaster why he was fighting so hard when it was obvious to everybody that the proposal was going to be tabled without a vote. And Lemaster looked at him, gave him that steely-eyed glance of his, you know, like everybody's disdainful father? And he said, 'You're against the rule. That's enough reason for me to be for it.' Kellen said, 'Don't make this personal'—or something like that. Lemaster was still looking at him like he was an interesting species of rodent. He said, 'It's not personal. It's official. I just think you're a dangerous man.' Words to that effect."

"Did anybody else hear this exchange?"

"I don't really know. Could be. The hallway was pretty crowded. I mean, they weren't shouting or anything, they were both pretty civil, but I don't think they cared about being overheard."

Bruce weighed the tale. Too thin, he decided. Even combined with what else Art had told him about the night of the murder, it was just too thin. "I see," was his only comment.

A hiatus, each playing a bit of poker with the other.

"If you don't need me any more, I'd like to get my bag and head home—" Art began.

"Wait."

"I'm tired, Bruce." The sullen child was back.

"Just one thing more."

He sighed and looked around as if expecting help. In the course of their walk, a gray twilight had crept over the campus. The frigid wind promised worse to come. The professor thrust his soft hands into his pockets, looking balefully at the director of campus safety, and it occurred to Bruce that Art Lewin was a dreadfully unhappy man.

"Sure, Bruce, sure. One thing more."

"When we were in your office, you said that you'd want to kill Kellen Zant."

The youthful eyes widened. "Well, I didn't mean it seriously. It was kind of . . . I was just trying to make a point."

"Do you think you could elaborate?"

"It's not a secret, Bruce. I went over this with the investigators. If you want to find a motive, just track down the husbands of all those wives he seduced. One of them is bound to be angry enough." A pause. "Or hurt enough."

Bruce saw it. Remembered the photograph on his desk: two children, no mother. He glanced down at Arthur's left hand. No wedding band, but an indentation where one used to be.

"You're divorced."

"That's right."

"Did Kellen Zant have something to do with it?"

Art Lewin glanced away again, his Adam's apple bobbing as he coped with whatever was stirring in him. His baby face was flushed and wounded. "You could say that."

"Kellen . . . slept with your wife?"

"Stole my wife."

"What?"

"A little miscalculation on his part." A shrill laugh, half sane. "Carol left me, babies and all, to chase after him. It wasn't part of his calculation."

"Your wife left you for Kellen Zant? When was this?"

"Oh, nine, ten months. More. Almost a year now, come to think of it."

Bruce frowned. He had heard nothing of this from any of his

sources, not a whisper. He said, "Now, Art, let me understand this. Your wife left you for the man, and you still played chess with him? Every Friday afternoon?"

"It was only the man I hated. I didn't love his mind any less."

This was too much for Bruce to process, so he put it aside for later consideration. "So . . . your wife . . . Carol . . . what did Kellen do when she said she was leaving you?"

"Kellen? What do you think he did? I told you, he was commitment-shy. He sent her back. Said that wasn't the deal."

"He sent her back . . . to you?"

Art nodded. "She came banging on the door, the middle of the night, the day after she walked out. Crying, miserable, telling me she made a big mistake. I thought it was funny. I laughed my head off. I let her in, but the next day I told her I was moving out."

Bruce's head was whirling. Somehow he could not picture the laughter. Then, looking at the young man's sad, greedy face, he could.

"You let her in but you moved out?"

"No. I just told her I was. I wasn't going to, not really."

"I see," said Bruce, but he didn't. "Maybe I should talk to Carol. Where is she now?"

"Home."

"Home? Like, her parents'?"

"No, Bruce. Not home like at her parents'. Home like at our house. That's why I have to go. Carol will have dinner waiting."

"But I thought you were . . . uh . . ."

"Divorced. Right."

"Then how on earth—"

"We're just divorced, Bruce. That doesn't mean we can't live together. Doing it this way is a sensible exercise in rationally managing risk. There are no legal impediments if either of us wants to make a change, and, in the meanwhile, Carol and I have all the benefits of marital life. Sometimes she'll want to stay out all night with somebody else. Or I will. Or we both will." His winter pallor brightened in blush. "Then, you know, my mother-in-law takes care of the kids. Well, no, she's not my mother-in-law any more, is she? I don't think there's a word for it. My estranged mother-in-law? I don't know. Anyway, the point is, Carol and I are both free to see other people. If we want to do it, we do it. In that sense, what happened with Kellen has been good for us. I think you could say it has had a liberating effect on our rational faculties. We're no longer bound by any artificial barriers. We can make choices with better information. We've become more efficient in the pursuit of happiness." Art Lewin's head was bobbing, his adolescent face was smiling, his voice had grown louder, and he seemed scarcely aware that Bruce at his side was trembling with a baffled fury. "You know, lots of people who aren't married live together. It's the coming thing. I'm not even sure there is a rational case to be made for traditional marriage any more. Without external pressure, religious or social, to compel marriage, no rational, welfare-maximizing individual would enter into one. As a matter of fact, at the rate the numbers are increasing, we can expect—"

Art Lewin was still deep in his own maunderings as Bruce, unable to bear any more, slipped away into the shadows. He had decided: campus life was not for him.

The young economist had said there was no rational case to be made for traditional marriage, and a part of Bruce Vallely hated him for that. Bruce could have offered a perfectly rational case, although he suspected that a scholar trained in the modern way would never understand. For Bruce, the case in behalf of marriage consisted of a single beautiful word:

Grace.

CHAPTER 19

A DISTURBING COMPLAINT

(I)

BACK IN HIS OFFICE for a few precious minutes before hurrying home to beat the storm, Bruce put in a call to Rick Chrebet. There were only so many remaining favors he could call in, but what he needed, he needed. For a change, Rick was at his desk, and, yes, they had interviewed Art Lewin at length before everything stopped, and, yes, they had picked up on the remark about Jamaica. Yes, they had checked it out: they had not, said Rick, quite lost all of their competence since Bruce left. And, no, he was not in anybody's computer for anything that weekend or anytime soon: no Jamaica, no Caribbean, no air travel, no hotel, no car rental, no cruise ticket, nothing. Zant was just back from a trip to Dallas and Atlanta to make presentations for his consulting clients. On the way home he had stopped in Arkadelphia to see his uncle. The week after the murder, the economist was supposed to have gone to Los Angeles to visit another client, but had not yet made his reservations: the client's corporate travel department had been waiting to hear from him. "First class," said Rick, awestruck. Zant had also booked tickets, buying early to save his hosts the fare, for an April conference at the University of Chicago, where he was supposed to deliver a paper on the optimal level of adultery.

"Seriously," said Rick.

One more thing, he added, voice dropping. Zant had recently used his E-ZPass, his digital toll card, on expressways in Massachusetts. But no hotels or motels had hosted him, and none of his Upper New England friends had seen him.

A puzzle, said Rick.

Bruce agreed. "Now, Kellen Zant did a lot of consulting work."

"True," said Rick.

"Do you know what he was working on when he died?" A long pause, two old colleagues sniffing each other out. "Is it a state secret, what he was doing?"

To Bruce's surprise, his sally brought forth no answering laugh, even the mirthless one that would tell him he wasn't being funny. Instead, the silence continued, as though Rick Chrebet was weighing sad options his old partner could not imagine. When Rick spoke, his usually dry voice dripped reluctance. "It was a robbery, Bruce. You know that, right?"

"I read the papers, but—"

"We're not looking into his consulting work, or his private life, or anything else." Words slow and painfully clear. "We're looking for an armed robber who shoots his victims in the head. Period. An official statement will be out soon."

"Suppose it wasn't a robbery. Suppose—"

"Other avenues have been considered. They're closed now."

"Does that mean—"

Rick was implacable, even if amiable. "We've known each other a long time, Bruce. I know how your suspicious little mind works. I know you must be thinking, double-tap, back of the head, it looks like a professional hit. And you must be thinking, whatever Zant was working on, he must have scared somebody important. But you're wrong, Bruce. Those possibilities have all been ruled out."

Bruce considered. They had been partners forever, friends nearly as long, and knew how to send messages without ever letting on. Rick had used the passive voice. He did not say he or his people had chosen not to try the other avenues. He said they were closed—implying that someone else had done the closing. So Bruce answered, every bit as carefully, "Bear with me for a moment. Okay, it was a robbery. I accept that. I'm just trying to tie up some loose ends."

Rick laughed, humorlessly, and it occurred to Bruce that his old partner, usually tumbling with mirth, was genuinely perplexed, even miserable. "You're not a cop any more, Bruce. Loose ends aren't really your department."

"These loose ends are. It's a university matter. I'm not . . . working the case."

Again the answer was a long while coming, and Bruce wondered what invisible line he had crossed. *He must have scared somebody important.* In the outer office, somebody was shouting about a basketball game, a big upset. Rick said, "Sorry, Bruce. His work is a dead end. That's our conclusion."

"Who concluded it?"

Still the slowness, words dragged upward like heavy treasure buried in a tomb. "I really can't get into those details, Bruce."

"This really goes that high up? Is that what you're saying?"

Another hush on the telephone. The predicted snow was spattering the window, except that it was mostly rain. What flakes there were melted before they could stick: sort of like the official investigation. Bruce wondered why his partner had been so forthcoming at first, but slowed the flow of information once they reached the topic of Kellen's work.

"I'm sorry," said Rick at last, and Bruce knew better than to press. He had already asked for, and been denied, access to the Audi and to Zant's house. If he asked too many favors, even Rick would reach a point when the word *no* might become too easy to say.

"Okay. Just one more thing."

"Sure, Bruce," said his golfing buddy, but the arid voice carried a note of warning.

"They say Kellen Zant was a bit of a ladies' man. They say he particularly liked married women."

"That's not a question." Impatient now, the favors plainly at an end.

"You must have interviewed some of the, ah, husbands involved."

"And wives. What's your point?"

"Were any of them . . . Did you ever focus on one of them as a suspect?"

A hiatus on the other end. Paper rustling. Voices in the background. Had Rick put the telephone down? No. He had unplugged his headset and was whispering directly into the mouthpiece. "That's over the line, Bruce. I can't discuss that."

"Come on, Rick. This is me."

"Yeah, Bruce, it's you. Are you gonna punch me in the face if I don't talk?"

"I never did anything like that and you know it."

"Some of the guys you dragged in here sure thought you might." A heavy sigh. "Matter of fact, I seem to remember that a couple of them filed civil-rights complaints."

"What? That never happened!"

"I think it did."

"What is this, some kind of joke?"

Although Rick was no longer on the headset, his voice was as distant and dry as before. "A couple of the complaints are in process now. Maybe they were filed after you left the force."

"There's rules. The department would have to give me notice."

"Must have fallen through the cracks."

Bruce ran a hand through his short, brushy hair, trying to get his mind around what could only be a threat. "What are you telling me, Rick? Am I under investigation?"

A beat. The voice came back, not so harsh. "I'd watch myself if I were you, that's all I'm saying."

(11)

BRUCE BADE GOOD NIGHT to the second-shift staff, just filtering in, a dispatcher and a sergeant in the building, a pair of patrol cars on the move, three officers and one administrator for a campus of several hundred acres: the agony of the balanced budget. Six more cruisers and a trio of vans were behind a wired gate, awaiting the day shift, and the day of more money. He pushed through the double glass doors and out into the parking lot. He never left the Mustang in the space reserved for him, because backing up and turning around were too difficult. With his wife passed on and his children grown, worrying about scratches in the smooth red bodywork was one way to fill the need to fret. He opened the door and smiled grimly, remembering all the years of opening the passenger side first for Grace, who declared herself utterly liberated except on the issue of . . . well, who gets to go first.

And thinking about Grace put an itch in his mind, something to do with Kellen Zant and his car—

He stopped. He felt watched.

Swift eyes that had known jungle darkness and desert glare ranged across the shadows that lay beyond the far end of the lot, where the university property ended. The border was marked by a sprinkling of small houses, a couple of disused factories, and, farther on, a slowly rising hill at the crest of which developers hoped to create a luxury subdivision. Sight is drawn to movement in the inkiest of nights, but Bruce, gaze impeded by the yellow gleam of the lamps that illuminated and, in theory, protected the parking lot, saw nothing.

Something.

A wisp of movement in the woods near one of the houses, a fold in the darkness like a brief thickening of the very air.

Gone.

An animal. A gust of wind. Imagination, born of stress: he knew that malady, too.

Yet Bruce Vallely was a man who would rather trust his instincts than interrogate them. If he felt watched, somebody was watching. But no amount of patient waiting was able to conjure afresh that strange twisting image in the woods.

Bruce shook his head, then stood still again, looking at his hand. He was still holding on to the wide-open door of the car. The itch in his mind was back. He thought about handing Grace in, as her people used to call it, securing her door before opening his own.

Of course.

He realized what had bothered him during his interview with Nathaniel Knowland. What had the div student told him about the night he saw Kellen Zant?

There had been a woman with him, a skinny phantom, a black woman with a British accent, wearing what might or might not have been a white rain slicker. They had climbed into Zant's gold Audi TT on Town Street, across from the stadium.

The woman drove, Bruce remembered. And Kellen Zant got in first on the passenger side.

Bruce had pressed the young man, and he had not backed off this particular detail.

Kellen Zant, the great ladies' man, not only allowed the stranger to drive his car, but did not hold her door before seeing to his own.

Slipping behind the wheel of the Mustang and starting the engine, Bruce felt twin theses forming. One possibility was that Kellen was too distracted, or too angry, to be polite. This struck him as unlikely. Politesse was not choice but training. Either the habit of opening doors first for the ladies was so ingrained that it survived one's moments of passion, or it was not. Very well, in the generation that had spawned Nathaniel Knowland, or the generation looming just a few years beyond it, such pleasantries meant nothing, or might even be taken as insults. But Professor Kellen Zant was of a different time.

All of which led Bruce, as he steered past the cemetery toward Royal Road and, beyond it, North Elm and home, to his second possibility: namely, that Kellen Zant got in first because his companion told him to.

And why would he do what she commanded?

Well, that would depend. But one fact of which both police officers and, say, Secret Service agents are agonizingly aware is that, unlike most coats and jackets, a loose, voluminous rain slicker is an excellent place to conceal a hand holding a gun.

CHAPTER 20

AN EVENING VISIT

(1)

Sunday night.

Kellen Zant's blocky, modern house was surrounded by trees, set back from the road on three-quarters of an acre in Hobby Hill, one of the priciest, and oldest, neighborhoods in Elm Harbor. The house was "cold," in the jargon, meaning that the police teams had been in and out so often that there was not a shred of untainted, or unlocated, evidence left inside. But Bruce Vallely was not sitting in his Mustang on a side street around the corner because he was searching for the critical clue that would solve the case. He was there because he wanted to get a better sense of who this man was, or had been; and spending an hour or so wandering a house, studying furniture or the arrangement of food in the kitchen or the selection of prints and photographs for the walls, was his favorite way to get inside the heads of those no longer around to answer his questions. The tricky part was that he had no official standing, and his liaison at the police department had turned down flat his request to go inside. There was no owner to ask. Kellen Zant had left no will, and his estate would be tied up for months if not years. So Bruce made an old-fashioned sort of plan.

He would break in.

He reasoned that the alarm would be off, with nobody either to pay the bill or to set the code, and that the neighbors would not consider it strange to see a man, even a black man, playing with the front door— well, the back—because so many evidence techs must have gone through the place that by now local residents must surely have decided to shut the curtains and ignore the noise.

And there was something else.

Bruce had spoken to a man whose home backed on Zant's yard, a retired classicist named Bischoff, who insisted that he had seen two people enter the house, via the back door, the night Kellen Zant was killed. And what was interesting was that he swore they had gone in at a quarter past eight precisely, the same time that Nathaniel Knowland had spotted the economist on Town Street, outside the stadium. Bischoff was certain because he had been up in the bathroom taking his medication, according to his rigid schedule. He even pulled out his time chart to show it to Bruce, then drew an analogy to something in Ovid that Bruce had never heard of, to say nothing of read. Thinking it over, Bruce supposed it was possible that Nate Knowland had the time wrong by a few minutes, or, possibly, Zant had left earlier than young Knowland thought, and he and his female companion had hurried up to Hobby Hill, a drive of only five or six minutes. But why would they have snuck around to the back door, arriving, as Bischoff insisted they had, not from the driveway but through the trees? Bruce had asked the classicist whether he had shared his story with the police, and he said yes, and produced the business card the officer had given him—Janey Wei, whom Bruce knew, a rising star in the department—adding that she had promised to get back to him, but never had.

So now Bruce had his car parked in line with the trees through which, said Bischoff, the intruders had come. The intruders who entered the house after Kellen Zant left but before he was dead—because, once he was dead, the police might show at any minute—but who could have made the decision only if they knew he would not be interrupting them. To emerge from the woods at the spot the retired professor had indicated, they had to have crossed another lawn. There were several to choose from, and Bruce doubted that anybody had seen anything. But the decision entailed a certain risk, and he wondered what they could have wanted so badly that they would chance getting caught.

He climbed out of the Mustang, lock-picking tools in his pocket, and walked along Hobby Road, where massive, brooding Victorians competed with massive, brooding brick Colonials for the prize of most dourly expensive home in the city. Not many black residents out here. If he remembered correctly, other than Zant there was only one, a single woman who was a partner in a local law firm. How did they manage out among the white folks, these lone pioneers? He could not guess and decided not to care. The job. Focus on the job. It was night, just past eight, for he wanted to see the street the way it was when the intruders made their sally into the house. Lights were on in almost every house. Family rooms or dining rooms looked out on the lawns. How on earth had the visitors slipped by, especially on a snowy night, when movement would show against the backdrop of solid white?

The risk was enormous, sneaking across a lawn at so early an hour of the evening, when one parent arriving home late, one teenager putting out the trash, one dog making a ruckus, would spell disaster.

Then he spotted a possibility.

On the corner, one of the largest homes was under renovation, and looked as if it had been for some time. True, the lot did not back on Kellen Zant's, but once Bruce slipped behind it he found that the tree line that connected the back of all the properties along the street was sufficiently thick that one could, with a modicum of caution, move under cover from one lot to the next until reaching a path to the economist's house. Bruce did exactly this, and, even moving slowly to avoid unnecessary noise, he took no more than two or three minutes to do it, not least because the path was already marked, at least to his experienced jungle eye: marked by bent twigs and broken branches, to show the passage of humans, first inward, to enter the house, and then, when they were finished, outward again, on a slightly different course, blazing a fresh trail.

The classicist, Bischoff, had seen what he said he saw.

Bruce checked his tools. Trevor Land would be astonished at Bruce's enterprise, but this was the only way he knew to pursue the case. He did not expect to find evidence of who had committed the crime. He sought only evidence of who Kellen Zant had been. He would be in and out of the house swiftly and undetected, and Trevor Land would never have to know.

(11)

HE CROSSED THE BACK LAWN by moonlight, having learned long ago that nature almost always provides enough illumination if you just let your eyes get used to it. An indentation in the heaping snow was a swimming pool, covered for the season. The walls of the house were vertical wood siding, painted gray, with casement windows. Thirty or forty years ago, when the place was new, the design must have been the latest thing. It took no more than ninety seconds to pick the lock, and he was right, the alarm had been shut off, not even set to a "watch" function that might have beeped to signal the door opening and recorded the intrusion in some computer out in Kansas or Karachi. He did not flick on a light. He stood in the kitchen, adjusting to the richer darkness indoors. Glowing smears in the shadows were the fluorescent fingerprint powders so beloved of today's investigators. Bruce still preferred the traditional basic black, perhaps because of the seriousness it connoted.

The kitchen was stainless steel and did not get much use. Dishes and cookware were the latest thing, and gleaming. Cookbooks had unbent spines. Zant liked to put on a show but did not like to cook, and, evidently, rarely had anyone cook for him. Beneath each sparkling-clean gas burner was a tray made of wrinkled aluminum foil, presumably a habit the economist had brought with him from the South, hardly ever seen these days. In the nearly empty refrigerator he found another: the open box of baking soda to absorb odors. A spill on the shelf told him that the police had searched inside the package, and perhaps taken some powder as a sample. The police, or the other intruders: the ones who dropped in before the police. Why the powder? What were they looking for?

Worry about it later.

Bruce moved out into the hallway. Living and dining rooms were furnished with a strange mix of new heavy pieces and sleek Scandinavian designs that had been in fashion twenty years ago. Zant could afford to change with the times but obviously had not wanted to. Yet, from what Bruce had learned, the economist was hardly wedded to the old ways. Perhaps he had chosen not to buy new tables and chairs because he lacked the time to invest; or, more likely, because by preserving the furniture he was preserving something else.

The question was what.

He continued through the first floor. Everywhere there were books. They had been taken down and put back, by a sloppier hand than Kellen Zant's, for the professor liked everything clear and neatly organized. No doubt the police had done some searching, but what really impressed Bruce was that whoever had entered the night Zant was shot had also done their search with care, leaving few traces, not wanting subsequent, more official investigators to come across a wrecked house that might lead to a more extended official investigation.

First tentative conclusion: those first, unofficial searchers had been professionals.

Second: they had known or guessed that, in the absence of serious clues to indicate a break-in, the search for the killer would be closed down.

Bruce found the economist's study, and, on the walls, the expected collection of degrees and awards and photographs. Lots and lots of photographs: plainly a man in love with his own image. The filing cabinets had been rifled, and he was willing to bet that everything that dwelt even remotely on Zant's finances was gone. He saw no checkbook or Rolodex or address book, his usual tools for reconstructing a life, and supposed they were tagged and sealed in the police evidence room. In the old days, Bruce would have had bank and telephone records to examine, but not as unofficial investigator and official lackey to Trevor Land.

No matter. He would make do.

The desktop was arranged to make space for a computer, but none was present: presumably the detectives had borrowed it to analyze the hard drive. Not plausible, however, that it would be the only one. A man like Kellen Zant would also carry a sleek notebook computer. Art Lewin had two or three. Bruce made a note in his old-fashioned leather-bound notebook to inquire whether one was found. About to leave the room, Bruce noticed a thick sheaf of pages still on the printer, perhaps the last work the economist had produced, probably in draft form. A yellow light was flashing, presumably because the device was no longer connected to a computer. If the pages had been left by both the police and the intruders, they likely possessed no evidentiary significance, but he was a methodical man and so lifted them anyway, flipping through, pausing here and there. Three separate academic papers in progress, from what he could tell, none thin. He examined the first— jointly authored, he noticed, with Art Lewin.

> . . . but, because the relatively successful liberation of women has made marriage less economically necessary for women, and thus

less attractive to them, one would predict that fewer women would marry, or, among those who do marry, that fewer would remain married. The data bear out both predictions. . . .

Revolted at the reduction of matrimony to analysis of data, Bruce shuddered. Then he collected himself—what else would one analyze?—and flipped farther through the packet.

. . . of course either the first-price auction or the all-pay auction will yield the same long-run convergence if players adopt strategies enabling them to learn from the results of previous plays. This is true whether or not the bidders' preferences are convex. If however the players participate in only a single iteration of the auction, the benefits to the auctioneer are likely to be greater under . . .

This time Bruce almost smiled in the musty darkness of the study. Academics had so many ways of saying "Bow down before my brilliance." That article, too, he put aside. The next one gave him pause.

. . . but no trace of Gina's body was found for days thereafter. Although to this day the evidence points to young DeShaun, for years ever after rumors circulated through the town like winter wind. . . .

Bruce frowned. Odd that Kellen Zant should be looking into this old case. And the words hardly sounded like Kellen Zant's academic prose. They sounded . . . adolescent. He flipped back to the title page and understood. Instinct, instinct. Already guilty of breaking and entering, Bruce reasoned that theft of a twelve-page paper was a lesser offense, especially a paper not authored by Zant. He slipped the pages into his pocket.

A last look around the study. Why had the police taken the computer? General principles, or did they have a particular goal they had yet to share with the university? Or might it have been whoever broke in the night Zant died? Bruce shook his head. For a moment the ego wall caught his attention, a peculiarity he could not quite name—

He stopped, peering out into the yard. He thought he had seen a light, a brief flicker, like a signal, but although he waited and waited by the window, there was no repetition.

He went upstairs.

Three bedrooms, none particularly spacious or modern. One looked unused, another had a distinctly feminine cast, with dead flowers in a vase—the only flowers he had seen in the house, so Zant was no fan—and, atop the dresser, a scattering of powders and creams. The drawers were empty. The closet was empty. Had a woman been staying here? If so, had she cleared out her things before or after the murder? And why leave the cosmetics? Because they're messy if you're in a hurry. So either she was in the house after the murder, clandestinely, or, if before, she left in a rush. The police had asked themselves the same questions: fingerprint powder glowed brightly in the darkness. Bruce made another note in the book. Flipping back, he made tick marks next to two lines in his interview with Arthur Lewin, Professor Zant's protégé.

Instinct. He took two of the jars, one an exotic and, to look at it, expensive moisturizer, the other a foundation powder with a silhouette of Africa on the label. He stuffed both into plastic bags he had brought along and slipped them into his pocket. Maybe the substances would be traceable, and, in the unlikely event that the detectives returned, a couple of missing vials might not be noticed.

Finally, he tackled the master bedroom.

More Scandinavian furniture, including a dresser so battered that one corner was supported by a dusty economics textbook. But Zant had money. The twin closets were jammed with enough fancy duds to clothe half of Hollywood on Oscar night. The top dresser drawer held racks for tie clips and cuff links, but the container was empty. Odd. In the next two drawers, underwear, socks, pajamas, sweaters, athletic togs, everything pressed so perfectly his eyes ached. In the bottom drawer, family albums, snapshots, old report cards, a meaningless jumble.

In the bathroom, an empty medicine cabinet. The police would have taken it all. The tiles were the same age as the house, grout missing and some of them sprung, but the surfaces gleamed. Nothing was hidden beneath. Maybe Zant just didn't care about his surroundings, as long as they were clean.

But he flew first-class, stayed only at four-star hotels, and dressed like a Rothschild. Or a rock star.

Bruce shook his head, was about to leave the room, then returned to the dresser.

That bottom drawer drew him, the photos. No better way to get acquainted. But he would need to use his light. So he sat on the floor and slid the flashlight beneath the bed and turned it on, then sorted through the albums and pictures by the hidden beam. Family. A preteen Zant with an older couple, presumably the aunt and uncle who raised him. The son in California he never saw, photos at all ages. Kellen Zant receiving various awards, Kellen Zant delivering various lectures, Kellen Zant at various graduations, Kellen Zant shaking hands with various dignitaries. Something odd about all this.

Then he grasped it.

No photos of Kellen Zant with any woman his own age. Not his ex-wife, not a girlfriend at an amusement park or a cotillion or even one of those silly sets of three snaps from a machine in the drugstore that everyone above a certain age seems to own. Portraits of himself at all ages, but he was not merely the star of the show. He was the whole performance.

Bruce sat on the floor, trying to work out the reasoning. He imagined Art Lewin next to him, explaining that not preserving photos of past girlfriends was a rational means of maximizing the chances of pleasing present ones. After all, nobody wanted to wake up in a strange man's bed and go through his things and discover mementos of ex-lovers everywhere.

Made sense.

The other possibility was that the economist's ego was of sufficient size that it would never occur to him that there might be a grace to be found in the warm contemplation of past romances, even those that ended badly. Bruce's pastor, Morris Young, liked to say that there was not a single person we would meet in our lives who was not both worthy of and in need of our lifelong prayers; and of whose lifelong prayers we ourselves were not both needy and worthy.

"So analyze that, Professor," Bruce said, speaking aloud for the first time since entering the house.

He put out the light, returned the albums to their places, and stood by the window, this time looking out on the front and side of the house, because he thought he had seen another flicker. But his sharp eyes could pick out only the playful moon, teasing him with reflections from the shiny frozen snow.

(1 1 1)

BACK DOWNSTAIRS IN THE KITCHEN, preparing to depart, Bruce paused again. The scene was nagging at him. He took a last, quick, professional glance around the room, looking for something amiss. The polished crockery. The gleaming stainless steel. The nearly empty refrigerator. The gourmet gas range, rarely used, because Zant rarely cooked. Bruce looked again. That was it. The trays of wrinkled foil Zant had stuffed beneath the burners, to catch spills and keep the surfaces clean. The old-fashioned Southern touch, so incongruous in the modern kitchen. Even if the economist had been raised that way, why bother if you never used the burners? Why break up the clean, shiny, modern lines? Bruce stood over the range top. He lifted the burners and, one by one, the foil coverings beneath. On his third try he found it: a thick wad of paper. Why hide it under a burner, where it might accidentally be burned? Because nobody would think of looking there; and because you could burn it up yourself in two seconds if need be.

The papers were folded over twice, and Bruce, opening them gently, hunched on the kitchen floor, using the flashlight to examine his find.

First item. A carbon of a typed report by an insurance claims adjuster, an estimate of the cost of repairing a badly damaged car, dated early March 1973. The insurance company he recognized, and knew it was no longer in business. He did not know about the body shop, but its address was in Scottsville, a washed-out factory town some miles northwest of Elm Harbor, and nowhere near Tyler's Landing. No indication of who owned the car. Only a policy number and claim number.

All right, a transfer of money from an insurance company would be the sort of evidence an economist would find useful. But what was it evidence *of*? Where on earth had Zant found it? Why was it hidden so carefully, as if nothing could be more precious?

Second item. A yellowing police report from Tyler's Landing, addressed to the first selectman, date and signature both torn off. A summary of recent activity, perhaps as part of the budgeting process. Several sentences were underlined:

The numerous reports of Negroes driving through town in recent weeks may be well-founded. Officers stopped one Negro near the Town Green last month. His identification said he was an Air Force general, and he reported that he was just passing through. Another the same night turned out to be a congressional staffer. Possibly some of our more "liberal" townspeople have been entertaining them.

"And hello to you, too," muttered Bruce, who could not for the life of him understand why black people moved to the suburbs.

Third item. A small page torn from what must have been a notebook or journal, the jagged writing overlarge and smeary, a man's hand, picking up in the middle of one sentence, and ending in the middle of another:

. . . but according to Deputy Nacchio, none of her friends reported seeing her that night. Deputy Nacchio also reported that around nine that night she knocked on the door of one of her teachers, a Mrs. Spicer, and asked to use the telephone. That report was later . . .

Perfectly unenlightening. He supposed he would have to find out who exactly Deputy Nacchio was, or had been, for the paper was old and crumbling.

All right. He had to know more about what Kellen Zant was up to when he died. Talking to Art Lewin had not yielded enough.

Bruce refolded the police statement and the insurance report, slipping them along with the journal entry into his notebook. The foil he wrinkled afresh and replaced beneath the burners, hoping to leave no sign. Still he hesitated. Yes, he had found what everyone else had overlooked, but still the back of his mind tickled. He had the sense that his attention was gliding past the obvious. In his mind he worked backward through the house. A police report, a diary entry, and an insurance claim, hidden from prying eyes. A drawer-full of photos of Kellen Zant by himself. A spare bedroom yielding signs of recent female occupancy. A study crammed with books and the usual academic ego wall. Furniture far less grand than what the economist could afford. A confusing jumble, although Bruce already knew he did not much like the man who had created it.

"Time to go," he said aloud, and had a hand on the knob of the kitchen door when he realized what else he had missed.

He returned to the study, to the display of photos on the wall.

There. Kellen Zant in formal attire, at a reception of some sort, smiling as he received a plaque from Bill Clinton. Lemaster and Julia Carlyle stood in the front row, applauding.

Okay, so what?

Bruce skimmed along and found another. A newspaper shot of Kellen Zant jogging to raise money for AIDS awareness. And there, also running, separated by no more than two or three other participants, was Julia Carlyle.

And another: Kellen Zant, in casual dress, at a cocktail party, laughing at a joke being told by Johnnie Cochran. The several faces laughing beside his belonged to Spike Lee, Skip Gates, Charles Ogletree . . . and Julia Carlyle.

Yet another: Kellen Zant delivering a lecture at a church full of upturned, expectant black faces, on the occasion of some major civil-rights anniversary. And there, in the front row, beaming up at him, was Julia Carlyle.

When his survey was done, he counted seventeen photographs displayed in the study, and Julia had edged her way into fully eight of them. Here was the economist's secret shrine, disguised from the clever eye of casual lovers, and professional searchers, too. No other woman seriously in evidence. Zant had selected for his wall no shots that included close-ups of women unless they could be cropped to give prominence to Julia.

And not only that.

Bruce was ready to bet that the Scandinavian furniture that Kellen Zant lacked the heart to junk dated from their days together. Perhaps he had left it in storage during his brief foray to Palo Alto, and briefer marriage, but, on returning east, he had uncrated it again. The economist turned out to be hiding a sentimental streak of frightening size. Bruce had no idea whether the feelings were reciprocated, but one thing was clear: Art Lewin was wrong.

Two decades after their breakup, Kellen Zant had been obsessed with his ex-lover Julia Carlyle.

CHAPTER 21

THE ANSWER

(1)

"How have you been, Julia?"

"Good. Good."

Bruce Vallely nodded solemnly as he sat across the table from her in the smoky tavern on Route 48. Gray winter New England light dribbled in through cheaply tinted windows. It was half past two. Only a handful of customers. Julia had warned him that she would have only a few minutes: she wanted to be home before the first school bus arrived at three. She was determined to squeeze their conversation into as small a temporal space as possible, and, had Bruce not been Grace's husband—or widower now—and had Grace not been a Sister Lady, Julia likely would have refused to see him at all. Service as first lady of the university had a few perks after all.

"How's Vanessa been holding up? I heard about what happened. I'm so sorry."

"She's doing better, thanks."

"And the rest of the family?"

"Everybody's fine," said Julia, bewildered. So far, the "urgent" meeting, in this odd venue, had been idle chitchat. She could not tell whether he was circling toward a destination or whether they had somehow passed it. In the meanwhile, she could not seem to stop uttering banalities; nor, for that matter, could he. She glanced around, hoping not to see anyone who knew her, because the meeting felt strangely like an assignation. Julia remembered—and supposed Bruce must, too—the night the two of them first met, in the days before she set up housekeeping with Lemaster, when a younger and somehow rawer

Bruce Vallely, along with another officer, answered a call to her little student apartment in an Elm Harbor walk-up after a burglary, and she flirted with him without troubling to check his left hand for the wedding band that he wore even now, a year after Grace's passing. Bruce was offended and did not try to hide it, turning cool and businesslike and in a great hurry to depart. Years later, she learned to appreciate that reaction, although at the time it wounded and embarrassed her.

"And your husband? How has he settled in?"

Julia was surprised at her own nervous giggle, a holdover from her biracial childhood in Hanover, when giggling had been a form of self-protection, enamoring her to blacks and whites alike.

"Lemaster? He's going strong as always." She remembered that Bruce technically worked for her husband, and decided to remind them both. "He loves the job. Loves it. I guess he kind of hit the ground running."

Bruce smiled. "He's had a few controversies already. So I'd say he's settled in nicely."

"Yes, he has," she said, mystified.

"He's an exceptional man," said Bruce, his solemn tone suggesting that she jot this down in case it was on the exam. "You're fortunate to have each other."

"Oh, well, thanks. And Grace . . . was wonderful, too."

A thin smile. Julia had the sense that she had said the wrong thing but was not sure why. Mona and Granny Vee had not really trained her to the etiquette of talking about a dead friend, least of all to said friend's husband.

"Yes, she was," said Bruce, tonelessly.

"She was lucky to have you," she heard herself saying, and blushed.

"I was blessed to have her."

To this there was nothing to say, so Julia said nothing. At the next table somebody was telling a ribald story very loud, but Julia caught only snatches. Her uneasiness grew. They were conspicuous, she decided, leaning in close at a corner table, the only black couple—ah, people—in the room. Mona had raised her to value reputation above most things. She wished he would get to the point and release her.

Bruce, either unaware of her growing distress or unconcerned, nevertheless had his answer ready, as though this was the point he had waited the past ten minutes for her to make. "Grace was a wise woman, Julia. Well, you know that. She was nervous when I took this job. She appreciated the extra income, but another part of her wanted to head to South Carolina. Maybe I should have done what she wanted." Bruce voiced this sentiment without rancor or self-contempt. He was a plain-spoken man, accustomed to a linear way of thinking, merely stating facts: around the campus, a rarity.

"She always supported you, Bruce. Whatever you chose to do."

"I know that, but thank you. And she used to tell me, if I was going to do it, then do it well. I've tried to follow her advice." He nodded and, leaning forward, folded his enormous hands on the table to show her that they were approaching the nub of the matter. "Julia, listen. Let me explain my position here. I am the director of campus safety. I am depu-tized, I have powers of arrest, just as my people do. But I lack the authority, except within certain very narrow limits, to investigate. The university police are a crime-preventing force but not a crime-solving force. Okay?"

"Okay," said Julia, more mystified than ever. He seemed to be resuming an argument the beginning of which she had missed.

"Our charter makes that very clear. If we come across evidence that warrants serious criminal investigation, we turn it over to the city or state police."

"Okay."

"Now, within those limits, I would like, if I could, to ask you a couple of questions about Kellen Zant."

Probably the sudden change in room light and temperature was her imagination, Julia told herself. The coincidence of the sun's choosing just this moment to drift behind a cloud and the wind's selecting the same instant to rattle the windows would be too great.

"What kind of questions?"

Bruce smiled to say she needn't worry. "Nothing complicated. I'm just tidying up a few loose ends. But I realized I never met the man. Maybe you could help me out a little, tell me what he was like."

"I thought the case was closed. It was a robbery. That's what it says in the papers."

"As I said, I'm really just tidying loose ends."

"Can't you just talk to the police? Get their reports?"

"Let's just say the reports are inaccessible. Reports from the Land-ing, reports from the Elm Harbor police, reports from the state police. I have their conclusions, a couple of memos, three or four pages each. But that's all I can get. No raw interviews. No investigators' notes. Only the conclusions."

The scientist in her followed the equation. "Usually you'd get more?"

"Usually." Another beat. "They give me what they're required to give me, but usually I can get more, either as a courtesy or through a back channel."

"So what's different about Kellen Zant?"

He puffed out a lot of air, evidently deciding whether to shed the final veil. The fire exit smacked open, somebody having leaned on the crash bar. Two heads peeked in, students from the high school looking for an after-school drink, immediately made Bruce for a cop and Julia for a teacher, former professions but close enough, and vanished again. "The truth is, I don't know what's different. I want to find out."

"I'm sorry, I'm not following."

Bruce sighed, stretched his long legs, looked around the room. The swinging stainless-steel door to the kitchen opened. He seemed to sense the act a split second before it occurred. A middle-aged woman of the paler nation, dressed in a pink uniform, emerged with napkins in a brown paper wrapper and began to refill the holders on the tables, preparing for the evening rush. She watched the two of them incuriously, then returned to her work. Evidently satisfied, Bruce shifted his gaze back to Julia.

"For some reason, Julia, they seem to have been ordered to keep away from me."

"Seriously?"

He nodded, not at all put out. "I'm not sure what's going on. Maybe it's some sort of bureaucratic snafu. I don't know. But, in the meantime, I have to do a lot of work to catch up. And, to start with, I'd like to know more about Kellen Zant and his work."

"You should interview his friends." Her voice sounded too brittle to her own ears, but the cat-and-mouse game he seemed to be playing suddenly disturbed her. Where was he taking this?

"He didn't have a lot of friends, Julia. Colleagues, sure, and I've talked to them. But not friends. As a matter of fact, some people told me that you might be his best friend."

Her world rocked, as she remembered running into Kellen that final time at the mall up in Norport, and their argument—

"I hardly knew him these last few years," she said.

"Really." A statement.

"Yes, really."

"The night he got shot, he told someone that he was on his way to Jamaica. But nobody can find a hotel or airline or cruise ticket in his name." She sensed that the sudden roughness of affect was a stratagem, intended to shock and so to get her talking. "I think it was a code. A message of some kind. Jamaica stood for something else."

"I have no idea," Julia said, a shade too quickly, and felt again that peculiarly sleepy sensation she used to get when Kellen would come on to her. Jamaica. Jamaica. She nibbled her lip. "No idea," she repeated, trying for an innocent, Marian-the-Librarian quality.

"There's some question about what he was working on when he died," Bruce said after a moment. "You seem to be the only one he would have trusted with his secrets."

"Me?"

"Everybody says so."

"Well, everybody's wrong." She tried another diversion, even as it occurred to her that many a successful interrogation probably consists entirely of subjects' trying to throw you off the scent. "A lawyer looked me up. Tice, Anthony Tice. He said he was working with Kellen. Maybe he'd know."

Bruce stared. Julia stared back. Someone dropped a dish and somebody else laughed, but Julia never turned. Facing down Mona all these years had taught her a thing or two about avoiding the seduction of being first to break a silence.

At last Bruce dropped his eyes to his notebook, less a concession than a change of plans. Whatever avenue he had intended to pursue in the conversation, he was about to take a detour. Before he opened his mouth, however, Julia threw in another twist. Feeling deliciously mischievous, she added, "Oh, and there's a woman named Mary Mallard, in Washington. She said she was a friend of his. You could talk to her."

"The writer?"

"That's what she says." Julia hesitated, then pressed on. "Bruce? Do they know anything about Boris Gibbs?"

"Hit-and-run," he said, still writing. "Why?"

"I just . . . I knew him. We worked together." And he had something to tell me, just like Kellen did.

"I know that," said Bruce, and then, without looking up, struck back. "The other thing, Julia, is that I would like to talk to Vanessa."

Again Julia's world rocked. First Chrebet, now his ex-partner. "Vanessa? Why? About what?"

"About Kellen Zant."

Julia was already shaking her head. "Come on, Bruce. Vanessa doesn't know anything about Kellen Zant. Why would you want to talk to her?" A shudder. "I won't have her upset, Bruce. Not about this, not about anything. She sees her therapist two days a week."

"I thought you said she's okay." Spoken swiftly, like a cross-examiner.

"She will be, if the rest of you will just leave her alone."

He pondered. It struck Julia that he was genuinely concerned, but perhaps she was simply projecting. When he spoke, he chose his words cautiously, like a rock-climber who knows that one wrong selection means a long way down. "It isn't my intention to upset her, Julia. But there are a few details I'd like to check. Remember, Kellen Zant was a member of the faculty, so his murder does come, technically, within my mandate to protect the campus." She felt his urgency lashing at her but kept her face stone. "And, besides," he said, "it's important that I talk to Vanessa. There's information I can't get anywhere else."

"What kind of information?"

"For one thing, why a copy of her eleventh-grade term paper was sitting on his printer."

(11)

IN HIS TIME, Bruce Vallely had seen plenty of witnesses fighting not to squirm or shift their gazes, trying to project a confident innocence quite different from what they felt. He saw it in Julia Carlyle now, any number of small nuances by which the body indicated nervousness, even fear. From the moment he had spotted Vanessa's name on the title page, he had suspected that he had struck pay dirt that the other searchers had missed, and now he was certain of it. He watched Julia now, cornered and uncertain. Bruce did not much care for her, or any of the growing number of well-to-do black parents who vanished with their offspring into lily-white suburbs at their first opportunity, but he thought he understood her: she was dragging her children toward her own childhood. She was a mother, she was protective, and her fear, he knew, would only make her all the fiercer in battle.

So he had to assuage it.

He said, "Nobody suspects Vanessa of anything. Nobody thinks she was involved in any way. I want to make that clear." But her eyes said he had not made it clear enough. "This is my problem, Julia. I can't do my job unless I can figure out what Kellen Zant was working on. Now, you tell me you don't know. Let's take that as true. His friends and colleagues don't know. And yet there are people out there trying to find out, which suggests that whatever he was working on mattered to somebody." Bruce had to restrain the urge to quote Rick: *He must have scared somebody important.* "Now I discover that he had a copy of your daughter's term paper. And it wasn't a photocopy from a library or somewhere. It was printed from his computer, Julia. I don't see how that's possible unless she e-mailed it to him or gave him a disk. That means she knew him. Not only knew him, but was in close enough touch with him to—"

Julia interrupted, so sweetly that Bruce knew the sugar was fake. "How do you happen to know what was on his printer?"

"I saw it."

"Oh, really? Does your unofficial tidying up of loose ends include breaking into the private homes of the faculty?"

Bruce was too old a hand to take umbrage. "Maybe it was his office printer, Julia. I'm intrigued that you would think it was his house."

She glared.

"Please understand, Julia. I'm not trying to hurt Vanessa or your family. But I have to know why she gave him her term paper."

Without warning, Julia leaped to her feet. "I'm sorry, Bruce. It's late. I have to get home for the kids."

Bruce stood, too, towering above her, but she was not cowed. "Julia, wait a minute. Hold on. I didn't mean to imply—"

"Bruce, I'm sorry. The answer is no. Just no. No ifs, ands, or buts. No, you may not talk to Vanessa, or any other member of my family. Not about that night. Not about anything."

"Julia—"

The defiant mother, determined to protect her child. "We've known each other a long time, Bruce. I loved Grace, and she loved you, so I wouldn't hurt you for the world. I'm not going to mention this to

Lemaster. But if you make any attempt to speak to my daughter, about any subject, if you ever raise the question of Vanessa and Kellen Zant again, with anybody, and I hear about it, I will definitely tell my husband, and not only will you get fired, we will come down on you with all the influence we have. And, around here, Bruce, that's an awful lot of influence. So remember that," she finished, more lamely than she meant to.

Bruce was staring. Not frightened but certainly astonished. And, again, he seemed to her oddly pleased. Julia knew she had said too much, gone too far, a Veazie family trait. But this was hardly the moment to back down.

"Just remember that," Julia repeated, because Bruce was not saying a word. She pointed at their coffees. "I assume you'll take care of this," she added. "I think I can find the way out." And, trembling—more with fear than with rage—she stormed from the room.

She had survived. That was what Julia kept telling herself as she hurried home in the Escalade, her show tunes turned up loud to drown the fear. She had survived, her daughter had survived, her family had survived. The official investigation was closed, Tony Tice and Mary Mallard had nothing to go on, and Bruce was skimming the surface, worried about who had killed Kellen, not seeking a deeper truth. He was not concerned, as everybody else seemed to be, about what Kellen might have uncovered that got him killed. Bruce did not care about the dirt Astrid had tried to dig up. He was not interested in the possibility that, unlikely though it seemed, plagued her through the late hours as she lay sleepless in her gigantic house: that thirty years ago, when he was a student, the man who was now President of the United States had committed a terrible crime; or that the man who was now president of the university was helping him cover it up.

(1 1 1)

BRUCE WAS IN his beloved vintage Mustang, cruising back toward Elm Harbor. He had forgotten how good it felt to be a cop instead of an administrator. He had accomplished exactly what he had set out to accomplish. He had never expected Julia Carlyle to let him interview her daughter. But her responses had told him that she knew perfectly well that there was some sort of extracurricular involvement between

Vanessa and Kellen Zant. What its bounds were, he did not know, and did not really care. That it existed was enough.

He mentally toted up the evidence he had gathered. Julia Carlyle had once been involved with Kellen Zant, and the relationship was said to have scarred her. Julia was often seen in his company even in recent years. The economist, moreover, was obsessed with Julia, and was quite open in his disdain for traditional marital boundaries. As for Vanessa, her connection to Zant was the sort of thing that no West Indian father of Bruce's acquaintance would have tolerated for an instant. Add to all that the simple fact that there had long been bad blood between Kellen Zant and Julia's husband. As to the mysterious black woman with the British accent—well, Bruce was pretty sure he had the answer to that one, too.

Streaking down the highway, Bruce Vallely marveled at the possibility, the growing likelihood, that Zant's death was no robbery, and had nothing to do with his work. No doubt the crime was committed through intermediaries layered on so thick that the instigator might never be caught. But all Bruce's instincts told him that Lemaster Carlyle had arranged for the killing of Kellen Zant.

PART II

SUPPLYING DEMAND

Supply Curve—In economics, a graph showing how supply of a good or service varies according to the price offered. Supply curves usually slope upward, meaning that a greater demand for a product, by raising prices, will produce a greater supply. If the demand cannot be met by existing producers, new firms may be attracted into the market.

CHAPTER 22

SEMI-PRECIOUS

(1)

CAMERON KNOWLAND ARRIVED on Thursday, rolling merrily along the drafty halls of Kepler Quadrangle, dodging the falling plaster and the crumbling cardboard storage boxes crowding every passageway, until he found his way to Julia's small, neat office with its aging furniture, its gorgeous spill of mid-December sunshine, and its distracting cacophony of sound from Hudson Street, which ran, it sometimes seemed, within mere inches of her desk.

Her door, as usual, was standing open, a tradition that went back to the founding of the divinity school, something to do with avoidance of sin. Latisha, the tenacious full-time assistant Boris Gibbs had wanted her to fire, was off on some errand, so Minnie Foxon—the lazy part-timer Boris had wanted her to keep—announced him, her airy tone and averted eyes informing the world she would rather be doing anything else. But this was one of those days when Julia felt the same way, wondering how she herself had ended up here, a biology teacher who only half believed in science settling at a divinity school that only half believed in God.

"Up here anyway," Cameron boomed, for he was the sort of small, tubby man who creates space around himself by the radiation of sheer power. "Meeting with Claire Alvarez. Your dean," he added, in case Julia had forgotten.

"It's always a pleasure," lied Julia, mystified by the unexpected visit. "What brings you to my end of campus?" She tried for coquettish, probably managed arch: "I would have thought you'd stick down the hill with the seculars."

She projected as much warmth as she could, given that the man was technically Lemaster's boss, and so, of course, hers too. Actually, her mood was grim. She had just returned from an overlong lunch with Suzanne de Broglie and Stanley Penrose, who were trying to persuade her not to cut the program that sent two students to Latin America each summer to study liberation theology firsthand, building houses, teaching school, organizing workers, and generally participating in the global war against the forces of reaction. Julia tried not to let on that she knew the program was doomed because of the way her husband, in unguarded moments at home, made fun of it.

"Not actually in Elm Harbor on business," said Cameron, whose use of verbs tended toward the forgetful, like a man who had learned the language from e-mail. His flat blue eyes were angelic with sympathy, as if he was suffering for a pain she would soon experience. "In New York to see some money people. Came up to settle some kind of trouble my boy is having. Harassment by a campus cop. Don't remember the details. Probably exaggerated. My Nate does that." He crossed pudgy legs. His dove-gray suit was so skillfully cut you might easily have mistaken him for buff instead of fat. "Thought I'd take a stroll up to Kepler because I always hear the sob stories, how nobody cares to fund God any more." Julia was not sure her dean would ever choose quite those words, but elected for once a prudent silence. He glanced around her office. "Wanted to see for myself," he added, dubiously. "Not much of a God man myself. Still, might be ways to help."

"That would be lovely."

Julia meant this seriously, but Cameron frowned as if suspecting an insult. He was in his early sixties, came from nothing, and, from his splendid castle in San Marino, near Los Angeles, ran the family of mutual funds he had founded almost forty years ago. He seemed wonderfully energetic, despite his roly-poly form, and affected a delightful breadth of gesture that filled the air with possibility, with energy, even with hope: you had the sense that this was a man who commanded resources, and could solve all your problems if you only gave him the chance.

"Stuck my head in the chapel. Scaffolding. What's that all about?"

"A piece of the roof fell in."

"Mmmm. Heavy symbol." He strained the other way in the hard wooden chair, eyes now on the biblical scenes in the leaded glass windows. "Faculty still up in arms? Adopting resolutions? Think Lemas-

ter's the tool of the alumni? Going to put an end to multicultural-
ism or something? Suppose they think we should just give money and
shut up."

The swift change of subject caught Julia by surprise, and she heard
herself offering too many explanations. "That's all blown over. The
media exaggerated it anyway. It was just a handful of professors.
Besides, you know Lemmie. He'll charm his way out of—"

"Good. Right." Julia realized, too late, that Cameron had not really
been asking a question. "Let me tell you why I'm here."

"Certainly," said Julia, smiling, but worried about how long this
would take, because she had only another hour to finish the day's work,
if she meant to beat the school buses.

The Senior Trustee read her mind. "Don't mean to take too much
of your time," he said, glancing at his watch to show her whose time he
valued more.

"It's just, I like to be home before my kids."

Cameron nodded. "Don't you have a couple in college?"

"One. Our oldest. Preston."

"Liking it?"

"I think so. He's in grad school now." At twenty. "He's thriving."

"Don't you have a daughter who's applying now?"

Of course they did, and Cameron knew it. He must also know of the
confusion attending her applications, given Vanessa's difficulties over
the past year. So this was just campus one-upmanship.

"It's still pretty early in the process," she said cautiously.

He scarcely heard. "Know what I've been doing the past couple of
years?"

Getting richer. Ripping off investors. Protecting your children from
the consequences of their actions. "I'm afraid not."

"I help out the President with fund-raising, especially in the West.
Help out the whole party." It took Julia a moment to process this intelligence, because she had thought he meant the president of the university. "Don't mean to brag. But it's possible I'm the best fund-raiser they
have."

"I see," said Julia, who did not. He could not be asking her for
money. He had a better chance of predicting the date of the Second
Coming.

Not that she necessarily believed in the Second Coming.

"Thing is, Julia, I don't think your husband is being reasonable."

This sat her up straight. "Reasonable? About what?"

"The election coming up. Most important in decades. Need to pull out all the stops, or the liberals could win. Lemaster's a smart man. Must see it. But he won't help."

"What kind of help did you have in mind?"

"Awkward to talk about, but I tend to speak my mind." Uncrossing his soft legs, leaning forward, crowding her in the tiny space behind her desk. "Simple, really. Lemaster has known Senator Malcolm Whisted for more than thirty years. College roommates, et cetera. Whisted always struck me as a pompous so-and-so. Rumor is he has a lot to hide. Could be some of it has to do with his college years. And Lemaster—"

Julia let out a hoot of laughter. She could not help herself. Déjà vu all over again, as Yogi Berra put it. Same question. Same answer. "My husband is a very principled man, Cameron."

"Principles be damned," said the money manager, perfectly serious. His fingers rested on the edge of Julia's desk. "Not just some election. This one *matters*."

"I'll tell you why I laughed before. Would you be surprised to learn that somebody from, ah, the other side recently tried to get Lemaster to turn over dirt on your guy?"

"I'm not a bit surprised. The liberals will stop at nothing to gain control of the country. They'll make it unlivable, believe me. Especially for business. That's why Lemaster has to help." Raising a hand to forestall her reply. "Don't worry. Easy to do it quietly. Nobody would have to know the information came from Lemaster. Could use an intermediary, for example—"

Julia felt nervy, jangly, ready to attack. She had always hated overheated rhetoric, and refused absolutely to participate. When people talked this way, even people with whose positions she agreed, Julia invariably gravitated toward whatever camp they were opposing. Back in college, after discovering that Mona liked to call her "Jewel," the other black students christened Julia "Semi-Precious," mocking what they saw as her refusal to get involved in the causes they considered important.

"Lemaster turned the other side down, Cameron. He'll turn you down, too."

"Already did. But you should get him to change his mind. Make him see that it's in his interest." The Senior Trustee was on his feet. His pale eyes flicked over her, lingering once more where they should not. "In your interest, too, Julia. Get him to change his mind."

"I hardly think it's my place to—"

"We'll fix some of this." Waving vaguely around. "Find the money somewhere. Don't worry." Smiling suddenly. "Julia. Say. Don't happen to know what your friend Kellen Zant was working on, do you? When he died?"

Startling her into truthfulness. "Ah, no. No. I've been wondering myself."

"Tell you the interesting part, Julia. Called me up. Not two weeks before he died. Wouldn't talk to an assistant, insisted on the big boss. Company hired him before, do a little consulting work. Designed this market game to let our analysts bet on which way stocks are going to move, get points if they're right, lose 'em if they're wrong, and nice rewards at the end. Real salesman, that Zant." Words rich with admiration. And relish. "Had some fresh information, he said. Swing the balance in the campaign. That's what he said. Wouldn't say which way it would swing. Clever bastard. Said it was for sale. Sale, Julia. Imagine that. Putting a price on the future of this nation!"

"You turned him down?" she said, very attentive, waiting for him, like Mary Mallard, to mention the Black Lady.

"Told him we'd talk next time I was back east. Supposed to have breakfast the morning after he got his head shot off." A handshake like a swift thunderclap. "Listen. Love home, right, Julia?"

(11)

JULIA WAS EDITING A MEMO when old Clay Maxwell stuck his head into her office. He had been her favorite professor twenty years ago, although she had been anything but his favorite student. "I guess you heard the news," he said.

"What news?"

"About your husband's cousin. Astrid Venable."

"What about her?" Panic. "Is she all right?"

"Whisted fired her this morning. Something about unauthorized opposition research." A shrug of Clay's carefully apolitical shoulders. "He gave a nice little speech, too, all about how he planned to run a clean campaign, but I'm sure there's another reason. Nobody would be fired for what Astrid is supposed to have done. I mean, that's all they do these days, isn't it? Candidates? They dig up dirt."

(I I I)

LEMASTER WAS ABLE TO GIVE his wife ten minutes that afternoon in his capacious Lombard Hall office, right before the provost and vice-president for finance, who usually managed to depress even their irre-pressible president, and right after the leaders of a student protest movement demanding that the university divest from companies doing business wherever American troops served abroad—not realizing that there existed no more than a dozen or so countries in the world where no American forces were present, few of which possessed a hard cur-rency to invest in.

"I had nothing to do with it, Jules. You're crediting me with too much power."

"You said you talked to Mal. To get him to call her off."

Lemaster nodded somberly. "I did exactly that. I didn't complain or make demands. I suggested that he get Astrid to slow down a little on the oppo research, or the story would become not whatever she dug up but the fact that she was digging."

"And that was all?"

The charming elfin smile. "There wasn't need for anything else. Or time. I got my point across, and Mal said he would look into it. Then he had to go to some meeting. We talked for, oh, five minutes. Six or seven at the most."

Julia frowned, sure she was missing something—not in her hus-band's explanation, but in Malcolm Whisted's. But trying to work it out by force was like trying to breathe by grabbing air. She said, "Have you talked to her?"

"Of course."

"And how was she?" Julia prompted.

Lemaster, as so often, answered the question he wished she had asked instead, for he valued being one up, and on anybody in the vicin-ity. After his selection last spring as president of the university, he had granted the obligatory *Times* interview. The reporter had asked what he planned to do about charges that the campus administration was insufficiently diverse, with none of the top jobs being held by anyone not white. Lemaster, offering his most supercilious smile—Julia had been there, and saw it, and cringed—had answered that what he planned to do was accept the post. The reporter, unamused, perhaps even feeling patronized, had spun the quote to make it look as if the new president was insensitive to the issue, and Lemaster, before even receiving his first paycheck, had been forced to write one of those humiliating *I-didn't-choose-the-best-language-to-make-my-point* letters to the editor. Only his wife knew how it had pained him. But nothing in the experience had changed him. He still could not stand not being the smartest person in the room, and searched constantly for the opportunity to prove it. Night after night, at official dinners and receptions but also at home, Lemaster proved afresh his genius at the casual, complimentary put-down.

Especially when Kellen was around: then her husband's juice of intellectual competitiveness seemed to flow with special vigor, and Kellen's ego flashed right back, as though the ancient male blood-competition over mates had, in their generation, been transformed into a jargon-ridden, name-dropping, erudition-proving version of the dozens. The economist seemed to push her husband's buttons, probably on purpose; and Lemaster, for all his charm and placid grace, knew how to use his tongue to slice you up and leave you bloody on the floor.

Now he said, "Astrid assured me that she doesn't blame me. Probably that is not true. I would think she would surely blame me, whether fairly or not. It would seem, ah, anomalous of her to blame anybody else."

"She could blame herself," Julia pointed out, knowing from her husband's posture that her time had expired. "Or she could blame the Senator." Lemaster only shrugged. "It's possible, Lemmie. That's all I'm saying. What she did—tried to do—didn't seem that serious. Not at the time. There has to be more to this than meets the eye."

"I'm sure there is," said Lemaster, his gaze straying to the report he had to read to prepare himself for the budget meeting.

At the door, allowing him his softly possessive kiss, Julia asked, "What about Cameron? Are you going to get him fired, too?"

"I didn't get Astrid fired, Jules. I told you." Paging through the document. "Anyway, Cameron's a little big for me to take on." He laughed. His wife did not.

"Lemmie?"

"Yes, Jules?"

No choice but straight at him. "The night he died, Kellen told somebody that he was on his way to Jamaica."

"Maybe he was."

"No plane ticket, no hotel reservation."

"Well, then, it's a matter for the police."

"Not any more," said Julia, for the investigation, as Chrebet had predicted, had reached its end.

"I suppose not." Lemaster kissed her again, the report stuffed beneath his arm. A rising hum of conversation from beyond the stout oak door told Julia she had overstayed her welcome. His highly organized working day was running behind. "Why do you bring up this Jamaica business?"

"I was wondering if you had any idea—"

But his face told her he didn't, even if he wished he did.

"Jules?"

Pausing, hand on the door. "Yes, Lemmie?"

Gaze down on the report again. "What do you think of Bruce Vallely?"

"Bruce? Why do you ask about Bruce?"

"I understand he's exploring other options," said Lemaster, not looking up. "I wondered whether we should try to persuade him to stay."

Julia swallowed, shuffling her feet, feeling the way she did back in high school when a guidance counselor accused her of lying about the theft of her purse to get another girl in trouble. "Ah, well—that's up to you, I guess."

Brilliant smile. "Thank you, darling."

(I V)

BACK AT KEPLER QUAD, Julia rushed through her work. She cautioned a student who was missing too many classes, and counseled a student whose boyfriend had stopped calling. She read files of applicants and did her best to keep track of her assistants. She tried several times to get in touch with Astrid, imagined her in her townhouse near Capitol Hill, stalking back and forth, smoking like a chimney, ignoring the constantly ringing phone.

Or maybe it was only Julia's call Astrid was refusing to take.

What do you think of Bruce Vallely?

She picked up a pencil and spent a little time working anagrams with "Shari Larid," the name Tony Tice had asked her about, because word games were what Kellen liked. Her results—*Hard liar is? Dial Harris? Rash rail id?*—were unsatisfying. Shari Larid had not turned up in any Internet search, but maybe Julia was spelling the name wrong.

Two-thirty: time to pack her bag for the day and beat the buses to Hunter's Heights. About to leave her office, she had a thought. Bruce Vallely had found a copy of Vanessa's term paper on Kellen's computer. The term paper came in two varieties: the original she had turned in, for which Ms. Klein had delivered the dreadful grade, and a revised version, a working draft, featuring some of the additional research her daughter had done. If she knew which version Kellen had possessed, she might know more about his relationship with Vanessa—even though, sooner or later, despite Dr. Brady's strictures on cross-examining his patient, she would have to ask directly, just as Rick Chrebet suggested.

In the bottom right-hand drawer of her desk, hidden among folders with various forms that students needed, Julia kept her Vanessa File—her collection of everything from clippings about the fire to the washed-out newspaper photograph of Gina that once adorned Vanessa's dresser. The file also contained both versions of the term paper.

Except that it did not.

When she drew out the folder and opened it, only the newspaper cuttings about the fire remained. Everything else was missing.

She would have blamed Tricky Tony Tice, but the evidence was otherwise: all over the olive-drab folder, like blood smears after a murder, were fingerprints in mushy brown chocolate, left by the late Boris Gibbs as he rifled her desk.

CHAPTER 23

MIRROR, MIRROR

(1)

IT DELIGHTED VERA BRIGHTWOOD no end that the sport utility vehicle that smashed poor Boris Gibbs to smithereens up in Norport was her very own, stolen two days before from her house on Pleasant Road. Down at Cookie's, she told her regulars, and anybody else who wandered in, about the hours she had spent with the detectives, after nobody had cared when she first reported the car missing. About time they paid some attention to the crime wave in the village, she said. The number of assaults in the Landing had doubled over the past year, she announced, and for once had her statistics right, even though she omitted to mention that the doubling took the cases from two to four. But Vera was just about the only source of news in town, and, as Lemaster pointed out with a smile when Julia complained, failing to mention the details that made the numbers less impressive was a habit shared by pretty much all the media.

Julia spent a couple of afternoons on Main Street, roving from shop to shop, collecting stories, sifting rumors, seeking truth. Beth Stonington, the top Realtor in town, who had sold the Carlyles the land on which Hunter's Heights was built, insisted that nobody could look at one of the town's few remaining waterfront lots without her hearing about it. And, no, she said when Julia pressed, thinking Boris might have had the story wrong: Kellen Zant had not viewed any of the houses on the market. She would have heard.

Because he was black, Julia thought but did not say.

Carrie Bissette, evening manager at the CVS, had never met Kellen Zant, but had seen a great deal of Boris Gibbs. People said they used to have a thing. And, no, she assured Julia gravely, Boris had never asked her about Zant. Greta Hudak, who ran the tavern bearing her name, told Julia what she had told the police, that a tall black man who did not live in the Landing had been in once or twice for lunch but she could not pick out his photograph. Julia asked how she knew he didn't live in town. She would have remembered, said Greta. Danny Weiss, who ran the struggling local bookstore, had sold Zant a volume on antiques a week or so before he died. Lurleen Maddox at Luma's Gifts told her that Kellen Zant had indeed stopped in, the same day he purchased the book.

"Did he buy anything?"

"Just a little toy mirror," she said, with sour disapproval of his parsimony.

(11)

AND SO IT WAS PLAIN that Kellen was telling her something. He was buying mirrors, delivering mirrors, trying to give mirrors as gifts, even though he died before he could accomplish his plan. He had wanted her to follow his trail, like a night creature, leaving his spoor along his path through the Landing, signaling Julia in a way she was no doubt supposed to find both irresistible and irrefutable, and she marveled that she had heretofore been unaware of his presence in her town. It was as though the Main Street merchants conspired together to keep from her the simple truth of what Kellen had been up to.

But what was he up to?

Inventory risk. The dark matters.

Still Julia could not work out how Kellen thought he would blow the lid off the presidential campaign. The most plausible guess was that he had evidence that the President of the United States, while a junior at the college thirty years ago, had killed Gina Joule and hidden that truth all these years. In the panic of her confrontation with Bruce Vallely, she had actually credited this possibility. Now, in a calmer moment, she felt as if accusing the President, even in her mind, was to slip into someone else's paranoia. Besides, there was no reason it had to be Scrunchy. After all, Lemaster had not been around Hilliman Suite to keep order: he had spent the spring semester of 1973 studying at Oxford. Any one of his roommates—Scrunchy or Mal or Jock

Hilliman—could have done any sort of mischief without Big Brother, as they used to call him, finding out.

Vanessa, however, remained adamant in her insistence that DeShaun Moton was the killer. On Sunday, Julia took her daughter out to dinner at Greta's and pumped her for more.

"I told you, Kellen and I never talked about it."

"Never?"

"Well, he asked what I was working on. When I said it was Gina Joule, and that it was clear that DeShaun did it, he complimented me on being willing to take unpopular positions." Her fork clattered, because her hand was trembling. "Creepy pervert."

"Why didn't you tell me this before?"

"Tell you what?"

"That you told him about Gina?"

Vanessa seemed unable to think of an answer to that one, or at least unable to articulate it, for she dipped her head and hid her face behind her braids. Her hand shook harder, and she put down the fork. Outside, the night was crisp and clear. Cars drifted through yesterday's snow with majestic unconcern.

"Honey?"

"Yes, Moms?"

"Did you give Kellen a copy of your term paper?"

She smiled in reminiscence, like an old woman thinking back on her youth. "He promised to help me get it published. He was creepy. He just wanted—well, you know what he wanted." She sliced a piece of salmon. "I e-mailed it to him." Chewing. "But he never got back to me. I guess it wasn't good enough." Her face went into its fall. "You know, Moms, he could be pretty cruel. Your Kellen."

"I know, honey." Covering both her hands at once. "I know."

Driving home, Vanessa squinting over calculus homework on her lap, Julia turned the sequence over in her mind. Maybe. Maybe not. Say Kellen is hanging around Kepler, hoping for a glimpse of Julia, meaning to cause trouble. He runs into Vanessa, and, pleasantly surprised, he teases her for a bit, probably as a way to tease Julia by remote control, possibly because Vanessa herself—well, anything was possible. He visits the div school another day, and there's Vanessa again, working in the library on her research. Maybe he flirts with her. They talk. He learns about the paper. About Gina. Does he extrapolate? Do the calculations himself to discover that the white teenager died while Scrunchy and the others shared Hilliman Suite? Or did he know already, in which case Vanessa was simply a source of additional information? Either way, Kellen is intrigued and looks into the matter further, and discovers— what?—the President? Did he die because of who he decided was guilty? Did Boris die for the same reason?

Julia shivered, partly with worry, partly with relief: Vanessa had recently announced she was giving up on the paper.

"Honey?"

"Yes, Moms?" Writing furiously by the glow of the map light, equations sprawling over the page.

"You're sure it was DeShaun? Absolutely sure?"

"Uh-huh."

"No evidence of anybody else?"

"Nope." Vanessa flipped to the back of her math book, checking her answers, and, frowning, began a massive erasure. She had missed a step. "I mean, somebody could fake some evidence or something," she continued, starting the problem over. "You know. Try to frame somebody." She smiled and nodded to herself. Now she had the equations right. "But I can't see Kellen doing that."

"Why not, honey?" said Julia, marveling at how Vanessa, as usual, stayed a step ahead.

"Because framing somebody would require . . . passion. Commitment. And you know what? You'd have to really hate your victim to take the chance." Vanessa was in the next chapter, working a new problem. "I mean, who would Kellen hate that much?"

(I I I)

AT HOME, LATER, Julia bolted awake. Half past one. She had been dreaming, as she often did, of stumbling through snowy trees, pursued by some furious nightmare creature, snarling that she was not as nice as people thought. Up ahead was sanctuary, but the dream always ended before she found out if she reached it or not. What had tugged her to wakefulness this time was a high-pitched keening. The sound had stopped, so maybe it was part of the dream. Beside her, the president of the university snored on. Julia settled back down, then sat up again. No. No dream. There it was again, faint, but Julia's hearing was, like her daughter's, exceptional: they both played piano. She swung her feet into slippers, tugged on her favorite tattered robe. She tracked the sound to Vanessa's room. She put her ear to the door. A kind of squealing hum, vaguely tuneful.

The sound stopped.

She was still deciding whether to knock when the door whisked open. Vanessa, in pajamas and bare feet, was already talking before Julia had a chance to ask.

"There's this really cool Web site that I found that lets you download these funeral dirges from different cultures? You can't do it with earphones. You need the speakers to get the feel." Julia peered past her daughter. The room was a mess, clothes and papers and books mounded everywhere, but she could pick out, here and there, the remote Bose speakers scattered around. Eight, she vaguely recalled. "I turned it down low, and I'm sorry if it was too loud, but I'm kind of glad, too. We can listen together. You'll *love* this."

"Tomorrow's a school day."

"I'll sleep in French class. Sit down." Drawing her mother in, shutting the door. Julia moved a dog-eared book about the battle for Stalingrad and sank into a chair. When Vanessa bent over the desk, Julia identified the laptop, hidden behind a wall of Perrier bottles and glittering CD cases. A tune came on, mournful and sweet. Chanting. Vanessa began, slowly, to slide her bare feet from side to side. "They dance to these, Moms," she explained, shrugging prettily, smiling. "That's what I was up to when you knocked on the door. Nothing nefarious. This one is from the Ewe people of Ghana. They have this special dance for the death of an elder. I don't know all the moves, so I made most of them up." She closed her eyes and lifted her slim arms and began to shimmy. A moment later, Julia was on her feet, the two of them dancing together to the funereal moaning, dipping and swaying and twirling as they struggled to remember, and to forget. Vanessa clicked. Another came on, more up-tempo, no accompaniment, just a faster keening. Julia whirled and whirled, because movement was real and death was a fraud and if she could only whirl fast enough nobody would ever have to die. Vanessa, laughing, was explaining what culture the dirge was from, and how outside of the West most cultures danced at funerals, but her mother was lost in the music and the movement, hardly listening, whirling and whirling as she felt oddly joyful tears running down her honey-colored cheeks, because Kellen might be dead, Jay and Granny Vee might be dead, but she was alive, she was here dancing with her daughter, and they were going to make it right, they were going to start over, they were going to—

"And this one is my favorite," said Vanessa.

Silence.

Julia stopped twirling. She waited. Nothing happened. Vanessa stood hunched over the desk, fingers poised and trembling on the mouse, but unable to click. She struggled and struggled, finally turning helpless eyes toward her mother.

Julia crossed the room, lifted her daughter's hands, squeezed them between her own, and held Vanessa close until whatever had frozen her melted into sobs.

And she realized, as she thought of Vanessa's tears, and the trauma Vincent Brady said she was repressing, that she no longer had any choice. She had to do exactly what Mary Mallard and Tony Tice wanted her to. She had to work quietly, but she had to work. She had to find out what Kellen was working on when he died—not for Kellen's sake, but for Vanessa's.

And perhaps, she realized, for her own.

CHAPTER 24

THE HORSEMEN

(1)

EVEN IN HIS SPECIAL FORCES DAYS, Bruce Vallely had rarely worked alone. He was trained to be part of a team, and a teammate was what he needed now. Julia Carlyle would have been best, but he would take what he could get. So, on a pretext, he enlisted Gwen Turian, his no-nonsense, by-the-book deputy, whose formal rank was lieutenant, and who, perhaps influenced by Hollywood, insisted on being addressed by last name only and calling her boss, even to his face, simply "Director." Late Friday morning, he stood in the lobby of the building that housed his minuscule staff, stamping filthy snow from his boots as he struggled to shrug off the remaining tension of having been present, by rule, when the state narcotics squad served a warrant at one of the dormitories, where drugs were being sold by a pair of weak-eyed political-science majors whose parents were, unfortunately, not well enough connected to get Trevor Land on the phone. One of the students had leaped from the window in his panic, breaking a toe, and Bruce knew he would be dodging complaints of police brutality for the next month or two. He had just picked up mail and messages from his cubbyhole when Turian materialized beside him, tall and skinny and nervously distant, blue serge uniform draped like the wrong stage prop.

"Good morning, Director," she said stiffly, handing over an envelope. "I have the research you ordered."

"Thank you, Gwen."

The lieutenant frowned, perhaps because in the films she would have been just "Turian." The gun at her hip was larger than what the rules specified, and it seemed to Bruce that the extra straps could not possibly be regulation. But the uniform itself was something of an affectation: by university tradition, patrol officers wore blue but supervisors wore business attire. She seemed reluctant to go, and, as he turned toward his office, she followed.

"Is there a problem, Gwen?"

"May I speak frankly, sir?"

"Of course, Lieutenant," he said, and her hard green eyes lit up. Unlike Bruce and most of the others, Turian had never been part of a real police force.

"Sir, this information—is it part of an authorized investigation?"

"Why don't you let me worry about what it's part of, Gwen?"

"Yes, sir. Only, I had to use a back channel to get it, and I had to tell them something—"

Alarm. "What did you say?"

"That the university was facing the possibility of litigation because of an old case. I'm sorry, Director, it was the best I could come up with."

Bruce smiled. "Excellent work. That was well done . . . Turian."

"Thank you, sir," said his deputy, unsmiling back.

(1 1)

THE CAR belonging to the Vehicle Identification Number on the insurance form Kellen Zant had hidden in his kitchen was a Jaguar XKE, or had been, for the adjuster had declared it totaled. The owner had been a Jonathan Hilliman. Bruce sat at his desk, frowning. The name was familiar.

He swiveled to face his monitor, ran the name across Google, and had the answer in a fraction of a second: Yes. Jonathan Hilliman— "Jock," everyone called him—was an alum, a scion of the Hilliman family, whose money was about as old as money gets. The Hillimans lived behind walls of money, like whoever it was in *Gatsby*, and rarely emerged except to have buildings named after them. Jock, a bit of a playboy, had died three years ago of a heart attack. He left no heirs— but there were plenty of Hillimans still around.

So what? Why did Kellen Zant care so much about Jock Hilliman and his automobile accident? And why did his name resonate in Bruce's head? But Gwendolyn Turian, in her zeal to get her duty right, had appended a note; reading it, Bruce remembered a smidgen of the briefing he had received when hired. On the top level of one of the university dormitories, commanding majestic views of the skyline and water, was Hilliman Suite, a fantastic four-bedroom affair far swankier than any other campus housing. The Hilliman family had built it fifty or sixty years ago, and provided substantial funds for its upkeep, with the proviso that, whenever a Hilliman was in residence, he (in the old days always a "he") would have use of the suite, and could select his own roommates.

That explained why the name Hilliman tickled at Bruce's head. But why had it tickled at Kellen Zant's?

Back on Google, he tried searching for the Hilliman name alongside the economist's and came up with nothing of any substance. Something buried, then.

He thought back. What had driven Zant? His ego, obviously. His need to escape his past through accumulating material possessions. Fine, but a cliché. He remembered the photographs in the economist's study, half featuring Julia Carlyle. Another sort of drive.

Why not?

He searched for intersections between the late Jonathan Hilliman and the name Carlyle, and his screen lit up with thousands of hits. Perusing a couple, he swiftly had the connection, although not the one he expected. The two names occurred mainly in profiles of the great Lemaster. Of course. The Fabulous Four, the Four Horsemen, the many other names they were given, or gave themselves. In college, they had been a frat boy, a campus politico, a three-sport star, and the grind who set grade-point records. Today the three survivors were a President, a Senator with his eyes on the White House, and Lemaster, who succeeded at everything he tried.

The Horsemen.

Turian had appended a profile of Jock Hilliman that ran in *The New Yorker* back in the nineties, when all four were busily making their names. Bruce skimmed the article, not sure what he was looking for, letting the words form impressions:

I think Mal came up with the name . . . only later did we become roommates . . . a truly odd quartet . . . amateur trouble-makers . . . soon had a bit of a reputation around the place . . .

others began trying to join but I always said no to an increase in membership . . . from my father that the better portion has to stick together . . . I decided the group should be allowed to die when the last of us graduated . . . Students and faculty alike began to respect . . . Hilliman Suite was not exactly party central but we held our own . . . kind of a four-man secret society . . . built on trust . . . shared pretty much everything . . .

No new members allowed: Lemaster would have liked that part, Bruce decided. An exclusive white club to go with all the exclusive black ones he would later join: the better portion sticking together.

Back to the story. He flipped the pages, fascinated.

. . . each had a specialty . . . Lemaster was determined to finish first in the class, because it had never been done by a . . . missed out by a half-point when he got a B on the final in an advanced calculus course . . .

Bruce smiled, lost for a moment in admiration of the man he still half suspected of involvement in the murder of Kellen Zant. Fighting to finish first, he nevertheless takes advanced calculus rather than some survey course where he could phone in for an A. Skimming to the next page, Bruce stopped again, and read the text carefully:

The university admitted its first class of undergraduate women in our final year, and, like the other senior boys, we achieved a rapid Nirvana. Before that, we fulfilled our needs, you might say, each according to his proclivities. Lemaster was very discreet, dating a quiet young lady from the Catholic women's college up in Norport. Mal was heavily involved with a slightly crazed graduate student in anthropology who had big plans for blowing up the world and starting over. As for me, well, they accused me of having a new woman every week, or perhaps I should say a new girl, because age was a matter of indifference. My own specialty was seducing the innocent teenaged daughters of members of the faculty. . . .

Bruce read no more. He leaned back and rubbed his eyes. What had Zant thought himself on the track of?

The innocent teenaged daughters of members of the faculty.

Like the overprotected Gina Joule? Because, by all accounts, the teenager led a sheltered, rule-bound life, severe even for that era. Had Jock Hilliman, in the interview, meant this as a joke? Because, if not, the mystery surrounding the night Gina vanished might be simpler than it seemed. Bruce pulled out the copy of Vanessa's term paper he had taken from Kellen Zant's house. Gina had just turned seventeen. She had fought with her mother, marched out of the house, stopped in at Cookie's for ice cream, then evidently wandered around the Green until DeShaun picked her up. A woman named Janet Spicer, one of her teachers, now deceased, had a house on the Green and saw her climb into the stolen BMW with DeShaun. End of the story.

Or was it?

He went to his safe, shoved aside the gun he was not allowed to carry on campus unless he was in uniform, and pulled out the other materials he had taken from Professor Zant's house. A diary page:

Deputy Nacchio also reported that around nine that night she knocked on the door of one of her teachers, a Mrs. Spicer, and asked to use the telephone. That report was later . . .

Later *retracted.* Wasn't that the word that would have appeared had he found the next page? Or was the word *confirmed?*

Bruce worried the problem around in his mind. Perhaps the facts were no more than they seemed. Say that Jock had somehow pierced the protective shield Gina's parents built around her and managed to meet her, even seduce her. She told her friends at Cookie's she would walk home but, really, was meeting her secret lover, Jock Hilliman. Perhaps the fight with her mother was even a ruse. It was Valentine's Day after all, and Gina surely wanted to see her boyfriend. So she stopped at Mrs. Spicer's house to call Jock—no cell phones in those days!—and he picked her up in his Jaguar. The Jag was wrecked, according to the adjuster's report, a week after Gina Joule vanished, and in Scottsville, nowhere near Tyler's Landing. But a report, as the policeman in him knew, was only a piece of paper.

All right.

Suppose, for the sake of argument, that the Hilliman family, with its money and power, had the report fudged. Bribed the adjuster, the body shop, the police, whoever was necessary. Then the connection was plain. Gina Joule died after climbing into the Jag that night, and somehow the secret had been kept all these years.

That had to be what Kellen Zant had discovered. That was the reason for the secrecy. Kellen had learned that the university, through one of its most prominent alumni, was connected to the death, whether accidental or intentional, of Gina Joule. He wondered how many knew. And how many were covering up.

And his excitement faded as swiftly as it had built. The hypothesis was wrong. Nobody would kill Kellen Zant to hide the facts behind the murder if the murderer was dead. And Jock Hilliman was, indisputably, dead.

Shared pretty much everything.

Was that it? Was that the key? That the Four Horsemen had "shared everything"?

Might "everything" not have included the Jag?

Except that witnesses saw Gina on the Town Green talking to DeShaun Moton, sixteen years old, who indisputably stole a car in the Landing that night, and, a few days later, was chased by the police, and caught, and slain.

Case closed.

The trouble was, the other witnesses just saw the teenagers talking. Only Janet Spicer claimed to have seen Gina Joule climb into the stolen car. And DeShaun was not named as a suspect in the slaying until after he was killed.

Bruce turned to Vanessa's term paper once more. Merrill Joule was among the most popular professors on campus. And one of the best connected. His wife was a cousin of Cicero Hadley, then president of the university. Gina's godfather was a minor Lombard Hall functionary named Trevor Land.

What had Nate Knowland said? Bruce leafed through his notebook. There. Nate had overheard Kellen Zant and the unknown black woman talking about Lemaster Carlyle on Town Street the night the economist was murdered, and, in particular, had heard Zant whisper that the university president was too big for them to take on.

Bruce walked over to the window, which looked out into the drab lot where the university stored the fleet of recycled school buses, repainted in the college colors, that wheezed around the campus in a parody of efficient transport. Ordinarily the lot was also home to snowplows of all sizes, but the state had been cursed with an unexpected thaw, and the plows were all out failing to clear the slush. Oh, but he was tired of New England winters.

Gina was seen with a black man.

And the Horsemen shared everything.

No wonder Julia Carlyle had warned him off with such adamance. She knew or suspected the same truth that Bruce did.

Lemaster Carlyle. Too big for Professor Zant to take on.

But murder? Unless Kellen Zant possessed some evidence far more persuasive than the fragments Bruce had found beneath the burner, the reaction seemed . . . extreme. On the other hand, murderers, in his experience, rarely acted rationally.

The telephone rang, his direct line, and the caller ID displayed his least favorite extension.

"Chief Vallely? Trevor Land here. Merry Christmas and so forth. Wonder whether you might pop by my end of the campus on your way home."

(I I I)

THEY SAT IN PLUSH EASY CHAIRS in front of a fireplace that, by a miracle, still worked, possibly the last one on campus, probably a violation of the fire code. The flue must have gone years between cleanings, because the air was smoky. The secretary wanted first to talk about the raid on the dormitory this morning, murmuring about how this would surely "redound to the detriment" of the school's reputation. Bruce told him that he considered the raid a mistake, and had issued a strong protest on behalf of the university.

"And how might one have handled the matter differently, I wonder? Drug sales and whatnot."

"I would have arrested them elsewhere on campus between classes. No risk of harm."

"Quite." The lidded eyes hid whatever the secretary thought. "But our state's attorney has to face the voters, Chief Vallely, whereas you do not. Bashing the university—trashing, whatever—may not be good police work, but it is good politics. Especially when she has so much egg on her face over the Zant matter."

"Yes, sir," said Bruce, now that the true subject of the meeting had been broached. The smoke from the illegal fireplace was making the shadowy room dimmer.

The secretary stated his needs. A review of Bruce's progress. The details of his interviews. But Gina Joule had been Trevor Land's god-daughter, and the cop in Bruce was not about to give up all the information he had collected.

"I'm still fairly early in my inquiry," he said.

The secretary nodded, scarcely listening. Bruce could barely see him through the haze slowly filling the room.

"Thing is, this Zant has raised more than a few hackles. Not sure what the problem is, really, why everybody's up in arms, but everybody is. Alums on the phone every day. Have two dead professors now, not one, so it's hard times, Chief Vallely. Hard times for the school we love. All right, Gibbs was an accident. Zant was a robbery. Still, don't believe in the Easter Bunny, sort of thing, do we, Chief? Men of the world and so forth. But a little early to man the lifeboats, Chief Vallely, don't you think? Can't let the school suffer, can we? All pull together, kind of thing. Truth. Leadership at the top is weak at the moment. Well, all right, not his fault. Business with his daughter and so forth, unfortu-nate, but one of those things. Professors up in arms over this or that. Not really the best moment to go to the president for decisions. Your chain of command runs through the vice-president, but she'll just ask the president anyway. Doing the man a bit of a service, I should think, if we don't bother him with these concerns. Better bring everything to me instead." Bruce's eyes were tearing from the smoke, but Trevor Land seemed to tolerate it just fine. "Needs must, Chief Vallely. Insti-tution cannot be allowed to suffer. Try to keep a lower profile. No harassing the professors, they don't like it and they complain. Students, same. This Knowland. Father's been in to see me. Mustn't antagonize the alums. Look into the Zant thing, yes, but without making noise. Have a lead for you," he said, and paused to swirl his brandy.

"I'd be grateful," said Bruce, swirling but not sipping his own snifter, for his late wife had made a teetotaler of him, and he was not about to go back on anything he had promised her. They were now at the real point of the meeting. Outside the long, high windows, a sink-ing sun spread shadows of unseen buildings across the snow-shrouded lawn.

"Yes. Well. Final point, Chief. Final point. Other reason alums are on my back. Not just the scandal, as it turns out. Some of them had business dealings with Zant. Research, consulting, I don't know what all. Happy with his work, most of them, and so they should be. Brilliant man, all accounts. But a few of them, Chief Vallely, seem to think he took something that belongs to them."

"Something like what?"

The secretary dropped his clever gaze to examine the brown liquid in his glass. "Wouldn't know, really. Corporate secrets. Inside information. Formulas. Not one's field, Chief. But, whatever he took, they're rather desperate to have it back."

"Can you tell me if the item was something physical—a notebook, say, or papers maybe—or the sort of thing a man might carry around in his head?"

"Wouldn't know, really. Alums not terribly forthcoming, I fear. Want it both ways. Get the item back without saying what it is. Detective work. More up your alley than mine."

"Perhaps if I could talk to these, ah, these alums—"

"Out of the question, Chief Vallely. Confidential sources, sort of thing. Trust me, because I've known 'em forever."

Bruce effaced himself, easy enough in the cavernous office. "I see," he murmured.

"If you find it for them, Chief, one rather thinks they'll be grateful. Write your own ticket, sort of thing." That lift of a finger, so like a Roman emperor. "Word of advice. Don't ever cross the alums, Chief Vallely. Power corrupts, sort of thing. True as morning. Not bad people, really, the alums, but rather accustomed to getting their way." The clever eyes sparkled with glee. "They do tend to get their backs up when they don't get what they want."

"I see," said Bruce again, his own back rising in anger.

"Not the sort of people you'd want to cross, I think," said the secretary, and poured a fresh tot of brandy. A small shake of that clever head, then the conspiratorial smile with which Trevor Land closed every meeting. "Alums," he said, and drank.

(I V)

DRIVING HOME after the strange meeting, Bruce began to sense Kellen Zant's grand design. Why would Zant steal something from a client? Something of value? Not for the money: according to Rick Chrebet, the economist had a couple of million comfortably banked when he was killed, and more in his pension plan. Yet he was an economist, and saw life in terms of transactions and efficiency. The only reason to take the risk of theft was to obtain something he could not buy with money. So the item was not for his own pleasure; he had taken it for its trade value, bartering it in exchange for something he could not buy with money.

Bruce had an idea what.

He wondered whether the secretary saw what he saw. Probably. Trevor Land played the egregious fool but was in fact one of the most devious men Bruce had ever known, and the director of campus safety doubted his own ability to outguess him. The little man had to have figured out what Zant was up to.

Trevor Land had doted on his goddaughter Gina. Everybody said so. If Zant's work was intended to discover her killer, the secretary had every reason to keep Bruce on the trail.

Wherever it might lead.

CHAPTER 25

THE FLUTTERING

(I)

IT WAS HEFTY TONYA MONTEZ, chief Sister Lady of Harbor County, who provided the clue, and although in truth she had no earthly idea that she had done so, afterward, when reporters arrived to tote up the damage and decide whom to blame, she preened as though she bore the principal responsibility for the less scandalous of Julia's subsequent decisions. And perhaps, in a sense, she did, for Kellen used to tease that gossip played important regulatory functions, less because of the information it contained than because of the information it omitted: people would avoid certain disapproved behaviors in order to avoid being gossiped about.

Not that Tonya was a gossip. Oh, no. Ladybugs buzzed high above such pursuits, and, to demonstrate their contempt for gossiping, often handed around, chuckling, the silly stories less disciplined members of the community were busily spreading. So when Tonya, on Tuesday, swung by the huge house at the crest of Hunter's Meadow Road just after the dinner hour, gossip was the last thing on her mind. Naturally. Tonya lived a good eight or ten miles away, at the western edge of the county, far from the heart of whiteness, but made the trek anyway, as a faithful Sister Lady should, for the sole purpose of reviewing with Julia in person what had happened two weeks ago at the meeting to plan for their chapter's presentation at the Grand Orange and White Cotillion up in Boston just after Christmas—certainly not to soak up the latest gossip about the crazy daughter to pass along through the Elm Harbor end of the Clan.

By the time Tonya rang the bell, and was surprised when the heavy front door was flung happily wide by little Flew, Julia was, as Granny Vee used to say, in no mood. Lemaster was supposed to have come home early to help her frame a rather nice piece of Afro-Cuban art she had picked up at a gallery in the city. Always dutiful, always game, her husband had reminded Julia of the broken antique picture frame she had bought at a small discount from Frank Carrington a few months ago, meaning to repair it later. It looked about the right size, said Lemaster: they would do the work together. Probably she should have suspected that he would send Flew in his place. Lemaster had been a workaholic at the White House and the federal courthouse and the law school; he had been a workaholic back when they were students at Kepler, determined, as he told her in the divinity school library one afternoon, to allow no book within his reach to go unread. Julia had found herself utterly enchanted by the absurdity of this conceit. That she knew the brilliant young lawyer who thought he had a vocation to the priesthood intended to enchant her did nothing to diminish the effectiveness of his strategy. No coincidence, probably, that they made love for the first time the same night: in the basement stacks of the Kepler Library, after closing, because that was where Lemaster was to be found, and, after the finding, one must make do.

"A couple of rich alums unexpectedly in town," said Mr. Flew, apologetically, who spent more and more time at the house, even when his master was absent. Julia, grudgingly, was coming to accept him as a mysterious but established part of the family's life. Now and then he would even stay over in the guest room, Lemaster insisting, after one late meeting or another, on not forcing the young man to make the drive back to his condo in town. Julia was far too well bred—or far too kindhearted—to object, and even was learning to put up with the fussy way he seemed unable to pass the Thermador range without grabbing the rag and the special polish and cleaning the black glass top until it sparkled. She could not quite work him out. He was a slender, tow-headed sprite, with impressive degrees and work experience on four continents, considerably overqualified for the post he held, hoping, said Lemaster, to move on one day to run a small nonprofit, and content meanwhile to flit along in the great man's shadow. But Julia was not content just now. With anything.

Indeed, until the doorbell sounded, Julia had spent most of their two hours in the makeshift workshop in an unused bay of the four-car garage complaining about Mary Mallard, who kept on calling, and busily informing little Flew of her intention—having no husband present to hear her tirade—to do something about her, fast.

"I'll take care of it," said the sprite, and, in her current emotional state, she imagined for a moment that he meant Mary, not the doorbell. Julia nodded, wiping sweat from her brow. The work was harder than expected, not least because the compound joints in the old, softening wood were separating and had to be repaired. Flew, fortunately, possessed a native cleverness with the proper functioning of objects, and caught on swiftly to the proper angle for inserting the hypodermic full of hide glue into the joints as Julia pressed the wood together. Then, while she continued holding the pieces in place, he applied the masking tape.

"Thank you," said Julia.

Jeannie, who had been watching the project, and watching Jeremy Flew, on whom she now harbored a tiny crush that she imagined was her secret alone, hopped to her feet and said, with perfect mimicry of his rising dulcet tone, "I'll take care of it."

"Let Mr. Flew take care of it," said her mother.

A moment later, Flew was back, informing Julia, as a good butler might, that "Ms. Montez" had arrived, and was waiting for Julia in the solarium.

"I'll finish up here," he said.

And Julia, by now utterly bewildered at what could be driving her husband to keep sending this stranger into their home, mopped her forehead with a cloth and decided to let him.

"Come with me, honey," said Julia to her youngest.

Jeannie said, gazing at her hero: "I'll finish up here."

"You should go with your mother, Jeans," said little Flew, and only then did her daughter hop down from her perch and scurry into the kitchen.

(I I)

TONYA HAD BROUGHT a bottle of wine, a nice Napa Valley Chardonnay, because wine was what Julia liked, and, besides, the word among the Sister Ladies was that Julia had lately grown morose, and Tonya hoped, if not to cheer her, at least to soften her up. So they sat in the living room and sipped the wine (fruity but a little too much oak, judged Julia, who had learned her oenology from Mona) while Tonya, a soft, spreading woman of generous curvature and a generous nature, chatted about every topic under the sun except the one she wanted to most. Jeannie had slipped away, probably to watch Mr. Flew. Tonya moved on to Ladybugs business, reminding Julia in her foxily officious tone that everybody was supposed to have attended the meeting at Alice Henner's house (*and, oh, honey, the weight that girl can't seem to get off since the second baby*), which was also the deadline for turning in the money for the tickets, members and guests only.

"I mean, you are going to the Cotillion, right?" Tonya's bright doe eyes kept straying to the foyer, perhaps hoping that the unspoken topic would put in an appearance. But the unspoken topic was upstairs doing her homework, or instant-messaging Janine Goldsmith, now plain Smith, or perhaps was posting to her blog, Gainful Nonsenses, although it remained to be seen whether Vanessa would hold her readers once she left the world of real-life murder and returned to her usual dreary fare of medieval chants, the history of warfare, and the oppression of the adolescent. The anagram of the site's name, which kept popping up if you navigated there, was SINFUL SANE N.E. SONG—"N.E." for "New England." Julia did not consider the title particularly clever, and Lemaster hated all blogs on principle, but Dr. Brady pronounced himself encouraged by his patient's use of the word *sane*.

Lemaster's principle was that blogs had been invented since his youth.

"We're going to the Cotillion, yes. We never miss it." And this was true. The Orange and White was, for the Clan, the social event of the year, and, if no longer as important for the debutantes who "came out," the ball still allowed the elite to remind one another, amid the clamor and waste of their secret segregated existence, that they were real, and made a difference. "But I told you I'd miss the meeting," Julia went on. "Remember? We had dinner at the White House."

Tonya covered her mouth. "Oh, honey, I couldn't go telling the Sister Ladies that, could I?"

"It's not a secret dinner, Tonya. The President and Lemaster go way back."

The chief Sister Lady laid a soft, unwanted hand on Julia's thigh. "Yeah, well, you don't wanna go spreading that around either."

"I don't?"

"Our people don't *like* the President, Julia."

"Is that right?" said Julia. She had voted for the other guy, just as Tonya had, but Veazie women were not quite pushable-around. "I must have missed the directive from Blackness Central."

Tonya, about to snap right back at her, noticed the smile twitching at the corners of the crooked mouth, and smiled back instead. "All right, I come on a little strong. But, honey, I do need to make sure you're going to the Cotillion. That's why I'm here. To make a personal plea. I mean, your family practically founded the thing."

"What does that make me? An exhibit?"

"Come on, Julia. You're the life of the party."

A smokescreen, Julia reminded herself. On the other hand, most of the others probably had turned in their money on time, because the Cotillion was a matter of the utmost seriousness: almost as serious as the endless debates on whether to amend section (e)(3) of the bylaws to change *those* to *these*, or whether Bitsy Farnsworth wore the same dress to the formal reception on the second night of the regional conference in Syracuse last month as she wore two years ago, or—silly woman!—just a dress that looked the same.

"You don't have to plead with me, Tonya. We'll be there, I told you."

Flew popped his fair head in. The framing was all done. Where would Julia like it hung? Yes, indeed, the library was an excellent choice. He knew just the perfect spot, right above the period Hepplewhite: he could take down that unfortunate Escher print. Would she mind terribly if Jeannie helped? The child had such a splendid eye. Oh, and he had done some Brie and so forth for the two of them. By the way—turning to Tonya with a little bow—who was this delicious creature anyway? Why had they never met before tonight? They would be the best of friends, he said to the chief Sister Lady. He was certain of it.

"Who on earth was that?" said Tonya, flushing, when they were alone again.

"Jeremy. Mr. Flew. He works for Lemmie." Rainbow Coalition had wandered in and sat on her haunches amid the tall plants beneath the bay windows, still as ceramic. Outside, the floodlights illuminated the lawn as it sloped toward the reservoir. Lights of distant houses glittered on the other side. "He's a kind of . . . factotum, I guess. Most people just call him Flew."

"But what's he doing here? Didn't you say Lemaster's at the office?"

"Well, yes, but—anyway, Jeremy's here." Rumors. All she needed was more rumors.

"He's a little strange, isn't he?" Stuffing her mouth full of cheese and crackers all the same. "Tell you a funny story. I was over at Sandra Maxson's house for a committee meeting the other day. Alice Henner mentions this lawyer, Tice I think his name was, dropped by her office, wanting to ask her all these questions about Kellen Zant, what he was working on. She threw him out, of course. She'd do it, too, with that temper. Then Patrice Pomeroy goes, 'Really? Me, too.' Bitsy Farnsworth, the same. Not that Bitsy has an office. All she does is sit around and spend her husband's—"

"Are you telling me that Anthony Tice is talking to all the Sister Ladies?"

Tonya covered her round, teasing mouth with a soft brown hand. The nails glinted a quite remarkable shade of pink. "Oh, I wouldn't know about all. Some." Tonya was the principal of an elementary school and liked to be precise. "So, what are you telling me, honey? You know the guy?"

"We've met."

"Sounds like it didn't go well."

"He asked me the same thing," said Julia, hiding in the crowd.

"Well, I'm still waiting for my turn." Another nibble, surprisingly dainty, on a cracker. "It's not like you don't have enough on your plate, Julia. It's been rough. I know that. My kids envy Vanessa. They think her life's a thrill a minute. They don't have a clue. I know it's hard. Everybody understands, honey, but people are starting to talk. They say, Julia thinks she's better than everybody else, and that's why she doesn't come. Now, I know that's not true, even if nobody else lives in a palace. Still, believe me, honey, if it was up to me, you could come and go as you please. But it's not, is it? The bylaws do set a minimum annual attendance requirement. Half the meetings. That's only six a year. You can do that. There's people waiting in line to get in," she lied. "I'm not criticizing, honey, but you could be suspended. The good news is, there's a provision for waiver in the case of hardship, under 10 (b) (5), assuming we have the consent of a majority of the executive committee and then a majority of those present and voting at the next meeting of the whole following—"

Julia searched for a place to interrupt, for a Ladybug in full flutter is as inexorable as winter wind, and about as warm and fuzzy.

"Tonya, stop. Wait. Stop for a minute. You have to tell them. Tell everybody. Anthony Tice is trouble. They need to stay away from him."

A wolfish grin, waiting for the inside information. "Why do you say that, honey?"

"Take my word for it."

"You can give me a clue."

"Please, Tonya. You'll have to trust me. But nobody should say anything to him." She hesitated over the next words. "Especially if he asks about me."

"Is he gonna do that? Ask about you?" In her excitement, she hopped up from the sofa and, unbidden, sat down on the piano bench, fingering the keys, creating what Julia's piano teacher used to call a broken chord. "You mean, like, about you and Kellen?"

"Please don't do that," said Julia, feeling foolish, and uppity.

"Don't do what?"

"Don't play with the piano."

"I thought you meant, don't tease." She played a few awkward notes from *The Sound of Music*. "This is what you like, right? Broadway?"

Julia's agitation grew. "Stop, Tonya, okay? Please."

"Wait, wait, I remember. I remember. Duke Ellington played this piano."

"Well, he did."

Irritated, Tonya closed the cover. "You're really particular, did you know that?"

"Runs in the family," said Julia, probably by way of apology.

"So—is he?" On her feet, searching for her jacket. "Going to ask about you and Kellen? Is that what he's up to?"

Julia shuddered to think what stories were being told. "Tonya, come on. There wasn't any me and Kellen."

"Oh, really?"

"I mean, not in years. Not since long before Lemmie."

They were at the door. "Julia, honey?"

"Hmmm?"

"Is everything okay with you and Lemaster?"

Stunned again. "What kind of a question is that?"

"I was just wondering."

"But why would you ask something like that?" Shivering with indignation. "Tonya, really!"

"Nothing. Forget I asked."

She turned away.

(III)

LATER THAT NIGHT. Julia was in the basement, straightening up, because the house was not quite recovered from Jeannie's slumber party last night, celebrating the start of winter break. Under Lemaster's regime, each of the children was responsible for the behavior of his or her own friends, a rule, he said, that got the incentives right. Jeannie's friends, all of the paler nation, had left a considerable mess behind. Mona Veazie would have criticized their raising in her daughter's hearing, and Julia was half tempted to do the same. She found paper plates of pizza, forbidden down here, and spills of soft drinks. DVDs and video games were scattered everywhere, many out of their packages. The state of the bathroom did not bear mentioning. She could have waited for the twice-a-week maid service, but had learned from her mother never to let a mess lie around, and the lower level was, unquestionably, a mess. Jeannie, as her drive for self-perfection grew, made an unfortunate point of playing only with the children of the well-placed families of the Landing, either those with money or those connected to the university.

Julia scrubbed and picked up and vacuumed. She stripped the futons, then walked into the guest room to do the same for the bed and fold-out sofa. The room was decorated with posters of Broadway musicals, but only those with black themes or black casts, a collection she had begun in Manhattan back when Kellen used to tease her about her show tunes. Broadway, said Kellen, was the music of white America. *There are three things you always seem to be running from*, he would say. *Your people, your past, and your God.* But here in the basement bedroom of Hunter's Heights, surrounded by Ethel Waters and Lena Horne and Paul Robeson and Eartha Kitt and half a dozen others, Julia assured herself that he was wrong. Here were her people. Here was her past.

She wondered what Jeannie's friends thought of the posters.

And Astrid, who always used this room.

Your people and your past.

Julia sat down hard on the bed she had just stripped.

History, Frank Carrington had said, repeating what Kellen had told him when he bought the cheval mirror. *He said you would like it because you love history.*

Was it possible—

Show tunes. Tonya had teased her, as Kellen used to, as everybody did, about her taste for Broadway show tunes. All her friends knew what she loved.

She turned to look at the poster of Lena Horne.

Jamaica, Kellen had told someone the night he died. He was going to Jamaica. Nobody had found a plane ticket or a reservation. Nobody knew what he meant. But now Julia did.

The famous title song of the musical *Jamaica*. Famous, at least, among those who knew the history of African Americans on Broadway. Lena Horne singing about the little island on the Hudson.

Lemaster, in the div school speech Kellen had mocked, calling Kepler "an island of transcendent clarity in a sea of secular confusion."

Kepler Divinity Quadrangle, a little island . . . on Hudson Street.

That was Kellen's message. A message for Julia's ears alone. Maybe she was his Black Lady after all. The night he died, Kellen had visited the divinity school, and if he wanted nobody else to understand his message, that implied that he had hidden something there, somewhere, for Julia and Julia alone to—

"Mommy?"

Perfect Jeannie stood in the doorway.

"I was gonna help you clean up. Those other girls left such a mess down here." Clucking her tongue, exactly like Granny Vee, who died twenty years before Jeannie was born. "Oh, you're done." Miming surprise. "I guess I'm too late. Oh well."

She scampered off.

CHAPTER 26

PERSONA GRATA

(1)

BRUCE VALLELY WAS UNHAPPY. He was busily preparing next year's preliminary budget for submission to the provost. The tricky part was that he had received, just last week, a memorandum informing him that his department was facing a budget cut of 2.5 percent, part of the university-wide effort to trim operating costs in the wake of declining investment income. Yet his instructions were explicit: he was to find the cuts without laying off any officers, postponing "vital" equipment acquisitions, or weakening "net campus security." Maybe Penn and Teller could work this trick, but Bruce himself had no idea how to do it. Still, he was the boss and this was the job, so he sat in his drafty office with a yellow pad on his desk, testing various permutations of numbers, none of which added up.

He glanced out the window at the fleet of university buses in the lot, painted in the school colors. Several were caked in snow. Christmas was coming in a week and a half, and Grace would not be there to make it special.

First time ever.

He shook off the mood and bent to his yellow pad once more, playing with numbers on the calculator to figure out how to meet the provost's impossible demands. He had an image, albeit dim and distant, of how state legislators and members of Congress must struggle to put together a budget in an era of limited resources. Never again, Bruce promised himself, would he assume that politicians had an easy job. The media, along with ordinary voters, gave them a terrible time, but

the truth was, they were asked to achieve the impossible; and, occasionally, did.

His mind was not on his work. Not this part of his work.

His mind was on the case.

Earlier this week, enlisting a friend from Temple Baptist, where he
and Grace used to worship and he occasionally still did, he had found
the source of the jars from Kellen Zant's guest room: makeup products
manufactured by a small black-owned firm in Detroit, sold only by
one beauty shop in the city, where, as it happened, Julia Carlyle was a
regular.

All right, another black woman could have bought it and left it in
the guest room. The trouble was, Kellen didn't date black women. He
dated white women.

Except for Julia.

Yet Bruce could not imagine Julia Carlyle sneaking in and out of
Kellen's house on Hobby Hill, and not just because she would almost
certainly have been seen. More to the point, she just did not strike him
as the type. Such behavior would seem, in her Clannishness, beneath
her.

Another black woman? With a British accent?

Very strange, and getting stranger.

Bruce forced his attention back to the budget. He was still fiddling
with figures when the receptionist buzzed to say that Rick Chrebet was
on the phone.

"We better meet," Rick said.

(11)

"IT'S NOT PERSONAL," said Rick Chrebet.

"That's a relief."

"Seriously, Bruce. It has nothing to do with you."

The thaw was memory. The weather had turned wintry again.
Bruce Valley shoved his famous hands deeper into the pockets of his
overcoat, wishing for his parka. The two men were descending the towpath that bordered the fetid Harbor Canal. Reeds four feet high separated the frozen mud from the water. On their right, up the slope from
the path, ran Deepwater Street, where, ten or twelve feet above their

heads, cars scuttled past, seeking a shortcut to avoid rush-hour traffic. In theory, the land abutting the canal was a park. In theory.

In practice, it was simply raw, and deserted.

The department wits used to say that God put together Rick Chrebet with the little that was left after he made Bruce, for Rick was—everyone in the squad room could recite the litany—shorter, thinner, slower, cooler, and paler than his partner. Back when the two were rookies together, twenty-odd years ago, one might also have said that Rick Chrebet was blonder, but the decades had sprinkled both heads equally with a salty gray. Now Bruce had retired and Rick, just passed over for captain, was on the verge of doing the same, except that he enjoyed the work.

For a few minutes, there was no sound but the tread of feet over snow: one pair heavy, one pair light, one pair heavy, one pair light, the rhythm as steady and predictable as an old friendship.

Finally, Bruce said, "If it's not personal, what's going on? There's no investigation of anything but a robbery. Everything else has stopped."

"Tell me something I don't know."

"It's robbery? That's the final verdict?"

Rick had been carrying a long stick. Now he tossed it into the reeds, disturbing whatever lived there, because there were ugly flurries in every direction. "I told you this was coming."

Bruce raised his face to the battered afternoon sky. A bright smudge suggested that the sun still lived out there somewhere. "Nobody will talk to me all of a sudden."

"I'm talking to you." It occurred to Bruce that his former partner was very angry. "Never mind. I know exactly what you mean."

"So—what's going on?"

His partner eyed him. "Why are you so interested in this? You're retired."

Bruce knew better than to trot out the "loose ends" explanation this time. "I'm under some pressure here, Rick. My employers want to make sure every 't' is crossed, every 'i' is dotted, so on. You know how it is."

But Rick Chrebet was not saying whether he knew how it was or not. "Look, Bruce. This is very hush-hush. And people aren't very happy about it." A pause. "I hear Ben Church threatened to resign. And Janey Wei threw a hissy fit."

Bruce tried to picture little Janey losing her temper, couldn't.

"What were they so mad about? What happened?"

"Look. We follow orders, okay? From higher authority. Let's put it that way. Now, a couple of days after the murder, the cops out in the Landing were running in circles, but Ben and Janey had a couple of leads. They were making a nice case. They—well, never mind the details. The point is, they were making progress, right?"

Their walk had carried them to the muddy edge of the water meadow. Tall grasses seemed weedy and offending.

"So—another day goes by, and Janey and Ben develop a little more information, and they have an interview they want to do. Not a suspect or anything, but a lead. Somebody who might point them in the right direction. They want to interview this individual, but it turns out to be a little bit sensitive, for . . . well, reasons. They have to get certain permissions. They see the people they have to ask for permission—this is where your higher authority comes back in, right?—and then they wait and wait, and maybe two days later, three, an order comes down. No interview. No speculation, not to anybody. Then, a couple of weeks later, no investigation either. No more work. Call it an armed robbery, close the case, and turn over all the notes, all the files, sealed and signed. Want to know why?"

"Yes."

"So do we. Janey and Ben especially. All we know is, the state's attorney herself made the call. One rumor said it was the feds. Another said she was worried about next year's election with this case hanging over her head. Anyway, higher authority tells everybody on the force to stand down. From now on, we only look for people who might have wanted to steal his wallet and his keys. And that's the end of that."

"And Ben and Janey . . ."

"Hey, Janey's got little kids now, so does Ben, even if he never sees them since the divorce. Mortgages. Retirement to save for. I mean, Bruce, look. Okay, it's a little high-handed, but robbery does make sense. Maybe it even *was* a robbery. People will accept that verdict. They'll skin us alive for not finding the perpetrator, but they'll believe the motive."

They were near the end of the towpath. A rusty bicycle barred the way, the brackish water dark and unwelcoming where, when Bruce was a boy, he and his older brother used to launch their canoe. Even the floating ice looked polluted.

Bruce said, "Theresa Pappas—the state's attorney—she's a good friend of the Carlyles, isn't she?"

Rick shrugged. "One thing I learned in this investigation is, except for Kellen Zant, just about everybody is Lemaster Carlyle's pal. Oh, some people are a little bit intimidated by him, because he knows pretty much all the movers and shakers. But, either way, nobody wants to say a word against—" He stopped, and clapped his old partner on the back. His face was pinched. "Bruce, look. That's not why I wanted to talk. Whether we're ordered to call Zant's murder a robbery or something else isn't your problem."

"Then why?"

"Because—just between you and me and the wall?—you're not exactly what we'd call persona grata these days, if that's the phrase."

"What are you talking about?"

"We've had some problems. Evidence vanishing from custody. Even Zant's cell phone, believe it or not. So Mrs. Pappas has put a hard lid on. The order isn't just that nobody's supposed to talk. It's very specific." Rick's buggy eyes were pained but determined. "One person we are specifically not allowed to talk to is a certain Bruce Vallely, director of campus safety."

Sheets of ice floated on the old canal. On the other side, in the section of town known as Outer Elm, patient developers had dredged the area nearest the shore and built condos, shopping malls, playgrounds, a boardwalk. All white, by happy coincidence, an ethnically cleansed paradise in the middle of the city, and quite reasonably priced: mostly third-generation immigrant families.

"Seriously?"

"Actually, Bruce, it's worse than that."

"Worse how?"

Rick Chrebet still had his hands deep in his pockets. His breath described pale arcs in the frigid air. "They know you've been running some kind of private investigation, Bruce. They know you were in Zant's house. I'm not in Mrs. Pappas's confidence—not on something like this—but the word is, they're considering a case against you for obstruction."

CHAPTER 27

AGAIN THE COMYNS MIRROR

(1)

JULIA BEGAN HER TASK methodically but also impulsively, the same combination that had carried her to so much success in life, and so much failure. Mary Mallard and Tony Tice both seemed to think that Kellen had turned something over to her. The surplus he intended to capture. The inventory he did not want to hold. Aside from his cryptic messages and the occasional unwanted gift of fudge, Julia could only think of one object Kellen had recently arranged to have delivered to her.

The mirror.

The silver-and-tortoiseshell hand mirror by William Comyns of London that Granny Vee had given her not long before she died, and that Kellen had evidently kept next to his desk for twenty years.

So, late Tuesday night, as the house slumbered, Julia took the mirror from its place atop her small desk in a corner of the bedroom and carried it down to the kitchen, a long, grand room with trendy and pricey black granite counters that looked gorgeous in the showroom but, when darkness fell, seemed to suck all the light out of the air. Kellen, at a party Lemaster gave for black faculty five years ago—one of his few visits to Hunter's Heights—had remarked that the counters reminded him of the Clan, tough and dark and sturdy, proudly and determinedly preserving all that was useless in African America.

Julia had told him to leave her alone.

Now she laid the mirror under the reading lamp next to the computer that sat on the kitchen desk. She had cleaned and polished it, but not with the effort it needed. She should take it to a professional, she decided, turning it over and over. Come on, Kellen, she said in her mind. If I'm your Black Lady, then talk to me. Why did you give me the mirror? What does the mirror mean? The mirror, the surplus, the inventory risk. And Jamaica. Why did you go to the div school that night? She could find no pattern, make no sense. She ran her fingers over the delicate filigree on the back, the clusters of leaves along the edges, the emblem of the sun in the middle, the royal decorations surrounding it. She felt her annoyance rise hotly, not only because she could not fathom its significance, if any, but also because Kellen had taken such poor care of the mirror, allowing the tarnished surface to get so scratched up that she could hardly make out the famous *W•C* hallmark any more, because of all the—

The hallmark?

She put the mirror down again, focused the bright light. The Comyns hallmark was a "W" followed by a "C," with a small circle between them, raised about three-quarters of the height of the letters. It was hidden in the design, but any expert would know where to look. But this hallmark was not just scratched. It was obliterated.

This was not wear and tear. It was purposeful.

She turned the mirror upside down, and saw it at once. The letters had been . . . altered. Altered in a way that only someone who knew the hallmark was there would even notice; and nobody but Julia was likely to know.

The "C" was turned around the wrong way, the long curve bisected neatly by a horizontal slash. As for the "W," the left-hand slope was worn away, and the middle part of the letter, which pointed upward, had been turned on its side, to point to the right.

It made no sense.

Oh, yes, it did.

It was a *mirror.*

Julia smiled. She already knew what Kellen had done, but carried the mirror into the powder room to be sure. She held it up to the mirror, and, sure enough, viewed closely, but only through a mirror, the hallmark had been changed. No longer did it read *W•C.* Now it read *E•K.*

Her smile faded. What, or who, on earth was *E•K*? Eddie Krueger? No, his name was Freddy. Edward Kennedy? Ernst Kaltenbrunner?

Elegant Kellen? Perhaps she had misunderstood. Maybe she had read the new hallmark wrong, or maybe she was working too hard, reading heavy symbols into normal wear and tear because she wanted them to be there. Nevertheless, because she was organized, she took several shots of the mirror with her digital camera, both in the mirror and lying on the counter, several of them close-ups of the hallmark, and downloaded them to her laptop, then sent them along the Internet to Kodak, where she stored digital images.

Patience was not natural to her, but if the mirror was a message, Julia knew she would, given time, figure it out.

(11)

EARLIER IN THE DAY, she had asked Latisha call Joe Poynting, who hurried over, worried, no doubt, that the dean had discovered a rule making him ineligible for the grants he was seeking to support his research in Bologna. Instead, Julia turned facedown the memo pad on which she was still working out permutations of "Shari Larid," then shut the door, a rarity, and swore the young man to secrecy. Then she asked her question.

"You work late in the library every night. You're there till closing, sometimes later. What I need to know is if you ever saw Professor Zant."

"In the Kepler Library?"

"Yes."

Joe nodded. "Sure, I saw him. Sometimes at night, sometimes in the late afternoon."

"What was he doing?"

"Research, I guess. I didn't ask."

"I meant, what did you see?"

The student sat with his knees together and his hands in his lap. Julia sensed he had not much liked Kellen. "He was usually going in or out of the archives."

Confirming Vanessa's tale. Except—

"How often did you see him in the archives?"

"I'd say at least once a week."

Of course. Kellen came over to the div school after Julia left for the day, meaning that he was not dropping by just to annoy her. Nor was he just looking for Vanessa, who had visited the archives perhaps five times in the past year. No. Kellen Zant had been at Kepler because he was working on a project of his own.

In the archives.

(I I I)

LEMASTER WOKE when his wife crept back into the master suite and, when she slipped into bed beside him, reached for her. Julia was willing to be reached for. She was jangly, worried, confused, a little frightened, and ready for physical reassurance of the reality of their shared life. Lemmie made love the same way he did everything else: thoughtfully, dutifully, and fully master of himself and all around him. He was male enough to take pride in her pleasure, but far too self-aware to imagine there might be virtue in occasionally surrendering his control. Sometimes, at a tender moment, she would catch his gaze, the somber brown eyes watchful and patient, Lemaster thinking only of her needs, when a bit of male selfishness might have turned pleasant to thrilling. Now and then she caught herself wondering what if anything truly lit her husband up; for she had never, in all their years together, seen him truly lose control.

Julia had fallen for him within a week of starting divinity school, when she watched him take over a lecture hall where a visiting philosopher from Cambridge was hectoring the intimidated audience on why God was necessarily the author of all evil; Lemaster stood up to him when even most of the faculty seemed cowed. She loved his brilliance, the way he had set academic records as an undergraduate, and gone on to star in law school and in the legal profession, before quitting in mid-career to try to determine whether he had a vocation to the ministry. She loved his softly charming assurance, the preternatural calm he brought to every situation, even bed, providing the antidote for the exhausting excitement of Kellen Zant. And she loved the way that their engagement rocked the Clan, because Lemaster Carlyle, whatever his virtues, was not really one of *us*, dear. And then he turned out to be an Empyreal. An Empyreal—weren't they all dead, or dying? Weren't they practically bankrupt? How could Julia, whose grandmother had founded Ladybugs, marry a mere Empyreal? And, of course, he was a West Indian, and dark-skinned, for the hardy prejudices from the old Harlem days still lurked around certain unmentioned corners.

Now, sex finished, she clung to him, wondering what secrets he was truly carrying, what he had refused to disclose to either Astrid Venable or Cameron Knowland, what he knew about those old days in Hilliman Suite. Lemaster, a Catholic school boy, had bound himself in the tight strictures of principle and obligation, and Julia supposed she loved that in him, too, even though virtues like loyalty and discretion could get in the way of finding truth.

"You're a good man," said Julia, kissing his shoulder as he slept. She pressed closer. "A good man," she said again, hoping it was true.

CHAPTER 28

DEFYING GRAVITAS

(1)

THE DIVINITY SCHOOL ARCHIVES WERE entered through a kind of antechapel, complete with wrought-iron altar screen, at the southmost end of the high-ceilinged reading room of Kepler Library. Julia stepped inside the library as rarely as possible, but on Wednesday she strode briskly across creakily uneven wooden floors covered by an insufficiency of aged carpet. Scaffolding hid one wall. The rest were high with books and windows and portraits of the great preachers and theologians who had been graduated from Kepler. Most of them looked disappointed. Here, Bibles of all versions. There, the works of the great theologians; or summaries of the works of the great theologians; or computers to find summaries of the summaries. A couple of students glanced up incuriously. At the iron bars, a listless receptionist pretended to check Julia's university identification. Then Julia descended a metal stair and was inside the holy of holies, where, at the moment, nobody else was burrowing. The div school's collection of sermons and pamphlets and holograph letters, many possessing inestimable value, operated as a "closed" stack, meaning that you filled out a search request, then waited in a small workroom for the archivist or one of his assistants to bring the materials you needed. You did your reading on one of several tables scattered around the room. Nothing could be removed from the archives, but if you were a regular they provided you a rolling cart to hold your papers while you attended to such frivolities as classes, family, or sleep. To preserve the precious trove, the air conditioners and dehumidifiers kept everything bone-dry throughout the year, and Julia, standing there amid the long tables, study carrels, and movable gunmetal shelves on little tracks, knew her skin would itch the rest of the day.

Think.

Joe Poynting said he had seen Kellen in here several times the past few months, usually in the late afternoons or at night—that is, when Julia, with her early afternoon departure time, would be unlikely to spot him.

The archives.

So what was he doing?

Julia moved toward one of the trolleys, fingering a stack of blue folders, each bound with brown string. The labels told her somebody was researching homilies delivered in French churches in the days of the Paris Commune. Didn't sound like Kellen's taste. The next trolley held pre–World War II financial reports from what was originally known as the Federal Council of Churches. Maybe Kellen was doing economic history—

"May I be of assistance, Dean Carlyle?"

Julia dropped her hand to her side like a child caught at sin, spinning around with the old Hanover grin on her face, and found herself staring into the ghostly, glittery countenance of Rod Rutherford, Kepler's librarian and chief archivist.

"I didn't see you," she said. "I'm sorry."

"May I be of assistance?" he repeated, the formality in his greeting a symbol of respect less for Julia than for tradition.

"I'm very sorry to disturb you," she said, mimicking, unintentionally, his sepulchral tone. "But I had a question."

"I see."

"An important question," she continued, a bit stupidly.

"Important. Well."

"May I speak to you privately?"

"By all means." He led the way into his whitewashed cubicle, furnished with cheap metal furniture because Rod Rutherford did not hold with spending library money on anything but books. She sat across from him and spoke for several minutes, shivering in the artificial chill, editing and amplifying, but offering, Julia thought, a reasonable version of the truth.

"I really wish I could help you, Dean Carlyle," said the librarian when he had heard her out. "But I'm afraid what you ask is quite impossible."

"All I'm asking is what files Professor Zant might have looked at."

"Alas, I am unable even to confirm that he was ever here." Roderick Ryan Rutherford favored her with an unapologetic smile. He was a creepy, cadaverous man, pale as any cave dweller, fussy and disdainful, who had the unnerving habit of materializing behind you in a hallway or parking lot when you had been certain a moment earlier that you were alone. Julia did not know him well, for her work rarely brought her into contact with the library or the archives, both of which were run by the librarian, and both of which had fallen within the purview of the late Boris Gibbs. As a matter of fact, still sensitive about her uneven record as a student, she rarely ventured into the once-grand reading room, and had not entered the open stacks since the day she dropped out. She had toured the archives just after her arrival as a dean, and had come back a year and a half ago to introduce Vanessa, who would be doing research here. "Much less am I able to confirm what materials he may or may not have drawn from the collection," Mr. Rutherford was saying.

"Would anybody else know?"

"Oh, dear me. I am not saying I lack the information you seek, Dean Carlyle. But it is impossible for me to turn it over to you. Quite impossible." Raising a finger, making a circle, as if to remind her of a wider world. "Rules, you know."

"Rules?"

"Surely you believe in rules, Dean Carlyle." Ghostly hands washing each other like a greedy undertaker's. "Without rules, man lives in anarchy. And a library cannot bear anarchy. Still less can an archive."

"Yes, but—"

"Such records are entirely confidential. As deputy dean, you are surely aware of Rule 22-C, relating to privacy of library records, adopted by the faculty senate in 1973, following the congressional passage of the Buckley Amendment, and subsequently ratified by the trustees of the—"

"Try to understand, Mr. Rutherford"—he liked formality—"how important this is. I can't tell you all the reasons, but—"

"No doubt it is a matter of life or death." He sounded entirely unpersuaded. "But I serve, by necessity, a different muse. A library is the repository of knowledge, Dean Carlyle. A place of preservation. In an earlier era, the work of preserving knowledge was respected. No longer. Knowledge is today coincident with desire. Nothing unpleasant is permitted to be true. The Dark Ages are once more upon us. We therefore preserve our function by insisting upon the rules. Those who insist on playing by other rules play elsewhere."

Sitting across the archivist's desk as he glowered at her, Julia wondered whether she might be dreaming this unexpected impediment. She had not anticipated such opposition, but held her temper, pondering. It was not because of her color, she consoled herself, not entirely persuaded, for she often felt, even on so flagrantly liberal a campus as this, that certain doors—intellectual, social, reputational—swung wide only for the denizens of the paler nation. But Roderick Rutherford condescended to everyone. He always left her feeling less ignored than chilled: his whispery way of turning his head half away when speaking gave her the creeps.

She decided to begin again.

"I'm not asking for much. I know that Professor Zant was down here several times, late at night, the month before he died. All I'm asking—"

"Late at night? Dear me, that could have nothing to do with us. The archives close at half past five, you know, six days a week. On the seventh day we rest. That's a joke."

Neither laughed. On the wall behind his narrow head hung a dour portrait of a famous New England abolitionist. Two yellowy windows high up were at ground level, and barred. Feet passed in sepia shadow. Nothing else in the chilly room gave a hint that the sun was shining.

"Well, my understanding is that Professor Zant was down here later than that."

"I don't see how that would have been possible, Dean Carlyle. I lock the doors personally. Mrs. Bethe has a key, of course, but would hardly return to let someone in without authorization. I suppose the campus police could get in, although I daresay they'd make a great ruckus, not knowing the codes for the alarm."

"Surely Claire Alvarez would be able to—"

"Dear me, no. Dean Alvarez possesses no key, and has no knowledge of the codes. I believe that only Mrs. Bethe and myself know the codes."

"So—what do you do if somebody wants to work late? Suzanne de Broglie is here at night all the time."

"Professor de Broglie tells us what files she wants, and we leave them for her in the main reading room. She signs them out at the desk, takes them into the faculty library, does her studying there. Of course we would not make such an arrangement for just anybody, but the good professor is unusually respectful of our collections."

"Did you make an arrangement like that for Kellen Zant?"

Again the hands slid over and through each other like separate things doing unnatural battle. "My dear Dean Carlyle, I couldn't possibly say."

She thought furiously. In Rod Rutherford's library, paper records existed and mattered. Computerized information was disdained. Everything was written down, for Roderick Ryan Rutherford might or might not have believed in God, but he believed in the old days with the fervor of the recent convert.

"All right. You can't tell me what files he requested. But if he was here, you'd have his signature. He'd have to sign in or out."

"No doubt."

"May I see those records?" Controlling, barely, her exasperation.

"Oh, no, Dean Carlyle, I'm afraid there is no question of that. Again, Rule 22-C governs the matter entirely. It was adopted after five months of debate. I hardly think we are free to change it."

"Mr. Rutherford, please." Holding up both hands against this flooding bureaucratic tide. The archivist fell silent, but his expression of distress never softened. "I'm not some jealous div student trying to find out if my boyfriend was really in the archives that night or not." Although in her day she had played that role, too. "This is related to . . . to, ah, to what happened to Professor Zant."

"Yes. A most unfortunate business."

"Then you understand why—"

"Do you have a subpoena? Any sort of court order?" Glancing down at her hands as if hoping to find one. "Some other form of authorization?"

She shook her head. "No, but I'm sure you see that—"

"In that case, I am so very sorry, Dean Carlyle. I cannot possibly be of assistance."

A thought struck her. "Suppose I were to return with the director of campus security?"

"Safety, I suppose you mean. The director of campus safety." A bony finger dimpled his chin, and the translucent brow furrowed still more deeply. "Yes. Well. Alas, Dean Carlyle, unless the director arrived carrying pertinent authorization, he, too, would leave empty-handed."

Shaking his long head to emphasize the point. "No court order. No authorization. Most irregular, Dean Carlyle. You really should pay more attention to the rules."

One last chance. She swallowed her pride. "Mr. Rutherford, you know who I am. You know who my husband is."

"Indeed. And may I say that I am quite unimpressed with the muttering against him from all corners."

"Ah, well, thank you. I think." Gathering herself. "Mr. Rutherford, if the president of the university were to give you a direct order, surely you—"

Lifting a powdery palm to stop her. "Dean Carlyle, allow me to disabuse you of a common error. I fear that I am not in the employ of your husband. Nor is any member of the faculty. The position of university president is more, ah, hortatory than supervisory, at least with respect to the academic mission. In any case, Rule 22-C binds me absolutely."

About to say more, Julia saw the futility. It was like arguing with a poorly programmed machine. Lemaster loved libraries, books, traditions, but Julia would take the Internet any day. She turned and stalked toward the exit.

"Dean Carlyle." Softly.

Over her shoulder, not wanting to look at him. "Yes, Mr. Rutherford."

"I suggest that you study the rules. Perhaps you will discover a pertinent exception."

Enough was enough. The line from pettiness to condescension had been crossed. But when she spun around to lash him with her tongue, she was alone in the hallway.

(I I)

SHE FED THE CHILDREN AND LEMASTER, describing her day as uneventful, and then was back in the Escalade, storming into Elm Harbor once more, still edgy and frustrated from her confrontation with Rod Rutherford. She arrived just past seven-thirty at Kimmer Madison's house, a lovely old Victorian on Hobby Hill, where the ad hoc committee to draft the neutral statement on abortion was holding another impromptu gabfest and wine-tasting, to consider the possibility of getting some work done. Julia contributed a nice Saint-Hilaire Blanquette de Limoux, a gift from Mona, the great Francophile. Kimmer and Regina Thackery gossiped about other women with their words, and about Julia with their eyes. She had guessed from little hints dropped over the past week that a version of her meeting with Bruce Vallely had spread among the local Sister Ladies, and it occurred to her, for the first time, that Lemaster might actually be lucky to belong to a dying men's club that had only four hundred members, as opposed to Ladybugs, whose chapters fluttered all over the United States, and in sixteen foreign countries as well. Julia met their curious eyes, wondering what they had heard. Because nobody would say anything to her directly, she did not know how many erroneous assumptions were making the rounds. And, sitting comfortably on the sofa, talking Washington politics and recent films, while Kimmer's six-year-old son scampered noisily around the first floor, Julia was too much a Veazie to just ask.

So she sat and suffered and in the back of her mind played with an idea that had been teasing her all day. Every now and then, she checked her watch surreptitiously, but it was close to ten before she could decently take her leave. Julia helped an unsteady Regina Thackery down the slippery front walk. Fresh sleet was falling. "Can you make it home?"

"You had as much as I did," accused Regina, quite cross.

Julia hid a smile. Actually, she was a cautious drinker, and had managed to hold her consumption to one glass of the sparkling wine, enough to fortify without impairing the judgment.

"I seem to be walking reasonably straight," she said.

"You walk your way, I'll walk mine."

"Maybe I should give you a ride."

"You're not everybody's mommy, Julia."

Regina shoved her away, but, as Julia the onetime science teacher could have told her, the reactive force shoved back. Regina tumbled onto the grass. Julia tried to help her up, but the younger woman snatched her hand away. "Don't you have enough trouble with the daughter you already have?"

Stung, she soldiered on. "I'm worried about you, that's all."

"This is America, honey." Eyes sizzling, Regina was on her feet: teetering, to be sure, but definitely on her feet. "You don't tell me what to do. Play by your own rules, okay? And I'll play by mine."

Julia, stunned, did not snatch her friend's keys as planned, and allowed Regina to slide into her Acura RL and streak off down the icy road. Julia stood there, watching her go. Regina's last, furious objection had opened a new door.

"Oh, Kellen," Julia said to the frosty air. "Oh, Kellen, you clever, clever bastard."

Climbing into the Escalade, she remembered to say a quick prayer for Regina's safety, just in case somebody was listening. But mostly she focused on her destination, and the bold absurdity of what she was about to undertake.

The rules, she told herself. It was time to make her own rules.

(I I I)

THE SLEET HAD TURNED to plain snow. The night was moonless. Julia climbed from the Escalade in the brooding shadow of Hilliman Tower, where lights burned in a few offices, even at half past ten. Her key card admitted her to Kepler through the side door, and as she stepped inside she wondered whether Kellen might have been here so late that he needed digital permission to enter; and who gave it to him. You're insane, she lectured herself, in Mona's voice. Absolutely insane. Now we know where Vanessa gets it from. They're going to lock you up.

In the dimly lighted hallway, her footsteps echoed like cell doors slamming. She could not remember the last time she had been inside the divinity school at this hour, and doubted that she had ever been here at this hour alone. In her office she watered the plants and fussed with her perfectly arranged desk and picked up a couple of memos she had to study for a meeting tomorrow with Iris Feynman, papers she had left intentionally to provide an excuse for her return, on the off chance that somebody noticed she was there, or perhaps checked the digital records.

Back out in the hall, she encountered a trio of exhausted students, arguing vaguely about Kierkegaard, as astonished as Julia herself by the nighttime presence of the dean of students. She offered a cheery good night and ostentatiously left the building. She put the memos in her car, glanced around, and then, giving herself no chance to think, padded off into the snow, not down the steps to the side entrance this time, but around the back, where plowed snow was still heaped beneath the windows of the deserted common room. She crouched against the aging brickwork, ignoring the chill on her legs, and found what she was looking for: the well leading to the basement windows.

The windows she had seen set high up in the wall as she sat in Rod Rutherford's office.

From the archivist's perspective, they were sealed and barred, but some of the students appointed the dean of students their confessor, and a couple of months ago a young woman had sat in Julia's office and, after swearing her to secrecy, confessed to sneaking into the archives late one night to deface a portrait of a former professor accused of sexual harassment.

"How did you get in?" Julia had asked, marveling proudly at the young woman's chutzpah.

And so the student had explained. She used to work in the archives to pay her tuition, and had noticed, while filing papers in Rod Rutherford's office, that the screws on some of the bars were loose. After that, whenever she found herself alone, she would climb on a chair and spend a few minutes working on them. The stonework was a hundred years old, the bars probably half that, and they came loose with surprising ease. She left them hanging so that they would appear to be in place, then pried the cover off the latch so that it would not seal properly but the damage would be invisible from below.

"All this so you could draw a mustache on poor Professor Millikan?"

"It wasn't a mustache."

No wonder Roderick Rutherford had sent the portrait off for cleaning, without ever quite saying why.

Had the librarian noticed his intern's secret entrance? Evidently not: when Julia leaned down into the window well and shoved, the glass swung open with a surprised pop. She hesitated and then, taking a last look around, lowered herself into the well. Snow caked around her stylish boots. Then, refusing to consider the consequences, Julia took a cue from Broadway, for Regina's lament about following her own rules had reminded her of Elphaba, the anti-heroine of the musical *Wicked*, who sang about how she was through playing by the rules of someone else's game, and how it was time to close her eyes and leap.

After so long and placid a marriage, it felt good to be taking risks again.

She closed her eyes and leaped . . .

(IV)

. . . AND CAME DOWN IN A HEAP, her head missing a file cabinet by inches, and immediately she saw her error. She had not brought a flashlight. She also had not considered how she would get out again, and, looking up at the hanging window, wondered whether some special corner of Hell was reserved for the truly stupid. In the soft, snowy glow from the window, she found the switch and turned on the fluorescents, reasoning that nobody would be standing behind the div school peeking at the basement to see whether the lights were on; at least nobody who knew that the archives were locked and alarmed at five-thirty, six days a week, because Mr. Rutherford rested on the seventh.

She tried to figure out whether it was breaking and entering to sneak into the closed stacks of a building to which she had every right of access, twenty-four hours a day.

Never mind.

Close your eyes and leap.

The cabinets in Rod Rutherford's office were all locked, but his files were not her objective. She stepped out into the workroom. The archives themselves were locked up for the evening too, but they were not her objective either. Not tonight. She crossed the pitted linoleum floor to Mrs. Bethe's little hutch, where Mr. Rutherford's assistant filed request forms in long gray boxes behind her desk. The boxes were neatly stacked but otherwise unsecured, and Julia paged swiftly through them.

No request form from Kellen on the last night of his life.

Frowning, she went back, page by page, the work not particularly difficult, because the divinity school archives, once Kepler's glory, actually got little use.

Julia worked her way past November and into October.

She finally found a request with Kellen's name on it from the middle of the month. She held it up, looked, then looked again, to make sure the name was Zant. Paging back, faster and faster, she found several more, almost all of them seeking documents from the same collection. Volume so-and-so, folio such-and-such, of the Merrill Barnes Joule papers.

The same collection Vanessa had used a year ago in writing her disastrous term paper.

Julia sat down hard on the desk, staring sightlessly across the low room, the roar of the air conditioners drowned by the roaring of blood in her head.

Now she knew for sure what all the fuss was about, what Astrid had wanted, and Cameron Knowland, and Tony Tice, and Mary Mallard. She knew what surplus Kellen had been trying to capture, and what inventory risk he had tried desperately to spread. What she had suspected was confirmed. At the time of his death, Kellen Zant had been investigating the death of Gina Joule.

And, no matter what Vanessa thought, Kellen had believed that his answer would blow the lid off the election.

CHAPTER 29

THE INVESTOR

(1)

LEMASTER CARLYLE WAS the sort of man who collected acquaintances rather than friends, but Marlon Thackery, Sister Lady Regina's husband, was as close to him as anybody in Harbor County. Marlon had been a successful money manager at a New York firm, and had been hired by Lemaster's predecessor to run the university's endowment. He was a tall man, taller than Bruce Vallely, but so thin you feared a harsh word would break him in two, and so hopelessly unassuming that if you passed him on campus, head down and shoulders hunched as he slouched about his business, you would take him for an African American of the working class, hurrying off to his job in a sub-basement somewhere, the sort of fellow who kept out of view. Even in his bright, modern office in a glass-walled tower downtown, with a splendid view of beach and ocean, he seemed an interloper, sitting behind the wrong desk, and Bruce kept waiting for the boss to come in and take his place.

Marlon said, eyes on the glass desktop, "Lemaster loves his wife. Why would you think he didn't?" His voice was scarcely above a mutter, but he was by all accounts a financial genius. Golf trophies stood here and there on shelves, and photographs of his lovely wife and three angelic daughters at all ages filled the extra space, so he could not possibly spend all his time folded into himself like this. People said he was a fantastic father. "That's a really weird thing to ask."

"I didn't say he didn't love his wife. I asked about how he and his wife met."

"Well, I think it's a weird question."

"It's part of filling in Professor Zant's background. That's all. So, please, Mr. Thackery. Humor me."

Still the money manager was unable to lift his eyes. They strayed to one of the several computer monitors in view, but Bruce was at a loss to guess what the charts and numbers meant. The door stood open, and every now and then minions came rushing in, dropping off vital memoranda. The semi-private firm that handled the university's investment accounts ran to thirty-six employees on two floors, but seventeen billion dollars is a lot of money.

"Lemaster's not an easy man," Marlon Thackery finally said. "Julia's Julia. She's a sweetheart. Everybody knows that. Lemaster is focused. Controlled. Sticks to the matter at hand. He's an immigrant," he added, as if that explained everything. "He grew up with nothing, and now the world's at his feet. Law. Politics. Both parties are after him to run for office. Senator. Governor. Do you know how many corporate headhunters call every month? How many investment banks? He could have been chief executive officer of— Never mind. He holds all of this together by holding himself together, and he holds himself together because of the marriage. Julia might not always know she's his rock, but she is. The marriage is everything to him, because without it he could do nothing."

Bruce caught an undercurrent, then wondered if he had imagined it. "You said the marriage is everything. Not Julia. The marriage. Like it's a symbol or something."

"I meant Julia."

No, you didn't. "They met as students," said Bruce.

"Divinity students. Right. Lemaster was an Assistant United States Attorney—that's when we met—and then a Wall Street lawyer. He quit, traveled the world, spent a year in Africa, went home to Barbados, came back, did some volunteer work in Brooklyn, then decided he might want to be an Episcopal priest. He enrolled at Kepler, met Julia, dropped out, got married. He joined the law school faculty. The wandering stopped. He settled down. And, after that, you know, the judgeship, the White House, everything else."

That was it. Had to be. "When you say he settled down—"

"I mean his career. Hold on." He tapped some keys, clicked his mouse. "Sorry. Have to jump in fast on those."

"Just his career?"

"What else is there?"

"What about his personal life? There had to be women before Julia."

"Obviously," said Marlon, tight-lipped now, fully engaged, and Bruce knew he was near the heart of whatever was being defended.

"He met Julia when he was—what?—thirty? How long did you know him before that?"

"Probably five years. Six."

"Did he have a lot of women?"

Back at the keyboard. No doubt currency was fluctuating somewhere. Marlon Thackery, eyes glued to the screen, spoke out of the side of his mouth. "That isn't really your business."

"Does that mean you're not going to tell me?"

"Yes. It means I'm not going to tell you."

Had the investigation been official, or Marlon Thackery less prominent, Bruce might have tried browbeating. But facts were facts. He glanced at the rolling water and selected a more delicate course. "You said Lemaster settled down after Julia. You said he used to wander—"

The chair swiveled back. "He doesn't wander any more. He would never cheat on his wife. Not the Lemaster I know. Please don't suggest such a thing. Frankly, such a statement is defamatory. I wouldn't be surprised if it's actionable. You're not official. You can't use that defense."

"I'm not making any such statement. What intrigues me is that you're so quick to deny it. I ask you about how he met his wife, and you tell me he's done with wandering. You tell me Julia is his rock." Bruce turned to a fresh page of his notebook, but only for effect. "I think you're suggesting that his social life before Julia was more . . . complex. Is that fair?"

A pause. "Complex. Yes."

"For all those five or six years you knew him before they met?"

A longer pause. "I suppose."

"Do you know who he dated in college?"

"Is this really related to what happened to Kellen Zant?" The sleepy eyes briefly flashed fire. "Or is this some private vendetta of yours?"

"Humor me," said Bruce again, controlling himself with an effort, and Grace's whispered encouragement. "I know it seems distant."

"It's not just distant, it's in another galaxy."

"What about in Washington? His year and a half at the White House?"

"What about it?"

"His family stayed here. Do you know why?"

"I imagine they didn't want to disrupt the children's education. What kind of a question is that? You have to be careful, Bruce. Very careful." Something pinged, and he turned to the computer again. "You do realize I'm going to tell Lemaster about this conversation," he said, out of the side of his mouth. "I just want that to be clear."

"Of course," said Bruce, who had expected nothing less. Probably he was trying to rile his president a bit, before their inevitable interview. But Thackery was right. He no longer had any official standing, and had to tread lightly. "I wouldn't ask you to do anything else."

"Good. Because I wouldn't." Another longish wait, after which Marlon Thackery answered a different question. "I didn't know him then, but I understand he was seeing a young woman from the Catholic university. This was long before Julia, of course." The humorless eyes came back up. "This conversation is making me uneasy, Bruce. Why are you so interested in what Lemaster did in college? Or with whom? First Kellen Zant, now you."

"Are you saying Professor Zant asked you about—"

"Listen to me, Bruce. We've talked about you, Lemaster and I. He's not really sure what you're up to. I'm not really sure what you're up to. And I have a feeling you're not really sure what you're up to. But I'll tell you one thing. Lemaster Carlyle is not a man to cross. And do you know what? Julia Carlyle is not a woman to cross. They protect each other, Bruce. Fiercely. They protect their family. Fiercely."

"What are you trying to tell me?"

"I analyze numbers for a living and make predictions. So let's take a look." Hunching over the pristine desk. The computer bleeped, but he ignored it. "Lemaster's cousin causes trouble, and she's gone. Cameron Knowland causes trouble, and, just between you, me, and the wall, he's in trouble with the White House and maybe even planning to step down as Senior Trustee. Anthony Tice causes trouble, and I understand the Bar is investigating his conduct in a couple of cases. I'm just warning you. Why are you looking at me like that?"

Bruce stood up. And Kellen Zant caused trouble, too, he shouted, but not quite aloud.

(11)

BACK AT HIS OFFICE, Bruce watched the blowing snow and tried to get the numbers straight in his head. The hope that the name "Gina Joule" might have dropped from Marlon Thackery's lips had been in any case something of a long shot. Yet the visit had not been wasted. The money manager had warned him that Lemaster might sue, and had hinted that he could lose his job. And Marlon was the second person, maybe the third, to warn him about what happened to people who crossed Lemaster Carlyle. Yet none of this suggested violence, just the ruthless use of connections, of influence, of whatever tools happened to be at hand. The line between getting the Bar Association to investigate a lawyer who would not stop harassing your wife and hiring a killer to take care of her ex-lover was as bright as a line could be. Nobody stepped over it by accident.

He put his notebook aside and delved into his messages. One of his officers had broken his wrist playing basketball, and looked to be unavailable for tomorrow night, when he always sent three to the campus rink for the hockey games. He would have to get somebody else. Crowd control was important inside the rink, and traffic control was important outside. On hockey nights, the city wisely banned parking all along Town Street, and—

Wait a minute.

He pulled the notebook back, paged to the front.

Nathaniel Knowland's statement: *We were out on Town Street, I'd say, ah, eight-fifteen, eight-thirty, something like that. We were out on the street, trying to decide what to do next, and that was when we saw the car. The gold Audi, the one Zant got killed in, parked right on the street.*

Not possible. The Audi could not have been parked on Town Street, not after the game started at seven-thirty. Not with an officer patrolling the street all night and a tow truck on five-minute call.

Nathaniel Knowland had lied through his teeth.

Wherever he had seen Kellen Zant—if indeed the young man had seen the professor at all—it was not out on Town Street climbing into the Audi.

Trevor Land, having been dressed down by Nate's daddy, had warned Bruce to stay away from the witness henceforth, but Bruce had never taken terribly well to warnings. He reached for the phone, but Nate Knowland's answering machine said that the spoiled little rich boy had already left for the holiday.

CHAPTER 30

AGAIN OLD LANDING

(1)

SHE DECIDED TO GO see Frank Carrington again, because she liked him as much as she did any of the merchants along Main Street, and because he liked minorities and had talked to Kellen three days before he died, but mostly because of a fact she remembered from Frank's background—and because he had been nervous the day she came to visit.

Julia thought she knew why.

Meanwhile, they both pretended Julia had come on her usual errand. The cheval Kellen had bought was still in the back of the store, but now Frank had a nice early-nineteenth-century Federal mirror with painted nautical design, one she had seen in a Winterthur Museum book and admired. She had asked him to keep an eye out.

"It's been in a private estate for years," said Frank, unwrapping it on the counter. "My customer's the daughter. Mother died. She's been cleaning out the house. Pretty valuable," he lied.

"Mmmm."

"She wants a quick sale. I bet she'd bargain."

"I'm sure." She felt his eyes as she studied the mirror. His hands were shaking again. They always were, but today seemed worse. Illness? Nervousness? He hovered. Sometimes it seemed to her that Frank watched her too closely, and this was one of those times. She ignored his gaze. She noticed the patina and asked what it had been cleaned with. Alas, Frank did not know. She pointed to some touch-up paintwork on the white oak frame and asked if it was original. Alas, Frank could not be helpful. He was not, as he often proclaimed with proud humility, an educated man, but during his years in the trade he had learned not to make representations or warranties. You went into his shop, you examined his wares, and what you saw was what you got. If you lacked the eye, that was your problem.

"I think the paint was added later." Cagey, cagey. She wanted the mirror. She wanted answers, too. Sometimes life really could be about getting both.

"I wouldn't know."

"That would reduce the value."

"If you say so."

She calculated furiously, and made a take-it-or-leave-it offer, as she had learned from Granny Vee: *Never bargain,* Amaretta had preached. *Walk away politely but walk away. That's the way to stay rich.* Only with Kellen had Julia failed to heed this advice. Walking away had been impossible. Tessa had been forced to drag her. But this time, she promised herself—this time, she would walk away from Kellen. She would. She promised.

Just as soon as she got a few answers.

Frank pleaded other customers and high expenses, but Julia refused to budge, and, in the end, he yielded, because he knew, as she did, that the price was fair.

As they shook hands, Julia said, in as casual a voice as she could manage, "People say you used to be a cop."

"A deputy," he said at once, not lifting his gaze from the credit-card machine, which was the dial-up kind. "A long time ago."

"Thirty years ago."

A pause.

"About that."

"When Gina Joule was—"

He swiveled, a statue on a plinth, hands folded for prayer. "Sign here, please," he said. His hands trembled.

"I just wanted to ask—"

"I know what you wanted to ask."

"Frank—"

"We don't talk about it."

"Who's *we?*"

He tore off her copy of the credit-card slip, handed it over. "You're a newcomer, Julia. Not an old Landinger. Now, I like you. I like your family. I'm glad you're here. And you know I think we need more minorities. But there are things"—he glanced toward the front of the store, where, a month ago, Jeannie had broken the porcelain train station; today Julia was alone—"that it's not safe to talk about."

"Not safe?"

"I'm not a brave man," Frank said, and dropped his head again to prove it.

Julia stepped in front of him, crowding his vision, making him look at her. "Frank, listen to me. You said you know why I'm here. I'm here about Gina. About what happened that night. You were a cop. A deputy. It's not like the Landing has a lot of crime. You must have worked the case." His wary eyes watched her. "Everybody says DeShaun Moton did it. The way you're reacting now, I get the idea you don't think that's true." Shying bonelessly away, he shook his head—in refusal, not denial. Julia clutched his shoulders, wishing she could shake it out of him. "Frank, please. This isn't just curiosity. This is—it's important. I have to know."

He hesitated, biting hard on his lower lip in agonized indecision, then crossed to the door and flipped the sign from HI, WE'RE OPEN! to BE BACK SOON! Then he beckoned her toward the back room. Julia, seeing that he was doing all the things you should never do when trying to avoid attention, worried about what unfortunate rumors might next fly through the chatty little village, but followed nevertheless.

(11)

THEY SAT AT A WORK TABLE drinking coffee. Chilly breezes sliced through a cracked window, but Frank Carrington, Yankee frugal, was not about to turn up the heat. Putting on an extra sweater was your job.

Frank came straight to the point, the reluctant penitent who had decided to confess all.

"You're right, Julia. I worked the Joule case. Everybody did. Look. The whole force in those days was a constable, two dispatchers, and three deputies. It was us, the state boys, a couple of detectives they loaned us from the city. There was pressure. Political pressure. The newspapers. In those days we didn't have so many professors. The town was . . . poor. Oh, sure, there were the big houses on the water, but mostly it was farmers and, on Main Street, a little bit of trade. We're kind of far from the city, and we weren't fashionable yet. So you see the problem. A little girl gets killed? The daughter of one of the few university types we have? Yes. There was pressure. Plenty of it. Old Arnie Huebner was constable in those days, and Tommy Highsmith was his boss. Tommy had been first selectman since Moses brought the tablets down from Sinai, and he must have been pushing eighty, but in those days the Landing was Tommy's town. And Arnie would come in every day and tell us how Tommy was complaining. And the Joules, well, they were pretty well connected. The governor would call, some people from Washington—you get the idea. They'd pressure Tommy, Tommy would pressure Arnie, Arnie would pressure the rest of us."

He was working on his second cup of coffee. Julia had barely sipped her first. He had offered her a sticky bun that also looked like it had come down with Moses. Outside the window, afternoon wind swirled yesterday's snow.

"Local pressure, too. The president of the university. The Lands. Gina was one of theirs. And the Whisteds—"

"Whisted? As in, Senator Whisted?"

"Sure. You know the Senator was a student in those days, right? Well, his family was pretty prominent politically in this state. You know that. What you might not know is that Merrill Joule was his godfather. Mal was close to the Joule family. Used to have dinner at their house a couple of times a month. Well, after Gina died, he was one of the loudest of the voices yelling for justice. He must have been—what?— twenty-one? He organized search parties, I mean until her body washed up. Then, after we found her, he'd be on the phone five times a day demanding action. Did this for about a week, and then I guess somebody must have called him off."

"Called him off?"

A tired shrug. Frank swallowed more coffee, pulled a sour face, then glanced toward the front shop window with such unease that Julia half expected the bad guys to burst in. "Well, he stopped bothering us. That's all I know. But we kept looking. As a matter of fact, we didn't really do anything else but work the Joule case."

A beat.

"That's the official story, anyway. And maybe it's partly true. I mean, yes, there was pressure, and plenty of it. But there's more. Julia, you know, the Landing—well, you probably think it's kind of a conservative town, and it is. Back in those days, well, if anything, we were more conservative. I like to think nowadays we're conservative in a useful way.

But back then, well, we were conservative in a bad way. And, well, there's no good way to say this." The antiques dealer was in motion, as if the table had become too constricting, and the back room too small. He was prowling the shelves, peeking here and there as if to find the rest of his tale.

"They didn't want to solve it. There. They didn't want to, Julia. They focused on DeShaun almost from the minute he was shot. Nobody else. Just DeShaun. There were rumors of a boyfriend, but we didn't track those down. And there were other leads we didn't check out." Frank had found a perch, swinging long legs as he sat on a bench, jammed between a couple of New England–style sewing machines, one of which might or might not have been a genuine Shaw & Clark "closed pillar" model. "All we did was concentrate on DeShaun. That's what they told us, and that's what we did. And Constable Huebner, well, he was mad about the whole thing, but what was he going to do? It's a good job, constable, especially in a little town like this one, with no crime. So he went along."

Julia said, "Who's 'they'?"

"They?"

"You said they didn't want it solved. You said they told you. I'm assuming that the same they told the constable what to do. Who were they?"

The words came out flat and uninflected, as if forcing themselves between unwilling lips. "I don't know. None of us knew. But there was pressure. We all knew that. And the constable said—"

On his feet again, facing away from her, face pressed against the window. "It was a day just like this," said Frank, and at first Julia thought it a non sequitur. "Snow pelting down like somebody was up there pouring it. We were in the squad room. That's what we called it. It was kind of a joke. Really what we had was this little corner of the town hall, down in the basement, in the back. Must have been about four, because I was just coming on shift. Arnie was there, and Ralphie Nacchio—he's dead now—and the day dispatcher, Cheryl Wysocki. She moved to Florida, I think. Anyway, it's just the four of us there, and Arnie's been at this meeting for hours. He comes in out of the storm, and he tells us, okay, that's it, put the chairs back on the tables till next time. It was one of his expressions. He meant the hunt was over. This was, let's see, um, three or four days after the black boy got shot. Four days, maybe. He came in and stood there dripping all over the floor and told us it was over, and how it was time to get back to business as usual. And Ralphie, well, Ralphie always had this mouth on him—he asked Arnie exactly what business was that. Because Ralphie was the one who'd heard those boyfriend rumors that the state boys never did anything about. And Ralphie had other leads, too. He was a good cop. Anyway, Ralphie said, um, if we're not in the business of solving murders, we shouldn't be in business. Arnie gave him this look he used to have if he thought you were being insolent? Like he might pick you up and put you through the window? Arnie said, the last time he checked, he didn't follow Ralphie's orders. Well, so Ralphie shut up. I respected Arnold Huebner. But this one was too much. Arnie was a good man, but in this case he was following orders, and the orders stunk. Call me a moral coward if you want. I didn't argue, but I still couldn't be a part of the force any more. Six months later—seven—I quit. Ralphie left the next year. And that was the end of that."

"No," said Julia, the analytical part of her mind trumping her flaming red fury. "No, Frank. That's not the end of that."

"It's all I know," he insisted.

"I don't think so. You still can't meet my eyes. There's something you're not telling me."

"Julia—"

"There's more to the story. And Kellen Zant knew what the more was, didn't he? Maybe he even asked you about it, when he came in to buy the cheval."

Silence, but the chin lifted briefly before the antiques dealer swung away toward the window once more.

"Come on, Frank. Why did you tell me all this?"

"Because it's time, Julia. It's time for the lies to stop. It's time for the town to pay."

"The town?"

Rich with pain and rimmed with fear, the eyes met hers once more. "Arnie kept a diary," Frank said. "And, well, I think he wrote down all the reasons he thought DeShaun didn't do it. Maybe he even wrote down who he thinks did do it. And I'll bet he wrote down who pressured him to say it was DeShaun." He paused. "Nobody knows what happened to the diary, Julia. People around town know he kept one, but nobody knows where it is. Not even his boy. Mitch. Ten, twelve years ago, Mitch offered some kind of cash reward if anybody came up with it. No takers." He glanced around the shop as if expecting to find the diary on the shelf. "Me? I think it doesn't exist any more."

"Why?"

"Because it hasn't turned up. See, Julia, ask yourself. Somebody puts pressure on Arnold Huebner to drop the case. Arnold Huebner's diary goes missing. If I was the one who put the pressure on and I got my hands on the diary, I'd just burn it. I wouldn't keep it around."

Julia remembered Tony Tice outside the restaurant, telling her about the item his client was trying to buy. She said, "Did you tell Kellen Zant any of this?"

Frank swung back from the window. "Any of what?"

"About the diary?"

A slow shake of the head, as if the idea was new to him. "I'm sorry, Julia. It's like I told you. Kellen Zant didn't come to the shop to talk about Gina. He came to the shop to buy that antique mirror."

At the door, her carefully wrapped purchase in her arms, Julia had a final question. "What if the person who had it wasn't the same person who put the pressure on?"

The dealer spread his soft hands. "I don't think I follow you."

"The diary. Arnold Huebner's diary. Maybe whoever closed down the investigation didn't find it. Maybe somebody hid it to keep it away from . . . from the bad guys."

"I guess that's possible." He sounded skeptical. "I don't know, though. Because, if it was me who had it? I'd have made it public. Cleared that poor black boy's name."

"I can think of two other possibilities," said Julia, mostly to herself.

"What are they?"

"Maybe it's still hidden, and the good guys haven't found it yet. Or maybe—"

But she stopped herself. She was not about to offer the worst possibility of all, that Kellen had somehow gotten his greedy hands on Arnold Huebner's diary and, instead of clearing DeShaun, had auctioned it to the highest bidder.

"Maybe you shouldn't come around for a while, Julia. A fella could get into bad trouble, talking about these things."

(I I I)

JULIA MARCHED OUT THE DOOR, the newly purchased Federal mirror from the Winterthur book under her arm, intending to hit Cookie's before it closed, and hit instead a patch of black ice at the bottom of the steps. Her feet went out from under her, the mirror shattered on the sidewalk, and her head would have hit the nearest wall had a strong hand not chosen that moment to grab her.

What happened next was confusing.

Mitch Huebner, broad and red-faced and boozily unshaven beneath his watch cap, had firm hold of her shoulders and jerked her to her feet, then saw who she was and got up in her face, thick finger waggling, demanding that she stop spreading all these lies about how he had broken her lights and refused to pay. Julia, dizzy from the fall, and dizzier from the coincidence of meeting him immediately after hearing Frank's story, at first had literally no idea what Huebner was talking about. He said that it was hurting his business, that he never in his life had refused to pay for damage he had done, but he resented being pressured to pay for harm he had never caused, and his words were all gibberish to her, sheer gibberish.

Then Mitch stopped and turned away and said what sounded like "Oof!"—exactly the way they used to write it in the comic books—and Jeremy Flew was between them, palms raised toward the larger man as if to make peace, but also effectively holding him away from Julia—at some risk to himself, she realized, should Mr. Huebner decide to take a hammy fist to the little man's slender face.

"Please leave Mrs. Carlyle alone," said Flew reasonably. "We don't want any trouble."

"Who the hell are you?" he demanded, confused. Bleary eyes measured Flew, then flashed at Julia. "I'm not making trouble. She's the one making trouble."

"Please do not put your hands on Mrs. Carlyle again."

"She's telling everybody these lies—"

"Please," said Flew again, the voice of sweet reason in the middle of the wintry street. A couple of passersby had stopped to watch the fun. Julia, every bit as bewildered as Mitch Huebner, had no idea where on earth the sprite had materialized from.

"This is a private conversation," Huebner snapped, and tried to push past, but Flew moved with him, keeping between the adversaries.

"Please do not do this, sir."

"She's libeling me!"

"I believe you mean she's slandering you," said Flew, still smiling.

So Mitch Huebner put his hands on the little man instead, sweeping him aside in a rage, except that the bigger man wound up sitting on the frozen sidewalk, Flew still standing there with his hands up and out. Huebner started to get up, and Flew shoved him down again. It seemed to take little effort. His smile never wavered.

"Who the hell are you?" said Mitch again, but with less force. He was so large and, to those in the Landing, so scary. Thirty years ago, he had been the great bully in the local schools: Landingers still trembled when they told the stories. But here he was, sitting on his derrière, obviously in no hurry to try getting up again. Julia felt for him.

"A friend of Mrs. Carlyle's."

"Well, you better not touch me again."

"Please stay away from Mrs. Carlyle," said Flew again, like an automaton.

Julia said, "Jeremy, wait."

"I'm just trying to—"

"Let him up."

The little man stepped hastily back, and Mr. Huebner climbed to his feet. He jabbed an angry finger at Flew. "You try that again, you little bastard, we'll see who winds up on top."

"No, thank you," said Flew, with a polite bow. But he remained between the larger man and Julia, and she saw something in the playful eyes that frightened her.

She said, "You're right, Mr. Huebner. I'm sorry."

"You what?"

"I'm sorry to have accused you falsely. I'm sure you didn't break my lampposts, and I was wrong to tell anybody that you did. Please forgive me. I hope that you'll be taking care of our driveway for years to come."

She shook his astonished hand, his huge paw swallowing her tiny one.

"I'd like to ask you a question if I could."

"What question?" he asked, sullen eyes still on Jeremy Flew.

"It's about your father—"

"What about him?"

"I was wondering if you ever found his diary."

Violence rose in the puffy red eyes, and Flew, sensing the recharged atmosphere, moved closer. But Huebner only glared at her, then turned on his heel and stalked off.

Escorting her to the Escalade, little Flew broke out in paroxysms of nervous laughter. "I never did that before. I've had self-defense classes for years, but I never got to use them. Know what? I can see why people go to war. It's fun!"

"When you win," muttered Julia, who had seen humiliation and its close cousin, murder, warring in Mitch Huebner's eyes before she sounded retreat. But Mr. Flew just went on laughing his delighted executioner's laugh, and Julia, slogging through the snow, forgot to ask how on earth he had shown up just when needed. She was too busy wondering who exactly her husband had invited beneath their roof.

And why.

CHAPTER 31

FRIENDLY ADVICE

(1)

THE FOLLOWING AFTERNOON, Senator Malcolm Whisted spoke at a campaign rally on the edge of campus, a risky decision in the middle of final exams, but the only time he could squeeze in a visit to his home state. He made a total of four appearances in that one day, not counting his informal tea with the political-science students, his own major before he had gone into the State Department, then graduate school, then a university sinecure of his own, then electoral politics. That night the Senator dined at the home of his old friends Lemaster and Julia Carlyle. The event was carefully not styled a fund-raiser, because Lemaster and Julia were hosting in their dual roles—as president and first lady of the university, and also as dear old friends of Senator Malcolm Whisted and his wife, Maureen—and could not, in either role, be seen as partisan.

Said Lemaster.

To the surprise of the meteorologists, the weather held, so everybody came. Once the renovations on the presidential mansion were complete, the Carlyles would entertain on campus, but for now a dinner at home meant Tyler's Landing. The guest list at Hunter's Heights was forty-two strong, not counting aides. Food was served buffet style. There was lots of eating on laps as the old roommates, very loudly, traded stories. Most of the guests were faculty, who mostly fawned over the Senator, perhaps jockeying for places in the forthcoming administration, perhaps merely exulting at the thought that the forces of the Antichrist might shortly be driven from the White House. Some were the dignitaries of Elm Harbor. Some were Carlyle acquaintances from the Landing, because to try to find "friends" would have taxed their abilities. Back in grimy, dilapidated Elm Harbor, which Julia had been in so great a hurry to leave, neighbors of several colors had been on their doorstep with casseroles and freshly baked cookies the day they moved in, and, through the process of reciprocal invitation, the Carlyle family had made friends. Six years on Hunter's Meadow Road, where the houses stood continents apart, and Julia had learned the names of perhaps two families in the near vicinity. Here was the secret segregated truth at the heart of integration. No vandalism was committed. No crosses were burned. No epithets were uttered. The family was not attacked. It was simply ignored.

But, for Malcolm Whisted's dinner, suddenly everybody wanted to come. Mostly people crowded around the guest of honor, who, like all successful politicians, possessed the gift of seeming to lavish every bit of attention on your little question or concern even when his mind was on tomorrow's speech or this morning's *Times* editorial. His aides kept coming over to whisper: another competition between the roommates was over who would be called away to the telephone the most times. Across the foyer was a library equipped with a private bath, so that it could double as an extra guest room. Senator Whisted had converted it into his temporary office for the evening, a place to take his calls or answer questions from his aides. As the evening wore on, he spent more and more time closeted inside.

Julia moved dutifully from group to group, wishing Lemaster were beside her instead of across the room doing the same thing. In the bay window near the piano, Suzanne de Broglie from the divinity school was explaining dreamily to Donna Newman, doyenne of Landing society, how no moral person could support the blood-for-oil hegemony of the current Administration. Out in the solarium, Marcus Hadley, a law professor and old crony of Lemaster's, was lecturing Gayle Gittelman, the county's leading criminal-defense lawyer, on how support for school vouchers among poor black parents in the inner city should be ignored, for it was simply evidence of careful racist brainwashing. Julia, who had loved the darkly joyous Clannish boister of Harlem parties when she was a little girl, had come to hate the confident white preachiness of the campus parties to which her status required her to go.

Now and then Lemaster smiled at her across the room as he worked it, or even kissed her as he passed, but Julia saw nothing straight just now, and suspected her husband of putting on a show for his guests.

At some point in the evening, as Julia struggled to extricate herself from a conversation in the corner of the living room about how the family could in good conscience worship at a crazed right-wing congregation like Saint Matthias, Jeremy Flew tapped her on the shoulder and asked to borrow Mrs. Carlyle for a minute.

"The Senator would like a word with you," murmured the little man, turning her over to one of the Senator's people, who knocked on the library door. Inside, Malcolm Whisted was sitting atop the desk, tie loosened, one long leg swinging, his elegant wife, Maureen, sagging exhausted in an armchair.

Maureen said, "Thank you for having us to dinner, Julia."

"It's our pleasure. And our honor."

"We really need to get together more often. You need to call us next time you're in Washington." Using *need* like a command. "We can't let it be this long again."

"I agree," said Julia, trying unsuccessfully to watch them both.

A look passed between the pair. The Senator said, "I'd like to explain about what happened with Astrid."

"Oh, no, no, you don't have to—"

"I run only clean campaigns, Julia. No other kind."

"You need to understand that," ordered Maureen, perfect political wife and, some said, the brains of the outfit. "You need to remember what kind of man my husband is."

Whisted glared at her, but contrived to turn it into a fond gaze before Julia could be sure. His voice had the tone and conviction of the answer to a reporter's question. "Astrid Venable worked hard for us. I wish her all the best. But she wanted to dig up dirt on our opponents, and we don't do that." Eyes still on his wife. "We're the good guys."

"I understand," said Julia, hands massaging each other nervously behind her back.

"And we ask our opponents for the same courtesy," the Senator said.

"Of course."

"Nobody's a saint, Julia. Everybody has secrets in the past. I do. You do. Everybody does."

She went very still.

"What my husband is saying," Maureen explained, unnecessarily, eyes tightly shut, "is that we all had our wild periods." She brushed graying hair from her forehead. She had slipped off her shoes. Long ago, before her husband got into national politics, Maureen used to tell people she could read palms and auras. One night, at a party in the Hamptons, she had read Julia's, predicting decades of warmth and joy. "I can't imagine why anybody would try to dig those things up. You have to realize it has nothing to do with how a man would govern."

"Campaigns should be about ideas," said the Senator.

"Not about personalities," added his wife.

"About the future."

"Not about the past."

"About who a man is now."

"Not who a man used to be."

A knock on the door, an aide poking his head in. The Senator said they would be another minute, and the head disappeared. Everybody was in motion. The Senator was straightening his tie, Maureen was slipping on her shoes, Julia was backing away. Somehow Whisted had her hand in his and pumped it twice, then continued to hold on, dark, sincere eyes burning into hers. "Let's keep the campaign clean," he said, and slipped out to meet his admirers.

Maureen lingered. "Julia."

"Yes, Maureen."

"My husband is a good man. You need to know that."

Julia felt tired and, unaccountably, afraid. She had thought it was Scrunchy. If it was one of the Horsemen, it was Scrunchy. But now she was less sure.

"I know that, Maureen. I promise."

"He had a youth. We all had a youth."

"I understand."

"Julia, listen to me." Taking both of Julia's hands in both of hers. Maureen was a tall woman, in small ways endearingly awkward despite the surface elegance. "Nobody cares about what anybody did at that age. Most of us did things at that age we wish we hadn't. My husband did things I'm sure he wishes he hadn't. But he would never hurt anybody. Never."

"Maureen—"

"My husband is not a wealthy man, Julia." A sudden smile, like unexpected treasure. "The Whisteds have always believed in public service."

"I understand," said Julia, who did not.

"I'm sorry about Astrid. Truly sorry. Please don't hold it against my husband. It's going to be a tough campaign. Astrid understands."

"Believe me, Maureen, I don't hold anything against your husband."

"Good. I'm so glad." A long look, as if considering how much to tell. Then a polished detour. "Call me when you're in Washington. We need to spend more time together."

"Thank you."

"Or if we can do anything for you. Call."

"I will." She tugged but could not get her hands free. "Thanks."

"It's the Landing," Maureen explained, eyes hammering at her. Her flesh was slick and warm. Julia squirmed. "I remember from when we lived here. The Landing affects people. The things that happen here are always so—"

She stopped, hugged, went out.

(11)

IN THE FOYER, Julia said goodbye to the Senator and his wife and, rubbing her eyes, watched as the tide drifted out, the last few stragglers among the guests draining toward the door. The Senator wanted her to stop. As simple as that. Malcolm Whisted wanted Kellen's surplus to stay buried, and so did his wife.

Which meant—

"So—you heard about Tice?" Marcus Hadley was suddenly beside her, white and hefty and confidently judgmental. His family had been around the university even longer than the Lands. His uncle had been one of Lemaster's predecessors as president. His grandfather had discovered a famous dinosaur fossil. Back when Marc and Lemaster were professors together, they used to run a competition—a serious one, with rules nobody else understood—to figure out which of the two was the most brilliant member of the law faculty. "That lawyer? The one with the commercials?"

"Tony Tice?" she said, as foreboding rose.

"Right. Lemaster told me how he bothered you."

Julia realized that she had been holding her glass all this time. She handed it to a waiter, feeling the room waver. "What about him? What did he do now?"

"Beat up his girlfriend. Gayle Gittelman was telling us."

"What? He did what?"

"Tice. Tricky Tony." Eying her. "He's been arrested."

CHAPTER 32

DENNISON

(I)

THE FOLLOWING MONDAY, Julia and Lemaster drove up to New Hampshire to pick up Aaron at Exeter, where the fourteen-year-old was marvelously popular, perhaps because of his considerable charm, or perhaps because his father was president of a university where a not-inconsiderable number of the school's graduates hoped to matriculate. They had decided to do it together, but conversation during the drive was more muted than usual. Preston had called the night before from Cambridge to announce that he would not be home for Christmas. He and his latest girlfriend were heading to Mexico. Julia was stunned. None of the children had ever missed Christmas. She pleaded. She argued. Preston was, as always, immovable. She decided to detour and see him, but Preston told her not to bother: they were leaving on the early flight.

Tonya Montez, chief local Sister Lady, liked to say that parenthood was the process of watching your children slowly lose interest in you. With her eldest, that process was already over.

They drove by his apartment anyway, just to be sure. There was no answer at the buzzer. "I suppose he already left," said Lemaster.

"I suppose," said Julia, worried, secretly, that Preston was ignoring them. She wished she knew why her firstborn so determinedly avoided his parents. If wishes were horses, Granny Vee used to say, then beggars would ride. Around Preston she always felt like a beggar.

Leaving Cambridge, they headed across the bridge into Boston and stopped at a row house in the endless maze of narrow, crooked historic streets of Beacon Hill. Parking is impossible but Lemaster eventually managed the miracle, squeezing the Mercedes into a spot that looked, at first glance, large enough to hold a child's bicycle. He pumped his fist, because beating the odds was his hobby, and she kissed his cheek, because congratulating him was hers. The sky had the flat, hazy look that comes only from heavy smog or heavy weather. Their feet slid on the bumpy, cobbled sidewalk, the stones slippery because not every homeowner was equally diligent in clearing the seasonal mess. The houses were of stout brick, cramped and expensive. Few had lawns of any consequence. Windows opened directly into the street, like they did in many parts of Europe; walking past, you caught glimpses of neighbors sleeping, shaving, dressing, embracing, the full spectrum of activity among the newly wakened. Julia felt newly wakened herself. For the first time in years, she was taking risks. She would find Kellen's evidence and save her daughter: unless, of course, her pride led to a fall, which she admitted was always possible.

The house was just like all the others, except that it sat on a corner lot and had slightly more than a postage stamp of a yard, guarded by a low wrought-iron fence in need of painting. Standing on the front step, they had an excellent view down the hill toward the Boston Common and the Public Garden. The brass knocker was an eagle, easily a hundred years old. A tall nurse of improbable beauty admitted them and whispered in a Haitian accent that Mr. Dennison was doing a little better today. Better than what? Julia wondered, but dared not ask. The nurse led them straight along the narrow hall to a chamber at the back of the house that could serve as dining room, parlor, or game room, because Bay Dennison, back in the day, had run a high-stakes poker game at which the powerful could do their dealing well beyond the scrutiny of the press; except, of course, for those members of the press who were invited to play.

The old man was in his wheelchair, wrapped to mid-chest in blankets, ignoring the view. He had lost weight to his several illnesses—his body was guilty of as many transgressions as the doctors chose to test for—but retained an insolent heft across the shoulders and a determined set to his jowly yellow jaw that reminded you of the power he had once wielded in American politics. Usually he would have a gofer present, but he fired them fast and, according to Lemaster, was between assistants just now. On the rolling table before him were scattered page proofs for the forthcoming third volume of his best-selling autobiography, and when they entered, he was hunched over, pencil in hand, furiously correcting the prose, obviously excited at the opportunity to spew more venom, although God alone knew who was left for him to skewer.

"With you in a minute," he snapped without turning.

"Take your time, sir," said Lemaster, and Julia glanced at her husband, who looked ready to stand and wait all day if commanded. He responded this way to nobody else. In fact, she had never heard him refer to another living soul as "sir." She had never fathomed all the dimensions of her husband's relationship with the man. But thirty-odd years ago, Representative Byron Dennison had started a far younger Lemaster on his path to professional glory, spotting the boundless potential in the summer intern, taking him beneath the same capacious wing that had launched so many other careers in the same generation of African America, opening doors, smoothing his path, and, as the years went by, making sure he stuck to it.

Unlike most of them, Lemaster never forgot.

"Not much time left," the old man countered, scribbling hard with the red pencil. Peeking over his shoulder, Julia saw that he was now chasing the ghosts of his former friends in the civil-rights movement. Just what the country needed.

"You'll outlive us all, Mr. Dennison," said her husband.

"Only if you're all planning to go in the next six months."

"You should try to think positive."

"Give me a reason." He turned a page and returned to his agonistic scribbling. "Anyway, thinking positive didn't help Zant, did it? Poor bastard. I thought they were all through lynching our people down your way."

Lemaster smiled behind his mentor's back. "I brought Julia."

The head came up, the chair made a circle, and a welcoming smile spread over the ravaged gray face, flesh hanging in loose folds as if ready to peel. One of the eyes was faded and wheeling, but the other was bright and sharp as ever. "So you did. Not that you ever deserved her. She's too good for you, Little Master"—which was what Dennison always used to call him, and therefore still did. But Lemaster loved him, and they all knew it. In two months it would be time for the old man's birthday party, still a raucous affair attended by hundreds of movers and shakers, an event Lemaster had never missed, and nowadays helped organize. "How about you, Julia? Had your fifteen allotted affairs yet? Because you should be looking for somebody better, gorgeous creature that you are. If I were married to Little Master here, I'd have left him

years ago. I don't know how you put up with him. You're a saint. A mar-
tyr. They'll give you a statue. Listen, you can have mine. They're
unveiling my bust up at the Capitol. Stupid-ass amateur idea. I'm not
going. They said, It's a short walk. I said, Do I look to you like I can
walk? Amateurs."

"It's good to see you, too, Bay," she said, smiling back, because he
never expected any response to his bombast, and he had commanded
her, years ago, to use his nickname, one of his many tricks to keep
Lemaster in his place. He tried to keep all his protégés in their places;
what made Lemaster different was his willingness to stay there, a trait
Julia admired in him, even though she could not quite say why.

"How's your mother?"

"Thriving."

"Still in France? Robbing the cradle?" Because Mona lived near
Toulouse with an Englishman called Hap, twenty years her junior—
short, said Mona, for *happiness*.

"She says she's not coming back until we're a democracy again."

Bay Dennison never precisely laughed: more a bray of delight,
amused and condescending, as if he alone saw the world authentic and
whole. "That'll be the day." Another guffaw. "So, any new books on the
way?" He waved at the sheets on his rolling table. "I have to judge the
competition."

Julia shook her head. Mona had not published a volume in over a
decade, although her furious essays still found an audience in the more
marginal publications of righteously hating left anger. "You'll have the
stores all to yourself, Bay."

"I dated her once. Maybe twice. You were just a little girl." The
good eye lapped at her as a younger man's might. According to Lemaster, the worst of his tumors was behind the bad one. "Did she ever tell
you?"

"Yes, Bay. You told me, too."

"We went to the White House. LBJ was President. Danced all
night. Lyndon danced with her, too. Wouldn't let her go. And poor
Lady Bird leaned over to me and said, 'I don't mind him dancing, but
why does he have to slobber all over her?' " Dennison laughed, so his
guests laughed, too. The story had appeared in the second volume of
his memoirs. Most historians and Johnson insiders thought it no truer
than the rest of Bay's angrily exaggerated memories, many of which led
to furious denials. But he wisely protected himself from liability by

defaming only the dead. "I liked LBJ. People hated him for Vietnam, but he was the best of them all. Did the Civil Rights Act. Great Society. Voting Rights Act. Knew how to sit in a back room and drink whiskey and make deals. If you shook his hand, he'd keep his word. That's what matters, Julia. Keeping your word." A sly glance at Little Master, as if expecting an argument.

"I agree," said Lemaster, right on cue.

Still Byron Dennison addressed himself only to Julia. "Know what the problem is nowadays? We haven't had a real drinker in the White House since Nixon. Don't know how they get anything done without the stuff. No wonder they're all at each other's throats. Too much tee-totaling down in Washington, if you want my opinion."

"You could be right." We visit the dying to seek their permission to go on living, Granny Vee used to say. Maybe that explains why we agree with whatever they tell us.

"I liked Nixon, too. He'd do you a deal. Just lock up the silver and keep your hands on the table."

"So you keep telling me, Bay."

"Sit in my lap."

"I can't. I have to watch my blood pressure." Dennison laughed, the sound spluttery and wet, and Julia, smiling to make sure he knew her mood was gay, voiced the question his earlier comment had sparked. "Did you know him, Bay? Kellen Zant?"

He slapped the table in mirth. "Everybody knew that old faker."

"Faker?"

"Mau-Maued everybody into hiring him. Made a fortune off of being the official, true-blue, certified Negro economist." The good eye swiveled her way. Lemaster stood mute, a spectator at the play. "I liked him. Yeah, he was a faker. But he was my kind of faker."

"I don't understand."

"Sure you do. Zant would call up some corporation and say, 'How come you don't have any black consultants?' Then he'd threaten to go on television and make a stink about how they didn't have any. And guess what? They'd hire him."

Despite her husband's presence and her respect for the old man, Julia could not keep a certain stiffness from her voice. "He was good at what he did. Those models to calculate the proper valuation of options—"

More laughter. Like most men accustomed to power, Byron Dennison valued his own opinions above other people's facts. "He *was* good at what he did. And what he did best was making money for Kellen Zant. I know he *said* he was doing it for his client. I know he *said* he was doing it for the people. But he was *really* doing it for Kellen Zant."

"I'm just saying—"

"You don't have to defend your boyfriends to me, Julia. I told you I liked him."

Cheeks flaming, Julia tried to answer, but the old man grabbed her wrist, stopped laughing, and tugged her close to whisper in her ear.

"Trust your husband," he murmured, dying breath hot and moist.

"I try," Julia said, very surprised, as Lemaster busied himself examining his mentor's ego wall.

The grip was iron. "Try harder. It matters."

After that came the part of the visit Julia hated. After ritual hugs, and ritual drinks, and ritual questions about the children, she was politely but firmly banished from the house. Bay Dennison studied his protégé's face and told Julia to return in an hour. Knowing this moment would come, she had worn loose pants and sneakers. And, after an autumn spent far too close to Cookie's, she could use the exercise. So she left the two men alone. This was their element, scheming together. Bay Dennison had been for many years supreme leader of the Empyreals, and Lemaster, through the two decades she had known him, had never made a major decision without consulting his mentor first. The Empyreals might be a good distance from the top of the heap, but the connection still mattered, and her husband nurtured it.

She wondered what decision he was making now.

Julia stopped in a deli for a bottle of water, and then walked through the Public Garden, finding it surprisingly crowded. There was old snow on the ground, but the temperature was in the forties, perfect walking weather. She stayed on the main paths, crossing each bridge several times, striding hard past the statues and monuments, because she was working out, not sightseeing, working hard because she was out of shape. The third time Julia passed the greening statue of the abolitionist Wendell Phillips, Mary Mallard was sitting on the bench, smiling at her.

"I'm full of surprises," the writer said.

MARY HAD HER SNEAKERS ON TOO, so they walked together. She lit a cigarette, but Julia made her put it out.

"You've changed," said Mary, adjusting her scarf.

"I certainly hope so."

"I like you this way. You have your shit together. You make eye contact. You're confident. You even walk differently."

Julia had to laugh. "All that in a few weeks." Then: "What are you doing here, Mary? You obviously followed me."

"From Elm Harbor? That would take some fancy driving, not to be seen."

"All right, you're a fancy driver."

They were passing the swan boats, stacked and covered for the season. On the shore, a bevy of children played an intricate game of freeze tag, watched over by nuns. "I'm here because you need help, Julia. You can't do this alone."

"I've been walking alone most of my life."

"I mean, track down what Kellen was working on. It's obvious that's what you're up to. Obvious to me, anyway." She waved a hand. "And that accounts for the aura you've got these days, too." She laughed alone this time. She even had her own water bottle, and swigged deeply. "Seriously, Julia. You need my help. I can keep you out of trouble. Save you from mistakes. Share my resources. My expertise."

"Mary—"

"And I can tell you things you can't possibly know."

"Like what?"

They had reached a set of boulders. Mary sat while Julia stretched. "Like, I'm not the only person who followed you today."

Julia's first instinct, quite irresistible, was to glance wildly around, although she had no idea what, or whom, she was looking for. Her next was to glower. "You made that up."

Mary shrugged. "Maybe I did. Maybe I didn't. That's the point. You wouldn't even think to wonder. And if you did wonder, you wouldn't know what to look for."

"And you would?"

"Of course. The kind of books I write? I pick up surveillance now and then."

Along with hubris and paranoia, Julia thought, but did not say. Mary was right. She could not do this alone. More to the point, she didn't want to. A partner would be wonderful. The question was whether Mary Mallard was the right one.

"Tell me exactly what Kellen told you."

"This really is a new you, isn't it?"

"Come on, Mary. You're auditioning for a place. What was Kellen up to? What did he say?"

The writer sighed and gazed off toward the pond. The *Make Way for Ducklings* sculpture glistened darkly in the bright winter sun. Clearly Mary wanted that cigarette, and Julia took a perverse pride in denying permission. "Kellen came to see me a few months ago. We had met when I interviewed him for my book on the corporate accounting scandals. Kellen earned a ton of money from his lectures, and he lectured on the scandals, and, well, anyway, we met. He loved capitalism, wasn't worried by its excesses, believed markets could mostly regulate themselves. And he loved to argue. I learned not to disagree with what he said, because winning meant so much to him. And, yes, if you're wondering, he came on to me a couple of times, but, well, that was never going anywhere." She put her hands flat on the rock, tilted her head back, closed her eyes to take the sun. "So, anyway, he called me last summer and said he had come up with something that would interest me. I suggested we have a drink the next time he was in D.C., which we did, about a week later. Late July, I think, because I go to Maine in August. He told me about Gina Joule. I'd never heard of her. He told me the story, and I told him there are a million stories like that one. I wasn't interested unless there was a book in it, or at least an article. He said this was different. This wasn't just some black boy lynched for allegedly killing a white girl. This was a black boy who died in the place of somebody who mattered. That was Kellen's term. Somebody who mattered."

"So you got interested."

"A little. Not too much. Given what I do for a living, people peddle these tales all the time. But then he told me about Hilliman Suite, and who lived there, and I got very, very interested. He said he was pretty sure he could prove that one of the guys from Hilliman Suite was at least dating her, which would already blow a hole in the official story, and maybe blow the election wide open. He said with enough time he was sure he could prove more. He said he would put it on the market.

He would do an auction to capture the surplus. An all-pay auction, he said. I didn't know what that was, but it didn't matter. I asked why he was telling me. I don't pay for information, I said, even information that can blow an election wide open. He said he needed somebody who knew how to present things. He wanted me to write up his findings for this auction. I told him that wasn't exactly the business I was in, but, believe me, Julia, by now I was hooked. I wanted that story. The trouble was, he wanted me to swear never to tell a soul. Well, I make my money by writing about what I learn, not by keeping it secret. We argued for a couple of weeks, and then he said he would send me a teaser, so I'd know he was on the level. In September I got a photograph in the mail. No return address, by the way, and no note, but the postmark said Elm Harbor."

"What was in the photo?" Julia asked, because Mary had paused and was pursing her lips, perhaps drawing on the imaginary cigarette.

"It was a young man on a sofa asleep. That was all. A young man, late teens, early twenties, asleep on a sofa. I called Kellen, I told him this didn't help. He told me if I could identify the young man he would identify where it was taken. So I did. It didn't take long, because I knew who he was investigating. It was a photo of Senator Malcolm Whisted when he was in college. When I told Kellen, he sent me a note, with an address on it in Tyler's Landing. I looked up the address at the time the Senator was a student, and, sure enough, it was Merrill and Anna Joule's house."

"That's not much to go on."

"That's what I told him. Same thing I told you at the funeral. The fact that Senator Whisted slept at her house once didn't prove anything. The Whisteds knew everybody. Kellen asked if it would matter if he told me young Mal was drunk at the time. I said no. In college everybody's drunk all the time. Kellen laughed. He said that's why it's called a teaser."

"And that was it?"

"Not quite." Mary pursed her lips, wanting that cigarette badly. "He said the whole case really proved why nonrivalrous consumption was almost impossible."

"Spell that for me."

Mary did, and loaned Julia a pencil and paper to write it down. "It means—" the writer began, but Julia held up her hand. She did not want Mary's explanations. Or her biases.

"Thanks." Julia looked at her watch. "I have to go."

"Lemaster's with Bay Dennison, right?"

"You're very good at this, Mary."

"Hey, I don't need you to tell me that." She stood up. "So, do we have a deal?"

"No."

The white woman's face fell. "But I told you—"

"Mary, listen. You're half right. I do need help. And I can certainly use yours. I'd love it if you signed on. But if you do, you have to know that it's my project, not yours, and the information I give you will be the information I choose to give you." She considered. "And you can't write anything without my permission."

"Are you sure you and Kellen weren't married or anything? I mean, you talk just the same."

"Oh, and one more thing. We get Christmas season off."

Mary was appalled. "You know, Julia, the Iowa caucuses are in two months."

"If you can solve the mystery without me before then, you're welcome to it."

"And here I thought I was the bitch."

Julia smiled. This being-in-charge business was fun.

CHAPTER 33

'TIS THE SEASON

(1)

CHRISTMAS SLIPSTREAMED PAST the family like a billboard beside
the highway, first a distant glimmer, then looming closer and larger,
then suddenly full and bright and cheery and easy to read, but blink and
it is in the rearview mirror, beyond the curve you just passed, and gone.
Astrid and her children came to town, the hatchet having evidently
been buried between the cousins, and even went to midnight mass at
Saint Matthias, where, following the service, Lemaster showed an
unaccustomed lack of tact, complaining to anyone who would listen
about the Nativity scene near the altar. He objected, said Lemaster, not
to the blond whiteness of the Baby Jesus or the decidedly Aryan features of Mary and Joseph, but, rather, to the presence and number of
the wise men, the Magi. Matthew's Gospel, he argued over coffee in the
parish hall, did not specify the number of Magi, but did note explicitly
that they visited the child (not baby) Jesus at his house—not, as tradition has it, in the manger where he was born. The shepherds, not the
wise men, were led to the manger. The senior warden, pale as a cadaver
and nearly as animated, murmured in his funeral tones that tradition
was what kept people Anglican, but Lemaster was unmoved. Tradition
was one thing, he said. Defying the Gospels was another.
  Riding home, the Escalade bravely holding course around the slick
curves, Lemaster fulminated to his wife, and to part of his family—
others rode with Aunt Astrid in her Lincoln Navigator—on the matter
of the church's resistance to what seemed to him the plain truth. When
her father finally paused for breath in the vast family quiet, Vanessa, in
the back, leaned forward between the plush bucket seats and asked

sweetly whether it was really likely that Dads alone had it right and everyone else, who had followed the tradition for centuries, right down to those who celebrated, *con mucho gusto*, Three Kings Day, had it wrong. Before he could answer, she continued, "It's like Saint Paul's journeys in the first century. We don't know all the places he went. The Bible doesn't tell us. But tradition fills in the answers, right? The tradition teaches that he went to Spain, it's unbroken and pretty much unchallenged, and so we say, yes, okay, he probably went to Spain. So— what's wrong with accepting the tradition that there were in fact three wise men? After all, it's not as if the Bible says there was some other number."

Lemaster started to reply—gently, as he always did when Vanessa spoke—but he stopped because he noticed, the same time everyone else in the car did, that her mouth was still moving although her words had dried up. When they arrived at Hunter's Heights, Jeremy Flew, who seemed to have no home of his own, had eggnog waiting, delicately spiked, and he helped the children leave cookies and milk for Santa. Four young people then scurried for their bedrooms to allow the grown-ups to wrap the gifts—none of them from Mona, who always forgot, and apologized later. Julia tried to send Vanessa to bed, too, but her daughter, pronouncing herself too old for such nonsense, refused. Instead she sat in the kitchen drinking one Diet Sprite after another and rereading a dog-eared book about Roman military strategy.

"What are you doing?" Aunt Astrid asked at one point.

"Reading."

"I mean, why do you spend so much time reading about war? When we should all be working together for peace?"

Vanessa never looked up. "Getting ready," she said.

That was how they spent Christmas Eve.

(11)

BRUCE VALLELY SPENT THE LATE AFTERNOON of Christmas Eve at the shopping mall in Norport, although not shopping. He sat in the Mustang convertible with the top up, in a far corner of the parking lot, talking to Rick Chrebet, whose family thought he was picking up a few last-minute gifts. Rick kept saying he was risking his pension if he got caught. But he passed along some of his notes anyway. Back home, Bruce marveled at the amount of work Rick had managed before the investigation had shut down. He had even determined, by a similar but not identical path of reasoning, that Lemaster Carlyle was a possible suspect. Rick, less impulsive than his former partner, had also troubled to obtain an item that Bruce had overlooked.

A copy of Lemaster's résumé.

One look sent Bruce's theory of the case out the window.

Gina Joule had disappeared in February 1973, during Lemaster's junior year.

The résumé was explicit and unambiguous: *January–June 1973, study at Oxford.*

When the university reopened for business after New Year's Day, Bruce would check the dates to be sure the résumé was accurate. But he knew already that it would be. Unless the future president of the university had rushed home to the States just in time to kill Gina Joule and fly back to England, Lemaster could not have done the deed. That did not mean that he could not have murdered Zant, but it reduced the likelihood considerably.

Bruce would be forced, against his inclination, to look to other possibilities. He put away his work and went out into the living room where Laurie, his daughter, home from college, was decorating the tree.

(I I I)

ON CHRISTMAS DAY, hidden in the down news cycle, Cameron Knowland quietly cut all ties to the President's re-election campaign. His office released a letter, scarcely noticed by the media until another week had gone by, in which he apologized handsomely for "engaging in practices that might have given the appearance that I sought to discover scandalous information about leading candidates of the other party." The White House statement thanked him for his service over the years, as well as his friendship to the President, but did not suggest any regret at the parting of the ways. Astrid knew before the rest of the family, because somebody text-messaged her and somebody else called her. On December 26, the story got a minute and a half on the evening news. Astrid watched, a sickly look in her eyes. Julia had intended to ask how she had heard these rumors about Lemaster's hiding dirt, but, seeing the woman's genuine sorrow, dared not. The next day Astrid and her children left for home. That night, Julia watched Tessa's show. The onetime roommates had made their peace after Tessa's little betrayal of Julia's confidence. They always did. Julia would never stop being grateful to Tessa for saving her life, and Tessa would never stop counting on her gratitude. Tonight Tessa was talking about the possibility that the two dismissals, Astrid Venable and Cameron Knowland, each an important cog in a political machine, signaled an outbreak of civility, a welcome change from the campaigns of recent years.

Julia worried that they represented an outbreak of something else. She did not know quite what. What she remembered was how, even though Lemaster had said Cameron was too big for him to take on, she had heard him late the same night on his cell phone: . . . *man had the infernal temerity to march in and threaten my wife in the middle of my campus. I won't put up with it. Yes, I know. I know, but I don't care. I won't stand for it. Do I make myself clear? And not this Tice either, asking about my wife all over the place. I will not have this in my city. Is that clear?*

Julia had meant to sneak up on her husband and hug him out of his recent glooms. What sent her reeling back to bed to pull the covers over her head, was, once again, his use of the possessive pronoun.

CHAPTER 34

THE LOOKING-GLASS WORLD

(1)

THE FORTY-THIRD GRAND NEW ENGLAND Orange and White Cotillion was held as usual at a fancy Boston hotel a few days before the new year began: cocktails, then dinner, then dancing, sometimes until dawn, the upper crust of African America letting its collective hair down as, cool and successful, it regarded itself with approval. White America knew nothing like it, and nothing about it. Ladybugs had started the tradition, first in New York, then in Washington, now in eight different regions around the country, back when the presentation of young women to society by the great and near-great families of the darker nation actually mattered, and there was no place else to do it. Nowadays fewer and fewer of the teenaged girls had any interest in playing the debutante. But the Grand Orange and White Cotillions went on. Members of Ladybugs still wore the traditional white gowns accented with something orange, and their guests—once upon a time it had been husbands only—wore white tie, although Julia, standing in the ballroom with Lemaster and Marlon and Regina Thackery, spotted two or three couples in which both partners wore white gowns, the outcome of two years of vehement argument.

"I think Bitsy's wearing the same dress as last year," said Regina, their contretemps in Kimmer's driveway quite forgotten.

"It's a new one," Julia assured her. "I was with her when she bought it."

"Well, it looks like the same one, and I know I've seen that purse."

"Last year she wore backless."

"You call that a back?"

Lemaster and Marlon meanwhile had drifted into a knot of the well-to-do men of the New England branch of the nation, six or seven of them gazing benignly over the crowd as if recognizing the differences in class: not like the old days, when the Clan was small and hard to enter. Lemaster was doing his thing, telling raucous jokes that kept the whole bunch of them tittering, captains of industry and politics and the arts captivated by the wit he never displayed at home. On occasions like this, Julia often felt they had passed through the looking glass into a magical world in which Lemaster was a charmer rather than the affectionately distant man who shared her bed, and she herself was the center of other women's attention and envy. Now, as Regina gossiped on and on, Julia strained to overhear the men's conversation, fascinated as always by her husband's ability to enthrall. She heard nothing but the laughter.

"They should be dancing," said a voice next to her. "And so should you."

Julia turned, and smiled, because Aurelia Treene, in her mid-seventies, remained one of her favorite novelists, and one of her favorite people, even though they saw each other only at events like this. Aurie was tall and slim and gentle, with a quiet, sober-eyed authority that told you she had seen it all. She and Mona had been cronies and rivals in Harlem, back in the day, although Aurie hailed from Tennessee. She used to visit the house on North Balch Street at least once a year. Nowadays she lived in Maine.

"How's your mom?"

"Thriving."

"She's a great lady." The dance floor was crowded and the band was loud, but Aurelia never raised her voice. A cone of silence seemed to have descended over them. "There's still a lot she can teach you."

"I know." Julia sipped her champagne. Aurie's delicate hands were empty. She chose an orange shawl to complement her gown. She had arrived unescorted, and had danced a few times, usually with surprised and flattered women, most of them married. "We just don't see each other often, and you know how she hates to talk on the phone."

"That's very sensible of her, under the circumstances."

"What circumstances?"

"With what's been going on."

This time Julia turned toward her. "What's been going on?"

Aurie grinned and tapped the side of her forehead, as if to signal that

Julia must know perfectly well what she was talking about. A waiter came by with a tray of champagne flutes. Julia took a fresh one. Aurie took one too but did not sip. She changed the subject. "You must be very proud."

"Proud?"

Pointing with her glass. "Of Lemaster. It's a huge honor. Huge. It's bestowed on so few men."

"Well, of course. Although being president of the university has its complications, and some members of the faculty seem ready to string him up, it's been—"

"That's not what I mean."

"What do you mean?"

Aurie's hand gave Julia's shoulder a quick, clawlike squeeze. "Come on, Julia. I have a lifetime's worth of sources to draw on. You don't have to keep your secrets from me."

"What secrets?" An awkward grin. "What am I forgetting that Lemmie's accomplished? Because the list is so long"—oh, how she hated being the dutiful wife, hated it!—"that it's not easy to keep track."

"That he's the Bubba."

"He's what?"

"The Bubba. So the family tradition continues." Another squeeze, harder. "You don't have to pretend. Sure, outsiders aren't supposed to know, but I do have my little pipelines into the frats."

Julia shook her head in sliding confusion. Maybe it was the champagne, because she felt like the moron at the genius convention again. "I'm sorry, Aurie. I don't have the slightest idea what you're talking about."

"So what are you saying? That he told you the real name? Not Bubba, but what the Empyreals really call their second-in-command?" A thrilling shiver. "Now, that's delicious, Julia. Truly delicious. What did he tell you? Come on. Share."

Julia stared. "Are you saying that my husband is the . . . the second-in-command of the Empyreals?"

"You didn't know? Oh, Julia, don't tell me you have one of those old-school types, follows all the traditions, outsiders can't know what's going on, et cetera."

"Lemaster's as old-school as they get."

"So he's doing the successor? The whole business?"

"Successor?"

"The Empyreals recruit them young. Well, you probably know that. A lot of the members groom their own sons. Of course, Bay Dennison didn't have children—" The patent surprise on Julia's face stopped her. A mask dropped over the writer's elegant features, just like that, as if she and Lemaster were indeed part of that secret, looking-glass world but Julia remained an outsider. "Well, it doesn't matter. Congratulations. But, please, forget I mentioned it."

In the corner of her eye, Julia spotted Lemaster coming toward them, waving and smiling, obviously ready to dance again for his fans. Aurie looked ready to depart. Julia said, "Wait. Wait a minute. Tell me one thing."

"One." She sounded annoyed, probably at herself, for letting the cat out of the bag.

"I think the reason Lemaster didn't tell me is probably that Empyreals are old and dying." Watching Aurelia's face. "They are old and dying, aren't they? An unimportant, minor social club, not even mentioned when people list the prestigious ones? I am right, aren't I, Aurie? Aren't I?"

"Of course they are."

"You're sure?"

The novelist glanced at the approaching Lemaster, then smiled at Julia in radiant dismissal. "Oh, you are so cute. So cute."

Aurie kissed the tip of Julia's nose, and returned to her entourage.

(1 1)

THEY HAD THREE ROOMS in the hotel, one for the parents, a second for Aaron, and a third shared by the girls, for Vanessa had prevailed in the latest battle of wills with her mother and had not been among the young women formally presented tonight. Julia and Lemaster went upstairs around one in the morning. Lemaster went to bed. Julia made mother's rounds. Aaron was on his cell phone. Jeannie was asleep, but Julia sat up watching a silly comedy Vanessa loved, glancing intermittently at her youngest to be sure she did not wake and listen to the horrifically foul language; although perhaps she was absorbing it anyway. Julia and Vanessa stretched out on the bed, holding each other the way they used to. They talked a bit and laughed at the movie a bit, and then Julia jerked her head up to find Vanessa snoring and the digital clock informing her that it was close to three.

She crept back to her room, put on her nightgown, crawled between the covers, trying not to wake her husband.

He woke anyway.

They kissed and petted a bit, but proved too tired for anything energetic, so instead she left her head on his shoulder while he stroked her neck and shoulder the way she liked. They talked about the dance, and about faculty politics, and about what Preston might be up to in Mexico. Then Julia asked why he hadn't mentioned to her about being elected—she was not sure what the right word was—the Bubba.

"We're sworn to secrecy, Jules. You know that."

"But you told me Bay Dennison used to be the . . . whatever you call the head of it."

"The Grand Paramount. Sometimes known as the Author." He laughed in the darkness of the hotel room. So did she. Another tradition of the darker nation was these fantastic titles. "There. I told you an Empyreal secret. Happy now?"

She kissed him. "So—you are the Bubba?"

Another station break before the news resumed. "Yes, Jules. I am. Now, please. We can't discuss any more."

"Can you just tell me what 'Bubba' is short for? Aurie said there's another name, a name used just among insiders." Silence. She tried again: "Well, then, tell me how long you serve."

"Ten years."

"Why so long? I've never heard of anything like that."

"Because we're patient people."

A drowsy interlude. It felt nice to learn a few of her husband's secrets, even if she sensed the deeper, more fascinating secrets hiding just beneath them.

"Lemmie?"

"Hmmm?"

"Can I ask you an important question?"

"Those weren't important?"

She refused to be deterred. "Aurelia said the family tradition was continuing. What did she mean? Is there an Empyreals chapter in Barbados?"

Again he made her wait. "Aurelia has a big mouth," he said.

"What did she mean, Lemmie?"

"I wouldn't know, Jules."

"Then what about the successor? Have you picked one?"

Silence.

"Then tell me something else. Are the Empyreals really old and dying? Aurelia laughed when I told her that. Remember how upset Mona was when I told her we were getting married? She wanted a man from one of the more prestigious clubs. That's what she said. She was furious when you wouldn't leave the Empyreals for the Boulé or the Guardsmen. Remember? We laughed at the idea that she took the social scene so seriously. We laughed, Lemmie."

"I remember."

"But were we right? Or are there aspects of Empyreals I don't know about?"

"Of course there are aspects you don't know about. We don't talk to outsiders, and you, my love, are an outsider."

So much for that line of inquiry. Still not ready to surrender the delicious campfire stillness, she tried another.

"Lemmie?"

"Hmmm?"

"Remember the year Gina Joule died?"

"Was murdered." Hard and unforgiving.

"Yes." She squeezed him gratefully for that one. "The year she was murdered. When you got back from England, in, what? May?"

"June."

"Were people still talking about the . . . murder?"

"Not much. Not really."

She hesitated. "What about Mal? Or Scrunchy? Did they talk about it?"

"I don't really remember."

"What I mean is—"

"It's after three, Jules. We have a long drive tomorrow." He slipped free of her and rolled away, leaving her alone in the chilly darkness.

CHAPTER 35

A FRIENDLY CONVERSATION

(1)

"IT'S GOOD OF YOU to make time to see me," said Bruce Vallely with a smile. This was only his second time in the president's office, and he wanted to put no foot wrong, especially after his embarrassment with Marlon Thackery.

But Lemaster Carlyle was as friendly as one could ask. "Not at all, Bruce. It's the least I can do. May I say again how sorry I am for your loss."

"Thank you."

"How's Laurie? She's at Penn State, isn't she? Star of the track team?"

"Something like that."

The president smiled and nodded. He consulted no notes. Instead of seating Bruce across from his massive desk, he had waved him to the sofa, and a sprightly assistant had brought tea. It was the first Tuesday in January, 2004, and the university was barely back in session. "I understand she wants to be a veterinarian. Is that still right? And Brucie? Still the terror of the Navy? Wasn't he serving on a submarine?"

"Yes, sir. USS *Michigan*, in the Pacific Fleet." Lemaster was good at this. Bruce had to give him credit. He reminded himself that he had to be on his guard. The president remained a murder suspect, even if nobody but Bruce and maybe Trevor Land suspected him.

"Didn't follow his father into Special Forces?"

Bruce was surprised. Lemaster's eyes glittered at his little coup. Nobody's service record had "Special Forces" written on it. Somebody would have to know where to dig; and have an insider to do the digging. "No, sir."

"So—what can I do for you, Bruce? I understand this is about poor Kellen."

"Yes, sir."

Lemaster poured out. "Trevor told me that you're helping. I think that's a splendid idea."

Bruce was not sure many people outside the movies actually said the word *splendid*. "Just doing my job, sir."

"You can dispense with the 'sir,' Bruce. This isn't the military, and our wives were close." He crossed his legs and sipped his tea, the very picture of relaxation. "I'm glad you're looking into this, Bruce. I don't believe that robbery story, and I'm sure nobody else does either. I'm hoping you'll come up with some answers."

Bruce had his notebook out. "Can you tell me why you don't believe the robbery story?"

"Maybe instinct. It's too convenient."

"Convenient?"

The president snorted. "The man gets shot on the eve of a meeting with our Senior Trustee? Who tells me Kellen had some information that would be useful in the election? Yes, Bruce. I think it's too convenient."

"Do you know which side the information was supposed to help?"

A stiff shake of the head. "No. I don't think Cameron does either, but you're free to ask him."

"Can you describe your own relationship to Kellen Zant?"

"We didn't have one. Long ago, before Julia and I married, she and Kellen had a close personal relationship. I'm sure you know that. Since then, well, our work did not bring us naturally into contact. Most of the time that I was a law professor, Kellen was teaching at Chicago or Stanford. He came back to town just before I went on the bench, but he was in the econ department. Then, when I was away, I was . . . away."

"I understand that Kellen Zant and your wife remained friends."

For the first time, Lemaster Carlyle deflated a bit. "I suppose."

"Did that bother you?"

"That they were friends? I suppose." The smile faded, but Bruce quickly saw that his quarry was not, as he had thought, put out. The smooth features became earnest. "Bruce, listen to me. This all stays confidential, right? You see, the trouble is, when Kellen and my wife had their close personal relationship, he hurt her very badly. He was in most ways an abusive man. Not physically, I suppose. But there is such a thing as emotional abuse, and it can be just as wounding. My worry was that he would manage to hurt my wife again."

Bruce nodded and made a note. Then he asked, without looking up, "Do you have any reason to think Professor Zant was hurting her?"

"I'm not sure I follow."

But Bruce was sure he followed just fine. "I mean, in recent years, say. Since Kellen Zant returned to campus. Had he hurt your wife in any way?"

"I hope not." Leaning back again. "I'd like to think I would have heard about it."

Bruce noted the careful wording, the lack of a clear denial, but decided, rather than pursuing it, to file the dissimulation away for future reference.

"I just have a couple of questions about the night you found the body."

"Of course."

"You stopped the car because you had an accident."

"The embarrassing answer is yes." A rueful shake of the head. The phone buzzed several times, but Lemaster ignored it. "All right, it's a sharp turn and there was a storm. Still, I've been driving that road for six years. I never missed the turn before."

"Did anything special happen to make you miss the turn? A deer in the woods, something like that?"

"I'm afraid not. I have no excuse."

"You didn't slow down because you saw the body in the ditch?"

Again the bonhomie vanished, and the icy careerist peeked out, the friend of Presidents of the United States and billionaires. "I understand why you need to ask that question, Bruce. I was a prosecutor. I know how the process works. Let me save you some time. I didn't kill Kellen Zant. I didn't arrange for anybody else to kill Kellen Zant. I didn't know his body was there when I had my accident. All right?"

"Yes, sir. I wasn't going to ask those questions."

"But you wouldn't be doing your job if you didn't wonder."

Bruce allowed that one to slip past him, for he was bureaucrat enough to recognize that there was no right answer. "Just one more thing, sir, if I could."

"Please."

"According to people who were there, you left the dinner that night three times to take calls on your cell phone."

"Sounds about right."

"The thing is, I'm told that ordinarily you're quite scrupulous about not answering your cell during a meal, especially an official meal, except for emergencies. May I ask who called you, and whether there was an emergency that night?"

He ticked them off on his fingers. "One call was from my daughter, who was out at the movies. She wanted to arrange a pick up time. One call was from the White House. I always answer when the President calls—the big President—but this time I told him I was busy on college business and asked if I could call him back." The look on Bruce's face amused him. "Yes, people do that. He's just a person."

"And the third call?"

Lemaster Carlyle frowned. "I only remember two. Are you sure there were three?"

"That's what I'm told."

"Well, I'll consult my records and see what I can find out." Smoothly, magically, Lemaster had moved Bruce to his feet and across the office. They shook hands. "Thank you for taking this on, Bruce. Really. We all appreciate it."

Bruce fired his last arrow. "Oh, I almost forgot."

"Please, Bruce. That's an even older game."

They laughed together, but it was plain that the president's good humor was fraying at the edges, which was probably what Bruce intended. The sprightly aide was back, his job plainly to usher the visitor out. It occurred to Bruce that he had seen him before, but he could not work out where. "Those cell-phone calls. Were they on your personal cell or your university cell?"

A frown. "I'm sure my daughter would have called my personal phone. Probably the White House, too."

"And the third call?"

"I told you. I don't remember a third call."

(I I)

BACK AT THE OFFICE, Bruce went over the notes of his interviews. Yes, the witnesses agreed, Lemaster had taken at least three calls, and one witness thought four. Two had been short, which would account for the pick up time and telling the President of the United States he would have to call him back, a feat of confidence or hubris that left Bruce breathless. The third call had been a long one. Everyone agreed on that, too.

Bruce longed to be official. To possess subpoena power. To be able to get into telephone records, bank accounts, credit reports, all the places where people leave their lives lying around. But he had no status. He was doing his bosses, and his university, a favor. All he could do was ask questions.

That is, he could ask questions when he could find witnesses.

In the back of his notebook were people he still had to see, including Nathaniel Knowland, who had lied about spotting Kellen Zant the night he died, and had not returned to school for spring term. He had interviewed Carol Lewin, who could prove she was out of town the night Zant died. But he was running out of witnesses.

For some reason, Rick Chrebet's warning was tugging at his mind: evidence had vanished from police custody, including Kellen Zant's cell phone. But why? Surely the phone company's records carried all the information anybody could want. Cell phones. Wait. Flipping back a page, he noticed a possibility he had overlooked. The first two calls Lemaster Carlyle had received the night Kellen Zant died were on his personal cell phone. Suppose, just suppose, that the third had been on his official one.

Bruce pulled out his campus directory. Sure enough, the office of telecommunications fell under the domain of the secretary of the university. He placed a call to Trevor Land.

"I was wondering, sir, if you could obtain the call records for a particular cell phone."

"Oh, well, Chief Vallely, I doubt whether the pertinent regulations—"

"I'll take that as a yes."

CHAPTER 36

HUEBNER

(1)

JULIA HAD ALWAYS KNOWN that Mitch Huebner was out there, as Granny Vee used to say, but until she stepped out of the Escalade in the dooryard of his lonely shack in the East Woods, she had not realized that the word *crazy* was too mild. She stood, looking around in wonder. He had a dog, of course, a filthy black monster named Goetz, who growled and drooled and stank when he was in the cab of the plow, and who huffed at her now, restrained by a choke chain that looked to her untrained eye too thin to hold him if he really got going. Cords of wood stood in haphazard piles, some covered neatly with tarps, some scattered on the ground, perhaps struck by a drunken plowman.

The house itself was one story, of dark wood, with two cracked windows on the side facing her, and holes in the wall dabbed with creosote or tar. An unfinished totem, carved from a heavy log, stood next to the door, a face to frighten the devil himself. A cross lashed together from two large branches and painted gold was bolted upright on the roof, giving the grim house something of the look of a backwoods church in the Bible Belt, only without the raucous joy. Mr. Huebner's truck was missing, but the body of an old Ford pickup sat on blocks, and Julia could tell at a glance that he cannibalized it for parts for the one he drove. Mr. Huebner was the sort of man who would only ever drive a car that he could fix himself. She had heard him lavish a special seething disdain on the new generation of auto mechanics, who plugged engines into computers to find out what was wrong with them, and downloaded patches from the Internet, while political Lemaster, who prided himself on being able to get along with anybody, nodded severe agreement.

Julia did not want to be here alone, but did not see that she had much choice. The children were in school, except for Aaron, who had another week of vacation. Lemaster was out of town. She would never have a better chance to find out whether she was right, whether Kellen Zant had come here and picked up the diary of Arnold Huebner, long dead, who had been town constable when Gina died.

Mindful of Goetz, who bared his teeth and snarled and spewed frothy strands of saliva but made no other move, Julia inched toward the house.

"Nice doggie," she murmured, having read somewhere that talking this way actually worked. "Good doggie. Nice doggie. Good boy."

The dog snapped at her, but from a safe distance. Maybe he was a scaredy-dog.

"Good doggie. Yes. Yes. I'm friendly, see?" Holding up her hands so the beast could see their emptiness. She wondered whether he could smell cat on her, and what difference it might make. "Good boy. Nice doggie."

Goetz lowered his massive head to his hairy paws. He was shivering, perhaps from the cold, although his pelt was very rich. The doghouse off behind him looked far too small. He peered at her, tongue dangling from his mouth.

"Yes. Good doggie. Good boy."

She had reached the door. A snow shovel stood beside it, the wooden handle so grimy and old it might have been a museum piece. Mitch Huebner had cleared a path, but a narrow one. She knocked, because there was no bell, and because she had already guessed that he was not home, which was probably what she wanted.

"Mr. Huebner?" she called.

No answer. She peered through the smeary glass, but it was like looking into someone else's dream, for all was shadow, shot through with hints of whitish motion. She shivered.

"Mr. Huebner? Are you here?"

Nothing.

"Mr. Huebner. It's Julia Carlyle. I'd like to talk to you."

A harder knock. Something moved in the woods, and the dog's head snapped around to look. So did hers. An angry bird had been disturbed, a red-tailed hawk from the look of it, and Julia tried to remember whether hawks went south for winter. She wondered, if they did, why this one had decided to stick around. Julia waited, but the snowy trees were quiet. She peered down the sodden dirt track along which she had driven but saw no sign of life. Snow crunched loudly out among the trees. The Eggameese, she thought irrelevantly.

"What do you think?" she asked the dog. "Is your daddy here?" Which is what they used to call dogs' owners back in her childhood.

The animal glared, thick tongue pinkly lolling.

"Are you here by yourself?" She knocked again. "Mr. Huebner, I only need a minute."

No answer.

She hesitated, glanced around. Goetz watched passively, breathing hard. She wondered how old he must be. She wondered whether he was even a he. She wondered what Anthony Tice was doing. She wondered if Bruce Vallely was still working on the case. She wondered why both campaigns had targeted the same dirt, and which of the bad guys did it. She wondered whether Lemaster loved her or was simply doing his duty by her. She wondered just about everything she could think of, in fact, except why her hand was turning the knob, and why her instincts, usually right, had assured her that the door would be unlocked, which of course it was. She called Mr. Huebner's name, but it was all for show.

The toe of her boot touched the threshold.

Without a warning growl, the dog charged. The only sound was the sudden snapping as the thin chain broke.

(11)

LEMASTER HAD ONCE SAID, partly in mockery, partly in awe, that Julia was like an insect, able to think with parts of her body other than her brain. Actually, he had made this observation on a long-ago tender morning in their marriage bed, but Julia, creature of instinct, knew that the same uncanny speed of choice afflicted her in everyday life. So she did not decide that there was no time to rush into the house and shut the door, she knew it already, when Goetz was still resting placidly in the dooryard, knew it the same way she knew which discs were in the changer in the Escalade, and which blouse Jeannie had on at breakfast, information toward which she would never cast her focus unless she turned out to need it. She could not outrun the dog, she could not evade it, she could not hide behind some barrier. She lacked sufficient time to come up with a plan. There was only the shovel, already seized tightly in her gloved hands, for she had swept it up without thinking at the first hint that the dog was in motion.

Julia spun in place, nearly losing her footing as the beast leaped at her.

She swung the shovel hard, like the softball player she had been at Hanover High, and made firm contact with the creature's head.

It was like hitting solid rock.

The shovel stung her hands, and Goetz was knocked off course, onto the porch, where he shook his snout, scrabbled for purchase on the ice, then turned, dribbling furiously, and came at her a second time, growling now. She suspected that she had wounded only his pride.

In a panic now, Julia swung a second time, missing the head and smacking the upper torso.

The dog howled in pain but kept on coming. Heavy paws pressed her parka, and, with the bulk of its weight leaning into her, the creature tipped her over. Julia screamed. She and Goetz both hit the ice with the same shivering thud and, for an instant, were equally stunned. The blade of the shovel was between her face and the dog's snapping jaws. The fall left her dizzy, but hot, fetid breath was in her nose and mouth, waking her as sharply as any smelling salt. The wild black eyes hated her as the snout kept pressing at the shovel, the beast too stupid to realize that it could just nose the metal aside. Sooner or later, Goetz would work it out by trial and error. Julia had known panic, but not like this. Her heart seemed ready to attempt an escape without the rest of her body.

She tried to jerk upward, but she was too small, or the angle was too narrow, or, most likely, the dog was just too big. She freed the hand that was pinned beneath the shovel, but this only gave the monster a target, and he lunged for the fingers, teeth sinking into the glove. She yanked instinctively, and the glove came off in the dog's angry mouth, the thick cold-resistant fabric confusing him, sticking in his teeth. He snapped and snarled and pawed at his own jaw, and Julia pulled a leg out from under him and kicked up, hard. Goetz tried to stay atop her but skidded again, and she rolled out from under. She tried to get to her feet, but the porch was too icy. Then he was on top of her again, this time on her back, and no shovel to protect her, nothing but the parka, and the fabric was too thin and his jaws were too close, and she screamed and slapped at him awkwardly and thought she heard a shout but it was probably her own and anyway Goetz was not slowing down so she just screamed again—

And the gunshot came as a complete surprise.

(111)

THE WEIGHT WAS GONE. Julia lay there, heaving in terror, briefly unable to move.

"Stupid bitch," somebody said, which got her blood flowing again, and she rolled over, the panic yet shuddering through her though she was still ready for an argument, until she saw Mitch Huebner gazing sorrowfully at his dog.

Goetz wasn't hit. At least Julia didn't think so, although with all that thick black fur it was not easy to tell. But he was cowed—no, she, *she* was cowed—crawling back toward the canted doghouse, the shotgun cradled loosely under Mitch Huebner's arm having done its work of scaring her off.

He was standing on the running board of his pickup, the dented yellow plow pointing toward the shack as though meaning to push it over, and he still had not looked in her direction. He shut off the engine, and she waited for him to slide the gun back into the rack above the seat, but he didn't. She noticed for the first time that several of the stickers on the glass behind the driver's headrest bore the names of organizations squeezed so narrowly into the right-hand margin that they made the National Rifle Association look like the National Council of Churches. He climbed down from the truck and made a great show of walking over to the doghouse, where Goetz continued to sulk, until her master crouched above her, murmuring some words meant to soothe, and gave her what Julia first thought was a bone, then realized was a hamburger. The dog sat up fast, offered that near-smile that dogs present when they want to be liked, and proceeded to tear into the meat with all the gusto she no doubt would have preferred to demonstrate by tearing into Julia.

"Sorry about the dog," said Mr. Huebner, standing a couple of feet from the porch now, still not looking at his visitor, an apology the last thing she expected, for in her mind she had already laid out a cover story or two. "Breaks every chain I put on her. Gonna hurt somebody one day. Never was much on self-control." A heavy sigh. "Suppose I should have her put down, but I love the old hag."

"You could do a fence," Julia suggested, sitting up and rubbing her bottom, sore from her collision with the ice. The adrenaline rush had her breath ragged. He never asked if she was all right.

"I could at that. Costs money, though."

"You have to do something about her." Huffing, huffing. "Like you said, she could hurt somebody."

"Doesn't have much in the way of teeth no more."

"They looked pretty sharp to me."

"Nearly had to shoot the stupid bitch." A shake of his head. The bill of his checkered hat hid his expression. "Never had to do that before. Guess you musta really spooked her."

"She's dangerous."

"I don't get many visitors. Wasn't expecting one today." Raising his eyes at last, the shotgun still cradled beneath his arm. His face was its usual bristly red, as though he had for the past few mornings preferred drinking to shaving. He wore old jeans and hunting boots that had a lot of miles on them, and a windbreaker, as though to prove that his roots ran too deep in the loamy New England soil for a little chill to scare him.

"I didn't mean to barge in. I couldn't get you on the phone. I knocked, and, well, the door just opened, and then she—"

"She wouldn't do anything unless you tried to go inside."

"Well, I—"

"Did you walk in my house, Mrs. Carlyle?"

Caught by a white man, the thing she hated most. Mitch Huebner had her dead to rights. He also had a shotgun. Her mouth flapped for an instant before she got the words in the right order.

"Maybe I put a foot in."

"Maybe you did at that." He lowered the barrel. "Way I was raised, we used to call it trespassing."

A beat. She realized that he was waiting for her to return grace for grace. "I'm sorry, Mr. Huebner. I didn't mean to. Your door was open."

Maybe the cold Yankee eyes forgave her, but not by much. "Can I do something for you, Mrs. Carlyle?"

"Uh, well, yes. I wanted to ask you a couple of questions, if you have a minute." Julia shivered. Some of it was aftershock, some of it was fresh fear, some of it was cold. Her fingers in particular were chilly. She wondered where Goetz had tossed her bitten glove.

"Not about the lampposts. I'm not the one who knocked them down, Mrs. Carlyle." Surly but emphatic. "I've hit a lamp or two, a mailbox here and there over the years, even a wall that was buried in the snow. I know what it feels like. I didn't hit your lights."

She smiled for him, not an easy performance with her teeth chattering with cold and adrenaline. "I told you before, Mr. Huebner, and I'll tell you again. I don't blame you for the lights." She rubbed a bruised elbow. "I know you didn't knock them down. I'm sorry I ever thought you did."

A moment, and now it was his turn to think. She had reassured him. What else did he want? Then he shrugged, and clomped onto the porch. "Come on in if you've a mind," he said, once again not looking at her. Mr. Huebner seemed a little too nervous, even with the business of the lighting fixtures out of the way, and Julia sensed that he had few women visitors, other than, perhaps, the kind who hung out in the bars at the seedy end of Route 48.

Following his lead, Julia Carlyle stepped over the threshold, and into his madness.

Everything was wrong. Subtly but certainly wrong.

In the stone hearth she saw not only burnt logs, but long, soot-darkened knives, which Mr. Huebner had evidently been heating. Above the mantel was a grimy mirror, but the grime seemed in some way a matter of intention, as though a child had daubed the surface with a marker. Perhaps he usually kept the mirror covered: a moth-eaten blanket, once blue, lying on the unpolished wood floor looked just the right size. The windows, except for the one in the door, were shuttered, and each one had a sprig of some weed—heather?—stapled across the opening. Crosses were daubed in black paint across the shutters. Enough handguns and rifles and semi-automatics lay around the room to start a small war and probably to finish it. A pair of lawn-sized Madonnas stood on either side of the front entrance like the alarm system in a video shop. Tightly closed doors presumably led to the kitchen, the bathroom, perhaps a bedroom, although it looked to her like Mr. Huebner usually slept on the old red leather sofa, beneath a blanket festooned with more crudely drawn crosses. A banner along a side wall called for white power.

Oh, this was a great idea, Julia.

In the middle of the room, Mr. Huebner stripped off his gloves and tossed them, along with his hat, onto a table. He picked up a bag of Oreos that might have been around since last season, top folded in with a dutiful child's care. "Can I offer you something?" he said, still not looking at her.

"I'm fine," said Julia, standing very still and feeling very prissy, and very afraid. The front door stood wide open. He had not asked her to close it, and if he did, she would dash for her car, for she would rather tangle with Goetz again than face Mitch Huebner with the door to this crazy little room closed. His madness was a live thing, burning within him, and, standing even this close, she felt she could inhale it like secondhand smoke and, in time, grow sick herself.

"So—what did you want to ask me about?"

"Well . . ."

He followed her glance toward the white-power flag. He chuckled. "Hey, don't let that bother you. It's just to scare her away. It doesn't mean anything."

Julia felt herself stepping into the cool, prickly stream of impossibility. "Scare who away?"

He scowled at her, eyes flat and shining yet empty, the eyes of a dead thing you pass on the road at night. "I think you know the answer to that, Mrs. Carlyle. Otherwise you wouldn't be here."

Julia fought the urge to lick her lips. Outside, the wind shifted. The dog howled, and the breeze tickled the small of her back even through her parka. She would not ask. She absolutely refused, even unconsciously, to ask.

And so, unsteadily, she returned to her text. "You . . . you knew that professor who got killed. Kellen Zant."

"Is that so?"

"He came to you. He wanted your father's diary."

"Maybe." He folded strong arms. He had not removed his windbreaker, and, for all Julia knew, could be hiding another gun or two in there. "What's it to you, Mrs. Carlyle?"

Again her eyes shifted, taking in the grimy mirror, the covered windows, the religious symbols scattered around the room. None looked new. "Your father was the constable when Gina Joule was killed. The Joules made a stink for a while, and then the case was closed. DeShaun

Moton did it. Everybody agreed. Your father was at the press conference." She watched his face. "Of course there were the riots afterward, and the Landing got a bad name for a while. The scandal ended your father's career. It pretty much ended the Huebners in the Landing. Before Gina died, the Huebners were pretty prominent. Afterward, your father"—she did not want to say that Arnold Huebner drank himself to death, although, according to Vera Brightwood, he pretty much had—"well, he was in disgrace. Your sisters both left town. You stayed around, but you moved out here, where you wouldn't have to worry about . . . about . . ."

She trailed off, looked around the room with fresh eyes.

"All of this. It's for Gina, isn't it?" Prickle, prickle. Even as she pronounced the words, Julia knew she would never believe them. What mattered was whether Mr. Huebner believed them. "She . . . bothers you. Haunts you." Julia waited, but Mitch Huebner was rough New England stone. "Why? Because your father named the wrong killer?" She pointed at the Madonnas. "You're hoping to scare her away. The crosses. And that's garlic, isn't it? On the windows."

The shotgun came up fast, and Julia got ready to run, but he was only breaking it open to dump the remaining shell into his palm. "What if it is?" he said, looking down.

"Your father never believed it. He never believed it was DeShaun. Not really. He wrote it down in his diary. That's what this whole thing has been about. What Professor Zant was looking for. Your father's diary." She tried to remember what Frank had said. "There was a powerful family, wasn't there? Protecting itself. Kellen told you he could prove it, and in return he wanted that diary."

"He might have wanted it, Mrs. Carlyle, but I couldn't give it to him. It's lost."

"That's what everybody thinks. I'm not sure I believe it."

"I put out a reward—"

"I heard. But I think the reward was cover. I think you had the diary all along, but you pretended not to, because you wanted to stay out of trouble. I think Kellen persuaded you to give it to him. Maybe he promised to do justice. I don't know. But I think you gave him the diary, and that's why he was so certain he knew—"

"Knew what, Mrs. Carlyle?"

"Who really killed Gina Joule."

(I V)

JULIA REFUSED TO SIT in the house, and Mitch Huebner refused to leave the property, so they compromised on the front porch, where she kept a wary eye on Goetz, who lay curled and sulking near her broken chain. They both held Buds, because Julia did not want to alienate him by refusing. Whenever he guzzled, she sipped.

"Tell you something funny, Mrs. Carlyle. Nobody ever asks me anything. They all think I'm crazy, they think I'm dirty, and they know I'm from the wrong part of town. So everybody's always wondering what really happened that night, and none of them ever ask me anything. When your Vanessa came to talk to me a year, year and a half ago, she was the first one in a long time, Mrs. Carlyle. Maybe I was a little rude. I didn't tell her much. I didn't owe her. What I did tell her was how my daddy was almost run out of town when he couldn't find who killed little Gina. In those days the Landing wasn't like it is now, all the university types, executives, like that. We were just a little farm town. When the Joules moved in, well, we probably had two or three professors, and they all lived down near the Town Green. We needed them, Mrs. Carlyle. Their influence. Their money. Back in those days, the richest man in town was Mr. Brightwood—Vera's dad—who ran the bank. But the little bit he had wouldn't count for much in any kind of big city, or even in Elm Harbor. So the Joules were kind of a big deal. So were the other professors."

Mitch Huebner possessed a big man's laugh but with a raw sadness underneath. Wind teased snow from the thick, lonely trees.

"So, anyway," he resumed, "the town fathers already had this dream, to turn the Landing into what they called a bedroom town. Get the commuters to move in. Most of us thought they had their heads up their proverbial asses, but that was the dream. If Gina had been local, everything would have been fine. But she was the daughter of a professor, Mrs. Carlyle. See why it matters? If the Landing couldn't solve it, how could we get the commuters to move in? So, sure, the Joules put all kinds of pressure on. Well, who could blame them? Merrill Joule called in every favor he knew. He knew the governor. The president of the university—man named Cicero Hadley in those days, the one who did all the civil-rights business—well, old Cicero was close to the Nixon people, so the feds put the pressure on, too. Mrs. Joule, well, her family owned newspapers, and they sent people to do a big story."

Julia again thought back on Vanessa's work. "There was never any big story. A little mention, maybe, in a couple of the state papers, and that was it."

Mr. Huebner nodded, and chugged. Julia took a dainty sip. She had always hated beer, but found the sensation less bad than she remembered. The winter woodland sounds soothed her. She wondered if she was mellowing with age; or if the beer was creating the pleasant buzz.

"That's right, Mrs. Carlyle. The big story never ran. The way I heard it from my daddy, Merrill Joule had a change of heart. His daughter was dead or worse, and embarrassing the town wouldn't bring her back. The Joules never really believed that the black boy did it. Merrill decided to keep up the pressure to find out what happened to her, but not in such a public way. He was a liberal, Mrs. Carlyle. The old-fashioned kind. Not this lifestyle crap. The kind who believed in sacrifice, helping the less fortunate. The town was poor in those days. Not like now. And Merrill Joule didn't want his own tragedy to make it poorer. Mrs. Joule, well, she promised to set up a trust fund in Gina's name to send children from the Landing to college. But before she could do it, she . . . well, she had her troubles."

This, too, Julia recalled from Vanessa's paper. After her daughter died, Anna Joule took a year to travel in Europe. Upon her return, Anna rapidly deteriorated, spending the next decade of her life in a series of mental institutions, insisting that her daughter spoke to her at night. As for Merrill, he took his own life, or drowned by accident, in the middle of the night, at the town beach, five years after Gina died there.

"Tell me about the diary."

"I am telling you about the diary." Mitch Huebner struck a philosophical tone. The man continued to surprise her, and she wondered whether what people assumed to be his politics and his seeming lack of interest in matters intellectual were a pose. "You see, Mrs. Carlyle, you're judging by what people around the town say. But they don't say everything they know. Not to you. Not to your Vanessa. You're outsiders. Not just because you haven't lived in town very long. Also because . . . well, because you weren't here when it happened. You look at any town in New England, Mrs. Carlyle, and you'll find a line down the middle. On one side are the people who don't know the secrets. On the other are the people who've always been there, who hold on to the town's history like the roots that keep the trees standing. Cut away the secrets—make them public—and the whole town withers and blows away with the next nor'easter." He put his beer down, cocked his head to the side. "And there's another reason, too. Another reason people won't tell you the story. Don't take offense, Mrs. Carlyle, but you're also not . . . white."

"What difference does that make?"

"It just makes a difference. I'm sorry, Mrs. Carlyle, but that's life."

She forced upon herself an uncommon calm. "What's the secret, Mr. Huebner? What are the Landingers hiding?"

Another long swallow. He was on his third beer, possibly his fourth. Julia was working on her second can, even though she did not quite recall finishing the first. "Yes, Mrs. Carlyle. You're right. I used to have my father's diary. Turned up ten years ago in a file cabinet in the basement of the town hall, with a bunch of my daddy's junk they were gonna throw out. But I don't have it any more. I gave it to Zant, like you said." Raising a hand before she could ask the obvious question. "I don't know what he did with it. And I never read it. I never even opened it. Call me a coward. The truth is, I didn't want to know. What my father always told me, though, was that Gina had a boyfriend. A college boy she was seeing."

"I heard that, too," said Julia, vaguely disappointed. "Is that what's in the diary? The name of the boyfriend?"

He nodded, watching the woods. "Most likely. But there's something else my daddy told me, Mrs. Carlyle. The night Gina died, there was this witness who saw her get into the car with DeShaun—"

"Mrs. Spicer. Her teacher."

"Right. Mrs. Spicer. Changed her story." He waited for Julia to say she already knew this part, too, but this time she had more sense. "What my daddy told me was, he went around to her house later and got the truth out of her. Seems Gina did ring her bell that night, just the way Mrs. Spicer said the first time. Not only that. Gina asks if she can make a call. Half an hour later, forty-five minutes maybe, there's a mighty sporty looking car in her driveway, and two guys inside."

"Two!"

"That's right. Two guys. College age. White. One of them rings the bell, but Mrs. Spicer sees the other one in the car. And Gina, well, she hugs the one guy but then, when she gets outside—Mrs. Spicer is watching through the window the whole time—when Gina gets to the car, she looks like she didn't expect the other guy to be there. They have words, Gina and her boyfriend, and she looks mad, but she gets into the car. Last time anybody sees her." Mitch Huebner shrugged, swigged more beer. "My daddy asked why she changed her story. Mrs. Spicer said she was afraid. My daddy thought that some money might have changed—" He stopped, cocked his head. He had heard something she had missed, out there in the woods. "Did you come out here alone, Mrs. Carlyle?"

"Yes. Yes, of course." She turned in the direction of his gaze, saw nothing more than the thrilling, silent beauty of any snowy wood. "Why?"

"Are you sure?"

"I'm sure, Mr. Huebner."

He eased the shotgun from its position by the door onto his lap. He said, "Somebody's out in my woods, making a hell of a racket trying to stay quiet."

"Kids—"

"Kids don't come out here, Mrs. Carlyle. Mitch Huebner is crazy. Mitch Huebner is a right-wing nutcase. Mitch Huebner eats kids for breakfast. They're scared of me."

Julia looked off the other way but saw nothing. "Deer—"

"Or visitors from Mars. No, it's a human somebody. But, if he comes too close, Goetz'll take care of it." He made a quick hand signal, and the massive dog bounded uninjured to its feet and was lost in the snow-capped trees. "Where was I?"

"Ah, what your father told you about the night Gina Joule disappeared."

Mitch Huebner nodded. "I knew Gina. Not well. A little. I must have been, oh, thirteen, fourteen when it happened. I would see her around town. I'd notice her the way thirteen-year-old boys everywhere start noticing the pretty girls a few years older. Never saw her with a boy. Because of those parents. Not that they didn't love her. But she was the only one they ever had, and they had trouble having the one, and they used to protect her like she was the most precious creature on God's earth. Most of the boys around here, well, they were scared to try to date her. Gina was a real beauty, but Merrill Joule was a terror. She could have had all the boyfriends she wanted, that's how pretty she was."

Julia hid her smile behind another sip of beer. What a crush Mitch Huebner must have harbored. "You sound like you . . . thought highly of her."

"It wasn't just me, Mrs. Carlyle. It was everybody. People just naturally liked her. Maybe it was because"—he shook it off, then seemed to catch her thoughts, because he tipped his grizzled chin to the side and shook his head. "Now, don't get me wrong. I was from a different side of the tracks. Sure, my daddy was constable, but Gina was university, and town and gown don't mix." A smaller sip. "Anyway, my daddy told me once that it's true what they say, you can't fight City Hall. The thing is, Mrs. Carlyle, back in those days, there was still such a thing as people so big you couldn't touch them. Not like now, when the press goes after every politician who can't keep his pants on. No, in those days—" He stopped again, leaping to his feet, gun in hand, and she turned in time to hear an angry shout in the woods, and Goetz barking. "Let's go see who's out there," he said, hurrying down into the snow.

Julia followed, not because she wanted to go into those woods, but because she wanted to hear the end of the story. They stepped into the trees, mostly conifers, so tall and thick that the sun slowly vanished. It was like walking at twilight, even though it was the middle of the day.

"Is all this your property?" she said.

"Keep your voice down," he whispered, following his dog on surprisingly light feet.

"But who—"

"Please, Mrs. Carlyle. Trust me."

They reached a clearing. Goetz was there, tail wagging happily. Trapped beneath her paw was a gleaming black loafer, owned by a man with very large feet. The toe had been nibbled. Mitch Huebner crouched, lifting the shoe with the barrel of the gun. "Huh. Looks expensive."

"Yes, it does," said Julia distantly.

"Want it? I don't have much use for these fancy shoes."

Julia shook her head. She wanted nothing to do with it. "Neither do I," she said.

Mitch Huebner shrugged and threw it deeper into the woods, but Goetz thought he was playing and immediately fetched it.

Back at the house, she said, "Mr. Huebner, listen. What you were saying about Gina—"

"My daddy said you have to pick your fights, and it would be better for all concerned if he picked a different one."

"You found the diary ten years ago."

"That's right, Mrs. Carlyle."

About the time one Horseman was running for his first term in the Senate, and another for his first term as a governor.

"Did you tell anyone you had it? Ten years ago, I mean?"

An unfathomable shrug.

"But you gave the diary to Kellen Zant. And never saw it again."

"Uh-huh."

She hesitated over the next, obvious question. "Why does it matter that I'm not white?"

Mitch Huebner shook his head. Remonstrance? Refusal? Or just good old-fashioned Yankee reticence?

"Was it"—admitting to herself the final horror—"are you saying . . . the boyfriend . . . the college boy . . . was he . . . black?"

"The boys who picked her up were white."

"I need to know this, Mr. Huebner. I *need* to know."

Still the stony silence.

Sinking fast, Julia tried again. "And only Kellen knew who she was seeing that night."

He nodded, busying himself with a sudden urge to polish the fender of his truck with a dry and dirty rag. "See why I don't want to know?" He tossed the rag into the back seat. "They killed him for it."

"I see."

"I think it's time for you to go, Mrs. Carlyle."

"I guess it is." Her voice was wooden. Too much was happening. Lemaster had not been in the country, she reminded herself. Even if he knew her—and Mitch Huebner had not even confirmed that the boyfriend was black—he had not been in the country. "Thank you for your time, Mr. Huebner."

A moment later she was in the Escalade, but no sooner had she started the engine than he appeared beside her window, smiling uneasily, holding a small package.

"What's this?"

"It's from Professor Zant. He said to give it to you."

Fear and fury mingled. "To give it to me? And you waited till now?"

"He said to give it to you if you asked about my father's diary. And only if you asked about the diary." He stepped away from the car, unsmiling. "Time for you to go," he repeated.

She drove half a mile into the woods, keeping her eyes peeled for a man missing a shiny new loafer. A natty dresser like Tony Tice, say: she had heard he was out on bail. Then, seeing no one, she pulled to the side of the road and opened the package.

Of course.

Another mirror.

Or, rather, a piece of one.

It was the cheap mirror he had bought at Luma's Gifts, the price tag still on the handle, broken jaggedly down the middle so that it reflected only half her face, which seemed appropriate. And a business card—A. W. ACME, LAND SURVEYORS, it read—and, below, in Kellen Zant's zagging, left-sloping hand, "—*Secretary?*"

Oh, this should be a big help.

She turned the card over, and found a note in the same writing:

My dearest sweet J—Bring the mirror to the straight man. And if you have trouble finding Shari Larid, take a train. Always, K.

More of his word games. Utter gibberish.

But beneath the mirror was pay dirt. Two yellowed pages torn from the missing diary. Julia looked up and down the road, settled in, and began to read.

CHAPTER 37

TWO MEETINGS

(1)

JULIA KNEW ACME LAND SURVEYORS because they had done some of the drawings needed to get the approvals for Hunter's Heights, a lengthy process in which the Landing threw up one fresh obstacle after another until Lemaster visited the first selectman with his friend Jerry Nathanson, managing partner at the biggest law firm in town, who kindly estimated the town's likely cost for a litigation the Carlyles were bound to win. The village caved, the house was built, and, for a while, Tyler's Landing was awash in envy. That Lemaster and Julia possessed so wonderful a house and such a paucity of local friends had given Mona a shiver of nationalist delight the first time Julia told her the story, while strolling the vineyards behind her mother's house in Plaisance-du-Touch: *You should be happy*, Mona announced, *that you've got something that the Caucasians want and can't ever have. Outside of the Oprah Winfreys and Tiger Woodses of the world, not many of our people can say that.* There was even a word for it, Mona announced, one that Julia suspected her mother of inventing on the spot, although it later turned up in several of the great woman's essays: *Afrofactophilia*. The word, said Mona, warming to it, referred to a desire by Caucasians (as she, like Lemmie, was careful to call them) for *objets* collected or produced by the people of the African diaspora, another favored bit of jargon. *They hate us but they love our precious and pretty things*, she explained. *They covet.* Then she looked at her daughter through the eyes of the coquette and, for a dizzying moment, Julia thought she understood a small part of why her mother had always and only chased after white men. *And sometimes they covet our precious and pretty selves.*

As Kellen had coveted Julia, and insisted, even after his death, on drawing her into his world.

She found Acme in a converted barn at the wrong end of town, and chatted with Amy Warren, who was the "A.W.," using only her initials and mostly employing men, because women in her field were considered a joke. And Amy, as it happened, did indeed recall Kellen Zant, and had even told the police after he died. He came in only once, she said, and told them he was looking at waterfront properties and might need some studies done.

"Gave him my business card."

"And then what?"

"Never heard from him again."

Because Kellen was not really surveying a lot, Julia decided as she drove back to town, any more than he was really building a house. He was, once more, throwing up a smokescreen. Or sending a signal. The house was not the point. The signal was the point, and, once more, Julia suspected that she was the target. Everything scribbled on the business card meant something, and Kellen had imagined that Julia would figure it out.

(11)

SINCE THE BACK OF THE CARD was obscure, she started with the front. After all, the secretary of the university was named Land—a weak connection, but the best she could manage. They met for tea at the faculty club, but, alas, Trevor Land confessed, he barely knew the man, so many professors nowadays, and everybody so busy. "Progress. All for it, oh, yes. Publicity or perish these days. But does rather get in the path of our scholarly endeavor, Dean Carlyle."

She muttered what must have been agreement.

The talk turned to the no-confidence motion some of the faculty were pressing, an attack on her husband motivated, it seemed, by a number of forces, not least his decision to impose a merger between gender studies and women's studies, as recommended by his budget task force, but even more so by his close friendship with the occupant of the White House.

"Lemmie says it won't come to a vote," said Julia.

"Wouldn't know about that. Not a member of the faculty senate.

Not a political man, Dean Carlyle. Live and let live, kind of thing. Care about the institution." A shy smile. "Think your husband's rather the best thing to happen to the institution in decades."

She smiled back.

And then he surprised her. "I understand, Dean Carlyle, that you and Professor Zant were friends, after a fashion."

"After a fashion," she agreed, cautiously, hiding her swiftly growing unease behind a finger sandwich.

"Only ask because he had friends and supporters among the alums. Lots of them. Anything they can do to help, one need only ask."

"Help what?"

"Anything that might arise, Dean Carlyle. Anything that might arise."

Plainly he was waiting, leaving the onus on Julia, who finally plunged. "Gina Joule was your goddaughter."

"Indeed."

"I think Kellen Zant might have been looking into what really happened that night." Silence. "And, ah, there are these stories in the Landing. Old stories. That maybe the official version of that night's events—"

His palm, chalky and commanding, arrested her comments. "Not really the sort of thing one enjoys talking about, Dean Carlyle."

"I understand. But you were as close to Merrill Joule as anyone." When the secretary did not see fit to dispute this, she was emboldened. "Senator Whisted was Merrill Joule's godson. I was wondering how well he knew the family."

"The Whisteds are the sort of family who make a point of knowing everybody, Dean Carlyle. Rather helps in politics, one would imagine." She sensed the distaste in his cultured voice. "No doubt the young man would have been over to the house for the occasional dinner, kind of thing."

"So he knew Gina?"

"I would imagine so."

Confirming part of Mary's story: the photo. "Did he have an opinion on, ah, whether the official story was true? If that young black man was the, ah, killer?"

"One hardly wants to argue with the police. Still, family first and so forth. Rather think one would do anything to protect them, kind of thing. Still, not one's job to punish, thank you very much. Told Merrill the same. Anna. Young Whisted. Vengeance won't bring her back, kind of thing. Better to build up than to tear down."

"Young Whisted? As in Malcolm?" The secretary sipped, but said nothing. Julia put down her cup and glanced around the faculty club, but nobody was listening in. "The only way you could have had that conversation was if Merrill and Anna and Mal Whisted knew who did it, and if that person was still alive."

"You'll want to meet Chief Vallely."

"Bruce? Whatever for?"

"Talk to Chief Vallely," he repeated. He sipped his tea and made a face, telling the world that everything that changed grew worse. "I believe the chief may be looking into Professor Zant's death, kind of thing. Wouldn't be surprised if he can answer the rest of your questions."

"We already met, and, frankly, I didn't appreciate the way he—"

"Dear me, look at the time. Always pleasant to see you, Dean Carlyle, but work won't wait. Meeting out your way this afternoon, as a matter of fact. Happy to give you a ride home, sort of thing. But I suppose you would have your own transport, wouldn't you?"

When she left the faculty club, freshly worried, she did not notice Bruce Vallely across the street in his red Mustang.

(III)

FOLLOWING JULIA CARLYLE was a minor and occasional part of Bruce's investigation. He did not expect her to suddenly pull over to the side of the road, reach into a rotting stump, and pull out whatever Kellen Zant was working on. Or, if she did, there was no reason to think she would do it during one of the three or four hours a week that he had committed to the surveillance. Still, one never knew. However small the odds that she would stumble on the answer to the puzzle while he had her in view, they were even smaller if he never followed her at all.

The Escalade, hulking and powerful yet somehow smoothly purring, was easy to follow along the city streets. She was not heading for the expressway. She seemed to prefer returning home to the Landing the long way around. He stayed a comfortable block and a half behind her, close enough to catch her if she made an unexpected turn, far enough that she was unlikely to detect him in her rearview mirror.

She left the city limits and cruised into the town of Langford, and Bruce slowed further, putting more space between them, because the traffic was lighter. Langford seemed to be all strip malls and gas stations. Julia was driving very fast. He had heard that she liked to sing while behind the wheel, and wondered what kind of music she preferred. There was a rumor that Lemaster liked hip-hop. He found that one difficult to swallow, but tastes had a funny way of—

Somebody else was following her. A small white sedan. Had he not slowed, he would never have noticed. But when Julia pulled over to her usual gas station to fill up the gas-guzzling SUV's enormous tank, the sedan pulled into the parking lot of the fast-food restaurant across the way. Bruce did not even slow down. He went straight past, parking at a small office building, where he could see the Escalade in his side-view mirror.

All right. It made sense. There were lots of people interested in whatever Kellen Zant had been up to. The more of them who believed that he had left whatever it was to Julia Carlyle, the more likely it was that she would pick up a tail.

He assumed that nobody was out to harm her. The point had to be to find whatever she intended to find.

Action.

The white sedan came sailing past him, pulling the same trick as Bruce, following from in front for a while, but doing so less smoothly. The driver pulled to the side a couple of blocks down the road. Bruce saw his face, and was so stunned that he almost missed the Escalade when it came along.

He put his car into gear and followed.

He recognized the driver of the white sedan. It was the sprightly little aide who had ushered him in and out of Lemaster Carlyle's office.

CHAPTER 38

AGAIN MAIN STREET

(I)

ARRIVING BACK IN THE LANDING after her cryptic conversation with Trevor Land, Julia parked on Main Street just as the snow began to fall. She stepped out of the car, planning to dart into Cookie's for a quick fix, which she would disguise, as usual, with purchases of gifts for others, and Jelly Bellys for the jar on Lemaster's desk in Lombard Hall. She was burning with anger.

Bruce Vallely. Did Trevor Land really expect her to talk to Bruce Vallely? The same Bruce Vallely who, with the slightest encouragement, would winkle out Vanessa's entanglement with Kellen? And who, according to Sister Lady Regina Thackery's account of Bruce's interview with her husband, had been asking a few questions too many about Lemaster?

Julia thought maybe it would be better if Bruce Vallely took an early retirement. Oh, he was a nice enough man, she told herself as she hurried along the sidewalk, struggling toward calm. Bruce was hulking and socially clumsy but did not seem to have a mean bone in his body. Grace had certainly adored him. But the risks involved in any sort of collaboration—

Cookie's was closed.

Odd. Vera Brightwood had not taken a vacation in living memory, and she was never sick. Lemaster liked to say she got rid of germs by bestowing them, in the form of her diatribes, upon her customers.

Julia checked her watch, but it was not yet two-thirty, and the candy shop was usually open until half past four. Vera took Sundays and Mondays off, but today was Friday. The front step had been shoveled and salted, and, as Vera was too cheap to pay anybody else to do it, she must have done it herself, meaning that the store had been open earlier in the day. Julia knocked, then peered through the glass just to be sure, but the shop was empty. Puzzled, she walked three doors down to Luma's Gifts to ask Lurleen Maddox, Vera's only friend, whether the Landing's leading gossip might have suffered an accident or a death in the family.

Only Luma's was closed, too.

Julia stood on the sidewalk, nibbling her lip. Was it some special holiday in the Landing? No, because the florist was open. So were Greta's Tavern and the real-estate office and the bookstore and the CVS drugstore that stood on the lot once occupied by the grand house in which Anna and Merrill Joule had raised their daughter. She glanced across the street. The antiques shop was closed. Had Frank left town, driven by his fears? Then where were Vera and Lurleen? On impulse, she headed for the bookstore, because Daniel Weiss, the former professor of Shakespeare who ran it, was Lemaster's frequent ally in chasing down antiquarian books. Danny might know what was going on.

But the assistant manager told her that Mr. Weiss had left early today. He said he had a meeting.

"Oh, right," said Julia, inventing poorly. "I forgot. Danny and my husband were getting together for lunch."

"Really? Wow. Maybe there's been a mix-up. I thought Mr. Weiss said he had to see Miss Brightwood."

Out on Main Street again, Julia considered. Why was she worrying? It was not her job to ferret out the friendships among Main Street shopkeepers, and if a bunch of them wanted to get together on a Friday afternoon, it was none of her business. She was a member of a couple of Landing social clubs herself—the Caucasian Squawk Circle—and knew their penchant for testing loyalty by scheduling meetings at peculiar times.

But Julia was arguing against her own convictions. As she slid behind the wheel of the Escalade, she conceded that the coincidence was simply too large.

Trevor Land, who just happens to be Gina Joule's godfather, tells her he has to drive out to the Landing this afternoon for a meeting. And suddenly, along Main Street, a clutch of longtime Landingers also vanish—for a meeting.

I'll tell you another thing I heard about your friend Kellen, Boris Gibbs had told her over lunch. *A few people out in the Landing were pretty angry with him.*

Julia took a breath. Maybe she was just being Mallardish, seeing conspiracies everywhere, but as she sat in the Escalade drumming her fingers on the wheel, she decided that she had to know.

Instinct told her where to search.

Julia drove north, away from Main Street, quickly leaving the village proper. She watched her rearview mirror. The houses were increasingly scattered on wooded lots, and then she crossed a narrow bridge and was in the more rural northern half of the Landing, broad fields of perfect white, punctuated by enough stone walls and farmhouses to inspire an army of New England poets.

The snow was turning to rain.

She was taking the long way around, she knew, but that was because she had spotted a car on her tail and wanted to see if he, or she, would stay there. The Escalade breasted a hill and the car was still there, a quarter-mile back. She zipped through a stand of conifers, and when she looked back the car was still there. She turned off the main road onto a barely plowed track and stopped, quite boldly, waiting for her pursuer to pass, cell phone at the ready just in case.

Nothing.

Julia drummed her fingers, watched the road, watched the clock, watched the sky shift from slate to gray. Heavy frozen drops pelted the car. At last she decided she had been mistaken and pulled back onto the road. Five minutes more and she was surrounded by trees again. She found Pleasant Road. Snuggled in the woods near the end of the cul-de-sac was the dull-red saltbox belonging to Vera Brightwood.

Julia never slowed down. She made the wide turn, fishtailing on the slippery tarmac, and sped the other way.

In Vera's driveway were three or four cars. One of them was Frank Carrington's Ford pickup. Another was a blue Infiniti she had seen at Hunter's Heights half a dozen times. It belonged to Trevor Land.

A few people out in the Landing were pretty angry with him.

Maybe all the angry people were finally getting together.

(11)

JULIA BEAT THE SCHOOL BUSES HOME by a hair and listened to Jeannie burble about her day while Vanessa chanted upstairs. The dean called to discuss next week's conference with the Lombard bean counters, but Julia, deep in a discussion of the details, nevertheless sensed within herself a rising lack of interest in the affairs of the divinity school. She kept peeking out the living room window as if expecting the meeting at Vera's house to conclude with an angry march up to Hunter's Heights. She thought of calling Lemaster, who was down in Washington, but was not sure what to tell him. She e-mailed Mary Mallard, outlining the possibility that some of the older Landingers were up to something, then fed the children and sent them off to do their homework. Up in the master suite, she curled on the bed with Rainbow Coalition, poured herself a glass of wine, and turned on an old movie. When she opened her eyes, it was almost eleven.

Jeannie had put her perfect self perfectly to bed, but Vanessa was down in the kitchen, sitting at the shining black counter, a bowl of Cheerios beside her, rushing through homework she had started much too late. Julia stood at the sink, mind weaving tangled skeins of conspiracy, trying to frame the question that only one person in all the world—the person sitting in front of her—would not think insane. But before she could ask, Vanessa spoke.

"Oh, Moms, while you were asleep? You got a message from Mary. She says it's important."

"From Mary?" Julia was surprised. Like Mona, the writer avoided the telephone for anything of substance. "Mary Mallard?"

Vanessa nodded, furiously polishing a French translation. "Uh-huh."

"Did she want me to call her back?"

"It wasn't a phone call."

"Are you saying she came to the *house*?"

"No, Moms, no." The start of a grin behind the braids. Vanessa, like Kellen, liked her verbal fun. "It was an e-mail."

"She *e-mailed* you? I don't *believe* this."

"No, Moms. She e-mailed *you*."

"You read my e-mail?"

"You should really change your password more than once every couple of years."

Julia's voice was flat with anger. And fear. "How much have you read?"

"Enough to know you're wasting your time. DeShaun did it. Nobody else. Just DeShaun. Remember I'm like the world's leading expert on Gina Joule." Vanessa's nose never lifted from her book. In the night quiet, her tone was placid and soothing, the voice of adult authority. The ensuing explosion came as a shock. "So why can't the two of you just mind your own business? It was *DeShaun!* Why can't you leave it alone? Why are you letting this woman push you around? You used to leave *everything* alone, so leave this alone, too!" Vanessa was shivering, but forced a trembling calm into her words. "Anyway, the e-mail said Mary found this witness who— never mind. You can read it."

"Why are you so upset, angry, honey? What's wrong?"

"Nothing." She turned a page, pretending to read. "So, what's next? Looking for Shari Larid?"

Julia put an unsteady hand on Vanessa's shoulder. "You can't be a part of this, honey." Stubborn, fuming silence. "I'm serious. It's for your own good."

"Who wants to be a part of it? You and your creepy friends."

"Just promise me you'll stay away from this." A kiss on the forehead. Still Vanessa refused to look at her mother. Then Julia, remembering, reared back. "And don't you ever read another person's e-mail again! You know better than that!"

"It was DeShaun." Her litany. She sagged, exhausted. Dr. Brady warned the Carlyles, often, to make sure Vanessa got enough sleep. "You're wasting your time."

"It's not that I don't trust you. But I think I'll change my password."

"Good idea."

Julia sat in front of the computer, clicked, frowned. "Honey?"

"Hmmm?"

"Can you show me how?"

CHAPTER 39

COMMON PRAYER

(I)

ON MOST SUNDAYS, the Carlyle family attended mass up in Norport at the Church of Saint Matthias the Apostle, an Anglican congregation that had, in the view of its defiant rector, turned its back on apostasy. The Episcopal diocese begged to disagree, and the ensuing litigation over who owned the church building had yet to be resolved. When the name of Lemaster Carlyle was first floated as a possible president, the campus paper sent a reporter to attend services at Saint Matthias for several weeks running, then ran a story asserting, in considerable outrage, that the rector, Father Freed, seemed to consider the Bible to be the divinely inspired Word of God. Two professors from the divinity school were quoted on the dangers inherent in such a view.

The two Sunday-morning services drew a racially integrated congregation, a mixture of Caribbean immigrants raised in the Anglo-Catholic tradition, who found the ways of the American branch incoherent and slovenly—male parishioners showed up without ties, the priest faced the congregants across the altar instead of turning away, toward the Lord, when consecrating the wine and bread, and, oh, by the way, what was this nonsense about female bishops?—alongside the sturdy edge of the white upper crust, scattered survivors of old New England families who had yet to make their peace with a Book of Common Prayer that had been revised a quarter-century ago.

Lemaster drew his energy from tradition. For him, the very idea of "church" captured a continuing institution entrusted with custody of the historical teaching of the apostles—the "deposit," as traditionalists still called it—of which the believer, living out his transitory life in faith and fear, dared not alter a single stroke. As for the children, Saint Matthias was the only church they knew. Julia never let on that the cloying smell of the incense, unvarying from season to season although mercifully absent from Ash Wednesday until the Easter Vigil, always seemed to transform the music of the organ into the unnerving soundtrack of the old Dracula movies with Bela Lugosi, which she used to stay up late on Saturday nights to watch on the black-and-white television on her dresser, a synesthesia she dared not confess to her husband, lest he deem her insufficiently pious. It would be wrong to say that nothing meant more to Lemaster Carlyle than the celebration of the Eucharist at Saint Matthias, but the number of things that did was small. Lemaster, for all his outward liberalism, ran a traditional household. What he wanted, he got. And so it was, on the third Sunday after Christmas, that the Carlyles braved an ice storm that made driving an adventure in order to travel up to Norport for the eleven o'clock high mass.

(11)

THE RECTOR, spotted hands spread before him, solemnly recited the traditional call to the altar, as specified in the 1928 version of the Book of Common Prayer, for Father Freed and his dwindling flock would hear no word of any other. "Ye who do truly and earnestly repent you of your sins, and are in love and charity with your neighbours, and intend to lead a new life, following the commandments of God, and walking from henceforth in his holy ways: Draw near with faith, and take this holy Sacrament to your comfort; and make your humble confession to Almighty God, devoutly kneeling."

With a great shuffling silence, the congregation slid off the benches and onto the red leather kneelers. The Carlyle family, as it had done for years, also assumed the position, as absent Preston, the household wit, used to call it.

Except for Vanessa, who, sniffling, remained seated.

Her father, head bowed next to her, frowned and plucked at her sleeve.

Vanessa shook her head and snatched her slim arm away. On the high altar, twin candles flickered as though in a breeze. Someone sneezed. Someone moaned.

"You have to confess, honey," Lemaster hissed.

"No."

"You can't receive the Sacrament if you don't make your confession."

"Then I won't."

Her father made a face. "But that's the whole point of the Eucharistic Prayer."

"I know."

"Vanessa, what's wrong?" he said, still whispering, but now others were looking, not only Julia and the children, but judgment-eyed Mrs. Galloway in the pew right in front of them, and the surviving members of the vast Traynor clan just behind. One of the few things Lemaster hated, his wife well knew, was committing a faux pas before a white audience.

"Nothing," snapped Vanessa, loud enough to be heard at the altar. Jeannie looked on in astonished delight.

"Vanessa," Julia began, rubbing her arm. "Honey, come on."

Louder: "Honey, come on."

"No!" Vanessa cried and, leaping to her feet, shoved past her father, into the aisle, and down toward the vestibule, or, in Anglican-speak, the narthex. Julia started to rise and follow her, but Lemaster waved at his wife to stay put. She assumed that he meant he would go, but he simply bent his head over his neatly folded hands where they rested on the back of the next pew ahead and resumed his silent prayer of repentance. Julia mimicked him, closing her eyes against the beckoning tears, begging God to forgive her, and Vanessa, and Lemaster, too.

Then the loving fury of motherhood took her. She stood and, not bothering to explain herself to her husband, slipped into the aisle and followed her daughter.

(I I I)

"I CAN'T TAKE COMMUNION ANY MORE," Vanessa told her after they had walked in silence for a few minutes down the snow-crusted main street of Norport. A few cars wheezed along, but the business district, such as it was, was basically deserted.

Julia nodded as though this information was the most obvious commonsense point on the face of the globe. She wondered what Lemaster was doing, and why he had not followed. Leading Jeannie to the altar rail by now, she imagined.

"Okay," she said.

"Aren't you going to ask me why?"

"Do you want me to ask you why?"

"Oh, Moms, don't do that. I get enough of that from my shrink."

Conceding the point, Julia tried to slip an arm around her daughter's shoulders, but Vanessa wiggled free.

Julia said, "Okay, tell me why you can't take Communion any more."

"Because I'm not in love and charity with my neighbors." Waving her hands up and down the street. "That's what the prayer says, right? I'm not in love and charity and—"

Again Julia tried, and failed, to hug her. "Oh, honey, they don't literally mean love and charity with all your neighbors."

Vanessa stiffened. "No? What do they mean, then?" As Julia fumbled for an answer, her daughter slumped again. "Never mind. I'm sorry, Moms. Look. I . . . Look. It's not your fault, okay? It's just"—for an instant so small Julia later wondered whether she had seen it, Vanessa's eyes welled up; and then were dry again—"I can't do it any more. Never again."

"That's why they put the confession before Communion, honey." Julia, whose belief in the details of the Anglican tradition tended to be uneven at best, was weary of the dialectic. Yet she sensed the nearness of the trauma about which Vincent Brady had warned. "Even if you can't tell me, you can still tell God."

"Look, I don't want to talk about it, okay? Can we just not talk about it? Why do you people always have to talk about everything?"

Sometimes Julia found herself riding her high horse before she knew she had climbed aboard. "By 'you people,' I assume you mean your father and myself."

Vanessa had stopped in front of a cheap little deli which seemed to leave the meat in the window when it was closed, which struck Julia as a poor idea, and probably a violation of about sixteen provisions of the health code. "I mean everybody. Everybody always wants to talk. They all want me to talk. But there's things you just can't talk about!"

"Can't talk to me? Or can't talk to anybody?"

"Why do you get like this?" Vanessa cried, spinning away once more and stumbling down the block. "Look. I don't want to go to church any more. I don't want to confess any more. I don't want to talk to God any more."

"You don't believe in God?"

"I didn't say that. I just said I don't want to talk to Him. No more—"

She stopped and hurried off, Julia striding fast to keep up with her taller daughter.

"Vanessa, please. What happened?" Successfully managing a hug this time, except that it was like hugging a wiggling snake. "Did somebody do something to you? Kellen? Is this about Kellen? Stop it! Vanessa!"

"Look, forget it, okay? Forget what I said. I'm sorry I walked out of church. Just forget it."

Julia had a temper, too, although she had learned, under Brady's guidance, to keep it in check, especially around Vanessa. But sometimes it was so hard. She said, as gently as she could, but more harshly than she wanted, "Vanessa, I love you. I would march through fire for you. Now, you know that. I don't know what's bothering you, but, whatever it is, I just want to help you. I want you to be happy."

The speech, as she had feared, clunked. "Happy! You want me to be happy!"

"Yes, darling. Of course I do."

"Then tell Senator Whisted to get out of the race."

"Do what?"

"They're gonna nominate him, right?" The swift tears again, appearing, then vanishing. "Well, don't let them do it!"

"Honey—"

"Dads can do anything, right? He can get people fired with a phone call. If he tells Whisted to drop out of the race, he'll drop out of the race."

Julia stood shivering in the wind, hands in her pockets, unwilling to surrender to the voluptuous possibility that the mystery was solved. She had wanted it to be Scrunchy, but now the evidence pointed the other way. Kellen had sent Mary the photograph of Mal Whisted. Maureen Whisted had warned Julia that everybody had bad secrets in their past. Mitch Huebner had gone hunting for his father's diary ten years ago—around the time of Mal Whisted's first campaign for the Senate. Now here was Vanessa, the self-proclaimed expert on the case, who insisted that DeShaun was guilty—and yet thought Malcolm Whisted should drop out of the primaries.

Julia spoke gently, but unrelentingly.

"Does this have something to do with Gina?"

Vanessa lifted her chin, and the wide mouth started to move. For a brilliant moment, Julia thought her second-eldest was going to explain. Then Vanessa shook her head. "Look. It wasn't even my idea, okay? He told me—"

She covered her mouth and shook her head, wind picking at her jacket. They were close, so agonizingly close. Julia spoke gently. "Go on, honey. It's okay."

Vanessa tried. She lifted a palm as if to display the answer and said, again, "He told me to try—"

Again she stopped.

"Who told you, honey? Who told you what?"

"It doesn't matter, Moms. It's not important."

"But honey—"

"No." Hands out in front of her, palms downturned, the sign of abnegation Vanessa had employed even as a child. She could be as unyielding as her Barbadian father, and living with the both of them sometimes seemed to suck the oxygen from the air. "It's over, okay? Just leave it alone."

Be firm but loving, Brady had said. *Don't cross-examine. Never press her into a corner. But do not forget for a moment, and don't let her forget, which one of you is the child and which one is the parent.*

"All right, Vanessa. We don't have to talk about it. Not just now. But we are going back inside." A hint of steel to remind her daughter that the Harlem side could be as tough as the Barbadian.

"No."

"What did you say to me?"

"I said no. I'm not going."

More steel. "Vanessa, I'm not taking a public-opinion poll here."

"And I'm not stating an opinion. I'm stating a fact. I can't go in there."

Then she calmed down. "Look. I really can't be in there just now. I'm sorry. I'm not being disrespectful. But I can't go back in there. I just can't. Please don't make me."

Julia studied her child's troubled face, saw moisture welling in her eyes, felt the mistiness in her own. Oh, Vanessa, what's wrong with you? What's happening? "Then I'll stay out here with you."

"You don't have to do that."

"I want to."

"No. No, it's okay." Touching her mother's coat, the gesture at once affectionate and dismissive. "Really. You go back in. Maybe you can still get a wafer."

"Vanessa—"

"I'll be fine, Moms. Honestly. I promise not to burn anything, okay?"

"That's not what I was going to—"

"Moms, look. I'm a big girl. I just want to be alone for a few minutes, that's all." The eyes implored her. "Please, Moms. Trust me."

She knew what Lemaster would say, but, this once, it was not his call. Vincent Brady had suggested that they show more faith in Vanessa, and Julia decided to give it a try. "Okay, honey. We'll be out in fifteen minutes. Maybe less."

"I'll meet you at the car."

"Promise?"

Vanessa clapped her mother on the shoulder. "Don't worry. I said I'll meet you. And I will."

"Okay."

But she didn't.

It was another ten hours before they tracked her down.

PART III

CLEARING THE MARKET

Market Clearing—In economics, the process through which markets seek equilibrium, as supply grows to meet increased demand, or as demand shrinks because of high prices. Most economists accept that market clearing occurs with little need for outside intervention, but many believe that, absent regulation, today's complex markets often will not clear efficiently. Debate remains fierce on whether intervention tends to make markets work better or worse.

CHAPTER 40

AGAIN BOSTON

(1)

"I TOLD YOU not to have kids, Julia," whispered Byron Dennison, agony tautening the powerful face.

"Oh, Bay, you did not." Cleaning his mouth with a cloth napkin. Much against his formidable will, he was back in the hospital, and helpless, several bodily systems having decided simultaneously to err on the side of failure. No doubt his family members would be flocking to his side, if he had family members. Politicians and celebrities had shown up long enough to have their pictures taken and lie about their deep affection for the cantankerous old so-and-so, but the deathwatch had been left largely to a tiny handful of acolytes, most too busy with their careers to do much watching. Lemaster had been up three times this week. "All you said was that there are two kinds of people in the world, people who are parents and people who have fun."

He coughed, and laughed, and sputtered. A hand jerked but went nowhere in particular. His suite was private, and fancy, and expensive, but still smelled of all those things we avoid hospitals to avoid smelling. Though his body was dissipating, his single good eye sparkled, and his clever mind seemed sharp as ever. "And do you have fun? You and the Little Master? See? I was right." He shifted position. Julia helped with the pillows. She had just returned Aaron to school and was detouring to Boston for a couple of days, specifically to see Byron, but also to meet Mary Mallard. "He loves you, Julia. You have to remember that. He loves you as much as he can. Listen to me. He's a wounded man. Hell, we all are. The Little Master's a wounded man, I'm a wounded man. All right, you're a wounded woman, but it's different for women. You're allowed to be wounded. We're not."

"That's a little bit outdated, Bay."

"I'm a little bit outdated. Lemaster's a little bit outdated. He's eight years older than you are, Julia. Those eight years are huge. He's a different generation. Don't let yourself forget that. And here's the biggest difference between men then and men now. We don't wear our wounds like medals. We wear our medals like wounds. Do you understand?" The left side of his mouth did not close properly. She cleaned it again. "When I say he loves you as much as he can, I mean that. He would never hurt you. Never. You or the children."

"Anybody, in the right situation—"

"You mean the wrong situation. And he's not just anybody. He's Little Master. He's a man so caught up in duty and obligation that he doesn't have a spare minute to think of who he is. If he betrayed you, you'd know the next day. He wouldn't be able to function. You're his wife, but I've known him a lot longer than you have. You keep the Little Master's world together, Julia. End of speech."

And it was. He drooped, his eyes fluttered, his breathing grew harder. One of the many monitors changed the rate at which it was beeping, and she wondered if she should call the nurse. He was permitted only one visitor at a time, but nobody was waiting, and, besides, Bay had asked her to stay awhile.

She said, "Do you need anything?"

"Just a bribe for Saint Peter." Julia smiled. The good eye sought her out. "See? See? That's the kind of thing I could never say to the Little Master. He hates jokes about his faith."

"He can be a little . . . pompous."

"Balls. The Little Master isn't pompous. He just doesn't have a sense of humor."

"Bay—"

"I know. I know. This other business." His hand rose abruptly, dropped onto hers. She held the cool flesh, pressed it in her warmth. "My advice is to forget about it."

Julia was surprised. "Forget about it?"

"Listen to me. You have your daughter to take care of. You have your little one. Your job, your marriage—a million other things to do. There are people who waste their lives trying to get a little bit of leverage to influence a political campaign." His cough was hollow and wet and rattling. "Leave that work to them, Julia."

"I'm not thinking about politics. I'm thinking about justice."

"Justice." Not quite a sneer but almost. "Let me tell you something. People who want justice cause more horror in the world than all the rest of— Never mind. Never mind. I'm old. I'm mostly dead. Ignore me."

Ignoring him was the last thing Julia wanted to do. She craved his advice mostly because he was, unlike most adults her own age, a grown-up. Outside the wide windows, the afternoon sun was setting in a clear, perfect sky. "If one of the candidates killed that little girl—"

"You know what Lincoln said? In politics, the statute of limitations should be short."

"Come on, Bay. We're not talking about having sex with the wrong woman or fiddling on your taxes. We're talking about somebody who killed a teenager and covered it up. And if one of them did it, even if he's a Senator or President—"

"If. Maybe. Might have. Possibly. A source says. That's what's wrecking our democracy, Julia. Everything's conditional. Everything's a rumor. But it's on television or it's on the Internet, so it must be true. At least, if it helps our side, it's true. If it helps the bad guys, why, then, it's dirty, nasty partisan politics, isn't it?" To her astonishment, he managed to sit halfway up. One of the machines launched a loud protest and persuaded a second to join in. "If you have facts—not rumors, not ideas, not guesses, but actual facts, evidence—then take your facts to the authorities. The FBI. The CIA. I don't care who." He settled again, exhausted. "But if you don't? If all you have is rumor, innuendo, unnamed sources, all that crap? Don't take it anywhere. Forget about it. That's my old-man's advice. You can ignore it for free." He closed his eyes.

Hiatus, because the nurse came in and fiddled and fussed and started making notes with a stylus on a handheld computer. Bay flirted without enthusiasm. The nurse smiled tiredly. The break was welcome, at least to Julia, because she did not know what to say. The authorities! Well, of course, Bay would think that, having long been part of the power structure himself. Julia remembered, when she was at Dartmouth, how the black students, herself included, would sit around and condemn any members of the darker nation who wielded real influence, on the insidious theory that their success was itself evidence of their disloyalty.

Representative Byron Dennison, in particular, was whispered to have powerful white backers, rich men who furthered his career, never mind that there was no other way to get into Congress. But now, when Bay mentioned the authorities, Julia's first panicky thought was of Vanessa, whose relationship with Kellen the authorities would surely explore. Beyond that, Byron Dennison seemed to be taking Lemaster's side in a dispute Julia and her husband had rehearsed a dozen times. Her husband's faith in officialdom had over the years been a matter of occasional contention between them. Julia, like so many raised to privilege and prospect in African America, sensed within herself a reflexive suspicion toward the apparatus of government. Perhaps it was the influence of Mad Mona, who continued preaching to her many acolytes that the United States was the source of most of the world's evil. Perhaps it was the influence of the public-relations trade, which, in one of her many other lives, Julia had thought to ply. Or perhaps—as Lemmie himself always seemed keen to argue, no matter how he wounded her— it was Julia's way of identifying her own fortunes with those of the less fortunate among the community, with whom she had had almost no contact while growing up in New Hampshire and precious little since.

When the nurse was gone again, Byron Dennison settled back, breathing with difficulty.

"Bay?"

"Still with you."

She licked her lips and wished she had a way to moisten her throat. "The thing is, Bay, I can't go to the authorities. I can't." Her voice was, momentarily, faint. "I'm sorry."

"Your call, not mine. I told you, ignore my advice if you want." This time his cough was dry, the sound inestimably worse. "Tell you another secret. If the girl won't tell you where she was, well, she has her reasons. Smart girl. Always liked her. So she slipped the reins a little. Well, that's what Thoroughbreds do, Julia. And your Vanessa's a Thoroughbred. Good genes. Never mind. Don't listen to me. I'm tired."

"Bay—"

"Hush. I'm sleeping."

"No, you're not."

He smiled, eyes still tightly shut. "Where did you say you found her? A dance club?"

"Actually, it was the director of campus safety. He found her at a club. Her friend Smith—Janine Goldsmith—picked her up from the church and drove her to the train station. Vanessa went to New York. She won't say where. She says she didn't find what she was looking for, but she won't say what she was looking for. She took the train back, she took a taxi to the club—"

"Maybe she just needed a break."

"Maybe." Julia steadied herself. She had lost her temper severely. So had Lemaster, but at Dr. Brady, not Vanessa. He planned to fire the man as soon as they could line up a new therapist. "But I don't think so. I think it had to do with— Never mind. The point is, Vanessa is seriously grounded. She can't see Janine, can't talk to her, instant-message her, anything." Julia stopped, because the room was wavering and the machines were roaring in her ears, but probably it was her own blood. "Anyway, Bruce Vallely tracked her down at the club, dancing with guys twice her age. She said she just wanted to have a little fun before she got too old. The fun Gina never got to have." Again she needed a moment to collect herself, remembering how all Vanessa would say was that she had no choice. "Oh, and she was underage to be admitted to the club, even if she didn't drink anything. I imagine by now Lemmie's had their liquor license pulled."

"Good for him."

"You taught him that, didn't you?"

"Taught him what?"

"About power. How to use it. When."

The good eye rolled open. Sweat stood out on the gray flesh. "I told them all. Use power any way you want. Get rich. Help the poor. Whatever. The important thing is to use it and keep using it. If you leave it lying around, somebody else will pick it up. Power has to be used, or it's not real." Cough. "If you use it, people decide you're a powerful person, they get accustomed to doing what you want, and that gives you more power. Just don't ever start trying to use it for justice. People are real, justice is abstract. Abstract is when the killing starts."

Julia, the empiricist, hated abstractions, which was one reason she had hardly ever stepped inside a classroom since starting work at the divinity school. Chafing as she listened, she nibbled her lower lip. "Bay, ah, the only other thing is—"

"Don't tell Little Master what we talked about. I remember."

"I'm sorry to put you in this position, Bay. Especially now."

"I'm the keeper of lots of secrets, Julia. That's what people like me do for a living. We keep secrets." A gurgle. "I'm outdated. I was taught you take your secrets to your grave. People today, give them a secret, all they can think of is which reporter to call first. No integrity. No honor. And, God knows, no loyalty. Can't keep their mouths shut. Just want to see their names in the paper, even if their names are 'unnamed source' or 'person with knowledge of the situation.' Reporters are just as bad. Have it backward. Seem to think the fact that somebody won't go on the record proves he's telling the truth. As if an honorable man betrays the trust of his colleagues. Sorry. End of speech. Ignore me."

She had scarcely heard him. "It's just that Lemaster is under a lot of . . . strain. I don't think he'd understand why I have to do this."

A quiet, labored guffaw. "Don't worry, Julia. I understand. Now, listen to me. Are you listening?"

"Of course." Squeezing his hand, because she was suddenly not sure Bay could see her.

"If I were you? What I'd want to know?"

"Yes?"

"Not *where* my little girl spent those hours in New York. *Why* my little girl spent those hours in New York. I told you, she's smart. And she's single-minded, like her mother. I wonder if she had any—"

The eye closed again, and he slept.

(11)

"WHAT EXACTLY DID KELLEN TELL YOU about his Black Lady?" asked Julia. She and Mary were sitting in a booth at a Cambridge restaurant across the square from the Inn at Harvard, where Julia was staying overnight. She had tried without success to reach her son Preston and had chosen the hotel to be near him, but had a shrewd suspicion that he was not answering the phone until she left. "Before he got himself arrested, Tony Tice was interviewing Ladybugs. Presumably he thinks one of us must be the Black Lady."

Mary picked at her grilled-chicken-and-arugula salad. It was not on the menu, but she had charmed the waiter into creating it. Like many heavy smokers, she ate with care. The students crowding the next table were reassuringly raucous. Mary had assured her that the best place not to be overheard was a crowd.

"Only that the Black Lady was helping him with his research. Oh, and that she was one of his old stories." A tight smile. "Don't worry, it couldn't be your Vanessa, because Kellen said the Black Lady had been around awhile and seen things."

Julia chewed thoughtfully on her sloshy burger. "That's the other reason you thought it was me? Because I'm one of his old stories?"

"Unless he's slept with another Sister Lady." She saw Julia's face. "Sorry. I'm pretty blunt."

"I'll say."

Mary lifted a bite of arugula on her fork, then thought better of the urge and returned it to her plate. "But then I decided I was wrong. It was pretty clear to me that the Black Lady who was helping in his research and the New York girlfriend who would take on the inventory risk for him were two different people."

"One of his old stories," said Julia, an idea beginning to form, although not one she was prepared to share with Mary. "Now tell me about Tice's connection to Kellen," she commanded.

"You're really bossy, do you know that?"

"You have no idea," said Julia, thrilling secretly to the new her, much more like the old her than the one who shared Lemaster's bed and board. Semi-Precious was gone. Jewel was back.

"Well, all I know is what Kellen told me. Tony had a client who was interested in bidding for the surplus. I got the idea that the client was on the shady side, and if Kellen could prove what he thought he could prove, well, you can see why it would make sense."

"People say Tony's clients are Mafiosi or terrorists or—"

"Or a coalition of Texas oilmen or Silicon Valley tycoons. They're every bit as dangerous, Julia. Every bit as corrupt." Mary was entirely serious. "Don't be fooled by arbitrary labels telling us what's legal or illegal. No matter who his clients are, anybody who'd pay for the surplus is dangerous." She stirred her salad, managed to find a mushroom of which she approved. "I mean, somebody killed Kellen. And maybe your friend Boris, too. God knows who else."

Julia nodded, although not in agreement. She stuffed a French fry into her mouth. She heard wild conspiracy theories in her inner-city beauty parlor and on Kwame Kennerly's radio show, and it was easy to forget that white people, too, were capable of believing anything.

"Did Tony go to Kellen initially, or did Kellen go to Tony?"

"Good question. I asked Kellen the same thing. Unfortunately, he never answered," Mary said, shoving her salad aside. "The thing is, Kellen told me he was planning an auction for his inventory. What he called an 'all-pay auction.' Do you know what that means? I had to look it up. It's an auction where you pay your bid whether you get the item or not."

"Why would anybody do that? It's nuts."

"No, it isn't, if you think about it. People will bid less, because they know they lose the money if their bid isn't the highest. So, if you can guess other people's bids, you'll get the thing for less in an all-pay auction than in the other kinds. The crazy part was Kellen thinking once he started putting out feelers the whole thing would stay secret. Are you done?"

Julia grinned. She understood. Five minutes later, they were strolling through the chilly night across Harvard Yard, most of the gates now locked at night, windows brightly lighted in the massive Georgian dorms. Mary was working on her second cigarette already.

"I've met a couple of times with Bruce Vallely," Julia said. "Trevor Land suggested it. And you know what? He's not so bad. He's clumsy, but kind of nice."

"Hubba-hubba."

Julia elbowed her. "Cut it out. He's actually shared some useful information. I've even put together a sort of chronology."

"Tell."

"On the night she died, Gina was seen talking to DeShaun. Okay. But here's the thing. One witness—a teacher—said she saw Gina alive after she was supposed to have gotten into the car with DeShaun. Then she changed her story. Said she was mistaken." Julia shivered. "According to Mitch Huebner, though, she didn't just see Gina. She let Gina in her house to make a phone call. Half an hour later, a sporty-looking car showed up in the driveway with two young men inside. One of the guys got out. Gina argued with him, but finally the three of them drove off. And that was that."

They walked in silence for a moment. Then Julia resumed.

"So—who were the two boys? Well, Mitch Huebner says Gina had a boyfriend she used to sneak out to meet. And Bruce says Jock Hilliman's Jag was wrecked that night. By Jock's own admission, he made a specialty of seducing the daughters of faculty. In those days, even more than these days, that was a high-risk business. Not everybody would take to it. I would guess that Jock was the boyfriend."

"And Mal Whisted was a friend of the family."

"That doesn't mean Scrunchy couldn't have been in the car. We don't know which two they were." She nibbled her lip. "In fairness, it could have been Jock and somebody we haven't thought about."

"But you don't believe that, and neither do I." Mary's turn now. "I told you I found this witness. It's a guy from the President's class who says he's ready to go on the record. Lives out in the Midwest. He swears Scrunchy was at a frat party that night, had too much to drink, and fell asleep on the sofa. He slept there all night. The guy says he remembers because it was the Valentine's Day party, and Scrunchy showed up with a woman who left with somebody else and got all maudlin. So, if this guy's telling the truth, it couldn't have been Scrunchy in the car that night."

"Too convenient," said Julia.

"I'll say. Witnesses turning up just as people need them." She blew out more smoke. "Still, the guy didn't come to me. I tracked him down. I don't know, Julia. He doesn't sound like he's making it up."

"Did he use the word *maudlin*?"

"What difference does it make?"

"Call me prejudiced, but it just doesn't strike me as a frat kind of word." Julia's boots crunched agreeably through the snow. "And, by the way, how many of Scrunchy's frat brothers did you call before you found one willing to talk?"

Mary smiled. "And here I thought I was the conspiracy theorist." She moved to the next subject. "I've tried to find a source in the Hilliman family. But they're so secretive, they live behind so many walls of lawyers and retainers, I can't find a way in. I've talked to a friend of mine who wrote a book about them, and he told me he didn't have any good inside sources either. I don't think the Hillimans will do us much good." She hesitated. "I did find out something about your boyfriend, though. Hey, no need to get rough. About Bruce Vallely. When he was doing Special Forces in Central America, he beat some poor CIA guy within an inch of his life because the Agency didn't want to bring out an informer who'd been targeted by the death squads. He's a very protective guy, Bruce Vallely."

"Huh." Julia was not sure how she felt about that one. A glance over her shoulder. She felt observed. "Were you serious a couple of weeks ago? About how I might be under surveillance?"

"Sure."

"What makes you say that?"

The tip gleamed redly as Mary inhaled. "It's a feeling. When you're around people who follow people for a living—and I've spent a lot of time with them—you just get that sense. A couple of times, even in Harbor County, I've been around you, and you haven't noticed. I don't think I'm the only one. There are big people worried about what Kellen was doing, Julia. Powerful people. They want to know what you're up to."

"Last week, in the Landing, there was a car I thought was following me."

"I wouldn't be surprised."

"And there was all this top-of-the-line spyware on my computer—"

"Kind of makes my point, doesn't it? Powerful people, Julia."

"Any idea who?"

"I'm working on it."

"Are we being followed right now?"

"I don't think so. You can't ever be sure, but I don't think so." Blowing smoke through her nose. "College campuses are actually very difficult targets, my friends in the business tell me. Students sitting around doing nothing don't stand out. Adults do. If adults are on campus, they're headed someplace. Colleges belong to the kids now."

"I sure hope so."

"Because of your antics last month," said the writer, smiling. "That was pretty brave of you. Breaking into the basement of your own building. But, you know, Julia, you probably left your fingerprints everywhere."

"I thought it through. I think it's okay. My fingerprints have legitimate reasons to be in the library."

"On the barred window eight feet off the floor?"

"Okay, so I didn't think it through." The tickle of smoke in her nose set off the old craving. She was determined to resist. Students traveled in small knots, hoods up as they leaned into the wind. But Julia was from New Hampshire and Mary was from Maine, and neither was prepared to admit that the temperature was uncomfortable. "The thing is, I was wrong."

"Wrong about what?"

"Well, I have this student—Joe—who owes me a favor. I wanted to figure out exactly what part of the Joule papers Kellen had looked at, but I didn't want to arouse the suspicion of the archivist, who already doesn't like me. So I gave Joe the cites and asked him to go to the library and pretend he needed them for his own research. Which he did."

They turned into a cul-de-sac, retraced their steps to get out. Julia had the sense that Mary had led her this way intentionally, to check their back. Angry voices exploded across the Yard, a couple fiercely breaking up, at least for the moment. Back at Dartmouth, Julia and Kellen had endured several such shouting matches in the middle of the Green, hating each other so much they had to go back to bed to prove it.

"That was clever," said Mary. "Using a student, I mean. So—what were the cites?"

"They weren't anything. That was the funny part. Kellen had written 'Merrill Joule Collection' at the top of each request slip, but none of the numbers on the slips matched anything in the Joule papers. Joe thought this was odd, and he asked Mrs. Bethe—she's the archival assistant—he asked Mrs. Bethe if she could tell him what documents the numbers would fit. Only she refused. Said it was against the rules. He had to show a bona fide academic need for any collection he wanted to get into, and a sheet full of numbers wasn't a need."

"She sounds like a real treat. Want one?" Offering the cigarettes. Addicts hate to suffer alone.

With an effort, Julia made herself wave the pack away. "The two of them run those archives like the most important thing is making sure nobody knows what's inside. Rod Rutherford probably spends almost as much on security for that place as he does on books." Both women stopped. "You thinking what I'm thinking?"

Mary said, "Extra locks, alarms, bars on the windows, and a staff that doesn't trust anybody, can't be talked out of following the rules, and makes you leave a dozen written records if you ever do get inside."

Julia said, "The perfect hiding place for whatever you don't want found."

"Like, say, pages from Arnold Huebner's diary. And whatever other forms the surplus took."

"Perfect," Julia said again. A pause. "Except we can't get in."

"We can't. You can."

"How do I do that exactly?"

"I have no idea. But don't worry. You've pulled one brilliancy after another out of your hat the past few weeks. I'm sure you'll figure this one out."

Julia doubted it but played along. "And when I get there, what do I look for?"

"I leave that to you, too."

"Thanks a lot."

"Seriously. You're the one he left the clues for. Not me or Tony or anybody else. You're who Kellen left them for, and you're who can interpret them."

Julia put her hands on her hips. "And while I'm risking my neck sneaking into the Kepler archives and going through all ten thousand folios, or whatever they have, looking for a few loose diary pages, what exactly will you be doing?"

"Research. Interviews. Memos."

"In other words, nothing."

"Working hard on my book proposal."

"I meant, what are you going to do to help *me*?"

Mary made a dainty face, dimpling her chin with a finger. "Well, in high school I was a cheerleader." She laughed in the winter night. "Rah, rah."

CHAPTER 41

DARK MATTER

(1)

JULIA HAD NOT TOLD MARY EVERYTHING. Alone again, she steered the Escalade through the narrow side streets of Cambridge and parked at an awkward angle three blocks from the address she wanted, because no space was wide enough for her car. She knew that if she pushed the buzzer her son would find some excuse, so she dawdled near the entrance to the low building until a knot of students exited, slipping in as one politely held the door. On the fourth floor, she heard the raised voices before she reached the apartment. She knocked anyway, loud enough to be heard over the din. The door snapped open, and a twentyish redhead with teary bags under her eyes snarled, "What?"

Then Preston was there, small and compact and brilliantly complete, needing nobody, least of all a parent or a weepy girlfriend. "Well," he said. To the girlfriend: "Believe it or not, this serious hottie is my mother." A silence everybody waited for somebody else to break. "I guess you can come in."

The living room and kitchen were filthy, and Julia was not invited to inspect the rest. "Megan isn't much of a housekeeper. Well, what do you expect? She's a historian, not a scientist." He had his father's devastating smile, but his eyes were New England winter. "Oh, right, I forgot. You're not a scientist, either, are you, Ma? You're a *biologist*. A biologist-*theologian*."

They sat on opposite sides of a rickety table. Megan served coffee and stale croissants, then made herself scarce. Julia attempted small talk, even told Preston how she missed him, but he treated conversation like an indulgence to be shared only with your peers. In her son's presence she felt uncertain, even inferior. Mary Mallard would not have recognized her.

"What do you want, Ma? You didn't come to shoot the breeze. If you'd called I could have saved you the trouble."

"Do you hate me that much?"

"I don't hate *you* at all," he said, savagely, and Julia could hardly miss the point.

"What is it about, Preston? This thing with your father?"

"What are you doing here, Ma?"

Julia realized that she made her son as uncomfortable as he made her. They possessed no natural way of relating to each other. She remembered him as a small boy, the way he reveled in her hugs upon every fresh accomplishment. Everybody used to say that Preston would always be his mother's son, and Vanessa her father's daughter. Like most generalizations made by adults about the young, this one had proved false.

She said, "Did your father ever talk to you about his fraternity? The Empyreals? Maybe about . . . being his, ah, successor?"

"Of course." His interest gleamed, but he was waiting for her to play a better card. "Like a feudal lord with his firstborn son. Right of primogeniture."

"And you said no?"

"I'm not interested in that crap. The old families. The traditions. All that bullshit." Megan was weeping in the next room, but Preston was too puffed up with pride to notice. "I'm trying to discover the dark matter, and he's worrying about the darker nation."

"Dark matter?"

"The fundamental stuff of the universe. The equations predict— Never mind, you wouldn't understand. What do you *want*, Ma?"

Excitement. *The dark matters*, Kellen had said. "Right now, I want you to tell me what dark matter is."

"Seriously?"

She nodded.

"There isn't enough matter in the universe. That's what. We can only detect like one percent of the matter and energy there should be. That's what the equations tell us. Gravity, background radiation— everything's off. So, this other matter, the matter we can't find, is called dark matter. They used to think it was dead stars, or maybe neutrinos, but those have been disproved. Some physicists will tell you it's just a myth, but most of us think it's real stuff. It's out there somewhere, or maybe in here, passing through us all day long"—animated now that he was talking about his work, waving his hands back and forth like a man treading water—"and we just can't detect it. Get the idea? Just beneath the surface. We can't find it, but we know it has to be there. And, Ma, the thing is, the universe we see? It's such a tiny part of what's real. It's so thin it's almost an illusion. If we could find the dark matter, then we'd really know what's going on."

That had to be it. What Kellen wanted her to understand. The dark matter was down beneath the surface: *what's really going on*. And Preston had made the allusion for her, unasked. Dark matter. Darker nation. The Empyreals had popularized the phrase *darker nation*. What swirled around in plain sight was the illusion. The dark matter, the hidden hand of the Empyreals—that was the secret reality.

But what was that hidden reality? What were the Empyreals *doing*?

(11)

PRESTON COULD HARDLY WAIT to get her out of the apartment. He said he had to go to the lab, and perhaps he did. In the kitchen, Megan was raising a furious clatter. At the door, Julia turned to her son.

"Your friend seems very nice."

"She's just a diversion."

Ouch. "I miss you," she said. "We all miss you."

"How sweet, Ma."

Another misfire. She tried again. "You said you don't hate me. Does that mean you hate your father?"

Malice rose in his face, hot and sure. He seemed about to answer, but, with his father's discipline, decided to wait and discover her plan before refuting it, just as he used to wait out his opponents when he finished third in the United States Junior Chess Championship. "I gotta go," he said.

"Is that why you never come home, Preston? Because of whatever your father told you about the Empyreals?" She swallowed, closed her eyes and leaped. "What did he tell you?"

"No, Ma. That's not the reason."

"Then what is? Why are you having this feud?"

"It's not a feud. We just don't like each other." His face told her the subject was closed. Julia knew not to press: people said Preston resembled his mother, but the firmly locked set of mouth and eyes, the *I-have-decided*, was entirely Lemaster's.

"All right, Preston. All right." Wondering whether any of her children would ever confide in her again.

Her son's tone grew gentler. "Hey, how's Nessa? How's she holding up with all this Gina business going on?"

"She's remarkably strong, given—" Julia covered her mouth. She had almost missed his error. "What Gina business? What do you know about what's going on, Preston?"

"I'm just making sure she's all right. Running away and all."

"And who told you about that? Or that it had anything to do with Gina?" Julia answered her own question. "Vanessa did, didn't she, Preston? You're never in touch with anybody from the family, except you seem to know what's going on with Vanessa. Not phone calls, they'd show up on the bill." She saw the computer screen the night Smith had slept over, Vanessa hastily clicking away the instant messages when her mother walked into the room. "All right. You're in touch with her. She tells you things. And—and you tell her things, too, don't you?"

"I love my sister," he said defensively.

"I bet you do. I just bet you do." Julia was angry. At herself. She felt like a fool not to have seen it. *He told me to try*, Vanessa had said. "This Gina business—that's what you just called it. Except you forgot to tell me that this Gina business was your idea from the start. A year ago Vanessa had a different topic. A month later she announces she's looking into what happened to Gina. And who would have put the idea into her head if not you?" Her son said nothing. "What happened, Preston? Something made you stay away from the topic and then tell your sister to go for it. What was it?"

"It was an interesting topic, Ma. That's all."

"No, Preston. That's not all. You're like your father. You never do anything just for the hell of it. You always have a reason." She read the impatience in his handsome face. "What made you tell your sister to change her topic?" Although by now what she meant was, *What makes you tick?*

"I wouldn't hurt Nessa for the world."

"Hurt her? Her obsession with Gina didn't start until the paper you told her to do! That's what's hurting her!"

"I'm done talking about Gina, Ma." A swift, boyish grin. "Now if you'll excuse me, I have to go lie to my girlfriend for a while. You must know what that's like."

"What's that supposed to—" She saw it then, and, for a rich moment, her anger matched his own. "Kellen Zant was here, wasn't he? Maybe he shared some old stories about your mother. Then he asked you what I'm asking you. And you told him—what?"

"That I don't believe in ghosts or Santa Claus or convenient little black boys who show up just in time to get blamed for killing cute little white girls."

"Your sister seems sure—"

"I told you, Ma, I'm done talking about this. Done." He blew out a lot of air. Julia knew that the next concession would be his last. "But I'll tell you about Dad."

"What does your father have to do with—"

"Not Gina. The Empyreals. You asked what he told me." He shifted his weight, looked at his watch, glanced over his shoulder, then seized her arm and drew her physically into the dimly lighted hall. "You know in the Bible? How Satan takes Jesus up on the mountain and shows Him the kingdoms of the earth and says He can have it all if He'll just fall down and worship the devil?" Preston stepped back into the apartment. "That's Lemaster Carlyle, Ma. That's your husband. The devil."

"But what does that mean?"

"Just what it sounds like. Tempting me with earthly authority. What the fuck am I supposed to do with earthly authority? I'm doing important work, Ma. Using the blue horizontal branch stars to study Lyman alpha absorption in quasar spectra." But he was mocking her, and they both knew it. "Please don't come by without calling again. It's not polite."

He shut the door.

(III)

VEAZIE WOMEN NEVER CRIED, so Julia blundered along the snowy streets, forcing her mind to work the data, because she had gotten everything from Preston that he would ever give. It was Kellen who wanted her to hear it. That was what she reminded herself. Kellen wanted her to hear Preston's tale, and if she lacked the details, at least she had the outline. Every Empyreal was supposed to groom a young successor, and

Lemaster had tried to recruit his elder son. But Preston had rejected his blandishments. The disagreement was not the source of the hatred her son so carefully nurtured toward his father; it was the result. Had Lemmie then moved on to Aaron? But Julia had pressed him on the way up to Exeter, and was sure he knew nothing.

Rejected by Preston, Lemaster would have tried somebody outside the family.

A young black man. A student? A former law clerk? She shook her head. The possibilities were too scattered, and her information was too limited.

Dark matter. The hidden power in the universe. Lemmie insisted that Empyreals were no more than an insignificant Harlem men's club. Aurie implied that they were more, and now so did Preston—with Kellen's implicit endorsement.

Tempting me with earthly authority.

Authority over what? What on earth could the Empyreals have to do with Kellen's surplus? The research about Gina Joule?

We can't find it, but we know it has to be there.

You know what, Preston? I feel exactly the same way.

She had overshot the car by two blocks, probably on purpose, and now, doubling back, she saw a woman who had been behind her turn just as suddenly, fumbling in her pocket for a cell phone. Maybe she was answering an unexpected call. Maybe she was following Julia's utterly undisguised trail. Maybe Mary Mallard's paranoia was playing with Julia's mind. She hesitated. But the Escalade was in that direction, straight past her. She walked faster, toward the woman, who stood near a shop window, head down, chattering into the phone. Julia drew abreast. Panicky eyes met panicky eyes.

Julia managed a plucky smile as she passed. "You'll have to do better than that," she said.

Startled, the woman took a step away. Then her fear softened. She reached into her pocket once more and pulled out not a gun or a knife or the bill for the coach lamps on the driveway but a couple of crushed dollar bills.

She handed them to Julia.

"I hope this helps a little," she said, and went back to her call.

CHAPTER 42

ANOTHER WALK
ON THE BEACH

(1)

"ALL I TOLD HIM," said Lemaster, puzzlement etched on his troubled face, "was that people like Byron Dennison could help him in his career. He laughed. I had never heard Preston laugh so hard. He said they couldn't help him, because they knew nothing about science. When I tried to explain that this was not the point, he told me he didn't have any interest in my kind of life. That's what he called it. My kind of life. He didn't explain what that was supposed to mean."

They were in the Mercedes, on their way home from another campus event: the opening dinner of a conference for out-of-power foreign-policy analysts. "You should have told me," said Julia, eyes shut as she leaned into the leather. To her own ear she sounded timid. Back in the Landing, Julia was feeling less confident than she had led Mary Mallard to think; or perhaps it was that Mary buoyed her in a way that her husband did not. "So—what's the plan now?" Sitting up. "Do you recruit Aaron?"

A long Lemaster silence as the Mercedes purred through nasty winter rain. "Our traditions somewhat constrain me," he said at last. "For the moment, I have no protégé."

She took a small shot. "But it doesn't matter, does it? In a few years the Empyreals will have folded up, right?"

"Sooner or later, Jules, we're all folded up."

At the house, Vanessa was slaughtering her aunt in Scrabble, for Astrid had rallied round loyally in the crisis. Julia reminded her daughter that it was a school night, and Vanessa answered serenely that formal education was habit, not necessity. But she went up to her room anyway.

"Astrid and I have some business," said Lemaster in a warning tone, and Julia said she had planned to turn in early anyway. She checked on Jeannie, then padded into the master suite.

From the bathroom mirror, a haggard countenance glared. Fresh lines had been graven into her oval face, or maybe she was noticing for the first time. Her eyes were wide and waiflike. Her formerly smooth lips were bruised from nibbling and twisted from frowning, just the way her mother used to warn they would be if her Jewel didn't smile. She supposed the worry was aging her fast, because she felt drained of energy. The only time she could remember a face like this looking back at her had been the night she took that bottle of pills; and in those days Julia had been just twenty, immature enough to be certain that pain of a particular depth constituted a unique feature of her existence, never experienced by anyone else, and thus incomprehensible beyond her own mind.

Yesterday, at Kepler, Julia had snapped at an astonished Iris Feynman for no good reason. Iris had remarked after a budget meeting that Julia seemed exhausted, and Julia replied that she was tired of being the one everyone else counted on for smiles. When Clay Maxwell dropped by an hour later to tell stories, as he often did, about what the div school had been like in its golden age, Julia told him she was too busy, not troubling to mention what had mainly kept her busy so far that morning had been berating herself for being rude to Iris. And then the dean had called to ask whether Julia had made her peace with Tony Tice—

The voices from downstairs were louder.

Astrid was yelling. Well, she did that.

"Starting next week," her husband murmured sleepily, later, "Mr. Flew will be here pretty much full-time."

"Here?" Clinging to him, more wakeful than she wanted to be. "You mean, in the house?"

"Uh-huh."

"Why, Lemmie?"

"Rearranging things in my office. Lots of papers to go through. Just for a few weeks."

"Well, we can all look forward to that," she said, and lay, worrying, awake.

(11)

IN THE MORNING, Julia returned to the beach to walk with her husband's cousin. She carefully did not stop on Main Street. Since her unnerving experience after her tea with Trevor Land, she had stayed away from the village proper, doing her shopping, to her family's surprise, among the hoi polloi at the strip malls along Route 48. The trouble was, she could not look at the façade of Cookie's or Old Landing or the bookstore without wondering what the proprietors had talked about at Vera's house that afternoon, and if the secretary of the university had gone with them. She had come to view the winter as a fastness protecting the Landing and its secrets against outsiders like herself. The chill seeped into your bones, slowed you down, and finally stopped you altogether—unless, of course, you left town. She had considered that option, going so far as to ask Lemmie whether the work on the presidential mansion could somehow be sped up.

"If you don't mind the roof falling in."

The truth was, much as the Landing had come to unsettle her, the campus, too, had stopped feeling like home. She was taking yet another day off from work. Iris Feynman had warned her that some people around Kepler were beginning to mutter that Julia, as first lady of the university, was taking liberties. Claire Alvarez assured anyone who inquired—said Iris—that a divinity school should not be a place where people were punished for tending to the needs of their families. But Clay Maxwell called to remind her that when the dean poured it on thickest she was at her most disingenuous. Julia told him that if somebody else wanted the job she would willingly give it up.

This time when Julia and her cousin-in-law reached the gate, nobody stopped them, the guard hardly looking up from his comic book, perhaps because everybody in town had heard about how not even the wife of the president of the university, who lived in the Landing, could get onto the beach. Kwame Kennerly had talked about the incident on his radio show for a month. Of course he never said who his source was, and though some in town suspected Julia, she would never have done so underhanded a thing, even though she had been more than happy to spread the word among the Sister Ladies. If a couple of them had chosen to pass it on, well, that was not Julia's doing: Ladybugs were, after all, against gossip.

Astrid, now in the Washington office of a New York law firm, teased Julia that she should make her husband earn some money—because Lemaster, whose salary as university president was just shy of a million dollars, was the family pauper.

Julia changed the subject.

Yes, said Astrid. Her original source had been Kellen Zant.

Yes, she said again, to the next question, she had seen Kellen shortly before he died, but not, Astrid emphasized, that night.

As a matter of fact, Julia prompted, Astrid had seen him often: "Those were your cosmetics in his house, weren't they?"—for Bruce Vallely had shared a few tidbits from his investigation, in an effort to win her cooperation.

"Unless they belonged to one of his other women."

"You came to town to see him? And didn't tell us you were here?"

Astrid snorted. "So that you could do what?"

Julia, astonishment and jealousy warring, let that one go.

It was possible, said Astrid, that someone could have seen them together. They were careful, but everyone makes mistakes. Still, she had not been in Elm Harbor that night, and, in any case, she did not understand how some racist little white boy would be unable to distinguish a Barbadian from a British accent.

And, yes, she said—Julia feeding her one softball after another, to make it easier—yes, Kellen had contacted her, not the other way around.

"It started maybe six months ago. He said he had material that could affect the outcome of the election. Naturally, I'd be interested. Any right-thinking American would be. To get rid of this crowd, I would use any means necessary. I had to be in New York on business; he took the train down. We had tea at the Stanhope, where everybody whispers anyway, and the bastard pulled a fast one. Number one, he told me he wanted money. He was not about to let me capture the surplus value of his labor, he said, which I took to be some kind of silly economics joke. I told him it would not be fitting to pay for opposition research, and it would look bad in the papers. He was a greedy little prick, wasn't he? He said in that case he would keep it to himself."

Astrid was smoking, and Julia stayed upwind. Gulls looked interested, as if a cigarette might be a type of food about to be discarded.

"Number two, he refused to tell me which side would be hurt by the evidence. He said my side was going to lose anyway, so it wasn't that big a deal. He stood there and said if I begged him, if I said pretty please, maybe he'd tell me. What made him so evil?"

"Did you beg him?"

"I slapped him in the face."

"In the middle of the Stanhope?"

"On the sidewalk."

"Well, he brought that out in people."

Astrid glanced at her as if suspecting an insult, then smiled wanly and tossed her cigarette into the water. Julia, revolted, turned her head.

"Number three, he told me that there was more to the story. Then he offered to buy me dinner. Well, he could be a charmer. I guess you know that." She shook herself physically, as if throwing off the memory. "One thing led to another."

"Your relationship—"

"It wasn't a relationship. Don't put some formal construction on it. We slept together now and then. That was all. I'm sure Kellen saw other women, the bastard." A moment's uncertainty, but when Astrid spoke again she was perfectly calm. "I didn't know, Julia. About the two of you. Kellen kept your secrets, just in case you wondered. We had fun together, Julia. I won't deny that. But now, looking back—I wasn't his type. He liked them white and clingy. I think sleeping with me was just a way for Kellen to get one up on you. I think he hoped you'd find out."

But I'm not white, Julia almost protested—although Kellen had always said he loved the honeyed skin she often hated. *On the other hand, I sure was clingy.*

"It only lasted a couple of months," Astrid was saying. "It was over by, oh, September. Then he called me in November to ask if I was still interested. This was the Wednesday before he died. I thought he meant interested in him, but Kellen was talking about the information. He wanted to meet in New York. Well, I was through with all my crying by then, and I didn't want to start over. I told him to say what he had to say. That made him uncomfortable—he said his phone might be tapped— but finally he said if I wanted the material I had to put in a bid, fast. He said he planned to sell it within a day or two. He was setting up an auc- tion, and I'd have to get in my bid right away. And he said—well, he said if anything happened to him I might get a chance at the material anyway." She took a new cigarette from her pocket, then changed her mind and shoved it back. She snorted. "I told him I'd think about it. Two nights later, he got his head shot off."

Sell it within a day or two. Walking back to the car, Julia turned the phrase over and over in her mind. *Sell it within a day or two.* He was supposed to have breakfast Saturday morning with Cameron Knowland, she remembered. But they had not met yet, and therefore he could not be confident that a deal would be reached.

Within a day or two.

"Julia?" said Astrid.

"Just thinking. Sorry."

"Do you notice that no reporters are digging into the President's college years? I hate this kind of conspiracy of silence. You should call your old roommate. Tessa. Tell her to find the scandal."

"Call her yourself," said Julia, more coldly than she intended. But a part of her was furious, for reasons she dared not contemplate.

"I would." Matter-of-factly. "But nobody takes my calls any more."

"I'm sure that's not true." But she squeezed Astrid's hand anyway, just in case it was.

Kellen had called the Senator's side on Wednesday and planned to see the President's side on Saturday, which meant that whoever he was seeing on Friday was not on either side. Mary was right. Somebody else was interested.

Somebody, maybe, Kellen met that night.

The other bidder, who for some reason had turned on him and—

Julia stopped.

Sitting on the hood of the Escalade was Tony Tice.

(III)

"Would you mind getting off my car?"

His handsome head was tilted up toward the brilliant winter sun. He said, "Aren't you going to introduce me to your lovely friend?"

"Tony Tice, Astrid Venable. Tony here was recently arrested for beating up his girlfriend. And if he doesn't stop following me around, he's going to be arrested again."

"I'm out on bail, and it was a setup. No way is it going to trial."

Julia summoned her coldest voice. "I'm sure."

"And, as far as arresting me again is concerned"—he hopped off the car and stood in the snow like a monument to his own permanence—

"well, three years ago I sued the campus police and won. I'd love the chance to sue the Landing, too."

"Do you get some kind of kick out of following me? Because I think that was your shoe Mitch Huebner's dog chewed up."

The lawyer did not bother to answer. He reached into his jacket, but the bulge was only a cell phone. He studied the screen. "I wanted to give you a last chance to cooperate with me. I'm afraid my clients are unhappy."

"Last chance before what?"

"Before I file suit against you." Still smiling. But Julia sensed the desperation behind the words. "A replevin action. A suit to make the defendant return the plaintiff's property that the defendant is unlawfully—"

"I know what *replevin* means," she lied. "What property?"

"Whatever Zant left. It's rightfully mine, Julia. Or, rather, it was sold to my clients first. So you don't own it. My clients do. You can give it to me now, or you can wait for the court to order you."

His phone rang. He listened, then said, "No, she's here. I'm talking to her now. Yes." He put the phone away. "Sorry."

"Who was that?"

"Do you really want to force me to sue you, Julia?" Spreading his hands. "Think about it. In the depositions the whole story would come out. The Black Lady, your prior relationship with Zant, Vanessa, everything. Do you really want your kids to read all that in the papers?"

Astrid spoke for the first time. "Run him over," she said.

CHAPTER 43

A SMALL REQUEST

(1)

BRUCE TOOK THE CALL from Gayle Gittelman as he sat at his desk perusing the personnel file for Jeremy Flew, which the reliable Turian had obtained under another pretext. Flew was thirty-two years old. He had come aboard last year with the new president. He possessed an undergraduate degree from Michigan State, a couple of years of graduate work at the Georgetown School of Foreign Service, followed by eight years at the State Department, one year at a consulting firm of which Bruce had never heard, and now assistant to the president of the university. Bruce looked for a connection with the school and did not find one. He looked for a connection with Lemaster and did not find one. The file contained no letters of reference. The résumé listed a pair of retired foreign-service officers. Flew's health and life insurance forms listed no dependents.

What Bruce found most intriguing was the service at State. "Various foreign postings" was the entirety of the résumé description. Bruce Vallely was familiar with such gaps in the official record. Anyone obtaining Bruce Vallely's own record would discover a similar gap, for much of the work he had done during his Army Special Forces service in Central America during the Reagan years remained forevermore undiscussable. He wondered what undiscussable work Jeremy Flew had been up to, and where; and whether, on the night Kellen Zant was shot, he might have initiated an undiscussable telephone call to Lemaster Carlyle—telling him, for example, where to have his "accident."

All right, it was all speculation. Bruce admitted that, even if he was not prepared to admit what Marlon Thackery insisted—that his continued concentration on Lemaster Carlyle smacked of a vendetta. He was not seeking to vindicate his parents—so Bruce insisted—and was not driven by his resentment of the elite of African America. No. All he was trying to do was discover what happened to Kellen Zant.

Fortified by his reaffirmed certainty, Bruce once more opened Jeremy Flew's personnel file, and that was when the receptionist buzzed to say that Gayle was on the phone.

Bruce knew Gayle in the casual way that senior cops always tended to know the top criminal lawyers in town. Mutual admiration between a longtime detective and an attorney who represented with considerable success many of those he arrested was not possible, but, certainly, he recognized both the quality of Gayle's mind and the seriousness of her purpose. She had never been one to waste other people's time.

So he took the call.

"A client of mine wants to talk to you, this morning if possible," the lawyer said. "I have to warn you, it's a little bit tricky, because he's currently awaiting trial."

Kwame Kennerly, he guessed, because the radio personality was constantly being arrested for protesting this or that. "About what?"

A moment's hesitation, as if, even now, Gayle Gittelman wished her client would make a different choice. "He asked me to tell you that he has information about what really happened to Kellen Zant."

"Why isn't he trading with the state's attorney?"

"If he tells you, be sure to let me know."

Then Gayle told him her client's name, and Bruce reached for his jacket.

(11)

ANTHONY TICE WAS GOING to tell Bruce as little as possible, and seemed delighted at the prospect. He was, in Bruce's mind, the opposite of Gayle Gittelman, an opponent for whom he harbored neither respect nor admiration. Tony had always been the sort of attorney who could not cite client privilege without a small chuckle, for he was not so much asserting a solemn duty as drawing the winning ace from his sleeve. "You know how it works, Bruce," said the attorney, using first names because he pretended to be everyone's friend when he was really very much the opposite. "I couldn't stay in business if I passed around my clients' confidences. I wouldn't have any clients. I'd be disbarred," he concluded proudly. "You understand, Bruce. I've checked you out. I know your background."

Bruce nodded to say he indeed understood. They faced each other across a conference table in Gayle Gittelman's office. Gayle herself was absent. "Is that why you asked to see me?" His face was stone. "You're asking me to help you get out of your current mess?"

"No, no, no, nothing like that." The white teeth gleamed in a thick, enticing smile. "I know this kind of frame-up, and I know how to handle it."

"By harassing Julia Carlyle?" Because Lemaster had been on the phone to Bruce just hours after the episode, demanding that he warn the man off once and for all. The university president had been so angry that Bruce had half expected him to ask if anyone would rid him of this troublesome lawyer, or however it went. "That struck me as a very panicky thing to do, Tony. You must be in serious trouble."

"Why would you say that?"

"First you're arrested. Then you bother Mrs. Carlyle. Now you want my help. Sounds to me like desperation."

"The reason I was arrested," said the lawyer indignantly, "is that I was making too much progress. I was getting a little too close to finding what Kellen had hidden."

The lawyer laid his hands on the table, wrists close together as if waiting for the cuffs. Bruce wondered whether Tricky Tony was really so confident of his ability to beat the rap. The clever eyes flicked across Bruce's hard face. Bruce had arrested all kinds: the ones you knew could never do the time, the ones you suspected would find God on the other side of the bars, and the ones who would spend their whole sentences plotting revenge, emerging at the end even more evil than when they went in.

Anthony Tice he placed in the last category.

"If you say so," said Bruce after a moment.

A feral grin. "Now, Bruce, I know what you think of me. I know what everybody thinks of me. Of my . . . clientele. But that's why Kellen came to my door. Because of the clientele that everybody hates."

Bruce nodded and said nothing. In his experience, when a man wanted to confess, he confessed, not just to an interrogator, but to whoever happened along: bartender, girlfriend, stranger on a train.

"Kellen had in his possession something of great value and wanted to know what a certain client of mine would bid for it. I talked to my clients, who thought it over and asked for proof. Kellen gave them what he called a teaser. A page from a certain diary. Well, my clients were impressed. There was a little bargaining, some back-and-forth, and at last a deal was struck. I was not a party to the deal, Bruce. I was only the broker. Naturally, a broker takes a cut."

"Naturally."

Tony frowned but could evidently find no insult in the tone. Bruce wondered if he was the sort of powerful white man who minded being interrogated by a black one. But it was the lawyer who had extended the invitation.

"The trouble began," Tice resumed, "when my clients came to me and said they'd heard from certain friends that Kellen was offering to sell to others the same item he'd agreed to sell to them. My clients are patient men, Bruce, but this naturally annoyed them. They met me, told me to remind Zant that they had a deal. They don't like welshers, my clients."

"So you met with him. Kellen Zant."

"I met with him. And he laughed in my face. He said there was going to be an auction, and my clients could bid along with everybody else. I told him they don't do that. He said in that case he would find another buyer. He had one coming into town the next day, and they might just make a deal."

Bruce rolled a pencil back and forth on the table, for he had found that drawing the suspect's focus often aided the urge to talk. So did a good hard slap in the face, so he said, not looking up, "Did your clients kill him? Or did their lawyer do it for them?"

"My clients had no reason to hurt Kellen. Neither did I. They wanted what he was selling."

But it occurred to Bruce that the lawyer was being too clever, that the story he told was too easy. Kellen Zant was no fool. He would not have made a deal with men like the ones Tice represented only to break it for a profit. Tice's clients had rather unpleasant ways of exacting damages for breach. More likely, Tricky Tony had told his clients that a deal had been reached before Zant had agreed. Maybe the lawyer had already taken his cut. No wonder he was worried.

"Your clients must be getting desperate, too," Bruce said.

"My clients are not men who get desperate." Looking down at his hands. "They're men who make other men desperate."

"And are you desperate? Is that why you called me?"

"You have to understand the way my clients think, Bruce. They set themselves an objective and head straight toward it. Very military. Very organized. Very mission-driven. Your kind of people, Bruce." The cockiness was returning. "I think maybe you could help them."

"You're joking."

"The thing is, Bruce, so far I've persuaded them to hang back. Not to do anything directly, just to wait and let events shape themselves. Like I said, they're patient men. But they won't hang back forever. Sooner or later, if there aren't any concrete results, they might decide to take more active measures. And they're not the kind of people who will be deterred by such trivialities as who gets hurt along the way."

"They sound like a fun bunch."

"They're not. I assure you."

Bruce rolled his shoulders and had the satisfaction of watching the lawyer shrink away. "Why don't you tell me the rest?"

"The rest?"

"Zant told you he had another buyer coming into town the next day. That would be Cameron Knowland, I'm betting. Knowland and Zant were supposed to have breakfast on Saturday, but Zant got shot on Friday night. That means you saw Zant the night he died. That's when you had your argument. And that's why you're so worried. It's not just your clients you're worried about. It's the police, the actual police. Until the investigation got shut down, you were scared they would hear that the two of you were together that night and pin the crime on you."

"They'd never convict me. I didn't do it."

"Maybe not. But the arrest would ruin you." He folded his huge hands where Tice could see them. "So tell me the rest, Tony. Tell me what happened the night Zant died."

And so the lawyer did.

(111)

IT HAD SEEMED SO SIMPLE, said Tice. He called Zant at his office on Friday afternoon, and Zant agreed to meet him at five-thirty in the parking lot outside Hilliman Tower. He was a few minutes late, but he brought along another teaser. Another diary page, said Tony, where somebody had scribbled that the guard at the beach had developed a sudden case of I-can't-remember-itis. There was a lot of money floating around town, the unknown author had written, and then the page ended. Tony took the teaser but explained his clients' position nevertheless. Kellen, as Bruce had suspected, denied having made a deal. Tony said his clients wouldn't like that very much. Kellen thought it over, then told the lawyer to meet him back in this same parking lot in two hours—that is, at half past seven. Then he got into his own car and drove away.

"But you followed him."

"I tried to. There was a lot of traffic because of the hockey game. I don't know the campus that well. He turned into some alley, and when I got there he was gone."

So Tony hung around, cruising the area, hoping to spot the car. Twice his clients called to demand a progress report, and twice he assured them that he was working on it. By seven-fifteen, he was back in the parking lot, and the Audi was there. It was covered with a fair dusting of snow from the storm, and Tice realized he had been had. The economist must have circled the block, knowing he was being followed, and swung back into the parking lot, the last place Tony would look. So the lawyer sat in his car, watching both the Audi and the entrance to Hilliman Tower, and at seven-forty-five Zant knocked on the window of his car, surprising him. He had come up the other way.

"Which other way?"

"Downhill. I don't know. The arts center, the div school, lots of buildings are down there."

Zant told Tony to come for a ride. The lawyer climbed into the Audi, and they drove out to Tyler's Landing. Tice kept asking where they were going, and the economist kept saying not to worry, he just wanted to show him something. They hit Main Street around eight-fifteen, and that was when Zant's cell phone rang. He parked and told the lawyer to wait, then stepped out of the car to take the call. He was angry or upset. He did a lot of yelling. Even from inside, Tice could hear snatches. At one point Zant shouted, *You can't do that.* Finally, he said, *No, I'm in town, I'll come to you.*

Then, visibly shaking, Zant opened the door and told the lawyer to get out. There had been a change of plans, he said. He pointed to Greta's Tavern, across the street. You should go in there and get a cup of coffee or something. If I'm not back in an hour, call yourself a cab and forget tonight ever happened. Zant never came back, and the lawyer called a taxi.

"Did he say where he was going?"

"No."

"Or who was on the phone?"

"No."

"And you didn't tell the police any of this?"

He shook his head. "They never talked to me."

"But you talked to your clients, didn't you? Maybe called them from the car, while Zant was on the phone? Or from the tavern while you waited for your taxi?" Bruce nodded, confirming his own hypothesis. "You called your clients and told them it looked like he'd be tied up in the Landing for a while, and they sent somebody to search his house."

"I can't confirm that."

"You don't have to. And don't worry. I know you didn't kill Zant. Neither did your clients. He was too valuable alive."

Revived, the lawyer walked him to the door of the conference room. "You're right, Bruce. I'm in a jam. I need something to show my clients. You have to help. They say you're a dogged investigator. I'm sure you'll track down Zant's surplus."

"There is no reason in the world for me to help you."

"You don't want my clients to become active, believe me. I can keep them quiet if I can tell them you're willing to share what you find."

Bruce felt the delicious thrill of approaching combat. "I'm not afraid of your clients."

Tricky Tony laid a hand on his arm. "You're not the only person involved in this, Bruce. So think about it, okay?"

In the anteroom, Gayle Gittelman bustled over. "So did you get some useful info? Anything I can trade?"

"Your client," said Bruce, "is not a pleasant man."

"Yeah?" She got up on her toes and whispered. "Well, his clients are worse."

CHAPTER 44

THE NEST

(1)

To ROMANTIC DEMOGRAPHERS, to say nothing of restaurant critics, the city of Elm Harbor was deliciously multi-ethnic, offering, in a single block of Henley Street not far from the campus, Russian or Ethiopian or Korean or Italian or Irish or Malaysian or Greek cuisine: and that was just the north side of the street. "A lived monument to diversity," the mayor liked to say of the depressed metropolis over which he so corruptly reigned.

So ran the official story.

Residents of the Nest, the unflattering nickname of the worst of the city's trio of ethnically black neighborhoods, would tell a different story. The Nest began three blocks northwest of the campus and ran as fast as it could for about another ten or twelve—the border was as unreliable as the police patrols—and few students entered it willingly, other than a handful of idealistic undergraduate volunteers who tutored elementary-school children or ran Boy Scout troops, and who were as a result considered eccentric, or just plain foolish, by their fellows. To those who lived and generally died in the Nest—the Nesters, they had come to call themselves, probably in solidaritous self-defense—the city of Elm Harbor was demographically simple: there were the blacks and there were the whites, and no place, except perhaps for the welfare office and the courthouse, did the twain ever meet.

The Nesters believed that the rest of the city liked it this way.

Julia Carlyle did not share the Nesters' view of the city, but, although she would never admit it, even to Lemmie, she often shared the city's view of the Nesters. The Nest, for Julia, was a darkly dangerous spot, gangs of sullen hip-hoppers on every corner, ready to flash into violent action at any instant.

The empiricist was digging up her facts the hard way now. No choice, really.

Julia passed public-housing projects, squat and endless, red brick low-rises built forty years ago or more on the theory that the poor needed a kind of transitional residence on their way up into the working class. Mothers younger than Vanessa sat on the stoops with their children in bright blue strollers, taking the winter air and listening on earphones and flirting with the boys as though, having burdened themselves with a baby or two apiece, they were ready to try for more.

Between the housing projects were rows of single-family homes. Perhaps they had once been rather fancy. Now some were boarded up, and others had iron bars on the windows, and few showed much sign of life. In one of the yards, two boys who looked to be about three years old were enjoying a snowball fight. An inexpensive sports car blocked half the road up ahead for no better reason than that the driver had spied an acquaintance and wanted to chat. As Julia cruised by, their envious eyes followed the blue Mercedes, as did the music they were generous enough to share, their tastes not unlike Lemaster's, the bass cranked so high she could feel the beat pounding within her breastbone.

There were businesses, too, with cheaply lettered signs, most devoted to food, or nails and hair, or furniture rental, the triumvirate that evidently represented the principal needs of her people, because one found them everywhere. There were funeral parlors. There was a barbershop. There were churches galore, from AME to Baptist to a bewildering spread of nondenominational congregations to simple storefronts, in which some hefty woman with a calling—Lemaster's dismissive phrase—would set herself up as bishop and call her mission a tabernacle and be right in business.

There was the street.

Julia braked hard, having almost missed the turn, but the Mercedes was up to the task, cornering smartly without shimmy, and without burning any rubber. She found the address easily, a small, neat row house, layered in green paint and in considerable need of more, with the curtains drawn, and, in the yard, a plastic tricycle with only two wheels leaning against the low hurricane fence.

This was still the Nest, so she checked around the car before unlocking the door, then stepped smartly onto the front porch, keeping the Mercedes in view even though the alarm was on. A light-footed tread in the hallway answered her ring. A vertical window was set along one side of the door, and the curtain twitched. A dark face gazed out, and Julia offered her best smile, but the face was already gone. A baby wailed, though it might have been another house. She heard the ragged metallic clunking of a series of bolts and chains being undone, and it occurred to her that the windows possessed no bars. Lemaster claimed that one could tell a high-crime area by the barred windows.

The door opened, and Julia stifled a sound of surprise.

The woman standing there was a few years older than she, and a good deal prettier, as such things were classically measured, her skin smoother, her bones longer, her face more handsome. Her sober clothes, to Julia's experienced eye, were cheaply cut, her looped earrings inexpensive gold-toned, her flattened curls considerably over-done. Yet she carried herself with a certain casual authority, as though the world was a place she had with effort bested.

"May I help you?" she asked, her voice husky and cautious.

Julia managed, "I'm sorry. I was looking for, I guess, your mother."

"My mother?"

"I'm looking for Theresa Vinney. Uh, DeShaun Moton's mother." It occurred to her that this was likely DeShaun's sister, which might be even better.

"I am Theresa Vinney. I am DeShaun's mother."

A moment's re-evaluation. Everything Julia knew about life was wrong. But why could this woman not be DeShaun's mother? He had died at age sixteen thirty years ago. If she had been in her teens when he was born, she would be in her sixties now. Julia stared, stupidly. Theresa Vinney's eyes were wide, the surrounding flesh heavy with worry. Yes. Sixty at least. Julia decided that her earlier judgment had been a hallucination: the woman was less handsome than haunted, less regal than on edge.

"I'm so sorry, Mrs. Vinney. My name is Julia Carlyle. I . . . I work at the university. Do you think you might spare me a few minutes?"

"I'm not married." Frowning, as if waiting for eyes to roll. "You can call me Miss Terry."

Julia nodded respectfully. "I would really welcome a few minutes of your time, Miss Terry. I'd like to talk."

"About what?"

"About what really happened the night your son died."

(11)

THE HOUSE WAS CRAMPED and shadowy but clean. They sat in the front room, on the kind of furniture purchased from a discounter on credit, the fuzzy green fabric protected by clear plastic slipcovers of the sort hardly anybody used any more outside of the inner city. The walls were decorated with photographs of children and grandchildren and nephews and nieces in numbers sufficiently impressive that Julia, whose brother was long dead, had no idea how anybody could keep them straight. A brace of shiny sports trophies stood on a table in the corner like forgotten idols, and Julia had a shrewd instinct that whichever young people had earned them played no longer whatever they had once played so well. Miss Terry served instant coffee in mismatched cups, one the remainder of an old ceramic set, the other bearing the logo of a fast-food chain.

Just a couple of girls chatting, Julia had decided on the way over. That was how she would play it.

Except that Miss Terry was nobody's little girl.

Theresa Vinney admitted to sixty-one years on God's earth, in the course of which she had borne five children. She had six grand-children that she knew of, and a pair of great-grands. Julia tried to cal-culate the generations, but it beat her. Her boys, Miss Terry explained with disarming yet stern frankness, might well have given her more, but she didn't know and, she suspected, neither did they. The eternal empiricist did the arithmetic. DeShaun Moton was sixteen when he was shot dead. If she was telling the truth about her age, the tough, stylish, and quite beautiful churchwoman sitting across from her on the plastic cover that crinkled whenever she leaned forward to sip her coffee had given birth to DeShaun when she was fifteen years of age.

Julia had donated money to teen-pregnancy prevention programs, she had even supported, to her husband's cheerful disgust, condom distribution in the public schools. But she experienced the people she was helping only at a distance. Julia was no social worker, and not much of a volunteer—her job and her children kept her too busy. When Father Freed talked about giving over to the Lord one-tenth of your time, talent, and treasure, Julia usually decided that treasure was enough. For all her concern over the problem to which she, like many others, referred to as "babies having babies," Julia had never expected the problem to sit her down in the front parlor and serve her coffee.

"You're not from around here," said Miss Terry, her eyes flat with accusation.

"Ah, no, ma'am."

"You didn't grow up in town?"

"No, ma'am. I grew up in Hanover."

"Where's Hanover?" she asked, quite unembarrassed.

"Uh, New Hampshire."

The slow interrogation continued, Miss Terry's voice that of a doubting schoolmarm. "And where do you live now, Julia?"

"In the Landing," she confessed, miserably, the words burning like a fresh betrayal of her people. The Clan felt very far off.

"*Tyler's* Landing."

"I'm afraid so."

"Where they say DeShaun killed that girl." A pause. "Where they killed him right back."

"Yes, that's right. I'm so sorry, Miss Terry."

"They don't have many of our people out there."

"No, ma'am."

"How many?"

"I don't know exactly." But she was remembering how Beth Stonington, the real-estate agent who sold them the lot, knew the number off pat when they asked, as if a list circulated weekly through the town, updated to show departures and arrivals. Kellen Zant used to call it "Nigger-scan."

"Everybody's white?"

"Almost everybody."

Miss Terry nodded. Behind her head a framed poster advertised a long-ago exhibit at the university museum on the Underground Railroad. The popular magazines of the darker nation—*Ebony, Essence, Jet*—mingled on the floor beside her chair. Every year, *Ebony* listed

Lemaster Carlyle as one of the nation's hundred most influential black Americans.

Julia suspected he was in the top five.

"I've been out to your town a few times, Julia. I used to clean houses out there." A grimace. "I can see why the white folks like it. It's all neat and tidy, and none of our people. But for us? Our people? Tell me, Julia. Why did you want to live all the way out there?"

With her college girlfriends, with her Sister Ladies, with Mona, with Lemaster's family, Julia had rehearsed a hundred different answers to this question. Now, face-to-face with DeShaun's mother, she felt her glib and careful explanations sting her throat like thorns. "We wanted what's best for the children. You know. Good schools, things like that."

"Mmmm-hmmm."

"And I . . . I guess I like the New England kind of atmosphere."

"Mmmm-hmmm."

"But I guess, most of all, we wanted to raise the children someplace where we would feel they were safe."

This perked Miss Terry up. "Safe. My DeShaun was sure safe. Eight cops around him, he should've been real safe."

"That's what I want to talk about," said Julia after a slightly desperate pause.

"Well, I don't wanna talk about it." Eyes bright and challenging. "We sued, but we dropped the lawsuit years ago. Why do you wanna go digging all this up again?" An angry laugh. "Eight cops, and DeShaun is dead. I don't know that there's nothing else to say anyway."

The mother awoke. "Please, Miss Terry. I need your help." She thought of Frank Carrington, insisting as they sat in the back of the shop that DeShaun was innocent; and of Vanessa, insisting at Hunter's Heights that DeShaun was guilty. "I wouldn't bother you except for my daughter. She's in trouble."

Eyes narrowing, suspicion and sympathy mixed. "And how is digging up the past supposed to help?"

"A couple of months ago, they found a . . . a body in the Landing. A black man. A professor. I don't know if you heard about it." Miss Terry said nothing, her expression unyielding, determined to make Julia say the rest. "The man who was killed . . . the professor . . . I think he was trying to find out what happened that night. He thought DeShaun was innocent." Still the older woman sat like a stone. "Miss Terry, I'm the one who found the body, and my daughter . . . my daughter was doing research about DeShaun, and I think something that she found is driving her mad." There. The words were out. What Julia had never expressed so starkly, even to Lemaster, she had just confessed to this stranger who, even now, watched and waited. "Please. I have to know."

"What do you have to know, Julia?"

"Why you dropped your lawsuit."

CHAPTER 45

MISS TERRY'S TALE

(1)

To tell DeShaun's story, Miss Terry took a rambling course through her own. She had lived her life mostly in sin, she said, and in her time had done plenty of things of which she was not proud.

"I was born right down the street, in the university hospital, and I grew up in those projects they used to have, over in South Elm. The projects weren't all black in those days. We had whites in there, some other colors, too. My mother worked for the university. They called her a 'dietary specialist C' or some such, but we all knew she was a cook. My father was a janitor in the public schools. When he was a little boy, he used to shine shoes for the kids at the university. Know how it worked? No? He would stand under the windows of the dormitory with a bunch of other boys, and they would throw the shoes out the window, the students would, and the Negro boys would all fight over them. Then the boys—whoever won—would take the shoes home with them and clean them overnight and, in the morning, bring them to the side door of the dorms. They couldn't go in. In those days coloreds weren't allowed."

She settled back in her chair. "My father always said the most important thing was dignity. He was a janitor, but his shoes were always clean, and whenever we went visiting, anytime he didn't have to wear his uniform, he would put on his suit and his tie. He only seemed to have the one suit, the black, and the bottom was all shiny, but he wore it whenever he could. And a white shirt. He would walk up and down the block on his days off in his black suit and his white shirt. He looked like an undertaker, but the kids in the neighborhood, even the tough ones, they all respected him, Julia. They all did what he told them. This was back in the days when you could talk to your neighbors' kids if they were up to no good, you could grab them by the arm and shake them and tell them to get on home and not get sued or arrested or what-have-you."

Miss Terry paused, her smile of gentle reminiscence melting into something softer and sadder, a different set of memories tugging. She picked up a cookie from the foil tray, bit off a tiny chunk, put it back with the others. Julia, hating herself for her automatic mysophobic caution, made careful note of which one Miss Terry had nibbled, where she had placed it on the tray, which of the others it was touching.

"There were six children, and maybe it was too many for him, because he had a heart attack and died when I was eight. And we buried him in the same black suit. My mother we buried just two years ago. Eighty-seven years old. A tough lady, tried her best to keep the family together, Julia. But the times got a little wild, and most of us, the children, well, we got a little wild with the times. Not all of us. My middle sister even went to college—went to Hampton—Rebecca is her name, and she married a very sweet man. Rebecca's a schoolteacher now, down in Virginia, where her husband has people. And one of my brothers, Neebie, we called him—Benjamin—he got out of town the other way, he joined the Marines. He runs an auto supply now, up in the state capital. Those two got out. The rest of us, well, we stayed right here in town, got into trouble, one thing or another. I have a brother who died in prison. I have a baby brother, fifty-five years old, living on the street. And one more sister, the baby. She does one thing or another. Says she's clean now, but she's still out there on the street."

Julia thought of Hanover High School and the lives to which her teenaged friends, none of them black, had not unreasonably aspired: medicine, engineering, microbiology, law. Some wanted more than anything else to be mommies, but they envisioned—and generally had achieved—what Julia had, childbirth in consequence of a stable marriage. That was one way to grow up in this country. The other was what Miss Terry had described.

"I don't say that everybody winds up on the street," Miss Terry continued. "You listen to the white folks talk about us, they think everybody in this part of town is a pimp or a whore or using or dealing. Truth is, Julia, most people down here work for a living. It's hard, because there isn't any help except the Lord, but it can be done. It's just, a lot of folks, the kids especially, they can't do it."

Miss Terry took another bite.

Julia at last had the rhythm of the conversation, and she knew better than to stop the flow. So, much as she longed to, she did not interrupt.

"I had my children when I was too young to know any better. I didn't know how to raise them. I didn't know how to keep from getting what Momma used to call 'in the family way.' And I didn't use the sense the good Lord gave me, so I didn't know I was supposed to say no in the first place. I was wild, like my baby sister. She looked to me, Julia. To see how to behave. And I taught her every wrong thing there is. She messed up her life because she saw me mess up my life first."

"People make their own decisions," Julia interjected automatically, quite forgetting her own resolution of a few seconds ago.

"Huh. Is that what they tell folks out there in the suburbs? Because, down here on the plantation, we have this idea that we're supposed to be role models. Every adult is supposed to show every child how to act. Every older child is supposed to show every younger child how to act. My father told us that, over and over, before he died. And after he died, I didn't want to be a role model any more. I wanted to do my thing and not worry about anybody else. It was just like that basketball player—what was his name?—the one who said he didn't want to be a role model for kids."

"Charles Barkley."

"Barkley. Right. I always loved to watch him play ball, but, oh, Julia, he was just so wrong about being a role model. You don't get to decide. You don't get to choose. My baby sister, she did what she saw me do. And when I had children of my own, well, they did what they saw me do and what they saw all the other young folks do. I'm a church-woman now, and I wish I had done it earlier, early enough to help my own kids, Julia. But back then God and I weren't on speaking terms, except every now and then when I took his name in vain. And DeShaun, well, he was a wild little boy. He got wilder as time went on. I thought maybe I could handle him, because by that time I'd got myself saved. Still, without a father, I tried everything, but it was a war. I put him in Boy Scouts, I put him in that after-school program at the university, they got him a big brother, but after a while DeShaun just wouldn't go." A shudder as she remembered the next chapter of the story. "The sin of pride. I thought I could handle him, Julia. But I guess I must be a weak woman after all, way down deep inside, where it counts, because, no matter how hard I prayed, Julia, that boy was always too much for me. Oh, the devil was in him for sure. I was going to put him out of my house, he was just acting too much the fool and doing too much that was evil, but, before I could do it, he went and stole that car and got himself shot."

No tears as her story ground to its sudden and violent halt: instead, a defiant glare, as though daring her guest to sass her. Julia knew she had to tread carefully. "I'm sorry, Miss Terry. I only have a couple of questions."

"Julia, let me make this easier for you." Her voice was cold. "My DeShaun was an evil little character. He stole cars. He got himself arrested twice for assault. The night that girl died, he was in the Landing. I believe that. He knew the Landing because I used to clean houses out there. He stole a car that night. I believe that. They said he was talking to that girl down on the Green. I believe that, too. And, yes, we did sue. But we dropped the lawsuit. We didn't get no settlement or anything. We just dropped it. Are you satisfied?"

"No."

"Why not? What did I leave out?"

"You told me you believe DeShaun was in the Landing that night. You believe he stole a car that night. You believe he talked to Gina that night. What you didn't say was that you believe he killed her."

Silence.

"Nobody ever collected any forensic evidence, Miss Terry. Nothing linked Gina to that stolen car. We don't know she was ever inside." In the tiny, shadowed room, Julia leaned forward in her excitement, and watched Miss Terry flinch away. "I think you already knew all that. I think that's why you sued. Now let me tell you something you might not have known. After Gina Joule talked to DeShaun on the Green— after!—she showed up at the home of one of her teachers, not a hair on her head out of place."

More silence, but surging now, like the dark quantum foam before the Big Bang.

"I don't think you believe DeShaun killed that girl. I don't think you ever believed it. I think you filed the lawsuit because you didn't believe it. And I think the reason you dropped the lawsuit without a settlement was that somebody paid you off." Theresa Vinney made a snorting sound and shook her head but said nothing. "I think somebody else killed that girl, somebody powerful and rich. I think it got covered up. I think when DeShaun turned up it fell right into their laps." Julia could not bear Miss Terry's silence any longer. Her own anger rose, a mother's, righteous and pure. "I think somebody came to your house, maybe sat right here, where I'm sitting, and told you if you dropped the suit he'd give you—what?—ten thousand? Fifty? A hundred? How much did he offer you, Miss Terry?"

"Why do you wanna mess with this?" the older woman asked.

"I want justice to be done."

"Justice." Another derisive snort, this one reminding her of Bay Dennison. "Julia, I've buried three of my five children, one from drugs, one from AIDS, and DeShaun, and not a one of them saved. Now, my little DeShaun got himself shot after he stole a car. They say he killed that white girl, and our people were ready to tear the place apart. But I'm his mother and I dropped the lawsuit, and that kind of shut down all the protests. People went back to their lives. And here you are, sitting in my living room, drinking my coffee, telling me you just stopped by to let me know, in case maybe I was worried, that it wasn't DeShaun who killed that little girl, and then you insult me, you tell me I dropped the lawsuit because some black man came to my house and gave me money. I'm a churchwoman, Julia, not some money-grubbing little twist of tail. So—what I think, the best thing to do is to just let it go on the way it's going on. Everybody knows DeShaun killed that girl. Let's just leave it there." Jerkily, Miss Terry was on her feet. "And now, Julia, honey, I think I have a few responsibilities to handle down at the church, if that's all right with you. But I sure want to thank you for coming all the way over here to chat with me this morning, and I wish God's blessing on you as you drive on home to your nice suburbs."

Julia said, "I never said the man who paid you was black."

(11)

MISS TERRY SUGGESTED a little walk down three blocks toward her church, because she was worried, she told Julia as soon as they were out the door, about being bugged. The white folks, she said, didn't have much use for black folks who wouldn't keep in their place, and they had bugged the hell out of poor Dr. King before they shot him.

"You really didn't know he was black?" she said.

"Not till you told me, no."

"Well, I should learn to keep my stupid mouth shut."

The neighborhood knew Miss Terry, and respected her. Maybe they had been raised by mothers who shouted at them, because that was how she communicated with everybody except Julia, bellowing at the top of her lungs for them to cut it out! And her holler, surprisingly, was enough. When she scolded small children for throwing snowballs at cars, they stopped; and when she chased off the fourteen-year-old drug dealers, they hung their heads and went. You have to earn people's respect, Miss Terry explained as they walked, her black plastic boots with fake fur lining swishing along the sidewalk. They have to know you'll do what you say. Again she sounded like Byron Dennison, and it occurred to Julia that the secrets of power must be the same everywhere, and powerful people all knew them.

Julia said she agreed.

"And you're really sure you want to get into this?" Miss Terry asked her as they turned down Third.

"Yes, Miss Terry."

"Because of your daughter. You mentioned that."

Julia sighed, weighing possible answers, and settled on the truth. "Yes. But that was only half true." Miss Terry's dark eyes questioned her. "The man who got killed out in the Landing. The professor. I, ah, I knew him. We were very close once. No. That isn't even the real reason." The churchwoman waited patiently. "It's also for my own sake. I guess I'm the kind of person—all my life, I've let people just take care of me. Protect me from the world. For twenty years I've been safe. Now it's time for me to pay back a little."

They crossed another street, Miss Terry waiting patiently for the light to change and Julia therefore waiting too, although waiting was not in her nature. Miss Terry waved a hand at someone she knew, then took Julia's arm. She pointed out a crackhouse. She pointed out a political party headquarters, staffed only during election season. She said, "Say you're right about what happened, Julia. I'm not agreeing with you. But say you are. Say we dropped the lawsuit for money. Everybody in town was following that case, Julia. There were those riots. So if we kept quiet about getting a little money, we must have had an awful good reason."

"I can see that, Miss Terry."

"Not greed."

"No, ma'am."

They reached the church, a blocky building that had been a warehouse. Now, painted white and fitted with long vertical windows, it was the House of Faithful Holiness, the words emblazoned in fiery red letters four feet high, along with the identity of the founder, almost as large, and his name wasn't Jesus. The ornate doors were shut tight, but Miss Terry led Julia through the large, nearly empty parking lot to a fire door set in the side. The interior was chilly, and Julia supposed they saved money by keeping the thermostat low during the week. The sanctuary had movable chairs rather than pews, and it looked to Julia as though it could seat, comfortably, close to a thousand people. She asked how many came.

"Most Sundays, four hundred. Five. Twice that Christmas and Easter."

"I'm impressed," said Julia, thinking of Lemaster's stubborn Anglican congregation, which counted it a small victory to welcome fifty parishioners, and a major miracle to break one hundred.

"No reason to be. It's the Lord's work."

"Uh-huh," said Julia, fighting the urge to nibble at her cuticle, and wondering why in the world Miss Terry had brought her here.

Passing a couple of neatly groomed parishioners, who greeted Miss Terry with what looked to Julia like joy, they made their way down a back hallway—the place was enormous—and wound up in a Sunday-school classroom. On the walls were scenes from the Bible and quotations from both Testaments. An attendance calendar, the names of the children running down the side, was marked with checks and minuses. In the Bible scenes, everybody was black.

They sat on two child-height chairs, facing each other across a low table.

"DeShaun didn't have a room like this to grow up in. This church didn't exist back then. None of my children were raised here. But most of my grandchildren started out either here or someplace like it in another church. Me, I didn't come to the Lord until I was advanced in my years, but most of the children from around here are raised in the church. They listen to the Lord's words every Sunday, they sing the hymns, they get themselves baptized."

Julia, about to say she agreed, decided not to interrupt.

"We have a ton of little children here, Julia. Most of the churches around here do, but this one especially. Their mothers bring them most of the time. Their fathers, I am sorry to say, are not very interested in what the Lord has to offer, although Heaven knows they need it. Most of them, well, they can't be bothered to marry the mothers of their children. Used to be, a young lady got herself pregnant, well, her father and her brothers would be on the young man's doorstep the next day looking to cause him some kind of trouble unless he did the right thing, and, a couple of months later, we'd have ourselves a wedding."

Julia blushed and dropped her eyes, remembering afresh how Lemaster's aunt had accused her of trapping him into marriage. Miss Terry didn't notice. "Well, those were the old days," she continued. "But, these days, Julia? We'd have to hunt around in the prisons or in the cemeteries. Or down on the corner. Most likely that's where we'd find the father. That's where we'd find the brothers. And they'd say, 'Get outta my face.' "

Julia wished she possessed her husband's gift for patience. She said, "Miss Terry, if we could just talk about DeShaun—"

"Julia, honey, that's exactly who I am talking about. You have to understand what we are trying to do here. We are trying to keep these kids in the church, because the church is the only hope most of them have. They go to school, and they can dress any way they want and they never hear about God but they hear about sex and they hear about being themselves and doing their own thing. Well, maybe for the white folks in the suburbs, it's okay to tell kids to do their own thing, to be themselves, whatever they learn out there. I wouldn't know. I only know that for our kids, it's a disaster, Julia. Just a disaster.

"Some stupid boy gets some silly girl pregnant, and the white folks say they don't have to get married and it's wrong to pressure them. We fall into line. We do what the white folks tell us. See, Julia, we're still basically on a plantation here. The white folks get to set the rules. The white folks say no God in the schools, so there's no God in the schools. The white folks say you can't tell the kids not to have sex, so they have sex. The white folks say you can't make them feel ashamed if they get in the family way, so nobody feels ashamed. Like I said, the white folks set the rules. And then they get to live in the big house. Down here in the fields? Nobody asks our opinion. So, we live on the street corner or we live in the Lord's house. Down here, there isn't any third choice."

Every word stung. Every sentence presented a proposition against which Julia longed to argue. But she dared not offend Theresa Vinney, not now when she was so close. She had to focus. "And DeShuan—"

"DeShaun chose the corner, Julia, and that's what killed him. He was wicked, Julia. From the day he came out of the womb, he wanted things his own way. He never took any telling, that boy. The night he died, I had told him already that I was putting him out of the house. The way it turned out, I didn't get the chance. Now, you want justice?" She waved her hand around, encompassing the ornate church with its huge sanctuary and many classrooms. "This is our justice, Julia. Not some fancy government program. This building. This building is all we have. And it's all we need."

Julia was about to object, but Miss Terry wasn't finished. Out in the hall, somebody was singing, off-key, a snatch of sixties Motown, but a sharp voice told the artist to shut up.

"Listen to me, Julia. Yes, we filed that lawsuit. Yes, we dropped it. Now, I'm not saying why. But I'll tell you this. God made a miracle here. We built this church. We built this school. We have some bene-factors. They send a nice check every six months, and every penny goes to the church and the school. We're growing every year. We're trying to teach our kids what the white folks don't want us to learn, like how much God loves them and the difference between right and wrong. We can't pay much, so our teachers aren't what you have out there in the suburbs, but we do the best we can." For a silly moment Julia thought she read accusation in the hard eyes, as if DeShaun's mother knew that her guest had once been a teacher, and was waiting for her to volunteer. But Miss Terry was only gathering her strength to resume the lecture. Her finger stabbed the air. "Now, DeShaun is dead, and if you go digging that up, well, no story in the newspapers is gonna bring him back. Putting some powerful white man in jail isn't gonna bring him back. But with this school, Julia, with this church, maybe we can save a few of our kids from going down DeShaun's path." Her voice softened. "You used to be some kind of teacher, didn't you?"

Julia bristled but kept her temper, the surface tension holding. "I taught in the public schools for—" She stopped, aware that she had missed the point. "How did you know I used to be a teacher? Kellen Zant told you, didn't he? The professor who got killed. He came to see you to talk about your son."

Theresa Vinney nodded. "This was, oh, last spring. Early summer, maybe. He asked me what you did, if some black man had paid me to drop the lawsuit."

"He asked about a black man?"

"That's what I said."

So simple, Julia realized. She should have seen it. Kellen's motivation was coming into sharper focus. Perhaps he was not, after all, just after money. Until today, Julia would not have guessed that the man who went around and sanitized the evidence after Gina died was black. Even now, she knew only because Theresa Vinney had let the fact slip. Kellen had the information before he arrived. Maybe he worked it out from the diary. Or maybe he knew because he heard it from—

"Miss Terry?"

"Yes, dear?"

"When Professor Zant asked you if the black man offered you money, what did you tell him?"

"That God had a plan for him." She patted Julia's knee. "Now, Julia, I am truly sorry about what your daughter is going through. I'll ask everybody in the church to pray for her. But what I think you need to do is go home and count your blessings. You need to take care of your own children, Julia. Let us take care of ours."

CHAPTER 46

TWO MORE MEETINGS

(1)

"I HAVE MOST of what you asked for," said Bruce Vallely. "Not all. But most."

Across the table, Julia Carlyle pulled a face. To Bruce she looked a little spoiled, or perhaps she had simply grown used to getting her way. He knew that Trevor Land had prodded her to talk to him. Julia, in turn, had offered to help him out, but insisted that they trade.

"Then we'll go with what we've got," said Julia. They were in Ruby Tuesday in the shopping mall up in Norport, and Bruce sensed the authority slipping from his fingers into hers. Not long ago, he had thought this woman weak and pampered, the prototypical Princess of the Gold Coast, the sort of whom, in college, his working-class crowd had made relentless fun. But there was steel beneath the softness. He remembered Marlon Thackery's warning about not crossing Julia or her husband. "Tell me what you have so far," she ordered, as if he worked for her.

Bruce almost smiled. "I couldn't find out much," he told her, sliding yet another envelope across the table for her collection. "As far as the public records are concerned, the Empyreals might not be bankrupt, but they're close. They own a clubhouse in Brooklyn. There are about ten liens on it. They used to own a nice piece of property in the Hamptons, where they planned to build a very ritzy black-owned country club. Foreclosed twenty years ago. They had a hotel in Atlantic City back in the fifties and sixties, but now the land is part of a casino parking lot, and the Empyreals don't own any of it. I don't think they're doing so well, Julia."

"Hmmm."

"May I ask why you wanted this information?"

"Yes."

He waited, then frowned. "Yes, what?"

"Yes, Bruce, you may ask. But I'm not going to tell you." She patted his hand, an instinct, because she used to be a dedicated toucher of other people, and found she connected better that way. "Thank you, though. I mean it. I called you because I couldn't think of anybody else."

"Does this have anything to do with your husband?"

"Sorry, Bruce. I'm not going to talk about it."

"He's an Empyreal, isn't he?" Bruce leaned across the table, he hoped more imploring than threatening. "Julia?"

She shook her head firmly. "Don't press me, Bruce."

Something in her eyes bothered him, and perhaps she saw something in his, because she dropped her hand to the table. She started drumming.

"All right," said Bruce. "Then it's your turn to give me information."

Except that she could not. No, she had not seen anybody or anything before stumbling across Kellen's body. No, she had no idea where he might have been going the night he was shot, or what "Jamaica" meant.

Bruce said, "He was at the div school that night, wasn't he?" A reasonable surmise after his conversation with Tony Tice, who had no doubt made the same guess. Bruce knew he was right when Julia, trying to suppress her reaction, reacted. "Why was he there, Julia? Did you leave something for him? Did he leave something for you?"

She shook her head, more in refusal than in denial.

He said, "And what about Gina Joule? Do you think it's likely that Kellen Zant was looking into the death of Gina Joule? Because that's the way it looks to me."

"I don't know."

"Had he tracked the killing to somebody high up? Is that why he was shot?"

She spread her hands and offered her crooked smile. "Really, Bruce, I couldn't possibly help."

"You can't do this without help," he said, but Julia was too busy doing the math in order to split the check.

(11)

JULIA TRACKED DOWN JOE POYNTING in the student lounge, where he was struggling to craft a practice sermon for his homiletics course. She wanted to know the definition of "nonrivalrous consumption," an economics term, and Joe was, once more, her muse.

"Consumption is rivalrous," he said, "when my use of a thing leaves less for you. Look out the window. See the gulls? They're fighting over a piece of food. When one of them eats it, his consumption is rivalrous to all the others, because they can't eat it. See?"

Julia nodded.

"Consumption is nonrivalrous when my use does not affect your use. Look at the gulls again. See the sun glinting off their wings? The rainbow effect? It's lovely to look at, and the fact that I'm looking at it does not reduce your ability to look at it. We can both consume it. Nonrivalrous. See?"

She saw. She thanked him.

The case was about nonrivalrous consumption, Kellen had told Mary, and sent her the photograph of Malcolm Whisted. Malcolm Whisted, who knew the family. It was beyond vicious to refer to a human being as being consumed, but perhaps that was what Kellen had in mind. If Gina had a single boyfriend, then the consumption was rivalrous. But if she had, say, more than one—then it was nonrivalrous.

That had to be what Kellen was trying to tell them. The two boys who picked Gina up that night in the Jag were planning to share her. Say Jock was the boyfriend. Maybe one of his roommates was getting a little jealous of what Jock was getting. And Jock, the most fun-loving in a fun-loving bunch, said, Sure, next time she calls, come along. We'll share her.

Share a human being, like a sex toy.

Nonrivalrous consumption.

Only Gina was not ready to be shared. Gina had fought back.

And lost.

She worried the problem around in her mind, and then, for the moment, forgot it. Inspiration had struck. The seagulls.

The sea *gulls*.

Kellen and his word games.

Julia pulled out the memo pad on which she had been scribbling hopeless anagrams of "Shari Larid," the mysterious substitute teacher nobody could track down. Of course nobody could find her. She didn't exist, except as a message for Julia's own ear. By describing her as a substitute teacher, he was giving an instruction. A larid was a kind of seagull, and if you *substituted* "Gull" in place of "Larid," you got "Shari Gull," which was an anagram of . . .

CHAPTER 47

SUGAR HILL

(1)

ON SATURDAY, the mothers of the Harbor County chapter of Lady-bugs gathered their smallest children—the Littlebugs—and decamped for Manhattan, where they lunched in the delightful space-age insanity of Mars 2112, then took in the matinee of *The Lion King* on Broadway. They went by car pool, and Julia, driving the Escalade, ferried Kimmer Madison and her son, Bentley, who was two years younger than Jeannie. Julia would have been grateful for the break from her worries, had the trip only been a break. But it was not. She had scheduled an unscheduled stop. She planned to spring it on her passengers on the way home.

Kimmer spent most of the trip into the city asking Julia to turn down the radio while she took another call on her cell phone, because for lawyers these days, as for other professionals, the office possesses no natural borders. In between her urgent conversations, she beamed at the two children ignoring each other in the back seat and murmured, over and over, "Who knows what the future holds for these two?"— because Kimmer, like Julia, came from one of the royal families of the darker nation, and worried about the future of the traditions.

The show was a hit even with the most unsentimental among the mothers—like Kimmer—or those who, like Julia, had seen it before, and the children clamored to stay in town for dinner, but the caravan loaded up despite the begging, and by half past five, all the cars were on their way out of town.

All but the Escalade.

Julia explained about the stop she had to make.

"If you have time," she told Kimmer.

"How much time?" Actually looking at her watch. Seeing that she was caught, she pulled an infectious smile. Kimmer was fun-loving and sassy and smart. There were two husbands behind her, and it was easy to imagine others waiting their turn.

"It'll take us half an hour out of our way. No more."

"Half an hour?"

"And you can wait in the car with the kids. I'll be, like, ten minutes once we get there."

"Where are we going?"

"Harlem."

"Julia, it's almost six."

"They don't close."

(11)

THE LAST TIME Julia Carlyle had seen the three-story townhouse at Edgecombe Avenue and West 145th Street, all her children had been with her, and happy. It was seven years ago, and Julia, accompanied by Tessa, was showing them through Harlem, spinning barely remembered stories in mimicry of Granny Vee. Despite her own reluctance, the kids had clamored, and so she had driven them for a quick goggle at the fabled Veazie mansion, not stopping to let anybody out, streaking past in the hope that none of them would notice how the once-proud structure, setting of so many of their mother's stories, had fallen into a dilapidated mess.

Squeezing the Escalade into a space that might have been shaped for it, she expected no more tonight. She knew it was a fool's errand, and yet she had to try.

Just in case she failed to solve the anagram of "Shari Larid," Kellen had arranged for Mr. Huebner to deliver the note. Take a train, Kellen had written, knowing his ex-lover's musical tastes: Broadway and the big-band sound, preferably as interpreted by artists of her nation. The translation was trivial: Ella Fitzgerald and Duke Ellington had made famous Billy Strayhorn's song about taking the "A" train to Sugar Hill way up in Harlem.

Sugar Hill, the highest point in Harlem, where, back in the day, invisible to the larger world, the elite of the darker nation, ensconced in apartments and row houses furnished as beautifully as those on Park Avenue, had looked down their noses at the middle-class Negroes in Strivers' Row, down around 138th Street, and, farther south, the lower classes crowding into what the denizens of Sugar Hill labeled, derisively, the Valley. Sugar Hill, where Amaretta Veazie held her fabled court, one among the "light-skinned Czarinas," as Adam Clayton Powell, Jr., called them—the matriarchs who ran the elite end of Harlem. Amaretta, an original Sister Lady; Amaretta, who had tried to limit membership in the Clan to a handful of the old families, the way her whole generation did, thinking the exclusivity a gift to future generations; Amaretta, who, like the rest of the Czarinas, failed. The darker nation proved too big and talented; or integration too tempting; either way, the Clan spread and thinned.

The townhouse where, according to legend, Ladybugs was founded. And where, back in the old days, Amaretta had kept her famous collection of mirrors.

Kellen had sent her mirrors, and reminded her of history, just to make sure she got the point.

How Vanessa had figured it out Julia was not sure, but this had been her daughter's destination, too, the Veazie townhouse. Julia was certain of it. Vanessa had realized before her mother did that the house was at the heart of Kellen's mystery, and wanted for some reason to visit it alone. The trouble was, Vanessa did not remember the address and was trying to pick it out by eye. Like most African Americans who had never lived there, Vanessa underestimated the sheer vastness of Harlem, the hundreds upon hundreds of square blocks. Searching Harlem was not like searching a tiny New England town. The chance of blundering by accident upon a single townhouse among all the streets and boulevards of what had once been the capital of the darker nation was virtually nil.

As Vanessa had discovered.

No wonder she had chosen to dance the night away instead, first at the club in Elm Harbor, and then, as only her mother knew, to the funeral dirges behind the locked door of her bedroom.

Why Kellen wanted her to go to Amaretta's house, Julia had no idea; but she was quite certain this was where he wanted her to go.

Julia climbed out. She asked Kimmer to wait in the car with the kids.

"You're going in there?"

"Ten minutes at most. They're probably not even home."

"Julia, come on. We're in the middle of Harlem." The lawyer looked around as if expecting an army of escaped convicts to show up, Uzis at the ready.

"Look around. This part is all gentrified now. We're perfectly safe."

"But—"

"Please. I need to do this."

The lawyer took a long look at Julia's face, then a longer look around at the neighborhood. She slid into the driver's seat. "I'll be circling the block," said Kimmer, who hated, above all things, sitting still.

Julia turned, and mounted the steps.

(I I I)

THE BUILDING WAS BRIGHTLY LIGHTED in the early winter night, tasteful curtains in the windows, bricks nicely pointed, the snow neatly cleared from the steps. A hallucination, Julia decided. Her disobedient brain had carried her back nearly four decades, to the days when she used to play, along with her brother and her cousins, on this very sidewalk, waiting for Granny Vee's maid to call them for dinner. But when she glanced over her shoulder, there was the Escalade, Kimmer struggling to maneuver the massive car out of the space so that she could circle the block. Turning back, Julia spotted the gleaming new buzzers, and realized that the elegant old house had been converted to apartments, one to a floor, including the basement with its walled-in rear yard.

Sugar Hill was coming back. Some of the hottest property in Manhattan: the *Times* said so, and so did her favorite real-estate blogs.

Great. The Veazie mansion was co-ops. What now?

She lifted the hand mirror she had stuffed into her pocket but saw in its dulling surface only her own reflection, brow furrowed uncertainly. Kellen had told her to bring it with her, but she could not think why. She was stymied. About to return to the car, she noticed movement on her right. A man stood in the first-floor bay window, smoking a cigar and watching her.

All right, fine.

She smiled and waved as though they were old pals, pointed to the door, and pressed the second button from the bottom, hoping it was the right one. The man vanished, and, seconds later, the front door gave off an electronic groan, a tumbler clicked, and Julia stepped into the lobby.

The pattern of orange and white tiles on the floor of the foyer was as she remembered. The wood walls gleamed with recent refinishing, mailboxes had been added, and in front of her, where the archway to the parlor should have stood, was a somewhat stronger door, reinforced with metal bars, and the same man holding it open, the same cigar in his hand, as he gazed at her questioningly out of a brown face so smooth and confident that she was reminded of Kellen. Behind him was a hallway, the door to his first-floor apartment standing open, smooth jazz wafting from beyond.

He said, "Are you Margot?"

"Me? Oh, no. No. I, ah, I used to live here. Or spend time here." She stuck out her hand. "I'm Julia. Julia Carlyle."

His handshake was moist and disappointed. "You couldn't have used to live here, Julia. I'm just the second owner of the unit." He frowned, glancing over her shoulder, perhaps searching for someone more important. "Are you sure you're not Margot?" A nervously apologetic smile. "It's a blind-date thing."

"My grandmother owned the place. The whole building."

"Retta Veazie?"

"Amaretta Veazie. Yes."

"I've heard of her. They used to call her Retta, back in the day." He drew on the cigar, stepped toward her, flicked ash out into the street, reminding her of Mary Mallard. In his pricey shirt and loosened tie, he looked bored and prosperous. "So, what can I do for you, Mrs. Carlyle?"

"I was in town on business, and I was driving by, and, well, I didn't know they'd done a conversion. I had to stop and see." She shrugged, aware that she was telling too much, as she always did when nervous. "I didn't mean to bother you. I just wanted to see what the place looks like now."

"Oh, no. No. It's no bother, Mrs. Carlyle. Do come in, please. I was just having a drink."

Julia hesitated. She sensed no attempt at seduction, and, after all, the whole point of this stop was to peek inside with the mirror now tucked into her pocket. But the certainties of half an hour ago were dissipating into a larger fog, and she no longer felt sure of her purpose. The mirror business was ridiculous. A mirror was glass and silvering and

—and the occasional Eggameese—

a fancy handle, put together by human beings in a shop or factory somewhere, not a doorway into the past or the future or the hidden supernatural world where everyone looked at things edgewise. To walk in would be to act the fool. No matter what she thought Kellen might have been trying to tell her.

She smiled and backed off. "No, thank you. I'm sorry to have disturbed you. Go back to your drink." The man in the doorway took a long pull on his cigar but never budged, sharp hazel eyes measuring her, and, even before she sensed trouble, Julia wondered how on earth he could have known she was married. "I hope your date gets here soon," she said, backing away faster. "Thanks again."

From deeper in the apartment, a familiar voice said, "Oh, you can spare us a few minutes, Julia. Come on in."

(i v)

CAMERON KNOWLAND BECKONED with a proprietary air that told her immediately that he owned the unit, and, maybe, the whole building.

"Well, this is a surprise," she said, because she had to say something.

"Not an unpleasant one, I trust."

"That depends on what we're all doing here."

Cameron smiled. Julia looked around. The ceilings were as high as she remembered. The pricey furnishings expressed a modern blandness that no amount of money could quite disguise as taste. The man who had smiled from the window was of the Clan: she sensed it in his manner of speech and of dress and in the way that he carried himself, without either the tragic slouching disdain of the young men of their nation, or the nervous confidence of those who were newer to fortune. He was probably a decade younger than she, and it became clear in the first minute that Cameron was the boss, and the black man his minion.

Not that she had harbored any doubt.

"I'm sorry for the melodrama, Julia." He perched on the edge of the long table. "I happened to be in the city on business. My people told me you were coming to town—"

"What people?" she said sharply.

Cameron smiled. "My people told me you were coming, and, well, you hadn't been up to Harlem since Zant died. I hoped this might be the occasion. I guessed right." His tone said he usually did.

"This is . . . yours?"

"It used to be Kellen's. Did you know that? He bought as soon as the building went on the market."

"How did you hear I was coming down?" she asked, tone still wooden. When Cameron just kept smiling, she tried another question: "Tony Tice. Are you his secret client?"

This at least drew a bothered frown. "A most disagreeable man. Certainly not. After Kellen died, Tice got in touch with me to suggest— Well, never mind. No, Julia. I have nothing to do with him and want nothing to do with him."

"Good," she said, and meant it.

The billionaire looked around the room. "This is a beautiful apartment. They tell me the whole townhouse was beautiful, back in the old days. Sugar Hill." He rolled the name around. "Until a couple of months ago, I'd never heard of it. But this was the heart of Harlem, wasn't it? Your Harlem. Your family. The other old ones."

"Yes."

"Don't be frightened, Julia. Nobody means you any harm."

"I'm not frightened." She rubbed her eyes. "I'm just tired of being lied to."

Cameron Knowland came down off his perch and crouched in front of her. "When have I lied to you, Julia? Have I told you one thing that wasn't true?" But she was a long way from persuaded. "We're after the same thing. Kellen's surplus. Look around. I bought this apartment from the co-op. I bought it with contents. Never mind how. There are ways. The contents were crucial. I wanted to keep it just the way Kellen left it. He spent a lot of time decorating, making sure everything was just the way he wanted. He was down here at least once a month. You didn't know that?"

"No, Cameron. I didn't know that."

"Well, he was. And do you know what's on the walls in the study?" He pointed at one of the doorways. "Pictures of you, that's what. Or you and him together. I think your ex had a serious thing for you, Julia."

He straightened. "I'll tell you something else. The pictures aren't only of you. Your children are there."

"My children?"

He nodded. "You can come look for yourself if you want."

And so she did, following him dutifully into the study, walls covered with fabric of dusty rose, her favorite shade. And, sure enough, photos of Julia alone, photos of Julia with Kellen, photos of Julia with her children, either blown up from magazines or snapped—so it now seemed to her—surreptitiously. Her trembling fingers touched a shot she remembered, all four kids wiggling on her lap, clipped from an *Ebony* magazine article about the grown-up children of a certain Harlem generation. Tears tried to surprise her, but the new Julia surprised them right back.

"I think he was getting this place ready for you," said Cameron from behind her.

"For me? What's that supposed to mean?"

"I think it was supposed to be a love nest."

She whirled around, ready to get in his face.

"No, no, no, Julia, no. Calm down. I'm not suggesting anything untoward, except in poor Kellen's imagination. I think he planned to get the place ready and then present it to you like a gift. He wanted you back, Julia. He was trying to fight for you."

Not sure whether to laugh or cry, she kept a stubborn silence. Yet, at the back of her mind, something tickled.

Cameron waved a hand. "You're wondering why I bought the place."

"Yes."

"Because I was hoping that the surplus is here somewhere. Hidden. The answer. A clue. Anything. The amount of time he spent here, I can't believe he didn't leave some sort of record behind."

"I thought you weren't involved with the re-election campaign any more."

He chuckled, his whole belly shaking with mirth. "Oh, Julia. Your husband's influence is vast, but it's not infinite. Men like me do what we want. We just prefer to do what we do in the shadows. Besides"—up on his feet now, roaming the room—"not everything has to be for somebody else. I'm not an altruist. I'd love it if the President won, but, if he doesn't, he doesn't. That's why I bought the place. Don't you see? If there's any way to find out what Kellen was up to, I want it. I want the evidence. I don't care which way the evidence cuts. If it's evidence that the President did wrong, then I'll bury it. If it's evidence against Senator Whisted, then I'll hold on to it and if he wins I'll use it, ah, to keep him from straying too far from where he needs to be."

That was it. Almost. Almost. She could even overlook the perfidy of his motivation in the realization that she was nearly home.

"Or, if it's evidence against the President," she said slowly, "you could still use it to make sure he didn't stray too far."

He folded his arms. "I suppose."

"But you don't have the evidence, do you?"

"Not yet."

She almost smiled. "Sorry."

"Julia. Come. You didn't drop in for no reason. Kellen left you some kind of message. A clue. You're searching for something." Waving his hand again. "Don't let me stop you."

"I'm sorry, Cameron. I really can't help you."

"I am entirely confident that you can help me. Take as much time as you need. Look around."

"I'm kind of in a hurry—"

The investor gestured, and his black minion appeared. "Please go outside and tell Ms. Madison that Mrs. Carlyle will be a few minutes more. Wait. Invite them in. Find the kids some cookies or something."

"We really have to go," said Julia, but the minion was already out the door. And, after all, Cameron was just good old Mr. Knowland, who, as Jeannie brightly put it, owned the university.

Pretty much true.

(v)

AND SO SHE LOOKED. She could have left. She did not think Cameron meant to stop her. She could have climbed into the Escalade, driven home to the Landing with Kimmer and the kids, and put Kellen and his surplus behind her once and for all. She did not. The urge that had led her this far—the urge to solve the mystery, not for its own sake but to save Vanessa—held her tightly in its grip. Kellen had led her back to her childhood, the days when Amaretta Veazie tried, as elite Harlem society faded around her, to maintain a salon, just the way she and the other Czarinas had back in the day.

There are three things you always seem to be running from, he had said. *Your people, your past, and your God.*

Kellen had led her back to her people, through Miss Terry, and into her past, right here in Harlem. She supposed God would be next, but could not see how.

"Julia?"

"Hush," she said, secretly gleeful at shutting up a billionaire.

It worked, too.

She stood in the front hall gazing into the long mirror—another cheval—and remembering, as a girl, watching Sidney Poitier and Harry Belafonte standing here to straighten their ties and collars before plunging into the waiting throng of a Veazie party. Once, when she was about five, the guest of honor was Martin Luther King, Jr. Another time Hubert Humphrey held a fund-raiser. And then there was the wretched day in the spring of 1972 when Mona, aided by her twins, swept a furious and unwilling Granny Vee into their Plymouth station wagon for the long ride to Hanover. Kellen, upon hearing that story, had said—

That was it.

She stepped away from the cheval and walked into the apartment, Cameron following her with his eyes, the children at the kitchen table eating ice cream, Kimmer hovering near them like a bodyguard. The minion was nowhere to be seen.

"I came up here with Kellen a couple of times," she said, not sure why she had decided to narrate, except that her instincts told her the story would distract. "When we were . . . together. I wanted to show him Harlem. But it was all different. This place was dilapidated. Boarded up. We snuck in anyway. Just pushed aside some plywood and climbed in the window."

I'm going to buy this place one day, Kellen had promised, standing amid the filth. *For us.* A kiss. *For you.* Another kiss. *And for our children.* A third. *It has too much history to waste.*

I hate history, she had said.

If I had your history, I'd love it, Kellen had answered—and that night went out to a meeting he had forgotten to mention and stayed away until morning.

"What else do you remember?" prompted Cameron from behind, his urging quite unnecessary.

"We must have come here twice when we were together, and we

broke in both times." She laughed. "They hadn't even replaced the boards. The second time, some homeless guy was living in one of the rooms. I wanted to go, but Kellen booted him out."

"Did the two of you ever come here after that?"

"No."

Yes. The final goodbye. Gathering the tatters of her Veazie courage, Julia had taken the train down to the city to tell the man who had wrecked her life that somebody else was on the verge of saving it. They met for lunch at Sylvia's—a Harlem legend, and one of his favorites—and Julia looked him in the eye and told him she was pregnant, and marrying Lemaster. She watched the emotions work in his beautiful face. Anger. Astonishment. Jealousy? She had never worked it out. All through the months Julia had spent dating Lemaster—even when she had lived with him—Kellen would now and then call or send a note, either wanting to keep her on a string or trying to pry her loose. Now, hearing her news, he took his time, then smiled, said congratulations, and leaned across the table to kiss her, lightly, on the mouth. Afterward they took the subway up to Sugar Hill for a last look around.

A month later, he accepted an appointment at the University of Chicago, never quite saying goodbye.

But that day in early 1983, they had crawled in through the same window, even though it was more carefully boarded this time. Kellen had crossed to the fireplace, where ornately carved woodwork was all that remained of the huge decorative mirror above. She turned. A new mirror was in place, but the woodwork was the same. On that visit in 1983, Kellen had pulled a Swiss Army knife from his jacket and carved their initials and the date into the filigree. Followed closely by Cameron, she crossed the room. She looked in the mirror and saw reflected back not a middle-aged woman stalked by an anxious billionaire but a nervously pregnant twenty-something who felt her life slipping into other hands than her own. She smiled, but her younger self looked close to tears.

Stop it, she mouthed.

I can't, she mouthed back.

Cheeks burning, Julia fingered the woodwork, careful to stay away from the spot. She remembered how Kellen had carved *KZ & JV*, and the year, 1983. Then he had tried, and failed, to draw her into a kiss considerably more passionate than the chaste peck they had shared in the restaurant. At the time Julia had been both proud and regretful of her newfound ability to refuse him. Now, like the hallmark on the Comyns mirror, the letters had been rubbed away, obscured, the scratches in this case shellacked into permanence.

"What did you find?" said Cameron.

"Nothing yet."

Intelligence, not luck, had pushed him to the top of his field. He pointed at the scratches. "What's this?"

"I don't know."

"It says *83* and then some markings." He leaned close. "I can't make them out."

"I don't think they're anything."

"Why would Kellen carve this? It has to mean something."

"What makes you think it was Kellen?"

She left the mirror and went over to the window opening on the back yard, where Amaretta used to make her sit on a wrought-iron chair for hours, practicing her table manners. Here, too, she studied the molding and reflections.

"Nothing," she said.

"Think," he suggested.

"I've tried thinking. I can't think of anything else."

She went into the kitchen, caressing Jeannie's shoulder as she passed. But everything here was new. She opened a few random cabinets anyway. The dining room had preserved aged dentil molding, which she pretended to study. She examined the woodwork in both bedrooms.

She shook her head.

"What about all those mirrors he tried to send you?" Obviously the Senior Trustee had done a lot of homework. "They must mean something!"

Julia shook her head. "I thought he meant them to lead me here. But I don't see anything I . . . recognize." A sad shrug. "Maybe I misunderstood. Maybe you did."

"You're not trying to say—"

"There's nothing here." She turned to face him. "It's over, Cameron. I can't find it. You can't find it. If there was anything to find, it's hidden someplace else. I'm done."

"Done?"

"Done looking. I've had enough. I have a family to worry about—"

"You can't stop now!"

"I can, and I will. I'm tired of this. Kellen wasn't a good man, Cameron. You're welcome to keep looking if you want. But I'm through."

"Right. Right." Scarcely listening, so bright was his fury. If she could not help him and could not obstruct him, she was irrelevant to him. He was still fuming as she collected Kimmer and the children and went outside, where the black minion had spent the past half-hour guarding the car. She had what she had come for.

(v i)

"So THAT WAS the great Cameron Knowland," murmured Kimmer as Julia popped the locks. The street was dark but refreshingly quiet. "Why did he want to meet you in Harlem? I mean, it's not like an assignation, right?"

"It's a long story."

"With Saturday-night traffic, we've got hours and hours."

"Maybe another time." She was scribbling frantically, drawing the curves she had memorized that Kellen had carved beside the *83* in the wainscoting. The squiggles were quite elaborate, with serifs and curlicues everywhere, to make reading them backward difficult. But Julia, who had brought her mirror, had no trouble. *BCP*, the carving, reversed, now read. Since Kellen had done nothing to the numbers, she assumed she should read them as they were. *BCP 83.*

She did not know for sure where Kellen had meant her to look next, but this time, at least, she had a theory.

"Mommy," said Jeans, tugging at her sleeve from behind.

"Don't worry, honey. We're going home now. And you can sleep all the way."

"No, Mommy, that's not what I'm talking about. Look. Look!"

She glanced where her daughter was pointing, at a small park across the street. Kimmer was already on her cell phone again.

"What am I looking at?" she asked her youngest.

"He was there, Mommy!" Jeannie was thrilled and concerned at once. "He was! He's gone now, but he was there!"

"Who was?"

"Jeremy!" Kicking the back of the driver's seat to illustrate the stupidity of the question. "Mr. Flew! He was over there on the bench!"

Julia laughed nervously, aware of Kimmer's scrutiny. "Oh, honey, he works all the way home in Elm Harbor. I'm sure you imagined it."

At least I hope you did, she thought but did not say. Maybe Jeannie had spotted Jeremy. Maybe not. Certainly Julia had suspected for a while that she was being followed, and not only because Mary Mallard said so. She had felt the scrutiny of perfect strangers, like hot breath on the back of her neck. Perhaps some of them worked for Cameron Knowland. If she was going to complete her task, she could not afford to be tracked. Heading down from Sugar Hill toward Madison Avenue and the bridge across the East River to the Bronx and on to New England, Julia had a fresh idea. Ideas seemed to plague her constantly since what Mary called her liberation and Lemaster called something odd going on with her; and some of the ideas were pretty good. This time Kimmer's incessant yakking had inspired her. Cell phones. Something about cell phones. According to Bruce Vallely, Kellen's cell phone had vanished from police custody. Tony Tice, like Kimmer, seemed unable to put his down. Julia thought back to the night Janine Goldsmith had slept over, before Vanessa was, as she liked to say, Smithgrounded. Julia had caught the two teenagers playing with a device to clone cell-phone numbers, constructed from plans they found on the Internet.

Cell phones. Of course.

She wondered if Smith had ever tried to build . . . Hmmm.

CHAPTER 48

SAFETY IN NUMBERS

(1)

SUNDAY NIGHT was yet another committee of Ladybugs, and this time nobody pretended not to be interested in how Julia's family was doing, and Vanessa in particular, the Sister Ladies smothering her with their fluttery concern. Julia finally pointed the Escalade toward home well past ten. Exhausted by their swarming attentions, she wanted nothing so much as to tumble into bed.

She drove through town. She hardly ever took the expressway, especially at night, preferring the relative coziness of city streets. But the city streets were empty. Furtive flakes snuck through the bright cones of her headlights as if embarrassed to be falling so thinly. Later tonight they would be back, proudly, trillions of buddies in tow. Safety in numbers: the same theory that still fortified Ladybugs and Empyreals and the dozens of other groups to which middle-class African America aspired. Once upon a time, when the most professionally successful among the darker nation were yet segregated out of white social life, the fraternities and sororities and clubs had filled the need to rub shoulders with people of similar education and attainment. Today, even with most formal barriers gone, black Americans at the top of their professions seemed to feel the need from time to time to slough off the personas that brought success in the wider, whiter world— and to escape the small whispers and slights whose existence they secretly feared—and hang out instead with the successful of their own nation.

Safety, still, in numbers.

And Julia Carlyle, who had grown up surrounded by white kids in Hanover, whose closest friends most of her life had been white, and who lived now in Tyler's Landing, the heart of whiteness, felt the same tug.

Julia stopped for gas as usual at the Exxon station on Route 48 in Langford—she loved her car, but it seemed to need a tankful every two days—and set the pump, then went inside for a cup of foul coffee. She was alongside her car, pulling out her phone in defiance of the warning sign, when the skinny man in the windbreaker climbed out of the sedan that had pulled in seconds after she did and asked if he could talk to her for a minute.

"I'm in a hurry," said Julia, in her mother's voice, for she assumed, although her accoster looked not at all penurious, that she was about to be hit up for money. She stopped pumping at once and hung the nozzle. She declined the receipt. "I'm sorry," she said, reaching for the door.

"I only need a moment, Mrs. Carlyle."

An instant's astonished paralysis at the sound of her name, and an instant was all the stranger needed. He put a hand on her arm. She pulled free.

"Don't touch me." It occurred to her that the stranger had chosen a moment when no other car was in the station. His thick mop of hair was an uneasy brown. He wore a diamond stud in one ear. "Who are you?"

"I only have a few questions."

"I don't have any answers."

"I'm afraid I'm going to have to insist."

"Leave me alone," she snapped, and opened the door, fast. The man grabbed her arm again, more firmly. Stunned, she struggled, but his grip was iron. He was dragging her away from her car. She threw her coffee in his face, and cocked her arm for a good hard slap, except that by now the man was on his knees, not from the pain of the scalding coffee, but because Bruce Vallely had him in an armlock.

Bruce stepped back and the man stood up, hands at his sides, not saying a word.

"Where did you come from?" said Julia, surprised and appalled. Safety in numbers indeed. She was trembling, and had already decided, incoherently, never to stop for gas again in her life.

"I thought you were staying away from reporters," said Bruce.

"Reporters?"

Bruce nodded. The light snow settled in his bushy hair. One hand was on the stranger's shoulder. The other was out of sight. "This gentleman is a reporter. Tell Mrs. Carlyle you're a reporter."

"I'm a reporter," the stranger confirmed, tonelessly. In a perfect world, Julia would have noticed something amiss. But pounding adrenaline warps the judgment. Besides, she was growing tired of journalists as a breed and lately had not even returned Tessa's calls.

"We're going to have a little talk, this gentleman and I." Bruce gestured toward the man's car, and the brown-haired man drifted toward it. "I'll find out who he works for, and make sure you're not bothered again."

"Wait," said Julia. "What are you doing here?"

"Buying gas."

"But—"

"If you'll excuse us, we have to be going."

After the two men drove away in the stranger's car, Julia finally spotted Bruce's Mustang, in the parking lot of the long-closed florist across the road.

(11)

SAFELY BACK HOME, having calmed herself with two glasses of a playful Monterey white Riesling, Julia decided to act on the impulse that had seized her when, in Harlem, she had noticed how Kimmer could not put down her cell phone. Tony Tice, Kimmer's fellow attorney, could not live without his either. Julia had been about ready to chalk up Gina's killing to Malcolm Whisted, but Cameron Knowland's determination had set her back. She would have to talk to Mary, who said she had discovered startling information of her own. The two women would meet in a few days. Meanwhile, Julia found Vanessa in the kitchen, sitting at the shining black counter, a half-eaten apple and a glass of milk beside her, nose in a volume of Emily Dickinson from the school library.

"Gina was right," said the teen, not looking up.

"Gina?"

"I always thought Dickinson was overrated, but she's not. She's a *genius.*" She turned a page. "Or she *was*. I was never into poetry all that much, but listen to this."

"Honey—"

"Listen." She had found what she wanted:

> "*Exultation is the going*
> *Of an inland soul to sea,—*
> *Past the houses, past the headlands,*
> *Into deep eternity!*"

Vanessa ran her fingers over the verses as if memorizing their feel, then slipped a cloth marker into the book and closed it. "I'm going to post it on my blog," she said, and, swiveling on the counter stool, brandished the volume like a fire-and-brimstone preacher holding her Bible. "This woman understood death."

Julia searched for the appropriate words. "I'm so glad you've found a—"

"Heroine," her daughter finished. "Don't worry, Moms, I don't expect to start communing with her spirit anytime soon."

"Oh, ah, well, good."

For a few minutes, Julia busied herself at the sink, scrubbing what needed to be scrubbed, rinsing what needed to be rinsed. These late hours still belonged to the two of them. Lemaster and Jeans slumbered upstairs, Mr. Flew in the basement. Vanessa, perhaps sensing that her mother wanted something, stayed at the counter, reading and clucking. Julia waited until she could wait no longer.

"Honey?" Casually, casually, barely glancing up as she wiped the countertops. "You remember that electronic toy you and Janine were playing with last month? The thing that, ah, that cloned cell-phone numbers?"

Color flooded Vanessa's smooth cheeks. She was ready to get very angry indeed. "You told us to stop, and we stopped, okay? And we weren't playing. It wasn't a toy."

"No, no, I understand. I understand." Holding her hands up for peace. "I'm not criticizing you, honey. I want to ask you about, ah, another device that I bet Janine has got lying around somewhere."

"Smith."

"Right. Smith. Until the violence stops."

"No, that's the vow of silence. Her name is a protest against consumerism and regimentation."

"Oh, right. Right. Sorry." She put down the rag, leaned back against the counter, and explained to her daughter what she had in mind. Vanessa shook her head several times, then, finally, said, "Those things aren't illegal. Well, they are some places. Most places. And, well, this state is one of those places. This whole country, actually."

"Does she have one? That's all I want to know."

"Why?" Defiantly. "What are you going to do if she does?"

"Borrow it. But without her knowing."

Vanessa's brow crinkled in thought. "What do you need it for?"

"To sell to Hollywood. To worship in my spare time. To decorate the mantelpiece. What difference does it make what I want it for?"

"I'm just asking." Sharply, followed by a sulk. "You don't have to jump down my throat."

Julia softened. "I'm sorry, honey. Let's just say it's my ace in the hole."

Her daughter thought this over. "How?"

"How, what?"

"How are you going to borrow it without Smith knowing?"

"Oh, that part's easy. You're going to borrow it from Smith, and I'm going to borrow it from you."

Vanessa immediately shook her head. "I can't borrow it. I'm Smith-grounded. I'm not allowed to see her. I'm not allowed to talk to her. I'm not allowed to IM her or e-mail her or text-message her or anything. I'm not even allowed to sit next to her in the cafeteria. Ergo, I can't borrow it."

Julia put her hands on her hips. "Vanessa Amaretta Carlyle, I have known you since the night you came out of my womb, squealing and fighting all the way. You are a Veazie from your beautiful braids down to your lovely brown toes. You always do everything your own way. I refuse to believe that you've followed all those rules just because we told you to, and I wouldn't be terribly surprised to learn that you haven't followed any of them." Lifting a hand to forestall a squawked objection. "Now, listen to me. I don't care if you've broken the rules before or not. I'm giving you a dispensation now. Be discreet. Don't let anybody know what you're up to. But borrow the thing from Smith and get it to me."

The teen's mouth was hanging open. "And I bet you don't want me to tell Dads, right?"

"I'll deal with your father."

"Yeah. I bet you will."

"What's that supposed to mean?"

A sudden smile, like winter's thaw. "It means I like this new you. I *love* her."

Julia smiled. "You know what, honey? I love her, too."

(III)

THAT BRUCE HAD HAPPENED UPON Julia Carlyle being accosted by the stranger that night was attributable at least partly to luck. He did not follow her every evening. He was one man, he had a whole department to run, and every minute he stole for the Zant case was a minute he could not spend on a more productive endeavor. Surveillance was most intrusive of all, which was why he indulged in it rarely. On the other hand, Tony Tice's warning about his clients becoming active worried him. And the lawyer was right. They would not bother to go after Bruce. If they chased anybody, it would be someone who could actually give them information.

Like Julia Carlyle, who Tice believed to be Zant's Black Lady.

He had tracked Julia to the meeting at the home of Tonya Montez, then met some friends for dinner and still been back in time to catch her as she left. He had decided to follow, just to see if her back was clean—in particular, if Jeremy Flew was in the picture—but had spotted the stranger instead.

Bruce had watched, and waited, and finally intervened when he saw the man grab her arm.

The stranger had stopped resisting once he felt Bruce's gun in his back, for he had no way of knowing that the university's rules did not allow any campus officer, even the director, to carry a gun if not in uniform; or that what he felt in his back was only a wooden tube. They parked in a municipal lot, hidden by yellow school buses. The interrogation was unpleasant. Once Bruce found the gun in the stranger's waistband, he would have turned the man over to the police, except that he also found a syringe and a set of plastic handcuffs. Bruce gave him-

self a moment. This was not some ruffian, out to put a scare into Julia
Carlyle. This was a man who intended to take her along.

Tony Tice's clients were indeed becoming active. The stakes of the
game had changed, and he had to change them back, fast.

Bruce dropped the man he had interrogated at the university hospital, flashing his credentials and spinning a tale, knowing the stranger
would not contradict him. From the Mustang he called the lawyer to
say they had a deal. If Bruce Vallely were to get his hands on Kellen
Zant's surplus, he would deliver it to Tony's clients.

CHAPTER 49

AGAIN THE COMYNS MIRROR

(I)

MARY MALLARD CAME AND WENT, leaving behind information every bit as startling as she had promised. According to her sources, the President of the United States and Senator Malcolm Whisted had recently had at least two and possibly three off-the-record meetings. Leaks would soon be published, said Mary, to the effect that they were discussing foreign policy, both men wanting to look presidential and nonpartisan. But Mary's sources said no aides were present, and the meetings were long.

In return, Julia told her about encountering Cameron Knowland in New York. She kept to herself what she had found there. She had never told Mary about the Comyns mirror either.

After Mary left, Julia checked the family calendar. One of the meetings had occurred when Lemaster was in Washington. But when she asked, he repeated Bay Dennison's dictum that a rumor was not rendered more likely to be true because the rumormonger refused to give his name.

"That's not a denial," Julia had said.

"I didn't hear an accusation," he answered calmly.

Meanwhile, she had been searching for BCP 83. Kellen had promised to send her back to her God, and Julia guessed that BCP stood for the Book of Common Prayer. But when she checked all the copies in the house—both the 1928 version favored by Lemaster and the more modern texts used by nearly all Episcopal churches—no notes or cards or photos fell out of page 83, or any other page. She spent an afternoon back at the Kepler Library, sorting through every edition of the book she could find, in every available language, but came away disappointed. She even found herself making excuses to visit the offices of div school colleagues who might have a copy on their shelves. She would stand there chatting with Suzanne de Broglie or Clay Maxwell about faculty appointments or the state of the physical plant, and pick up, as if idly, any Book of Common Prayer in sight.

No luck.

One afternoon, Julia arrived early for a meeting with Claire Alvarez, who was held up at a campus event. An assistant invited Julia to wait in the dean's office. Claire stepped inside a few minutes later to find her deputy on the rolling stepladder, pulling down from a high shelf in a glass-fronted cabinet the aged copy of the prayer book to which every dean, by long tradition, added a new *dédicace* before passing it on to the next. Claire Alvarez expressed no surprise. She smiled beatifically, the only way she ever displayed anger, and, remarking that she, too, drew inspiration by reading from time to time what others had written there, plucked the book gently from Julia's fingers.

But Julia held on long enough to establish that there was nothing stuffed inside.

As their meeting ended, the dean put a hand on Julia's shoulder and said, her voice dripping sweetness and affection, that people had told her that the dean of students seemed to have missed quite a few days of work lately. Not that anyone took attendance, naturally, but was everything all right at home? It was? And with Vanessa, too? Yes? Marvelous, Claire Alvarez assured her, just marvelous. Oh, and, by the way, should she happen to have the chance, she wouldn't mind, would she—only if it comes up in conversation, naturally!—but perhaps she wouldn't mind mentioning to her husband that the div school was still hoping that Lombard Hall would look favorably on the request for a supplemental capital appropriation to help with the chapel roof?

That same night Julia drove up to Saint Matthias, because the church was open late for the weekly prayer meeting, and, feeling foolish, spent over an hour afterward straightening up the books in the pews—*no, please, I don't need help, I can handle it, thanks!*—still without result.

Another day, at Kepler, she pulled Suzanne de Broglie aside after a faculty lunch, because Suzanne spent more time in the archives than any other professor. Suzanne, always impatient around actual people, cut her off before the question was finished. The sub-basement, she said. That was the level of the stacks used least. The sub-basement.

Now it was Friday night, and Julia, still agitated, settled at the piano, because the other way she relaxed was to play. Jeannie was sleeping over with friends, and Lemaster was out of town again, so it was just Julia and Vanessa in the house. Vanessa had her door closed and, very likely, her earphones on. She would not be disturbed. So Julia did a couple of finger exercises and then began to play. Not classical this time but her beloved Broadway. She did a medley from *The King and I*, and another from *The Sound of Music*, stopping here and there because the instrument seemed to be in need of a tuning. She remembered Tonya Montez sitting at the keyboard and wondered whether the chief Sister Lady might have damaged something when she slammed the lid. She grew irritated. This piano was worth a fortune. Duke Ellington had played it, often. And Tonya had treated it like a—

Wait.

Was it possible?

Julia went upstairs to the master suite, opened the drawer of her vanity, pulled out Granny Vee's mirror, the one Seth Zant had returned to her after Kellen held it hostage for twenty years. She turned on the lights around the dressing mirror, held up the William Comyns to examine its back. Yes, as she had thought before. The *W·C* hallmark had been scratched out, replaced with backward letters that, translated, were *E·K*.

Granny Vee's mirror. *E·K.*

Duke Ellington's given names, as jazz fans and everyone of a certain age in the darker nation knew, were Edward Kennedy.

Edward Kennedy Ellington.

Back down in the living room, she examined the piano. She did not pause to ask herself how Kellen could have gotten into the house to hide whatever he hid. Knowing he had done so was enough. This was why he had come to the house the night he died. He wanted to retrieve whatever he had left here, but saw the sitter's car, panicked, turned, sideswiped the lamposts on his way to the road.

Julia began to search. She looked inside the piano bench, but there was only the sheet music. She looked under it. She looked inside the piano. Under it. In every cranny. And saw nothing. Not a scratched message, not a piece of paper, not a photograph.

Nothing.

Julia stood up, frustrated and sweating. All right, she had erred. Suppose she had the $E \cdot K$ right, but not the piano. Could Kellen have meant Amaretta's Harlem townhouse, where the piano used to sit? But she had just been there—

A footfall behind her.

"Dance with me," said Vanessa, her voice soft and caressing. "Like you did last month. I liked that."

"It's late, honey. I think—"

"Just for a little while? Please?"

How could she refuse? So dance they did, in the family room, gently, as smooth jazz played. Probably they wept a bit, but neither discussed it. When Julia at last tiptoed into her bedroom, it was well past one. She used the bathroom and hung up her robe, and found on her pillow a long white envelope. She remembered her daughter's long-ago habit of leaving little scraps of paper around to tell Mommy she loved her.

That girl, said Julia to herself, smiling.

Then she noticed the bits of tape hanging off it and bits of shellac hanging off the tape.

"Is that what you were looking for?" asked Vanessa, who had crept up behind her again.

(11)

"YOU FIND EVERYTHING," said Julia, frustration and admiration mixed in her tone. As a small child, Vanessa had spoiled more than one Christmas Eve by gleefully announcing that she had discovered where Mommy and Daddy had hidden the presents. Finally, they had stopped hiding them at home.

"Most things," said Vanessa complacently.

"Have you—"

"Read them? Uh-huh. It's pages from some guy's diary." She took the envelope from her mother, but only to pull out the sheaf and hand it over. "All the reasons DeShaun couldn't have done it. Like how Gina's prints weren't in the car, or Gina's blood, and how the fact that somebody saw them talking doesn't mean she ever got into the car. Look at the last page." Julia, reading fast, had found the place already.

"See what he says there? He wanted to investigate some more, but they wouldn't let him. He said he and his deputy went to this meeting, and at the meeting they ordered him to stop." She had to stop for a moment to allow her mouth to catch up with her mind. "Only the thing is, he doesn't say who was at the meeting. I don't know why you care," Vanessa continued, one hand trembling. "It was DeShaun. Anybody who says it wasn't, is lying. I'm like the world's leading expert—"

"Why are you so adamant, honey?"

"I'm not adamant. I'm right."

"You know I have to check. I have to be sure."

Voice suddenly small: "I know."

Julia read the pages for a third time. Nothing new here, except for one tiny phrase.

Julia looked at her daughter. The braids had fallen in front of Vanessa's face so that her voice seemed disembodied. "Moms? Are you okay?"

Julia said, "This changes everything."

CHAPTER 50

HOUSE OF TOYS

(1)

FRANK CARRINGTON LIVED in a pretty but exhausted Victorian not far from the Town Green—the spot where, in the official story, poor DeShaun Moton had picked up Gina Joule the night he supposedly murdered her. Julia stood on the front step. Icicles dangled from aging gutters. A part of her knew she should not be here, especially with Vanessa in tow, but the teenager had refused to wait in the car. Julia was feeling like a bit of a teenaged sneak herself. She had picked her daughter up from Smith's house, where she had gone, secretly, to borrow the device that now snuggled in her mother's purse. She could not afford to wait another day, because Old Landing wore a CLOSED sign, and Vera Brightwood said Frank was leaving town.

"I just stopped by to see Shirley," she lied almost before Frank had the door fully open: Mrs. Carrington had taken a bad fall on the ice two days earlier, providing Julia with the necessary excuse. "How's that ankle?"

"It's better." Glancing past her to Vanessa, who stood fidgeting on the walk. "I've sent her to her folks in Vermont." Inclining his head. "I think I might follow her."

"Why?"

"I warned you, Julia. I told you there are things I shouldn't talk about. Well, you made me talk about them, and—well, there are people who aren't too happy with me. Let me put it that way." He caught her look. "Oh, no, don't you worry. You're married to the great Lemaster Carlyle. Nobody can touch you. But everybody can touch me."

Julia asked if she and Vanessa could come in for a minute anyway, and he told her that he had nothing more to say. Then he let them in anyway, as she had known he would, because she was his best customer, and because he was the sort of man who could be pushed.

"Mind the toys," he warned, leading them into a low room in the back of the house.

"Toys?"

"Uh-huh."

They turned out to be toys of war. Model airplanes, tanks, ships, painted soldiers in their neat and—Julia suspected—precisely correct ranks. Dominating them all were the displays, the maps and battlefield dioramas that lay everywhere, their terrains painfully worked to include hills and little green trees and roads and rivers and crisp cards that gave places and dates, alongside little plastic markers to represent armies and navies.

Julia, who loved peace, was aghast.

But she asked anyway, to be polite, and Frank grew increasingly excited as he took them on a tour of the many battles he had never fought but obviously would have handled better than the generals in charge—Thermopylae, First Manassas, Second Manassas, Waterloo, the Bulge, and others that she forgot again a moment after he pointed them out—while Vanessa, who Julia had hoped would impress, stood like furniture, imprisoned by her shyness. He moved figures around on the boards with loving fingers.

"Very impressive," Julia murmured.

Then the three of them sat around the room drinking Diet Cokes. In the middle of the floor, Frank seemed to be working on his most ambitious project yet, a diorama that took up most of the floor. Paints and bits of card and plastic armies were scattered all over the rug, and Julia envisioned poor Shirley trying to get him to straighten up after himself.

"So, what can I do for you?" he finally said. "Because, I told you, I'm all through talking about Gina Joule."

Vanessa perked up at the name, then lapsed into her torpor once more.

"I've found part of the diary," said Julia.

"Seriously? Arnie's diary?"

"Yes."

He nodded, and almost smiled. "So you should take it to the police. The papers. Get the truth out."

"Unfortunately, I don't have enough of it to do that. But the part that I have does raise an interesting question." She glanced at her daughter, who seemed to be dozing. "You told me last month that the day Arnold Huebner announced that the investigation was closed, he went to a meeting. He didn't make his decision until after the meeting was over. Remember?"

"I remember." But the haunted look was back in his eyes. He was the best source she had, perhaps the only source left alive, and something had him terrified.

"In the diary, Arnold Huebner says the same thing. That there was a meeting. But he doesn't say who the meeting was with." When this did not draw him, Julia went on. "You know, don't you? You know who he met with."

"The first selectman. That's no secret."

"Who else was there?" Stubborn silence. "In the diary, Arnold Huebner says 'they' told him to stop. Not just one person. At least two. So who else told him? Come on, Frank. I've read it over ten times. You know what else? Arnold Huebner didn't write 'I' went to the meeting. He wrote 'we.' And you were his principal deputy. Not Ralphie Nacchio. You. I think you were at that meeting, Frank. I think you know who ordered Arnold Huebner to drop the case. I think that's why you're afraid, but it's also why you've looked for the diary all these years. You admired Arnold Huebner and you watched them make him bend. You want whoever really killed Gina brought to justice. You just didn't want to risk your family to do it. You needed a proxy. You needed me—"

Vanessa suddenly covered her face, telling Julia that she had gone too far, even before Frank Carrington exploded.

"You have no right! No right!" He was on his feet, the formerly mild visage splotchy with anger and fear. In his hand were the small-bladed, long-handled scissors he used to trim plastic for his toys. He looked ready to stab somebody. Instead, he put the shears away and pointed at the door. "I want you out of here. Right now. Just go, Julia. I mean it."

"I wasn't trying to—"

"I told you I'm not going to talk about it. I haven't talked about it for thirty years, and I'm not going to start now. No, Julia. No more arguments. You're too persuasive. Keep your mouth shut and go. Just go."

Julia protested and cajoled, but Frank escorted his guests to the door, his fury crackling in the air like heat lightning. He said he would be leaving for Norwich, most likely tomorrow, and was never coming back to this horrible town. Silent Vanessa turned her head away, as if offended, or hearing sounds they had missed.

On the doorstep, chill wind nipping, Frank forced a calm into his voice. He was no less angry, but he was in control. "I'm sorry I yelled at you, Julia. But I don't ever want to hear from you again."

"I understand," said Julia, defeated. "I'm sorry."

"Bad times in the Landing. That's all."

"I understand," she said a second time, because she could think of nothing else. She had thought Frank Carrington a pushover, but fear can do amazing things.

Vanessa stood beside her, embarrassed at the failure of their mission, and by her mother's obvious intimidation. The teen cast about for a way to turn defeat into victory, as the generals she admired always figured out how to do. Suddenly Gina was beside her, first time in ages, signaling urgently for her attention, and Vanessa, after an initial period of trembling resistance—*If you look at those things too long, you'll turn into one of them!*—turned to listen. Gina got up on her toes and spent half a minute or so whispering in her ear, until Vanessa finally nodded.

"Mr. Carrington? May I use the powder room?"

The former deputy sighed as if to say this always happened in the end, then pushed the door wider, and pointed down the hall. "Second left," he said.

Vanessa turned to her mother. "I'll only be a minute."

"I'll wait here, honey."

Worried about her. Naturally. Vanessa said, "How about if you start the car and get the heater going?"

"I'd rather wait."

"She'll be fine," said Frank, annoyed.

"He's right, Moms. I'll be fine. I promise. But you have to wait in the car." She leaned over and kissed her mother on the forehead. "Trust me," she said softly. "Please."

(11)

VANESSA HURRIED into the powder room—she really did have to go—and heard the front door slam, and the antiques dealer's booming voice commanding her to let him know when she was done. She stood in front of the mirror, adjusting her braids, listening to Gina's further advice, and stoking her courage. You are here, Gina was saying. You might as well find out.

Then she stepped out. "Mr. Carrington?" she called.

Voice from the family room studio again, no trace of welcome. "I assume you can find the front door."

"I just wanted to ask you one more thing."

"I have nothing more to say. I'm sorry."

Vanessa stepped down into the room, where the antiques dealer was brushing blue paint into his diorama as a river took shape, bowing in like a topped V, and another river, already painted, bowed back toward it, and Gina murmured that she could do this one, she could, yes, and she heard Frank Carrington's voice wanting to know why she was still here, and she looked and looked and raced through the hundreds upon hundreds of maps stored in the amazing memory that no one ever respected because they did not respect what she put in it, and at last a light went on and the student-who-could-have-been whispered from deep inside her, *Volga.*

He was growing angry again, and squaring to throw her out, but she kept her eyes down.

"What are you staring at?" he demanded.

Vanessa pointed to the bottom right-hand corner of the diorama. "The terrain is wrong."

"What did you say?"

"It's too green. There shouldn't be trees or grass. Most of it was barren."

His eyes grew wide, fear and fury mixing. "Miss"—had she been male, it might have been "boy"—"I hate to say it, but you don't know what the fuck you're talking about. Excuse my French."

She moved closer, fingers still extended. "This is the Kalmyk Steppe, isn't it? Due south of Stalingrad."

"Is that so?"

"This is Operation Blue, summer of 1942, when the Germans are winning. I *loved* that one." A sliding motion of her hand. "The Fourth Panzers, curling south and then shooting north again, and nobody to protect the Steppe except some sailors rushed in from Siberia or someplace."

"There were tanks. T-34s."

"Just sailors. Marines, maybe. No tanks."

"Barbarossa," he said, eying her. "Not Blue."

"No. By summer it was Operation Blue. If Hitler had just gone after the oil fields and not insisted on taking the city, he might have won the war. Thank God he was such a military idiot."

"How do you know all that?"

Vanessa allowed herself a grin. "I guess I like to read."

"About war?"

"Yes."

"Famous battles? All that?"

"Uh-huh."

Frank Carrington did not really smile—she did not think his facial muscles ran to that—but he did grunt and twist his face in a grimace that might have meant delight at discovering a long-lost relative or dismay at learning that the tests were positive. "Funny hobby for a girl."

Vanessa nodded. "At school they all think I'm nuts."

"Funny thing. In the village, they think I'm nuts, too."

She searched for an appropriate response. Gina, who loved Emily Dickinson, supplied it. "Then there's a pair of us," Vanessa recited from Gina's dictation. "Don't tell."

(111)

OUTSIDE, IN THE ESCALADE, Julia began to grow nervous. How long did it take to use the bathroom? She wondered whether she had been wise to leave Vanessa alone. She worried the problem over in her mind. Usually so decisive, Julia could not figure out whether to ring the bell again or not. The sun passed behind a low winter cloud and took her confidence with it. She shivered and turned the heat up and pressed the button to direct more of it to her legs, even though the cocooning warmth made her drowsy. The familiar dream came, fleeing through winter woods, a fearful night creature nipping at her heels—

A tapping on the window, like claws on a corpse.

Julia started, then shook herself awake. On the passenger's side of the car, Vanessa stood impatiently, stamping her feet against the cold.

Odd how Julia did not remember locking the doors.

"What were you doing all that time? I was worried about you."

"We talked."

"About what?"

"What we went there to talk about."

"That meeting?"

Vanessa nodded. "But first we talked about Stalingrad."

Julia's foot hit the brake, but the Escalade was still in the driveway. "About what?"

"Stalingrad. Worst battle of World War II. Maybe of all time. Ended in the winter of 1943, and probably turned the war."

"Oh." A pause while each waited for the other. "Ah, and what did you decide about . . . Stalingrad?"

The answer was a long time coming, and echoed, sepulchral and distant and touched with tragedy, as if Vanessa was orating at a funeral a long way off. "That the only human lives we really believe are precious are the lives of the people we know well. Everybody is willing to sacrifice other people's lives."

Julia, stung, took a few seconds to realize that this was not a slap at her personally. She decided to let it go. "I see," was her only comment.

"You don't believe that, do you?" A smirk? No, no, just the usual sardonic innocence by which Vanessa evaluated the world outside her own mind and perceptions. "Or you don't think you do."

"I believe every single life is precious," Julia said quietly, but firmly.

"Even unborn ones?"

Oh, Heaven! Oh, help! Vanessa never asked her mother's opinion on matters of morality, and Julia, none too certain of her own ethical perceptions, preferred to keep it that way. "I, ah, I'm not entirely convinced that those are lives."

"Father Freed says they are."

"People have different opinions on that question," said Julia, fighting her way out of a conversational corner into which she did not remember backing. "Even different religions have, ah, different opinions. And that's why, uh, why nobody has the right to, uh, to impose . . . ah, their view on a disputed issue. . . ." She ran down. She had lost the thread. It all seemed so clear and obvious, sitting around Kepler lamenting the assault on the most fundamental of all human rights, but, sitting in this too-hot car with her brilliant and inquisitive daughter, Julia found everything muddy and uncertain. She said, voice trembling, "Maybe we should, ah, talk about this another time."

Vanessa seemed unaware of her distress, but Julia suspected that she was concealing her perception, for this child saw everything, a fact Lemaster seemed not to understand. "Okay," she said.

They were passing the Town Green. Light afternoon flurries had started to dance across the windshield. "Vanessa?"

"Hmmm?"

"What did Mr. Carrington tell you about the meeting?"

"He got a lot nicer after he found out I knew Stalingrad. I helped him with his diorama. He had made a few mistakes."

"Mistakes?"

"Terrain. The name of one of the towns. The route the Sixth Army took. He had them crossing the Don *south* of Kalach, if you can believe it."

A quick glance. Who was this precocious child? What else went on in that brain that she hid from public view? What had God wrought in this creature?

And where did *that* thought come from?

"What else?"

"Oh, he knew a lot more than I did." Unlike most smart teenagers— or most smart adults—Vanessa was able to admit this truth with no embarrassment, perhaps because she met the species so rarely. "I learned a lot about war. He even gave me a book to read." She held up a well-thumbed volume by somebody named Keegan. "He said I can keep it if I want."

"Vanessa—"

"Did you know that a lot of the movies are wrong? Archers couldn't shoot through armor, so, a lot of the time—when cavalry wore armor?—the only real point of attacking them with arrows was psychological. The impact and the noise. No real harm. Just fear."

Frustrated by this circuitous disquisition, Julia asked, directly, "What happened at the meeting?"

"I was *getting* to that," said Vanessa, as if it was the less important part of the conversation. "The meeting was the first selectman, and Sheriff Huebner, and Mr. Carrington, and a black man."

"A what?"

"A black man. And he seemed to be in charge." Julia's face went gray, but her daughter continued merrily on. "Tall, broad across the shoulders, a little overweight. Skin almost yellow. He never gave his name, but Mr. Carrington thinks he might have been a congressman. Moms, are you okay?"

No, she was not okay. She was furious at being misled, and frightened out of her wits. But she kept her voice calm. "I told you I didn't want you involved."

Vanessa was tart. "If not for me, you wouldn't know any of this."

Maybe I didn't want to know, said Julia, but not quite aloud. She decided to drive back to Boston in the morning to ask Byron Dennison to his face what he was doing in the Landing ten days after Gina Joule died, and, for all Julia knew, in Elm Harbor a year later, persuading DeShaun's family to drop the lawsuit.

But the hospital called that very night, to say that Bay had fallen asleep again—for good.

CHAPTER 51

MONA

(1)

IN THE SECOND WEEK OF FEBRUARY, over the fervent objections
of her husband and for the sake of her daughter, Julia Carlyle flew to
Paris, where she spent the night at one of those delightful little hotels
that dot the side streets, and took the morning train south for Toulouse,
where Hap, Mona's live-in companion, waited in the aging red Renault
18 GTX. He was a slumping, shuffling man in his fifties, with rounded
shoulders, as if from decades of hard labor, and the cheerless when-
will-it-end smile of an exhausted headwaiter. He jerked his way
through the cranky five-speed manual gearbox as if it was an old enemy,
making little conversation as they darted through suburbs and into the
countryside, slipping through copses of trees and between endless
fields. Julia was grateful for the chance to doze and watch the view and,
mostly, to consider and reconsider how to approach the mother who
had omitted a big chunk of the family story.

"She'll be pleased to see you," Hap ventured at one point.

"I bet she will," Julia snapped, which shut him up for a while.

The house was small and ragged and stuccoed, with red tiles on the
roof and red awnings covering some of the windows and metal frames
from which awnings were missing covering the rest. The garden,
mostly brown, was sprinkled with an unexpected snow, and she wondered if she had somehow brought it with her. The foyer was a reddish
marble. So were the frayed carpet runners. Every time she visited, Julia
felt she was overdosing on the color, and wished Mona would redeco-
rate: not that there was money for such frills, because Mona, lacking
the good fortune to be married to a frugal first-generation immigrant,

had spent her years doling out her inheritance to anyone with a cause or a sob story or cute eyes. The house backed on the woods. Two downstairs bedrooms opened onto a walled garden where faded tiles, wobbly wrought-iron furniture, and a desiccated fountain warned you that life dried up in the end. Dying vineyards lay just over the rise. Mona had once thought to produce an income, before discovering that they yielded a particularly inferior variety of grape.

"She'll be down in a minute," said Hap, with an air of depleted apology. "May I offer you anything?"

"I'm fine," said Julia, whose mother loved to make her wait.

Mona had the master suite upstairs, Hap slept in what must once have been the maid's room next to the kitchen, and Julia would have the guest suite at the other end of the house. On the rare occasions when she visited with one or more of the children, they shared the suite, far closer to Hap than to Mona, and Julia had yet to recover from the rejection. This was her mother's world.

Mona appeared at the top of the stairs, small and pert, wrapped in a robe, sneezing noisily into a handkerchief. She smiled an uncertain welcome, because Julia would not have made the trip for the sheer joy of familial reunion. Mona allowed the expected hug but turned away before Julia was quite ready to let go, citing as excuse whatever virus was pummeling her thin body, even if her true reason was different.

"You've lost weight, dear."

"No, I haven't. I've put on five pounds since last year."

"You always did keep careful track. Watching that figure of yours so hard. And the boys watched it, too." She sneezed, then caught her daughter's mood. "Well, you were a flirt back in those days, dear. You were. I'm not saying you're one *now*."

The other thing about Mona was that you never knew what angle, in her sweet, unassuming way, she might choose for her attack.

"It's good to see you," Julia offered, but Hap appeared with tea and crackers, protecting his beloved Mona from the burden of response. Julia went off to unpack, and sulk. Over dinner, Mona moaned. She moaned about how the proximity of Airbus was driving prices up. About how terrible it was that so many Americans were coming to town these days to "hunt" at the Safari Parc. About how the United States was the world's leading sponsor of terrorism. About how she liked the way the French did not allow Muslim girls to wear head scarves in school, and she wished America would confiscate them too, along with all the crosses and little red-white-and-blue flag pins. She moaned about everything she could think of, except the issue that had brought her daughter to France. She rambled with the nervous energy of the condemned prisoner who knows that when the words stop the reckoning begins . . . and swiftly ends.

Julia asked her about the old days, probing, pressing, enticing. But missed the mark.

"The Empyreals were always a very *odd* fraternity," Mona said as she struggled ostentatiously up the staircase, delighting in her ill health. "This was back before their collapse, of course. Before the bankruptcy and everything. Oh, but they were a treat! They were limited to four hundred members nationwide. Four hundred colored gentlemen of quality is what the charter used to say. Everyone knew how exclusive they were, but they never bragged about it. As a matter of fact, dear, back in the day, members were not even allowed to admit that the group existed. They were never the most *showy* men. Never the *smoothies*. The quiet, successful types who never had a word to say at the parties." Halfway up, voice trailing behind her like steam from the engine of memory. "I'll tell you something, dear. I couldn't have seen it at the time, but you know what they were like back in the day? The Empyreals? Like a quiet, sullen kid at school who isn't in a clique and never talks to anybody and doesn't have any friends, the kind of kid you don't even notice until the morning he shows up with a hunting rifle and decides to make the world pay attention."

She went to bed.

(11)

IN THE MORNING, they drove up to Montech to look at the water slope, which was as so often under repair, the powerful tractors sitting idle. The tractors pulled a wedge, the wedge made a huge wave of water climb the slope, the wave carried small boats, or a barge in which you could ride, seeming to defy gravity and common experience. Mona liked to tell the story of the day the rubber tires had slipped the tracks because of an oil leak, tilting the tourists on their way up the slope, and maybe spilling a few into the filthy water, but Julia, who had ridden the slide in the eighties, when Mona brought her and the baby Preston to France just after the construction was done—and just after Jay died—

did not know whether to believe her mother or not. So many of her memories, especially of Toulouse, were happy ones, and for some reason Mona took unadorned pleasure in spoiling them. The slope was called by the French *La Pente d'Eau*, a name Julia loved for the way it rolled on the tongue. The whole thing remained one of the technological wonders of the world: where else could you watch water flow uphill?

If only Julia knew how to climb her mountains so easily: twenty-four hours in Plaisance-du-Touch and she had yet to get to the point.

Mona had yet to encourage her.

Hap had packed a picnic lunch, and the two women walked the forest for a while, choosing the paths on which they were marginally less likely to be crushed by onrushing cyclists. Whenever Julia visited, she expected to find that Mona had suddenly aged; only it never happened. Mona, well past seventy, possessed the same skinny energy Julia remembered from her childhood, when, in search of the right chapter of the right group of the children of the Clan, she had driven Julia and Jay all over New England: Providence for a Christmas party, Boston for a cotillion, Springfield for a junior prom. Although Granny Vee had been a serious clubwoman, and the Veazies had been in on the founding of a Greek-letter group or two, Mona had always been more a hanger-on, clinging by her thoroughly nibbled fingertips to every possible solution to the problem of raising her children in Hanover while living out her dictum that her children's friends must be drawn mostly from the darker nation; and, despite her egalitarian pretensions, she meant what Granny Vee would have called the better half of the nation.

It was just past noon, and the tall trees stood amid tiny circular shadows like dark puddles. Julia remembered vaguely that Montech lay in a floodplain, and most of the trees were scattered in smaller copses, but here the woods were thick. The smell in the air was water and reeds. After half an hour of their nearly silent ramble through the chilly afternoon sunshine, Mona pointed to a small clearing near a still pond.

"There."

Julia grinned, working at it. "That's the same place we always stop."

Her mother grinned back. "You know what a conservative I am."

So they sat on handy stumps and ate their sandwiches and listened to hidden animals, some of them human, scurrying through the undergrowth. In the distance a motor hummed, men shouted, a horn honked.

Mona said, "Something's on your mind."

"Uh-huh."

"Is it your Lemaster? Is he mistreating you again?"

Julia made a swatting motion, even though there was no fly. "Lemmie's an angel, Mona. I keep telling you that. He would never do anything to hurt me."

"I read the papers, dear. The *Herald Tribune* says that he's on the short list for Attorney General."

"I can't talk about—"

"For these people. He'd actually work for these people. I don't think I'll ever understand people like him."

Black people like him, she meant, echoing Astrid.

Julia leaned back, hands on the wood, tipped her face upward to feel the sun, wondering if God was up there, or out there, watching, listening, already knowing how it turns out in the end. She found Mona easier to bear when she did not have to gaze into those tiny, dark, loving, pleading, righteous, crazy, hurtfully helpful eyes. "I won't discuss Lemmie with you, okay? I won't." Firm, but careful not to raise her voice to her mother, on the off chance that the Ten Commandments might be true. "That's not why I'm here, Mona."

"Then why are you here?" Plaintive. "What do you want? You always want something."

"Mona—"

"It's true, dear. There just always turns out to be an agenda. I know, I know. You just want advice. You'd think you didn't have any friends to talk to."

A breeze plucked at the sleeve of her heavy jacket. Julia tried not to bristle. Mona did not actually believe any of this; she simply wanted her daughter to reassure her: Yes, yes, I value your advice specially. But Julia had tired years ago of flattering her mother. If her presence in France, as her confused family suffered back home, was not proof enough of Julia's devotion, she had none to offer.

"I just want to talk, Mona," she said, all but strangling on the intemperate words held forcibly in her throat. She found herself still unable to come to the point. "Can we do that? Just talk?"

"We are talking," said Mona, touching her daughter's knee. "Isn't this talking?"

"No, Mona. No. You're doing what you always do. You're talking. I'm supposed to sit still and listen."

"Well, excuse me." Wounded, putting a hand to her throat. "There's no need to shout at your mother."

"I'm not shouting." But she had been, for Mona had intentionally provoked her. Every conversation with the great Mona Veazie was a minefield of righteousness through which you crawled at your own peril. Usually you could survive if you just did not touch American politics. If you stepped on that particular trigger, the world exploded.

"Raising your voice, then."

Julia rushed on, to forestall the likely litany of complaints, all the little ways Julia, who still mailed her two thousand of their precious dollars every month, had hurt her over the years. "Mona, please. Listen. I need to ask you some questions." The next words came hard, but she knew what peace with her mother demanded. "I need . . . I need your help. It's about Vanessa."

Mona's smile was brilliant, and satisfied. "Well, why didn't you say so?"

(111)

"I've told you and told you, you're too hard on that girl," Mona interrupted once she had, or thought she did, the gist of her daughter's inquiry. "You shouldn't be raising her out there with all those white kids to begin with. I've told you, if the race is going to survive, each of us will have to have—"

"More black friends than white friends. I know, Mona. I know."

"But you're not doing anything about it, are you? Vanessa's friends are all white, aren't they?"

"Not all—"

Mona's eyes glittered with satisfaction. "I know. I know. She does Jack and Jill, she used to do Littlebugs, there's some black kids in that church of yours. She told me, dear." Raising a small hand to ward off the objection. "But they don't count. They're not her good friends. Her good friends are white kids from the high school."

"It's the same way you raised me," Julia snapped, hot and, as her mother probably intended, distracted.

"And you shouldn't be repeating my mistakes," Mona counseled, very pleased.

For a moment they fought without speaking. Julia prodded the picnic basket with her toe. Twin cyclists zipped past—male and female, she thought, but the glimpse was brief, mostly of dark hair flying beneath bright helmets. Down near the canal, children were laughing. The day had started clear and fine but was beginning to cloud over; or perhaps it was only her mood that was changing.

"Mona, listen to me, please," said Julia at last, not looking at her mother. "Yes, I've made mistakes with Vanessa. With the others, too. But I don't want to talk about my mistakes. Not today. I want to talk about history."

"History?"

"I ran into your friend Aurelia Treene last month at the Grand Cotillion. And do you know what she told me? That my husband was Bubba of the Empyreals, and she said he was carrying on the family tradition. But Lemaster's a first-generation immigrant. So she must have meant the Veazie side of the family." She paused. "Tell me, Mona. Was Grandpa Vee an Empyreal? Was Preston Veazie maybe even, ah, the Bubba of the Empyreals?"

Her mother laughed. "Why, yes, dear. He was."

"And when were you going to tell me?"

"I'm not sure it's ever come up in daily conversation. I wasn't hiding it from you," Mona hastened to add. "There just was never a reason to discuss it."

"Well, then, discuss this. When I married Lemmie, and you were upset about him being an Empyreal, it wasn't because they're small and unimportant, was it?"

Silence.

"Come on, Mona. I'm not letting you out of this." At last she lifted her gaze, but Mona was an old hand and kept a poker face. "This Gina Joule business that Vanessa's obsessed with? The Empyreals were involved somehow in the aftermath. I want to know how. And why. I want to know what your old boyfriend Bay Dennison was doing there." Still her mother waited. "I'm only asking because I have this mess at home, and I think Aurie was trying to tell me that they're related. Come on. You know something about them that I don't. I think it's about time you told me."

"Told you what, dear?"

"Who the Empyreals really are."

CHAPTER 52

THE EMPYREALS

(1)

"YOU HAVE TO PICTURE what it was like, dear, back in the day. When we truly lived as two nations. The darker nation. The paler nation. The Empyreals invented those terms, dear. Or popularized them, anyway. They were such a big deal, the Empyreals. Back in the day." They were walking again, along the path as it meandered through the trees. Water gurgled just out of sight. A fresh chill had settled, and Julia supposed they might get more snow. "Back when all these groups were being founded. So few of our people had education, but those who did, well, they'd study physics or Greek or Confucius, and the only job they could get would be on a loading dock in some big city, or maybe, if they were lucky, they could be undertakers or schoolteachers. All these brilliant, professional, educated men—some women, but mostly men—and the white world shut them out. So, naturally, they wanted to associate with others of their own kind. A lot of these clubs came out of that background, dear."

"Looking down their noses at the rest of their people."

"Maybe so. Maybe so. Let's not judge them, dear. Not yet. The point is, they had difficulties. Lots and lots of difficulties. The clubs were a place to forget all that, to try to create a space where you could have intellectual talk, or at least talk to people who had seen as much as you had."

Julia was too tired for this. "Mona, please. I didn't come all this way for a history lesson. I don't want to know how these groups got started. I want to know about the Empyreals."

"Because of your Lemaster. Because he's the Bubba."

"That's not the only reason."

"What else, dear?"

"Ever since I talked to Aurelia, there's been this story from my childhood I haven't been able to get out of my mind. This was in Hanover. November 1972. I remember because Nixon had just been re-elected. Granny Vee was living with us then. You had some people over to watch the election returns that night. I was a kid, but I remember how the rest of you sat there, watching one state after another fall to Nixon, and you all had the same look on your faces, like you'd been kicked in the—well, kicked pretty hard. Remember that night?"

"Of course I do, dear. We were a family in those days. I still had you both. You and Jay, dear." She smiled and brushed her fingers over Julia's slim shoulder as if trying to decide whether to give her a hug. "And, my goodness, I'm surprised you remember. We had a regular party. There weren't but a few of us on the faculty in those days. Black people, I mean. We were depressed. We were mad. We all got together and got drunk." Her wide mouth turned down in disapproving memory. "And you remember that? How old were you, dear? Four? Five?"

"Twelve." One child in the world, and Mona could not remember her age. Julia fought the urge to bristle. "The thing is, Granny Vee got tired. You made me take her up to bed. On the way out of the room, she said the strangest thing. Now, I know, Granny Vee wasn't all there in those days, and I haven't thought about it in years, but lately I haven't been able to get it out of my mind. She said it just goes to show you that the Clan should stay out of the election business. She said the Clan should have learned its lesson in '56. What were they talking about, Mona? What happened in '56? What happened in '72?"

"The Republicans won by a landslide both times. That's what happened."

"No. That's not what she meant. She said, 'They backed the wrong horse, as usual.' You told her to hush, but Granny Vee wasn't so easy to quiet down. I got her out into the hallway, but she was still yelling. She said they kept trying and kept messing up. And she said, 'The Paramount is such an idiot.' "

The path split, and Mona selected the more overgrown fork. The forest closed tightly around them, blotting out what little warmth the day offered. As the old woman danced on ahead, Julia found herself hurrying to keep up. "You heard wrong, dear," she called over her shoulder. "Granny must have been talking about Perry Mount. He was a Harlem boy—you met him, but you were little, you wouldn't remember—but poor Perry wanted so badly to have influence. He was involved in one of the other campaigns, not even McGovern's. His man didn't even get nominated. Poor Perry backed the wrong horse. That's our history, dear. The Negroes are always backing losers. That explains why we're where we are."

"She didn't say 'Perry Mount.' She said '*the* Paramount.' "

"I'm sure she didn't."

"She did. That's exactly what she said." Julia had caught up with her mother on the path. "And then she said—she said, 'They should have listened to Preston.' I wondered for years what she meant. Then, the other week, Lemmie told me that the head of the Empyreals is called the Paramount, and it was all clear. She was saying the Empyreals backed the wrong horse because their leader was an idiot. They were involved in the election, weren't they?"

"Oh, well, electoral coalitions are complicated—"

"Mona, stop it. Stop. No more games. No more hiding. Tell me." Mona's cocky hazel eyes never shifted, but they did now. Julia pounced. "Come on, Mona. Granny wasn't making general statements about the race. She was being too crafty. She was teasing. She thought she was telling secrets." A frown. "And she said one more thing, Mona. I don't think you heard it. I walked her up to her bedroom, the way I did every night. When I got her in bed and all tucked in, she said they needed either a new author or a new plan. I didn't know what she was talking about. But it wasn't the darker nation. She said 'they,' not 'we.' And the head of the Empyreals isn't just known as the Paramount, is he? He's also known as the Author. I think Granny Vee was talking about the Empyreals. I think they were trying to do something about the election, and it didn't work." Her mother reacted. Definitely. Squirming as she hurried on ahead. "What was it, Mona? What did they do?"

"Nothing that concerns you."

"I'm not a child, Mona."

"You are, in some respects." Holding up a slim hand to forestall any protest. She was making one of her speeches. "Maybe you're right, dear. No knowledge is ever sinful, is it? Secrets are the only thing that keep us apart in this world. The not knowing. That's the danger. We're reasoning creatures, dear. We're designed to breathe the truth. We need it to live. When the truth we crave is hidden away, we'll breathe the lies to keep from smothering." The pale eyes grew somber. "All right, dear. Never mind. You want to hear the story, I'll tell you the story. But, believe me, Julia Anne, you'll be sorry you ever heard it."

(11)

THEY HAD REACHED ANOTHER FORK. Mona blinked owlishly, peering in both directions, a fist at her mouth, and it occurred to Julia that her mother was not sure which path to take. A part of her was prepared to wait and force Mona to ask for help, but before daughter could decide how long to make mother suffer, she had stepped past the hesitating old woman, laid a hand on the shrunken shoulder, and selected the left, which led slightly uphill, toward a clearing. As they climbed, Mona seemed to relax, and the words flowed easily again.

"It was 1956, just as you said. I was living at home while I did some graduate work at Columbia. Now, the thing you have to understand, dear, is that in those days the most powerful black man in the country—Negro, we said back then—the most powerful Negro in the country, and maybe the most famous, was Adam Clayton Powell. You met him. You were a baby. You wouldn't remember. You used to see his first wife on the Vineyard. Never mind. The thing is, Adam, well, he had so much influence, he got Eisenhower to desegregate military bases and movie theaters, all of this back before the Supreme Court decided *Brown*. An amazing man. He was the pastor of Abyssinian Baptist Church on 138th Street, same as his father had been. He was also a member of Congress for years and years. A Democrat, of course, although in those days, dear, there wasn't anything wrong with being a Republican. I think most of the Clan probably voted Republican. Not most Negroes. But most of the Clan. Well, things were different. But Adam was a Democrat. And then, in 1956, he stunned the whole world by endorsing Eisenhower for President. The Democrat was dear Adlai Stevenson. A sweet, sweet man. Didn't have much of a chance, you understand, but you never knew. Especially if he could line up the whole Negro vote. It wasn't like now. In those days, the Democrats didn't have the Negro vote locked up. They couldn't take us for granted and give us nothing in return, the way they do today. Our leaders were smart enough to do deals with the Republicans sometimes, instead of just calling them names and guaranteeing they'd never listen to us. Never mind. The point is, Adlai was trying to get the whole Negro leadership behind him. And then Adam said he was going to endorse Eisenhower. Took the poor Democrats completely by surprise. Naturally, Stevenson wanted to meet with Powell. They had a secret meeting. Guess where?"

"Granny Vee's house?"

The slope was steeper now. The going was hard work for Julia, harder still for her mother, but neither wanted to be the first to call for rest. If Mona was disturbed at how Julia, by interposing an answer to the rhetorical question, had spoiled the drama of the moment, it didn't show. "Exactly, dear. At the Veazie townhouse on Edgecombe Avenue. Right there in my father's study. Your grandfather was not only host but also referee. I was dating a man named Eddie in those days, and we were going out that night. We were in the foyer. We heard bits and pieces of the conversation. Adam said he was tired of endorsing a party that was so beholden to its Southern wing that its platform couldn't give even a lukewarm endorsement of the *Brown* decision, and a party that ran the Congress but couldn't pass a federal anti-lynching law. He said if that was the best the Democrats could do he'd try the Republicans. Adlai said if he got elected he could change all that, but Powell wouldn't budge. I think it was plain to Stevenson that the meeting was just for show, that Powell never had any intention of negotiating. He was for Eisenhower all the way. That's what I thought, anyway. Then my father caught us listening in the foyer. He got mad and slammed the door." Mona smiled. "You'd never have been in that situation, would you, dear? Listening in the foyer? In Hanover, you always made sure your young man waited for you. You liked that, didn't you? Leaving your young man alone downstairs until you were ready to make your entrance. And they waited. You had them eating out of your hand. You always liked that, didn't you? Guys falling all over you? You were such a terrible flirt in those days. Never mind."

Julia, boiling, kept her peace.

"That night, Eddie and I talked about it. He heard a little bit of the meeting, too. And we decided, the two of us, that Powell had another reason. It wasn't just about the lynch law, or if the Dixiecrats had too much influence in the party. No. He was too passionate. Powell was no fool. He must have known Eisenhower had doubts about civil rights, and Stevenson didn't. But Powell was determined not to endorse the Democrats that year, no matter what Stevenson offered him. And Eddie, well, he had a theory about why that might be. He said,

'Maybe Powell doesn't like who else is backing Stevenson.' As simple as that."

They had emerged from the tree line on a ridge overlooking farm-land and clustered toy villages. Mona had reached her limit. Julia knew it at once. Her mother's hands were trembling.

"We can stop for a rest if you want."

But Mona was too deeply into her story to consider it. "So, anyway, I asked my mother. Granny Vee. This was a few days later. We were getting dressed, probably on our way to a Ladybugs thing. A wake, I think. We were wearing orange and white, because, well, when a Sister Lady dies, you dress for her wake in Ladybugs colors. All right, you know that already. I forget sometimes. Never mind. I asked her. Amaretta. She gave me this look, Julia. I know, when you were little, you used to say I had these looks I'd give you, like you were just the lowest of the low. My how-could-you-let-me-down-this-way look. I remember. Well, I used to tell you, I got it from Amaretta. Only her looks were worse. She looked at me like just by asking the question I had betrayed the Clan. And you know what she said to me, dear? She said, 'We had to give it a shot, dear.' That's what she said. That's all she said. And, yes, I know, maybe she was just talking about the meeting. Trying to make peace in the Democratic Party. But that wasn't the impression I got. I got the impression that she was talking about some-thing bigger. And for Amaretta, only one thing was big enough to qualify for that kind of—of worshipful abstraction. Not God. Not America. Not Harlem, or the darker nation. The Clan. Only the Clan. There wasn't any other 'we' for Amaretta. I got the idea that what she was trying to say was that the Clan had gambled and lost. That the Clan had made some kind of big bet on Adlai Stevenson, and Adam Clayton Powell had spoiled it."

Julia shook her head. "Then I don't see what the big deal is. The Clan supported Stevenson. He lost. So what?"

"I don't think the Empyreals are dying at all, dear. I think they're doing just fine. Secretive as ever, but going strong."

"You're saying that all of this about how they're old and unimportant—it's some kind of cover story?"

"I just think they're up to something. They were always up to something."

"Something like what?"

They had started back down the slope. Mona took short, almost mincing steps, and now Julia had to work hard not to drift on ahead. "I'm an old woman, Julia Anne, and you shouldn't take me too seriously. But Aurelia's information was wrong. Your grandfather wasn't the Bubba. Or he wasn't just the Bubba. Later, he became the Grand Paramount. He ran the thing for ten years, before Bay Dennison. And it's all supposed to be a big secret, but Preston had no secrets from your grandmother. And let me tell you what Granny Vee told me, years later. They've always been obsessed with the Presidency. The Empyreals."

"You mean, wanting to influence him?"

"No, dear. I mean, wanting to pick one." The forest thinned around them. Mona was near the end of her resources, and of her story. "About that night in '56. Granny Vee told me the Empyreals ran Stevenson. That's the way Amaretta put it, that they ran him. He was their man. They didn't just support him. They had some kind of influence over him. And again in '72. Not McGovern. One of the other Democrats. But something happened and he didn't get the nomination. You see, Julia, your grandfather had this idea that the only way to get anything from the Caucasians was to use their own tools against them. They would never do the right thing out of conscience, he said. They would only do it out of self-interest. We had to own a candidate, he told your grandmother. The same way the powerful Caucasians did. We needed a man who would do our bidding not because his conscience bothered him but because circumstances left him no choice."

"Blackmail," Julia breathed. "You're talking about blackmail."

"I don't know that for sure, Julia Anne. It's possible. All I know is, the Empyreals developed this idea that what they needed was to own powerful Caucasians, to put them into positions where they would have no choice but to help our people. That was Grandpa Vee's idea. At least I think it was."

"Are you saying the Empyreals owned Adlai Stevenson?"

A long moment's hesitation, Mona's aged eyes gazing into the mirror of her youth. "Adlai was a good man. A decent man. A man of integrity. I don't think it was possible to own him." Focusing on her daughter again. "No, dear. I'd be very surprised if the Empyreals owned him. But it's possible they thought they did." A sad chuckle. "Those connections go way, way back, dear. The old families. Ours. Theirs. Black and white. Decades. More. It didn't all have to be coercion. Some of it was more . . . mutual self-interest."

Julia perked up. "Are you talking about passing? That some of the old white families are really old black families?" She could scarcely take it in. "Is that what you mean?"

Mona shook her head. "Oh, no, no, dear. Not at all. Oh, it could be. It's possible. Back then, conditions were just so terrible. If you had the chance to flee from the darker nation and join the whiter world—yes, it could be. But that isn't my point. I'm just saying that there could be commonalities of interest. Old white families and old black ones might wind up working together. Don't assume it's the Empyreals alone." That laugh again, like a nervous spectator at a tragedy. "I'm an old woman, Julia, and an old fool. You shouldn't take me too seriously. The mind plays tricks at my age." Wobbly on her feet now. "I'm tired, Julia. I have to get back and get to bed."

"We're almost at the car."

"I don't want to talk any more."

"Please. Just one more thing."

"Take your hand off me, Julia Anne."

"I'm sorry. Sorry." She had not realized that she was holding her mother's arm—gripping it, really, tightly, in anger, the way she used to squeeze Kellen's when he looked at her the wrong way, or didn't. "Mona, please. Just tell me. You're saying Empyreals used to gather information on powerful people, and they'd use it to—to improve the condition of the community? Is that what you're saying?"

"That's what Amaretta told me." Mona shook her head. "I don't think anybody really knows."

"But it has to be true, Mona. Byron Dennison was in the Landing a week and a half after Gina Joule was killed, pretty much giving the orders. Why else would he be there?"

"I was a married woman by then, dear. Living in New Hampshire. I wouldn't have any idea."

"Come on, Mona. You used to date him. Are you saying he never mentioned some kind of plan?"

The smile was once more dismissive and grandmotherly. "If Bay Dennison was the kind of secret manipulator you seem to think, dear, why would he let himself be seen? It's all very strange."

They were at the car. Mona asked her daughter to take the wheel, and Julia, who never drove a stick shift except when she visited her mother, agreed. The car jerked and shuddered all the way back to the house. Mona never complained. Her eyes were tightly shut, and if she was not actually asleep, she was happy to pretend to be.

(I I I)

JULIA WOULD NEVER KNOW FOR SURE. Lying abed that night, searching for a comfortable position on the ancient, sagging mattress, Julia marveled at how much of the life of the darker nation took place behind a veil of ignorance. Of the existence of the old families, with their money and education and tradition, most black Americans and nearly all white ones knew nothing. Of the secrets of their exclusive fraternities and sororities, outsiders knew far less than they thought they did. Of the Empyreals, most exclusive of all, nobody knew a thing. It all swirled through her mind. The Grand Paramount. Adlai Stevenson. Bubba. Kellen Zant, promising to blow the lid off the election, then being shot. She dozed, half woke, half dreamed, shuffling the events of the past three months.

And then she saw it.

Not all of it. There would be plenty of loose ends to tie up. But, lying there in the overheated guest room on the first floor of her mother's crumbling manse in Plaisance-du-Touch, Julia Veazie Carlyle saw the shape of the Empyreals' plan, and understood at last what Kellen had thought he knew. The only question was whether he was right.

She slept poorly, and dreamed of snow.

(I V)

LEAVING MONA IN THE MORNING was more difficult than Julia had expected, not because mother showed remorse but because daughter was shot through with it. Mona offered no assistance in apologizing. She behaved as though yesterday's argument had never taken place. Over breakfast, Hap hovering as usual, Julia suddenly saw her mother as both more and less than she had always imagined. Mona was old, she was weakening, she was dispirited. Hap took care of her, and Mona, whatever her liveliness in youth, was of an age when being cared for was all she really wanted.

And what was so terrible about that?

"I'm sorry, Mona," she said, hoping not to sound wooden.

"For what, dear?"

"For the way I . . . talked to you yesterday. I'm sorry."

"Hormones," her mother said, as she used to when Julia was a teen and they were at each other's throats. Only Mona laughed.

Over the meal, Hap played referee, careful to ensure the conversation turned to nothing that might further upset his beloved. Afterward, Mona pronounced herself exhausted. "I'm still glad you came, dear."

"So am I."

Julia walked beside her mother along the short hall with its cracked parquet. The door to the master suite needed paint. She wished, idly, for the winning lottery ticket, so that she could care for Mona as she deserved. Then the empiricist took charge, reminding her that wishes were not horses, and most people in the world lived a good deal worse than this.

Mona took her daughter's hands, pressed strengthlessly, smiled. She said, "You shouldn't listen to me, dear. At my age there is a certain tendency to ramble. And to know everything."

"I thought seventy was the new fifty."

"Is it? Because just now it feels like the old ninety."

"I love you, Mom," Julia blurted.

Mona looked vaguely pleased, the way we are when we hear that a distant relative has remarried. "I love you also," she said, the hazel eyes still far away. "Now, listen to me, dear. I have no idea what's going on in . . . America. I don't understand the country. I don't know if I ever did. But I do know this much. It's not a good place for our people. Negroes. The darker nation. African Americans. Not a good place. Never was and never will be." She held up a hand to forestall her daughter's objection. "You're part of the Clan, dear. It feels to you like a kind of freedom. But it's like that mirror over there." She pointed. "The people in the mirror aren't free at all, are they? They just do what the people on this side of the mirror let them do. We move, and they move the same way. We talk, they talk. We stop, they stop."

"I think Lewis Carroll wrote that already."

"Listen to me, dear. What Granny Vee told me, about the Empyreals? About their grand design? You're right. She wasn't herself. I have no idea how much was fact and how much was fancy. Fantasy, even. But, Julia dear, if it's true? If the Empyreals aren't dying? If they're hiding in the shadows somewhere in the mirror where you can't see, plotting and plotting, trying to make the Caucasians do what's right?" An exhausted shrug. "I'm just wondering, dear: who's to say they're wrong?"

Abruptly, she released her daughter's hand and, closing the door behind her, retreated once more into her chosen exile.

(v)

UNSATISFIED but knowing she was doomed to remain so, Julia finally departed, Hap returning her to Toulouse and the station as she puzzled pointlessly over his true relationship to Mona. At the barrier, he hugged her clumsily and handed her a shopping bag, the forgotten Christmas gifts for the children, wrapped beautifully. Julia asked him to thank Mona, but suspected he had bought them himself, and recently. The train left fifteen minutes late: for France, a national disaster. The ride was six hours, and once more she slept most of the way, swatting away the efforts at conversation from a friendly young American couple who sat across from her and resembled closely the lovers she and Mona had twice passed on the path in Montech. In Paris, she stayed at the same hotel, and suddenly the clerk behind the counter and the man reading the newspaper in the lobby and the smiling elevator operator seemed part of a single vast conspiracy. The boy who brought her breakfast kept eyeing her sideways as she stood in her robe waiting for him to finish, and she wondered whether it was her legs that drew his admiration, or if somebody owned him.

Leaving the country turned out to be harder even than leaving Mona. She saw the officer's eyes widen when he ran her passport beneath the scanner. A guard led her to a small room off the main floor, where two uniformed women went through her luggage, under the watchful eyes of two men in business suits, one of them from the American embassy, who said he was there to safeguard her rights but kept his eyes on the table. The women went through her cosmetics and dirty underclothes. They even unwrapped the tardy Christmas presents, which turned out to be unimaginative touristy gimcracks. The only thing they did not search was her person—they seemed willing, but the man from the embassy forestalled them—and that was a good thing, because it was on her person that Julia had hidden the contents of the long manila envelope she had found squeezed into the shopping bag among the gifts.

Finally they allowed her, with Gallic reluctance, to depart. The man from the embassy apologized, and snapped at them in French, but Julia remembered that the American ambassador was one of the President's most trusted cronies. As if in recompense, the airline bumped her to first class. She dozed for an hour, restraining her natural tendency to rush, because they could still be watching. Then she took herself off to the restroom, where she withdrew from their hiding place the three pages from the envelope. She read through the legal document for perhaps the fifth time since last night. Back in her seat, she returned the pages to their envelope and slid the envelope into her carry-on. She rang the flight attendant, and they discussed what wines were on board: this being Air France, there was a nice selection. She drank two glasses before her hands stopped shaking.

The document was a confession to the accidental killing of Gina Joule on or about February 14, 1973. It was signed by Lemaster's third roommate in Hilliman Suite, the late Jonathan "Jock" Hilliman.

CHAPTER 53

ARRIVAL

(1)

BUT LEMASTER DID NOT BELIEVE a word of it. After all these years, she could distinguish the cool sobriety of admiring surprise from the gentle rationality of cautious skepticism. He had met her outside security, smiled and waved, and handed her a flower Jeannie had made in school that told her how much she was loved. Now, in the car, she had told him bits and pieces of the tale, wondering at last how far she could trust him; and how far he trusted her back.

"Those men are friends of mine," he said gently when his wife was done. "I want to make that clear. Well, you know already, but I want to emphasize it. I might be biased, but I've known all three of them for more than thirty years. Well, less for Jock, seeing as how he's no longer with us."

Julia looked at him as the Mercedes purred through the night. Mileposts clicked past on the Hutchinson River Parkway, small and shining green in the headlights, sharply etched against the trees and endless white beyond. She had called him before boarding the flight, asking him to cancel the limousine and meet her at the airport. She asked him to come alone—that is, without Mr. Flew. She did not want to say why over the telephone, and, for a blessing, Lemaster did not inquire. But she knew the time had come, as Granny Vee used to say, to make a clean breast.

Or moderately clean. She had told her husband about being searched, and knew from his reaction that the American observer would soon be transferred to a post in some mosquito-infested backwater. She had told him about the confession but had omitted, for the moment, the Empyreals, on the theory that he would refuse to talk about it.

"Are you saying I shouldn't believe it?"

"Don't you think it's terribly convenient, Jules? Your mother just happens to have a signed affidavit by Jock Hilliman lying around in case you ever ask." He sighed and shook his head, the way he always did when he mentioned Mona. "And as for Mal and the President, well, yes, okay, they're not perfect men. They've done things they should be ashamed of, yes. Terrible things." He hesitated. "The kind of things Astrid wondered about. Mal and Scrunchy are equally . . . guilty. They're not saints or angels. They're fallible, sinful human beings, the way we all are." A firm nod of the head, as if to drive the point home, perhaps to himself. He turned around, one palm lifted in open appeal. "Terrible things, Jules. Both of them. And, yes, things about which they have sought my advice from time to time. Things I can't talk about. But, Jules, what you're suggesting isn't a venial sin or a childish prank. You're talking about murder. Or, if it was an accident, maybe manslaughter. Still, the taking of a human life. The most profound crime on the books of any civilized society."

She pinched her nose and rubbed her eyes, wondering if her brain was especially logy after the rushing back and forth over the Atlantic, or whether perhaps her husband was being especially opaque. Was he going to discuss the evidence or not?

"Jules, look. I can't imagine any of them doing what you're suggesting. Not now. Not then." He changed lanes to pass a slow-moving minivan. His tone remained calmly affectionate. For once the raging hip-hop was not in evidence. The radio was tuned to classical music. "And if one of them ever did something like that, maybe by accident, I think he would have been so suffused with guilt and horror that he could scarcely have functioned. Everybody would have known something terrible had happened."

"You weren't here," Julia reminded him. "You were studying at Oxford. This was February. You got back in June. That's four months to calm down."

But she had run up against the stubbornness in him, the Everest needing freshly to be climbed. "All right. Granted. I'm not omniscient. I could have misjudged them. They could have fooled me. If they did, well, the obvious answer is that Jock did it." He tapped the envelope resting on her lap. "You have his confession, and you seem to believe it's genuine. From what you tell me, his Jaguar was wrecked the night Gina died, and Bruce Vallely thinks his family covered it up. So, if I'm wrong, the chances are I'm wrong about Jock." Julia sat perfectly still in the tropically warm car, saying nothing, the doubts assailing her, the carefully worked hypothesis falling to pieces under the assault of her own uneasiness, for her great skill was decisiveness, not confidence. What kept her going was her suspicion that Lemaster's doubts were assailing him, too. "All right. But then take the other point of view. Jock's confession is too convenient. Then you're back to the theory that it was Mal or Scrunchy. That means one of them, and Heaven knows how many other people, have spent all these years successfully hiding a murder committed in college. And could have known where to hire a gunman to kill Kellen Zant when he got too close to the secret." The smile was back, not the warmly delicious welcome to a more peaceable world with which he had seduced her two decades ago, but the brash and even cocky scholar who was never wrong, and wanted you to know it. "So, yes, Jules, one possibility is a secret conspiracy to hide a terrible crime all these years. But surely this is where we might apply Occam's razor. Let's not introduce unnecessary entities. Let me suggest a simpler explanation for what you found—even though it leaves Kellen in a less flattering light."

Julia knew her husband could feel the swift tension in her—had even stirred it deliberately. She waited for him to knock her argument down, the way he always did.

"The conspiracy could be a lot smaller, Jules, and it could have nothing to do with what really happened thirty-one years ago." His eyes were locked on the road ahead. His small, competent hands moved on the wheel with quiet authority. "Your evidence comes from three sources. Kellen Zant, Mona Veazie, and this Mary Mallard. Correct?"

"I guess so. Yes."

"And which one of them is widely considered a reliable source?"

This got to her, as perhaps it was supposed to. "All right, smarty. If the three of them conspired together—God knows how—then why did they do it? What's the object of the conspiracy?"

"Money," said Lemaster.

"What?"

"Money, Jules. Think about it." He pulled smoothly into a rest stop and stated his needs imperiously to the insolent white clerk, who began to fill the tank. Lemaster turned to his wife, touched her on the cheek with such soft and surprising affection that she gasped. "Jules, listen to me a minute. No, listen. The men you're talking about—not Jock, but the others—if they're associated, even by implication and innuendo, with the murder of a teenaged girl, well, their careers are over."

"Are you saying that Mary and Kellen and Mona were planning blackmail?" she spluttered. "Manufacturing evidence? Spreading rumors? Using me and Vanessa to help?"

"I know it sounds far-fetched. I'm not saying I believe it. But I think it's a lot more plausible than this guilty silence of thirty years, which would have had to involve so many people that there's no way it could have stayed secret. I'm trying to envision how large the cover-up would have had to be, and I can't even fathom the numbers. Plus, there's the matter of planting evidence to implicate DeShaun Moton—"

"I don't see how one conspiracy is worse than the other," she said, sullen and, as perhaps he intended, confused.

"Not worse. Less likely."

"Then how do you explain Anthony Tice? Astrid? Astrid said Kellen had evidence that would—"

"Change the outcome of the election. Yes. But that would be true even if the evidence was manufactured." He paid the rude clerk and even gave him a fair-sized tip, because the Lemaster Carlyles of the world tip everyone, even if the currency is not always cash. He pulled back onto the highway. "I'm not saying I believe it. I don't know what to believe. I'll tell you what I do believe, though. I do believe that Kellen was up to no good. I do believe that Tony Tice was up to no good. And now I believe that this Mary Mallard is up to no good, and I'm going to have to do something about her." His tone grew fierce. "I'm sick of this. Not of you. Of them. Nobody treats my wife that way. And not just my wife. It's time for the Caucasians to stop, Jules. I don't care how powerful they are. The era is over when they can just—"

"We're being followed," she said.

(11)

IF YOU LOOK CAREFULLY AT NIGHT, headlights are distinctive. These had the bluish tint of xenon and were set closer together than on most cars, suggesting something low and sporty. A pair of fog lights shone between them and lower down. The trapezoidal pattern could hardly be missed. She had seen it as they left the airport, and again on the Van Wyck, and even a couple of cars back in the toll line at the bridge. She had seen the same set of lamps hanging back in the shadows of the rest stop. There comes a time when coincidence is not coincidence any more. Having told her husband, she nibbled on her knuckle, the way she had as a child until Mona painted it with iodine, and waited for him to deride her.

He said, "How long?"

Julia, astonished, sat up straight. "What?"

"How long have they been following us?"

"Since JFK. They were in the gas station too. Lemmie—"

"Which one?"

"The xenon lights—"

"Got it." He slipped smoothly into the passing lane and accelerated. Relief caressed her. "Why didn't you tell me before?"

"I thought you wouldn't believe me."

"Silly." He reached over and mussed her hair, then floored the pedal. The Mercedes leaped ahead, the speedometer inching toward ninety, the car barely shuddering. Julia turned her head. The other lights were falling behind. She looked ahead and cried out. A sharp curve beckoned, and he tapped the brake, then hit the gas again, and the car, fishtailing only a smidgen, did as commanded.

"Lemmie, slow down!"

"Hold on."

"We'll get pulled over—ah!"

Before the car following them reached the curve, Lemaster threw the wheel over hard right, surprising another driver he cut off, and then the other driver, too, was left behind, and he streaked down the exit ramp. They were off the parkway and on city streets somewhere in Westchester County. As she caught her breath, he tucked them neatly beneath the overpass so that the car was invisible from above, waited ten or fifteen seconds—an eternity at high speed—then proceeded past fast-food restaurants and service stations until he saw a small bar.

"Let's get a drink," he said.

"Lemmie, we should call somebody."

"No, we shouldn't. Come inside. We have to talk. And, believe me, we'll both need a drink."

She looked at his face. Had being followed upset him so much? Or had he been humoring her again? "Lemmie, what is it? What's wrong?"

His smile was soft and assuring. Again he touched her face, and when he spoke, she knew why he had been so warm since meeting her, why he had been so gentle in arguing with her about the conspiracy, even why he had cooperated in eluding a car he did not for a moment believe was following them.

"There's been an accident," he said.

CHAPTER 54

AGAIN HOBBY HILL

(1)

"BIT OF A SURPRISE, Chief Vallely," said the secretary of the university, standing in the doorway of his elegant Victorian on Hobby Road. He was wearing shirtsleeves, his tie loosened, and, on his feet, comfortable slippers. "One values one's privacy. Don't actually remember inviting you, kind of thing. Perhaps you might be so good as to explain the meaning of this visit."

"It couldn't wait," said Bruce, and meant it.

"Don't actually follow, Chief Vallely."

"I wouldn't be here if it wasn't urgent, Mr. Secretary. Now, please, may I come in?"

Trevor Land thought it over for a moment. It was just past eight on Friday, and Bruce had been parked down the block for the past hour, waiting for the secretary to arrive, then giving him a few minutes to settle in. He had no choice. Every cop knew that witnesses were more likely to be rattled when you took them by surprise. But being rattled and being accurate were not the same thing.

At last the secretary stepped aside. The foyer was wide and nicely appointed, the furniture heavy and old and, to Bruce's untutored eye, valuable. Oil paintings of country scenes filled the walls, both here and up the staircase. To Bruce they mainly signaled money. Trevor Land had lived alone since his wife died nine years ago. Bruce smelled rewarmed food beneath the redolence of furniture polish, and realized that he had interrupted the old man's dinner.

"I'm sorry if this is a bad time, Mr. Secretary—"

"Assume you have your reasons." He led the way into a small study, walled in rich, dark wood, nicely bound first editions on the shelves, more landscapes on the walls. "Do have a seat, Chief Vallely."

He did, settling on the sofa because the chairs in front of the desk looked rickety and expensive. A heavy wooden chess set stood on the low table, the pieces set in a complicated position.

"I've just come from Nathaniel Knowland's apartment," Bruce began, and Trevor Land erupted—which is to say, he pouted and tilted his head and set off at a slow murmur that Bruce had to shut up in order to hear.

"Not my way to tell a man how to do his job. Still, one rather expects one's reasonable requests to be honored. Correct me if I am mistaken, Chief Vallely, but I believe you and I had a conversation about young Knowland. Father came to me—you remember—and asked, as a favor, if we would kindly leave his son in peace. Well, alums are who they are, and one does not want to cross them without an excellent reason. One presumes, therefore, that you had one. Because otherwise one hates to imagine the consequences."

"I fully understand, Mr. Secretary. And you're right, I would not have visited Nathaniel Knowland's apartment without a good reason. But I had one." Trevor Land nodded indulgently. By choosing the sofa, Bruce had forced him, for the sake of politeness, to take one of the armchairs, thus denying him the intimidation associated with sitting behind a desk only slightly smaller than the one in Lombard Hall. "I had to go because I realized that his story wasn't true. It couldn't have been. There was a hockey game, so there was no parking on Town Street the night Professor Zant was killed." He gave the secretary a moment to let this sink in. "Therefore, the professor could not have been seen there, getting into his car. And if Knowland and his friends had actually been on Town Street that night, even drunk, they would surely have noticed that no cars were parked there, so they would have made up a better story if they needed one."

"Fascinating observation, Chief Vallely."

"Actually, it isn't. I must have been an idiot not to work it out sooner. Nathaniel Knowland was nowhere near Town Street that night, and he did not see Professor Zant. Not on Town Street. Not anywhere. That's the reason he couldn't take his story to the police. They have more resources to check it out. They could have tracked down his imaginary friends. They would have punched holes in the story in an hour, but because I have to work alone, it's had me chasing my own tail for three months, trying to figure out why Zant would have been there."

"Fascinating chain of logic, Chief Vallely. And did young Knowland confirm all of this speculation for you?"

"You know perfectly well he didn't. He's back home. Taking the semester off."

"Pity, that." Trevor Land pursed his bloodless lips. He seemed imperturbable and immovable, one of the great elms that gave the city its name, roots so deep in the frozen New England earth that it would take a bomb to blast him off his feet. "So, really, you can't confirm your chain of logic, can you? It remains speculation. Pity."

Bruce shook his head. "It's not speculation. It's the only explanation that makes sense."

"Nothing against guesswork, mind. Reason, speculation, imagination, all part of one's intellectual faculties." His thoughtful eyes were on the landscape behind Bruce's head. The sconces were astonishingly bright, perhaps as an aid against failing eyesight. "On the other hand, Chief Vallely, reason is not really the same as fact, is it?" A stern shift of the head, something between a nod and a dismissal. "Now, tell me, please, why would young Knowland go to all that trouble? Making up a story like that, then running off?"

"I don't think he did."

"Say again, please."

"Nathaniel Knowland did not make up the story," said Bruce, leaning across the ornate coffee table dividing them. "He just repeated it."

"Then one naturally wonders, if young Knowland didn't make up the story, kind of thing, who did?"

"I don't know who made it up. I do know who told Nathaniel to tell it to me."

"And who might that have been, Chief Vallely?"

"You."

(I I)

THE SECRETARY OF THE UNIVERSITY, a man of class and breeding, remained as icily calm, and distantly amused, as at any time Bruce had seen him. He simply made the familiar chewing motion with his small, prim mouth, and said, "Fascinating idea, Chief Vallely."

"It's supported by a chain of logic."

"One rather thought it might be."

"May I share it?"

"Please." Folding his hands in his lap like an attentive student.

"Let's begin with the proposition that Nate Knowland lied. He lied elaborately. Now, why would he do that? Not to protect himself from the authorities. If he hadn't brought up the whole story of Professor Zant on Town Street, the authorities would not have paid him the slightest bit of attention. So the lie was to help someone else—not to help himself, or not directly." Bruce rubbed his hands together in satisfaction. "The question, then, is who would gain from my believing that Professor Zant was seen on Town Street that night, in the company of a black woman with a British accent. The first answer—the obvious one—is that the killer gains, if Professor Zant was actually somewhere else at the time, somewhere the killer has to hide."

Even Trevor Land's furious objections had the ring of calmly confident and very old money. "Surely, Chief Vallely, it is not your intention to suggest that I—"

"Killed Kellen Zant? No, no, Mr. Secretary. Nothing like that. Please. Allow me to continue." Settling again. In the hall, a grandfather clock ticked loudly. "No. As I said. My first thought was that the killer wanted me to think Zant was in one place when really he was somewhere else. Why not send me chasing a mythical black woman with a British accent, and figuring out where the two of them had driven off to? But then it occurred to me that the killer, if covering up the crime were his principal motivation, would be taking an enormous risk. Nathaniel Knowland is not exactly the soul of discretion. He might share the story with his friends."

"Perfectly well reasoned, Chief Vallely."

"Therefore, I realized that the story must have a different purpose than simply to mislead. The details actually matter. To explain why, I should tell you that I was already skeptical of the story, precisely because of those details. In particular, Nate Knowland seemed entirely too confident that Zant got in the car first, the mysterious black woman after. I don't think that was part of the original story. I think that was Nate's own embellishment, and once he added it, backing away became difficult, even when it was obvious I had doubts."

The secretary was fondling one of the knights, which had been captured and removed from the board. A plaque on the wall celebrated
forty years of service to the university.

"Might one ask why you had doubts?"

"Because Kellen Zant was a well-known ladies' man, by all accounts
an amazing charmer. Such a man would hold the door for the lady."

"Changing times, Chief Vallely. Not always for the better, but
changing times nevertheless. One believes in courtesy, but we live in an
age when it has become rather passé."

"True. But Kellen Zant grew up in a small Southern town, where
manners matter more, and—anyway, I was skeptical. That was one
detail. But two others, which at first I fully believed, were more important. First, the black woman with the British accent, and, second, the
location—that is, Town Street. I think those details were improvised
with great care, and entirely for my benefit. The black woman with the
British accent was an especially clever touch, because it would play to
my, ah, prejudices. I would naturally assume that Nate Knowland,
being white, would not be able to distinguish easily a British accent
from a Barbadian one. I was meant to think that the black woman walking with Professor Zant that night was Astrid Venable, the cousin of
Lemaster Carlyle."

"Might one ask why the inventor of the story would want you to
think that?"

"I can imagine two reasons. Astrid Venable was, at the time, a senior
aide to Senator Malcolm Whisted. If she was implicated, even by
rumor, in Professor Zant's death, that could hardly help the Senator's
presidential chances. Second, it places Zant's death a little bit closer to
the throne."

"The throne?"

"By extension. If Astrid Venable's implication in the murder could
hurt the career of Senator Malcolm Whisted, it would surely devastate
the career of Lemaster Carlyle."

"Then what you are suggesting, Chief Vallely, is that whoever
invented the story intended to harm one career or the other?"

"I think it's possible, yes. So, naturally, I thought of Cameron
Knowland, Nate's father, and a big booster of the President. Perhaps
Cameron, working through his son, took advantage of the murder to
hurt the Senator."

A moment while the two men pondered. Bruce's eye fell on the chessboard, the armies, one black and one white, locked in eternal combat. Whenever one battle ended, you set up the pieces and started another. All at once he felt terribly tired.

"Fascinating notion, Chief Vallely. Trouble is, doesn't quite square with the facts. Cameron Knowland was Lemaster's biggest booster for the job, one. Stuck with him through the shaky early months, two. And, three, Chief Vallely, one happens to know that the two of them are friends of very long standing."

"Yes, Mr. Secretary, I thought of that. And, besides, Astrid Venable denies absolutely that she was in Elm Harbor that night. She knew him, she saw him socially for a time, she spoke to him two days before, but did not see him that night. As it happens, she seems to be telling the truth, since she was at a forum on the media and politics that night at the University of Texas. You might have seen it on C-SPAN." Bruce smiled. "And so I decided that the lie, assuming it was a lie, could not have been intended to bring down Lemaster Carlyle. Possibly Astrid Venable, possibly Malcolm Whisted, but not Lemaster Carlyle. And that leads me to the second of the two details I think were manufactured for my benefit."

"And what detail is that, Chief Vallely?"

"The location. Town Street is just two blocks from Hilliman Tower, where Zant had his office, but it also forms the rear boundary of Kepler Quadrangle, the divinity school, where Julia Carlyle is a deputy dean. Julia Carlyle also happens to be Kellen Zant's ex-lover, and he remained obsessed with her to the day he died, as I was bound to discover. I think whoever invented this story wanted me to consider the possibility that Kellen Zant was on Town Street because he had been at Kepler that night. Why doesn't matter. I was meant to begin thinking of the two of them, Kellen Zant and Julia Carlyle, and speculating on the possibilities."

"Really, Chief Vallely, this is becoming rather lurid." Holding up his smooth white palms as if to prove his innocence. "To be sure, sexual freedom, wave of the future, and so forth. One happens to be rather libertarian. To each his own, me. But Julia Carlyle happens not to strike one as the sort of woman who—"

"I agree with you, Mr. Secretary. I agree. The point is, whoever manufactured the story wanted me to think along those lines."

The pout was back. The secretary's eyes ranged over the bookshelves. Perhaps the answer was there. "And do you seriously accuse me of being, as it were, the manufacturer?"

"No, Mr. Secretary. I don't think you invented it. I think you passed it on. You needed an eyewitness you could coerce and I could browbeat, preferably one with a powerful father you could sic on me, to make me even more dogged once I imagined the rich alums didn't want me on the trail." When this brought no denial, Bruce plunged confidently on. "Then, having suggested the story in the first place, you could monitor my progress, and make sure, through your constant doubts, that I would continue to believe it to be the truth."

"And how precisely would I have coerced young Knowland? Given that he does indeed possess, as you nicely put it, a powerful father."

"Because of the powerful father. That's my whole point." Bruce stayed on the sofa with an effort. He wanted to be up and striding, but the secretary might take it wrong. "Nathaniel Knowland was a marginal student, far too busy having fun to take his classes seriously. At the same time, he was worried about disappointing his father. As his grades got worse, he worried more. I think you gave him some sort of reassurance. You made a deal to keep him in school. He takes the semester off, then comes back in the fall with a clean slate."

"Which leads us back to where we began, Chief Vallely. Even if one grants for the sake of argument your quite extraordinary hypothesis, one would now need to imagine the existence of an individual possessing, you will excuse me, sufficient influence to recruit me to his nefarious plan, as well as an incentive to mislead you, both as to the involvement of Astrid Venable and to the possible relationship between Kellen Zant and Julia Carlyle."

"That's correct." Now to the point. "I'm here tonight because I have to confirm, urgently, whether what I have said is true. I'm not at liberty to tell you why, but the game has turned dangerous. There are some new players. We have to dispel the lie once and for all, or . . . well, people could get hurt."

Trevor Land's eyes narrowed. He seemed to be calculating: this much advantage with this choice, that much with that choice. Campus politics shifted and swirled, but the secretary was a survivor. He had served four university presidents, two of whom had left involuntarily. He had never even stumbled.

"Very well, Chief Vallely," he said at last. "Let us assume that I believe you. Have you such an individual in mind? An individual with the proper motives and the proper . . . connections?"

"Yes, Mr. Secretary, I do. And I believe you know exactly who I'm thinking of."

Grinning now, more sardonic than amused. Plainly, Trevor Land had decided. "Why not tell me anyway?"

"Lemaster Carlyle."

"Fascinating notion, Chief Vallely. And why, pray, would the president of the—"

Bruce's cell phone rang.

He ignored it.

"That reminds me," said the secretary. He was on his feet but waved Bruce to sit still. He took an envelope from his desk. "The phone records you asked for." Handing them over. "And now, if you will excuse me, Chief Vallely, I believe this meeting is at an end. One must return to one's dinner before it gets cold. Just keep up the good work, Chief. Keep along your present path."

On his way back to the car, Bruce returned the call from his deputy, Turian.

A professor had been badly injured, she said, voice shaky. Another hit-and-run, at an office park in Langford, not far from the border with Tyler's Landing.

"Who was it?"

"The chief of adolescent psychiatry at the medical school. A man named Brady, Vincent Brady."

CHAPTER 55

IMPERFECT INFORMATION

(1)

"How's Vanessa taking it?" said Mary Mallard.

"I'm not entirely sure." Julia stirred her coffee. They were sitting in the bagel shop on the corner of King and Hudson, where, as Mary had pointed out at the White House, Julia used to get together with Kellen for a quick bite. "She's very . . . inward. She doesn't let people know what she's thinking. She has so many faces, so many layers, no matter how many you peel down, you're never all the way to the core."

"Maybe her core's her own business. Maybe the world should keep out."

"Maybe so."

"Children need plenty of space," said Mary, with the authority of a woman who has never raised one.

"Maybe."

"And the police say it's an accident?"

Julia nodded, more uneasy than ever. It was Tuesday. She had a luncheon meeting at Lombard Hall, which was why she and Mary were limited to coffee. She wanted to skip it. She had told Mary nothing about the Empyreals. "His secretary says his briefcase is missing, but the police seem to think he was robbed after he was hit."

"A lot of hit-and-run accidents around the campus these days." Mary drummed her fingers, squirmed around on the bench, and in several other ways signaled that she was ready for a cigarette. Outside, the sun beat brightly down but the temperature was in the teens, and the wind chill was worse. "Julia, look. You're not in any danger. Your family's not in any danger. If they wanted to get you, they'd have gotten you." She let this sink in. "If Brady was an accident, hooray. If they wanted his briefcase, then they must have wanted something *in* his briefcase, and I'm willing to bet it was his files on Vanessa. They want to know what she told her psychiatrist, because they want to know what Kellen told her."

"I don't think Kellen told her anything. She didn't know what he was working on."

"They're keeping their distance, Julia. They're worried. Whoever really did it—whoever really killed Gina—is scared that it's going to come out." A quick smile, then the brisk look Julia had come to know so well. "But back to business." She tapped the envelope. "I agree with Lemaster. This confession is awfully convenient."

"I suppose."

"Notice that it's a photocopy?"

"So?"

"I'm wondering how many copies are around." Drumming those fingers. "And why your mother had one lying around to give you." Drumming, drumming. "It could be some kind of device to use when somebody gets too close to what's really going on." The fingers mercifully stopped. "The question is, how many people have copies? And why did your mother give you one?"

"That's not one question, it's two."

Quite appropriately, the writer ignored this dig. But she walked right into the next one. "What aren't you telling me?"

"Most of the details of my life," said Julia, with brio.

Mary did not even crack a smile. "Let me tell you something. I have another book project I could be working on. A very nice little exposé of lobbyists and slush funds on Capitol Hill."

"Maybe that's what you should do, then."

"Seriously?"

"Lemmie thinks I should stop."

"But you don't." She lifted the envelope. "You don't fool me, Julia. You're planning something nefarious and maybe illegal. I want in on it."

"I'm going back into the archives."

"Why?"

"In case the confession is a lie. Like you said, it's awfully convenient." She drummed her fingers. Now Mary had her doing it. "I only have a few diary pages. Not enough to pay for. Or kill for. There has to be more. I'm betting that's what Kellen hid in the library."

"When are you going?"

Julia shrugged.

Mary said, "You've figured out some of Kellen's clues, haven't you?"

Another shrug.

The writer was sanguine. "You don't trust me yet, do you?"

"I don't know when I'm going." A pause. "But I don't think I need your permission."

"So—what are you saying? I'm a cheerleader again?"

"Rah-rah," said Julia.

(11)

JULIA WAS HOME IN TIME to meet the school buses, Jeannie tumbling into the house with her usual perfect energy, Vanessa trudging upstairs as if she carried the weight of history on her narrow shoulders: over the weekend the anniversary of Gina's death had passed unnoticed, and this morning over breakfast Vanessa had made a fuss about it. Jeremy Flew, still rearranging Lemaster's study, had taken over the kitchen to make a special dinner, and Julia decided to let him.

Jeannie insisted on helping, and Julia decided to let her.

She waited until she heard Jeremy's patient instruction and Jeannie's insouciant giggling and then, with the two of them fully occupied, went up to Vanessa's bedroom for a chat. Vanessa was lying flat on her back on the bed, eyes closed and earphones in place, silently weeping as she listened to her funeral dirges. Julia rolled the chair from the desk and sat, worried eyes on the recumbent figure. She could not imagine how it must feel to have your therapist injured and nearly killed. Gently, she tapped her daughter on the shoulder. Vanessa's eyes flew open, the fearful, startled look frightening to see, until it melted into a smooth smile. She slipped off the earphones and sat up, pulling a book from somewhere, but Julia could see the tracks of the tears.

"I was just resting my eyes," said Vanessa. "Homework."

"Are you okay?"

"Uh-huh."

A long few seconds passed.

"Honey?"

Nose in her book. "Hmmm?"

"May I ask you a question?"

"I think you just did."

"Very funny." Julia inched closer. "Listen, honey. Did Kellen ever mention to you . . . somebody he called the Black Lady?"

Vanessa turned a page and, quite leisurely, reached for her Perrier bottle. Swallowing seemed to take her a very long time. "I thought we weren't supposed to talk about this stuff any more."

Julia bit her lip. She was trespassing on foreign territory, and did not even know whose forces patrolled the border. "And I thought we decided that Veazie women aren't interested in other people's rules." Pause. "Like Elphaba."

"No."

"Not like Elphaba?"

"No, Kellen never mentioned the Black Lady. Sorry, Moms."

About to creep out of the room in disappointment, Julia caught the ghost of a smile on Vanessa's winsome face, and realized that the teen had placed the ghost of an emphasis on Kellen's name. She glanced over her shoulder but the door was still closed.

"What are you trying to tell me, honey?"

"That Kellen never mentioned the Black Lady."

"Kellen never mentioned her." She had it. "Somebody else did."

Turning another page. "Uh-huh."

Again she and her clever daughter had reached the sixty-four-thousand-dollar question. She forced a gentle patience into her tone. "Who, honey? Who mentioned the Black Lady?"

"At Kellen's funeral."

"Kellen's funeral," Julia repeated, thinking, Mary Mallard, which would mean talking to Vanessa had only led her in a circle. A second later, she remembered that Mary and Vanessa had never been alone together at the funeral. "Somebody mentioned the Black Lady at Kellen's funeral." In her head she reviewed the players: Kellen's ex-wife, Nadia; Kellen's uncle Seth; the crowd at Seth's house—

"Uh-huh. Remember how I hung out with the kids and they told me the old stories about Arkadelphia? You got mad when I told you the one about the Civil War? Well, they have this legend down there. They have these colleges, really pretty, we saw them, remember? Well, there's this legend about one of them. There was a student whose boyfriend kind of dropped her for another chick." She rolled her tongue around in her mouth, face momentarily rippling, as she thought, perhaps, of Casey, who had not called in a while. "And, anyway, the legend is that she threw herself off the bell tower, and her ghost has haunted the campus ever since."

"And that's the Black Lady?"

"Right. They call her the Black Lady of Arkadelphia."

"Part of his past," Julia whispered, mostly to herself, wondering how she could have missed something so obvious. Had one of his women actually succeeded in doing herself in? She would have to arrange an excuse to travel back to Arkadelphia, although how she would know what to look for—

"Oh, and, Moms?" Vanessa, still reading, had rolled onto her stomach, a signal of dismissal every bit as unmistakable as Lemaster's habit of swiveling to face his computer. "There's one other thing."

"What's that, honey?"

"The Black Lady? She's white."

(III)

SHE STOOD in the living room window, beside the Steinway, watching the nightly parade of headlights along Hunter's Meadow Road, far more cars than could ever be justified by the still relatively small number of homes on the hill. She had always imagined that not a few carried curious townspeople wanting to see the grand house the black family had built, perhaps to gawk, perhaps to mock, perhaps simply to try to understand this strange new phenomenon of African-American wealth: because, as far as white America knew, nobody black ever had money or education before, say, affirmative action.

And maybe some of the cars were keeping an eye on her. Julia knew somebody was out there, watching and watching, waiting for her to come up with Kellen's surplus, ready to snatch it from her hands and spirit it off to—well, to somebody else. She knew because Mary had told her, and because of what had happened in Paris, but she also knew because she could sense it, the way New Englanders can sense, in the sudden soft change in the direction of the winter wind, the faint whisper of clouds unseen because they are over the horizon, and the rising storm to follow, although the sky is crisp, gorgeous blue.

She was trying, with what resources she possessed, to work out a way around the surveillance that she sensed but never saw. Borrowing Smith's little device, now safely in the glove box of the Escalade, was a part of her plan.

Now she had to plan afresh.

The Black Lady was white.

Julia felt like a fool.

For weeks now, she had been trying to track down Kellen's partner in crime, the woman he had called the Black Lady, not realizing that the Black Lady was busily tracking her. Thinking herself clever, Julia had been out-thought by her white shadow, fooled by her assumption that the Black Lady was black, and a Sister Lady; and that the Black Lady would never be so sneaky as to throw off suspicion by mentioning the phrase.

Steeling herself, she went down to the basement guest room.

Little Jeremy Flew, fully dressed and wide awake, had the door open before she knocked.

"Good evening, Mrs. Carlyle," he said, utterly unperturbed.

"May I talk to you for a moment?"

"About what?"

"It's more a who than a what."

"Consider my inquiry suitably corrected." Not quite smiling.

"Remember how you kept Mr. Huebner away from me that time on Main Street?"

"Of course."

"Well, there's somebody else I want you to keep away from me."

"I think you may misunderstand precisely what I—"

"Please, Jeremy. I know why you're here. I don't think I like it, but I do understand it."

"I see," he said after a moment.

"Now, will you help me? Please?"

"Perhaps." Careful eyes glittered pale and guileless. He meant the word literally. She wondered if he had to check with somebody first. "Who is it that you wish kept away from you?"

"A woman named Mary Mallard."

CHAPTER 56

AGAIN NORPORT

(1)

"Rick Chrebet is on vacation," said Bruce Vallely. "He'll be back next week. I trust your question can wait until then."

In Ruby Tuesday again, Julia being demanding and mysterious at the same time. She wanted him to persuade his former partner Lieutenant Chrebet to answer a single question for her. Although she refused to tell Bruce what the question was, she plainly thought the answer would blow the top off of . . . well, pretty much everything.

"You'll still arrange the meeting?" she asked.

"Of course."

"All right, then," said Julia, as if everything was settled. "Now, tell me about Dr. Brady."

"What's there to tell? It was a hit-and-run. An accident. Except you obviously don't believe it. Neither do I." A beat. "So maybe you'd like to tell me what they were looking for?"

Julia hesitated, obviously torn, then let slip a small nugget. "Vanessa doesn't know anything about what's going on. I want to make that clear. She doesn't know a thing. But some people think she does. A file was stolen from my office, and, well, maybe—"

"You're saying somebody tried to kill Vincent Brady to get a look at his files?"

Julia shrugged and took a bite of her burger. She was endorsing no theory.

"But why try to kill him? Why not just break into his office?"

"Vanessa has a new therapist. Sara Jacobstein is her name. We filled out all the paperwork to get her files opened for Sara, only to discover, according to Dr. Brady's office, that a lot of the files are missing. No sign of burglary, nobody tripped the alarms."

"You're saying Brady had the files with him. In the briefcase."

"Maybe."

"Why would he be carrying them around?"

She grinned that crooked grin. "That's why there's cops. To answer questions like that. Maybe he was studying them. Maybe he was selling them. Maybe anything."

Saying goodbye in the parking lot, Bruce tried again. "You can't do this by yourself, Julia."

"Do what?"

"Please don't play games. There are issues here you don't know about. There are interested parties. Kellen Zant set off a firestorm. Not just politics. Much more. I would hate for you to—"

He stopped.

They stared at each other for a long moment, and then, coloring, both looked elsewhere.

"Bruce?" she said, as they parted.

"Yes, Julia?"

"Who was that man? The one who bothered me at the Exxon station?"

"A reporter. I told you." He seemed suddenly in a hurry to be free of her.

"For what publication?"

"One of the tabloids. I don't remember."

"Well, thank you." A friendly hug. "For everything." She looked up into his eyes. Hers, he realized, were more gray than brown. "I need you to do me one more favor." A crooked grin. "It's a big one."

"What's that?"

"Stop following me."

"What?"

"I want you to stop following me, Bruce. I'm perfectly safe." Stepping back, fully in charge. "Just wait for my call."

(11)

BRUCE WATCHED HER from a distance as she climbed into the Escalade, a small, smart, competent woman, fiercely protecting her family. She did not want anybody looking into Vanessa's connection with Kellen Zant. That was why she insisted on doing it all herself. That was why she wanted Bruce to keep his distance. At least he hoped that secret was all Julia was protecting. The alternative was that she was protecting whatever Zant had discovered; or, worse, protecting whomever he had discovered it about.

He wondered if she knew that Jeremy Flew was dogging her tail rather more often than Bruce himself; and whether she knew as much about Flew's background as he did.

And whether she knew that nobody seemed to know where the little man had been the night Kellen Zant was shot.

"Be careful," Bruce called, very softly.

It was plain to him, although Trevor Land had never directly admitted it, that Lemaster was the author of the absurd story that Nathaniel Knowland had told him, with embellishments, about the night Zant was killed. The president of the university had somehow managed to get the official investigation shut down, and then maneuvered Bruce onto the trail instead of Rick Chrebet and his team. Why get the inquiry dropped only to have it started up again? Why did Lemaster want his director of campus safety following his wife around, searching for evidence of a link? The questions baffled him, and yet he sensed that the answer was right in front of him, hidden in the information he had already collected, and that if he could just stir things up a bit, the truth might fall into his lap.

CHAPTER 57

AGAIN THE LIBRARIAN

(1)

THIS TIME JULIA STRODE CONFIDENTLY into the workroom of
the archives, clutching the photocopies of Kellen's search requests. The
new me, she kept saying to herself, even as something inside her trembled at the thought of further rejection. This is the new me. She had
chosen late afternoon because morning was busier, and selected Mrs.
Bethe rather than Roderick Rutherford as her target because Mrs.
Bethe had been known every now and then to attempt a smile.

But not today.

"These citations do *not* match the Joule papers," Mrs. Bethe
explained, near breathless with wonder that anyone could think otherwise. "These items are all in *other* collections."

"I know that."

She handed the sheets back. "Then please write the names of the
proper collections on the indicated line. The rules require—"

"Yes, Mrs. Bethe, I know what the rules require. But since you have
the numbers, isn't finding the documents just a matter of going to the
indicated shelf and cubbyhole and taking them down? I mean, there's
no practical impediment, is there?"

Mrs. Bethe wore small-bore glasses, pearls, and a twin set. She had
assisted in the archives for a quarter century, and saw no distinction
between disagreement and insolence. "Wait here," she said, and
scooped up the search requests, providing Julia a moment of glorious
hope. Then she dashed it, marching across the small room into the
chief archivist's office.

Oh, great.

A moment later, Roderick Rutherford emerged and, rubbing his hands against each other as if he had been handling something dusty, crossed to her side as Mrs. Bethe returned to her hutch.

"Now, what can we do for you today, Dean Carlyle?"

"You can show me the files on this sheet." She passed over the page on which she had copied the folio and volume numbers. The librarian studied it briefly, eyebrows knitting, prim mouth working as if voicing them.

"May I ask why you want them?"

"Isn't it enough that I want them?"

"Oh, no, my dear Dean Carlyle, not at all. The archives are open only to scholars with a bona fide interest in materials available in our collection." He handed the page back to her. "I cannot permit you to examine any of these files without a legitimate academic reason."

Not again! "What counts as an academic reason, Mr. Rutherford?"

"Say you were writing a book or article that required you to—"

"All right. I am."

"You are what, Dean Carlyle?"

"Writing an article. An article about what happened to Gina Joule thirty-odd years ago. There. Now I have a scholarly purpose."

Rod Rutherford smiled rarely. Now that he was offering one, Julia knew why, and hoped he would not soon do it again. The smile was narrow and presumptuous, touching no other part of his face, which remained locked against her: the sort of bright, crazy smile we expect on the face of a little boy pulling the wings off a live butterfly for fun. Or a teenaged girl burning her father's midnight-blue Mercedes on the Town Green on the anniversary of Gina Joule's death.

"Alas, Dean Carlyle, the only difficulty is that I don't believe you."

"I beg your pardon."

"I believe, Dean Carlyle, that you are lying to me." Calmly. "There is no such article."

"Lying! *You're* accusing *me* of lying!"

The outburst stunned Mrs. Bethe, who was packing up her desk: that is to say, she cocked her head vaguely in the direction of the long work table, as if listening to distant music she was not sure she remembered. Without ever quite looking their way, she crossed to the heavy vault door guarding the archives, spun the lock, and set the alarm. Then she went out.

"That is correct, Dean Carlyle. I am accusing you of lying. Of course, ordinarily it would not be my business. But because I do not believe you have a bona fide scholarly purpose, I cannot comply with your request." Spreading his hands. "It is perfectly evident that you are still seeking to discover what documents, if any, Professor Zant might have examined. The pertinent rules forbid me to share that information. I believe I told you this already."

"Yes, you did, Mr. Rutherford. Rule 22-C, I believe you mentioned. Adopted by the faculty senate in 1973, after the Buckley Amendment."

"Correct, Dean Carlyle."

"The only trouble is, the Buckley Amendment didn't pass Congress until 1974. I looked it up. You told me to pay close attention to the rules, so I did."

The brows crinkled delicately. "Perhaps I made a mistake."

"I don't think so. You don't make that kind of mistake. Not unless you do it on purpose." From her shoulder bag she drew the university rulebook. She found the page she wanted. "And there's something else. Here's Rule 22. It has nothing to do with privacy, does it? It's about the two types of committees of the faculty, standing and ad hoc." Tapping the pertinent section. "And it only goes up to Part B."

"How distressing." His long pale hands made their washing motion again. "How terribly distressing."

Julia half smiled. "You're good, Mr. Rutherford. You're very good. I never would have guessed your whole story was a façade. But, as I said, you don't make that kind of mistake. You gave me that false information for a reason. I would like to know why."

He shook his head. "Alas, I cannot violate confidentiality. Whatever the pertinent rule number might be, I am unable to tell you whether Professor Zant was ever here, or what files he looked at."

"Just tell me why you made up that story about the rule."

"The rules, Dean Carlyle, exist for the benefit of the entire community. Of every one of us."

"I just—"

"And our families."

"Our families?"

He ignored her surprise. "And you have brought me no authorization? A subpoena, something like that?"

"No, I—"

Oh!

The straight man. Rod. Straight. Was it possible?

"Wait here," she said, in the most commanding voice she could muster. "Wait right here."

"Oh, dear me." A glance at his watch. "How the day does fly by. Five-thirty already. Time to lock up for the night."

"Five minutes," she said, and, without lingering for his answer, hurried back to her office. She opened her bag and pulled out the broken mirror from Luma's Gifts. Two minutes later, she was standing in front of him again.

"What am I to do with this, Dean Carlyle?" murmured the librarian, frowning down at the mirror she had laid on his blotter. "What is it, precisely?"

"You know what it is." So she hoped. "It's my authorization."

"That seems rather unlikely."

"Somewhere you have the other half. You're supposed to see if they fit together. Then you're supposed to give me what I want."

He shook his head, refusing to take the proffered item. "If indeed I were in possession of the other half, as you call it, I would hardly need time for study to see, as you put it, if they fit together. It would be obvious at a glance."

"Are you saying—"

"It is half past five, Dean Carlyle. The archives are now closed."

"Mr. Rutherford, you can't just—"

"I am afraid I must." He was on his feet, thin and imposing. "Sadly, Dean Carlyle, I am unable to be of further assistance in this matter. The rules about closing time are unambiguous."

"You can't just walk out on this conversation!"

"Incorrect, Dean Carlyle." Tugging on the heavy parka that emphasized rather than concealed his scrawniness. "I can do exactly that."

He pulled on his hat, turned off all the lights except the one directly above the table where they had been sitting, and walked out the door.

She stood, astonished.

The lock cycled. The red light came on.

The alarm was active. And Julia Carlyle was alone, locked inside the archives.

(11)

HER FIRST INSTINCT SAID ACCIDENT. Rod Rutherford, flustered by her demands, had followed his end-of-the-day routine, walking out the door precisely at half past five because he always did, except on Sunday, when he rested. But that was absurd. Surely a part of his daily routine was checking the archives to make sure nobody was hiding out to disturb the perfection of the preservation of knowledge.

So she swung the other way. He had left her on purpose.

Either way, the response was obvious. She banged on the heavy double doors leading to the stairs and called his name, then called for anybody—but of course nobody could hear her, because this entire end of the library would be deserted once the archives shut down.

Oh, great.

There would be no climbing out the window this time either. The bars had been repaired. She had already checked.

She clutched the reassuring techiness of her cell phone, only to discover, when she flipped it open, that down here in the basement, surrounded by metal beams and concrete, no signal was available. There was a phone on the archivist's desk but the handset was fastened down by a lock of a design popular in her own student days, when unpaid calls presented a significant budgetary problem, and Julia possessed no key. A glance out the door told her that Mrs. Bethe's phone was similarly secured.

Oh, this is great, Julia. Just great. The archivist has locked you in. Now all you have to do is sit down and wait for the Eggameese to come and gobble you up. Or for a bullet in your own stupid head.

She forced a calm on herself.

There had to be a reason for this.

First hypothesis: Roderick Rutherford was involved up to his manicured fingertips in the search for Kellen's surplus. Kellen was dead. Boris Gibbs was dead. Bruce Vallely had tried to warn her that if she kept this up she might wind up dead, too. So perhaps the Eggameese really was lurking out there, and she was next on the list.

She shivered and, back on her feet, banged on the door again, shouting. She already knew she could not be heard, but she could not bear not trying.

When she was all panicked out, she sat down again.

Second hypothesis: Nobody was waiting to kill her. Therefore, Roderick Rutherford had a method to his madness. Tomorrow morning, whoever opened up the archives first would find her, and she would have the librarian's job, and maybe see him in prison, too. Therefore, he expected her not to turn him in.

Why not?

She had an idea. Maybe they were on the same side. She walked over to the vault door and gave it a shove. The lights blinked angrily. All right, she needed the pass code to get in. An alarm on the outer door, a combination for the inner door, and only Roderick Rutherford and his assistant possessed both. Those were the rules, to prevent theft of—

The rules.

The rules?

What had he said to her? Rule 22-C. The nonexistent rule.

The panel had numbers and letters. She pushed 2, 2, C, then shoved the door.

Blinking red lights.

Okay, so that was a bad guess. But the archivist had lied about the year the rule was adopted as well as its number.

She tried 2, 2, C, 1, 9, 7, 3.

No result.

What else had he said?

It was adopted after five months of debate.

She entered 2, 2, C, 5. No. Then 2, 2, C, 1, 9, 7, 3, 5. No. She tried one permutation after another of the same letters and numbers, because standing here and punching possible combinations into the lock was at least moderately saner than hunching in the corner screaming her head off.

And then she had it.

Five months meant five numbers and letters in the combination.

She punched 2, 2, C, 7, 3. The light turned green. A metallic click, wet and heavy in the chilly silence. She pulled the handle, and the massive door swung easily in her grasp.

CHAPTER 58

AUTOMATIC LEVELING

(1)

THE LIGHTS WERE OFF, but she had armed herself with a flashlight from the librarian's desk. The windows in this part of the building were barred, too, and they gave on the parking lot, so, if she switched on the overheads, her chances of being spotted were not insignificant. She swung the beam through the darkness. It glittered off glass display cases holding valuable books and holograph documents, a touch she found amusing, given that nobody was allowed here. The elevator stood at the back of this weird little museum, an ordinary-looking door with a diamond-shaped glass window and a worn brass panel with one cracked plastic button and two lights: IN USE and NOT IN USE. The NOT IN USE light glowed faintly. One entered the elevator by opening the door manually, grabbing a handle, and sliding the gate aside. A silly system, hopelessly antiquated, but Claire Alvarez had not yet raised the money for the renovation. Closing all these contraptions behind her, Julia hesitated just a few seconds before pressing the button for the second sub-basement, where, according to Suzanne de Broglie, nobody ever went. Somewhere high up in the stacks, a motor whooshed and groaned. As the elevator creaked into motion, she thought she heard another sound, out in the workroom, but nobody could be there. The alarm would have sounded. She looked around the narrow elevator car. In her own student days, this part of the library had been part of the main stacks, accessible to anyone with a university identification. She remembered riding this same elevator to this same basement on another winter night, probably more nervous then than now, chasing down the great

Lemaster Carlyle, eight years her senior, who had said he would be working late.

After due deliberation, and a screaming argument with Tessa, she had decided to allow him to seduce her. Always impulsive, she had acted at once, and if he was in the library, well, then, the library would have to do—

Pay attention to business, she ordered herself sternly, for that was a thousand lifetimes ago. She licked her lips. The elevator was very slow. A peeling red-and-white sticker at eye level warned the unwary: THIS CAR IS NOT CAPABLE OF AUTOMATIC LEVELING. EXERCISE EXTREME CAUTION WHEN EXITING. Great. If I were the kind of person who exercised extreme caution, I wouldn't be here in the first place.

Clutching her briefcase with both hands to try to make them stop shaking, Julia Carlyle rode downward, watching the floors creak by on the other side of the gate, and experienced for an awful instant the illusion that the elevator was bearing her downward to Hell, full penalty for her sins, and that she would never see her family again. And then she thought, although this, too, must be her imagination at work, that the sound she had heard just before the elevator began its descent was the double door upstairs rattling open.

The Eggameese was coming for her, no question.

No. It wasn't. Only Rod Rutherford and Mrs. Bethe had keys. Rutherford had locked her in, and Mrs. Bethe would hardly come back to let her out. Therefore, nobody was upstairs. So stop it, Julia. Pay attention to business.

Red warning sticker or no, Julia stumbled as she stepped off the elevator. Everything went tumbling. Picking up her briefcase and the scattered photocopies, she noticed that the floor of the car was almost two inches lower than the floor of the subbasement. NOT CAPABLE OF AUTOMATIC LEVELING, indeed.

She closed the gate behind her and stepped out into the lowest level of the library stacks. A long time since last time. She paused, scenting the air, listening to currents, before deciding that she was alone.

She walked along the rows of battleship-gray shelves, her steps ringing on the metal plates of the floor, scarcely noticing the aged books and old pamphlets, the neatly stacked folios of sermons and reports and letters and diaries and minutes that constituted a remarkable history of religion in New England. She did not look at the items on the shelves. She looked at the letters and numbers. This was right. She knew it was.

Down here, in the underbelly of the divinity school, was where Kellen had hidden the missing pieces of his surplus. Covered by a code only Julia would understand, hidden in places only Julia could go. Unable to lure her out of her world during his life, the economist had ensured her presence in his world after his death.

There were moments when she thought his goal was not justice but spite.

"A little bit self-centered, Jules," she said, scaring herself with the accuracy of her imitation of her husband's gently correcting tone. "Not everything is about you."

"*Kellen* was about me," she answered him, words she would never speak to Lemaster's face. "Except when he wasn't," she admitted.

She was close. The numbers were starting to catch up with the forms in her hand. Dust was everywhere. There had been a time when the collection was in constant use, when scholars and students thought there was wisdom to be gained from reading the words of the great thinkers of the past, in the actual texts in which the words were laid down: on the printed page, not the computer screen. Nowadays nobody seemed to care about places like this any more—nobody but a handful of traditionalists like her husband, people who like to hold the reflections of earlier generations solidly in their hands, as a reminder, perhaps, that the edifice of morality and reason they have spent their lives building is less transitory than those who zip through ideas with mouse and keyboard might imagine. Solidity implies time: nothing that lasts is ever built quickly.

"Showtime," Julia said.

She had arrived at the first of Kellen's locations, a dusty corner of the collection of eighteenth-century sermons. She matched the letter and number and pulled from the blue folder a dozen tightly handwritten pages, ink faded, penned by an obscure—

A sound, in the shadows ahead of her.

Instinctively she swung the beam into the aisle, but saw nothing.

It was a bump. Julia was sure of it. The bump of a book falling from a shelf, as if, for example, knocked by a carelessly placed human hand. Not on this level, she decided. One floor up.

Somebody else was in here.

But when she shut off the flashlight and listened hard, there was only darkness and silence.

Enough of this flashlight shit.

She fumbled along the wall for a light switch, flicked it, then jumped back at the quick whooshing sound of a motor kicking to life.

Her heart rate and breathing returned to something close to normal as she realized that it was just the sound of the clankety elevator, summoned to some higher level of the stacks.

Nothing to do with her.

Except that the stacks were closed, the archives door was alarmed, and nobody was supposed to be in here but her.

All right. All right. Maybe the elevator was programmed to go back upstairs automatically. The motor stopped. The sliding manual door did not clank open: she would have heard it all the way down here.

She was alone.

Back to work.

Tucked inside an obscure sermon by an even more obscure eighteenth-century preacher, she found a trim white envelope like the one Kellen had taped beneath the piano. Wedged into an early draft of a forgotten monograph on Aristotle's concept of God by an unimportant religion scholar of a hundred years ago, she found another. And, snuggling puckishly inside the program from the annual student satirical show from the Kepler class of 1953, the year Kellen was born, she found a third.

She had just stuffed the third envelope into her bag when she looked up sharply at a footfall on the metal stairs.

"You must leave here at once," murmured Roderick Ryan Rutherford, ghostly face, twisted into a mask of disapproval, floating above her in the darkened stacks. "Surely, Dean Carlyle, you realize you are not permitted in the stacks unescorted. Such conduct is absolutely against the rules."

So was grabbing the archivist and kissing him on the cheek, but she did it anyway.

(11)

SHE WOULD NEVER KNOW WHY, Julia told herself, hurrying along the empty corridor toward her office. That Rod Rutherford had helped Kellen with his project was plain. He had transmitted the clues on her first visit, and then, when she returned with the authorization in hand, he had pretended to refuse her but left her inside the archives to go into the stacks. After a decent interval, he had returned to let her out again, and, although he refused absolutely to allow her to take the documents with her, he waited while she ran the photocopier—although he insisted on charging the copies to her university account. Her questions he politely but firmly refused to answer, citing confidentiality. When she departed, he was still inside, perhaps fussing around the stacks, putting everything back where it belonged.

Why had he helped Kellen? Rod's mother had been the Kepler librarian, first woman ever in that post, and he had helped out during the summers, developing his own interest in the field. He was too young to have courted Gina Joule, but not too young to have known her. Perhaps the Rutherfords and the Joules had been close. Perhaps the connection was more attenuated—or more obvious.

She would never know, and Mr. Rutherford would never tell her. Confidentiality. Loyalty. Secrets. Lies. Was the entire world run this way, or was this some special New England collegiate thing? For, other than her brief sojourn in Manhattan, when she had learned the names of perhaps two of her neighbors, she had never really lived anywhere else.

Perhaps partaking moderately of the archivist's paranoia, she locked both the outer and inner doors of her office suite, then sat down at her desk with only the reading lamp for company, and examined her finds.

The envelopes were conveniently numbered 1, 2, and 3 in Kellen's sloping hand, so she started with the first, which happened also to be the thickest. A series of letters from Merrill Joule to his wife, who had taken herself off to Europe after Gina's death. She read, and quickly became engrossed.

April 4, 1973

Dearest Anna,

I hope that this note finds you well, and that you and Margaret are continuing to profit from your holiday abroad. Nothing has changed here. President Nixon continues to duck and weave but I think he will shortly go down. At the university, the weather has lately been too cold for any demonstrations against the war, but with the arrival of spring I imagine we shall again see our share. Here in the Landing, matters are settling, and in the direction you predicted. I salute your wisdom.

Justice, I beg you to remember, comes in many forms. All our lives you and I have marched for a vision of justice that is distributive rather than retributive. Can we abandon that now, simply because a member of our family has died? The enemy is a bad system, not bad people. Eduard is right. Our task is not to seek further punishment but to improve the world to the best of our abilities. What is happening at that church is a good example. The important thing is to move on. . . .

That church: Miss Terry's? The justice *in many forms* proposed that they had—what?—forgone vengeance in return for something better?

Julia had no way of knowing how many letters had passed between the two before the next one Kellen culled from wherever he found them. But the tone had decidedly changed. Gone was the reassuring, almost condescending lord and master of the household, who barely acknowledged his wife's grief, or his own; in its place was a man given to sudden panic.

October 12, 1973

Dearest Anna,

   I have only a moment to pen this note. I am sitting in Ken Steinberg's office, and, yes, I know what you think of lawyers, but Ken is practically family, and, to be frank, I need his advice. The situation is changed. I am being watched. Yes, every paranoid believes this. But you know me, darling. I am not given to hyperbole. I am being watched. I feel their dark eyes on me even when I cannot see them. I sense their breath, passing nearby. They have done their part. They have pointed everyone in the wrong direction. They have obscured what should be obvious. I have given my word that I accept their vision of justice, and yet they do not believe I am going to keep my side of the bargain. I do not think they are able to break into the United States mails. Yet. But I urge you to beware. I believe you should extend your sojourn in Europe until I signal you that it is safe to return. . . .

Julia read the key sentences again. *They have pointed everyone in the wrong direction.* Manufacturing evidence? Manufacturing alibis? *I am being watched.* She shuddered. *I sense their breath, passing nearby.*

"I know exactly how you feel," she told the air.

The third letter was dated nearly five months later. Vanessa had written in her paper that Anna Joule took an extended European tour after Gina died. Evidently, Anna had taken her husband's advice.

March 7, 1974

Dearest Anna,
Destroy this letter once you have read it. I am afraid it is coming apart. Nixon's fortunes appear to be ours. Covering up is impossible. There is always an informer. Always. Again your wisdom was correct. Better to pursue the truth. I wish I had listened. Yet all is not lost. Unlike Nixon, we have options. Our friends have not deserted us. And here our lifelong struggle for justice stands us I think rather in good stead. We are good people, you and I. We are not monsters. We have made errors, but errors are not the same as evil, are they? Miscalculation need not pave the way to Hell—not if we have done the best we could with what we were given. We have done our best to ensure that our beloved daughter did not die in vain. If we are wrong, at least we have erred on the side of charity.

To place the letters in context, she opened the second envelope, which turned out to be more pages from the diary of the constable:

Neither of the college boys' alibis check out, but we're not to pursue it. Besides, with all this money floating around I can't trust anybody. Not even my own people. Not even myself.

Not enough. Surely this was not the sum total of Kellen's evidence.

With trepidation, she advanced on the final envelope. Another photocopy—

Julia's head snapped up. She heard the click of the outer door to her office suite opening, even though she was sure she had locked it. She remembered the sound of the elevator rising when she was in the basement, and how she had guessed it must be programmed to return to the main floor; only now did it occur to her that Rod Rutherford always took the stairs, and the rickety old elevator that served the archives was not likely to be capable of being programmed to do anything.

There was nowhere to run. She sat perfectly still, waiting for the Eggameese to come lurching through the door.

It swung wide, and Julia tensed.

"You're really something," said Mary Mallard, grinning. "I mean, you're good at this stuff."

(I I I)

JULIA WAS ALREADY ON HER FEET, shoveling everything back into the envelopes.

"What are you doing here?" she demanded. "How did you get in?"

Mary's smile faltered. "I take it you still don't trust me."

"I don't want you anywhere near me."

"What's the matter? I thought I was supposed to be your cheer-leader." Waving invisible pom-poms. "You know. Rah-rah?"

"I think I sent you an e-mail telling you we shouldn't see each other."

The writer grinned again. "Well, contrary to what you may have heard, I'm actually not all that easy to push around."

"So, Mary, what? You came up here and—what?—followed me around?"

"Sort of."

Julia shook her head. "How did you get in here?" Julia repeated, keeping the desk between them.

"In the building, that's easy. I waited for a couple of students to come out, and they held the door for me. Nobody ever thinks a girl is up to no good." She held up a key. "As to the office, well, I sort of picked your pocket in Boston, got the keys duplicated, slipped them back into your bag during our walk on the Common. Pretty cool, huh?"

Julia's mouth worked. "That's despicable."

"Okay, so I'm despicable, and I'm not charming. The kind of books I write, you learn to do a little bit of everything."

Julia looked past her, wondering what had happened to Jeremy Flew—or whether she had been wrong in her evaluation of his function.

"You lied to me," she said.

"About what?"

"The Black Lady. That was clever."

"What was?"

"Pretending that way." She had stuffed the envelopes in her brief-case. At the same time, she had palmed the chemical mace Lemaster made her carry. She had never used it before but was not about to let the materials pass into the wrong hands. She did not know who Mary was working for. She only knew she never wanted to see her again. "Now, please, Mary, I don't want to talk to you or see you any more. Please get out of here."

The journalist spread her hands wide, the ducklike face pouty. "I don't know what you're talking about, Julia."

"I'm talking about all that Black Lady bullshit. You had me conned from the start."

"No, Julia. I never conned you."

"No? Remember how you looked me up before the White House? Well, I finally got smart. I looked you up, too. Why didn't you tell me you're related to the President?"

Mary's face darkened. "You're joking, right? You got that from some idiot Web site. We're not related. We're like eighth cousins once removed or something. That means we probably had a common ancestor who signed the Declaration of Independence. Come on, Julia. By that logic, my family's related to pretty much all the Presidents." A desperate smile. "Yours probably is, too."

"Just go."

"What's in the envelopes, Julia? Who are you protecting?"

"Nobody. I want you to go."

Mary shook her head. "I can't do that. The Iowa caucuses are just a couple of weeks away." She pointed. "We have to use what's in there, Julia. We can't let some guy who wants to sit in the Oval Office get away with murder."

"I'm leaving now." Coming around the desk. "Please don't try to follow me."

"Julia, stop. Just stop. Tell me what's going on."

"Get out of my way, Mary."

The journalist reached. "Tell me what's in the—"

Julia maced her, dead in the face.

CHAPTER 59

FEBRUARY 1973

(1)

"You're lucky she's not pressing charges," said Lemaster.

"I had to protect myself!"

Her husband shook his head. He stood in front of the dresser, working with free weights. "We could probably have her arrested for breaking and entering. But the two of you have been palling around. No jury's going to believe she was assaulting you." He paused. "I don't even believe it."

Julia, nervous and sweaty and furious at herself, pulled the blankets over her head. She had never maced anyone before. She had assumed it worked like in the movies, the bad guy gasping, rubbing his eyes, falling against the wall as you rushed by. But Mary had shrieked, hands flying to her throat, her body convulsing even before she hit the ground, where she curled into a fetal crouch, dry-heaving and wet-heaving alternately until Julia stopped hugging her and apologizing long enough to dial 911. She had spent half the night in the emergency room, waiting for word.

Lemaster worked out in the mornings, before going to the campus. Julia was just now getting to bed.

"What was the big deal anyway?" he asked. "What were you two fighting about?"

"I want to know what happened the night Gina died. What really happened."

"I was in England, Jules. I wasn't here."

Julia jerked the blanket from her head and sat up. "Open my briefcase."

"Hmmm?"

"My briefcase."

Good-naturedly, he did, putting down his weights and, wearing his athletic togs, sitting next to her on the bed. He opened the slim leather valise. He found the envelopes. "These?"

"Look inside the envelope marked number three."

He did, glancing bemusedly over the pages from the letters and pages from the diary. His good humor faded as he reached the last document.

"No," he said.

"Yes," she said.

"This is impossible."

"No." She sat up. "Sweetie? I think it's time to tell me the truth."

He was holding a photocopy of a round-trip airline ticket. He lifted his gaze then to hers, and the tortured look made her want to hold him and protect him forever, just as soon as she finished never laying eyes on him again.

The ticket was London to Boston, dated February 1973, in Lemaster's name.

"You came for Bay Dennison's birthday," said Julia. "You've never missed it."

(11)

THEY DRESSED WARMLY and walked down the sloping back lawn toward the reservoir, boots crunching agreeably.

"I don't know all of it," said Lemaster. "I don't even know very much of it. Or I didn't. I know more now." He glanced at her. She kept her face as neutral as she could. "Yes. Yes. I came back for Bay's party. I had a day to kill first, so I came down to campus."

"To see your friends?"

"Actually, no. To check on the books and things I'd left behind in Hilliman Suite. I wanted to make sure nobody had disturbed them. My roommates had a habit of rearranging my things. They thought it was funny. I arrived on the night of the fourteenth, and nobody was home. I checked, and, by a miracle, everything was in place. I said hello to a couple of people around the dorm, but I was exhausted from the flight, so I went to bed, figuring I'd drive up for the party in the morning."

They had reached the fence. Lemaster grabbed hold as if to keep from falling in. His voice strengthened. "Then, about, oh, two, maybe three in the morning, I woke up. Or, rather, one of my roommates woke me. He said he was in big trouble. Something terrible had happened."

"Which roommate?" she asked, but she was ahead of the story.

"I asked what. He wouldn't say. He just said he was in trouble and—well, maybe they were all in trouble. He was drunk and crying and scared. Very scared. And, well, I was twenty years old, Jules. I wasn't sure what to do. I told him to get some sleep and it would all look better in the morning. He went off to bed. As for me, I got up, got dressed, got my things, got my car, got out of there. I drove straight to Boston. So, yes, I guess I abandoned him in his trouble. But, Jules, you know, my roommates were drunk a lot, and they were in trouble a lot, and they always asked me to fix it. They used to call me Big Brother. And I guess, well, I was feeling uncharitable. Here I was, back in the States for only seventy-two hours, and this guy wanted me to spend my first full day fixing some problem? No, thanks. I went to Boston for the party."

They were on the move again, walking along the fence. Julia was getting cold but was not about to interrupt.

"So that night was the party. At some point, I was alone with Bay Dennison, and I told him what had happened. I think I asked to talk to him. Maybe he just asked me how things were going. I'm not sure. Either way, I told him about my roommate. Bay thought it over, then said I should go back and tell him, if it was really serious, he should come up to Boston and tell Bay the story, and he would see what he could do. And I figured, Great, Bay's a fixer, this young man is connected, maybe I can help after all. So the next day—this is the sixteenth—I drove back to Elm Harbor, I found my roommate, I told him to go up and talk to Bay. I assured him that Bay could solve his problem. In those days, I thought Byron Dennison could do anything. And maybe he could."

"Did he go?" said Julia, when her husband paused.

"Yes. He went. I was back in England by then. I didn't know what the trouble was, and I didn't know how Bay had fixed it. But my roommate wrote me a letter to say that everything was fine, and he was in my debt. All I had to do was ask, and he would give me whatever I wanted. Now and forever."

Like dumping Cameron Knowland, Julia thought but did not say.

Like firing Astrid. Like shutting down an investigation or throwing Tony Tice in jail.

"When I got back in June, my roommates were unusually solicitous. If I was Big Brother before, I was Lord and Master now. It was strange. It was as though I had saved all of them, but in fact I didn't save any of them. I just sent one of them to see Bay. Still, they kept doing me favors, even unasked, and kept reminding me that they owed me, that I only had to ask, et cetera, et cetera. Naturally, I didn't turn them down, even though I was more than a little confused. I didn't know what they had done, or what Bay had done."

"The confession," Julia prompted, but Lemaster wanted to tell it his way.

"I graduated, I got a job, I got another job, I went to div school, I met you, we got married."

"You left out 'I fell in love.' "

"That was implied." They had reached the property line, deep in the winter woods, and were circling back the other way. "Anyway, by that time I was an Empyreal. A minor one. What they call a Legionnaire."

"They're not dying, are they?"

"No. Not really. They're—underground." He hesitated. He was now speaking not of his personal experience but of things he had promised never to disclose. "It's a part of their strategy, Jules. An important part. Staying in the shadows."

"What strategy?"

"To help our community. Jules, look." Walking faster, making her huff to keep up. "Let's take a hypothetical frat boy, a rich kid, well connected, at one of the top Ivies. His family plans big things for him. His only problem is, he develops this terrible crush on the seventeen-year-old daughter of one of his professors. And he's not the kind of kid who's ever really learned to resist temptation. His family has always been there to get him out of whatever jams he gets himself into. They can buy anybody. So he starts flirting with this—this kid. That's what she is, a kid. The thing is, she flirts back. And, after a while, the two of them start sneaking around together. All right, they never quite go all the way, as we used to say back in those days. But they do a lot, the frat boy and the teenager.

"Then, one night, one of his roommates wants to get in on the fun.

He says, 'Why should you be the only one who gets to mess around with her? We share everything. You should share.' Maybe they have words. Hypothetically. Or maybe the first frat boy is willing from the start, because—well, because he's spoiled to the point of utter amorality. So, that night, the two of them go cruising to go see her. It's Valentine's Day, but she has an easy way of seeing her boyfriend whenever she wants. She picks a fight with her mother and stalks out of the house. Simple as that. So, that night, sure enough, she and her mother get to screaming at each other, and our hypothetical teenager storms out of the house. Her boyfriend picks her up. Only there's two boys in the car, not one, and they've both been drinking. A lot. Maybe she's a little uneasy at this point, but she gets in anyway. They drive to the beach. There our first frat boy—her boyfriend—passes out in the car. The second frat boy, just as rich and spoiled as the first one, well, he wants to mess around. Maybe she cooperates at first. Maybe she fights all along. Either way, things go further than she planned. She tells him to stop. He won't stop. He's never had to stop in his life. His family has bought off a dozen girls by now. What's one more? So he gets rough with her."

They were back at the house. The patio furniture was covered in snow.

"So she runs," said Julia.

"Right. She runs. Hypothetically. It's the middle of the winter, and she runs away down the beach. There's a guard there. A teenaged boy. There always is. But, poor kid, she runs the wrong way. Not toward the guardhouse. Toward the water. Our frat boy chases her. He's drunk out of his mind, remember, and maybe she's had a few, too. He catches up with her just as she hits the water. Maybe they struggle. Maybe she just hauls off and slaps him, and he hits her back, a lot harder than he thought. Either way, she goes under. And she doesn't get up." He licked his lips. "Hypothetically."

"Right," said Julia, checking her watch. She had to go in shortly to make sure the girls made the school bus. "Hypothetically," she echoed.

"So now it's panic time. Our frat boy tries to revive her, but he doesn't know how. He gives up. He lets the water take her. Maybe he even gives her a push. I don't know. He jumps back in the car, he tries to wake his friend, but he can't. So he hightails it back to campus, because campus is safe. Campus is home. Campus is where you can call your family and tell them to come and fix what you did, except that this is a little more serious than seduction—which, although we forget, used to be a criminal offense. He finally gets his friend up, but of course doesn't tell him what happened. They stumble up the stairs, they get to the suite, and—what do you know?—their roommate who's been away is back. The one they call Big Brother."

"Their black roommate."

Lemaster smiled grimly. "So our frat boy wakes him up and starts babbling about how he's in a real mess this time, and a day and a half later Big Brother is back and tells him to go see this fixer up in Boston. Our frat boy goes. The fixer hears him out. Then he asks two questions. Did anybody see them at the beach? Only the guard. Does his roommate remember anything? No. The fixer says, leave everything to him. And, within twenty-four hours, he has a whole plan. Because by that time he knows that a black boy has stolen a car in the town. The plan is, the blame will shift to the black boy. But there's also a backup, in case something goes wrong. The drunken roommate, the one who slept through the whole thing, has to be persuaded that he did the crime, and that the frat boy in fact slept through it. The fixer sees him too, and gives him the reverse plan. We'll fix it so your friend gets the blame, he says. There's only one condition. They both have to sign confessions—"

"Why would they do that?"

"Because the fixer has them stuck between a rock and a hard place. Sign the confession and it'll be like it never happened, except that we'll always have the confession if we should, say, need a favor down the road. Or don't sign, and take your chances in court, bearing in mind that the fixer can testify against you, and he holds a lot of power in his hands. Maybe enough to beat the rich families. Certainly enough to give them a real battle. And, of course, in a battle, win or lose, the boys' futures would be destroyed. And families like that, the great future is what they're raised for." He looked at his watch, too. "Time to wake the kids."

"Lemmie, wait." She put a hand on his arm.

"What's wrong?"

"How long have you known this?"

The dark eyes were gentle now, at peace again, with himself and with her. "Only since I was elected Bubba."

"You mean, all these years—"

"I didn't know what happened. I suspected it had something to do with Gina—how could I not?—but I didn't know, and I didn't ask. And the interesting thing was, my roommates, well, they must have assumed I knew all about it. Because, all these years, whenever I've asked a favor, they've done it." Holding open the door. "Of course, I don't ask so many."

The children tumbled downstairs. Julia made Lemaster wait, for he liked to leave for work early. But they were not done, and both knew it. Jeremy Flew scrubbed the kitchen while Julia escorted the kids to the school bus.

(I I I)

"YOU'RE WONDERING what the fixer thought he was up to. I'll tell you exactly. He and his . . . club . . . have this theory. Their theory is that America gives nothing freely. They believe America won't cross the street to help a black man, not if it's not forced to. And so what they do, what they've done for a long time, is gather unflattering information about people in positions of power. Or people who might reasonably be expected to attain positions of power. Journalists and opposition politicians like to run with information like this, drive people out of office. Our hypothetical fixer considers this insanity. If you find some dirt on a powerful figure and use it to force him out of office, what do you have? A powerless politician and dirty hands, neither of which is useful. Better to let him stay in office, and let him know what you've got, and nudge him from time to time in the direction of justice. That way you have a powerful politician and clean hands, but he's still doing what you want. Not all the time," Lemaster added hastily. "You have to use it sparingly, or the system breaks down. But nudges. That's what they believe in. Nudges."

He caught the reproach in Julia's eyes. "Come on, Jules. How many times have you said to me that neither party really cares about the darker nation any more? How all the Republicans care about is cutting taxes and building up the military, and all the Democrats care about is abortion and gay rights? Isn't that what you always say, at least in private? Well, our hypothetical fixer and his club happen to agree with you. They don't think the identity of the party in power makes a dime's worth of difference in the lives of African Americans. All that matters to them is whether the people in power are people over whom they hold some influence."

"Do you agree?" she asked, voice very small. "Do you think he's right?"

"I see his point. Let's leave it at that." He was tying his tie. He could tell she remained unsatisfied. "Jules, look. Suppose you could prove who killed her. I don't think you could, but suppose it was possible, after all these years. Suppose you could prove it, make the evidence public, and put him in prison for life. Would that bring the dead girl back? Would that help our people?" A stern shake of the head, in case she had failed to guess the right answer. "No, Jules. No. This is the only way that makes sense. It's the only way in which justice actually accomplishes something other than allowing us to pat ourselves on the back. It's less emotionally satisfying—there's no catharsis—but it does some good for real people."

He slipped into his jacket, turned this way and that in the mirror, watching how the soft wool fell.

"Lemmie, no. You can't just stop there."

"I've already said more than I should."

"Please. There's Jock's confession. Did he really kill her? Or was he the boyfriend, just drunk in the back seat?"

"What difference does it make?"

"Your fixer might have been blackmailing two men for the same crime!"

"Twice the justice, don't you think?"

She shook her head. "I think it was Scrunchy. I think it was always Scrunchy. I think Jock's confession was the cover. What Merrill Joule called pointing everybody in the wrong direction. I think the reason Mona had one was that somehow, among the elite, there are people who know the truth, and if anybody gets too close, they're supposed to let them stumble on Jock's confession as a way to throw them off the scent." She stood up, still not dressed for work. "I think—if Scrunchy did it?—I hope he's suffering. He deserves to suffer."

"It doesn't matter who did the deed. Not really. I'll tell you something, Jules. They were all guilty. They were rich, drunken frat boys. All humans are mortal and imperfect, they grow up, and they grew into reasonably upstanding men. That's fine. But you asked me about the past. Fine. Let's talk about the past. They were monsters. They did what they wanted and assumed somebody else would clean up the mess. Because of who they were, somebody else usually did. They shared this attitude—most Caucasians do, at least in America, but the rich ones especially, no matter where they stand on the political spectrum—I see it every day on campus from the folks on the Left, and I see it every day in Washington from the folks on the Right—anyway, they had this attitude of being aggrieved. The world had given them everything, but they seemed to think they were due even more. Somebody had hurt them. Somebody had taken something they had, or denied them something they coveted. They sit around and reinforce each other's sense that the bad people are out there trying to steal their toys." He had crossed to the window. Fluffy snowflakes tumbled. In his mind he was far away. "And I'll tell you something else. I didn't create this plan. I didn't know anything about it. When I first heard about it—a year ago?—I thought it was—nuts. Illegal, certainly; immoral, probably; but definitely nuts. I even talked to some of the people on the Council about putting a stop to it. The Grand Paramount took me aside. Think about it, he said. A lot of effort has gone into this. A lot of thought. I still thought it was wrong, Jules. Now, though, I'm not so sure. Nowadays, when I look around, when I listen to what our elites babble about, in a country where solving the problems of race and class was once central to our politics, when I see how the paler nation has moved on to other issues and left the darker nation behind? Nowadays, I think our hypothetical fixer might have a point about America—"

He went out.

Julia, alone with her thoughts, was not prepared to deal with abstractions. She remained stuck on more concrete problems, such as who killed Gina Joule. She wondered who her husband was protecting. Confessions could be forged. Confessions could be coerced. No matter how much evidence pointed at Jock or Scrunchy, she could not get over the strong impression that Maureen Whisted, downstairs in the study the night of the dinner, was terrified that Kellen's inventory would prove that her husband had done it.

CHAPTER 60

COMPARATIVE AUTHORITY

(1)

BRUCE VALLELY WAS in a dark Buick Century, his official car, having found a parking spot on Hudson Street with a clear view of the entrance to the divinity school. He drummed his fingers on the wheel, watching the door through the fresh fluffy flakes because this was the only exit he had ever observed Julia using. He gave no thought to the peculiar racial inversion of the moment—a black cop wanting to find out why a white man was following a black woman—but had decided nevertheless that it was time he had a little talk with Mr. Flew. To ask him, say, to account for his whereabouts between eight and ten on the night Kellen Zant was shot. Or whether he might have been at the shopping mall in Norport the day Boris Gibbs got himself run over.

But, even more than he wanted to solve the crime, he wanted to figure out how on earth a man like Lemaster Carlyle wound up employing a Jeremy Flew; for the notion that Flew had tumbled into the job by splendid coincidence was too much to bear.

Action.

Julia came striding down the front steps in the company of a pair of students, who said their laughing goodbyes and trudged off toward the main campus. Julia stood for a moment, head moving as if to survey the street, and perhaps, consciously or not, she was doing exactly that. After a while, even the brain of an amateur senses surveillance. When her gaze moved over his car, he was careful to remain perfectly still, because ducking or turning his face away would only draw her attention.

She looked pale. Worried. Even frightened. Well, who wouldn't be, with all the burdens she was carrying?

At last she set off toward the lot, drawing her scarf tightly around her neck. She climbed the three steps up to the poorly plowed tarmac, slipping twice on her way to the Escalade.

Bruce turned to look at Kepler again, and, sure enough, there was little Flew, emerging from the side entrance, out of sight of the front door, circling toward the parking lot. Bruce had a quick decision to make. He could stop the presidential assistant right here and question him, leaving Julia to make her own way without the tail, or he could follow Flew as he followed Julia. But he had a hunch that Jeremy Flew, former roving consultant for the State Department, would spot him in traffic. Better to put an end to the mess right here. Still, Bruce was not about to underestimate his suspect. From the glove box he took his Smith & Wesson 64 and slipped it into his non-regulation belt holster. He opened the door slowly, for once thankful for the great white feathery silence of swiftly falling snow, and trotted along the buried pathway behind Kepler Quad.

Julia was almost at her car, head down, face pale, rushing and half stumbling, as if something had panicked her. He wondered if Flew noticed. He wondered if Flew was the cause.

Sprightly Flew, on the other hand, was taking his time, testing each step, worrying, perhaps, that too much haste would cause a commotion, and Julia would look around. Or maybe he was certain that he knew where she was headed, and therefore saw no need to hurry.

Bruce charted an interception course, and worked it perfectly, emerging from the shadows behind the granite fastness of the div school just as Jeremy Flew reached the snow-slick steps up to the lot.

"All right, Mr. Flew. That's far enough."

The small man stopped, but looked past him, toward Julia, who was climbing back into the Escalade. "What can I do for you, Mr. Vallely?"

"I think we need to talk."

"Not just now."

"Yes, Mr. Flew. Right now."

The elfin eyes shifted back toward Bruce, seeming to take his measure, then veered off to follow Julia once more. "I'm afraid I have urgent business, Mr. Vallely."

"Like following Julia Carlyle to see what she's up to?"

"Urgent business. I apologize."

Flew moved to go around him. Bruce, much larger, kept his bulk between the little man and the lot. "I'm afraid I'm going to have to insist."

"I don't believe you can keep me here, Mr. Vallely."

"If you're questioning my authority—"

"Not at all, Mr. Vallely. I quite understand that you have been charged with special duties. Nevertheless, I do not believe you can keep me here."

"Well, I'm not sure how you mean that, but maybe the easiest thing—"

It was very fast, and very unexpected, and, later, Bruce admitted that he must be getting old. One instant his hand was on the little man's arm, and the next instant the little man had laid him with surprising gentleness on his back in the snow. Stunned, Bruce took a crucial second to gather his wits, and the crucial second was all Flew needed. By the time the former detective scrambled to his feet, Lemaster's special assistant was halfway across the parking lot, sprinting for the white sedan Bruce had spotted before. Pulling his gun on the president's assistant in the middle of the campus was out of the question, and, besides, he had not been to the range in months. Judging the distance and the chances, Bruce headed not for Flew, or for the Escalade, which had just pulled out onto Hudson Street, but for the exit from the lot. You drove up to the gate and the pressure of your wheels pushed a switch that opened it. The process took a couple of seconds, and that would be his second chance to intercept Jeremy Flew.

But when Bruce stood to look back toward the parking lot, the white sedan was still covered in fresh snow, and the strange little man had disappeared.

(11)

FRUSTRATED, Bruce reviewed his options. Julia was gone and he had missed Flew. He could call Julia's cell phone, but what would he tell her? That she was in danger? He had no real reason to think this was true—if Flew had wanted to hurt her, he would have done it long ago—and, besides, if the warning turned out to be false, she would never trust him again. He tried nevertheless, but reached only her voice mail.

He left no message.

Instead, he decided to try to find out why she had left in such a hurry, because understanding her purpose might help him guess her destination.

Only Latisha was still in the suite. Foxon had left hours earlier. The young woman rose to her feet, eyes tinged with fear.

Awkwardly, he apologized for startling her. Then he said, "I need to know where Dean Carlyle went."

"She went home."

"Are you sure?"

Latisha pointed at the clock. "It's almost six. She had a faculty meeting. She hates to stay this late."

Bruce shook his head. He had seen Julia's face, and he knew, just knew, that she had been spooked. "What was she doing just before she left?"

"Why do you need to know?" asked the young woman, sensibly.

"I think she might be in trouble."

"Are you the cause of the trouble?"

"I hope not. I want to help her."

Latisha took her time thinking it over. Precious moments ticked past but Bruce was not about to rush her. Finally, she said, "You know who her husband is, right?"

"Yes."

"You know, if you're lying, he'll like ruin you."

"Yes."

Inside the office, Bruce searched with his eyes, not touching anything, waiting for any aberrant touch to jump out.

All he found was a business card, pinned beneath the keyboard to keep it from blowing off the desk. A. W. ACME, LAND SURVEYORS, it read, and below, in Kellen Zant's zagging hand, "—Secretary?" Bruce picked it up.

"Do you know what this is?" he asked Latisha.

Wide-eyed, she shook her head.

"You're Dean Carlyle's secretary." He pointed to the scrawl. "Is this you?"

"I'm not a secretary." Proud and frightened at once. "We don't have those any more. I'm an Administrative Assistant Class 3."

Bruce was thinking aloud. "You're right. I'm sorry. There aren't any secretaries at the university any more. Well, there's *the* secretary, of course—"

He stopped, the two of them staring at the card.

"Did Dean Carlyle get any calls just before she left?"

"She answers her own phone when she's here."

"Okay. Think back. Did the phone ring?"

A slow shake of the head. "It's been quiet this afternoon."

"Did anybody come to see her? A student? A professor?"

Another shake. "She had a student, like, two hours ago?"

"Please, Latisha. Help me out here. Anything you can remember."

"She was looking at that card? Like, doodling on it?"

Bruce looked again. Julia had drawn circles around each individual letter. Several circles. None of it made sense. "And nobody came to see her?"

"Nobody."

"All right. Do you know her e-mail password?"

The eyes went wide again.

"It's okay. I'm the director of campus safety."

"But we're not supposed to—"

"Latisha, please. Dean Carlyle—Julia—is in trouble. You know that. You're an intelligent young woman. You must have sensed that something's going on." Knowing his size intimidated her, he spoke as gently as he could. "Please. I'm trying to help her. You have to help me help her, and we don't have a lot of time."

It took less than a minute.

The last e-mail Julia had opened before rushing out the door had been from Vanessa.

The message read, in its entirety, "its a minus sign."

Bruce puzzled, then picked up the card and looked again.

Then he had it.

A minus sign. Another of those word games.

The secretary was Trevor Land. Take his surname away from the name, and it became simply A. W. Acme, Surveyors. So?

He said, "Do you know what else she was doing?"

Latisha nibbled her lip, as if afraid to get the boss in trouble. But she had gone this far. She turned to the computer, where Julia had left her Firefox browser open. She clicked a couple of times.

"This is what she was doing."

Bruce looked. The Internet Anagram Server, the site was called.

Julia had typed in what was left on the card after deleting the word "Land." Bruce nodded to Latisha, who pressed PRINT. The machine coughed out pages and pages of possibilities. He started working his way through them, but it was Latisha, starting at the back of the stack, who let out a little gasp.

She handed him the page, pointing at one line. The words were out of order, but in his mind he switched them around.

VERA WAS MY SOURCE, it read.

"Who's Vera?" he said.

"I don't know." Then she remembered. "Oh, the fudge!" She ran out to her desk, returned an instant later with a box, mostly empty, explaining her heftiness. "See?" The label.

Bruce looked at his watch.

He called the number, but the shop was closed. He called information, but Vera Brightwood's number was unpublished, and he lacked official authority. He called Julia's cell phone, but she must have been in a dead area. He called Hunter's Heights, but there was no answer.

"I'm about to feel very stupid," he said.

Latisha raised worried eyebrows.

He called Rick Chrebet.

His partner, just back from vacation, greeted him with: "If it isn't the pariah!"

But he listened anyway, then told Bruce to hold. Five minutes later, Rick picked up again, but only long enough to tell Bruce to call him back in ten.

Twenty minutes later, now in his car on the way to the Landing, Bruce finally got through to Rick. "I don't know what's going on. Units are on the way, and I'm heading out there myself. There's a report of shots fired at that address."

Bruce drove faster.

(111)

SHE FOUND most of the same cars in Vera's driveway, and knew she had come at both the wrong time and the right one. The doorbell played the opening notes of "The Star-Spangled Banner." When Vera opened the door, she just stood there staring and staring.

"You shouldn't be here," she said at last.

"Oh, yes, I should."

"Go away."

"I want to join the meeting."

Inside, a seeming infinitude of cats crawled along the hallway and stairs. The meeting was in the living room. The furniture was old and solid. There were sandwiches and soft drinks. Lurleen Maddox, from Luma's Gifts, sat sternly on a love seat. Danny Weiss, from the bookstore, perched edgily on an armchair. Trevor Land stood beside the fireplace, stolid and unblinking, a New England oak. And seated on a rocking chair by the fire, gazing on the rest as a king on his subjects, was a fortyish white man Julia knew she had seen before but could not immediately place.

"Bit of a surprise, kind of thing," said Trevor Land.

"I couldn't keep her out," said Vera.

"The jig's up," cackled Lurleen, who was half mad to begin with.

Julia looked around the cozy room. Nobody invited her to sit. For all she knew, she had interrupted a social gathering. Old friends. She remembered Mitch Huebner, warning her about how outsiders could never know the town's secrets. And Frank Carrington, who said talking about what happened to Gina could get him into trouble.

The five white faces all looked at each other, waiting for a leader to emerge. At last the stranger with the familiar face said coldly, "You should leave, Mrs. Carlyle. You should forget you were ever here."

It was the voice that did it. "I remember you. At Hunter's Heights. The dinner we gave for Senator Whisted. You were there. You're the one who replaced Astrid." She pointed at the others. "What is this? A little group to help you cover up what your boss did thirty years ago?"

"You really need to leave now," the aide said. "For your own good."

"Not until somebody tells me what's going on."

Again the crackling silence spun out. Danny Weiss finally said, "Julia, please. It's not what you think."

Lurleen cackled again. "It is too!"

Trevor Land said, "One does feel rather accused without evidence."

"I'm not accusing," she said. "I'm trying to understand. I want to know what happened to Gina Joule."

"So do we," said Danny Weiss, looking to the others for support.

Julia turned to Vera. "I don't know about everybody else, but you were helping Kellen, weren't you? You helped him get information about the Landing. Maybe you liked Gina, because—I don't know—

because she was in your shop the night she died. I think you're the one he called the Black Lady." She saw something in Vera's face. "It was one of his jokes."

Trevor Land said, "One hardly knows what to say—"

"Just tell me the truth. Please. I just want to know what you know."

"People could get hurt," said Danny.

"If you're thinking of the Joules, I already know they went along with the cover-up. What I didn't know until tonight was who the town was covering up for."

Trevor Land shook his head. "I knew young Malcolm well. He doted on that child. Led the search parties and so forth."

Julia said, "The line between doting and coveting—"

She got no further. Whisted's aide was on his feet. "You're not as smart as you think you are," he said, moving toward her.

"People know where I am," she gulped.

"How wonderful for them," he said, and, passing her, headed angrily for the door. Everybody watched him go.

"And the other thing is—" Julia began.

Then they heard the fortyish man shouting. "Hey, what is this? You can't—"

But evidently he could. The senatorial aide marched back into the living room, prodded by a rather drunken Anthony Tice, who was holding a gun.

"Looks like the gang's all here," the lawyer said.

(I V)

TRICKY TONY WANTED THEM to understand him. He was not a bad man, he said, waving the gun in a shaky hand. He just wanted to make sure that the government had to dot every "t" and cross every "i"—he was a little confused—before it took away anybody's liberty. But his clients, he said, were patient men. Very patient. And their patience was making him desperate. It was not his fault, he assured the frightened group, Julia sitting among them now like a full member. But he needed that diary, and he needed it now, tonight. His clients had let him know that he was out of time.

"Happy to help out," Trevor Land assured him, soft pink hands held high, as were everyone else's. "Man in trouble is a brother. Rather one's credo. Trouble is, not sure what diary you mean, kind of thing."

"Yes, you are," said Lurleen. For the first time, it occurred to Julia that maybe all the empty beer bottles were hers.

"We don't know where the diary is," said Whisted's aide. "We want it as much as you do."

"You're lying," the lawyer assured them happily. "If you didn't have the diary, *she* wouldn't be here." The gun waved vaguely toward Julia. "She's figured out all the clues, haven't you, Julia? And she doesn't want to get sued. So she's—"

A stone shattered the window behind Anthony Tice, who spun around and dropped into a crouch like a man who knows how to use a gun.

He called over the sill, "You think I'm scared of you, Bruce? My clients will eat you for lunch."

Silence from outside. Tice pulled out his cell phone, hit the push-to-talk button, and waited, but nothing happened. He glanced at the group, peeked over the sill, tried the button again. Nothing. He pressed a speed-dial button without any result.

He lifted the gun and fired three shots, very fast, through the window, the report quite loud in the narrow hallway.

"Bastards," he muttered, and tried the phone again. The Senator's aide chose that moment to stand up, but, even drunk, the lawyer was too fast for him, and had the gun centered on his chest in an instant. "Don't," he said.

Julia saw something, and leaped to her feet.

The gun immediately trained her way. "Sit," he began. But by the time he had finished the word "down," a small, lithe figure had hopped nimbly through the window, Tice was flat on the floor, and Jeremy Flew had Tricky Tony's gun in his hand.

CHAPTER 61

DEPARTURES

(1)

"That was interesting," said Julia. "Having an actual bodyguard. I never had one of those."

"Probably you never needed one."

"I'm sorry I maced you."

Mary Mallard, walking beside her through the grand lobby of the train station, managed a bitter laugh. "Not as sorry as I am." She hefted her overnight bag. "Are you sure, Julia? That he was only a bodyguard? Nothing else?"

Julia gave her a look. The two women slowed. Impatient passengers brushed past them. Sloshing water from boots and shoes made the floor dangerously slick. "What else did you have in mind?"

"Your boyfriend Bruce Vallely—"

"My *what*?"

"Sorry. Bruce. Your good buddy Bruce. He had this idea that maybe Jeremy Flew was up to no good. And, besides, why would Lemaster move a bodyguard into the house?" She held up a hand. "Wait. I know. You can't tell me, right?"

"Right."

"But I'm forbidden to write about him."

"Right."

"I think our deal gives you too much power."

"I think they're calling your train."

On the platform, Mary turned to her again. "Julia, listen to me. No, just listen. I think Tice is crazy. Just crazy. All right, he has clients.

They've been putting pressure on him—that would crack anybody up. But do you really think it's likely he killed Kellen? Think about it. His clients were buying what Kellen was selling. Why would Tice kill him?"

Julia shrugged.

"All right," Mary went on. "He could have run a car into Brady, or had somebody do it. He needed Brady's files to keep his clients happy. I'll grant that. He could have had the spyware planted on your computer. Maybe he bribed one of your assistants"—Julia had no trouble guessing which—"or maybe he broke in and did it himself. Just for trying to kill Brady, he faces years in prison. But, Julia, even if he did one, that doesn't mean he did the other, does it?"

Silence. A freezing winter rain peppered their faces.

"The police think they've got the killer. Tony isn't saying a word. But you don't believe it for a minute, do you? You think the killer's still out there. Somebody we haven't met yet."

But in her eyes were juicier possibilities. Your husband, said the dark, ducklike countenance. Your mysterious Mr. Flew. Maybe even you! Julia, staring back, had uneasy thoughts of her own. She had asked Jeremy why he had not intercepted Mary Mallard that night at the archives. He had pleaded other duties he was not at liberty to disclose. Maybe. But another possibility was that whatever world had spawned him was one through which Mary, with her network of intelligence sources, freely moved. Maybe they had met before, and owed each other favors.

And maybe paranoia was contagious.

Mary said, "I spoke to a colleague of yours. Suzanne de Broglie. Her parents and Gina's were best friends. Suzanne says her father told her that Merrill Joule made a deal with the devil. I think you know what he meant. But you won't tell me, will you?"

"You're going to miss your train."

"I'm not going to stop searching, Julia. Our deal doesn't cover facts I dig up for myself. This is too good a story now." Hugging her anyway. "Whether you help me or not, I'm going to find out who killed him."

"And write a nice book about it, right?"

"That's what I do." The writer hesitated. "I've also been talking to Tessa. She's told me a little bit about you and Kellen. Your history. And, Julia, I'm sorry—I never realized how hard this all must have—"

"I'm fine, Mary. Really." But she was wondering who else her old roommate had told, and marveling at how time ripens some friendships, yet can sour the best of them. "Tell Tessa I said hello."

Mary stepped onto the train. Julia stepped back. "Safe journey," she said.

"Julia, honey?"

"Hmmm?"

"If you do think the killer's still out there? If you do go searching?" She lifted her hands, waved imaginary pom-poms in the air. "Rah-rah."

(11)

VANESSA WAS WAITING IN THE ESCALADE. The two of them went to lunch at a place in the city they liked, what Lemaster called quiche-and-fern express.

Julia said, "Thank you, honey."

Eyebrows up, just like her father's.

"For what?"

"Well, number one, for being the wonderfully special person you are. Number two, for helping me out with Kellen's word games. I think you're actually better at it than he was. And, number three, for loaning me Smith's little device."

They grinned at each other. Julia had known all along that Tice could not be doing everything himself. Just keeping her in sight from time to time, while worrying about his own coming court case, would be too taxing. He must have had one or more accomplices. When Julia went to Vera's house to commend her on helping Kellen try to end the injustice done to DeShaun, and Tony burst in on them, thinking the solution to the mystery must be present, Jeremy Flew was there almost at once. Tony used his cell phone to call for help; or, rather, he tried to. To his dismay, he could not get a signal.

Smith had built a silencer, an electronic device that interfered with the ability of the cell phone to synchronize with the signal from the nearest repeater tower. As Vanessa had noted, silencers that worked by jamming were illegal in the United States; but the other types were less effective. Only by using a jammer could she be sure.

She had been certain that Jeremy, acting alone, could beat one man easily—and, in the event, he had beaten poor Tony Tice within an inch of his life, without ever seeming to work up a sweat.

I'm not going to ask where you got him from, Julia had told her husband.

I'm not going to tell you.

Although Lemaster denied absolutely that Jeremy was a bodyguard. He was just another aide, and if he happened to have some useful talents, so much the better. After Tice's arrest, Flew had submitted his resignation, effective immediately. Jeannie was devastated, and now insisted, as if in his memory, on being addressed only as "Jeans."

Now, sitting across the table from her elder daughter, Julia asked about how she liked her new psychiatrist, Sara Jacobstein, affiliated with the medical school and a family friend from their days living in the city, whose husband had been on the law faculty with Lemaster.

"I love her!" Vanessa burst out happily, and Julia believed every word. They went on to talk of school, and of That Casey, who was sniffing around her again, and of what she now thought about college choices—except that Vanessa said it would be better not to get her hopes up, but to wait and see who was going to let her in.

Sara Jacobstein was big on patience, said Vanessa.

And then, inevitably, they fought, the way that mothers and teen daughters do.

"I think it's time to tell me how Kellen got in the house," said Julia, softly.

"In the house?" Eyes wide, and far too innocent.

"To plant his little envelope underneath the piano or wherever he taped it. Were you there when he did it? Or did you just loan him your key?"

"No, and no."

Julia leaned forward. "Come on, honey. You can tell me."

Vanessa faded back in her chair, drew one knee up to her chest, began rocking slowly. "I am telling you. Why would I let him in the house, or give him my key? He was coming on to me. That's gross. I didn't want him near me." Her shudder of revulsion seemed utterly unfeigned. "I sure wouldn't want to be in an empty house with him."

"Then how did he get in?"

"I figured *you'd* know the answer to that," said Vanessa, and there was coldness between them once more.

(111)

TWO AFTERNOONS LATER, she met Bruce Vallely for coffee, quite openly, at the bagel shop in the middle of campus, the same place she used to meet Kellen. She waved unembarrassed to Alice Henner, a Sister Lady who taught in the history department, because somewhere during the past three months she had decided never to be embarrassed any more.

Bruce was the one who seemed uneasy.

Julia, after a few minutes of pleasantries, reminded him of his promise to stop following her. He assured her that his only interest had been keeping her safe from little Flew.

Neither one of them believed a word of it.

For a while, they sat and watched the weather go by, and Julia remembered how she used to teach her eighth-graders the difference between climate and weather by telling them to think of climate as everything available in the whole supermarket, and weather as whatever was in the shopping cart today. Her life right now was suffering from bad weather, she decided—but not necessarily bad climate.

Bruce said, "This has been fun."

"What has?"

"Getting to know you a little bit." He laughed. "Even if you are frustrating and bossy."

"You don't strike me as the kind of man who's easily bossed."

Then, seeing where this line of conversation was headed, they dropped it. Bruce asked a version of Mary Mallard's question: did Julia think Tice was the guilty party?

She answered with a question of her own: had he arranged for her to ask Rick Chrebet for the information she wanted?

"I've arranged it," he said, tone dubious. "I can't say whether he'll tell you what you want to know."

"He will."

"How can you be so sure?"

That crooked grin, so full of energy and confidence. "It's not widely known, Bruce, but I can be very charming when I put my mind to it."

Outside, Bruce watched Julia pull the Escalade into traffic for the drive back to the Landing. Gwen Turian emerged from a storefront.

"All done," she said.

CHAPTER 62

THE DUEL

(1)

THE FOURTH SATURDAY of February, Frank Carrington called to say he had a second Federal mirror with nautical motif, to replace the one she had broken, and Julia said she would come over that afternoon, because they had made their peace since the argument at his house. She arrived just before closing, because she had been ferrying Jeans between ballet and a birthday party, and also because she thought at closing they were marginally less likely to be interrupted. Parking, she glanced across the street, but Vera was away on vacation. Nobody could remember when she had last taken one. Lurleen Maddox, who had sold Kellen the cheap hand mirror, was just locking her door.

"Glad you could come," said Frank with his nervous twitter. "It'll just be a minute."

She stood by the counter, waiting, intrigued but not really surprised that Frank had never carried out his threat to leave town. He brought the package from the back room, unwrapped the mirror, and laid it on the glass for her to examine.

"It's cracked," she said. "Look at this."

"It's an easy repair."

They negotiated a steep discount anyway.

While Frank rewrapped the mirror, Julia said, "Can I ask you something?"

"Of course."

"I was talking to Rick Chrebet—the detective who worked on Kellen's murder?"

"Right. I hear they arrested that lawyer."

"Yes. But, Frank, I was wondering. During the investigation, Rick dropped by my office one day, and told me about some fudge I'd sent to Kellen on his birthday? And how Kellen sent the same fudge to my daughter?"

"Uh-huh." He turned back and took her credit card.

"Well, here's the funny part. I didn't send the fudge from Vera's shop. I sent it by campus mail. Nobody knew I sent that fudge but me and Kellen. And nobody knew Kellen sent fudge to my daughter but—Kellen. Even Vanessa didn't know who it was from."

He pulled out the receipt for her to sign. "Is that a fact?"

"Anyway, I asked Rick Chrebet how he happened to know about the fudge. Know what he told me?"

"Nope."

"He told me you told him about it."

Frank's pinched face came up, eyes squinty and moist. "Me? How would I know something like that? I only met the man that one time, when he came in the store to—"

"To buy the cheval. I know." Writing her name with a flourish. "All the same, it seems to me that Vera Brightwood couldn't have been Kellen's only helper in the Landing. Vera mostly knows rumors. He would have needed somebody who knew the facts, too."

"Makes sense."

"Say, an ex-cop who worked on the Gina Joule murder?"

Another nod. "Makes sense," he repeated, handing her the yellow copy of the receipt.

"That would be quite a formidable team. You and Vera and Boris Gibbs and Kellen, all trying to find that diary. To bring the real killer to justice. Clear DeShaun's memory."

"I suppose so."

"I think it's commendable."

A nervous grin. "I like minorities."

"I know that, Frank. But there's a couple of problems."

"Problems?"

Carefully, carefully, measuring the space to the door. He was on the other side of the counter. No way could he catch her if she bolted. "Number one, Four Mile Road isn't on any map or GPS. So whoever killed Kellen and left him there had to be local. That excludes Tony Tice or some phantom hit man. Number two, I now have most of the diary. I've read it, Frank. Arnie Huebner said he couldn't trust his own people, with all the money floating around. I think Arnie was afraid that one of his deputies might have been in on the cover-up. Maybe even took a bribe. That would give the deputy, if he's still alive, a pretty strong motive to kill Kellen Zant, even if he pretended to be helping. The deputy could maybe have asked Zant to pick him up on that Friday night, maybe to go out and look at a couple more clues. Kellen was a little worried. Maybe even suspicious. He tried to drop some materials off at the one house he knew in the Landing, but he couldn't quite work it. I think the deputy killed him, Frank. I think the deputy killed him, and took what evidence he had on him, and then, when he discovered the diary wasn't there, got a little panicky and maybe let slip to somebody who would care—me, for instance—that the diary was out there, waiting to be found."

Frank nodded. "You say you've got the diary."

"Uh-huh."

"Then let's go get it."

Her plan to run out the front had not counted on a gun.

At that moment the bell over the front door tinkled. They both looked up.

"Am I interrupting?" said Mary Mallard. Then she saw Frank's hand. "Oops."

(11)

THEY TOOK THE ESCALADE, so that Julia could drive and Frank could keep the gun pointed at her. He was still nervous, but he told little jokes along the way to ease the tension, none of them funny. Julia was kicking herself, and not only because she and Mary might both be dead in five minutes. She was the one who had assured Bruce Vallely that she could take care of herself. And she knew he was not secretly following. Out here on the back roads of the East Woods, traffic was so sparse that his car would have been visible a long way off.

Mary, sitting in the back seat with her wrists tied behind her, had started out on a tirade of don't-you-know-who-I-am, but had eventually subsided after Frank threatened to gag her. Julia was furious at her friend for showing up again, but Mary, on the scent of a story, was irrepressible.

"Where are we going?" Frank asked.

"You said you want the diary. I'm taking you to the diary."

Four Mile Road had several forks. No one who didn't know the area could possibly track them all. Frank knew the area. Bruce did not. Cell phones didn't work, and GPS systems had never heard of the place. Oh, this was a great plan.

"Where is it?" he asked.

"Well hidden."

"We better be there in five minutes."

"It won't take that long."

Mary said, "Don't give him the diary," although she could have no earthly idea whether Julia had it or not.

Frank said, "I told you to hush." He looked around, realized where they were. "Nobody lives out this way but Mitch Huebner." A light dawned. "You're saying Mitch Huebner had the diary all along?" He laughed. "That lying old bastard."

Julia did not answer. She took one fork, then another, driving deeper into the woods.

"What are you doing, Julia?"

Driving hard, she said nothing.

"Come on, Julia," said the former deputy. "This isn't the way to Huebner's. You missed the turn. Julia! What are you up to? Slow down!"

Instead, she sped up, the sturdy car leaping through drifts and rattling over ditches.

Carrington lifted the gun. "Enough is enough, Julia. I'm impressed. But, truly, there isn't any point. No more games."

"You're going to kill us anyway!"

"If you don't stop the car," he answered, calmly, "I think I probably will."

"Killing is a sin against God's gift of—"

"Stop the car, Julia."

"As you wish," said Julia, and, turning the wheel hard, floored the accelerator and slammed the Escalade into the biggest tree she could find.

(1 1 1)

THE WORLD WAS RENDERED DOWN to a crystalline simplicity.

Frank was stunned. Julia was stunned. In the back seat, Mary was moaning. She was not belted, but the side-impact air bag had likely saved her. Nevertheless, the angle of her leg suggested a pretty bad break. At the last minute, Julia had swerved the car into a skid, intentionally striking the tree with the side of the car rather than the front: but striking it hard all the same. The gas tank had ruptured, and the smell was intense. Mary's groans grew louder. Without speaking, Julia and Frank worked their their doors open and staggered around, trying to get their bearings. The former deputy, remarkably, had not lost the gun. Julia didn't care. She didn't want the gun. She wanted Mary Mallard's purse, and found it, on the floor of the car.

"All right, Julia," said Frank, breathing hard. "That was fun. Now playtime is over."

"Who's playing?"

"You didn't do that because you were scared. You didn't do it for fun. You did it because you know something, and you want me not to know it. What do you know?"

Julia said nothing. Stooping beside the car, she was scrounging in poor Mary's purse as gasoline puddled on the snow. She was remembering high-school science, and something Vanessa had told her after visiting Frank, about bows and arrows and armor.

"Stop faking, Julia. Get up from there. You're not seriously hurt." He saw what his captive was doing. "And get away from that purse!"

Julia stood up. She was holding Mary Mallard's cigarette lighter.

"My friend smokes too much," Julia said.

"What?"

"I want you to put down the gun, turn your back, walk into the woods in that direction"—pointing away from the trail—"and count to, oh, say, a thousand."

Frank shook his head, the gun steady. In his other hand was a flashlight he had pulled from some pocket—likely to prove useful now that winter dark was falling. His confidence was appalling.

"Do it," she said.

"Or else what?"

She flicked the lighter on. The dealer jumped back.

"Have you ever seen a gasoline explosion, Frank? How high the flames reach? How far away they sear? Have you ever seen that?"

"What are you going to do, Julia? Throw the lighter at me?"

"No." She held it higher, then pointed down at the gas that had run everywhere. "I'm just going to drop it."

Silence in the woods. At least between the two humans. Animals squiggled through the underbrush. Wind crackled the branches. The fuel continued to drip, drip, drip.

"You won't do it, Julia." But he did not sound so sure. "You want to burn up? You want your buddy in the car to burn up?"

"As opposed to what?"

"As opposed to telling me what you figured out just before you crashed the car, and telling me where the other clue is hidden in the woods, after which I vanish from your life." He smiled. "Or were you telling the truth about Mitch Huebner's house? Tell you what. Let's walk over there and see. If the diary's there, we call 911 for your buddy, and I'm gone. If it isn't, if you lied to me, well, that's another matter."

Julia shook her head. The hand holding the lighter shook wildly. In the distance she heard sirens. "No. You can't afford to let me live. I know too much."

"What do you know, Julia?"

"Too much," she said again. In the car, Mary was weeping from the enormous pain, and Julia knew that if this did not end fast she would break down in empathy.

"We're wasting time, Julia. Put the lighter away. Let's get the diary. Then we can get some help for your buddy."

"No." Stepping closer. "If you shoot me, it falls. You see that, don't you?"

He obviously saw that. He edged away.

"You're still too close."

"Julia, please. Think about it. You're not your husband. You don't see the world as simple, there's my way and the wrong way. The world is complex. You appreciate nuance. You're not some sort of comic-book—"

"I'm going to count to five, Frank."

The former deputy lowered his gun. He smiled. "Look, Julia. Even if you do know the truth—or think you do—if you go around talking about it, who's going to believe you? The world is too divided, Julia.

Nobody cares about 'real' truth. They only care about what helps their side, or hurts the other."

Another shake of the head. Julia refused to accept that the world was so cynical. There were people who believed in truth.

There had to be.

And Frank's worried eyes said he believed it, too.

"Go," she said softly. "Just go. Please. Get out of here."

"Julia—"

"I'm counting to five. Then I'm dropping the lighter."

"You wouldn't."

"One." Hand rock-steady again. The sirens said officialdom was minutes away. "Two."

"You won't do it. You won't kill your friend. You want to see your children grow up."

"I don't think you're going to let that happen. Three."

"Suicide is a sin," he tried, playing to Julia's other side.

"Four." Julia lifted the lighter high, astonished at the power throbbing in her arm. "Better get going, Frank."

"It's a sin against God's gift of life, and so is killing somebody else—"

"Five."

She opened her fingers.

Where Frank Carrington had stood was a patch of bare snow, and brush snapping.

Instinct made Julia grab for the lighter. Her natural clumsiness made her miss.

The lighter tumbled and spun and struck the puddling, running gasoline.

CHAPTER 63

THE SCIENCE QUIZ

(1)

To THE LAYMAN, and, sometimes, to the expert, scientific knowledge is little different from faith. It is believed in the absence of analysis, and often evidence—that is, we do not trouble to study the evidence ourselves but rely on our high priests to tell us what is so and what is not. And sometimes the high priests know no more than we do, yet their impassioned instruction forms the templates through which we view the world. If they are in error, so are we.

The lighter struck.

Flame, sudden and orange.

Spreading, leaping, hot.

Julia leaped back.

The fire flared, hissed, and then winked out, as Julia, former science teacher, had known it would. The high priests of Hollywood got it wrong every time, as every science teacher in America knew but dared not teach, because some fool would try. In the movies, cars crash and explode. Heroes shoot cars and they explode. Cars fall off cliffs and buildings and explode. In real life, gasoline hardly ever explodes unless confined, and, even then, only after the vapor has built up adequate pressure—but never if it builds up too much. Gasoline is difficult even to burn, especially in cold weather.

Frank Carrington had seen too many movies.

(1 1)

THE ONLY PROBLEM with Julia's theory was that it was incomplete. Because there was no explosion, Frank would soon be back. In a foul mood.

Julia decided not to wait around.

She hurried back to the car, but with the airbags deployed, it would not move. She leaned in close, took Mary's pulse, then kissed her on the cheek. The skin was slick with perspiration. The writer was no longer moaning. Julia did not know if she was conscious. She squeezed Mary's hand. There was an awful lot of blood.

"Listen to me," she said. "There are sirens. Somebody's on the way. They'll help you. Otherwise I'll send help. But I can't stay here."

An answering squeeze, the eyes briefly open.

"Go," Mary whispered.

"I'm sorry."

"This isn't going to make me more charming." She laughed. Then groaned. The eyes closed, and opened again. "Go!"

Julia went.

Frank Carrington had run off the way they came, so Julia decided to plunge deeper into the woods, and did, kicking and snarling through the high drifts, and higher underbrush. In two minutes she could no longer see the clearing. In three she was lost. Great. Just great. Exactly what she needed. For all she knew, Frank was circling back, and she would blunder into him trying to escape. She should have stayed where she was. Surely the sirens meant salvation.

Still she ran, and stumbled, and got up and ran some more, not sure where she was going, only sure she dared not stop, as snow trickled into her boots and into her collar and soon chilled her skin. She laughed or cried, both were the same; she had avoided death by gunshot and death by suicide, and here she was, asking to freeze to death.

She reached for her cell phone, but it was in the car.

The road. She saw the road. No, another road, the fork she had chosen not to take.

And heard the gunshots. A pair, echoing in the woods. A second later, animals and birds were in full flurrying flight. Julia reared around, deciding that she would follow the fauna, who would surely know, with their perfect sense of direction, which way was *away*.

It occurred to her that the gunshots had been aimed in her direction.

Frank Carrington knew where she was.

She ran. She ran from her past and toward her future, ran from the Clan and from the heart of whiteness and from the world of expectations and also the world of hope. She ran from her husband and toward her children, from her job and toward her dreams. She ran, feet seemingly skimming the surface, pelting through the forest, as the cold seeped into her bones now from all the snow that had sifted into her clothes, but still she ran and ran and ran.

And stumbled into a ditch.

She was still trying to squirm out of it when she heard, behind her, a crunch in the snow.

"Well, that was a lot of fun," said Frank Carrington, the gun firmly in his hand. "I always heard you were quite the science teacher."

CHAPTER 64

THE HEART OF WHITENESS

(1)

THE WORST PART WAS, as Frank happily pointed out, they were less than half a mile from Mitch Huebner's shack. Julia begged to get help for Mary first, but Frank told her it was her own fault for wrecking the car. When she tried to defy him, he promised that if she did anything right now but walk with him to the Huebner place, he would shoot her in the back and let her bleed to death, then go back to the car and do the same to Mary.

"That's inhuman," said Julia, unable to come up with a sharper line.

"Come on, haven't you read any history? It's very human."

So they marched through the snowdrifts on the forest floor, avoiding the roads, Frank now in charge, because he knew the way. The trek seemed interminable, and her feet were soon so cold she could not feel her toes, but it hardly mattered, because she was too scared to worry.

"That Zant was something, wasn't he?" said the killer. "Kept everybody guessing."

"He was something, all right," said Julia, but Frank was not in the mood for irony.

"He was a real character. A showman. I liked him."

"I noticed."

"I didn't have a choice, Julia. He'd worked it all out." He was suddenly furious, perhaps detecting her unexpressed objection. "I was a kid, Julia. I was twenty-four years old! You can't hold me responsible for what I did when I was twenty-four years old!"

"You were a little older when you shot Kellen," she said softly.

They marched, snowy trees slipping past, each hiding its dark, archival history in the night. Kellen, country boy that he was at heart, professed to love snow. He loved it for its randomness, he said. For the fact that it needed us to give it a reason. Nothing in Kellen's world had a purpose or meaning other than the one Kellen determined. All of creation was new and fresh to Kellen, because he did not care what any-one else thought. This quality of lightness, this casual rejection of con-vention, had once attracted her to him, because she saw it as rebellious and ideologically exciting, before admitting, after years as one among his companions, that Kellen was merely narcissistic; and, years later, that he was in some basic way evil.

"Here we are," said Frank Carrington, with the same mad joy.

They had arrived at the rutted path leading to the dooryard of the slanting, empty shack. Mitch Huebner, as she had expected, was off plowing.

"I haven't been here in years," said Frank. "Not since I had to deliver a check one day or the old bastard wasn't going to clear my driveway any more."

"I can see where paying for services rendered would be inconve-nient."

"You really don't know when to stop, do you?"

"Not lately, no."

Frank Carrington put a hand on her shoulder, slowing her down. His flashlight played over the yard, picking out the scattered cords of wood, the broken windows of the lightless shack, the doghouse . . . the doghouse. "What's that?"

"That's Goetz," said Julia, nervously.

"Dog?"

"Yes."

"Is that a chain?"

"Yes."

"I don't like the looks of him. Maybe I should shoot him."

She had recovered a bit of her hauteur. "He's a she."

They began to cross the dooryard. As they reached the steps, the dog growled. Frank glanced over his shoulder, let his light play over the chain, muttered to himself. "I should have shot him."

"Be my guest," said Julia.

"What, you have something against dogs?"

"Just that one. The last time I was here, she knocked me down."

She felt his cool scrutiny in the darkness, wondered if she had said too much. But Frank only laughed. "Tell you what. If you try anything, I'll feed you to her. How does that sound?"

Her shudder was genuine. "Let's go in."

They reached the door.

Julia carefully did not touch the knob. "It's usually unlocked," she said. "Do you want to go first?"

He said, "Do I look like six kinds of fool?"

"Are you sure?"

"Don't waste time, Julia. Open the door."

She nodded, and swallowed, and put her hand on the knob. Without her gloves it felt slimy, a live thing, twisting and squirming in her hand like a dying fish. She turned the knob, and pushed.

Silently, Goetz charged.

(11)

FRANK WAS VERY FAST. He turned and crouched and brought the gun across his wrist, sighting down the barrel, all of this in less than a second, and it would have been plenty of time, he would have blown the massive dog to bits, except that Julia spoiled his aim when she smashed the shovel against his ear: the same shovel that had so ineffectively shielded her on her first visit to Mr. Huebner's shack.

The former deputy was not wounded, but he was woozy, and both shots went high and outside, and he grabbed shakily for Julia's ankle, and was strong enough to bring her down, even as Goetz landed on his stomach. Another shot, and then he dropped the gun, and then he was shouting, and then he was screaming, it was awful, the worst sound she had heard in her life, and she covered her ears and crawled away, legs aching from the fall, wanting Frank Carrington to deserve what he got, wanting to be the force of earthly punishment and decision, wanting his flesh torn and mutilated by the dog for what he had done to Kellen, and to her family, and she prayed with all her might for the strength to will herself to hate her neighbor, to stand by indifferently, or even gleefully, as Goetz tore him to death.

And could not do it.

She could not let another mother's child die this way.

Up on her knees, she swung the shovel hard, and smacked it against Goetz . . .

. . . and it was not hard enough . . .

. . . Frank screaming and scrabbling and helpless . . .

. . . blood everywhere, spurting blackly in the moonlight . . .

. . . she had never seen a mess like this . . .

. . . she hit the dog again and again, like a woman in a fever, and maybe sometimes she slipped and hit Frank instead of the dog, and maybe sometimes she hit Frank on purpose, swinging and swinging, again and again . . .

Julia turned.

The dog was dead.

She sat down on the porch.

Finished. Done.

Or not quite: beneath the dog's battered carcass, something bloody and dangerous was beginning to stir.

Frank Carrington was alive, but when she looked into his eyes, something darkly inhuman gazed out at her. He spoke not a word but grinned shabbily, blood streaming from a badly torn face, and struggled upright, half dragging one foot at an impossible angle, and his dripping red hand again clutched, impossibly, the gun.

When, at last, his mouth opened, the empty, sepulchral sound was the voice of all her nightmares come to wakefulness.

"Julia," the thing said, gurgling and coughing. "Not nice."

He reached out with both hands, the gun shaking, but any hit would do, and Julia, her courage and strength running out, leaned back and waited for his demonic embrace.

Don't be a fool, Sis, said her brother, Jay, from deep inside.

She got up and ran.

(III)

FLEEING ON FOOT through snow leads only to the fool's freedom. Julia realizes this after she has run ten yards. In the crisp moonlight, her tracks stand out in bold black relief from the gleaming white crust of the field. Frank Carrington, if he can walk reasonably fast, will have no trouble following her trail. She has no time for analysis, so she trusts the instinct that has so often preserved her.

Instinct warns her to make for the trees, where the gloom will make her tracks more difficult for a man in a hurry to see. Her cell phone would be easiest, but it is plugged into its carrier in the Escalade. So the trees are her only hope.

Back behind her, she hears him shouting, and, perhaps, another car slowing, but she dares not tarry.

She has made it to the forest. One foot, other foot. She is flying past the trees, listening for pursuit, hearing only the night sounds of any woodland, the tiny animals skittering for safe haven, the breeze teasing the frozen branches. She runs. The forest is eerie and seems alive to her presence, aware and worried, uncertain whether she is friend or foe. But for her certainty that ghosts are all creations of obsessive adolescent girls, Julia would be certain that they are running beside her through the woods. When she turns to look, there is never anyone there, or anything: just a glimpse of moonlight prismed through the evergreens . . . and the distant glow of streetlamps.

Julia stumbles and realizes that she has hit a curb and is standing on tarmac. Suddenly, the trees are not woods at all, but just a thin green-belt dividing the houses looming before her from the road behind her. She has emerged into a subdivision she does not recognize, not really the high-end, cookie-cutter neo-Colonials built by white neo-Colonialists on a tract of land once owned by the native people.

Stop it, she tells herself, recognizing delirium.

In the eerie winter silence of the street, Julia decides that she can work out the racial irony of the moment later; for now, she is relieved to be out of the woods and near people, because people mean telephones, and telephones mean police. She races across the quiet road, barges up to the nearest door, a light-blue house with pretty curtains and a toddler's plastic three-wheeled bike half buried on the lawn.

Julia bangs frantically on the door, and then, realizing that a late-night knock might be misconstrued as scary, demurely rings the bell instead.

She waits, glancing warily over her shoulder.

Nothing.

She rings again, then bangs again, calls, tentatively, "Help!" and then the same again, louder.

After a moment, a worried pale face, glasses on and hair in curlers, peeks from behind the curtained windows next to the door. The frightened eyes are huge, magnified by the lenses. A child clings to the woman's leg.

Julia calls out, "Please, I need help," and then, when the face does not budge, she makes a hand motion to indicate a telephone and puts on the most charming smile she can manage with a walking corpse out there trying to kill her.

Eyes widening with alarm, the woman inside shakes her head. The child continues to cling to her leg. The woman makes a shooing gesture, then mouths the words so that there will be no mistake: *Get away!* she is silently screaming. She allows the curtain to fall closed, and Julia, backing, stunned, down the well-salted walk, sees her in the window of what she takes to be the family room, watching with desperate satisfaction the flight of the darksome intruder.

(I V)

REJECTED AT TWO MORE HOUSES, chased away by leaping dogs at a couple more, Julia has surrendered her dream that one of the homeowners, her fellow Landingers, might offer her shelter—warm fire, hot chocolate, maybe even a gun in the closet—while they await together the arrival of one of the town's few police cars. Instead, she has watched through windows as the residents turned fearfully away, as though she is a terrorist, or a disease carrier, or black. Julia hurries toward the entrance to the cul-de-sac, far now from the greenbelt. Perhaps she should throw a rock through somebody's window, on the theory that cowering owners might at least call the police for protection against a marauding Negro; but she has counted on sheltering in one of the homes, and does not dare risk hanging around waiting for the police to arrive, not with the Carrington-thing back there somewhere. Her cell phone is in the car. She is rushing, but not sure where she is rushing from, or to. Light snow has begun to fall, but, far more important, the wind has grown bitter. It is past ten, and this is getting ridiculous. She cannot possibly be so helpless in the middle of the town she has called home for the past six years. The moon, so bright half a lifetime ago, when she and Mary and Frank were riding along in the Escalade, has disappeared. She has no way to tell whether she is still being pursued, or, if she is, how close her pursuer might be. She only knows she dares not stop running.

For that is her posture now, a run, not a walk. Running through the crunchy snow in her high boots, certain at every step that she is about to take a spill. Leaving the U of houses, she realizes that the subdivision is larger than she thought, the identically cut wooden cookies going on for blocks. She must be in Cromwell Woods, the only development of this size in the town, named by some historically illiterate Anglophile builder for the regicidal Lord Protector who tyrannized England in the name of the people. She recalls that there are nearly a hundred homes in Cromwell Woods, priced to be affordable by the middling classes, and that the town fought like mad to keep them out.

Later, Julia. Think about it later. Concentrate.

You have to get out of here!

A subdivision in which you do not live is a bewildering and scary place, especially at night and on foot. You do not know the houses, or the trees, or the people. You do not know the names of the streets, which, in America, all sound the same: Belmont leads to Park leads to Colony. Never does a builder name a street Wojtyla or Montanez or Chen. It is as though all the nation, whatever its actual ethnicity, yearns to live in suburban Waspville. Julia Carlyle used to yearn, too; only, now that she does indeed live in Waspville, she finds it, in her moment of need, devoid of generosity, or, for that matter, of meaning.

She has stopped running, because she is so tired and because she does not know which way to go. Every street looks like every other street. Every time she thinks she has found the way out, she is curving back toward the trees, and Frank. Every time she thinks she has turned a new corner, she looks at the sign and finds she has been down this block before. Her legs tell her they have had enough. Her thighs tell her she is no longer entitled to give the orders in this body. It occurs to her that being shot by Frank Carrington is preferable to many other fates that could await her, like walking another step in this hateful weather. The snow is falling a good deal faster now, and Julia supposes that, were she to lie down right on the tiny lawn of the latest house to ignore her, she would shortly freeze to death. That might not be so bad.

She sits down.

Cold, but bearable. Over soon. At last.

Get up, Julia.

Go away. You don't exist. You're just a message from the other half of my brain. A throwback to atavistic times, when the left brain was not in charge. Julian Jaynes proved it, and I believe him. He was a psychologist, in case you don't know, and my brother and I were named after him.

Julian Jaynes was a very wise psychologist, but he was misled. Now, get up!

She gets up, if only to silence the voice. But now her pants are covered with snow that will shortly begin to melt from her body heat, soaking her legs.

"This better be important," she grumbles, but the voice does not answer.

She takes a tentative step. The chill wind batters her. Swaying on her feet, Julia looks around for Frank Carrington. Her weary body feels like a single congealed block of ice. She seems to be freezing from the inside out. She tries and fails to remember the word for this process. Her brain has had enough. She is so sick of this snow. And of this night. Maybe the best thing is to sit down once more and wait for the voice in her head to freeze to death.

Then she sees the worst thing she can imagine.

Frank has caught up with her. There he is, no more than a block behind, shuffling along the street. She tells her body to run, but her body is asleep. He drags toward her, foot twisting with every step. Nobody throws open a door. Nobody comes to her aid. She hears a shout, but it is only the angry wind.

She turns anyway, tries to run, manages only a step or two before she stumbles into the enfolding chill of the New England snow.

Frank Carrington looms over her, parka thick with blood, eyes ringed with joyful madness, gun hand flailing but pointing in her direction. Julia forces herself to her feet, determined not to go without a fight. She swings a strengthless hand at him, not sure whether she means to slap or punch. Either way, his head snaps backward very hard.

Then Bruce Vallely is holding her as she weeps, leading her away from the body lying broken-necked in the snow.

CHAPTER 65

THE ALL-PAY AUCTION

(1)

AND SO THE REPORTERS CAME TO TOWN, invading hordes rolling along leafy byways in search of the perfect interview, delighted at the opportunity to celebrate one of their own, who had selflessly placed her own physical body in harm's way in order to trap the sinister, Mafia-connected antiques dealer she had come to Harbor County to track down. They considered it rather unsporting of the heroine, Mary Mallard, to refuse all visitors to her private room at the medical center, the extra expense paid for by the university, in gratitude for her services—because the dealer in question, the late Frank Carrington, was responsible for the slaying of Professor Kellen Zant and the brief kidnaping of the wife of President Lemaster Carlyle, whom he evidently intended to hold for ransom.

The school's press office refused to make available for interviews either the wife in question or the director of campus safety, who had cracked the case, although some of the stories called him the chief of campus security, or some other variation. In the story's early days, accuracy was not a strong point; for that matter, it was not in the later days, either. Mary Mallard, the press reported, had suffered multiple fractures and internal injuries when, forced to drive the first spouse's black Escalade at gunpoint, she smartly and bravely smashed the car into a tree. Her refusal to be interviewed was seen, and envied, as an effort to keep the details private until the time arrived for the presumed book tour. The chief of university security—well, whatever his title was—had some sort of important supporting role, and the hordes clamored for his story, but, alas, he chose that moment to take his accumulated vacation, looking at properties in South Carolina for his coming retirement. As for the Carlyles, the invading horde besieged them for a few days. President Carlyle delivered a grateful and charming and witty statement for the cameras, but the invaders were otherwise kept at bay by a phalanx constituting the director of public information, a brace of something called Sister Ladies, plus the president's cousin, Astrid Venable, and his somber new assistant, Katie Chu, who practically moved into the house for the duration of the siege.

A few intrepid reporters, turned away at Lombard Hall, snuck into Kepler Quad to chase down Julia Carlyle, only to discover that she had resigned her position. A statement from the dean said how proud the school was to count Julia Carlyle among its graduates, and how delighted the school was for her service, marked by such integrity and courage. The statement made it sound like Julia had been to war. All inquiries were directed to Iris Feynman.

The refusal of the Carlyle family or Mary Mallard to discuss the tragic events of that chilly New England night (as one cable anchor put it) still left the hordes with plenty to plunder. In the village of Tyler's Landing, Vera Brightwood, proprietor of Cookie's and unofficial town historian and conscience, gave one interview after another. Many of Julia Carlyle's acquaintances from the city also had praises to sing, chief among them Tonya Montez, described by several print journalists as her close confidante, and by one evening news anchor as her cousin. Julia's dear, dear friend Tessa Kenner filled a lot of airtime, not all of it on her own show, and hinted that she knew a lot more than she was telling.

Meanwhile, the popularity of President Carlyle on campus was soaring. None of the policies that had caused faculty discontent had changed, but the, ah, well, the context was different. No longer was he the tyrannical monster established in office by the right-wing alums. Well, all right, he was. But he had ascended to a new status, that most beloved of campus figures, the victim—an *actual victim*, an African American whose family had been endangered by a racist white man. True, the Carlyle family was modeled along lines both sexist and heteronormative, and therefore not a desirable example for exaltation, but the victimhood was perfect. (Even those among the oppressed peoples who try to live by the culture's illegitimate norms are crushed in the end by the forces of reaction!) And so, despite the resistance of a few diehards, they allowed him to merge gender studies and women's studies. They allowed him to toughen rather than weaken the school's anti-drug policies. By the spring, however, when he proposed appointment of a committee to consider the desirability of returning ROTC to campus, the old battle lines would be redrawn: being a victim was one thing, but allowing the mildest trespass upon the sacred groves of academe by the most dangerous organization in the world was another matter.

None of the stories mentioned the President of the United States, a New England Senator who hoped to replace him, or an obscure Harlem men's club fallen on hard times.

And then there was the quieter drama, well outside the scrutiny of the press, discreet emissaries from people who knew people who were connected to other people, slipping into town to confer, ever so quietly, with the Carlyles, making sure all was well, asking if they needed anything, promising assistance with whatever might arise, and inquiring, quietly, whether, by the way, any rumors of allegations had come quietly to light over the past few weeks that might tend to cast this candidate or that one in a—

No, no, and, no, said the Carlyles. We aren't political. But if anything turns up, you'll be the first to know.

(11)

MEANWHILE, Vanessa Carlyle's new therapist announced that she would not be trying to "cure" the teenager of being a teenager. I'm somebody for her to talk to, said Dr. Jacobstein. At this point in our relationship, I'm not going to pretend to be anything else.

Then who's going to set limits on her? asked Julia, very surprised.

Actually, that's the job of her parents, said Sara.

And what about the trauma underlying her behavior?

It's over, said Sara. Julia was stunned. The psychiatrist's eyes were kind, but when she spoke she sounded like Lemaster. I would tell you if I could, she said. The rules don't allow it. All I can say is that the trauma was based on an error in perception. Something Vanessa thought was true. Now she knows it wasn't.

Julia asked if that meant her daughter was fine.

No, she isn't fine. She has plenty of issues to deal with. But she's tough. She's going to deal with them.

And Gina? Is she coming back?

A distant smile. We'll just have to wait and see, won't we?

Back home, Julia watched her daughter closely. Vanessa kept reading about wars and listening to her dirges, and, in the wee hours, still danced with her mother. When Julia asked if it was true that she was feeling better, her daughter hugged her and said, Thanks to you. Julia asked what that meant. Vanessa, eyes glowing, assured her mother that she would figure it out.

Meanwhile Jeannie, now known as Jeans, continued her search for perfection, but after a few days of puzzled pining, asked first her mother, then her father, why Mr. Flew no longer dropped by the house. He's moved away, they reminded her. Moved away *where*? she demanded, stamping a perfect foot, because she wanted to write him; and because she could not bear the thought that he had departed without saying goodbye. Julia did not know the answer, and Lemaster refused to say. Jeannie—Jeans—had always been able to charm her father, who at last agreed, reluctantly, to forward a letter if she wrote one. She wrote it, he forwarded it, and three weeks later she had an actual answer, addressed to her personally, posted from one of the more turbulent former Soviet republics.

He missed them all, wrote Jeremy Flew, but duty called.

As for the other children, the boys, Aaron wanted to come home, to rally round the family in the crisis, but his parents decided he should stay in school, and the headmaster assured them that Phillips Exeter Academy could protect him from the media: they had managed the miracle for others far more sought after. Preston did not manage to call, and when Julia finally reached him, he told her that he was on his way to Australia, where he would be spending most of the next year at one of the world's great observatories, and, oh, yes, one of the other grad students had told him something about how his family was in the news, but he had paid little attention, because they always were.

Will we see you before you go?

I'm leaving tomorrow, said Preston, but he always was.

Then, in the middle of March, after the reporters departed, the director of campus safety returned from his vacation, and Julia knew it was time for the next act.

CHAPTER 66

. . . THEN BEGGARS WOULD RIDE

"So, where do you go from here?" asked Julia Carlyle. "What's next for the great Bruce Vallely?"

He blushed and shrugged and dropped his strong, gentle eyes. The weather had once more turned bright and fair, as sometimes happened in a New England winter before the thick gray walls closed in again. They were seated where the whole thing had started, the tavern on Route 48. The same disinterested crowd, the same uninteresting food, the same garbled hum of meaningless conversation, the same sputtering snow, as if the weather could not make up its mind.

When Bruce said nothing, but lingered over his coffee, Julia said, "Are you really retiring? Is that what people do when they run out of space on the shelves for their medals?"

"I don't think they give medals for . . . what I did."

"They should," she said, and meant it.

"I broke a man's neck, Julia, and another man"—he searched for the words—"another man I treated the way God never meant his creatures to treat each other."

The reporter, Julia supposed—or whatever he really was—the man who accosted her while she pumped gas in Langford. She knew, now, that Bruce had worked out a deal of some kind with Tony Tice's clients, and she had even supplied the envelope from Mona, with contents, to enable him to pay them off. But she had chosen not to pry too deeply.

"Well I'm grateful." A playful frown. "Even though I told you not to follow me. How did you find me?"

"A transmitter in your car." He neglected to mention that Turian, his deputy, was the one who had planted it, while Julia and Bruce sat in the bagel shop. He had recommended Gwen as his successor, but Lombard Hall was moving at its usual glacial pace. "I'm pretty sure I broke the law," he added.

For a moment they were joined in silence, as dishes clanked and doors banged and the easy hum of human communication rose and washed over them. It seemed to Julia, from what she had seen and what Mary had told her, that Bruce rarely let the law get in his way. A few months ago Julia would have said her husband was just the opposite.

Bruce said, "So—how is Vanessa doing?"

"Sara says she'll be fine. It'll take some work, but she'll be fine."

"It's a resilient age."

"Oh, Bruce, Grace was right about you." Teasing, but meaning it. On her plate, shifting patterns of morning sunlight played their distracting game of tag. "You're really hopeless when it comes to kids, aren't you? No, Bruce, the late teens are not a resilient age. They're an age of impressionability, and an age when every poor grade or pimple or romance gone bad means the universe is about to collapse on itself. You know what Lemaster says? That the West invented adolescence when we had enough wealth that we didn't need teens in the workforce, but we invented it badly. We're like on model 1.2 or something. That's what Lemmie says," Julia repeated, her husband's name strangely awkward on her lips. She hurried on. "The truth is, Bruce, she's going through a terrible time. Vanessa is. She doesn't cry or have nightmares, that's not who she is. She dances to funeral dirges. She studies war. She laughs, she seems ebullient. But on the inside she's suffering. I know she is. I don't blame her. I don't know how I would have survived what she's been through."

"I see your point," he said in that slow, absorbing manner. The eyes refused to release her, and her frantic command to her own to drop was ignored. She felt itchy and uncertain. "Maybe she needs a change of scene."

"I thought I might take her to France for a while after graduation," she gabbled desperately. "She and Mona get along so—"

"That's not what I meant."

"I know it isn't, Bruce." The first thread of panic, weaving itself through her aplomb. "It's what I meant, though. Right now, it's the only change I can offer her."

She remembered another Lemasterism. "The world is the way it is. It's not some other way, it's this way. You know what my Granny Vee used to say? If wishes were horses, then beggars would ride. But they're not. Wishes aren't real. They're not related to . . . to . . ." She hesitated, confused by the brave pain in his eyes, and began to founder, to lose her place in a stream that was, just seconds ago, flowing smoothly in the right direction. "We're real people, Bruce. There are people who live inside the mirror, doing what they want, as if their lives are mere reflections, not real at all. And there are other people who live on this side of the mirror, who have to ignore those reflections, no matter how much they might glitter. That's being an adult, Bruce."

Julia waited. It was Bruce's turn now. She wanted him to declare his feelings so she could tell him that she had come to agree with Lemaster that duty mattered most. Wanted him to talk about how wonderful life could be so that she could talk about how she had already lived the life of one who is unreliable, and half killed herself doing it. Wanted him to talk about the future so she could talk about the future she planned with the husband who had saved her when she needed him, and who needed her now.

Bruce spoke gently. "All I meant was, maybe the move to Elm Harbor will be good for her." Julia stared. He still loved his Grace. She felt silly, and young, and romantic.

Bruce Vallely obviously did not.

"Actually," he said, "I came to talk about something else."

"About what?"

"About the night Kellen Zant died."

Julia braced herself, wondering what shocks were left. "Frank killed him. Frank Carrington. He didn't want the diary to come out. Then he decided he needed it to protect himself . . ."

She trailed off.

Bruce nodded. "Yes, I do think Frank killed him. And I think you have correctly stated his motive. But there is one piece of evidence that does not fit the pattern, and I think I need you to tell me what I should do about it." He pulled out the envelope Trevor Land had given him. "University telephone records," he explained, drawing a page from within. "To a particular cell number the night Zant was killed."

"I don't want to see this."

"I don't want to show it to you."

But he did anyway. The phone number was Lemaster's. A call was circled on the night in question, about an hour before they left the dinner in Lombard Hall.

Anthony Tice had called her husband.

Out on the street they awkwardly hugged. Both knew the meeting would be their last.

"May I ask one question?" she said.

"Sure."

She hefted the envelope. "Why didn't you give this to the police?"

He smiled that tired smile. "The investigation," he said, "is closed."

Well, that was true enough. Julia felt the New England winter slipping up from the ground and down from the sky, grabbing hold of her limbs with its familiar chilly tendrils, determined to restrain her from any foolishness. And it dawned on her, first faintly, then with growing forceful certainty, that she would never live anywhere else; that she was as firmly married to New England as she was to Lemaster; that her roots ran too deep in the soil, past the frosty surface and down into the soft, brown warmth that was turned up with spring plantings.

She said, or maybe blurted, "I'll miss you."

That warming smile teased the corners of his lips, he dipped his heavy head, and then, good soldier that he had always tried to be, without a further word of objection or farewell, Bruce Vallely followed his orders and marched off into his overdue retirement.

CHAPTER 67

THE ILLUSIVE CALM

(1)

JUNE. Everything calm again, everything except Julia, who had simmered and percolated through three months of pretending that life was
once more perfection. The renovations to the old mansion on Town
Street, just where Hobby Road begins, had been completed, and the
results, the architectural critics agreed, were breathtaking: Norm
Wyatt's finest work, the sublime and subtle merger of traditional and
modern, the hidden technological marvels, the attention to the smallest
curlicue of carpenter's Gothic on the rebuilt veranda in the back, and
the sweeping lines that made the house seem to rise from the landscape,
proclaiming itself to matter, even if, in truth, it was no larger than any
of the other aging great houses along this stretch of campus. Lemaster
had moved almost full-time into the house in April, excepting only
weekends and the odd weeknight, and the joke among the Sister
Ladies, that the perfect Carlyles were testing what life would be like if
they went their separate ways, was no more than half funny, because no
more than half false.

By that time, Mary Mallard had moved to a rehabilitation center in
Maine, nearer her mother, but Julia spent the spring driving up at least
once a week to visit, for each was trying still to inch toward the truth.
On one of these visits, Mary pointed out that Kellen must have had a
source inside the conspiracy in order to begin his investigations in the
first place; and Julia, although she had carefully screened from her partner the knowledge that the "conspiracy" had been undertaken by a
bankrupt Harlem men's club, suspected that Mary knew anyway. And
then, one bright spring afternoon as they walked the grounds, Mary

showed Julia a printout from the Internet Anagram Server. One was circled. Julia stopped and grew ashen.

"I'm sorry," said Mary.

"I don't believe it."

"I'm not sure that's the issue."

Mary was, in this instance, correct, but her correctness tautened their relationship, and the fresh tension turned out to be more than their partnership could bear.

So they became distant correspondents instead of the close friends they had perhaps hoped to be.

As soon as school ended, Julia and the children packed up the grand house on Hunter's Meadow and left the heart of whiteness to return to the city. Beth Stonington assured them, and everyone else who would listen, but mostly her competitors, that the selling price would be well north of two million, possibly close to three, given what was going on with property in the Landing these days. Why anyone would give up this idyllic existence to raise children in a dying city like Elm Harbor, neither Beth nor her friends and cronies could guess.

"It's Lemaster's job, honey, not yours," Beth had explained to Julia, but only after she was persuaded that under no circumstances would her client change her mind; for there was no point in queering the sale for the sake of idle curiosity.

"It's my job, too," Julia assured her solemnly, but Beth told everybody that the gray eyes were lidded and puffy, as if she had spent a lot of time weeping. "Probably just allergies," said the feistier among them, meaning it as a joke, although, as it happened, it was true.

So the family settled in. In the fall, Aaron would be returning to Exeter, where he was thriving. Perfect Jeans had been accepted into the fourth grade at Ogden, the principal feeder for Hilltop, the most exclusive private high school in town, and so, in the way such things seem to be decided these days, the brightness of her future was assured.

As to Vanessa, she had been admitted to some colleges, turned down at others, and left her deposit at one of the Seven Sisters, much to the relief of her parents. Then, without quite asking for permission, or even informing her mother and father until the deed was done, she arranged to defer admission, and announced that, upon turning eighteen in October, she was going to join Smith for a tour of the country, by car.

"You're not allowed to drive," said Lemaster.

"Excuse me, Daddy, but that won't really be your call," she answered with a firm politeness learned at her father's feet, and proceeded to quote at length a relevant passage from George Orwell on the Spanish Civil War, trying to prove that meaning is dynamic, categories changing as the facts do their daily dance: "The soldier who was running away wasn't a fascist, so Orwell couldn't shoot him. And the girl who's eighteen isn't a child, so you can't tell her what to do."

"I'm not talking about the law," he said testily.

"I am. At eighteen I'll reach my majority. I'm not a danger to myself or others. I can go where I want, do what I want, right? You guys raised me. Now you'll just have to trust that you raised me right."

"You're still my child—" Lemaster began.

"But not in the hierarchical sense. I have to honor you, the Bible says. But not obey. Not once I'm grown." She raised her hands, palms outward. "I'm not defying you, Daddy. I'm doing what I have to do. The same way you did when you decided to go to divinity school instead of biz school like your parents wanted."

"What does Dr. Jacobstein say?"

"To be sure and take my cell phone."

Lemaster, to his wife's surprise, retreated from abstract rules to the world of the practical: "Even if we do let you go, Smith doesn't strike me as the most reliable companion."

"Then we're a perfect match, because I'm not terribly reliable either."

She added that if they liked L.A. they might settle down there and look for work, in which case the deferment might be . . . extended.

"They won't wait forever," said her father, quite cross, and quite defenseless.

"They will for the right person. That's what you always tell me."

"Vanessa—"

"It's time to grow up," she said, and left, not specifying who among them needed the growth.

Later, Julia sat on Vanessa's bed as the teen lay on her stomach programming her portable DVD player. Rainbow Coalition perched contentedly on the windowsill, licking her paws. "You don't dance any more."

"I'm bored with dirges." She pointed. "I still have my war books, though. They're making the trip. So don't worry, Moms. I promise not to get completely cured without checking with you first." Before Julia could come up with a bright answer, Vanessa kissed her. "I'm joking. But seriously. Some of the books will also be going." She glanced at the cat. "I wish RC could go."

"Is Gina going, too?" Julia asked, timidly. As her daughter seemed disinclined to answer, she tried again: "Or was the trip her idea in the first place?"

Daughter turned to look at mother, face obscured by the swaying braids, but Julia was fairly certain she saw a smile. Then Vanessa returned to her work.

(11)

A FEW AFTERNOONS LATER, having postponed as long as she decently could, Julia drove out to the Landing. She took a quick look at the house, to be sure the grass was being watered and cut and the real-estate agents and clients traipsing through had not yet ruined anything, then drove down to Main Street. She parked her new Escalade near the Town Green, where Vanessa had burned her father's car, waved hello to a handful of surprised acquaintances, and crossed the street. At Cookie's, Vera Brightwood professed herself delighted to see her and began making up an order of cappuccino truffles without waiting to hear exactly what Julia wanted, and Julia let her measure and wrap and cheat the scales, while going on and on about what the university people, present company excepted, were doing to the town.

Julia said, "I wanted to talk about what happened that night at your house."

"What night was that?"

"The night they arrested Tice. That lawyer."

Vera smiled her greedy porcelain smile. She had been angry that night, after Julia accused her of being Kellen's "Black Lady," the secret source who had managed his search for the diary. But no source would have been better. Vera knew the byways of the town's history better than anybody. "I sued him," said Vera. "Did you hear about that? For what he did that night. I'm going to take him to the cleaners."

"I think he'll be in prison for a while first."

"Probably," Vera agreed.

"I just had a question."

"Mmmm-hmmm." Adding, also unasked, some Jelly Bellys for the jar on Lemaster's desk at Lombard Hall.

"How did Tony Tice know I'd be at your house that night? I'm sure he didn't follow me. The man who was, ah, protecting me would have seen to that. And Tice didn't live in the Landing. So how did he happen to show up?"

"I wouldn't know, dear."

"I was thinking you might. I was thinking that maybe the whole group of you had set out to avenge Gina. People everybody has down as—excuse me—shameless right-wingers, but you still didn't like that innocent black boy suffering for what some rich white frat boy did. I think everyone in your group encouraged Kellen Zant, once you found out what he was working on. Maybe some people helped him indirectly, but everybody helped. Then I think he double-crossed you. Instead of going after justice, he went after money."

"I have some wonderful cranberry-chocolate fudge."

"I don't think you're violent people. I think you were shocked when Kellen got shot. Shocked and scared. I think Frank Carrington was a member of your group, and I bet he acted as shocked as anybody." Julia pulled out the cash for her purchase, but Vera said it was on the house. "The night Kellen died, Frank had to know that he was about to close a deal to sell the diary. Well, how else could he have known except from somebody in your group? Senator Whisted's aide, right? Grew up in the Landing, wanted to get revenge for Gina the same way the rest of you did, and maybe heard from Astrid what was up, and told the rest of you, including Frank."

"We didn't want to hurt anybody," said Vera after a long think. "Gina was a good girl, Julia. Not like the girls who run around today. A good girl. Whoever did it deserves what he gets." She eyed her best customer, who was probably making her last visit to the shop. Her uneasy half-smile reminded Julia of Latisha, her former assistant, who had finally gained protected status under the collective bargaining agreement after Minnie Foxon, without explanation, requested a transfer to another department. "What Kellen was going to do to him. What you're going to do to him. Maybe what your husband is going to do to him." She turned away, began to measure out peanut brittle. "But you're wrong, Julia. We didn't know about the diary. Who would have told us? Yes, I suppose you're right, Mal Whisted's man would have known. Maybe he told Frank. He certainly didn't tell the rest of us."

Julia popped a couple of Jelly Bellys into her mouth. In the mirror behind the counter, a rose-tinted Julia pondered with her. What exactly was Senator Whisted's connection to the group? Helping them out or monitoring their progress? She had thought she had the sequence right: Frank kills Kellen to keep the diary secret, then kills Boris Gibbs when, after stealing the Vanessa File, Boris gets too close to duplicating Kellen's research. The story was perfectly consistent. But was it true? she asked her reflection, as Vera sliced and wrapped. Why wouldn't Frank have preferred to jolly Kellen along—or, if not Kellen, at least Boris—and then, when the diary came out of hiding, swipe it and destroy it?

The aide, Julia decided. Only Whisted's aide would have known that Kellen had the diary. If he did tell Frank, it would only have been in the hope that the former deputy would act—but how could the aide have known that Frank was implicated? Was it possible that the phone conversation overheard by Tony Tice the night Kellen died might have been not with Frank Carrington, but with an aide to a United States Senator, perhaps threatening a double cross that made Kellen rush to meet him—

But behind the mirror's surface was only a silvery reflection, and beyond that nobody could see.

Meanwhile, behind the shining counter, Vera Brightwood had perked up. "You know, Julia, I was glad when you built the house on Hunter's Meadow Road, and I hated it when people tried to stop you, because I've always been for that open housing thing—"

Julia said she had to go to work.

"The papers say you quit your job."

"I have a new one."

"Doing what?" said Vera, hungry for fresh gossip to pass on.

"Teaching science," said Julia.

Back in the Escalade, she turned her show tunes up high and drove toward the city, and the Nest, and Miss Terry's school.

CHAPTER 68

WINNER'S CURSE

(1)

ON SATURDAY THERE WAS RAIN. Julia returned to Kepler Quadrangle, but not to say goodbye. She had already endured the going-
away party, and had intentionally chosen the weekend for this
expedition because her former colleagues were unlikely to be around.
They were not bad people, but they were no longer her people. They
were Lemaster's people. Part of his campus. His city. His world. She
had escaped to the sanctuary of the divinity school after the humiliating
end of her tenure in the public schools, but sanctuaries have a way of
becoming prisons, and she had escaped again.

She was back for a reason.

She did not need a parking space because the div school was a block
from the presidential mansion, and she did not need a key because a
student held the door open. On the last night of his life, evading Tony
Tice and scurrying off to Kepler, Kellen Zant had probably gained
entrance the same way. He had vanished for almost two hours, then
reappeared. But what would he have been doing inside the div school at
that hour? The archives would have been locked. Classrooms, offices,
everything would have been inaccessible.

Everything except for the chapel, open all night.

BCP 83.

She had misunderstood Kellen's carving on Sugar Hill after all,
assuming that he was trying to tell her the name of the book in which
he had hidden the third clue. But the Book of Common Prayer would
not, without more, draw her back to her God, as Kellen had promised

to do. The answer was not in the pages. But the pages still pointed to the answer.

Julia entered the chapel through the heavy double doors to Kepler's main hall and stood in the nave aisle, letting her eyes grow accustomed to the gloom, because the storm had darkened the windows, clerestory and stained glass alike. In the corner, a young woman was praying and, intermittently, sobbing, but the onetime dean of students did not go to her aid because interrupting a prayer was bad form. The chapel was otherwise empty.

Julia walked toward the altar. On page 83 of the 1928 version of the Book of Common Prayer—the only one Lemaster allowed in the house—the priest has finished consecrating the bread and wine and is busily delivering it to the people. On the night he died, Kellen must have made this very walk. He must have had a spot all picked out, for emergency use. Maybe all those visits to the chapel had not after all been for the purpose of annoying her.

Not for that sole purpose, anyway.

Julia mounted the choir steps. The main altar, stout New England pine, stood directly before her, but she gave it only the most cursory examination. Kellen, to the last, had his point to make. The old high altar of brick and darker wood with its carved words from John's Gospel was built into the far wall, and used for almost no purpose, except, in classes on liturgy, to show future pastors what not to do. It was a relic of the days when priests in all the orthodox traditions turned their backs on the congregation when speaking *to* God, facing the assembly only when speaking *for* God.

Kellen must have found the symbolism impossible to resist. He was no God man, but of course his rival was.

Speaking to God.

With her back to the congregation, Julia stood in the middle of the altar, before the shining gold chamber where, once upon a time, the consecrated host had been reserved for future use. The chamber was locked. She felt along the cloth laid across the top—she no longer remembered what it was called—and came up empty. She glanced behind her before acting too foolish. The weeping student had departed, and Julia had the sanctuary—that word again!—to herself. She took a step back, measured by eye where precisely the priest would be standing as he moved from the bread to the wine, using her years of attendance at Saint Matthias, where Father Freed used only the high altar, as her guide. She stood a little bit to the right of center, then got down on her knees and reached up beneath the altar.

And pulled out a thick envelope.

She opened it, and went pale.

Not possible. Absurd. What she was looking at could not have been hidden beneath the altar because Kellen had it with him when he died. Time did not twist around. The dead did not walk. Such wondrous magic could not exist. Even here in the chapel of the divinity school, where generations of students and faculty had knelt in prayer to the Impossible, Julia Carlyle would not accept a supernatural explanation.

She was holding Kellen Zant's missing cell phone.

(11)

JULIA SAT IN THE ESCALADE, listening to her show tunes, watching the rain sluice across her windshield. She was out of breath and supposed she must have been running in confused terror, but at the moment she was a little vague on the details. She had hurried back to the presidential mansion and climbed into her car, and was heading toward a downtown office tower where her husband was addressing a coalition of local civic organizations. She parked the car, strode across the lobby in her jeans, and refused to stop when the doorman queried her, because she was no longer a stopper. On the top floor, ignoring the earnest pleas of the headwaiter, she walked through the restaurant to the large private dining room in the corner. Lemaster's unsmiling assistant, Katie Chu, assured her that the president had almost finished his remarks, but Julia slipped past. She stood in the back of the room, unsmiling herself. Several heads turned. She stood dripping on the hardwood floor, hair a mess, not worrying whether the guests might be murmuring that the first lady of the university was as mad as her daughter. Lemaster was at the lectern. His eyes passed over her but did not linger. He fired off a series of jokes, everyone laughed, and then he was pumping everybody's hand as he made his way past the tables. He kissed his wife's chilly lips, slipped an unwanted arm around her waist, and led her out of the room as Katie Chu stayed behind to make his excuses.

They descended in silence until Julia, knowing she could never win a battle of patience with her husband, grew tired of her own anger. She pressed her head against his shoulder. He stroked her sopping hair. "I found the phone," she said.

"I assumed you would."

"You knew? About BCP 83?"

"Cameron told me."

"Does he still think he can blackmail—whoever?"

Lemaster put a finger beneath her chin and tilted her face toward his. "I think he understands now."

"Because only the Empyreals get to do that," she suggested, but they had reached the lobby, and a couple of late arrivals who had missed the speech nevertheless wanted to shake the hand of the diminutive black scholar who was the most powerful man in the county. Her husband, like royalty, accepted the homage of commoners as his due. Julia wondered if he was also the most powerful man in the country. Or one of them. For a crazy moment she was bursting with pride, less for her husband than for her people, and, especially, for an unknown Harlem social club: the Caucasians, Granny Vee used to say, have no idea what we are capable of doing.

Together they walked out into the storm. Lemaster had ridden over with Katie Chu, so he and his wife drove home together in the Escalade. "What did Kellen really hide?" Julia asked, eyes closed as she leaned back in the seat, her husband's favorite music thumping hard from the speakers. "In the chapel. Before you moved it. What was there?"

"Nothing important," he said after a moment's consultation with that little referee in his head. "Kellen thought he had the final proof, but he was wrong."

"What was it, Lemmie?"

"What was what?"

"The proof. The surplus. What did he hide in the chapel?"

This time the wait was longer. Julia sat up. She supposed he was not going to answer. Outside the rain was falling harder and the wind was tossing over trash bins and lawn sculptures: summer's version of the winter storm that started them down this terrible road. She wondered how long Lemaster had been outguessing her, and how he made prevarication seem so natural and right.

"A train ticket," he said.

"I'm sorry?"

"That's what Kellen hid beneath the altar. A train ticket, one way, Elm Harbor to Boston, dated February 18, 1973."

Julia nibbled on her lip. "A way to prove which one of the frat boys went to Dennison for advice. The one who killed Gina."

"I imagine that Kellen thought so."

She asked the next question as casually as she could. "Whose name was on it?"

They were home. He pulled the Escalade neatly into the two-car garage, quite a bit smaller than what they had enjoyed out in the Landing, but they had junked the Volvo.

"What difference does it make?" he said at last.

"I just thought you might want to be sure you're blackmailing the right man."

"They were all the right men," said Lemaster, and climbed out of the car. Julia took several minutes to compose herself, and then, unmeekly, followed.

(I I I)

THEY SAT UPSTAIRS in Lemaster's new study, which occupied most of the third floor, Kellen's phone on the desk between them. Julia did not ask how her husband had come into possession of it. She did not want to know how deeply the tentacles of his unknown Harlem social club curled into the life of Harbor County, or the world beyond. She waited for him to tell her the story. She had no doubt that he would: otherwise he would never have left the cell phone in the chapel for her to find.

"I made a mistake," said Lemaster. He sipped the wine she had brought upstairs. "A natural one, I suppose, given the circumstances, but still a mistake. One mistake led to others, and, well, here we are."

Julia said nothing. Outside the window, as the storm abated, she could see the Gothic towers of the university farther up the hill. Her husband's campus.

"That Casey is a runt," he continued, toying with the sleek silvery phone, spinning it this way and that. "The backbone of an eel. That much was clear from the start. Sure, he might play the rebel poet to impress our daughter, he might pretend to be a nonconformist, but he isn't like Smith. He isn't like Vanessa. He would never break the rules, not in the middle of college admission season. He's too ambitious, Jules. All right, his mother is dean of the law school, but I'm president of the university. He wouldn't have wanted to get on my bad side. He knew perfectly well Vanessa wasn't allowed in his car. It wouldn't matter how she begged or what she promised. He would have said no. There is no way That Casey gave her a ride home from the movies the night Kellen was shot."

Julia's eyes snapped back from the window.

Lemaster nodded. "Remember when Casey told you Vanessa used to always run away when they went out together? I think he was trying to send you a message. You think so, too, don't you, Jules?" He did not wait for her agreement. "He was telling you that she ran away the night Kellen died. He didn't want to follow through on the implications, so he dumped it in your lap, and you decided—wisely—not to look any further. But we both know that's what happened. And we both know how she got home that night, don't we?"

She dropped her gaze to her lap. Her hands were trembling, just the way her daughter's did. She covered one with the other but could not make the trembling stop. A buzzing deep in her brain became a ringing all through her body.

Lemaster, meanwhile, had flipped open the cell phone. He turned it on, waited for the software to boot, then clicked twice, displaying the list of recent calls. He slid it in her direction and she leaned over, not wanting to touch it with her trembling fingers. She squinted, trying to make her brain work. The last call Kellen had ever received had come from a number Julia recognized: Frank Carrington's. The next-to-last was from a number she knew even better: Vanessa's.

"Look at the time," said Lemaster.

Julia did. Eight-seventeen p.m.

"That was the call Kellen took while he was on Main Street with Tony Tice," Lemaster said. "The call that made him put Tony out of the car. The call he had to rush off and do something about."

Julia found her voice. "But the way Tony told the story, it sounded like whoever was on the phone was threatening him—he was upset—and Vanessa had nothing to frighten him with—"

"Of course she did."

Of course she did. So simple. So clear.

Vanessa wanted something from Kellen that night, and, if she did not get it, she was going to tell her father about his attentions.

Still Julia could not get her mind around the whole thing. "But what would she—what would she want him to—"

She stopped. Time flowed backward. Mary Mallard, showing her the anagram. Back. Back. Vanessa's wild insistence in the kitchen of Hunter's Heights that DeShaun, and only DeShaun, had done the killing. Back. Further. Vanessa's insistence on writing a simply terrible term paper devoted to proving the same point. Back. Back. The burning of the Mercedes on the anniversary of Gina Joule's death, culmination of the madness that had come upon her almost from the moment she began to look into the events of that Valentine's Day night three decades ago. Flash forward again, Julia and Lemaster lying in bed the night that Janine Goldsmith slept over, Lemaster telling her that whoever killed Kellen need not have hated him to do it.

What else could it be? Julia had asked.

Lemaster's answer now rang like thunder: *Rational maximizing of self-interest.*

And another, more painful image: Vanessa, outside Saint Matthias on that horrible Sunday, pulling Malcolm Whisted's name from the hat, desperate to deflect her mother, who was circling closer to the truth. Julia said now, "Vanessa's blog. GAINFUL NONSENSES. It's an anagram."

"Yes. Of SINFUL SANE N. E. SONG."

"Not only that." She scribbled the words Mary Mallard had pointed out. GINA FLEES NUN'S SON. Lemaster's thick eyebrows did their bushy frown. "You went to Catholic school, Lemmie. And you were motherless. Get it? Nun's son?"

"I get it," he said softly.

"That's the reason. That's Vanessa's trauma. What sent her over the edge a year and a half ago." Julia tapped the paper. "She thought you killed Gina Joule." She picked up the page and tore it into strips, then got up and crossed the room to drop them into the shredder Lemaster kept conveniently nearby. "That was the trauma. That was the big secret. She was protecting you, Lemmie. The paper. The refusal to consider that it could have been anybody but DeShaun. The evidence is all over the place. She thought you did it."

"Preston put the idea in her head," said Lemaster, tonelessly. "And it stayed there until—well, until recent events."

Julia picked up the cell phone, pushing the button to light the screen afresh. She held it close to her face, staring, until Lemaster took it gently from her hand. He closed the phone, turned it over, removed the battery. From a drawer he took a hammer. He smashed the cover, removed the memory chip, and smashed that, too. He shoved the mess neatly aside. Perhaps in recognition of his wife's distress, he folded his hands over hers, and waited.

"And that's what this was all about. I thought you were protecting the President, or Mal Whisted, or the Empyreals and their stupid plan. But it was Vanessa." Her vision blurred. "You didn't want anybody to know that she was in Kellen's car that night. To threaten him. To make clear, if he told anybody her father did it, she would tell the world how he had—had"—she could not pronounce the words—"paid inappropriate attention to her. If anybody knew, they would have thought she— oh, Lemmie." Julia wiped her eyes. "You had somebody swipe the phone for you, maybe you got rid of the records themselves, in whatever bunker the cell-phone company keeps them in. Could you have done that, Lemmie? Do you have that kind of"—she searched for the word—"authority?" Julia was on her feet. She did not remember rising but had backed physically away from her husband, and stood now near the window, staring at him, horror and admiration mixing, terrified of his conclusion, loving him for his instinctive use of the power the Empyreals had placed in his hands—using it to protect his own. "Will you get in trouble? For—for misusing the power they've entrusted to you? The Empyreals?"

"I will if they find out." Finally he smiled. "Sit down, Jules. Sit down and pour us some more wine."

(I V)

"I CAN'T TELL YOU everything, Jules. Even now. But, yes, I have a little cache of evidence that I keep around. Not the evidence Empyreals hold on to, like the original of Jock's confession." Tapping the pages. "A few little items of my own. To keep my friends in line. My old college buddies. After all, if you think about it, they might kick at the bit one day, and try to get rid of me. Empyreals would never avenge me, you see. They are in this for the long haul. Their focus is the fortune of the darker nation, not the preservation of Lemaster Carlyle. So I've kept the cache around. Every year I lodge a fresh letter with our lawyer, telling him where it's hidden. Scrunchy knows that. Mal knows that. They're powerful men, but they keep away from me. And from my family."

"But Jeremy was here in case they didn't."

"Well, yes. He was. Or in case some of their people, unfamiliar with the rules, got a little rough. At first I just wanted him nearby. But after I realized how many people were poking around—well, yes. After that I mostly wanted him in the house, or covering whoever was out, when he could. And I took other measures, too. Never mind what they were."

Other measures. She saw it at once. Trevor Land. Gina's godfather. Trevor had been Lemaster's man from the start. Through Trevor, Lemaster had arranged for Bruce to get involved with the investigation, knowing that Bruce was dogged, that he would often be around Julia and even Vanessa until he got his answers, and that he would be a formidable presence against any threat. All of this without ever exciting attention by publicly hiring a bodyguard.

"So, if you kept it hidden," said Julia, "how did Vanessa find it?"

"At that time I kept the cache in my study. It was inside a locked cabinet. A month or so after Vanessa returned from France, I got home one night and the lock had been jimmied. I was in a panic, I can tell you. I thought Scrunchy's people had gotten in. Mal Whisted's. But no. Somebody had been through the pages, but only the plane ticket was missing. It had to be Vanessa."

"She finds everything," Julia agreed. But, inside, she realized that she was at last one step ahead of her husband. The piano. Kellen had never taped anything to the piano. He had not gotten into the house. Vanessa had purloined a clue from Kellen and hidden it there to provide an explanation for the Audi knocking over the lamps on the night he drove her home. She said, "So what happens now, Lemmie? You have your hooks in both men."

"True."

"But they couldn't both have done it. Jock drove the car. Mal Whisted was drunk, and probably doesn't remember a thing, but his family doesn't have the kind of money this conspiracy would have cost. And Scrunchy—well, he wasn't there, was he? But maybe he helped with the cover-up. That's your hook into him. Or maybe the Empyreals showed each of them some piece of manufactured evidence. And so, maybe to this day, they both think they killed her." Counting off the points on her fingers, admiring the cleverness even as she despised the act. "That was Bay's plan from the start. Get them all tripping over each other. Tell each of them, You did it, but we'll set up a cover, so the others will think it was them. Why not? After all, the Empyreals didn't know which one of them would rise the highest, but it was a nice bet."

"A very nice bet." He seemed sad. "All these years, all these decades, the Caucasians have assumed that they are in charge. The ideology of the Empyreals is that this need not be so. The darker nation can wield enormous power, as long as we hide our hand. Public power the Caucasians would never stand for. Hidden power they can do nothing about."

"But if the hand is . . . hidden . . . then why did Jock and Mal ever believe that the Empyreals had so much power?"

"I believe that when the police turned their attention to DeShaun, all three men were persuaded that the Empyreals could do what they promised. And what they threatened."

"And that was it. They signed the confessions. Stupid little college boys. They signed the confessions, the Hillimans provided the cash to spread around, and all these years, Mal Whisted has been sure you're covering for him. All these years, Scrunchy has been sure you're covering for him. Neither one of them knew the other was even a suspect. And of course they fired their assistants when they looked into it. You told them to, and they didn't have a choice. I must be an idiot not to have seen it. Oh, Lemmie! Of course you can afford to be blasé about the election! The Empyreals win either way!"

"Remember, Jules, I came into the plan late. Things are as they are." A pause as he stood up and went to the window. The glare did not seem to bother him. "So—tell me, Jules. What would you do? If you had the choice. What would you have us do now?"

"Take the hooks out. Tell both men they're free."

"I don't think that's going to happen. Number one, it's not my decision. I'm a relatively minor player in Empyreals, no matter what my title might be. Number two—well, there are a lot of sunk costs, Jules. We've gone too far to turn back."

"Lemmie, come on! The President—Scrunchy—he's innocent! So is Senator Whisted! They were drunk but they didn't kill anybody! How on earth can you say it's too late to turn back? You're blackmailing the wrong men!"

"I suppose we are," he said, finally turning back toward his computer. Tap-tap-tap.

She wanted to throttle the life out of him. She wanted to hug him forever. She wanted to grab the family and head for the hills. She stared at the man who had rescued her, a man who believed in duty rather than desire, twisted now by so many conflicting obligations that he no longer understood free will, especially his own. "This is wrong, Lemmie. Can't you see why it's wrong?"

"No, Jules. I cannot see why it's wrong." Glancing up at her at last, eyes weary. Stunned by a sign of actual physical weakness in her husband, Julia took a step back. "A few months ago, when you thought the President was guilty, you seemed satisfied—reluctant, but satisfied—that the course we had chosen would lead to the best outcome for our people. The darker nation. Have you changed your mind? Don't you see that the possibility of helping our people is the same, no matter who did the actual deed?"

She sank into the chair.

Her husband eyed her with sympathy. "I'm surprised at you, Jules. Surprised. Our opportunity to win justice for our people does not turn in any way on the actual identity of the culprit in a crime the world has long forgotten. We are avenging a far larger crime, Jules. Remember that."

Now she knew what frightened her. The confidence she had long admired in him, even when it swelled into pride, was really the zeal of the ideologue. All these years he had spent at the table deriding left and right alike had persuaded her that Lemaster possessed no politics to speak of, apart from an admiration of his own brilliance. Now she saw how wrong she was. His politics were the politics of pure and perfect righteousness. As his own favorite philosopher, Isaiah Berlin, had once pointed out, no cause has ever claimed more victims.

"But you can't believe it's going to stay a secret. Sooner or later, it's going to come out. Everything does."

"No, Jules. Not everything does. The world is full of secrets people manage to keep." Tap-tap-tap. "This one wouldn't have come out if Byron Dennison hadn't been so arrogant. He couldn't resist the temptation. He had to meet with the frat boy himself instead of using an intermediary. He had to go to the meeting in the Landing, for the pleasure of watching the Caucasians dance to his tune. He forgot about how our hand is supposed to say hidden." Glancing up at her. "Anyway, now it's hidden again."

"What about DeShaun?" she said. "Are you willing to let that lie remain out there?"

He said nothing.

"You wouldn't lose anything if you let it be known—leaked it somehow—that Jock Hilliman was the real killer. You wouldn't let

Scrunchy or Mal off the hook. They both think they killed him. They think the evidence of Jock's guilt is manufactured. They think those confessions you made them sign—"

"The Empyreals made them sign."

"—you made them sign," she repeated, "are enough. They'll be nervous, probably, to see the old crime reopened. But they'll both still be yours."

He shrugged.

"What kind of man are you?" she said at last, lungs aching as if she had attempted a very long climb. But she did not know whether she was climbing up or down. "Come on, Lemmie. Don't you care about the truth?"

"The only truth that matters," said Lemaster with solemn kindness, "is the truth of how much we can gain for our people." He looked at her again. "I love you, Jules. I've loved you since the first day of div school. But this plan is now my responsibility. I cannot turn away from it on the threshold."

She swayed in the long, bright room, overwhelmed, not knowing who he was. Had he lied to her a moment ago about being a minor player? His doubts seemed to have vanished, in the brilliant glow of a willed belief. He could always talk anybody into believing anything, and he had talked himself into believing that the Empyreals were right.

Probably just in the last ten minutes.

And the crazy part was, she saw his point. She didn't. Lemaster was right. He wasn't. The world cared. It didn't.

"Are you going to leave me now, Jules? Take the children, run to France, call the papers, ask them to rescue poor Scrunchy and Mal from the clutches of a bunch of old men from the darker nation, some tiny unknown Harlem fraternity that secretly controls the destiny of the nation? Do you honestly think anybody but the far-right fringe of the far-right fringe would even consider the possibility that it could be true?"

"I could try."

"Yes, you could. And I'll always love you, whatever you do." He spoke gently, the way we do with the very ill. "I want you to stay. I want you with me. If you can't bear it, I'll understand. But, please, Jules, understand my position. I have to do this work. If I have you with me, I'll do it better."

"And Tony Tice? Why were you in touch with Tony Tice?" But she had already figured it out. "He was playing both ends against the middle, wasn't he? This was your project now. You had to protect it. You and . . . and Jeremy Flew. The Empyreals sent him, didn't they? To take care of us, but also to keep an eye on things. You knew what Kellen was doing. You had Tony to tell you how far he got in his research, except that Tony thought the chance for a buck was too good to pass up. He cheated you." Another thought. "That hundred thousand he donated to the div school every year. Was that the Empyreals too? Oh, Lemmie! Did they buy me a job?" She swayed. And hardened. "I don't think Tony Tice will do much time, will he, Lemmie? You'll call somebody, and he'll get a sweet deal." She hesitated. "Bruce told me, Vanessa too, that Kellen started working on this project a year and a half ago. You were still at the White House. But the Empyreals needed somebody to keep an eye on things. To maybe run the whole project. And the best way to do that would be if you could be, say, president of the university. The most powerful man in the county. How did they do it? Did they have the Hillimans call Cameron? What was it?"

A warning tone when he finally spoke. "It was the search for justice. That's all."

The questions swirled. Did Frank Carrington really cause so much mayhem on his own? Had Jeremy Flew acted only as a bodyguard, or might he have played a more active role? And what about Kellen—how had he learned so much, so fast? Did he have a source inside the Empyreals? But she knew her husband would offer no answers. So she asked the one question that mattered most: "But who gets to make the call, Lemmie? Who decides when to use this . . . this influence? Who's *wise* enough?"

Lemaster stared at his wife for a long moment, then leaped to his feet and stalked around the desk. Julia cringed instinctively away, all her suspicions rising. He took her by the shoulders and frog-marched her into the private bathroom off the study.

"Lemmie, what is it? Let me go!"

"Look," he said.

"What?"

"You're the one who loves mirrors! Now, look!"

She turned. And there was the answer to her question, staring back at her, the secret burden theirs to share.

THE MANSION
OF ALL MOODS

(1)

SUMMER. Julia stood in a bay window at the back of the Mallard mansion south of Portland, Maine, watching the Atlantic through gauzy curtains. Waves rolled in, dark and majestic, patiently battering the boulders that today stood proudly against the assault and, in the fullness of time, like all that seemed solid and unchangeable, would crumble to dust.

"So—what am I supposed to do now?" said Mary Mallard from behind her. She was on the sofa, her bad leg stretched along the cushions. "Publish the truth? Tell me, Julia. What am I supposed to do?"

"You don't know the truth," said Julia after a moment. "Neither do I."

"We know the lies, though."

Julia nodded, said nothing. The house belonged to Mary's mother, and was furnished with grand Yankee bad taste. The rear lawn swept down to the seawall, where Evelyn Mallard, related to so many Presidents that nobody could count them, walked with Jeannie. Maine summer sunshine sparkled on their trim white outfits. Jeannie—no, Jeans, always Jeans now—Jeans was laughing, having found in this rich seafront colony south of Portland a whole new world worth charming with her perfection. Aaron, summering at a program down at Babson for future business leaders, had been up last weekend. Preston promised to bring Megan, or her successor, as long as Lemaster was not around, and Julia hoped he would. Smith and Vanessa had left early on their cross-country trip, because their parents lacked the will to stop them. The two (or three) of them telephoned intermittently to assure their families that they were fine.

Lemaster kept calling to say he would be up in a few days, and his new assistant kept calling to say he wouldn't.

"I've worked most of it out, Julia. Jock killed Gina, Whisted was there with him that night, and poor Scrunchy was at some frat party, drunk out of his mind. He was nowhere near the beach."

"Maybe."

"That's a big story, Julia. A thirty-year-old murder, a black boy blamed for it and practically lynched, and now it turns out that Senator Whisted was there when it happened. A huge story. But I can't print it, can I? I don't have hard evidence. I can't print that somebody somewhere suspects that maybe it might have been, et cetera, et cetera. You know and I know, but we can't prove a word of it." A pause to let Julia put a word in, but Julia didn't. The curtains snapped in a sudden sea breeze. Upstairs on the guest room desk was an unfinished letter to Julia's mother. She had tried writing to Lemmie, too, but could not think what to say.

Behind her, Mary was still talking, perhaps to herself. "Besides, we know it's the kind of thing they kill people over, isn't it? I mean, really kill them. If I printed it, they'd send somebody to kill me, wouldn't they?"

"Maybe."

"And that doesn't bother you?"

Julia remembered her conversation with Vanessa after they left Frank Carrington's house a million years ago. "Of course it bothers me. I think every life is precious." She nibbled her lip. "But, Mary, the thing is—"

"That's not what I mean." The journalist was impatient. "I meant, doesn't it bother you that Whisted will never be brought to justice? That he might make it all the way to the White House?"

"He didn't do it. Being asleep in the back seat isn't a crime."

"He was there, Julia. The voters should know that."

Julia surprised herself with her answer. She had been in Maine the better part of a month. Needing a confidant, and realizing how much Mary had worked out for herself, Julia had shared much of the story, omitting, however the roles played by the Empyreals—and her own husband. She had not seen Lemaster in weeks. Yet here she was, channeling his argument. She remembered his hand gripping her upper arm, making her face the mirror, telling her to look at who would make the decisions.

"Let me tell you about justice," she said. "If you could write about Mal Whisted—suppose he even did it, and you could prove it—what would happen? He'd go to prison, right? He'd get what he deserved. But where would that leave the darker nation? Why shouldn't the darker nation have the chance to get what it deserves? Lock up Whisted, and you get the satisfaction of knowing that a man who did a terrible thing thirty years ago is behind bars. And that's it. But leave him free to rise, maybe all the way to the White House, and you get this powerful ally to push his party in the direction it needs to go. You can give Whisted justice, or you can give African America justice. It's as simple as that."

"That's not simple, Julia. It's . . . amoral."

She quoted Astrid. "You can't win the war against evil with one hand tied behind your back."

"Do you really think America is evil?"

"No. I think America has a short attention span."

(11)

MALCOLM WHISTED HAD WON the primaries. The press still loved the story of the two college roommates squaring off for the Presidency, and, in the excitement, paid no attention to various low-level resignations from their staffs. Everybody was still trying to dig up dirt, discounting the other side according to political preference: *Your guy's military record matters! Looking at my guy's military record is gutter politics!* Oddly, nobody seemed to consider the two men's college years a fruitful field of inquiry—perhaps because the reporters and editors and activists had all had their own college years, and liked to think of them as comfortably, even passionately, off limits. Nobody even hinted at the perfect balance of terror, the possibility that an obscure Harlem men's club, membership limited by charter to "four hundred colored gentlemen of quality," held both men's futures in its hands, because it owned evidence that each had committed a murder, evidence each man fully believed, even though neither one of them had done the deed.

Patience can be a strategy all by itself, as Lemaster liked to say—
and, in this case, an Empyreal patience had won the day.

Julia had considered leaving her husband after that final confrontation, just taking the kids and going—somewhere. Her growing sense of
duty held her back—duty, and, vaguely, gratitude. Lemaster was a
stranger, but he had rescued her, after all, and had never betrayed or
hurt her. The stern, locked-in convictions in which he bound his life
did not, she had discovered, bind her equally. He lived his way and she
lived hers. They could accomplish this under one roof. They could ride
together through life. They had done it for twenty-one years, even
with her confused and lingering feelings for Kellen between them
like a sword. They could continue, and not only because Lemaster and
his Empyreals gripped the reins with such fearsome and oppressive
goodwill. Kellen had liberated her. Whatever his motive—justice or
jealousy—his search for Gina's killer, and his mad plan to drag Julia into
his scheme, had released her instead from the prison of other people's
expectations.

She enjoyed her new job, and not only because she was away from
Lemaster's campus. She was helping young people who served, too,
often, as props for politicians and as applause lines for activists. Everybody sympathized with their plight and everybody avoided any more
contact with them than necessary—everybody who could afford to,
anyway. Julia Carlyle, raised in New Hampshire, stood in front of the
tiny classroom at Miss Terry's school in the center of the most dangerous neighborhood in Elm Harbor, sharing her knowledge for no salary
to speak of, and loving every minute. She had even attended the occasional service at the House of Faithful Holiness, and come away from
her encounters, if not with her cup running over, at least with a heightened sense of the desperate needs of the darker nation, and the unlike-
lihood that either political party, left to its own devices, would ever pay
more than lip service to the moral imperative to meet those needs. Certainly in the heated presidential campaign shaping around her nobody
gave any serious consideration to what should be done about race and
poverty—not when there were *important* issues to confront. There
were always important issues to confront. Race and poverty could come
later. Maybe that was why Jesus had said the poor we would have with
us always: He knew where they would rank, even two millennia later, in
the list of political priorities. What Mona had said so long ago, quoting

some writer, resonated more and more strongly with Julia as the weeks flew past: white people were far more interested in the equality of their wives and daughters than the equality of their servants.

That was the other reason she had not left Lemaster.

She had stayed with him because she thought he might be right.

(I I I)

AT THE BEACH, later, watching Jeans frolic, darling of the Clan, Julia sat on a towel, straw hat and sunglasses shielding her eyes, and finished the letter to Granny Mo.

Dear Mona:

I have often wondered why, with all the world to choose from, you decided to raise us in New Hampshire. I loved every minute of Hanover, but you were never truly happy. We were nowhere near anything—anything, at least, of the world that formed you and your whole generation of our people, the world to which you wanted your children, at whatever distance, to remain connected. The summers were beautiful, but the winters were preposterous. The town was wonderful, but, like all New England, white.

Now at last I think I understand. To be a great people is also to be an old people, and to be an old people is to be a people with a past. In the past are great triumphs, but also great tragedies. Wisdom is knowing one from the other—and how to keep the secrets. I think you moved us to Hanover for the winters. Time covers truth like snow. The best part of New England life is that it is a very long time before the snow melts.

Love always,

Julia

She posted the letter in the morning mail.

AUTHOR'S NOTE

READERS OF *The Emperor of Ocean Park*, the novel in which Lemaster and Julia Carlyle first appeared, might remember the family as residents of a suburb called Canner's Point, not Tyler's Landing. For a variety of story-related reasons, I moved their house. As I explained in the author's note to the previous novel, Elm Harbor is not a thinly disguised New Haven, although I will say again, as I said there, that the two towns share a lot of the same ghosts. The same caveat must apply to any comparisons between Kepler Quadrangle and the Yale Divinity School. And of course it should be unnecessary to add, but probably is not, that whatever events might have inspired the story, it is only a story—a "what-if"—and makes no larger claim than that.

Neither Ladybugs nor Empyreals is a real organization, nor is either based on one. Nor are their members based on any clubmen or clubwomen of whom I am aware. I greatly admire the ability of the traditional clubs of the darker nation to preserve their traditions in an untraditional age. The story of the Black Lady is told around Arkadelphia, Arkansas, to this day, albeit with far more emendations and additions than the bare-bones tale repeated by Vanessa Carlyle in the novel. The Internet Anagram Server may be found at www.wordsmith.org but—fair warning—its powers are quite addictive. The Web site Gainful Nonsenses does not exist.

As of this writing, Dartmouth College does not offer a Ph.D. in economics, and therefore Kellen Zant could not have done his graduate work there. I could have placed his affair with Julia at one of the other New England Ivies, but the image of Julia tramping through all that astonishing campus snow was too perfect to resist. In 2004, the Iowa caucuses were held in the middle of January, but that was too early to make my story work, so I moved them, rudely, a little later. I have also shoved around, in I hope minor ways, certain other aspects of the pace of a modern presidential campaign.

AUTHOR'S NOTE

Lemaster Carlyle's argument about how man desires to create a God who needs man's advice is inspired in part by the discussion of Dostoevsky in David Bentley Hart's startlingly exquisite 2005 book, *The Doors of the Sea: Where Was God in the Tsunami?*—although Hart is not of course responsible for any holes in Lemaster's exposition.

I am grateful as always to my alarmingly patient literary agent, Lynn Nesbit. I have benefited enormously from the guidance and encouragement of my editors, Robin Desser and Phyllis Grann, who waited through the frustrations of the pace at which I delivered the manuscript, and protected the story against many poor choices. I would also like to thank fans of my hesitantly offered first novel, whose persistent demands for another kept me working on this one. I have also had the useful advice of the small circle of intimates who read all or part of the manuscript along the way, particularly my dear friends George Jones and Loretta Pleasant-Jones.

Finally, no words can express my gratitude to my wife, Enola, my most careful and critical reader, and our wonderful children, Leah and Andrew, the three of them truly God's gifts in my life.

June 2006

A NOTE ABOUT THE AUTHOR

Stephen L. Carter is the William Nelson Cromwell Professor of Law at Yale University, where he has taught since 1982. He is the author of *The New York Times* best seller, *The Emperor of Ocean Park*, as well as seven acclaimed nonfiction books, including *The Culture of Disbelief: How American Law and Politics Trivialize Religious Devotion* and *Civility: Manners, Morals, and the Etiquette of Democracy*. He and his family live near New Haven, Connecticut.

A NOTE ON THE TYPE

This book was set in Janson, a typeface long thought to have been
made by the Dutchman Anton Janson, who was a practicing typefounder in Leipzig during the years 1668–1687. However, it has been
conclusively demonstrated that these types are actually the work of
Nicholas Kis (1650–1702), a Hungarian, who most probably learned
his trade from the master Dutch typefounder Dirk Voskens. The type
is an excellent example of the influential and sturdy Dutch types that
prevailed in England up to the time William Caslon (1692–1766)
developed his own incomparable designs from them.

Composed by Creative Graphics, Inc.,
Allentown, Pennsylvania
Designed by Virginia Tan